River Town
Wellsville Ohio

David Navarria

The People Who Built America
The Story of a Town and Its People

What you are about to read is based on a true story from my mother's memoirs, diaries, and dictations. It tells a mature tale of three generations of families in a small industrial river town and the people in it as it grows to contribute to two world wars and provides many of the materials that built a great nation.

Far from a quick read, it is a deep and passionate story, including one of redemption, which illustrates the drives of the human condition and 'man's inhumanity to man.' through brutal stories of crime, lawlessness, and war. All names have been changed to respect the privacy of any remaining descendants.

River Town
Wellsville Ohio

This Book Is Dedicated
To The Memory Of
My Mother

Eleanora Puch Navarria

Sergeant, United States Women's Army Corps. (WACs) Dec.
1943-1945

*Asiatic-Pacific Theatre Ribbon with three Bronze Battle Stars,
War Service Ribbon, Two Overseas Service Bars,
Philippine Liberation Ribbon and Good Conduct Medal 44*

One of the first WACs
who paved the way for other women
to serve in the United States military

Thank you to —————————

My late mother for the patience, time, effort, and dedication she displayed while explaining the entirety of this story.

My wife, Grazia, without whose help this book would not have been possible, and her family in her native country of Italy, who provided me with and confirmed many missing pieces of my family's history both abroad and in the United States.

The people who took the time to provide me with so much valuable information about the town of Wellsville, Ohio:

Susan Koontz

Paula Krawiec

Mr. & Mrs. Jeffrey MacLean

Robert J. Berresford, dec.

Bonnie Berresford

Robert 'Bob' Lloyd, dec.

Nicholas Puch, dec.

Gerald DiLoreto, dec.

Frank Dalonzo

Barry Arbaugh

Tom Davidson

Eva Price, dec.

And

The Wellsville River Museum

The Wellsville Historical Society

The East Liverpool Historical Society

The Columbiana County Historical Society

The Jefferson County Historical Society

The many women and men, both living and passed,
who anonymously provided me with so much
valuable personal information.

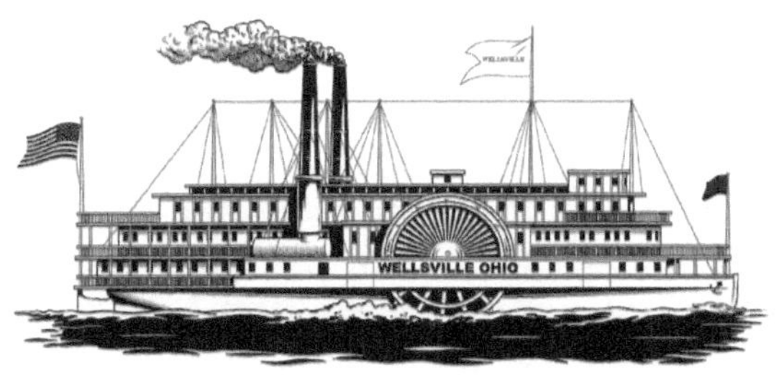

River Town
Wellsville Ohio

Forward

As the stories of this book took place in a very different time than 2024, with dissimilar social customs, it might be difficult for many readers to comprehend fully; it was indeed for me when I first learned about them. When I questioned my mother about some of that era's events in which the stories you are about to read occurred, including the violence, she answered, 'That was what happened.' So be it. I believe learning from the past is essential to create a better future.

I was 12 years old when I first learned about a family incident that had occurred with my great-grandparents. My mother, Eleanora, explained it to me in a way that was suitable for my age. As I grew older, I was interested in learning about something I couldn't fully understand, even as a young adult. In the mid-1970s, I began learning the full story of my family. That's when my mother began to dictate these stories to me. Work interrupted my outline of the story. My mother and I resumed our endeavor periodically throughout the 1980s and 1990s using recorded tapes and written notes. In 1992, I began outlining a

Continued

historical fiction book because the subject matter was personal and sensitive. In 2013, I began to obtain more specific and detailed information about the town of Wellsville and its historical significance. Work and life once again interrupted my efforts. My studies of the town and its surrounding area continued, and I clarified much of my mother's information. After years of preparing this story's history, it wasn't until 2023 that I dedicated myself to finishing this chronicle, which tells the hardships of both settlers and immigrants in Wellsville, Ohio, my mother's experiences during World War Two, and what men and women endured while serving in the allied militaries of two world wars. I adhered to my late mother's words on audio tapes and with the notes she dictated to me, her diary, and her personal memories.

As I followed her words as best I could, there was romance and sentimentality of time and place throughout, but also extreme violence and savage assaults on both men and women. I included those parts because they were part of her story and to give voice to those victims who suffered anonymously. As already explained, the story took place in an era much different than we know today, and I wrote it true to that period. I detailed this journey of my mother's family from when they first came to America and eventually settled in the small river town of Wellsville, Ohio.

I used creative non-fiction to bring the characters alive with dialogue and literal descriptions in this mature retelling of these stories, as explained to me by my mother, carried down by her mother and other family members. I researched the town, times, and places extensively to be historically correct as much as possible. The characters are real, but I changed all names to respect the privacy of any descendants of those mentioned.

————————————————————————***David Navarria***

River Town
Wellsville Ohio

Book One
The Town

Chapter One

Wellsville, Ohio 1890

Pip and Rollo

Rock boulders of a low mountain range followed the flowing snakelike water curves between them. The rhythmic current allowed tranquility while it nourished the soil, growing vegetation that fed all living things. It was the river that gave life to the Ohio Valley. Though having a disposition to change, that body of water would sometimes become temperamental and thus a force of nature to be reckoned with. Natives first inhabited the area just north of a great river bend. They traveled and traded by trails and water routes. George Washington and William Crawford surveyed land along the Ohio River as they navigated flatboats from Pittsburgh, Pennsylvania, in 1770. They noted 'good bottom soil' at a section of land called Yellow Creek. It was a southern part of what would later be named Wellsville, Ohio, after a steadfast settler named William Wells. The town grew and flourished.

Two suspicious figures emerged from the morning fog, walking briskly northwards along Main Street. One carried a long, thin object and a bag slung over his shoulder. They stopped at the corner of Third Street and Main and glanced to their right. The short road ended at the Ohio River, and the fog was even thicker closer to the water. The pair turned and walked slowly and cautiously down Third Street toward the end of the block as thick plumes of the gloomy mist rolled over them in the shadows of the dawning day. When a towering figure appeared out of the fog on their far left at the end of a building, the two characters came to a halt. They then began to creep slightly further.

A giant of a man shouted in a thick Irish brogue, "I thar! Who are ya now?" he couldn't see clearly through the dull haze of morning.

'Oh no! It's McElhenny,' thought Pip. Robert McElhenny was a guard at the Third Street Railroad Station in Wellsville, Ohio, and an intimidating figure. An immigrant from Ireland, McElhenny stood about six feet two inches tall and as muscular as a bull. Pip was scared to death of him. He thought of the ogre next to him as one of the grotesque gargoyles that graced Notre Dame Cathedral from pictures he had seen at the local library. Standing there guarding and ready to swoop down and devour anyone who approached his holy grounds, McElhenny was a fierce adversary. Pip and Rollo stood before him motionless. Even while biding such fears, they wanted to reach their objective, but they wouldn't be able to that morning.

"I'll ask again, who are ya now?" As McElhenny paused, he recognized who it was walking toward him. "So! It's the young lad Pip once more. And with yeh accomplice once again, are ya?"

"W-W-We're going the other way, Mr. McElhenny," replied Pip in a stutter. As his words parted his lips, he and Rollo immediately continued straight to the end of the block before the railroad tracks above the slope to the river. They made a sharp right turn and quickly walked toward the nearby riverboat wharf.

"Will are ya then? See that ya do!" Robert McElhenny, whom most adults called Bob, turned his back on Pip and faced the station. Knowing Pip couldn't see his face, he smiled and slowly began to walk back to the Third Street Station complex to fetch a cup of coffee. He passed between a couple of horse-drawn wagons tethered to a tree and proceeded along the back of the structure. That station was built in the early 1860s, back in the days of the C&P Railroad, and gradually became a symbol of the power of the railroad to the small town. The McElhenny family was among the Irish immigrants of the potato famine, which began in the 1840s. They arrived in America in 1850 when Robert was just two years old and eventually settled in the town of Wellsville, Ohio.

"Drat," whispered Pip. They were trying to go to his and Rollo's favorite spot. First, the two had to cross the railroad tracks past the lengthy building of the Third Street Station. There, they always sneaked down the slope to the bank of the Ohio River when the coast was clear. But that morning, they got caught by McElhenny, as they sometimes did. Now, they had to walk to the riverboat wharf, their second-best place. They could go there only if riverboats weren't docked or scheduled to be there. If so, there would be too much commotion with workers, unloading equipment, and horse-drawn wagons parked around the dock. They could see between the rolls of the thick morning river fog that they were lucky, and it was empty.

The heyday of the riverboats began to succumb to the railroads in the mid-1800s. The trains gradually grew to transport more passengers and goods. The steamer vessels maintained a presence in the river town in 1890. However, they no longer solely ruled the rivers as they had in their glorious days when Wellsville, Ohio, had the busiest port between Pittsburgh and Portsmouth. Back in the mid-1800s, Wellsville had two steamboat building yards. Other wharfs lined the riverbank from Seventh to Eight, crowded with boats, and the town boomed. Hotels flourished, with homes and stores built to accommodate the growing population. That was during the peak period of riverboat travel.

The young boy and his companion leisurely strolled the short distance along the side of the dusty dirt road of Riverside Avenue, careful to avoid any of the horse dung piled mainly in the center of the street. The pier was more of a walking path for passengers and unloading goods. The thick morning fog clouds slowly began their daily ritual to dissipate into puffs and swirls.

They resembled eerie figures as they slowly ascended to the heavens. The diffused early morning sun rose golden and struggled to shine between the evaporating mist lifting off the river, offering a kaleidoscope of magical colors as it did. Vivid hues blanketed the Ohio River Valley, forming a picturesque scene.

Engineers had dredged the dock long ago so the riverboats could align with the wharf. The two buddies could sit atop the far end of the short pier and cast a fishing rod. But a better option was to walk further down past the end of the plain berth. There, they could slide down to the river's bank, where the water pooled on opposite sides of the wood-planked, flat-topped pier. Sometimes, the current of the river trapped several fish. It depended on the height of the river at the time.

"C-C-C'mon Rollo," Pip stuttered in excitement. He tightened the leather leash on Rollo as they headed toward the harbor. Pip wore a long-sleeved white shirt and grey short pants with a button closure at his waist that morning. He sported high-knee socks and laced black boots. A short-brimmed straw hat topped off his outfit. His mother always insisted he wear a hat to protect him from the sun. He acquired his nickname from some older bullies at school based on Philip Pirrip, called Pip, from Charles Dickens's novel Great Expectations. In the story, Pip ranked low in society. Thus, the kids at school changed Douglas Nicholson II, Pip's real name, to suit their nasty needs of considering him low in their social hierarchy. And in addition to such cruelty, they also bullied Pip because he had a stammer. Pip was an eight-year-old loner, but not by choice. He was short, skinny, and weak, with dark blonde hair and blue eyes. Pip was a cute little boy—a perfect target for the tormentors at the Central School at Ninth Street, where he had just completed his second-grade year. That school housed elementary and high school classes in the same beautiful architectural achievement of a building. Pip had no friends except his dog, whom he considered his best friend. Rollo was Pip's mixed breed, part Bernese Mountain Dog and part Greater Swiss Mountain Dog, with a bit of Golden retriever mingled for good luck. At over

40 inches tall and a length of almost 50 inches, Rollo weighed about 115 pounds. His father gave the dog to his son as a surprise gift over a year before for doing so well in school. Rollo became a proud member of the Nicholson family as a seven-week-old pup. Pip named him Rollo after a famous Viking and Count of Rouen, who became the first ruler of Normandy. In addition to being Pip's best friend, Rollo served many titles, including First Knight of his Royal Medieval Army. All concealed in the castles, adventures, romances, and conquests of his scintillating imagination. The young boy lived inside that impregnable space to escape the terrors inflicted upon him by the bullies.

Many townspeople were amused whenever they saw the small boy pulled by such a big dog since Pip and Rollo traveled almost everywhere together. People would call out to greet Pip and Rollo. Nobody knew about the hurtful way that the young boy acquired his nickname when they used it. Others, especially family, would use his given name, Douglas.

Now that school was over that late spring morning, Pip and Rollo were getting ready to spend together every hour of what every young lad considered glorious summer days. Rollo was as gentle and friendly as a big teddy bear. He loved seeing people and being pet, especially under his chin. The exceptions to such time spent strolling about town were doing chores, going to school, and Sunday mornings when he and his family walked to the First Episcopal Congregation on Riverside, a short distance from the riverboat wharf. Once at the church, Pip tied Rollo to a tree nearby. Rollo rested there in the shade until the end of services. White Anglo-Saxon Protestants were the main religion and ethnicity of the town then, and Pip was a sixth-generation American with an ancestor who fought in the American Revolution.

As Pip and Rollo neared their fishing spot, they crossed the train tracks to survey the river's height atop the wide wharf. They climbed over a loading ramp set to the side and perched at the edge, looking down. Pip noticed a shoal of fish swimming

in a placid pool formed from the low water. "C-C-C'mon Rollo," Pip stuttered in delight. "C-C-C'mon boy!" Pip and Rollo jumped off the end of the dock and slid down the grassy
hill to the river's edge. "O-O-Oh, boy!" Pip was ecstatic as he
saw so many fish swimming around the isolated pond of water.
"A-A-Another conquest, Lord Rollo!" he shouted with glee as
he and his first knight, along with his brave army and cavalry,
descended upon their prey.

Rollo barked in excitement. Usually, Pip corrected him so as
not to scare away the fish. But that day, the fish had nowhere to
go. In a way, Pip felt sorry for them. But he would only take as
many as he needed. His father had taught him that the first time
when he learned to fish. Pip always complied with that rule, and
he baited his hook. One after another, Pip vigorously reeled in
six smallmouth bass fish.

As Pip assessed his catch, he decided to give a 14-inch two-
and-a-half-pounder to Mrs. Heely, his elderly next-door neighbor; Pip always gave her one. He would share another of the
same length and weight with his Aunt Ellen, his mother's older
widowed sister. As a young man, her husband died at the Battle
of Gettysburg during the American Civil War. After his death,
she relocated to Wellsville from Pennsylvania to be near her
sister. Two fish he saved for the Causwells, his next-door neighbors on the other side of his house. The remaining fish he would
bring home to his parents or divide them with anyone he met
on his way.

Pip packed the fish into his bag, and he and Rollo climbed
back up the grassy slope, crossed the train tracks, and resurfaced on Riverside Avenue. Some wagons assembled across the
street from the wharf. Pip also noticed a few near the train station. The Third Street Railroad Station was a passenger depot.
However, freight also came packed in some cars. There was
also an RPO, Railway Post Office, on many passing trains. That
was a specific mail car on the train. Most intercity mail in the
U.S. was postmarked and sorted by hand en route in those cars.
They used catcher pouches to pick up mail from small villages

where trains didn't stop. Catcher pouches were small mail bags usually attached to a pole assembly with a mail hook to 'catch' mail awaiting pickup from a moving train.

Many heavy crates also came by riverboat and freight trains unloaded at the wharf or the 12th Street Shop, a prominent railroad complex. Those grounds spanned from 12th Street to past 20th Street. The young boy and his dog often awaited the train's arrival at the Third Street Station. They always enjoyed seeing the passengers disembark and the commotion following a train arriving at the depot. At times, hundreds of people would gather on the station's platform—all paying homage to him, his loyal first knight, and the brave army of his imagination. Food and candy vendors assembled along with people who would eventually hold signs advertising hotel accommodations, bars, and restaurants.

Pip and Rollo began their journey home near Ninth Street and Riverside. On their left, they passed the Civil War Memorial with a large cannon facing the river. Across the street to the right was the famous Whitacre House Hotel. It was where Abraham Lincoln addressed a large gathering on his way to his first inauguration. James A. Garfield and Andrew Johnson also spoke from the front of the Whitacre House. The legendary Confederate General John Hunt Morgan stayed at the hotel under guard after being captured during the American Civil War. Though unauthorized by his superior, General Braxton Bragg, General John Hunt Morgan crossed the Ohio River and invaded the north in July 1863 during the aftermath of the Battle of Gettysburg. Credited with reaching the northernmost point of the Union States than any other organized Confederate force, he was captured at West Point, Ohio, a short distance from Wellsville. The general presented his sword not to the officers who caught him but to the hotel owner of Whitacre House Hotel, Thomas Whitacre, where the Union Army temporarily imprisoned him. Whitacre later left the sword to his heir. General John Hunt Morgan eventually escaped captivity but was shot and killed later in the war.

"Good morning, sir," shouted Pip to General Reilly, who was leaving his front door for his law office in town.

"Good morning, young man," replied the General, "Do you and Rollo have yourselves a good catch there?"

"Yes, sir. Would you like one?" Pip gave a big smile.

"No, no, but thank you, Douglas," the general chuckled. The young boy's smile was almost irresistible. "I have dinner plans tonight. You have yourself a good day now."

"Thank you, sir! You too!"

A former congressman, James William Reilly, led the 104th Ohio Infantry during the American Civil War. He was a strong supporter of the Underground Railroad before the war. General Reilly had a tunnel in his home to sneak ex-slaves into hay wagons and get them to safe places. The contested territory across the river from Wellsville was known as Western Virginia at the beginning of the war. Though the North ratified it as a Union state in 1863, both Union and Confederate sympathizers lived there, and it still housed slaves, which presented a danger to escaped slaves that went to Wellsville. There were also Confederate sympathizers in Wellsville who objected to the concept of Americans fighting Americans. Like many others, they wanted to avert war and find a peaceful solution through negotiations.

Pip and Rollo delivered the fish, and he received thanks and greetings from the people at the stops he made. His last delivery was home.

"Stay quiet and sit, Rollo!" Pip softly commanded his dog. He had plans to go back outside immediately. But first, Pip took his family's share of the fish and put it in a wooden icebox lined with tin. It stood near a shelf with other jarred meats and foods. A horse-drawn vehicle from a town ice house dropped off the ice that time of the year. Pip poured himself a glass of milk and sneaked some homemade butter cookies to accompany his refreshment. He flipped one to Rollo and then put some of the tasty treats in his pocket for later. Pip heard his mother upstairs, so he stepped quietly and carefully so his mother couldn't hear him.

"Douglas? Is that you?" his mother called.

"Caught!" Pip whispered to himself. "Yes, Mom, it's me, but I was just leaving."

"Wait there!" she shouted. "I'll be right there."

The young boy could hear his mother's light footsteps descend the stairs. Then she appeared. Martha Nicholson was 30 years old with a dainty, small-framed body. She was the average height of a woman. Martha had dark blonde hair and stylishly tied it in a bun. Her hazel-colored eyes stared sternly at her son. "Douglas, you promised you would straighten up your room." She had to hold back from smiling at the small boy's intimidated expression, his widened eyes looking up at her as he blushed; she loved her only child dearly.

Pip shuffled his feet as he stood, his eyes now looking down. "I started to, Mom, honestly, I did, but then I looked outside, and…well…" He glanced back up to meet his mother's eyes and continued, "The fish would be gone if I waited."

"Okay, Douglas, go upstairs and finish cleaning your room. Then I have a couple of errands for you to run for me," she smiled at her son, "and then you can go back out to fish."

"O-O-Okay, Mom!" Pip stuttered, then began to drag his feet a bit toward the stairway. Climbing the stairs, he realized the sooner he did the errands for his mother, the sooner he could get back out. Pip began to ascend the steps quicker, then stopped and turned his head back to his mother. "I caught a lot of fish, Mom. Wait 'til you see what I put in the icebox!" Then, he raced back up the stairway. "C-C-C'mon, Rollo," he shouted in a stutter of excitement.

Chapter Two

Messina, Sicily 1878 to New York City 1879
Luigi and Biaggio

From 1860 to 1880, diverse ethnicities of immigrants came to New York City, with far fewer Italians than those who followed in the late 1800s and early 1900s. After the unification of Italy in 1861, several Italians with aristocratic ties sought to invest in the larger cities of the New World. Most early Italian immigrants would stay in the larger cities throughout America to earn a living. Many of those immigrants who came between 1880 and 1900 went west to homestead. Some became vineyard owners in California

"**B**astardo!" Carmelo Mandanici shouted at Luigi Massaro.

"Sei un figlio di un bastardo," Luigi calmly replied. He said his words in perfect Italian, not the dialects of the peasants. It meant, 'And you are the son of a bastard.'

Like those of the Sicilian black olives of his homeland, Carmelo's dark eyes glared, resembling an animal claiming its territory. "Fino alla morte," he growled. 'To the death.'

"Come si desidera," said Luigi, again in a passive voice. 'As you wish.' He could see that his unassuming tone was rattling Carmelo, who rose and headed for his quarters of the university both young men attended.

After dawn the following day, several men stood in an open area of groomed vivid green grass near the Botanical Garden

Pietro Castelli of the University of Messina, Sicily. Seven horse-drawn carriages were parked close by. The coachmen stood beside their vehicles. One of them remained standing on the rear platform of the carriage to get a better view of the event. A surgeon, who also acted as a witness, was on hand.

Concetto Capizzi stood in as Carmelo's second in the duel. A second was someone who would assist, usually a friend of one of the duelers. He handed Carmelo a flintlock black powder dueling pistol with a ten-inch-long rifled barrel. It was loaded and ready for use. In turn, Salvatore Giorgianni, Luigi's best friend and second in the duel, handed Luigi the other pistol from the fine dueling set. Salvatore evaluated the working order of the weapon, loaded it, and handed it to his friend. Luigi gave a friendly nod to Salvatore.

"God be with you this morning, Luigi," Salvatore said in response to his friend's gesture. Both men removed their top hats and long-tailed suit jackets. Carmelo wore a grey vest over a white pleated fluffy shirt, baggy grey slacks, and brown booted shoes. Luigi, the better dresser, wore a dark maroon vest over a more stylish white shirt. He stood out with white tailored dress slacks and black short-length boots. The small crowd of spectators spread out to the side of the two young duelers. The witness shouted the rules to the two young men. Pistol duels were outlawed long before in Italy. However, they were still used as an honorable means to settle disputes among some royals and those eager to risk their lives to retain social honor. The two young men stood back-to-back amidst thick, gloomy fog clouds in the early morning of that late autumn day. When called, they would advance ten paces in opposite directions. Upon completing their steps, they would each fire the large bullets of their guns simultaneously.

The two young duelers received the call and began to count their paces as the fog slowly dissipated into dark twirls as a grim omen.

Luigi Giovanni Massaro was born an aristocrat in Messina, Sicily in 1858, three years before the finalization of the unification of Italy as a single state in 1861. His father was from a family of royals within the Kingdom of the Two Sicilies until his deposition after Italy's unification. About half of Italians can trace their roots to the Kingdom of the Two Sicilies following that period. It encompassed Sicily, Naples, and all regions up to the Papal State–about one-half of Italy then. The new king of Italy, Victor Emanuel II, recognized the title of the Massaro family of the former nobility of Sicily but not the former traditional precedence of leadership. Because the family retained title, money, and remaining land, Luigi would remain living in a privileged family. But only to a point–the feudal system in Italy was over.

Luigi was a tall, handsome, gentlemanly young aristocrat. He had a head full of black wavy hair with piercing dark blue eyes. Always dressed impeccably, he began attending the University of Messina in 1876. That university was founded in 1548 by Pope Paul III and was among the oldest universities in Italy. At the end of Luigi's second year at the university in 1878, he denounced Carmelo Mandanici as a cheat. Luigi discovered the hoax in sette e mezzo (seven and a half), an Italian card game similar to blackjack. Luigi had an incredible gift of being able to count cards, so he knew with certainty that Carmelo was cheating. Carmelo's father was from a family of higher rank in the old Sicilian nobility. Also, the Mandanici family had allied early on with the new king of the newly formed unified Italy. That empowered the Mandanicis more than the Massaros within the government.

Carmelo Mandanici was a short, slightly overweight young man who never cared about his attire. Usually partially unshaven, he was messy in everything he did, including his eating habits. His claim to fame was that of his father's position. With no social graces, he carved his way by bullying people using his family name. Carmelo had a bad habit of constantly cringing his nose. Combined with his black olive-colored shifty eyes, he looked like a rodent sniffing for its next meal. Carmelo Mandanici was an ugly individual, inside and out. Though it was a valid accusation, Carmelo took it as an insult only because he was caught and humiliated by a lower-ranking royal. In turn, he insulted Luigi's father about his lower social standing. He then challenged Luigi to a duel with pistols. Luigi had no choice but to accept the summons to such a contest to honor his family name, even though pistol dueling was outlawed.

Dueling with pistols did not always mean killing an opponent. In some cases, they were intended only for the satisfaction of honor and not to be mortal duels. Opponents would fire separately or together. In some cases, there was no intention of hitting the opponent altogether, allowing a neutral settlement to the dispute, both remaining gentlemen. However, this duel was to the death, as ordered by Carmelo Mandanici in his challenge.

So, after dawn, the two young duelers counted their ten paces and intended to shoot to kill. But Carmelo stopped short of his required paces, turned prematurely, and with a rat-like grin, he snarled and fired at Luigi's back. The large bullet grazed Luigi's left shoulder, and bright red blood stained his dark maroon vest and part of his stylish white shirt. Luigi instinctively fell to his left knee, pivoted his body while on one knee, and fired his pistol. He hit Carmelo directly in the center of his chest. A surge of blood spurted out of the immense hole as Carmelo's black olive eyes closed, his knees wobbled, and he fell to the ground. The bullet hit his heart or the aortic artery because blood remained pumping as Carmelo lay dead on the dew-moistened morning grass. His white, pleated, fluffy shirt became soaked with rich, dark blood. The surgeon rushed to his side and declared Carmelo dead.

The spectators were shocked at Carmelo's deceit and also the ghastly way the bullet opened his chest. A woman fainted. A younger coachman began vomiting from the gruesome site. Salvatore Giorgianni rushed to attend to his friend Luigi's wound. The surgeon intervened and told Luigi, "Sit still and let me assess your wound." As Luigi sat, the doctor opened Luigi's vest, saw it was not a deep wound, and said, "It affected only the surface of the skin." He packed the wound with cotton and wrapped it in cloth.

Salvatore was silent while the surgeon worked, and then he finally said, "You're lucky, Luigi, my friend." However, Salvatore immediately realized the consequences of his friend's deed as he glanced at Carmelo Mandanici's corpse.

Concetto Capizzi sobbed as he realized any treatment attempt for his friend Carmelo was futile. "You killed him!" he shouted. "What am I supposed to say to his father?"

Luigi wanted to shout out that Carmelo cheated in the duel like he did with cards but remained silent out of respect for the dead. But Salvatore intervened, "Your friend had no honor. You saw that."

"It won't matter to his father!" Concetto shouted. "You're a dead man, Luigi Massaro. That's for sure."

"You must leave immediately," advised Felice Massaro, Luigi's father. "Unfortunately, I'm powerless to help you now." Felice knew about family and honor and didn't discredit his son for his actions. In a way, he was proud of him for defending the Massaro family name. However, there were definite consequences to his son's loyalty, which caused the current predicament and upset the elder Massaro.

Since the late morning after the duel, Luigi sat and discussed the problem of Carmelo's death with his father and with Salvatore Giorgianni by his side. He covered every detail of the event while Salvatore filled in any details Luigi overlooked and attested to Carmelo's many other dishonorable deeds.

After patiently listening to both young men, Felice's first comment was, "The Mandanici family have no honor and are a disgrace to the old nobility. Good God, I know, but they now yield too much influence with Emmanuel's Senate at the Palazzo Madama." Felice's face grimaced at the thought of the northern royals who moved from Milan to Rome as a sign of empowerment over the Pope and the Church. Felice respected the Holy Catholic Church and the Pope. Contrary to Giuseppe Garibaldi, he objected to holding Pope Pius IX in exile. Realizing his pondering of that subject lingered far too long and known for restraining his anger, he continued, "We must get you to a safe place immediately."

Felice Massaro was a good man. Shorter in stature and small-boned, some regarded him to be physically weak. However, what Felice Massaro lacked in his bodily appearance was made up many times more with his intelligence, level-headedness, and kindness. Felice Massaro was a well-respected Sicilian aristocrat, even among his enemies. Many tapped into his wisdom for direction. But now his only son was in a situation he felt powerless to fix, and being in that uncustomary position is what troubled him, though he would never show it. "I have an associate at the Italian Senate of Parliament. He might be able to help me with this situation." Felice glanced over to Salvatore Giorgianni and said, "Salvatore, you have always been a good friend to my son, and I appreciate your help here. You may leave now with my blessings. Will you respect my wishes for my son's best interest, young Salvatore?"

"Of course, sir. I will not seek his whereabouts nor try to contact Luigi, and I pray for his safe return." Salvatore turned to Luigi, who rose to stand beside his best friend. "God be with you always, my dear friend." Then, the two young men embraced, recalling their childhood friendship.

"I will think of you always, Salvatore. No matter where I find myself. I will always remember you. Thank you for everything." Luigi stepped back from their embrace and forced a smile; a weak one was all he could offer at that sentimental time.

Salvatore understood that the conversation was now between father and son. He bowed before Felice Massaro, then turned and left. Luigi watched him go. A tear formed in his eye as Luigi understood that he would now be alone in the world.

After his friend's departure, Luigi sat back down and listened carefully to the elder Massaro while he spoke, "You must trust no one from now on. Use caution with all those whom you encounter. That fool Garibaldi has also inadvertently resurrected those mafioso savages once more with this so-called constitutional monarchy he helped build. Soon, those scoundrels will again domineer with their brutal ways," Felice was now clearly upset. "They will never suppress the mafioso; it has existed for centuries and always will. All the conquerors of Sicily were never able to subdue them. Mandanici might resort to employing the mafia to capture you. These are the reasons why you must leave this country. America is the safest place for you to hide. It is a grave injustice, but it is the reality of the circumstances."

Felice continued to explain his plan to his son, telling him he would give him a considerable amount of lira to take on his journey until he could resolve the problem. After the Italian unification, Vittorio Emanuele II established the unified lira. Luigi would carry some on his body and stash some in hidden places or compartments. He could exchange it at a bank in the country of his choosing.

"You must not write, my son. There will be an investigation," Felice sadly stated, hiding his sentiments and realizing that he might never see his son again. "Then it is settled. It would be best if you left tonight. You must go to Naples first, where I have friends that I can trust. One of them will direct you from there. I will give you their names and addresses. My trusted companions will help protect you until you can find a way to travel to America to blend into that country of vulgarians. It is a different place with entirely dissimilar customs, but you must go there." Felice frowned at the realization of losing his only son, if only for a while. But the prospect of losing Luigi forever frightened him. "Tell no one you plan to go to America. That is a secret between you and me. Use every safety precaution, my son. You are a rational and resourceful young man. I pray God be with you and protect you on this voyage until you return to your family here in Sicily."

Felice arose from his chair, and Luigi stood as a sign of respect. "Our family will find you in America when the time has come. We will use the best detectives to track you down, unlike the Mandanici family, who hold onto every lira they have. They would never spend the money to find you there. You'll be safe in America," Felice frowned at the reality of what was happening. "Wait one minute, Son." Felice left the room.

Felice returned in about ten minutes, holding two varnished boxes, one large and the other small. He put them both on the hand-carved dining room table where they had been speaking. Felice opened the large box first. It displayed a model 1874 Chamelot-Delvigne. The pistol was an officer's model six-round double-action revolver used by the French Army. Felice received it from a close business associate, and Luigi knew how much his father treasured it. Inside the box on the opposite side was a brown hand-made, customed soft Italian leather shoulder holster and straps. There were also four boxes of 11mm cartridges below the holster.

"No, Father. I can't."

"Don't resist me, Luigi. It's for your safety. You'll never know when you might need it," he sighed. "Wear it always, or this one." Felice opened the second smaller box, which revealed a pair of Colt House Cloverleaf model four-round pistols chambered in .41 caliber. The pistols were more concealable, each with a one-and-a-half-inch barrel. Alongside were four boxes of .41 caliber rimfire ammunition and two small leather waist holsters. "I'll tell your mother and sister that you went to Milan for me on an errand. Eventually, they will learn the truth."

Luigi was tall and well-built but inherited the same traits of intelligence, level-headedness, and kindness from his father. "Relay my love to them both and tell them not to worry. I will be fine and see them both again someday." Luigi pondered the agony of not seeing his mother and younger sister and their anguish when they discovered the truth of his departure.

Felice walked to his son and embraced him. He sobbed as he did.

Luigi Massaro left his hometown in Sicily at the age of 20. He followed his father's instructions and went straight to Naples. Luigi crossed the Straight of Messina, a small section of the Mediterranean Sea, by boat. He then traveled by train from Reggio di Calabria to Naples, Italy. Once there, Luigi looked up one of his father's associates. He chose the first on the list given to him by his father, reasoning that he must be the most important because he was at the top of the list.

When Luigi arrived at the address in Naples, he noticed it was a much more beautifully styled small palace than his home in Messina. Count Ciro DeRosa's home was built during the House of Bourbon rule about one hundred years before. The architect of that period spared no expense for the royal who commissioned him. A short but wide marble courtyard led to the large wooden double doors of the house. Statues adorned both sides of the pathway. Between each figure were sculpted bushes. A high black, ornamental wrought iron gate enclosed the entire property. Two armed guards stood at the front gateway. Luigi handed the sealed-stamped introduction papers his father had prepared to one of the guards, who immediately took them. He watched as the guard walked briskly to the door, opened it, and closed it behind him. The other sentry faced Luigi but did not acknowledge him. In less than three minutes, the gate guard called from the door to the other sentry attending Luigi. He told him to open the gate, and the other guard complied. Then he motioned for Luigi to follow him.

A house servant led Luigi as he entered a large foyer with beautifully crafted marble floors and extremely high ceilings with the surrounding edges designed in hand-crafted golden floral shapes. He followed the servant to a large, extravagant room embellished with bronze statues, priceless paintings, and ornaments. The high ceiling painted with holy figures resembled a small Sistine Chapel like the one in the Vatican.

Count Ciro DeRosa, of the old nobility of the Kingdom of

the Two Sicilies, was sitting on a hand-carved wooden uphol-stered chair. He had a full head of styled grey hair and dressed lavishly in the formal attire of a noble. He arose when Luigi entered the room. As he did, Luigi bowed before the imposing count as a sign of respect. "Count DeRosa, I am Luigi Massaro, son of felic. . ."

"Rise, my son," the count said as he interrupted Luigi's greeting. "I read your introduction. How are your father and mother, Giuseppina?" The count was an old friend of his father's and the first name on the list he gave his son.

"Very well, sir. My father sends his regards. My mother was traveling with my younger sister when circumstances forced me to leave." Luigi waited. His voice was shaky as he con-tinued, "I couldn't see them before I quickly departed." Luigi mentioned nothing about going to America, nor did his father in his introduction. He was merely looking for protection until he could find a way there.

"It's been far too long since I've seen them. Bless them both when you see them again," Count DeRosa said with a con-cerned expression. "And you will see them again. I'll make sure of it." The count gestured with his two arms apart, "I've been so busy with all these new political issues. Please be seated." He motioned Luigi to sit in a chair next to his. Luigi waited for the count to sit before he did.

"Thank you, sir."

Count DeRosa seemed bewildered. "From what your father wrote, you did nothing wrong." He shook his head back and forth. "The Mandanicis were always hotheads. As I already said, I will certainly take care of this." Then, he commanded a servant to bring some wine and food.

"No, thank you, sir. I've already had my dinner. But, thank you again."

"Such a crisis," the count declared as he looked at Luigi. "I would normally ask you to stay here at my home, but it might be too dangerous. The Mandanicis know that your father and I are good friends, and they might send someone to look for you here. Excuse me one minute, my son." The count rose, crossed the large room, and whispered something to a servant. It was not a short conversation. Count DeRosa's and the servant's expressions made Luigi recognize they were speaking about something serious, as if the count had ordered something special. Luigi made a point of not staring at the two men talking. Using his peripheral vision, the young man pretended to admire an heirloom he removed from the table.

After finishing his conversation with the servant, the count returned and sat beside Luigi as the servant hurriedly left the room. Count DeRosa told Luigi, "At least let us take some time to enjoy a fine glass of Sicilian wine before you leave."

"Yes, sir, of course." Luigi's heart raced, and his palms grew clammy. The count's actions seemed to be prolonging his departure, a thought that flickered through his mind, adding to his unease.

A different servant approached them with a silver tray, balancing a crystal pitcher and two matching wine glasses. "I'm going to give you the address of one of the finest hotels in Naples where I want you to go." Count DeRosa's eyes were stern as he spoke, and they stared directly into Luigi's dark blue eyes. "Stay there this night at my expense. Mention my name to the host when you arrive at the hotel. I will have someone take care of everything."

"You're too kind, sir."

Count DeRosa waved his hand in a gesture that it was nothing. "Remember, in the morning, I will send one of my servants to the hotel to bring you to someone who will help relocate you."

After the count and Luigi finished their wine, Luigi rose and bowed. "Thank you, sir, for everything." Then Count DeRosa escorted him to the door.

"I will have my servant call a coach for you. Stay well, young man. May God be with you."

"Thank you again, sir, for all your help." Luigi, a very perceptive young man, had a funny feeling but didn't fully understand why.

Luigi Massaro followed Count DeRosa's instructions and traveled by horse-drawn carriage to the hotel's address. He noticed a gentleman's lounge off the main hall as he entered. Several card games were taking place amidst smoke clouds from cigars and pipes. Tempted to go directly to the gentlemen's lounge, he followed the count's instructions and introduced himself to the hotel manager first.

"Yes, sir. I received notice from Count DeRosa," the dignified host confirmed. "I have one of our finest rooms available for you." The manager reached behind him and took something from one of the slots of a wooden rack. "Here is your key and room number. Would you like someone to escort you to your room?"

"No, thank you, but would you please have my luggage brought up?" He pointed to his things, except the one smaller strapped leather case containing his money and pistols camouflaged with some personal things also in the carry bag. That valise would remain with him always.

"Absolutely, sir, and enjoy your stay."

Luigi assumed the count had sent a messenger ahead to announce his arrival. That was probably what that mysterious conversation was about. It made him feel much safer. On his return to the smoking room, he noticed several well-dressed women sitting at tables and admiring him in the large main parlor. One beautiful young woman drinking a cup of tea smiled at him. She was seated beside an older woman. Luigi removed his formal top hat and bowed to her. The older woman didn't look pleased. The young, attractive woman blushed and waited for the young man to introduce himself. However, at that moment, between the presence of a lovely young woman and gambling, Luigi opted for a card game.

The gentlemen's lounge was smoke-filled and musty-smelling as Luigi strolled around the room, observing the tables of

card games. He finally chose one in particular. The table attracted him because of the characters involved in a game of sette e
mezzo. Luigi could tell that one player was a professional and
the others weren't. Unlike the seasoned player, the others made
too many foolish mistakes while the skilled player hustled
them. The daring young Luigi loved a challenge and presented
himself to that table.

"I am Luigi Massaro, gentlemen. May I have permission
to join your game?" The players unanimously welcomed the
handsome, well-dressed young man. They assumed he was
nothing more than a naïve but wealthy prey and would lose all
his money within 15 minutes.

The slick player rose from his chair, "I am Biaggio Giglio. It
is a pleasure to meet you, young man," he said charmingly. He
extended his hand and said, "Welcome to our game."

Biaggio Giglio, a heavyset man, was short and sported a
thick, waxed, curled mustache spanning at least six inches from
edge to edge over his upper lip. With the pleasant demeanor
of a card shark, he was undoubtedly a predator of the others
at his table. Luigi observed that Biaggio wore outdated, baggy
clothes and sported a derby hat, which he hadn't checked in as
the others, including Luigi, did before entering the room.

"Thank you, my good sir," responded Luigi as he shook the
man's chubby hand.

Luigi didn't want to win at the beginning. That would give
away his ability to count cards, which was considered unethical
in card playing and other games of chance. He pretended to be
a novice at first. After a few games, he began winning. "Must
be beginner's luck," he chuckled, "I don't play cards too often."

Biaggio let out a jolly laugh, "Surely so it must be." Immediately, he knew the kid was an experienced player. Then, he
concluded that Luigi could count cards. As the game continued, one player bowed out, and then another. Biaggio realized
that the young man counted cards with skill and grace as if it
were a gift from God. He had never seen anything like it. He
was amazed. After a third remaining player bowed out, Biaggio

invited Luigi for a drink in the parlor where they could speak privately.

Biaggio and Luigi sat at a table in the main parlor. Each had a large café espresso and a large glass of sambuca. Luigi always kept an alert mind when working on a business arrangement. So, he didn't drink anything from the large glass of the thick, clear liqueur. From the looks of things, it seemed that Biaggio also adhered to the same policy. However, Biaggio didn't have any reservations about eating while discussing business. He had just finished a second plate of biscotti cookies from the center of the table, all by himself.

Biaggio patted his robust belly, delicately spread his handlebar mustache with two fingers of each hand, and said, "I noticed you count cards very well." He waited for Luigi's expression before he continued.

There was none from Luigi, as he knew very well that the heavyset man was watching him closely and sizing him up. "Do I?" Luigi asked, bearing a slight grin on his face. He pretended to have no idea about counting cards. For all he knew, Biaggio could be a policeman. Perhaps a crooked one–the worst type.

"Here's the thing, young man: We both know you count cards quite well. It's a gift—one that I don't possess." Biaggio continued to watch Luigi's expressions. "I have a different method for gambling, and I do quite well. I also have a lot of experience and know quite a few people in the games—many connections, if you know what I mean."

"I see," Luigi casually answered. He noticed while playing cards that Biaggio was very talented. He could distract his opponents using charm. He also possessed swift hands. Those chubby fingers could fly while he was distracting the other players. Being fair-skinned, Biaggio obviously spent a great deal of time indoors. Of course, Luigi didn't display any emotions while Biaggio was speaking.

"I think it would be a good idea if I take you under my wing, so to speak. You know, teach you to play even better. I'll let you in for a third of the take. What do you say?"

"I say no."

"Don't be so hasty, my young man. You're good, but you need to learn a lot. I'll go up to a 60-40 split. Working as partners, we would always be winners," Biaggio reasoned. "I've been to America, and I have several connections there. You might want to visit that backward country. There's a lot of money over there." Luigi just shook his shoulders and said nothing. Though pondering the statement about going to America rose his interest, he wanted to ensure this man had no connections with those looking for him. "A gentleman like you could pretend to go there for business," Biaggio paused and gazed directly into Luigi's eyes. "Are you a wanted man?"

"Why would you ask such a question?" answered Luigi. "I do it for money. I enjoy the 'sport' of gambling," he joked.

"So, then, do we have a deal?" The robust man asked in a crude Napolitano dialect.

"Maybe, Signor Giglio," replied Luigi.

"Maybe?" Biaggio shifted his heavy body on his chair and leaned closer to Luigi. "Let me tell you something. . ."

Luigi cut Biaggio off midsentence because he spoke so close to his face. Luigi raised one hand and waved Biaggio to move back. The garlic on Biaggio's breath was overpowering him. "Please."

Biaggio complied without knowing why Luigi wanted him to sit back from where he was. Then, as he wiggled his large rump to slide back away from him, he continued where Luigi cut him off. "My fine young man, many would beg for an opportunity as this."

"Let me think about it," Luigi began to rise from his seat.

"Wait!" Biaggio yielded. "Okay!" 'The kid's a sharp negotiator,' he thought, not wanting to lose such an opportunity. "50-50 it is."

"It's a deal," answered Luigi with a smile. He raised his glass of sambuca and toasted, "To success in America!"

"Much success!" agreed Biaggio.

The two men exchanged room numbers and agreed to leave

for America. Luigi planned to arrange accommodations on one of the steamers leaving from a port in Naples, not realizing then that Biaggio had other travel plans in mind. Luigi intended to use a fake name so no one would follow him.

As Luigi passed through the hotel's main parlor, he noticed the beautiful young lady from earlier. She was still seated at the same table but alone. Earlier, he was preoccupied with gambling, but now he didn't mind a little female companionship.

"Good evening, young lady. How is it that someone such as lovely as yourself is sitting here alone?"

"I'm waiting for my chaperone, good sir," she smiled. Her smile was lovely, revealing beautiful white teeth as her voluptuous lips parted. She appeared cultured and wore a well-designed, fashionable dark blue gown. The young lady didn't wear a hat but had her dark blond hair pulled back tightly and swirled into a circular bun. It made her delicate features look more appealing and enhanced her dark blue eyes. Luigi was immediately attracted to her.

"My name is Luigi Dissaro," he said, using a fake name. "It is a pleasure to meet you, signorina." He bowed as he spoke those words. He could have used his real name, assuming such an elegant young lady wouldn't abide by any wrongdoings whatsoever. But he chose caution, as his father had instructed.

"And I am Countess Aurora Curti. It's good to meet you, Signor Dissaro."

"May I escort you to my room for an evening cordial, my lady?"

"I'm sure my 'la dama di compagnia' wouldn't approve."

"Does she have to know?"

The young woman blushed. She turned her head to either side, looking for her 'protector,' then said in a low voice, "Well, maybe just for a moment." The handsome young gentleman seemed refined, and she felt safe in his presence. Luigi bent and extended his arm to escort the young lady to his room. Aurora rose and took his arm. She could feel the hardened muscles of Luigi's upper limb flex as she did. It excited her, and her impure thoughts made her fair skin blush again.

The young gentleman said, "Countess, please come this way." Luigi led Aurora up the elegant swirled stairway to the second floor, and she gracefully stepped beside him like a gazelle, giggling at his subtle jokes and innuendos.

They chatted in low voices as they walked along the second-floor corridor. The young woman tittered again at some of Luigi's humor. But he suddenly stopped as they turned a corner and gently pulled Aurora back before the turn. "Stay here," Luigi quietly told her.

Luigi peeked around the corner, exposing just one side of his face to see. There were two men outside his room. One was a tall, burly giant of a man, and the other was short and thin. The large man wore a wool tweed cap, high-laced black boots, and a cheap suit that fit tight against his muscular body. The short man wore a high-styled top hat, a black-tailed suit jacket, and grey slacks with thin black stripes. He looked like an undertaker.

Luigi turned and softly told Aurora to remain quiet. Then he turned back to the two intruders. The large man held a small pistol, stood straight, and watched the shorter one use a knife as he tried to unlock the door of Luigi's suite. Listening carefully, he heard the one who looked like an undertaker mouth the words in a whisper, "We'll wait inside and kill him as soon as he enters. Make sure you use the knife. The gun is too loud."

'The count,' Luigi thought; he intuitively realized that the count had turned him in. He remembered when Count Ciro DeRosa had that long talk with the servant. Indeed, it was to send him ahead, but not for the reason Luigi thought. The count arranged his room at this hotel. "He set me up," Luigi whispered to himself. Count DeRosa was, without a doubt, loyal to the Mandanici family and not his father. The facts all came together. And Luigi wasn't wearing any of the guns his father gave him. They were in his room, a foolish mistake.

At that instant, the young man realized he had to kill the two men. The thought of such a brutal act made him feel queasy, but there was no other choice. It was either he or them. If he only subdued them, they would track him down and kill him before he left the country. If not, the pair of murderers would know he went to America and could even follow him there. Blood rushed to Luigi's face as he pondered the situation. He had to do it; there was no other way.

Luigi forced himself to remain calm and remembered noticing a hotel workman's toolbox outside one of the vacant room doors when he passed along the corridor a few yards behind him. Obviously, workers retired for the evening and planned the repairs of that room for the following day, yielding an idea that forced the young man back to look for tools that could serve as weapons. Not having the time to browse longer, a large pipe wrench and a long, pointed chisel promptly met his needs. Luigi reasoned that he first had to overpower the big man, the stronger of the two men.

The young lady looked terrified. "Who are they?"

"Robbers, I think!" Luigi didn't tell her the truth. "Stand back close to the wall." He didn't want Aurora to see what he was about to do.

Luigi ran as fast as he could, wielding the pipe wrench over his head. The two men couldn't see or hear him running on the soft carpeting as they faced the door. Using all his strength, he swung the wrench like a railroad worker hammering a spike. The heavy tool crashed onto the top of the big man's head. His wool tweed cap stayed fixed, but blood spurted from the sides of the wound, soaking the hat and forcing it to slide down slowly. Dark, rich blood ran down the huge man's face and streamed from his ears and nostrils before his legs buckled, and he crashed to the floor. His body jiggled in a gory spasm, giving it the appearance of being shocked by the high voltage of an electrical lightning storm.

The short man turned with a bewildered look just before Luigi's hands plunged the pointed chisel into the man's neck, lifting him onto his tiptoes. Dancing like a ballerina to Luigi's movements, the stabbed man gurgled as blood sprayed from his mouth. He struggled to grasp Luigi's arm, staring into the eyes of the man who was killing him until he lost all strength. The small man's external anal sphincter muscle relaxed, releasing feces into his grey-striped trousers. His bulged eyes finally rolled back as his legs gave out, and he fell to the floor as Luigi held his grip on the tool that was now a weapon.

Luigi had a look of horror on his face. The odor of death surrounding him was atrocious. The big man's body remained trembling, twisting with contractions, and bounced like a beached baby whale. His mouth was foaming, trying to speak. While still holding the spike, Luigi stooped over him and stabbed him in the neck; the man's big, hairy hand grabbed him as he did. Luigi pulled the claw off him, watching the large man's chest expand, and then exhaled his last breath, but his eyes remained open in a ghoulish stare. Both men lay bleeding on the dark burgundy carpeting of the corridor. Luigi gasped at the sight. His face was pale.

Luigi's thoughts of not wanting to kill the murderers tormented him as he ran back to the countess. He flung his precious bag over his shoulder. Lifting her quickly, she was as light as a doll. Luigi carried her in his arms and ran back down the swirled stairway, leaving her on a seat at the far end of the parlor. "Will I see you again?" asked the young lady, Aurora.

"Another time," Luigi called back. He quickly returned to his suite before anyone could see the crime scene. Luigi dragged the bodies into the vacant room under repair, packed his luggage, and left it in the foyer of his suite. He could easily pick them up in a hurry once he found Biaggio. Luigi did everything he could to keep his composure. Luckily, the blood stains blended well enough into the color of the carpeting.

Biaggio lay on the bed in his room in a deep sleep, probably from all the drinks and food he consumed earlier. Luigi could hear him snoring through the closed door as he pounded it. Finally, Biaggio awakened. Luigi listened as Biaggio stirred on his bed. He knocked on his door again. The chubby man was half asleep while opening the door. Shirtless, his belly hung over his underwear as he stood there wiping his eyes. Luigi had never seen so much hair on a human body. Biaggio's hair covered his shoulders, chest, stomach, back, and legs. He stood and delicately spread apart his mustache before he spoke. "What's so important? It's still nighttime." His glazed, tired eyes looked around, "Isn't it?"

"We must leave now," insisted Luigi. He spoke in a low voice but almost in a panic.

"Why?" Biaggio inquired in a stupor of drowsiness.

"Because I just killed two men!"

"What?" he exclaimed, his voice filled with alarm. "You did what? How?" The heavyset man's panic was evident as he hurriedly retreated into his room.

"Come inside!" Biaggio shouted. Then he covered his mouth and repeated the command, this time softly between his spread-out chubby fingers.

Luigi noticed that Biaggio waddled when he walked. He briefly explained his situation with the Mandanici family to Biaggio and Count Ciro DeRosa's ties to them. He had to trust somebody, but Biaggio wasn't carefully listening in his terror. Biaggio became red-faced from nervousness. "Okay, we must go! Immediately! No time at all to waste." He was undoubtedly scared. He quickly packed his only suitcase and was ready.

"Don't you want to gargle and quickly wash first?" Luigi asked him.

"No time! We must leave at once!"

"No ships are sailing from Naples in the morning. I already checked. We must travel north by train to Genoa," declared Luigi.

"No!" Biaggio yelled. Then, he covered his mouth and continued quietly, "I have a connection with a trade ship line here in Naples. One leaves this morning. I already reserved a room onboard before I went to sleep," Biaggio corrected Luigi, then stood straight with a proud expression for being so proficient.

Luigi was impressed but said, "I don't want to cross the ocean as a steerage passenger. Can't we find a better ship with private rooms?” Then he thought, “Did you give them my name?”

“Do you want to get caught while we rest comfortably and wait, Lord Idiot,” Biaggio teased. “No, it’s not like that. I know the chief mate. We will have a good room with food served in a dining room.” Biaggio was huffing as he spoke. “I’ve traveled to many places on ships like this one, even to America. It’s fine. We can probably find some gambling aboard. You’ll like it,” Biaggio smiled. “They don’t need names; they need money. Lots of it. Do you have enough money?”

“I have some,” replied Luigi. He didn’t trust Biaggio with the amount of money he was carrying.

“Okay, let’s go. I’ll make a good deal.”

“You can pay me back your share of the travel fee when we get to America.”

“Okay,” agreed Biaggio.

Luigi was impressed with Biaggio's ability to negotiate. The room wasn’t first class, as Luigi had always used, but second class. Other respectable passengers were also aboard.

“Why waste money on first class when you can travel like this?”

Luigi knew that Biaggio had no social graces and spoke with a strong dialect. But now he realized that the man he would travel with rose from the peasant class. Biaggio was in no way even a distant part of the nobility.

“At least we won’t have to make a run for it anymore,” said Biaggio.

“You’re overweight and sport a fine panzuto (belly in Italian dialect). You couldn’t run fast enough if we had to.” Luigi laughed after using the same dialect as Biaggio.

“You win again!” Biaggio said to Luigi.

Luigi and Biaggio were in a card game with three other passengers and two crew members. They all sat in a dreary oil lamp-lit cabin, the ship at sea on a cloudy and colorless day. Luigi and Biaggio developed various signals to communicate with each other during games. They usually allowed each other to win but sometimes let the others have a small victory to make the game look legitimate.

The ship Luigi and Biaggio traveled on was a returning iron hull cargo and passenger vessel. The steamship company had taken on more passengers to fill the void. Among them were steerage passengers, as well, but confined to the lower deck. The steamship weighed almost three tons, with two masts serving as auxiliary sails. Four cylindrical boilers powered the twin engines that turned the single four-blade propeller. They were almost to New York and only hit rough waters twice, but each for only a short time. Overall, it was a good voyage in the 12 days they had traveled so far. The ship was due to arrive in New York Harbor in two days.

On the voyage, after Luigi had time to compose himself, he dwelled on murdering those two men. It ate at his conscience. He was not yet 21 and was forced to kill three men. Luigi argued various points, both defending himself and condemning himself. He concluded that life is cruel and a man must be strong. However, Luigi pondered those thoughts for the entire sea voyage, except when he was gambling. Then, his mind had to be precise when counting cards.

"That's it for me," The discouraged man said. He was the last to bow out after the three-hour game. Luigi and Biaggio were glad as they were tired from the stress. Together, the working team won eight dollars during that game, a substantial amount of money. They had collected seven times that amount during the entire trip, which made for a very lucrative voyage.

They got to know each other during their time together. Oddly, it was a budding friendship. Besides Biaggio's table manners and dress attire, Luigi's main complaint was Biaggio's snoring. He wished he had a separate room but couldn't because of the circumstances. As it was an Italian vessel, the food was good but only acceptable to Luigi.

The young aristocrat didn't mention the two men he had killed at the hotel, nor did he speak about the circumstances that forced him to leave Italy. Biaggio never questioned his new partner about either of them. Luigi talked about life in the aristocracy, keeping Biaggio in awe.

"That's a lifestyle I only dreamed about," Biaggio mused. "My life's story is short: my father left home when I was six, leaving me, my mother, and my sister on the streets. They died; I survived." Biaggio's eyes faced downward in a daze.

"Sorry." It was the only word Luigi could utter in his shock, never realizing how hard the working class had it. In his past privileged life, nobody ever mentioned the subject of the simple people. Hearing this man's brief accounting of his past made him feel guilty.

"No need," Biaggio glanced up. "I used my God-given skills and did well for myself. I never asked for people's sympathy, ever." Then, his merry persona resumed: "Besides, we'll make a fortune in America working together. Perhaps I can become part of the nobility?" He roared a jolly laugh.

As they were on a cargo ship, it docked on the Lower East Side of Manhattan, not the West Side as passenger liners usually did. The United States Government detained steerage passengers. They had to wait for smaller boats to take them to Castle Garden at the Battery at the lower tip of Manhattan Island, where the United States Government processed immigrants during that period. They allowed first and second-class passengers to disembark.

Luigi and Biaggio stood together at the Eastside Harbor after they left the ship. They observed the Brooklyn Bridge in the distance, which had been under construction since 1869. Luigi was well over six feet tall and appeared about eight inches taller than Biaggio.

"Let's take a carriage ride," Biaggio spoke first after quietly watching the marvel of the bridge construction for a few minutes. "I want to talk to you before we go to my friend's hotel."

"About what? You can speak to me here."

"I'm tired. I'd rather speak somewhere I can relax," Biaggio complained.

"The only walking you did was to get off the ship. How can you be tired? All you did on the ship was eat and drink." Luigi raised one hand and pointed it to his chest, "I'm the one who should be tired. I walked along the decks of the ship twice every day. Plus, I exercised."

"Good! You're tired. You need to sit back and relax."

"Hey there!" Biaggio called out to a horse-drawn carriage.

"Ware to?" The coachman asked after he stopped. The driver sounded like an Irishman to Luigi.

"We justa wanna rida aroun." Biaggio spoke with a harsh, broken English accent.

"Come aboard then. Am not opening the dar for yeh, ya Majesty."

Luigi opened the door for Biaggio, and they sat side by side on the back seat of the carriage. Biaggio began speaking as soon as the carriage took off. "As I already mentioned, my friend in Pittsburgh claims that there is better gambling money to be had there than here in New York." He watched Luigi's expression as he continued, "They have a lot of steel and coal workers there. The city's full of laborers waiting to lose their pay. It's an open city." He noted that Luigi's facial expression hadn't changed, so he continued. "We have to make some money here to set up a place of our own in Pittsburgh, or we can work with my friend. He offered us a partnership."

"Okay," Luigi finally responded, "How much do we need?"

"Well, if we can make at least every day what we made on the last day of our trip here, we'd be fine in less than a year. We could set up a fine place."

"That's well over 50 American dollars a week. A lot of money!" Luigi emphasized the word 'lot.'

"Yeah, but we can do it if we stick to certain rules."

"Wait here, driver. I want to get out for a minute and see this," commanded Luigi in near-perfect English. His grammar was good, but he had a slight accent. Luigi studied English while he was at university, but he also learned it as a personal interest and practiced it from books he found on the ship voyage. He was a perfectionist and planned to speak the language fluently. He didn't want to lower himself to the status of a simple immigrant.

"Why are we stopping?" asked Biaggio

"C'mon, follow me! Driver, wait here for us."

"Ya won't skip out on me now, will ya?"

"No! We'll be standing right here." The driver saw that Luigi was well dressed and realized they were good for the money, so he complied and pulled over.

Luigi and Biaggio gazed at New York Harbor from the far southern tip of Manhattan. The sky was bright and clear as they stood at the Battery near the immigrants' processing place. Luigi had read many facts about New York Harbor. He began to explain some of them to Biaggio. "See the island way out there?" Luigi pointed with his finger. "That island is called Bedloe's Island. There is an abandoned military post on it. About a year and a half ago, the Americans announced it would be the place for the Statue of Liberty."

"What's a statue for liberty?"

"No, no. The Statue of Liberty," Luigi corrected Biaggio. "It's a gift to America from France. They must reduce it to individual pieces and pack it into crates for shipping. It won't arrive here for at least five years. First, they have to build the pedestal or base," he didn't know if Biaggio could understand the meaning of that word, pedestal. Luigi stood in awe, "It will take a while for the whole project to complete." Luigi looked in the far distance to the left, which led to the ocean and his homeland from which he came. Behind him was where his future lay before him. After pondering those private thoughts, he glanced back at Biaggio. Surprisingly, his new friend looked interested in the bits of information he just told him.

"How do you know all these things?" Biaggio seemed impressed.

"I read, Biaggio, I read." Biaggio just shook his shoulders. Luigi couldn't then know that the island next to Bedloe Island, Fort Gibson, would someday be the future site of Ellis Island, a new processing place for immigrants. "Let's go back to the coach," said Luigi.

Biaggio instructed the driver to go to an address on Mulberry Street. As the coach started, he told Luigi, "So, let me get back to the rules."

"I thought you might have forgotten them by now."

"I don't forget nothing," replied Biaggio in his peasant dialect. "Now, first, we can't stay anywhere fancy because we have to fit in with the Italian workers. My friend's place is perfect. Second, we can't show that we have too much money or we could get robbed. Thir. . ." Biaggio cut himself off after glancing at Luigi and seeing how his partner's eyes rolled upward. "Hey, Luigi, this is serious stuff."

"Okay, what's number three?"

"You have to dress like me."

"Never!"

"Luigi, you can't dress like you do. It will draw too much attention. You look like a royal or something."

"Actually, I am the son of a baron."

"You are, for real?"

"I explained my situation to you before we left."

"Yeah, but I never realized that you really are the son of a baron," Biaggio chuckled as he presented a humorous woman's curtsy while still seated in the coach.

"A kind of deposed one at that," explained Luigi. "We'll compromise with these issues."

"What does that mean?"

Luigi ignored the question and said, "By the way, we're riding in a horse-drawn carriage with lousy springs bouncing around on cobblestone roads. Do you call this relaxing?"

Biaggio laughed, "America doesn't have streets paved in gold like all the immigrants think, does it?"

Chapter Three

Wellsville, Ohio 1890

The Town of Wellsville

Wellsville's location on the Ohio River made it a significant town. It was the point on the river closest to Lake Erie. When the road to Cleveland was completed, it put the town of Wellsville in position for trade, even with the Great Northwest. That forced the birth of riverboat travel, and Wellsville was in the heart of it.

Pip held tightly to Rollo's leash and carried an empty canvas haversack-styled bag slung over his shoulder. Both headed north along Main Street to do the errands for his mother. Pip had to buy bread for dinner and ice cream for dessert. He also had to pick up a small package ordered by his father, which was now waiting at the variety store on Main Street. He and Rollo crossed Main at the corner of Eighth, careful of the wagons and carriages that passed by and the horse manure they produced. They waited for a man who rode by them on horseback.

Several men took on the job of cleaning the dung from the streets in the town. They brought it by wagons to the farms on the hills outside of town for fertilizer. Some farmers picked up the horse waste from the streets for their fields. Several people dried it into bricks used for heating sources.

Street signs were installed at intersections a few years before, and now there was talk of a trolley car line coming through Wellsville. "Speculation," Pip's father said one evening at dinner. "I'll believe it when I see it." Talk about trollies had been taking place for years. It was first mentioned in 1882 when politicians and business magnates proposed building a streetcar from East Liverpool, a larger sister town, to Wellsville.

Pip's father was a good-looking man with dark hair and blue eyes and stood about six feet tall with broad shoulders and a good build. He attributed his physique to hard work on the railroad right after he finished high school. Douglas Nicholson worked his way from a railroad laborer to one of the managers at the Shop on 12th Street, as people in town called it. In 1890, the average common laborer's salary was about $1.25 daily. Pip's father was making almost $4 a day. He had come a long way. A good, God-fearing Christian man, Mr. Nicholson wanted to bring up his only child to be the same.

Pip and Rollo continued down Main Street. They stopped at the variety store on their way to the ice cream parlor. Pip tied Rollo to a canopy support pole at the variety store and went in to pick up his father's package.

"Well, how are you today, young man?" the owner said from behind the counter. "Come to pick up your father's new things?" The store smelled of dried sawdust.

"Yes, sir," replied Pip respectfully.

"Tell your dad I'll put it on his account. Okay?" The older man smiled as he reached down to hand the string-tied package to the short boy, "How's Rollo doing today?" he asked while glancing through one of the windows at the front of the store.

"He's fine, sir," Pip answered, noticing a few kids outside playing with his dog as he spoke.

"You have a nice day, young man!"

"Thank you, sir." The bell above the wood-framed screen door jingled as the young boy left the store.

"Hi, Pip," giggled Margaret Myers as she twirled one of the long braids of her hair that hung from both sides of her head. The young girl was Pip's classmate. She stood taller than the small boy and had to look down as she spoke to him. Margaret had been playing with Rollo along with some other younger kids. She had a crush on Pip and always played with Rollo to strike up a conversation with the bashful young boy.

"H-H-Hi, Margaret," Pip blushed in embarrassment at his stammer. "I gotta go," he quickly said to avoid another clumsy struggle with his speech. Pip untied Rollo. "Bye!" he shouted as he and Rollo trotted away from Margaret and headed to do his last errand.

Just a couple of months before, the town had committed to brick paving Main Street from Third Street all the way to Nicholson's Lane, far uptown, past where the railroad shop complex ended. As he and Rollo walked, Pip noticed workers setting up supplies and equipment and preparing for the well-anticipated construction.

W.C. Bunting's Confectionery was located on Main Street, not far from Third. Ice cream was available there at wholesale and retail. It was the only bakery in town with fresh fruit baskets displayed in the front. The ice cream parlor was upstairs on the second floor. It was a meeting place for younger kids in 1890. That meant the older bullies were possibly there, and panic struck little Pip as he dwelled on that thought. His mind formed images of horrible things they would do to him if they discovered him. Those musings lay tucked away in that vestibule of his mind where he stored all such fears and anxieties.

Pip tied Rollo to a street lamp and picked up a loaf of fresh-baked bread. Then, he cautiously proceeded to climb the stairs. He was on the lookout for any of the older bullies from school. Standing on the last step, he carefully surveyed every direction. It appeared safe, so he went in and ordered a quart of ice cream to go. Pip anxiously waited, vigilant of any kids arriving. The attendant packed the ice cream, pushing it tightly to the top of a quart-sized jar. Then he placed the jar into a small burlap bag containing chopped ice, which the young boy put in his sack with his father's package and the bread he had just bought. Pip paid the clerk and quickly left.

Pip descended the stairs two at a time, but before he could untie Rollo, a hand appeared out of nowhere and grabbed Pip's shoulder. The hand belonged to Filip Aries, one of the older boys who harassed Pip. Sean McElhenny, the youngest son of Robert McElhenny, the guard at the Third Street Station, walked to the little boy's side along with Matt Carlson and Erik Olsson. Sean was large for his age, taking after his father, but Erik was even bigger and as strong as a mule. Unfortunately, God didn't bless the lad with too much common sense, and he had the misfortune of being somewhat dense. Now surrounded by four older boys, Pip was terrified, and tears began to run down his cheeks. Rollo fiercely barked while standing tall on his hind legs, fighting to pull away the leash wrapped around the street lamp.

"What's ya got in the bag, Pip?" laughed Erik. "Something for me?" The older and much bigger boy picked up little Pip, turned him upside down, and shook him. The haversack bag slid off the little boy's shoulder, emptying everything on the sidewalk. The ice cream jar broke, and Pip's father's package landed beside it. The loaf of bread slid off the sidewalk and into the street. It landed on top of a pile of horse dung.

"P-P-Please let me go," Pip pleaded with his stutter while crying.

"N-N-No!" teased Erik, imitating Pip's stammer. "Oh! Look! All your stuff fell. Look! You broke your ice cream jar, too!" Erik remained holding Pip upside down as the small boy tried to break free while dangling.

Sean walked over to the bread, which now lay near the curb. A passing horse had kicked it. The big boy picked up the loaf by its center, dipped one end into the warm, soft horse dung, and stirred it around. When enough manure was on it, he walked toward Pip and yelled, "Hold him still, Erik!" Then he painted Pip's face with the dung while the little boy sobbed. "Oh! I-I-I forgot the ice cream," once again mimicking Pip's stutter. Sean loaded the other end of the loaf with vanilla ice cream from the broken jar and added some to his artwork on Pip's face. "Now you have vanilla and chocolate ice cream." All the boys were laughing hysterically. But before Sean could put the dung end of the loaf into Pip's mouth, Rollo broke free of his leash. The huge dog charged at Erik, knocking him over. Erik quickly released his grip on Pip as he fell and dropped the boy like a hot potato. Then Rollo slammed against Sean, who fell on his butt. Filip and Matt were horrified and took off running down Main Street as Rollo went as wild as a bronc.

When Pip landed on the street, his face was directly in front of his father's package. He grabbed the package and got to his feet. "R-R-Rollo!" Pip shouted in a stutter, "C-C-Cmon, boy!" The little boy began running fast toward Eight Street as if he had robbed a bank, with Rollo following, his leash trailing behind him. Pip was frantic that the bullies were after him. His fear wasn't warranted because Sean and Erik were already past the Third Street corner by then, running as fast as they could. And Filip and Matt, with their head start, had also disappeared.

Pip stopped to catch his breath at the corner near where he lived. "Thank God, Rollo!" The little boy was huffing, still trying to catch his breath. "Good job, Sir Rollo!" he waited for a few seconds, still gasping for air. "You saved the day! Your reward will be great!"

Pip had already prepared his excuse to his mother for dropping everything. 'He tripped.' Yes, that was the best he could think of under so much pressure. Pip couldn't tell her the truth. His mother would go to their parents, which would worsen everything. He had to lie. Pip would acknowledge his sins before God but couldn't tell the truth.

"Douglas! What happened?" Martha appeared to be in shock. Her son looked like a raccoon with those dark and white colors smeared around his face. She sniffed the boy. "Is that horse poop?"

Pip shuffled his feet, widening his big blue eyes as he looked up at his mother. "I tripped, Mom." His eyes glanced down at the floor. "I lost the ice cream and the bread." Then Pip remembered he was holding his father's package. "But I saved this!" He held up the string-tied package.

"Douglas! Are you telling me that you tripped on horse dung

and ice cream at the same time?"

Pip thought quickly. "No. I tripped, and the ice cream broke and spattered on my face."

"Did those bullies do this? Douglas, tell me the truth."

"N-N-No! I tripped!" The little boy began crying. His mind created all sorts of tortures the big kids would do to him, the kind of things they always threatened to do if he ever told anyone.

Martha didn't believe her son but hated to see him so upset. "Okay, Honey, let's get you washed up in the tub. I'll get some clean clothes for you."

"You're not going to go to anyone's parents, are you?"

"No, Douglas, I'm not. We'll talk about this another time." Martha went to fetch clean clothes for her boy from the clothesline. After Pip bathed and changed his clothes, Martha advised him to lie down and rest. It broke her heart that her son was so small and couldn't defend himself. Martha knew those brats did this to her son, but she didn't want to worsen things. She would have to discuss this with her husband later that evening. Pip obeyed his mother and went upstairs with Rollo to get some rest. They both needed it.

"This is your reward for a noble deed, Sir Rollo." Pip handed the dog three butter cookies in a row that he sneaked from the kitchen. Then the two lay on the bed, Pip's arm holding his best friend.

After a long rest, Rollo's ears straightened. Pip knew that was always a sign that his friend heard something. Pip knew what it was. It was either a train or a riverboat. He ran down the stairs, opened the front door, and looked left far down to the river's north bend. He could see smoke plumes in the far distance over the hills. It was a steam locomotive traveling from the direction of Pittsburgh. From experience, Pip could tell it was less than 20 minutes away. He and Rollo had plenty of time to get to the Third Street Station. A passenger train was coming.

"Mom! Can I go back out now, please? I rested a lot." Only a train or a riverboat could get Pip out of the house that day after such a traumatic experience.

"Okay, Honey. But please be careful."

Chapter Four

New York City 1879 to Wellsville, Ohio 1890

The Way To Wellsville

Christopher Columbus, an Italian navigator sailing under the Spanish flag, was the first to charter a course to the New World from Europe. Giovanni Caboto (John Cabot) was an Italian navigator who believed in a shorter trade route to the East, like Columbus. He was sponsored by King Henry VII and sailed under the English Flag. Leaving Bristol, England, in 1497, he was the first to charter a course to the northern coast of North America. Juan Rodríguez Cabrillo, an Iberian maritime explorer, navigated the West Coast of North America under the Spanish flag. He explored what would later become California. The North and South American continents were named after the Italian explorer Amerigo Vespucci. He was the first to recognize North and South America as distinct continents, which was previously unknown. Other explorers followed, including Juan Ponce de León, Henry Hudson, and others.

"Good to see you again, Cumba," shouted Biaggio Giglio, his merry laugh boisterous, speaking his harsh dialect. 'Cumba' was a dialect for 'Compare,' a word for someone such as a best man at a friend's wedding, a friend who acts as a godfather at the Baptism of a friend's child, or other religious events. Sometimes, the term was used casually for a good friend or as a sign of respect.

"Maronna mia!" Giuseppe Pellettieri shouted back, "I haven't seen you since you baptized my son, Nunzio. My God, that was 15 years ago." He spoke in a heavy Napolitano dialect as he rushed to hug Biaggio. They embraced and kissed each other on both cheeks in the Italian tradition. "Annunziata, veni´ca!" Giuseppe shouted for his wife to come.

A short, slightly overweight woman in her early forties ran to Biaggio. "Biaggio! It's been too long!" Annunziata still possessed the face of an angel but now appeared tired. She also spoke in the same Italian dialect as her husband. She hugged Biaggio, and they kissed each other on both cheeks.

"You're still as beautiful as last I saw you," proclaimed Biaggio.

Annunziata put one hand on Biaggio's belly and said, "Hey, when are you having the baby?" Then she laughed and said, "It looks like you never miss a meal. I'm going to make you something nice for dinner."

"Oh, you don't have to go through the trouble."

"Hey, Biaggio, it's no trouble. I'm your cumma!" Annunziata glanced at Luigi and eyed him up and down. "Hey, is this good-looking young man your son?" Luigi's eyes rolled back, but he didn't say anything.

Biaggio straightened up, his jovial face became distinguished, and made the formal introduction, "Giuseppe and Annunziata Pellettieri, this fine young man is my second cousin. He's from Messina." Biaggio stood proud. "My nephew, Luigi, came to America to conduct some prestigious business for his family." Biaggio held up his arm and pointed his forefinger straight to symbolize the business's importance.

Luigi removed his top hat, bowed before them, and said in perfect Italian, not a dialect, "It's very nice to meet you, il signore e la signora, impressing the Pellettieris.'

"Such a gentleman!" exclaimed Annunziata. Giuseppe said nothing. He just examined the young man from head to toe. His young daughter immediately came to his mind, and the possibility of this tall and handsome young man sleeping under the same roof as her. However, after Annunziata kissed Luigi's two cheeks, Giuseppe came forth and did the same.

"He and I plan to stay in your hotel for a while. If you have a room available, that is," Biaggio said but in an asking manner.

"Oh, well, I think. . ." Giuseppe began to dissuade such an idea, but his wife cut him off.

"Of course, we have room," Annunziata stated. "We have plenty of rooms, especially for you two. Biaggio, you're like family." She glared back at her husband, his face reddening from suppressing anger.

"Thank you, my dear," replied Biaggio. Luigi said nothing but tipped his hat to the woman and bowed slightly, smiling in appreciation.

"Giuditta, Nunzio, veni´ca!" Annunziata yelled loudly for her daughter and son to come to her. They were both working in a back room.

Nunzio arrived first. He was a 15-year-old shorter boy with a well-developed upper body, probably from working and lifting heavy objects. "Si, Momma?"

"Biaggio, this is my dear son, Nunzio," Annunziata said as she introduced her son. "And this is your padrino, Biaggio Giglio," she said to Nunzio.

Nunzio smiled and ran to hug the godfather he had never met. "So good to meet you, Padrino," Nunzio uttered respectfully and sentimentally.

"It is a joyous occasion to finally meet you, my son," Biaggio pronounced as he handed the young man a five-dollar bill.

"No, No!!" Giuseppe and Annunziata screamed almost simultaneously. "It's too much money."

Luigi smiled slightly at the 'padrino' as he generously handed the young man the money. 'The cheapskate is buying his way to stay at this hellhole of a hotel. What a farfallone! (phoney) And I'll have to pay half,' he thought as he watched Biaggio's performance.

"I insist!" declared Biaggi. He gently spread his handlebar mustache with his fingers and stood proud. "He's my only godson. I should have come here sooner."

"Thank you so much, Padrino," Nunzio stood teary-eyed as he spoke.

"Grazie, Cumba," said Giuseppe. "I'll see that he spends it wisely." Annunziata was crying. The family was poor with a struggling business, and this was a fortune for the boy.

A beautiful young woman appeared as Luigi stood struggling to restrain himself from Biaggio's stage act. She seemed to come out of nowhere. Short and thin with black hair contrasting her fair skin, olive-green-colored eyes adorned the delicate features of the young woman's face. She was magnificent, and Luigi couldn't take his eyes away from her. He had never before seen a lovelier woman.

"Oh! This is my daughter, Giuditta," shouted Annunziata. "Giuditta, come here and meet these fine people."

Giuditta walked gracefully toward the small group. She quickly glanced into Luigi's eyes as she passed him. The beautiful young woman wore a long black dress with a white apron and black laced shoes with an inch and a half heel. Her father's eyes stayed pasted to Luigi, and he continually watched the young man's expressions. 'He's attracted to her,' he thought as he could sense the aura between them.

Annunziata introduced her daughter to Biaggio first. He kissed her cheeks and handed her three dollars. It was a considerable amount but less than what he gave her brother. Biaggio had to since she wasn't his goddaughter. It would have been disrespectful to Nunzio if he had given her the same amount.

Giuseppe and Annunziata began the same commotion until Biaggio raised his hand to silence them. "It's my sincerest pleasure!"

"Thank you, Zio!" Giuditta's face beamed, and her full lips parted, revealing the flawless white teeth of her heavenly smile. Luigi would have given her more money to relish her resplendent expression a little longer. He could only imagine living just another second of that loveliness.

Annunziata then introduced Giuditta to Luigi. She stood on her tiptoes and looked straight into Luigi's eyes. That one second seemed like a lifetime to the young man. Her body scent aroused Luigi. Then, she kissed each of his cheeks. He could feel the fullness of her lips on his face, which aroused him. Luigi returned the kiss in the same manner. Giuseppe knew it was a customary practice, but he noticed that Giuditta's eyes shined into Luigi's dark blue eyes for a few seconds after they kissed. That made Giuseppe's face turn red again.

The Pellettieri Hotel, located on Mulberry Street, was within the Five Points section of the Lower East Side. The neighborhood was part of Little Italy, an overpopulated, crime-ridden area. Little Italy began to take shape when the first wave of Italian immigrants arrived in the neighborhood of Five Points in the 1850s. Many reasons encouraged poorer Italians in the regions of southern Italy and Sicily to leave, at least temporarily. However, it began to intensify after the newly unified government in 1861. Disease caused by lack of medical care and a dirty, garbage-filled environment was rampant in Little Italy and surrounding neighborhoods. The tenement buildings were dirty fire hazards, with unrestrained lawlessness. Unattended fire outbreaks were a frequent occurrence. Luigi had to close his nose to the odor of horse dung and garbage when he traveled through the area's streets in a horse-drawn carriage to the Pellettieri Hotel. During the slow ride, Luigi told Biaggio he didn't think he could live there. Biaggio told him he would get used to it, but Luigi didn't know how he would survive in a slum like this. The police that patrolled that area were corrupt and composed of original Americans and Irishmen. Gangs of younger and older Americans, Irishmen, Jews, and other ethnicities, including Italians, looted the section. They caused havoc while robbing things from stores and the many various vendor carts parked along the streets. Some of them paid the police a percentage of what they stole. Others offered them sexual favors from young ladies in league with them.

Born in Laurenzana, Italy, Guiditta Pellettieri was taken to this neighborhood of New York City by her parents as a child. It was the only life she ever knew. Luigi Massaro felt a remorseful sentiment for her. He had grown up in a beautiful home and lived a life of luxury, which contrasted sharply with the existence this young woman and her family had known.

Luigi and Biaggio stayed in separate rooms at the Pellettieri Hotel to maintain their facade that they didn't know each other for the sake of card games. Being spared Biaggio's snoring was one of the two things Luigi favored about staying in the hotel: that and the presence of Guiditta. Giuseppe didn't allow gambling or prostitution at his establishment. Both vices were illegal in most cities. However, it was customary for such establishments to pay the police to permit those corruptions. The consensus was that holding back those manly needs was somewhat merciless, and the absence of those vices would lead to excessive fighting and violence. However, Giuseppe obeyed the law based on his moral convictions. That worked out well for the team of Biaggio and Luigi. Living apart from places gamblers frequented was perfect. However, they still went to a back room to hide whenever they interacted or had private discussions. They also ate their meals there for the same reason. Giuseppe prioritized serving excellent original Italian food, bread, pastries, and other sweets. They were also known in the area for making homemade beer, which Giuseppe learned in Italy. Biaggio felt like he was in heaven.

"Good day we had, my dear friend," said Luigi, puffing on a cigar while sitting at a table in a back room of the Pellettieri Hotel. He picked up the habit in New York over the last couple of years they had been there. The only exception was when the handsome young man was luring a woman. He knew from experience that most ladies of a certain caliber didn't like the smell. Luigi and Biaggio sat in the special corner that Giuseppe had set aside especially for them. It was their private place. That's where they ate and conversed. A small framed tintype photo of them hung on the wall there.

After arriving in New York, they noticed a small Photography studio as they strolled along upper Mulberry Street. Biaggio walked to the window. "Luigi!" Biaggio called his friend. "Hey, Cumba! Come here. Let's get a picture of us together!"

Luigi shrugged. "What for?"

"C'mon! Hey, you won't be young and beautiful forever," He laughed. "Look at me!" Biaggio spread apart his arms and stood posing. So, they went into the studio and had their picture taken. Luigi looked dignified as he stood erect, his arm bent with his hand inside his partially unbuttoned suit jacket. Biaggio had a cheerful expression, his head positioned back, accentuating his wide waxed mustache. And he appeared to be holding in his sizeable belly.

Luigi was now almost 23 years old. Because he sat so often gambling, he exercised daily to maintain his build and appearance. He and Biaggio fostered a good friendship during their time together. Due to the amount of money they made, they stayed in New York much longer than they had planned.

"Yes, indeed," agreed Biaggio, addressing Luigi's statement about having such a good day while Luigi puffed on his cigar and sat at a table in the back room of the Pellettieri Hotel. He spread apart his wide mustache with his fingers. "The last couple of years have been good to us." Surprisingly, Biaggio remained the same heavyset weight when they arrived in America. Even though he sat long, he didn't gain a pound. He attributed it to the exercise Fiona provided him in her loving arms.

Biaggio, already 43 years old, had met Fiona Kelly the year before, and a relationship quickly developed. They recently decided to marry. He felt it was about time. His fiancé was a short, plump, red-headed Irishwoman. She had fair skin and freckles. The marriage between an Italian and an Irishwoman would typically be frowned upon. However, Fiona had been estranged from her parents since they found her in bed years before with a young Jewish man. Fiona worked in a bar nearby that Biaggio frequented. His only regret was that she didn't know how to prepare Italian food. So, they made a deal: Annunziata would teach her to cook, and he would learn to speak English better than the 'muck' that Fiona called the way he spoke.

Once established in New York City with Biaggio's acquaintances, the team of Luigi and Biaggio had begun putting their chosen professions to work. Cheating at cards by various methods combined with Luigi's skill at counting cards, they began making much more money than they imagined right from the start. Of course, Biaggio never referred to it as cheating. Time and time again, he explained to Luigi, "My dear friend, what we do is mystifying. People pay to see such things by magicians at carnivals and side shows. It's merely our fee for displaying our talents—our gifts from God above!" To that, Luigi would not answer but merely roll back his eyes. Biaggio also taught Luigi the game of dice during their time together. They avoided the more glamorous areas of Manhattan where wealthier men gambled. There, they would be beacons to attract the wrath of more cultured Americans. Those established men would use their connections to eradicate Luigi and Biaggio immediately. The poorer neighborhood was a perfect place to blend in with local gambling. Biaggio considered it easy pickings from local workers who couldn't wait to take a chance to win money in Italian card games, primarily sette e mezzo or scopa.

Since the violent encounter at the hotel in Naples, Luigi began to practice with the revolvers his father presented to him as a parting gift. He was an excellent shooter on his university team, which is how he quickly targeted Carmelo Mandanici's chest dead center from one knee. Luigi always reflected on that duel in Messina that caused his current predicament. He also often thought about the problems it caused his family. And memories of his best friend, Salvatore Giorgianni, lingered in his mind. But now, he wanted to reacquaint himself with the specific model weapons his father gave him. Luigi would practice aiming in his hotel room. Occasionally, he would travel down to an abandoned pier and shoot a few rounds in the open area. Luigi ensured he was ready if anything like what occurred in Naples happened again.

Luigi's English improved during his time in America, and

one had to listen very hard to detect an accent. He sought companionship in the arms of several young women. When he did, Luigi traveled to better neighborhoods further uptown late at night for the intimacy of a lover. However, none were as appealing as young Giuditta. Luigi lusted her creamy white flesh and her gorgeous, petite but shapely figure. He had to have her, but he knew she was off-limits. Luigi spoke to Giuditta often over the last two years and knew she was attracted to him. But she was too young at the time. Yet, his passion for her led him. Little by little, that lust drew him like a spider to the web. Being in her company was like being in paradise, even in such a horrible neighborhood. However, it was only recently that they developed a stronger relationship. It began one day with a touch when her parents weren't around. The couple started to play gently with each other's hands at times. Once, with their fingers interlocked, Luigi kissed Giuditta's neck. It pleasured her immensely, but when Luigi tried to go further, Giuditta stopped him. But on the last occasion when they were alone, Luigi kissed Giuditta full on her lips. Then he slid the upper part of her dress down and revealed Giuditta's naked breasts. They were smooth and ivory-colored, firm with protruding nipples. They gazed into each other's eyes. Luigi kissed the side of her neck, and his tongue slid downward and licked the areola of one of her firm breasts. It drew a passion within the young woman that she had never experienced. Giuditta never knew a feeling like that existed. She lost control, grabbed Luigi's wrist, looked deep into his eyes, and stared at him. And finally, she pleaded, "Take me!" her voice was husky and seductive.

Luigi immediately stepped back to think quickly. His mind fought his bodily desires as he did. Luigi was soon leaving for Pittsburgh with Biaggio. At that moment, he knew he had to have Giuditta and could no longer wait. His lust won over any logic. But he knew he could not deflower this young woman without marrying her. Lifting her gently, he placed her on a table, tenderly raising her dress and removing her undergarments. His hands felt the soft flesh of Giuditta's loins, slowly moving them down to her lower abdomen and cleft of her womanhood. She screamed in ecstasy and repeated those words that Luigi couldn't resist, "Take me!" her voice deep and sensual. He lifted her legs close to him and penetrated the passion within her. Giuditta cried out, releasing joys and a satisfaction she never knew existed.

Afterward, as Luigi held Giuditta close in his arms, he told her, "You'll have to move with me to Pittsburgh when I leave." Luigi looked at Giuditta, waiting for a response. "Biaggio and Fiona are relocating there also, you know."

"Yes, I know," Giuditta replied. "I will come with you, but only as your wife, not before. You know I love you."

"Of course." Then, Luigi tightly held young Giuditta as the couple kissed passionately and repeated their lovemaking. Finally, the couple composed themselves.

Giuditta's majestic green eyes stared into those of Luigi's piercing dark blue. "I can't control myself when I'm with you. Marry me and take me away from this horrible place."

"I'll take you to paradise, my love," he whispered while caressing and kissing her naked body.

The days went by quickly as the couple waited to get married. Then, one day, Giuditta came running to Luigi. She was crying. "Amore mio!" she was almost hysterical. "I asked my father about us getting married an. . ."

"Wait! Why did you do that?" interrupting her, he looked at Giuditta bewildered. "I'm a man of honor. It is my place to ask your father for your hand in marriage!"

"I asked him because I couldn't wait to marry you."

"It's alright, but why did he say no? What happened?" Luigi comforted her in his arms.

"My father said I must marry Alfonso Delgetti," Giuditta waited until she composed herself, "He's a horrible man! He pinches my behind when my parents aren't looking," she hesitated, "and he fondles my breasts too," she bowed her head in embarrassment. "He whispers obscenities about what he's going to do to me, but I never knew I had to marry him! He's disgusting!"

"Is he that short, little old man who visits your father? The one who owns the importing company?"

"Yes," Giuditta sobbed. Papa arranged our marriage when I was 11 years old. I didn't know." She looked at Luigi appealingly with her stunning green eyes as if passionately urging his intervention.

"My God! He's much older than your father!"

"I know!" Giuditta began crying.

"Listen to me, my love. You and I will get married." It was painful for Luigi to see Giuditta so upset. "We'll do it right before we leave for Pittsburgh in about a week."

"Oh, Luigi!" her tearing eyes stopped crying, and she rested her head against his chest.

Luigi explained to Biaggio the entire story of what happened between Giuditta and her father. "Now Giuseppe will hate me for helping you take his daughter," Biaggio said with a miserable expression. "I never knew he promised his daughter to that old guy, did you?"

"No, never!" replied Luigi. "Annunziata might disagree with that arrangement because she likes me. I'm certain she does." Luigi was confident.

"It doesn't matter. Giuseppe made a promise to this man on his sacred honor." Biaggio looked upset. "Besides, you know that the man of the family rules over these types of decisions. It's the Italian way. It doesn't matter what Annunziata feels or says."

"We have to leave for Pittsburgh now; we already made more money than we planned."

"Yeah, it's time to leave," agreed Biaggio.

Late that same night, both men sneaked out of the Pellettieri Hotel. Biaggio was humiliated and could no longer face his cumba. They left money for the Pellettieris in the hotel kitchen. Annunziata would see it first thing in the morning. Then, Luigi and Biaggio checked into a different hotel for a few days before they left.

Luigi and his friend, Biaggio, planned a double wedding before they left. They went to Saint Patrick's Cathedral on Mulberry Street to arrange it. However, they learned that Italians were shunned there by the Irish. They made Italians observe mass and other sacraments in the Cathedral of Saint Patrick's basement, including marriage. This rule stemmed from Giuseppe Garibaldi, the Italian general. His hatred of the pope in Rome and the role he played helped create the unification of Italy. That caused the end of the Papal State in 1870 and put the pope in 'temporal limbo.' The Irish members showed strict loyalty to the Catholic Church and shunned all Italians for that reason. Luigi found that ironic. His family suffered shame because of Garibaldi. They hated him. And now he was treated this way because of him? It didn't make sense. However, he put aside his feelings and used his keen intuition to size up this priest who proclaimed those facts to him. He sensed that the Irish clergyman liked money as most did, so Luigi paid him handsomely to use the regular church upstairs for their marriages privately. The son of a baron would not be married in the basement of a cathedral.

Luigi and Biaggio gave their women enough money to purchase beautiful gowns for the occasion. Luigi also recommended that Biaggio buy himself a proper suit as well, which he painfully obeyed. Biaggio and Luigi stood as witnesses for each other on the ceremony day, and Giuditta and Fiona did the same. It was a beautiful ceremony. Luigi forewarned the priest to see that it was an extended High Mass with altar boys and another priest serving as an assistant. The clergyman was a little intimidated by the young man and willingly complied. Luigi eyeballed Father O'Brien sternly during the High Mass to make sure the dear priest didn't do a rush job.

"Let's celebrate!" Biaggio exclaimed after the ceremony.

The two newly married husbands took their wives uptown to a fine restaurant. In exquisite English, Luigi asked the maître de to prepare a special dinner for them with a bottle of 1860 Dom Perignon champagne. Fiona considered herself a bubbly character and liked her liquor, but she had never had anything as expensive. She was strictly a rye whiskey girl. Fiona was eager to try the good stuff, 'the bubbly,' just like her personality. Giuditta, on the other hand, had never had any alcohol, even though she helped make her family's beer at the restaurant. Now that she was married, she was eager to try some. After all, Luigi was going to take advantage of her erotically anyway. She smiled at the thought.

"To us!" Biaggio declared.

"Cento anni!" toasted Luigi. 'A hundred years!'

The newly married couple happily celebrated throughout the afternoon. All feasted on the fine food and luscious desserts and drank to their heart's desire. Fiona was used to drinking, but Giuditta got a little tipsy.

During the middle of the night after the wedding, Giuditta packed her clothes and sentimental things. She couldn't sleep anyway and had already said goodbye to her parents before retiring to her room as usual. They had no idea she was leaving them. Quietly, in the wee hours of the late spring morning, Giuditta departed the Pellettieri Hotel. As she walked to where Luigi told her to meet him, she looked back at the sign in front of the hotel she had known most of her life, then turned away.

Inside the closed carriage, Luigi whispered, "You are now Giulia." He used the Italian version of her name, not the dialect. "You are my lady, and from now on, I will call you Giulia." The two newly married couples traveled north on Mulberry Street in the carriage. Giulia smiled in her husband's arms as she left the only neighborhood she had ever known.

"Let's have one more go at either sette e mezzo or scopa!" Biaggio said to the others, exhausted from the prior day's excitement.

"I don't think so," said Luigi, "we're all tired, and we have to get going."

"C'mon, it will only take 15 minutes at best! We have enough time. Let's do it for good luck!"

"Okay! If you insist, Cumba," Luigi kidded his dear friend by using Biaggio's crude dialect.

"Good! I feel lucky!" Biaggio proclaimed while Fiona snuggled closer to her 'teddy bear,' the nickname she called her new husband.

The carriage man pulled over and waited for them as instructed. Giulia was too tired, and she remained in the comfort of her seat. Fiona still had a spark of life left in her, and she accompanied her husband into the bar. Luigi took his one personal leather bag and slung it over his shoulder. It contained most of their accumulated winnings and the money his father gave him in a hidden compartment. It was a precious bag. Luigi was careful carrying so much money, never telling anyone about it, and adhered to the premise that it was always better to be frugal with his money. His larger revolver, sheathed in the leather shoulder holster on his left side underneath his tailed jacket, was ready just in case anyone tried to rob him.

Biaggio asked to sit down at a table where a game of scopa was in play. There were three others at the table. Maintaining his typical jovial manner, Biaggio kept a big smile on his face. Fiona sat on a chair beside Biaggio, slightly back from the table but close enough to lean forward and keep her arm around her 'teddy bear.' Biaggio turned and whispered in her ear, "One game, and we leave." He smiled at her and turned back around to face the game. Luigi stood in the corner by the front door, watching the game.

The bar's front door crashed open, and a tall, husky Irishman tripped inside. The hard swing of the door almost knocked Luigi over. The drunken man staggered toward the table where Biaggio was sitting. "So there ya are, ya guinea bastard!" he spoke in a thick Irish brogue directly to a Sicilian laborer seated beside Biaggio.

"Go away, you drunk Mc," the man yelled back in a Sicilian accent. "You lost your money fair and square." The Irishman lost all his wages to the Sicilian earlier and had been drinking himself into a stupor ever since.

The tall, stocky Irishman, swaying back and forth as he stood, shouted, "You'll see ya guinea scum. I'll kill the lot of yeh!" Then he opened his coat, reached in, and removed a Colt Thunderer six-shot revolver. His hand wobbled as he pointed the big gun. The drunken man began to fire the double-action pistol. Large .41 caliber bullets flew carelessly in the direction of the Sicilian man. Those sitting at the table never expected it and didn't have time to duck. Luigi had to slide back the strap of his carry bag to reach his gun under his jacket. It took too long. Three bullets hit the wall, but another man at the table got hit in the shoulder. Then, a bullet hit Biaggio in the front of his neck, and blood squirted in a straight line. Luigi shot the Irishman three times in the center of his chest. The drunken man managed to get one round off before he swaggered and fell to the ground. That bullet hit Fiona in the center of her two eyes. Fiona's body leaned against Biaggio's, and her head lay back. Her eyes rolled backward and remained in a gaze. She appeared as if she was thinking. The Sicilian laborer sat unharmed.

Luigi ran to his friend. He kneeled by his side, put his hands on Biaggio's neck, and tried to stop the blood, angry at himself for not pulling his revolver fast enough. Luigi yelled out, "Someone go and get a doctor!" He turned back to Biaggio, whose eyes turned toward Luigi. Biaggio was struggling to say something. "Be calm, my friend, my dear, dearest friend." Luigi paused, his voice shaky, as he continued, "You've been like a father to me." Luigi nervously shouted again for a surgeon as tears ran down his face. Biaggio grabbed Luigi's arm and weakly pulled him near to him. Luigi leaned closer and put his ear next to his friend's mouth. Biaggio finally managed to whisper to Luigi, "Goodbye, my son," he grappled with speaking the words, "It was wonderful." Biaggio attempted to smile before he closed his eyes.

Luigi arranged a double funeral at the same church where they married. Fiona's and Biaggio's bodies rested in coffins at the foot of the altar. Biaggio wore the new suit that he had bought for his wedding. The thick waxed mustache over his upper lip looked different. Luigi walked to his friend and knelt before the coffin. He spread apart his friend's mustache with two fingers of each of his hands to fix it. Then he rose and returned to sit next to his wife, Giulia. Fiona wore her new wedding dress. Makeup covered her freckles, and rouge made her cheeks look rosy red. There was a slight food stain on Biaggio's suit, which happened when both couples celebrated their wedding feast just two days before. The memory brought a tear to Luigi's eye. Giulia sat speechless by Luigi's side during the service. She hadn't yet recovered from the shock of the deaths. She couldn't maintain a conversation and continually cried.

Luigi paid the priest handsomely to secretly bury the couple in side-by-side plots at Saint Patrick's Cemetery in Little Italy. The priest's rationale was that Fiona was Irish, and he gladly took the money.

It took months before Giulia was able to travel. Luigi took a suite at the Fifth Avenue Hotel for Giulia to recover. When she felt able to travel, they began their journey to Pittsburgh. First, they had to go to Philadelphia by boat and train. There, they would be able to go straight to Pittsburgh by train.

Giulia was never outside Little Italy in New York City, so she clung tightly to Luigi while experiencing things she had never seen. When the train rode over the infamous architectural wonder of Horseshoe Curve, she thought it was something from another planet. Giulia leaned closer to the passenger car window like a little girl. She smiled and laughed at the marvel that the Pennsylvania Railroad completed in 1854.

A tall, smiling black man served them their dinner. Giulia had never before seen a black man in Little Italy. Negroes in New York lived apart and in other areas from Italians. Giulia observed many different things as well. Never before seeing the outside world, her eyes explored the wonders of nature and the beauty of open spaces. The mixed-colored trees of the mountains in autumn contrasted with the deep blue skies as white puff clouds slowly swirled around the peaks. The sunset forced pastel colors upon the land that lay before. Thick grey smoke from the steam locomotive dissipated along the side of the train's window. Giulia was in her private wonderland and took pleasure in that marvelous place. She leaned over to Luigi and gently kissed his cheek. "Thank you," she softly said. Luigi was pleased that these things brought happiness to his new wife and took her mind off the tragedy. The killing of Biaggio was still on his mind. It always would be, but he kept a brave face for his wife.

After the long journey to Pittsburgh, the newlyweds rode in a horse-drawn carriage along the busy streets to a hotel in the city. They were both exhausted that late autumn evening of 1881.

In time, Luigi looked up Carlo Benedetto. He was Biaggio's friend and associate who urged him and Biaggio to go to Pittsburgh. Luigi showed up unexpectedly at his restaurant and bar one early afternoon on a mid-December day. It was a dirty hotel with a scratched wooden bar. Filthy workers sat and drank either whisky or beer. Bar girls and prostitutes clung to men, smiling and laughing.

Carlo Benedetto appeared very different from Biaggio. He was a thin man in his mid-forties of medium height with grey balding hair. Carlo spoke much better English than Biaggio. However, he still used the same Neapolitan dialect as his deceased friend. Carlo had a wife, Maria, and two children, a boy and a girl. Maria was pregnant with a third. Carlo became saddened upon hearing the news of his friend's killing. "I received a letter from him months ago," Carlo remembered. "He told me you both were coming. Maronna mia! Such a tragedy!"

"It was. Please don't speak about it when you meet my wife," Luigi frowned, "She has taken it very badly."

"Oh!" Carlo perked up. "Congratulations! You're a newlywed! I didn't know."

"Thank you," Luigi's eyes lowered. "Yes, so was Biaggio."

"He said he was getting married, but I never in this world thought he would do it." Carlo frowned again, saying, "Biaggio also told me how fond he was of you in the letter. He said that he loved you like a son." Carlo sighed. "Also, my old friend mentioned how good you are at card playing."

Luigi filled Carlo in on all the details of Biaggio's death and their time together in New York. They spoke while being served lunch. Carlo called for the waitress to bring a bottle of wine to their table. "Bastardo!" Carlo shouted, "And a drunken one at that! We don't have too many serious problems here," He explained to satisfy any uneasiness Luigi might have felt about his hotel and tavern. "Mostly steel and coal workers and other laborers. The kind of people who aren't smart enough to notice a quick hand or a card counter," he smiled. They also discussed how Luigi could get a start in the new city. Carlo was as helpful as Biaggio said he would be. "You can buy a place of your own, or you're welcome to become my partner," he mentioned in a friendly manner. "God knows I have too much business. Think it over. Either way, I'll help you."

"I don't have to," said Luigi, "Biaggio told me you are an honorable man and good at cards, and I always trusted him. My answer is yes." The two men shook hands and made a deal. It was 50-50 from the start. Luigi used the money he and Biaggio had saved in New York to buy in with Carlo and would pay half of the expenses to improve his hotel. He assumed Biaggio told Carlo how good he was at counting cards, not just a good card player. Luigi Massaro was ready to grow his business.

Many negroes settled in surrounding areas of Pittsburgh back in the days of the underground railroad. Abolitionists helped them escape, and they sought refuge there from the former slave owners searching for them. Eventually, many of them moved to the city to seek employment in the developing industries there. Those who did found more opportunities in Pittsburgh than in the rural areas. So, a surge of what would someday become termed as African Americans settled there in the 1880s. Many families worked hard together and began opening business establishments. Most blacks lived apart from the 'Americans,' as referred to, but some mingled with the ethnic immigrants.

In late December 1881, Giulia announced that she was pregnant. Luigi was ecstatic upon hearing the news and couldn't wait for his first son to be born. Luigi's mind was already preparing how many things he would teach him. Of course, he would become a gentleman and attend the best schools. Luigi planned to give him everything. On July 4th, 1882, Giulia delivered a beautiful baby girl with blonde hair and olive-green-colored eyes. Even though Luigi was expecting a boy, he loved this baby completely. They named her Giuseppina Annunziata Massaro. The baby's first name was after Luigi's mother. The middle name was after Giulia's mother. They called their baby Peppina for short.

The remaining year of 1882 went by quickly. Carlo and Luigi made more money than they ever expected. Biaggio was right to advise Luigi to relocate to this city. The two owners planned to improve the hotel. They hired pretty waitresses to serve and flirt with the hungry slobs who frequented their business. That gave the men incentive for the prostitutes that clung to them during card games. Later the hookers took the men upstairs to a room. Carlo and Luigi received a percentage of the fees. The women usually carried three-inch double-barreled Derringers in their garter belts to scare off anyone who didn't pay or tried to abuse them. They took care of themselves. But if things got out of control, a huge hired man stepped in with a wooden club to prevent serious harm to the ladies.

The improvements to the hotel made a big difference. It made lots of money from serving food, wine, hard liquor, and beer. Working miners and steel workers couldn't wait to throw away their money on gambling and whiskey after a hard day's work. There were occasional fistfights, but another hired man clubbed any fighters before anyone got seriously hurt. Everything was going well. They paid the Police to leave the hotel alone. Carlo and Luigi didn't want their wives to work or even be near a hotel like theirs.

At the end of the evening, at around 5:00 PM, Luigi would go home for dinner with his wife and daughter. He always looked forward to going home to his pretty wife and baby in their new house in Pittsburgh. He would return to the business after dinner but usually leave by 9:30 or sometimes 10 PM to be with his family. Carlo's brother-in-law, Alfonso Lorusso, Maria's younger brother, ran the hotel during the night. Unlike Maria, Alfonso spoke with a thick Barese dialect that many other Italians found difficult to understand.

Giulia was living a dream. Every day was better than the one before. She was learning to speak English a little better. Luigi guided her through the language. She sometimes became frustrated. "It's such a hard language to learn," she often said. But Luigi always continued to coach Giulia. In his heart, he felt she would never speak English well, but he tried.

Giulia made good friends with Carlo's wife, Maria Benedetto. Maria was a pretty woman in her late twenties. They went shopping often and shared recipes for delicious meals for their families. Luigi suggested hiring a maid to cook, but Giulia wouldn't hear of it. She didn't want a nanny, either. Giulia wanted to take care of her husband and daughter by herself. She was strict in the kitchen but a lamb in the bedroom with her husband. Giulia and Luigi were happy.

In January 1885, Luigi told Carlo that Giulia was pregnant again. Carlo's wife, Maria, was already about four months pregnant with their fourth. Now, the Benedettos had a girl and two boys, and their wives would be pregnant together.

"Hey! Luigi! This time, a boy, hey?"

"I hope so, but I love my little Peppina." Luigi stood proud. "Did you know that she talks already?"

"You're kidding!"

"Well, a word or two. Babble, you know. But sometimes, she doesn't shut up. I think she'll be talkative someday."

Carlo laughed, "You know something? You and I are doing really well in this business. You're very good at counting cards. I've never seen anything like it."

"And you're quick with your hands, just like Biaggio," Luigi remembered his old pal, "I wish he could see my little girl."

Giulia gave birth to her second daughter, Emanuela Carmella Massaro, in 1885. Little Peppina was fascinated by the new baby, and the three-year-old even tried to take care of her little sister. Emanuela's hair gradually changed from dark brown to solid black when she was two. Her dark brown eyes appeared almost black as well.

Little Peppina was a chatterbox as a young girl. Active, friendly, and very outgoing, Peppina always had a smile on her face and sang and danced for her parents. In addition to her performances, Peppina was daring. She climbed on chairs or piled books to get things from tables and higher pieces of furniture. Luigi called her his little firecracker.

Emanuela was quiet and distant from people, entirely unlike her sister, even as a baby. Emanuela cried often and had occasional tantrums. Emanuela didn't like people to hold her, and she struggled to escape the arms of those who did. She bore a natural frown and didn't smile or laugh that often. Giulia's and Luigi's two daughters had utterly opposite personalities. Giulia and Luigi loved both their daughters, but Peppina was the apple of Luigi's eye.

Giulia missed her mother and often thought of her family; sometimes, her emotions got the best of her. Her parents and Nunzio must have been devastated when they realized she had run away with Luigi. Giulia hoped the note she left for them comforted them in some way. When she left, her only thoughts and feelings were for Luigi. Eventually, she understood how important her family was to her. Giulia hoped they would forgive and welcome her back to visit someday. Other times, while enjoying everything in her present life and remembering that horrible neighborhood compared to how she was now living in luxury, she was glad she left. Still, she missed them terribly and wanted to send a letter to them. She knew one of her mother's friends understood English and would read it to her. Luigi would have to write it because she was illiterate. When Luigi had time, they sat together, and she dictated:

Dear Mamma,

I'm so sorry for leaving home the way I did. I love Luigi and wanted to be with him. We are married and have two daughters. Their names are Giuseppina Annunziata, age five, and Emanuela Carmella, age two. I want you to know that Luigi is very good to me. We have a beautiful house in Pittsburgh, Pennsylvania.

I hope you will let me visit you and Pappa someday. I miss both of you very much and think about both of you often. Please tell Pappa and Nunzio that I miss them and love them.

I love you, Mamma.

Love,
Giulia

Luigi wrote and mailed the short letter from a post office in Pittsburgh on his way to work the following day. He felt touched by the note, which made him realize his wife's emotional sacrifice. But he also knew getting her out of that hellhole of Little Italy was for the best.

Less than a month after Luigi mailed Giulia's letter to her mother, a letter arrived from an attorney in New York City. It had the words 'legal notice' at the head. It explained that Giuseppe Pellettieri instructed him to remove his daughter from any inheritance from her parents or the hotel. They wished no further communication from their former daughter. It said that if communication from Giulia Massaro to them or her brother persisted, it would be deemed harassment, and he would initiate legal charges. The notice was signed and notarized by Benjamin Goldman, Attorney-at-law.

After reading the document, Luigi thought, 'Hmm, Giuseppe hired himself a lawyer and a Jewish one at that. He must really be agitated.' Luigi opened all letters to their home, as Giulia was illiterate. Now, as he folded the enveloped letter and put it in the inside pocket of his jacket, he fought with the question of whether or not to tell his wife out of fear it would affect her terribly.

After days of struggling with how to handle that situation, Luigi gently broke it to his wife with a sugar-coated version of her father's feelings. He explained it to Giulia as a 'necessary precaution' to protect their son now that she was in a happy marriage and financially solvent. To his surprise, Giulia picked up on the true nature of the document and said, "If that's the way he feels, then so be it. I did what I had to do. I love you, Luigi, and not the ugly and weak 'vecchio' he wanted me to marry." She thought, 'That old man wouldn't have lasted one minute in bed with me. Maybe I should have married him and given him a heart attack,' she smiled openly. 'Then I could have collected his inheritance and then go with Luigi,' she smirked. 'No, my aristocratic Luigi would never have tolerated me sleeping with another man. That would have been 'disgrazia' to him.'

The Massaro's were a happy family, and everything went well until mid-1888. Luigi could not know that that day marked the beginning of his fall from grace. Carlo and Luigi discovered that Carlo's brother-in-law, Alfonso, was cheating them. A year after he began working, he started gambling at a place owned by the leader of a local small Italian gang. Alfonso was a young, naïve, inexperienced player and a natural-born loser. He borrowed from a small-time boss, Giuseppe Marino, to pay his debts. He didn't fully understand what type of man Giuseppe Marino was. The debt slowly escalated until Giuseppe sat Alfonso at a corner table across from him. Giuseppe Marino was short but had a large-boned, muscular build. His eyelids hung, giving him a hard, dead-eyed appearance. He spoke very slowly in a low, throaty Sicilian dialect and, without any emotion, told the young man to pay up all his gambling debts immediately.

The naïve Alfonso didn't take it seriously and told Giuseppe, "I can't. I don't have the money." He offered a hint of a smile.

That smirk might have been what set Giuseppe off, but he didn't blink at that response. He used those dead eyes to call over one of his goons, a large, brawny man poorly dressed in a baggy suit. Giuseppe nodded at him and motioned to Alfonso's left hand. Moving fast for a man of his size, the big goon pulled a switchblade out of his suit pocket and thumped Alfonso's forehead with his elbow enough to put the kid in a daze. Then, he spread apart the young man's fingers and used the sharp blade to chop off Alfonso's pinky finger.

Alfonso screamed in terror as the big guy dangled his finger in front of his face. "You got the money now?" Giuseppe asked slowly, his dead eyes staring into Alfonso's.

"I'll get it!" Alfonso screamed as tears rolled down his cheeks, blood flowing out of the stub that remained of his pinky.

"No," answered Giuseppe. "Now you work for me." He explained how a wagon would come every night, and his men would take liquor and supplies from Carlo and Luigi's bar. He also had to steal a quarter of the cash from the moneybox every night.

"Give it to the wagon driver only," Giuseppe said in that dreadful throaty voice, his dead eyes staring at Alfonso. "Next time you cross me, it won't be a pinky; it will be your balls or your life, and I ain't kidding."

Carlo and Luigi were making so much money that they hadn't noticed until it was too late. Luigi trusted the young man as he was Maria's brother and had Carlo's blessing. When Alfonso realized he was way over his head, he tried to leave Pittsburgh—a foolish mistake. Giuseppe Marino's men were watching him and dragged him from the train station, knocked him out, and threw him in the back of their wagon. When Carlo opened the door the following day, Alfonso's body hung upside down, a puddle of blood below him, his throat slashed. That's how Carlo and Luigi found out about the betrayal.

Eventually, Giuseppe used his connections at the police department to get Carlo arrested for gambling and prostitution. His plan had been to take over Carlo's and Luigi's business. He didn't target Luigi because he was a fellow Sicilian and sensed that he was a man to be reckoned with. He was out of business anyway. Perhaps another time, they could do business together.

Carlo and Luigi lost the hotel and everything in it. Not only were they out of business, but Carlo was also sentenced to five years in prison. The partners never used a bank, so all their cash in a hidden safe disappeared. Luigi only had the money his father gave him and a small amount of cash stashed in his house. Luigi had to sell his home in Pittsburgh quickly. He decided to move his family to Sharpsburg, Pennslyvania, a small industrial town five miles northeast of downtown Pittsburgh.

Giuseppe Marino approached Luigi with the same goon who had cut off Alfonso's pinky finger. In a thick Sicilian dialect that seemed grotesque to Luigi's ears, he asked him, "You wanna work with me? I could use someone like you."

Luigi was wearing his shoulder-holstered pistol under his suit jacket and ready to use it if necessary. He knew about these small Italian gangs that were popping up, trying to be like the mafia in Sicily. In Luigi's old country, the mafia was a dangerous secret organization. It was always part of the ruling class of Italy, even after unification. Here in America, they were nothing more than thugs impersonating the Sicilian Mafia at the time.

Luigi held his anger about losing his share of the business and looked directly into Giuseppe's dead eyes. He used his peripheral vision to watch every move Giuseppe's apparent enforcer made, then coldly said, "No, it's time for me to move on." He maintained his stare.

Giuseppe nodded, rolling his dead eyes back, signifying it was a shame. It seemed he feared Luigi more than Luigi feared him. Luigi didn't turn his back on Giuseppe. He stood firm and waited for him to leave, which he did with his goon following him.

Luigi felt defeated, something he had never been nor would accept. In late 1889, he bought a smaller home in Sharpsburg and relocated his family to a nice area of that town. Not wanting to spend money to buy a business, he began working out of different gambling parlors in the smaller town.

Giulia began to feel isolated from her husband. She learned what had happened and tried to lift Luigi's spirits, but it was futile. Giulia realized her husband was proud and blamed himself for their predicament. In Luigi's mind, he hadn't protected his family.

Giulia's friend, Maria, had to move in with her mother because her husband was serving time in prison. And Giulia didn't get to see her anymore. They could no longer shop together and visit each other. However, shortly after moving to Sharpsburg, Giulia became pregnant again. In 1890, Giulia delivered a son. Luigi praised the heavens; he finally had a boy! That event sparked Luigi. They named their son Felice Giuseppe Massaro. The first name was after Luigi's father. The second name was after Giulia's father. Luigi called his boy Felo for short. Little seven-and-a-half-year-old Peppina was a big help to her mother while caring for her baby brother. Four-year-old Emanuela quietly tagged along.

After the birth of his first son in 1890, Luigi was working on a game of Five Card Stud. Luigi mastered American card games during his years in Pittsburgh, as many Americans played in his former business. Three men had already folded. His remaining opponent, William, an American businessman, was working on a full house. He had three tens and one three showing. With three kings exposed, Luigi was going for a quad—four of the same cards—in this case, kings. They had continually raised the pot to about $1000, a fortune.

Almost everyone in the bar was interested. People were standing around the table in anticipation. The older, well-dressed businessman was confident that Luigi was bluffing. He knew he saw another king earlier in the game before someone folded. But the older man was wrong. His drinking interfered with his memory, and he raised the pot by another $100–all of his remaining money. Being able to count the deck, Luigi knew the grey-haired man had a full house, and Luigi held the last king turned face down under his cards.

"That's quite a bit of money," Luigi told his adversary, "I don't know if. . . ," he pretended he was thinking. "Well, it's only a game, isn't it?" he put down the $100 and raised another $200. Staring at his opponent with his piercing dark blue eyes, Luigi asked, "Well, William, what are you going to do?" ready to use one of the smaller guns he had tucked in his waist if the businessman was cheating.

Now, the businessman was worried, and he showed it. He didn't have enough money with him to meet the bet, so he nervously pondered. He knew Luigi was bluffing; the older man was sure of it. "I don't have enough money to meet the bet." William looked both worried and embarrassed. Luigi waited patiently as the American businessman appeared to be thinking intensely. William opened the collar of his shirt; he was sweating. "Well, I have this." After fumbling with papers in his briefcase, he pulled out a document—ownership of a hotel and passed it to Luigi.

Luigi read the document. "It looks real." Then he handed it to another player who earlier said he was a lawyer.

"It is real. Yes," the lawyer said while pointing to the legal stamp, "it is."

"What's the value of this business?" Luigi inquired.

"It's worth all the money on this table!" the older man hotly snapped. "The hotel is behind a train station and makes good money—a goldmine!"

"Are you sure you want to lose this?" Luigi asked with a hint of a smile.

"I don't intend to," the older man replied. "I know you're bluffing."

"Okay." Luigi allowed William to throw the document into the pot, and then he showed his cards.

"That's impossible," argued William as he lifted all the other player's cards who had folded. "But I'm sure I saw a king." He sat there in astonishment. Then he re-checked all the cards again.

"Sorry," said Luigi, asking William to transfer ownership to his name. William looked around the smoke-filled bar and reluctantly complied. "What's your full name?"

"Luigi Giovanni Massaro," Luigi proudly answered.

William raised his eyebrows and asked, "Could you spell that?" Then the man mumbled something under his breath.

Luigi asked the lawyer at the table, "Could you please witness the transfer of this document?"

"Gladly."

Everyone around the table was shaking their heads and talking as Luigi tucked the money and envelope with the document into his suit jacket pockets. One man said he had never seen a pot as large. Luigi attributed that good luck to the birth of his first son.

That recent win gave Luigi the jolt he needed. However, he wouldn't stop there. Luigi wanted to retain his former status, working longer hours and sometimes into the weary early morning hours. Luigi was growing apart from his family in an ironic effort to help them have a better life. The 32-year-old still exercised and maintained his physique, but the stress from the hours he worked put him under constant duress.

A few weeks after his last big win, Luigi was about to take an incredible pot of $1100 atop the table in another game at a different gambling parlor. It was another smoke-filled room that smelled like sour whiskey and beer. He just beat a man named Big Mike. Combined with what he previously won, this money would be enough to start a business again. However, this time, the loser was not as ethical as his past opponent. The fatigued Luigi, far too focused on the winnings, neglected to watch his opponent as he leaned over the table to pull in his winnings. His defeated competitor grabbed Luigi's wrist and held it down, revealing a Smith and Wesson six-shot revolver.

"Do you think I will allow you to take everything I have?"

asked the angry man as he pushed Luigi back and wiped the pile of money toward him with his free hand. A tired Luigi wasn't quick enough to have his holstered pistol ready. "Raise your hands!" shouted the man as he looked around the room to ensure no one interfered. Luigi obeyed; his dark blue eyes glared as Big Mike stuffed the money into his pants and jacket pockets. He sneered as he walked backward, constantly turning his head toward the door. Once outside, he got into a carriage and rode off with an accomplice. Luigi had been set up; Big Mike had a partner. Luigi lost everything he had except for his father's money, which was hidden in the cellar of his house. Luigi now realized that he was defeated.

The next day, Luigi looked closer at the legal document he had won. It was for a hotel in Wellsville, Ohio. Luigi had heard of the town. It was a smaller river town but booming with industry. At first, he thought about selling it and wanted to see how much it was worth. If he sold it, he might be able to re-establish himself in his business venture; that depended on how much the hotel was worth. But after much contemplation, Luigi decided it would be better to make the hotel he won into his workplace. What did he have to lose? So, he discussed the idea with Giulia, and together, they planned to move their family to Wellsville, Ohio, for a fresh start.

The family sold all their house furnishings, keeping only essential things. The Massaros worked feverishly to pack. Peppina had fun as she helped. The almost eight-year-old went from room to room and jumped on and off of different steamer trunks placed about in their home. Four-and-a-half-year-old Emanuela quietly helped out. By late spring, they were ready to leave. The Massaro family would travel by train from Pittsburgh.

Luigi finished preparing his wardrobe trunk. The last item he carefully packed was a framed photo that he always kept on his desk. It was the photo of Biaggio and him taken in Little Italy years before. In that picture, Luigi looked dignified as he stood erect, his arm bent with his hand inside his partially unbuttoned suit jacket. Luigi smiled as he reminisced about his friend and the time they shared. In the photo, Biaggio had a cheerful expression, his head positioned back, accentuating his wide waxed mustache. And he appeared to be holding in his sizeable belly. "Okay, my old friend Biaggio, let's do it again. I know that's what you would want."

Chapter Five

Wellsville, Ohio 1890
Settling in Wellsville

The railroad tracks ran along the river. Main Street was the primary thoroughfare, flowing with horse-drawn wagons, carriages, and carts. The Third Street Station was a passenger and freight station, and 12th Street was where the 'Shop' was located, with a locomotive turntable and roundhouse and work and shop houses spread out before the railyards. The Ohio River was an entity. It was the lifeblood of Wellsville. It fed and nourished the town, and at times, it punished it. The hissing and sputtering of smoke from chimneys, factory sounds, and the clamors of machinery and laborers hitting hammers at the 'Shop' and elsewhere were among the sounds of Wellsville as train whistles and toots from riverboats filled the background.

After spotting the smoky trail of the passenger train from the north, Pip attached the leash to Rollo, and they walked quickly along Riverside to the station. Bright white clouds slowly drifted along over the deep blue sky, the shining, yellow early afternoon sun peeking out in places. Rollo trotted at times, pulling the young boy behind him. Large horse-drawn wagons passed them and headed toward spaces around the Third Street Station. Buggies and smaller horse carts followed. The area near the station was filling up with people.

Pip and Rollo arrived at the station just as the big 4-6-0 steam locomotive revealed its nose and headlights nearby and ahead of them. The engineer carefully looked out the cab window on his right as high-pressure steam spurted from each side of the metal beast. Plumes of thick white and grey smoke floated from the stack and filled the area of that bright and sunny early afternoon. The train's pistons and coupling rods forced its wheels to stop and screeched against the steel rails. The locomotive slowly moved past the station building and stopped past Third Street. That way, the cargo cars behind the coal tender were exposed at the end of the street for unloading and re-loading shipping freight. The passenger cars aligned precisely with the lengthy platform of the station building.

Originally a hotel, the Third Street Station building was remodeled for the Cleveland and Pittsburgh Railroad Company (C&P) and finished its construction in the early 1860s. The wide, long freight and passenger station depot building housed a restaurant called The Beane House. There was a kitchen, a dining hall, passenger parlors, and a family room. The building accommodated almost 30-bed chambers and a reading room for railroad employees. The freight room handled and sorted some of the cargo for businesses and residents of the town. There was also a telegraph office and an express office on the premises. Railroad officials and their staff moved into the depot offices shortly after the completion of the building. The Train Master, railroad dispatchers, and other high-ranking department executives were all headquartered in the building. The only exception was the Superintendent, whose office was nearby on Fourth and Main Street.

Now managed by the Pennsylvania Railroad, about 16 passenger trains used the station daily. Some began and ended their schedules at the Third Street Station in Wellsville. There appeared to be well over 150 people on the platform that day in late spring of 1890. Amongst the commotion, candy, refreshments, novelty carts peddled their goods, and people holding or wearing large signs advertised restaurants, taverns, and hotels. The station was undoubtedly a busy and vital complement to the town and the Pennsylvania Railroad.

Pip and Rollo stood by a tree enjoying its shade while watching all the activities and excitement surrounding them. The puny young boy held his dog's leash as tightly as possible. Rollo stood on his hind legs at times, observing people.

The tall figure of Luigi Massaro emerged from the door at the end of a passenger car and stood on the small balcony outside. The golden sun reflected onto his face, transforming those chiseled features into that of a seraphic being. He then descended the few stairs to the station platform. Impeccably dressed in a suit and top hat, he turned and extended his arm to help his wife, Giulia, who wore a beautiful full-length, belted pale green dress and matching wide-brimmed hat with floral designs. She securely held their infant son, Felo, in her arms as their daughter, Emanuela, clung to her dress. Their oldest daughter, Peppina, excitedly danced and hopped as she climbed down the steps onto the platform.

Luigi diverted his attention to the wagons and carriages parked to the side. He walked toward them to get someone to bring his family and steamer trunks and packed boxes to the hotel he now owned. Giulia stood back and watched as her husband negotiated with the drivers. Emanuela remained by her mother's side. Peppina had separated from her mother and noticed a small young boy holding a large dog tightly. She began to skip in that direction. Rollo broke loose from Pip's grip and ran toward the little girl. He stood on his hind legs and started licking Peppina's face. The giant dog was much taller than Pepina's short stature.

"Hi, doggie," Peppina laughed as she petted the dog. "You're a pretty dog, aren't you?"

"R-R-Rollo!" shouted Pip. "C-C-Come here, boy!" he commanded excitedly, accentuating his stammer. But Rollo was preoccupied with the petite young girl. "R-R-Rollo!" he called again, but his dog ignored him. "I-I-I'm sorry," he said, walking to the young girl as he blushed from his stammer.

Peppina ignored the stutter and said, "Hi! I'm Giuseppina, but everyone calls me Peppina!" as she laughed excitedly, petted, and played with Rollo. "You have a nice doggie!"

"H-H-His name is Rollo. M-M-My name is Pip!"

"That's a funny name!" laughed Peppina. Rollo calmed down and sat by the short girl while she continued to pet him.

"My real name is Douglas, but kids call me Pip." The boy didn't want to explain how he acquired his nickname. He was just glad he didn't stutter that time.

"I like Douglas much better! Can I call you that?" Peppina gave Pip a big smile as she asked.

"S-S-Sure, yes." Pip blushed again.

"Do you live here, or are you visiting?"

Pip nervously explained to Peppina how he and Rollo always came to the station to see people get on and off the trains. He also mentioned his fishing spots but didn't tell her where they were, as he closely guarded those secret places. Peppina told him she and her family were moving into the hotel behind the station house. "Can I come fishing with you?" Peppina giggled.

Pip thought quickly: most girls he knew didn't like fishing. They always complained about bugs and worms to bait a hook. But this girl seemed different. She was friendly and had a spark of life that gave Pip a good feeling, and Rollo took to her right away, which was a good sign. Little Peppina seemed safe to him. "I guess so. But most girls here don't like to fish." He didn't stutter again.

Peppina practically cut off Pip's sentence and exclaimed, "I do! My Pappa taught me!"

Pip smiled, thinking he would never see her again, "Okay."

"Peppina veni´ca!" Giulia called for her daughter to come. "We're leaving!"

"Okay, Momma!" she yelled. Then she turned back to Pip and said, "Bye!" She gave him a big smile. "I'll see you soon!"

"Okay," Pip said as he watched the little young girl skip away toward her mother. He and Rollo watched Peppina board a carriage where her family was already seated. The little girl smiled again and waved to her two new friends while passing. Pip smiled and waved back, and Rollo barked once.

Chapter Six

Wellsville, Ohio 1890
The First Italian Americans in Wellsville

The Dutch settled in a section of northeastern North America and named it New Netherland. They introduced African slavery to that region. The English settled in Jamestown, and by 1650, they established dominance along the Atlantic coast and introduced African slavery to their land. The French were the first Europeans to explore what became known as 'Ohio Country.' In 1663, it became part of New France, a royal province of the French Empire. Robert La Salle explored northeastern Ohio in 1669. The British had made their way to Ohio Territory through their colony of Pennsylvania. Settlers built canoes and rafts to take them along the Youghiogheny River and onto the Ohio River. The British crossed the Allegheny Mountains as early as the 1720s, reaching the eastern edge of the Ohio Valley and pushing the frontier farther west into that valley. A part of that area would later form Columbiana County, where the town of Wellsville was settled.

Luigi sat with his family in the open carriage, traveling slowly to avoid bumps and potholes of the unpaved roads. A wagon followed behind, loaded with the packed boxes and steamer trunks. Peppina marveled and laughed as they traveled past the Metropole Hotel on Third Street. Luigi glanced back to check the wagon. Its wood-spoked wheels rolled over a railroad track spur, then another, bouncing the wagon as it did, to

Peppina's amusement. Her sister Emanuela sat wide-eyed with a stern expression. All the family's belongings remained secure. The hotel was not far from a large manufacturing complex and a steel mill.

Luigi stood outside with Guilia, who held Felo in her arms, assessing the front of the two-story hotel. The sun poised high and slightly behind them, forcing its vivid colors against the building, painting it with robust colors. Emanuela stood close to her parents as Peppina ran down the long side of the broad structure to the backyard behind the building.

"What do you think?" Giulia hesitantly asked Luigi, shifting Felo to her other arm. She knew her husband's spirits were low following his last card game and the robbery and hoped he liked their new home and place of business.

Luigi slowly walked along the front of the building as the drivers unloaded and carried everything inside the front door entrance. After Luigi paid them, they both tipped their hats in thanks for the generous tip. They offered the same courtesy to Giulia, saying 'ma'am' before boarding their wagons and leaving. As Luigi walked back to his wife, he replied to her question, "It's smaller than I thought and pretty close to that big factory," he said while pointing." He thought, adding, "But that might bring workers over to board and gamble. The outside looks clean and well-kept." Then he observed a few minor things that needed repair and pointed to them, saying, "Except for these." He smirked. "I'll look at the back later. Let's take a look inside."

"Peppina veni´ca!" Giulia called for her daughter. She feared the overactive girl might fall into a well or get hurt by hidden objects. They had no idea what lay behind the building. "Peppina!" she called again. Peppina returned to the front of the hotel, skipping as she did.

There was a musty odor as the family entered the building. It had been vacant for weeks since the owner lost it gambling in the card game. Except for accumulating dust, the hotel looked as good on the inside as it did on the outside. "The inside looks nice," Luigi immediately said as he turned his head to survey the layout. "I'll have to get some laborers to make some alterations, though." He was busy calculating everything he needed to make this place work.

A sizeable wooden drinking bar took precedence in the middle of the first floor, well past the main entrance. It was nicely varnished and polished, curved on both sides and ran to the mirrored wall behind it. It was a marvelous piece of workmanship. High-backed wooden matching stools complemented the aesthetic service counter. At each side of the bar were tables and chairs, presumably for eating, drinking, and gambling. At the left side of the bar was a polished mahogany check-in counter with wooden shelves set behind it. There were slots and small square openings built into the shelf setup for mail, messages, and other paperwork. On the shiny, varnished counter was an open log book of room occupants and a small brass call bell. At the top of the wooden counter, a sign read:

$1 a night includes one meal.
$3 a week includes one meal a day.
$1.75 room with bathtub and one meal a day.
Communal Bath 50 cents.
Laundry extra

Giulia looked at her husband, "Luigi, I want a wooden beer cask put behind the bar to siphon my homemade beer." Her mind was envisioning using her father's recipe for beer. "I'll need at least two." She handed Felo to Luigi and walked behind the bar. "Right about here," she smiled at him.

"As you wish, my princess!" he smiled back and advised, "It would be better to put them in the cellar and siphon the beer from there. It would stay cooler that way."

"Queen, you mean, and I agree." That made Luigi smile even more. Giulia's humor was raising his spirits. The prospects of the place filled his imagination and helped even more.

Behind the tables and chairs on the left side of the main floor was a wall partitioning a large kitchen with a water pump and a dishwashing and laundry area—a large doorway with a draped curtain allowed service to the tables. The considerable open space extended along the back to the other side of that floor. One room of significant size to the right of the kitchen near the center of the floor housed communal bathtubs separated by curtains. Luigi believed there was too much space surrounding the tubs–far too much that could go to better use. "We have to rebuild this back area. There's too much wasted space," he shouted to his wife, who stood on the other side of the extended area.

"Mama! There's a snake in the back!" Peppina excitably yelled as she ran back inside. Emanuela cringed at the words. Her younger sister was afraid of just about anything.

Luigi shrugged, "We have to do a lot of things. This place has been vacant for a while."

One doorway was at the right side of the wooden service bar, behind the table and chair setup. It led to a narrow hallway with four separate rooms. Luigi immediately recognized the rooms as convenient places where prostitutes would bring their customers. He knew the layout of many similar establishments where the hookers could do their work without disturbing other patrons on the upper floor.

Giulia was oblivious to such happenings since her parents never allowed such things in their hotel in the Lower East Side of New York City. Though outlawed in most cities and towns in the eastern United States, a customary payoff to local police usually rectified any problems. However, Giulia's father respected the law. She grew up in a clean, respectable hotel in a dirty, filthy neighborhood. Giulia was like her parents: very clean and organized. She intended to run her hotel the same way, having no idea of her husband's plans since she had never visited his and Carlo's place in Pittsburgh.

Luigi decided to make a partition for the tables and chairs on the right side of the bar. It would have an opening instead of a door. That would be a gentleman's smoking area, similar to the one where he met Biaggio in Naples. That way, it wouldn't draw attention to the gambling. He also planned to conduct prostitution, but a little more discreetly than at the hotel he and Carlo operated in Pittsburgh.

"The downstairs will be nice once we have workers re-arrange the floor," Luigi said as he and Giulia climbed the two-section fruitwood stairway beside the check-in counter, which led to the second floor. Luigi carefully held his baby son, Felo, as four-and-a-half-year-old Emanuela held onto the hand-rail and stepped carefully behind her mother. Peppina hopped on each step without holding on to the railing and followed her younger sister. The second floor was broad and accommodated assorted-sized rooms toward the back and additional rooms of various sizes on each side. One of the rooms on the side was beside the second-floor stairway.

All of the walls of that floor had in-wall gas connections with wall lamps. A piece of wallpaper slightly peeled away at one spot. It covered a little bulge of plaster that formed when workers installed the cast iron pipe after the building's erection when gas became available.

"We need a lot of plaster work, too," Luigi told his wife. "Wallpaper would look good downstairs."

Each room had a fireplace or a coal-burning stove and an oil lamp with an earthenware chamber pot under each bed. Six rooms had plain bathtubs with higher backs and circular bas-es that sat flat on the floor. Giulia knew from experience that the staff filled and emptied the bathtubs manually. She also un-derstood that hotel workers usually had to carry chamber pots downstairs. However, some guests threw the contents out of a window.

The rest of the family surveyed the rooms while Peppina ran inside and out of each room and then hopped back down the stairs to the first floor. She climbed back up to the second floor and jumped back down the steps again to the main floor. The two sisters would sleep together in a larger room with two beds on the second floor opposite the stairway. Luigi and Giulia would occupy the larger room across from them next to the stairway. It had a larger bed and enough space for a crib for Felo. That way, they would be away from the bar noise downstairs that Luigi expected to go on until the wee hours of the morning.

The Massaro family descended the stairs and decided to look at the sides and back of the building quickly. Remembering Peppina's warning about the snake, Giulia shouted to her, "Peppina! Stay with us!" Emanuela was frightened and wanted her mother to carry her. "You're too big now, tesoro!" Then, Giulia told Peppina, "Hold your sister's hand while we walk. We won't be long." The overzealous little girl always complied with her mother's wishes and took her meek sister by the hand.

"Where was the snake?" Emanuela asked her older sister in a terrified voice as she walked closely beside her.

"Way over there," Peppina pointed to the back of the yard to relieve her sister's fear. Really, the small garter snake had slithered along the side of the hotel.

A tiny building was to the side of the main building. Giulia recognized it as soon as she entered. It was a bakehouse with a large flat brick baking oven. Behind that building stood another communal bath and washroom. A water pump stood aside it.

Another tall, broad, small building behind the hotel housed six separate stalls of attached outhouses. Giulia assumed that cart workers had always emptied the soiled pots there. But because the hotel had been vacant for so long, water and waste had accumulated, probably from laborers passing by. "We have to get some workers to clean the whole outhouse shack thoroughly before we call the cart men," Giulia said. Human waste was politely called 'night soil' at the time. Workers called 'night soil cart men' had the unenviable job of shoveling the contents from the town's outhouses into carts during the night. They would dispose of the contents using different methods.

As the Massaro family began to unpack, the same locomotive in which they arrived blew its whistle, signaling it was getting ready to depart from the Third Street Station. It had unloaded its passengers and freight and reloaded new passengers and cargo.

Luigi turned to his family and said, "We all have much work to do."

"We need a complete staff," replied his wife, smiling.

Luigi nodded, "We'll get all the help we need, and this hotel will be ready as fast as I can," his mind thought of gambling and money.

Chapter Seven

Wellsville, Ohio 1890
Fishing Along The Ohio River

Boating was a means of transportation. By the late 1800s, it had become a leisurely activity, and people used water crafts for fishing. Many flocked to the shores of the great Ohio River to fish. Several of them brought along their families and made a day of it. More determined fishermen and women preferred to do it alone to avoid being distracted or scare away the fish. Either way, people had a marvelous time on the Ohio River.

Pip and Rollo walked past Cooper's Opera House on Main Street. They were on their way to fish at one of their favorite spots but had a late start. Pip originally began the journey along Riverside the quicker way but then realized he needed to buy more fishing hooks. So he and his dog turned onto Seventh Street and then walked along Main Street. Pip left his fishing rod and bag outside with Rollo as he went into the variety store to pick up the hooks, carefully looking for the bullies. After he untied Rollo, took his rod, and slung his fishing sack over his shoulder, the two anxiously continued to the Third Street Station, hoping that McElhenny, the guard, wouldn't see him that fine morning. Fog puffs were floating around at the station and much thicker by the river as usual. It was a rare morning that no fog would be by the water. It all had to do with the temperature. Early mornings were the coolest time of day. When cool air mixes with damp, warm air atop the water, the moist air cools, and humidity reaches 100 percent, forming fog.

As they turned right onto Third, Pip noticed people accumulating at the station platform. He pulled Rollo back, and they both slowed down, scouring the area for McElhenny. The guard was nowhere in sight, so Pip and Rollo stepped onto the platform and blended in with the crowd. It was a good idea; they would walk past the end and quickly cross the tracks. Nobody would notice them amidst the commotion, and no train was yet in sight. It was their lucky day.

Just as Pip contemplated their next move, he heard a voice cry out from the forming crowd. "Douglas! Hi, Douglas!" It was little Peppina calling to him. Rollo spotted her first and barked. His leash slipped through the young boy's hand as he ran to the petite girl. "Hi, Rollo," Peppina laughed as she hugged and petted the dog. "How are you today?" Her blonde hair glistened in the morning light that began peeking through the small clouds of morning fog.

The young boy trotted over to get his dog. "W-W-Wow, he really likes you! I've never seen him like this with anybody else before." Pip just shook his head back and forth in amazement.

"That's because he can tell I like him back." Peppina laughed. That's when Pip first noticed how pronounced Peppina's olive-green-colored eyes appeared when she smiled. She was standing next to her younger sister. A rectangular advertisement sign leaned against a station post behind the two girls.

"H-H-Hi there!" Pip said to Emanuela. But the smaller girl bowed her head and blushed. The curls of her dark hair swayed forward and dangled like springs.

"She's bashful," intervened her older sister. "Not like me!"

"T-T-That's for sure!" Pip stuttered but laughed as he did. He felt comfortable around Peppina.

"My Pappa calls me a firecracker!" Little Peppina laughed as her delightful eyes glowed.

It had been two weeks since the Massaros arrived at the hotel and when Pip last saw Peppina. She explained to Pip how much work they had done on the hotel in such a short time. Her

Pappa had hired some help, and it was ready for occupants. She showed her new friend, Pip, the large advertisement sign which was almost as tall as Emanuela's height, and it read:

Nice Low-Cost Rooms
Daily or Weekly
Food and Dining
Gentlemen's Smoking Lounge
Entertainment & Games of Chance
At Hotel on Second Street
Behind Station

"Whatcha doing today, Douglas?" Peppina inquired as she spotted the fishing rod he was trying to hide behind his back. Pip remained quiet. "Are you going fishing?"

"W-W-Well, I'm. . ."

"Can I come?"

"W-W-Well. . ."

"Please?" Peppina cut off Pip for the second time, smiled at Pip, and flashed her bright green eyes.

Pip had to think this out. It was his secret place, and no one knew about it except him. But he liked Peppina. He stood there thinking. Finally, he said, "Will you keep my fishing spot a secret?" The blonde-haired little boy was taking a chance, but for some inner feeling, he trusted the petite girl.

"I promise! I'll never tell another soul, cross my heart and hope to die!"

"Okay. But it's not a good idea to bring your sister. She's too small to climb down the slope to the river."

Peppina turned to her sister and said, "Emanuela, you must wait here for me. I won't be long and. . ."

"No! I'm afraid," she answered abruptly, cutting her sister off in mid-sentence, her eyes showing her alarm.

"Emanuela, you'll be five years old come the fall. You're a big girl now!" Peppina reminded her sister what their mother had said: 'Emanuela had to wait with the sign if her sister had to leave to use an outhouse or leave to get something.' She mentioned about not talking to strangers and staying where she was. "I won't be long. You're a big girl now," she said. "Here!" Peppina reached into her pocket and pulled out a box of candy for her little sister. "Do what I told you." Emanuela was too busy with the candy to answer.

Peppina followed Pip and Rollo, and the three crossed over the tracks at the end of the platform as planned. The young boy looked back, and everything was okay; no site of McElhenny. Nobody at all noticed the three figures crossing the tracks. People were too busy talking, reading, or eating. Peppina was wearing a long-sleeved, pleated blue dress that reached her knees. She had knee-length stockings and black-laced ankle-high boots. At the top of the slope, she untied her shoes and removed them and her stockings, leaving them next to where Pip had left his socks and shoes. Barefoot, she slid down the grassy slope to the river bank, where Pip and Rollo waited. Pip put his right forefinger to his lips to signal Peppina to remain quiet. She glanced at the river and couldn't believe her eyes. The young girl gasped and put her hands over her mouth to keep quiet. About three feet from the bank was a small recessed area of about six feet in diameter, probably cut into the river naturally. The depth there was much deeper than that of the river. About 40 fish swam trapped there. A mixture of smallmouth bass, largemouth bass, blue catfish, and walleyes struggled to escape to the river.

"I'm afraid they might jump," Pip whispered to Peppina. He handed her the rod and said, "Here, you go first."

Peppina took a worm from a pile that Pip had placed on a flat rock near the edge. He caught them earlier in the morning. She baited her hook and cast the line. Pip could tell she had fished before. "There's so many we could scoop them out of the water!" Peppina yelled out.

"That wouldn't be fair, would it?" Pip smiled as he watched Peppina holding the fishing pole and anxiously waiting. Then the rod tip bent and the little girl struggled but pulled out a nice-sized Largemouth Bass. "Wow! That must be an 16-incher!" He watched the small girl as she flung it onto the river bank.

"I wanna do it again!" Peppina cried out in laughter. Rollo stood erect and barked.

The two children remained sitting close together, and each took turns reeling fish out of the water. After almost an hour, Pip declared that they had reached their limit. They had more than enough fish for their families and, of course, the other people on Pip's regular list. They sat together, leaning back, and enjoyed the slight morning river breeze. Pip was more relaxed than he could remember. All his fears subsided. He didn't have a worry or a care in the world. Rollo had dozed off, and his big furry body lay beside them.

"Uh-oh!" Peppina remembered Emanuela. "My sister!"

"Let's go!" Pip said.

The two kids arose at once. Peppina grabbed the rod as Pip slung the loaded fish bag over his shoulder. The weight of it almost knocked him over. But he used all his strength to avoid embarrassing himself in front of Peppina. They climbed the grassy slope, as did Rollo, and quickly put back on their socks and shoes. A train was blocking the tracks. Pip learned from his father never to go between train cars. He held tightly to Rollo's leash, and they rushed down to Third Street past the stopped locomotive and crossed over the tracks in front of it. All three backtracked to the platform and hurried toward the middle, where they left Emanuela. They didn't see her at first. Peppina was worried. So was Pip, but he didn't show his fear because he didn't want to upset his friend. Then, Rollo pulled Pip in the direction of the advertisement sign. At the same time, the two kids saw the tiny figure of Emanuela sitting fast asleep. Her head was leaned over to her left, and her black hair curls dangled as she breathed deeply in her sleep. The finished candy container was still in her hand.

"Emanuela, c'mon, honey. I'm back." Peppina gently shook her sister until her eyes slowly opened.

"Your back already?" Emanuela said as she rubbed her eyes.

"Yeah, I told you I wouldn't be long."

The children and Rollo left for the hotel to drop off Peppina's share of their catch. They wouldn't have noticed a particular man in the departing crowd who had disembarked the train. The stranger was tall with broad shoulders and a sturdy build. He wore a black suit with a matching bowler hat, slightly pitched to one side. One suitcase stood by his feet. The large man had dark, shifty eyes, heavy black eyebrows, and a well-kept mustache. The bony cheekbones combined with the expression on his face are what set him apart from the others. The man looked fierce.

Chapter Eight

Wellsville, Ohio 1890

The Hotel

In 1890, there weren't that many Italian immigrants in the smaller towns around Wellsville. Italians came to America much earlier, though many of them had aristocratic ties. After Italy became unified, many ex-royals of the old aristocracy and those of the old feudal system had money to invest. The poorer Italians began migrating in the 1880s but went to larger cities for jobs. The surge of that nationality would not settle in smaller towns in abundance until around 1900. The few Italian immigrants that trickled into Wellsville at the turn of the century lived around the plants and industries and mixed in with immigrants of other nationalities. Many roomed near the Stevenson Company on First, Second, and Third Streets, eventually settling on Commerce Street.

After assessing his new hotel, Luigi Massaro immediately got to work, and his family moved in. Finally, after overcoming the mistakes of trusting people and leaving himself wide open for a robbery, this hotel was his means of redemption. It was a way to fulfill his dreams of his family living life like they did in Pittsburgh. He knew this place was only a stepping stone to a more significant legitimate establishment—possibly in an even bigger city than Pittsburgh. Luigi dreamed of being a businessman, a corporate mogul, or an industrialist like the people he read about. And he had the intelligence and character to do so.

Luigi painfully wanted to revive how he and his family lived before his fall. He told Giulia, "We're going to get back to how things were in Pittsburgh; I promise!" And that made his wife happy. But more so, she delighted in seeing his spirits raised. It reminded her of old times. Giulia never wanted to return to her way of life in New York and would do anything to ensure that didn't happen.

What began as a foundry to make steamboat machinery in 1836 later became known as The Stevenson Company. In the mid-1800s, when riverboat traffic was beginning to decline due to the expansion of railroads, the company started brick-making machinery. It was a large plant with smokestacks constantly pushing out large cloudy plumes. The company employed many people, some of them always drawn to an opportunity to win some money. And it was a short walk to the Massaro hotel.

Luigi had local workmen, some from the nearby Stevenson Company and the steel mill, make any repairs needed. He paid them to work day and night. Luigi bartered with some of those laborers to work for board and meals. He was a keen businessman. The Massaros made a better kitchen to serve more people and extended the dishwashing and laundry area. To provide good heat throughout the hotel in the cold winters of the valley, workers installed a new coal steam furnace. "I need a crew to do repairs out back," Luigi asked his hired men while they ate lunch. "Anyone interested?"

"Yes, Boss! I am," quickly answered one man. Everyone eating that afternoon shared that same sentiment. They liked working for Luigi, and as underpaid laborers, they needed the extra money and were happy to do the work. Luigi became viewed as a foreman.

"Okay, good. Give your names to Liam, and I'll work out the details. We have to repair the outhouse building, and I want to extend the carriage house and horse stable. There are other things, but like I said, I had better make a list. You men are doing a good job."

"Thanks, Boss!" And all the workers again shared that response. The men admired Luigi. He was fair, paid them good wages, and worked beside them.

Luigi had two gas chandeliers affixed to the ceiling above the gambling tables. Workers replaced all the wallpaper, drapes, and carpeting. The check-in counter was waxed and buffed. A photo of Biaggio and Luigi, taken years before, hung on the wall behind it.

Giulia hired kitchen help, waitresses, floor maids, and cleaning help. She managed that end of the business. The finishing touch was a new sign erected over the front doorway, which simply read, 'Hotel & Tavern.'

He had given the job of house supervisor to a tall, big Irishman named Liam Kelly, who always kept a large club nearby. Luigi considered him capable but hired another local named Roberto Barata as a backup. The Massaros were the first Italian-American family in town. Roberto Barata was a recent immigrant from Sicily and as big a man as Liam, though younger. Living in East Liverpool, he was the only other Italian in the area that Luigi knew of at that time.

Those men were armed, and a shotgun was always behind the bar. Luigi would take no more chances after he lost so much money during that robbery at a card game. He shoulder-holstered the larger Chamelot-Delvigne six-round revolver over his vest. Luigi considered that gun, given to him by his father, a treasure. Luigi wore it at all times. It reminded him of his father and his generosity. He also concealed one of the smaller pistols. Luigi always wore a dress shirt, vest, pants, and ankle-length dress boots around the hotel. He wore a dress jacket only during times when he left the hotel, along with his seven-inch tapered top hat. Luigi Massaro would not tolerate any problems at his establishment, and he made that known to Liam and Roberto.

Luigi also advertised the hotel, bar, restaurant, and 'gentlemen's games of chance,' which was nothing more than a more pleasant way of describing old, hard-lined gambling. He created posters and billboards and displayed them in public places. Luigi hired people to pass out trade cards at stores, and a small display ad went in the local newspaper. Of course, all these things were for the sole purpose of gambling, so he planned to carefully and thoroughly explain them to the local police with some cash in his handshake or donations, as he called them. The hotel was ready for business in two weeks.

Giulia's planned dream life was on hold for the time being. Unlike in Pittsburgh, besides taking care of her three children, she now had a full-time job–and a big one at that. She had to supervise the hotel, kitchen, and the staff. Giulia introduced her mother's food recipes and her family's homemade beer. Her daughters had chores, but she wanted them to socialize with other children. Giulia didn't want her children to grow up isolated in a hotel the way she did in Little Italy. She wanted her children to have fun but also learn responsibilities. They were allowed to go out after finishing their work.

Luigi allowed prostitutes in the bar as long as they dressed appropriately and maintained a subtle approach to their prey. He took a percentage of their take for use of the back rooms. Luigi also insisted that they carry Derringers and knew how to use them. He instructed them only to point them in a dangerous situation. Even though those guns weren't that accurate, they got their point across. The girls usually carried them in a garter belt as they didn't fully dress underneath.

Most people Luigi interacted with in town didn't know he was an Italian immigrant. His cultured presence, intelligence, and dignified mannerisms made Luigi Massaro captivating and likable. With his dark blue piercing eyes and how he mastered the English language, most townspeople assumed he was of British ancestry. The same went for his daughters. They were Americans and also spoke the language perfectly. It was Giulia who spoke with a harsh Italian accent. But she usually remained around the hotel directing work, and her beauty made up for any language shortcomings. Most men flustered around her like little boys. The girls did errands around town, and Luigi interacted with suppliers and took charge of other business activities. It was an expectation at that time that men conduct business. The

Massaro family blended well into the town of Wellsville, Ohio.

"Mama! I finished all my work. Can I go out to play?" Peppina's olive-green-colored eyes beamed in a way that her mother couldn't resist.

"Okay, Tesoro, you did your work, so you go."

"Thank you, Mama!"

"Wait! Who's that little boy I see you with? The one who gives you the fish?"

"Oh, that's Douglas. He's a nice boy, and he has the cutest dog."

"You bring him here. I want to meet this Doalis or whatever." Giulia couldn't pronounce that unfamiliar name.

"Okay, Mama. Oh! He doesn't give me fish. I catch them," she proudly said before running away.

Chapter Nine

Wellsville, Ohio 1890

Happy Times

Palermo, Sicily, was the center of the Sicilian mafia. The Sicilian mafia had been a powerful secret association for centuries. Sicilian commoners were so afraid of the mafia that they didn't even whisper the word mafia. Using their 'Omerta,' the Sicilian Mafia ruled through violence and terror. That code of silence was key to their success: nobody talked or knew who they were. They enforced everything with brutality and terror. People are always easily frightened when physically threatened. But there had to be a show of force.

"Hey, why you so skinny?" Giulia replied to Pip when the otherwise bashful boy introduced himself to his friend Peppina's mother, Mrs. Massaro, at the front of the hotel on Second Street.

"Mama!" laughed Guilia's daughter, "You're embarrassing him!"

After their first fishing expedition in late spring, Pip and Peppina had become fast friends. They spent most of their days together after they each did their chores. Peppina helped in the hotel in the mornings. She also cared for her baby brother, Felo, with whom she had a close bond. Rarely, Peppina's sister tagged along with her and Pip because Emanuela preferred to read and do things alone. Peppina loved Rollo, and he loved her back. The kids spent the Fourth of July together when their families brought them to the fireworks festivities when it got dark. Rollo sniffed Peppina out of the crowd and led his master to her. Peppina told Pip how, when she was younger in Pittsburgh, she thought the fireworks were in celebration of her birthday, which fell on that day. Pip had a big laugh at that. In a lot of ways, Peppina gave him the confidence he lacked.

It wasn't until August that Peppina finally convinced her timid friend, Pip, to come to the hotel to meet her mother. Even though Pip was frightened of meeting his friend's mother, he had to concede because he and Peppina wanted to go to the Shop down on 12th Street together. Pip's father offered to show the kids around the complex, but Mr. Nicholson first wanted Peppina's parents' permission. Mr. and Mrs. Nicholson had already met little Peppina. At first, they didn't even know that the fair-skinned blonde girl was the daughter of Italian immigrants. It wouldn't have mattered as they were both people who judged others, not where they came from but because all humans were equal in their eyes. The Nicholson couple, coming from hard-working families and valuing their immigrant friends, felt their son's new friend was a positive influence. They were also charmed by her cute and bubbly personality. So, on that hot and humid August day, Pip finally met Giulia.

"Can I go with Douglas, Mama?"

"Okay, you can go, but first, you gotta eat something." Giulia chuckled back. She had difficulty pronouncing the name Douglas, so after a few tries, the young boy told Mrs. Massaro she could call him Pip, his nickname. It was easier for her, but it came out as Pipa. "C'mon, Pipa, I feed you. C'mon, you need to eat more."

Pip tied Rollo to a small tree by the hotel's entrance, where the dog could relax in the shade. Then, he followed Peppina as Giulia led the children to a table and sat them down.

"You like lasagna, Pipa?"

Pip looked at Peppina, puzzled. "You'll like it," she laughed. "It's good!"

"Yes, ma'am," said Pip. "Thank you, Mrs. Massaro."

Giulia left the two and went into the kitchen. She already had lasagna and pizza ready for the afternoon customers and returned in a few minutes. Giulia made her lasagna 'the Italian way' with homemade pasta and Italian Béchamel sauce covered with a hearty Bolognese sauce. She didn't prepare it with ricotta and mozzarella like other countries that attempted that sacred recipe of her homeland.

Each child received a dish with a nice-sized piece of lasagna and a slice of pizza. Then, a small bowl with a mixed garden salad and homemade Italian dressing was placed in front of them. Pip's eyes almost popped out of his head, which made Peppina laugh.

"Mangiare, Pipa!" exclaimed Giulia. "You gotta get big and strong! Eat! Mangiare!" Giulia laughed and then left the kids to eat in peace.

"I never even saw these things before," Pip said as he sniffed the food's aroma.

"Eat! Like my mother said. You'll like it." Peppina laughed at her friend.

Pip started on the lasagna first. "My God, this is incredible!" Then Peppina showed him how to hold the pizza in his hand. "This is too!" he muttered his words as he was chewing. "I never had anything like this before. Ever!" he mumbled with a full mouth. Then, he kept quiet while he finished everything on his plate; fresh, homemade extra virgin olive oil dripped from his fingers as he feasted.

Peppina couldn't help but laugh and giggle as she watched her friend eat. "My Mama's a good cook, isn't she?"

"Good? She's unbelievable!"

Giulia returned holding a small sack and asked, "So, Mr. Pipa, you like my food?"

"Oh, Mrs. Massaro, this was so good! I never ate anything like it before in my life." Pip smiled assuredly. "Thank you so much!"

"Niente!" Giulia said. "You come here anytime! You're a nice boy." She smiled and said, "I try to get your name right next time. Here, bring this to your Papa. It's some pizza." She carefully wrapped two pieces in clean cheesecloth that Giulia used to make her ricotta and then placed them in a sack. She handed it to Pip.

"Oh, thanks, Mrs. Massaro. I know he'll like it."

"Okay, kids, be careful and have fun." Giulia was happy her daughter had a friend.

Pip untied Rollo and the three began their journey from Third to Twelfth Street, the location of the Shop complex entrance.

Just after the children exited, a large, well-built man dressed in a black suit with a matching bowler hat slightly tilted on his head opened the door. The children hadn't noticed him; they were too busy talking and laughing about their trip to the Shop. But Rollo growled a little as the strapping figure passed him. The man entered the hotel, his shifty dark eyes surveying the first floor's interior from where he stood.

"Can I help you?" Giulia called from where she was standing near the check-in counter.

The strapping guy raised one of his bushy, dark eyebrows to look at her, his expression somber, and grumbled something low. That and the man's imposing presence made a chill run up Giulia's spine. He ignored the petite, attractive woman and slowly wandered to a table in the gambling area of the large floor, pulled out a chair, and sat down sideways from the table. His right elbow rested on the table. The forefinger and thumb of his hand supported his rugged cleft chin, massaging it. The man continued to assess the surroundings.

Giulia noticed Luigi descending the stairway from the corner of her right eye. He was getting up from a long night of working the floor when all the drinkers and gamblers lingered to the early morning hours. That was also when most of the trouble occurred, which Giulia knew nothing about, as she and her kids were fast asleep, dreaming happy thoughts. But Luigi had experience from his time in New York, Pittsburgh, and

Sharpsburg. He was well-versed in America's dark and gritty nightlife and had the scars of failure that haunted him, but he grew strong from them. And he wasn't about to make the same mistakes as he had before.

"Luigi," Giulia called him in a frightful whisper. She said no more, just nodded her head toward the fearsome man in the black suit. It was customary for men to remove their hats indoors, but this guy's hat was still on and tilted. Luigi evaluated the situation and instinctively knew trouble was seated inside his hotel. Deciding how to handle what lay before him, he began walking toward the table where the man was sitting.

Luigi pulled a chair and sat directly across from the grisly figure. His dark blue piercing eyes stared into the dark, vile eyes of the man in the black suit. "What do you want?" he asked with direct eye contact. Luigi watched the man's every move, his six-shot Chamelot-Delvigne revolver secured in his shoulder holster, ready for use at a second's warning.

The stranger, who appeared in his mid-30s, turned slightly and observed Luigi closely, using his peripheral vision and not maintaining direct eye contact. He asked Luigi, "Will you speak the language of your country?" His voice was deep and raspy, and he used a crude Sicilian dialect.

Luigi replied, "Sí," realizing the man knew of him. How else would he know he was a Sicilian?

The man proceeded in his harsh vernacular: "I'm a paisano of you. My name is Lorenzo Ricci," he paused, "but you can call me Enzo." His cold eyes were now looking directly at Luigi, and he added, "I'm here just to look around."

"My name is Luigi Massaro. See anything interesting?" He gave a hint of a smile, sarcastic though. The man before him already knew his name and who he was. "Is there anything I can help you with to make your visit here more pleasurable?" Luigi could tell the man was packing a weapon of some type from the bulge at his waistline under his vest.

To that remark, Enzo's grave facial features gave a glimmer of a smirk, observing Luigi's higher-class usage of the language as that of an educated man. "No. But it's a nice place you have here."

"I want to keep it that way."

"Maybe I can help," Enzo replied while removing his bowler hat, revealing a completely shaven head that made him look even fiercer. Enzo Ricci had been a professional wrestler, and his bald head prevented his opponents from pulling his hair.

Luigi ignored Enzo's shaven head, which was uncommon in town, though bald and balding heads were. But Luigi had seen men with razor-shaven heads before. One of the shiphands on the sea vessel he and Biaggio had sailed on had his hair removed that way. Some seafarers did this to prevent hair maintenance and lice on long voyages. He decided to be courteous and humor this gruff guy. "Would you like a coffee?" Luigi turned to his wife, still keeping his peripheral vision on Enzo. He knew Giulia would still be there watching. "Due espresso per favore, amore mio," he politely asked Giulia, knowing this guy wanted Italian coffee, not the piss that the Americans drank. Luigi looked back into Enzo's eyes and asked. "How can you help me?"

"I'll be frank. I know about you from Pittsburgh. I came all the way from there to make you a proposition," Ricci answered.

The first thing that immediately came to Luigi's mind was Giuseppe Marino, the small-time boss who put him and Carlo out of business. This guy might be one of Marino's goons, or maybe he grew a brain and wanted something of his own. He had tracked Luigi from Pittsburgh for something. From the accent, he knew this guy was just off the boat from Palermo, Sicily, the center of the Sicilian mafia. Luigi also perceived the ways of the mafia in his home country. The Sicilian mafia had been a powerful secret association for centuries. Using their 'Omerta,' they ruled through violence and terror. That code of silence was key to their success. Nobody talked to the police about the mafioso who lived among them. They enforced everything with brutality and terror. Most people are usually easily frightened when physically threatened. But with the Sicilian mafia, there was always a show of force. 'Did Marino hire himself an old-world mafia enforcer?' Luigi wondered.

"What kind of proposition do you want to make me? I don't need anything."

"You need me. You might not realize it yet, but you need me."

Luigi chose to indulge him to find out his intentions. "Do we have any mutual friends from Pittsburgh?"

Enzo turned his face to his side and grinned. He didn't answer the question. Not looking directly at Luigi, he said, "I know you're a clever and good businessman." Then he looked straight into Luigi's eyes with an intimidating look and said, "And an excellent card player." Luigi didn't reply, nor did he show any emotion. He sat patiently, leering into the man's eyes. "I want to become your partner. I want half of your business." He mistook Luigi for a weak man.

Luigi knew what this guy was. Thugs like him were beginning to spring up in places in America, using the ways of the Sicilian mafia. But they mainly were small-time hoods, not the mafia of Sicily, an organized, indomitable entity. These groups were beginning to be known as 'Black Hands,' hoodlums that terrorized their own ethnicity. Newly arrived Italian immigrants couldn't bring their problems to the police because of the language barrier. Most didn't trust the police because of their experiences of dealing with corrupt law enforcement controlled by the mafia in Sicily. Though many had succumbed to the Black Hand in the larger cities, this was the first Luigi had heard of them being in smaller towns.

Enzo continued, "With me as your partner, your business will grow more than you can imagine."

Luigi kept thinking as he evaluated the man before him, remembering the cultural customs of Sicily, those of revenge and intimidation. Moreover, he knew the differences between the aristocracy and the commoners there. However, now he had a wife and three children and feared for their safety. Gone were the days when Luigi could defend his honor without harm as he did in that duel many years ago and in the hotel in Naples where he killed two men for his safety. But, Luigi would never show concern or fear to this man or any other. It was a sign of weakness to reveal such things. Possessing the traits of a true Sicilian and a nobleman, Luigi declared, "We're all walking over the fires of hell. I don't intend to fall in. Not yet," Luigi used an old Sicilian proverb, which was an answer that meant no to Enzo's proposal. Luigi was secure in the knowledge that he and both his hired watchmen could protect his place of business and his family. Liam Kelly and Roberto Barata would make excellent enforcers. In his early 30s, Liam had been a member of an Irish gang from Little Italy in New York City. He was arrested and escaped to the smaller town of Wellsville to seek sanctuary. Liam worked with Italians before in the Little Italy section of New York. He even understood and spoke some Italian. He had no apprehensions about working alongside an Italian. Roberto, about 25, insulted a Sicilian mafia boss and escaped for his life to America. He, too, had experience dealing with these *insetti*, as Luigi referred to them.

Lorenzo Ricci stirred in his seat, astonished that this man defied him. He had heard from Giuseppe Marino that this man, Luigi Massaro, ran from him with his tail between his legs. "Think about it!" demanded Enzo gruffly.

Luigi only nodded and remained seated while Enzo rose and scurried out of the hotel. Enzo had mistaken intelligence and strategy for cowardice. In Pittsburgh, Luigi realized that his business had ended due to the negligence of his partner Carlo in hiring an incompetent brother-in-law. It wasn't a time to fight then. But now, he would do all he could to protect what he had and didn't want another partner. Luigi knew Enzo would retaliate, but he would be ready. He smiled casually at the brute of a man leaving his hotel.

Walking along the beginning of Main Street that sunny and hot August afternoon, Peppina and Pip passed a stunning residence. It was a beautiful house enclosed by a wrought-iron gate.

"I love that house," Peppina blurted out. "I want to live in it someday when I grow up!"

"Me too!" said Pip admiringly. Rollo barked once.

"I think Rollo likes it too," the little girl said, and she and Pip began laughing.

Peppina mentioned that school was starting the following week, a subject that Pip dreaded. She brought it up as W.C. Bunting's Confectionery appeared ahead on the same side of the street. Kids would hang around there on that sunny day, eating ice cream and playing. The temperature always rose in the summer afternoons in Wellsville. But Pip forgot about the bullies when he was with Peppina. She had noticed how nervous her friend got whenever they went past that place, and Peppina surmised that the bigger boys were scaring him on purpose. She told him, "Douglas, they're not going to hurt you–not really. They can't when you think about it. They would be sent to one of those horrible reform schools if they did. And you have Rollo to protect you. You told me the story about how he protected you." She giggled at the memory of the tale when Rollo knocked over two of the big kids. "He would never let anything bad happen to you. They're bullies, and bullies are nothing more than cowards. My Papa explained that to me. Just look straight at their eyes and don't worry. That's what Papa taught me." Peppina gave Pip the confidence he needed. It made him feel more secure.

Just then, Margaret Myers, Pip's classmate, walked out of the doorway. Jimmy Brier, another one of Pip's classmates, trailed behind her. Jimmy was a bit taller than the girl he followed. "Hi, Pip!" Margaret gave a wide smile as she greeted the boy. "Hi, Rollo!" Her blonde braids were fixed in a bun in preparation for the heat. Then she noticed Peppina and frowned while rolling back her eyes. She was jealous of Pip's friend, and her tone of voice showed it. "I see you're busy today."

"Hi Margaret, we're going to the Wellsville Shop where my father works. He's giving us a tour," Pip proudly said.

"Well, have fun!" she said, looking coldly at Peppina.

"C'mon, let's go!" Jimmy said, ignoring Pip.

Peppina smiled at Pip and said, "You want to know something, Douglas?"

"What?" Pip looked surprised.

"You don't stutter anymore," she laughed. "You didn't just now and haven't for weeks."

"I didn't? Wow! I didn't notice. I mean…wow!" Pip just stood there, blushing at his surprise.

"It's great!" said Peppina, still laughing.

"I guess it's because I've been so busy I never realized. Wait until I tell my parents."

"I'm sure they already know, Douglas."

Pip just stood there, realizing how stupid what he just said sounded. "C'mon, let's go!"

The three characters continued their trip along Main Street. Telephone poles lined both sides of the street. They had begun to be erected ten years before by the Central District Telephone and Telegraph Company. Pip held tightly to Rollo's leash while shaking his head in disbelief that he never noticed he wasn't stuttering anymore.

"Well, anyway, I'll be going to the Catholic school at the church." Peppina pointed to the building across the street as the threesome neared Ninth Street. "My parents want me to go there, especially my mama. Papa does, too, but I think it's because he hates Garibaldi so much. I'm starting the third grade."

"Whose Garibaldi?"

Peppina explained her father's version of the general, Garibaldi. "Anyway, where are you going?"

"I'm going to fourth grade at the Central School," Pointing in the opposite direction of Ninth Street, "down there." Then Pip explained how he and his family went to the first Wellsville fair the year before, in 1889, to get off the subject of school. They passed by the roller skating rink between ninth and Tenth and continued.

"The brick paving is moving along," Pip said, pointing to

workers and the piles of bricks being stacked near the road by horse-drawn wagons. "My father says they'll finish paving Main Street pretty soon if everything continues on schedule."

The kids and Rollo stopped as they crossed 11th Street at the Ascension Church to their right. Pip pointed to the wooden structure and said, "They built that church about 20 years ago."

The Wellsville Yellow-ware Pottery was past the church between 11th and 12th Streets on Commerce Street. They decided to cross Main Street at the corner of 11th Street. After waiting for the passing horse-drawn wagons, carriages, and carts, they crossed the unpaved part of Main Street, careful not to step on any of the piles of horse dung. They then continued down Main to 12th Street, made a left, and walked to the end of the block where the entrance to the passenger depot and the Shop was. Construction of the Shop building finished just three years before, in 1887. That was the place Mr. Nicholson wanted the kids to meet him. He didn't want them to go unsupervised throughout the busy complex.

"Hi, Dad!" Pip spotted his father talking to another worker near the main entrance doorway. The man was much shorter than the towering height of his father, Douglas Sr., and somewhat heavy, especially at his midsection.

Smiling, his father said. "So, there you are, son." He turned his head to the other man and introduced his son. "Jack, you remember my son, Douglas."

"I sure do, but you're getting older now, young man," the heavy-set man gave a big grin. "And how are you today, Rollo?" He leaned over to pet Pip's dog, who was already sniffing around him.

"Hello, Mr. Carlson," replied Pip. He extended his arm and shook Jack's hand. Pip knew Jack's son, Matt, very well. He was one of the older kids who tormented him at school.

"And this is his friend, Peppina," Mr. Nicholson smiled at the young girl.

"Good afternoon, Mr. Carlson. It's very nice to meet you." Her pretty olive-green-colored eyes widely beamed while she spoke. "And it's good to see you again, Mr. Nicholson." The lively Peppina gave one of her big smiles and a giggle as she made a curtsey, like a ballerina after a performance, to the older men. Her head tilted back, poised appreciative; she looked adorable. Her parents taught her manners, and the little actress loved being in the limelight.

Mr. Nicholson couldn't help but chuckle and extend another big smile. "Well, it's good to see you again, too, young lady." He turned to face the other worker and asked, "Jack, would you look underneath that locomotive I showed you before? I'm heading off now to show these two young people around."

"This is for you," Peppina said as she handed Mr. Nicholson the sack. "My Momma sent it for you. It's pizza! Douglas and I already had ours." Rollo perched higher and tried for the bag, but Pip stopped him in time.

"Well, I'll be. I've only heard of it in books, but I never had it before." He noticed there were two pieces. "Hey, Jack! Come back here for a minute!" Pip's father called back to Jack Carlson, who was walking away to follow his orders. "Try some of this with me. It's pizza. Peppina's mother made it."

"Okay, but what's pizza?"

"Boy, this is good!" said Douglas Sr., and Jack agreed as they each took a bite. The pizza was still warm from the day's heat, and the extra virgin olive oil dripped from their fingers. "Very good!" Douglas Sr. mumbled, speaking with a mouthful, as his son had done while eating it. Peppina and Pip stood smiling as the two men enjoyed the treat neither of them had before. They remained silent as they ate. Rollo kept sniffing.

"Is your family I-talian?" asked Jack, accentuating the 'I' in the word. "Because I read that most I-talians don't understand English or speak with heavy accents."

"I was born in America on the Fourth of July," Peppina smiled. "My parents are from Italy, but my father speaks perfect English. He says it's important for someone to speak the language where they live."

"I see, young lady. Well, with your blonde hair and those big

114

green eyes of yours, I never would have known!" Jack smiled.

"You tell your Mom that I said thank you!" Mr. Nicholson finally said as he swallowed the last bite. "And tell her I never had anything as good before. But don't tell Douglas's Mom I said that," he laughed. "I think I'll be eating at your parents' hotel."

"So will I," said Jack Carlson. "You tell your Mom I thank her!" He smiled at little Peppina.

In 1853, the town abandoned its existing train station along Broadway. The Cleveland and Pittsburgh Railroad Company occupied the land between what would later be called Seventh and Eighth from Washington Street, past Commerce, to Broadway. That location housed freight and passenger stations, an engine house, and a turntable. Riverboat wharfs covered the Ohio River bank along Riverside between Seventh and Eight Street. When the railroad purchased land just past 12th Street, gradually, a series of maintenance facilities were built from that point along the river up to 18th Street. That complex would later be called the Wellsville Shop, casually referred to as the Shop.

The Wellsville railroad complex housed separate shops for machinists, carpenters, blacksmiths, boiler workers, tin smiths, an oil shop, and painters, among others. The railroad erected a larger roundhouse with a much larger turntable to accommodate larger steam locomotives. Wellsville was the central point of the railroad at that time and where all heavy repairs took place. A master mechanic oversaw that facility and other river towns in the area.

In 1872, the railroad purchased the old graveyard grounds at 12th Street and expanded the facility even more. It now housed a depot for passenger and freight with a telegraph office and an office for the Assistant Road Foreman of Engines. The two main tracks were diverted and curved close to the blacksmith shop and ran parallel to Main Street at 14th Street. The sorting and arrangement of loaded and empty cars extended the yard up to 25th Street at that time. When erected in 1897, the main Station building stood close to the tracks before the river. The

Third Street Depot remained the senior passenger depot, taking freight and packages for businesses and residents. The 12th Street Station received and sorted some heavy freight, gradually reducing riverboat usage from its inception in the mid-1800s. Now under a 99-year lease, the Pennsylvania Railroad owned and operated the railroad.

On that summer day, when Pip and Peppina arrived for their tour, Mr. Nicholson knew the kids would want to see the roundhouse and turntable first. That was the most impressive site at the shop, especially for children.

"Now, Douglas, I want you to take your friend by the hand and follow me and hold on tight to Rollo," Mr. Nicholson directed his son as he carefully led them through the safest passages there, waiting for slow-moving passing wagons at times and an occasional train pulling cars. Paths allowed workers to walk throughout easily. The children obediently followed the elder Nicholson as they passed between buildings with giant smokestacks, telegraph poles, and crossover bridges.

Peppina's face radiated with happiness as she walked and hopped at times, waving to workers and smiling as they waved back. Pip followed his friend's gestures and was having a great time in the busy railroad yard. He was especially proud of his father and showed it. Rollo barked at a few people, his canine way of saying hello.

Douglas Nicholson Sr., a mechanics manager, explained the giant mechanism of turning and housing steam locomotives. A few men were working underneath a sizeable 0-8-0 steam locomotive. One of them was Jack Carlson, who followed Mr. Nicholson's recent orders and led the small crew down in the pit of the turntable to look at the engine.

"It doesn't need service yet, Doug," Jack Carlson shouted up to his boss as he noticed him pass by. Douglas Nicholson Sr, a laborer before promoted, preferred to be addressed on a first-name basis. "But the rod bearings need to be replaced," Jack continued.

"House it, Jack, and schedule it for that. And give it a boiler wash and an oiling as soon as we have an opening."

"Aye, aye, skipper!"

Pip's father explained what those things meant and what it entailed. Then he took the kids inside the roundhouse, where they could see the giant locomotives up close.

"Wow! They're huge," laughed Peppina, and Pip agreed as he held tightly to Rollo's leash. "When I see them this close and together with other ones, I feel really tiny," she laughed again excitedly. "What do you think, Rollo?" The dog just tilted his head and looked at Peppina.

Mr. Nicholson showed them some of the shops. He brought them to where the trains emptied their coal dust and explained the procedure at the coal dump pits. Douglas Sr. described how the water filled the engines' boilers and where the coal chutes filled the coal tenders at an overhead trestle. Pip's father noticed that the kids were getting tired even though they denied it. To spare them an extra walk, he just pointed to the car sorting area and explained that operation from where they stood.

As the afternoon heat rose, Mr. Nicholson walked both children to his shop office, which was nearby, and sat them down. He opened an old ice chest, grabbed a cold bottle of his wife's homemade lemonade, and filled two ceramic cups. After handing the drinks to the children, Rollo received a large pan of water. The dog's tongue licked the pan dry, and then he curled up and laid down between Pip and Peppina.

After spending an hour and a half in the sun while seeing the Shop, Mr. Nicholson decided it was too hot for the young children to walk back on foot. He drove them and Rollo back to the hotel in a railroad-owned carriage.

"Thank you, Mr. Nicholson; I had a wonderful time!" Peppina indeed did and showed it with her magnanimous facial expressions.

"Thank you, Dad! I did, too!"

"You tell your mom I said thank you for the pizza, young lady." Douglas Sr. smiled before he drove off.

The kids spent the rest of the afternoon resting outside the hotel with Rollo in the shade of a tree.

Shortly after Lorenzo Ricci left the hotel, Luigi called Liam Kelly and Roberto Barata into a meeting in a back room on the first floor that he used as an office. Luigi considered neither of them especially intelligent, but they were both clever, focused on their work, always alert, and produced results. Most of all, they were loyal to him, and he trusted them. Luigi knew he had made good decisions by hiring them both. Men like Liam and Roberto were precisely what he needed to grow his business now and in the future.

Luigi was honest in his business dealings. He felt blessed with his ability to count cards and never considered that gift cheating, remembering how he and Baggio had discussed that topic often. 'Our abilities are gifts from the heavens above,' he recalled Biaggio's sentiments, 'we do nothing different than any other business or corporation in the world. Remember that always, my friend.' Luigi glanced at the photo of him and Biaggio now on his desk as he recollected that street wisdom of his old friend.

"This guy is going to do several things to us," Luigi predicted as he told them about his interaction with Enzo Ricci earlier. He used the word 'us' to include both of them as part of his place of business, which they regarded as respectful and made them feel comfortable. He never threw the fact that both were well-paid and employees beneath him. Luigi wanted to make them feel part of a family, and they did. Both men looked up to Luigi because of his wisdom, generosity, and, most of all, strength. They respected him as all the hotel employees did. Luigi was a good and strong man, someone to admire.

"Ricci's just a thug. He has no people working for him, only other punks he hires when he needs them. He's associated with another small-time hood named Giuseppe Marino. Still, he'll want to give the impression that he alone is powerful." Luigi was more observant of Ricci during his short meeting than

Enzo Ricci probably realized. "If Marino's involved, they most likely will hire some toughs from Pittsburgh to do these things. I assume it will be there because Marino has small-time associates over there. Here, he knows nobody and has no rapport with the local police. Ricci probably took the train from there by himself." His men chuckled at that notion. "He wants to be 'un grande capo,' what Italians call a big shot," Luigi said to amuse them further. "He'll start with something small to send us the message that he's coming for us, to scare us." Luigi wiggled in his chair, jokingly to simulate being afraid, but again using the word 'us' to show camaraderie between him and his two men. Liam and Roberto burst out with sincere belly laughs at their boss's gesture of fear. Then, Luigi became serious, leaned forward in his high-back padded chair, looked at each sternly, one at a time, and advised, "But don't underestimate him or anyone, for that matter. I don't want any of 'us' to get hurt!" Luigi leaned back and casually said, "If he approaches either of you with a proposition to betray me, don't brush him off. Act like you're interested and come to me with the information. You both know I'll reward you for your allegiance to me." Luigi noticed the expressions of gratitude on both his men's faces. "If his efforts get serious, we will eliminate him, one way or another."

As predicted by Luigi, Enzo Ricci's first move against him came from a small event. He sent a couple of guys into the hotel at night to disrupt the place by abusing two prostitutes. Ricci apparently didn't know that the women Luigi had hired were hardened and carried derringers in their garters under their dresses.

As the piano player entertained those in the bar, one of the hired hoods smacked a prostitute. Another young lady of the night spotted the trouble and immediately pulled out her small pistol as Luigi had instructed, firing directly at the grubby man from about ten feet away. The sound of the blast from the small gun penetrated throughout the hotel's first floor. Surprisingly, her aim with the usually inaccurate weapon was almost dead on, and the bullet grazed his cheek. Liam and Roberto were both alert and ready. Liam rushed over to the other hired thug and used his massive club to hammer him. The man's eyes crossed as blood poured down his face, and he fell to the ground like a dead weight. At the same time Liam was working on suppressing his prey, Roberto ran over to the one who had just had his cheek cropped by a bullet, the least of his problems. Roberto beat on him until his face was battered so severely he rolled over in a fetal position, sobbing like a baby. Liam and Roberto each grabbed one of the beaten men and dragged them outside near the tied horses and wagons. One taking the shoulders and the other the feet, Liam and Roberto flung them, one at a time, onto piles of horse dung.

Luigi remained seated throughout the quick altercation, observing his men at work. He rose from his chair at one of the gambling tables. "Everyone!" he called out in his robust voice, "Everyone! I apologize for the disruption and the inconvenience. A round of drinks is on the house." The men roared in gratefulness as the two waiters and one waitress began taking orders. Luigi raised his glass to Liam and Roberto as the two men appeared in the doorway after dumping the two lifeless bodies. "To my two guys! Thank you for your dedication to this fine establishment and for keeping us all safe! Heroes!" The men and women cheered. "And to Sandy," Luigi turned to face the young prostitute who fired the small pistol, "the young woman with such amazing aim!" Luigi had undoubtedly sent a message back to Enzo Ricci. The following morning, the two battered men were gone. Evidently, someone either picked them up or took them to a doctor for treatment.

Giulia managed and worked the kitchen. Helpers operated alongside her there and in preparing the beer for the bar. That was an enormous and successful contribution. She had recently met an immigrant woman named Luisa D'Angelo from Pittsburgh. Giulia put her in charge of the hotel cleaning staff.

"Luisa!" Giulia called her helper. "I want to show you how I make bread." Giulia reasoned that Luisa, being an Italian, might also be able to help her in the kitchen. She needed better help there but was careful who she hired. All of her helpers were Americans who knew nothing about Italian food. She could test Luisa on making bread to see if she knew how to cook and bake the way most Italian women did.

The two women walked outside to the bakehouse, each carrying a tray of raised bread loaves ready to bake. Inside the small structure were pieces of wood simmering over a flat brick surface. Giulia took a small rake and removed all the burnt ashes, revealing glowing bricks. "Watch me," she instructed. Giulia took a large handful of flour and sprinkled it all over the bricks. Then, she laid each loaf on the searing bricks, keeping them apart. Surprisingly to Giulia, Luisa knew the same method and even the exact time they were ready. Giulia smiled, "So you're a bread baker, hey?" Now she had a good kitchen helper.

Giulia also had help serving breakfast, lunch, and dinner. Other waitresses and waiters dealt with the night crowd. Luigi supervised every aspect of the hotel, from ordering all supplies to seeing to repairs. He was a natural-born manager. His biggest asset was the gambling area, where the house always made the money. Luigi knew that liquor was the main component of keeping the hotel alive; it was its lifeblood. Liquor made money, and it fueled gambling. So when Roberto reported back that Enzo Ricci approached him, Luigi was all ears.

It happened when Roberto Barata walked to his apartment on First Street two days after the first incident at the hotel. The robust figure of a large man appeared out of the fog in the early morning before Roberto arrived home. At first, he put up his fists to defend himself, looking around for other accomplices of the man. Then a distinct raspy voice came out of the mist saying, "Don't worry, I'm not gonna hurt you," he said in his thick Sicilian accent. "You and I are paesanos. I don't want to hurt a fellow countryman." Enzo pulled out a machine-rolled cigarette and offered one to Roberto, who declined. Enzo lit his cigarette and inhaled deeply, afterward casually saying, "I have an offer for you. A way you can make some money." He walked closer to where Roberto was standing. The younger man remembered what Luigi had told him. He would remain loyal to his boss but didn't want to seem too anxious to take Enzo's offer.

Enzo was closer to him now, and Roberto told him, "Not too close!" He studied his opponent carefully, grasping how accurate Luigi's prediction was. 'A brilliant man, my boss is,' he thought, 'I would never cross him,' his mind quickly wandered. "I work for Luigi Massaro," he said.

"I know. I know. But I can be a help to him." He took another deep puff from his cigarette and continued, "He just doesn't realize it yet." Ricci blew out the smoke and observed the young man before him. 'Young punk doesn't know anything,' he surmised. "I could double his profits within a year. You would be doing him a favor, and he doesn't even have to know you helped me."

"What do you mean?"

"Well, I'm going to steal his liquor shipment from Pittsburgh." He watched Roberto closely, thinking how that would severely damage Luigi's business. "I know your boss, and he's smart enough to understand how important liquor is to him. He gets all his booze in large shipments to save money. He's shrewd!" Inhaling again from his smoke, Enzo exhaled and said, "Losing that much money will bring him to his senses."

Roberto recalled how Luigi had brought up the importance of liquor supply to a bar. "He is smart; he won't let you just take it." Roberto played his role well for a younger man.

"Right!" After another quick draw from his cigarette, Enzo continued, "That's why he's going to make someone go on the ride like he always does. I want it to be you." Enzo smirked, "Yeah, I know about the ride-along with all the liquor deliveries. I've been watching your boss's activities. I don't know where he does it, but he sneaks someone onboard at some point." Full of self-pride, he told Roberto, "All you have to do is take a punch. You know, to make it look real. I'll make sure it's a light one. Then, you drop your shotgun or whatever weapon you carry and get paid $100," Enzo grinned, "That's a fortune for a young guy like you!"

"It is a lot of soldi," Roberto raised his eyebrows, pretending to be very interested. "What if he hires someone else to guard the train car like always?"

"Make sure it's you. Luigi has to leave one of you to watch the hotel. You seem to be a resourceful young man. Tell him you should personally go because of the importance. You know, with all that happened at his bar the other day and all." Then Enzo thought and added, "Make sure it's not the Irishman, or I'll take care of him." He grinned again. "You don't want that, do you?"

Roberto was smart enough to know that if he declined this offer Enzo would kill him before he walked into his home. An accomplice of his was probably hiding in the fog. He had too much information. But Roberto had to make his performance look real and pondered. "How do I know you'll pay me that much money?"

"Because I'm a man of my word!" Enzo appeared to get angry and added, "And because I would never kill a paesano unless I absolutely had to." He dropped the cigarette from his hand and used his black leather boot to extinguish it.

"Okay! But I never want Luigi to know I betrayed him."

"You got it, kid!" Enzo explained the plan thoroughly and then reached out his hand. Roberto shook it, carefully ensuring Enzo didn't pull any fast moves. 'Young punk took my bait,' thought Enzo, 'I would never pay this bastardo that much money. Stupid kid. He'll get paid with his own blood in the freight car before his body is dumped outside for the animals to feed on him.'

Roberto asked Luigi for a private meeting the next day. He reported everything to him about the hijack, especially cautioning Luigi about Liam's safety. Roberto told him Enzo's words, 'I'll take care of him,' to mean he was going to have him killed or seriously hurt if he picked Liam to go. Luigi understood that, and also, by targeting liquor, Enzo Ricci could cripple him. Luigi had to make careful plans. "Thank you, Roberto. I'll let you know what to do." He then sat back in his chair, thinking about a plan.

In the wee morning hours on the day of his liquor delivery, Luigi remained at the hotel and didn't go to sleep. He had sent both Roberto and Liam by horseback to Pittsburgh ten minutes earlier to get inside the freight car.

"It's going to be a rough ride, Men. Remember that," Luigi warned them before they left. Luigi acted as general, giving orders to his subordinates and carefully explaining how to handle the situation.

"Are you sure you don't want one of us with you in case he sends someone to the hotel?"

"He won't do that. He'll focus all his attention on the train. As I said, he only has a handful of thugs, and we took out two already. Nobody will want to come back here. Besides, he thinks Liam will be here." Luigi was sure of himself.

"At some point, probably close to Pittsburgh, he'll stop the train," Luigi paused, thinking, "I obviously don't know how, but be prepared at all times. I believe it will be closer to the city because Enzo Ricci knows people there to help him," Luigi mused. "And it's the perfect place to sell it." He thought, 'He'll probably sell it to Giuseppe Marino, that bastard who ruined my business there.' But he didn't tell the men what he was thinking. "Be prepared because Ricci's not stupid enough to stage a hold-up. No, he's going to stop the train another way." Luigi pondered. "Possibly staging an emergency or blocking the track, or somehow by pretending to be an official of some type. Anyway, that's what I think, but expect anything."

Luigi evaluated his employees. They were loyal men. "Get on the freight car right at the liquor distributor. The usual guards get on later, so they won't see you get on, but look closely anyway. Be careful, guys. I don't want to see either of you hurt. And you know I'll reward you both handsomely, but most of all, I want you to realize how much I appreciate your commitment. Thank you both." They nodded in reply.

"Don't worry, Boss. We'll take care of this guy once and for all," Liam said, and Roberto nodded in agreement.

"Be safe, men!" and they rode off on horseback. Both men held long lead lines, the extra horses Luigi told them to take trailing behind them as they rode off. The men galloped through open areas of the countryside to make up for the lost time riding slower through paths.

Luigi had instructed his men to ensure nobody was watching or following them. Liam and Roberto ferried their horses to West Virginia, cutting across that state's panhandle. Then, they rode hard and fast along the country trails of Pennsylvania and arrived at the distribution center well before the freight car departed. After putting their four horses in a local stable, they watched in seclusion as the laborers loaded the heavy crates into the large boxcar. Liam and Roberto jumped into the boxcar when no one was looking. They had checked their weapons to ensure they were loaded and ready before entering the darkness in the rear of the closed freight car, where they hid behind stacked crates. They had two six-shot Colt double-action revolvers and a pump shotgun a piece. "Okay, we're ready," Liam whispered to Roberto as they sat on a crate behind larger boxes. They remembered their positions for when the doors opened. In the light of day, their eyes would have to adapt quickly to the sudden change from darkness.

The foreman closed the doors and whistled to have the boxcar attached to the train. Liam and Roberto had settled in for the trip. However, less than ten minutes into the ride, the train, still traveling slowly, came to a crawl and then to an abrupt stop. Luigi's men were ready. They each carefully felt their way in the dark to opposite sides of the door so as not to be seen when it opened. Liam put his ear to the side of the car to listen to what was said outside. He could only hear mumbling. Then he heard a man's voice yell, "Now!" The next sound he and Roberto heard was the latch sliding. Next, the door slowly opened, revealing the harsh light of the early day. The two men waited inside the boxcar. Now, they could hear the exchange of words.

"We need to remove all these crates as evidence," a familiar raspy voice said to a railroad worker. Roberto carefully slid his face and peeked outside for two seconds. It was Enzo Ricci speaking. Three big and rugged-looking men were standing around four horse-drawn wagons. Ricci had a single revolver tucked into his waist belt. Roberto used four fingers to signal to Liam how many men were outside. Liam waved Roberto to go, and both men jumped off the train, each holding their shotguns. Both simultaneously pointed their weapons directly at Enzo Ricci.

"Hold it now!" shouted Liam. "Don't make me have to shoot ya, now," he said in his Irish brogue. The two railroad crew members ran back to the locomotive for safety.

Enzo Ricci stood dressed as a Pinkerton guard, with a fake badge pinned to his uniform and credentials in his hand. He raised one thick eyebrow, looked at the two men, and shouted, "Punks!" Enzo didn't appear to be alarmed. Looking directly at Roberto, he said, "I knew you were a lying, untrustworthy bastardo!" The red lantern he used to stop the train was on the ground by his side.

"You just stay still," Roberto yelled back in his Sicilian dialect. "Or we'll blast the four of you!" He held his shotgun high, pointing it at Enzo.

"No! You guys drop your guns!" a throaty voice shouted at Roberto's side. It was Giuseppe Marino himself. His short, muscular build pointed a double-barreled shotgun at Roberto. Neither Liam nor Roberto had noticed him. He had hidden out of harm's way to the side of the train. His giant goon stood on the other side of them. Poorly dressed in a black baggy suit, he pointed a similar shotgun at Liam. Looking at Roberto, Marino told him, "I knew we couldn't trust you. You're loyal to that asshole boss of yours."

"Say your prayers," said Marino. "It's time to go to bed."

As Liam and Roberto stood nervous but proud, ready to

meet their maker, a blast rang out, then another. Roberto and Liam quickly felt around their bodies as a reflex. They were unharmed. More blasts sounded, one after the other. Enzo Ricci lay face down; a shotgun round had obliterated his shaven head. Giuseppe Marino was on his knees, his hands in the air to surrender. What sounded like a pistol shot finished him off.

Marino's goon got hit twice but was still running and grunting at the man who shot him. Another single pistol shot slowed him in his tracks. He staggered, muttering something in Italian before falling to his knees. The goon tried to get up but fell to his side. His legs jiggled as bright red blood foamed in his mouth, and his hands clutched his neck as he choked. Luigi Massaro slowly walked up to him and used his boot to roll the giant of a man over on his back, sliding the shotgun away from what resembled a wounded grizzly bear. Watching him choke to death and remembering his brutality, he softly said, "Die, Bastardo. I won't put you out of your misery." His face now as red as a beet, eyes bulging in horror, Marino's goon took his last gasp of life. He was the guy who cut off Alfonso Lorusso's pinky finger and later killed him back when Luigi lost his business in Pittsburgh. 'A fine finish for you, my friend,' Luigi thought, looking at the body of a truly evil person.

The three wagon workers held their arms high, shouting, "We're only workers! We're only workers!" They remained unharmed. Two Pittsburgh policemen walked from the tree-lined area where Luigi Massaro had stood a few minutes before.

Luigi had waited about 15 minutes and followed his men. However, his journey went directly to the police station. Once there, he spoke to a cop he knew from his days in Pittsburgh, knowing he wasn't on Marino's payroll. That policeman assumed where the incident would occur as Marino's men had previously done other jobs there but never got caught. Marino had paid policemen on his take to turn a blind eye those few times. But Luigi and the police followed the train unseen, riding by horseback to the side of the tracks along the city streets. When they spotted the wagons just outside the city, they immediately rode into the wooded tree-lined area and waited.

Liam and Roberto had no idea that Luigi was following them and looked at him in amazement. "What? Did you think I would let you both get hurt?" Luigi smiled. Speechless, his two men just shook hands and hugged their boss one at a time, still bewildered. "Let's sell those horses you stabled," Luigi laughed, "the boxcar is safe, so we're riding home in style! I'm buying us tickets on a nice passenger car—and the drinks are on me!"

Chapter Ten

Wellsville, Ohio 1891-1893

Growing pains

The town of Wellsville was continually growing. Electric street-lights were used for the first time in the town during the first week of 1891. Developed in Cleveland, Ohio, in 1879, North America's first successful arc light system began distribution. Made from carbon arc, they had glowing carbon tips to produce most of the light. However, carbon arc lighting systems caused fires, especially indoors, because of the open sparks. In addition, someone had to trim the lights, a term for adding new carbon rods every night. Later, a different type of carbon was used to allow the lights to burn throughout the night. It was a flame arc type, and it produced more carbon vapor and lasted much longer without trimming so often.

By early 1893, most kids still called Douglas Nicholson II by the nickname he had been labeled as Pip, except for Peppina. His only friends were Peppina and his dog, Rollo. The three of them spent most of their available time together. Peppina gradually brought Pip out of his self-inflicted prison. She helped him escape that shell he hid in and made him into the boy who would someday become a man. The confidence and companionship she provided even cured his stammer.

Mr. Nicholson finally succumbed to the realization that trolleys were a reality. However, He had been right about so much political bickering and money passed around before the decision. Surprisingly, a Cleveland-based company won the rights to build over some of the most prominent leaders in East Liverpool. When the streetcar line from East Liverpool to Wellsville began being built, politicians proposed merging the two towns. Riveling politicians of the time crushed any possibility of that happening.

"Finally!" Douglas Sr. yelled, quoting his copy of the local newspaper, "The streetcar construction is moving along rapidly!" Since they settled the agreement on September 4, 1891, he expected something to stop its progression. But now it was happening. Martha just smiled as she listened while doing her sewing. Her husband's emotional outbursts about politics always amused her. Their son was reading. He and his dog, Rollo, sat on the floor closer to the fireplace, where a small wood fire glowed.

"I can't believe it's really happening," Pip said to boost his father's morale. Rollo had no opinion. He just remained sprawled out before the warm fire.

"Well, it is, son," Mr. Nicholson let out a joyous chuckle as he replied. "I can't believe it either, to tell you the truth. A long time coming." He laughed quietly as he shook his head.

The East Liverpool and Wellsville Electric Railway officially opened on December 17, 1891. There was a grand ceremony between politicians who mostly disliked each other. They shook hands and made speeches complimenting themselves in front of their constituents to acquire future votes. The streetcar line was an instant success and ran from East Liverpool all the way down to 18th Street in Wellsville, the location of a turntable that turned it around to go back.

Giulia Massaro was finally learning to pronounce the name 'Douglas.' Her version was far from perfect but close enough to be understood. Douglas appreciated that she made such an effort. He became fond of his friend's mother as she did of him. Giulia began to think of Douglas as a member of her own family. The young boy had many meals there during the remainder of 1890 and into 1891. She attributed his sudden increase in height to her cooking.

"You see? Mr. Douglas." She enjoyed jokingly calling him Mr. before his first name. "You're getting bigger! I told you that you gotta eat!"

Peppina giggled because she knew how much her friend loved her mother's cooking. "Mama made a different type of pizza today. I helped her. I'm learning to cook," her beautiful eyes sparkled from being so proud of herself. "And ravioli, too!" Her eyes gleamed once more.

"C'mon now, you and Peppina, come inside and sit down," Giulia called. "Emanuela veni´ca!" she shouted for her youngest daughter.

Peppina and her friend sat across from each other, ready for their afternoon meal. Rollo sat obediently by his master's side. Giulia took a liking to Pip's dog and allowed him inside only before or after the lunch rush hour was over. She felt sorry that the dog had to sit outside in the heat of summer or the cold of winter. The hour right after noon was when workers and laborers from factories, stores, and businesses came in to eat. Emanuela walked slowly toward the table and sat away from Rollo; she was afraid of the dog.

Giulia brought a wooden baby highchair for Felo and set it next to the table. Then, she returned with a specially prepared dish for her one-year-old son. "Peppina, help your brother eat if he doesn't." But Felo did a decent job of eating alone with his hands. He was already bonded with Peppina as she helped care for him the most between his sisters. The baby could also probably sense the bubbly personality of his older sister. And he also seemed to like Pip, waving his hands and laughing whenever he saw him.

After each finished their ravioli bowl, Peppina wanted to help her mother bring the other food. Giulia hadn't yet allowed her eldest daughter to carry heavy trays of hot food; she didn't feel she was quite ready. Giulia brought the larger tray with two dishes of pollo alla diavola. Peppina helped by carrying a small-er tray with two medium-sized bowls of insalata di giardino con pomodorini secchi. Along with the salads she brought were three slices of pizza and fresh bread baked earlier that morning. Emanuela only wanted pizza and quietly sat as she ate it.

"I love your Mom's ravioli," Pip smiled. "Is that chicken in the big plate?"

"It's called pollo alla diavola. It's chicken with my mama's homemade recipe of mixed spicy peppers seasoned with differ-ent types of herbs with a special tomato sauce." Peppina was teaching Douglas words in Italian, and she made him practice the names of food as well. The little girl made her friend sound out and enunciate each word. She giggled when he made a mis-take and then corrected him.

"And that?" Pip motioned to the salad. "What are those red things?"

"Okay, that's called insalata di giardino con pomodorini sec-chi. It's a garden salad. Mama picked the romaine early from the garde. . ."

"What's romaine?" Pip cut off Peppina midsentence.

"It's a lettuce. You've had it before, but Mama didn't cut it fresh when you had it the last time." Peppina looked directly into her friend's eyes. "It's not polite to cut someone off before they finish their sentence, Douglas," she said in a ladylike man-ner.

"I'm sorry."

"It's okay," Peppina giggled at her sanctimonious way of teaching Pip proper etiquette, even though the young boy was always well-mannered. Her father, Luigi, firmly insisted that his children adhered to the same manners and proper behavior he learned as a child. "The red things are the sun-dried toma-toes."

"Wow! They are good! really, really good!" That day in the late summer of 1891 was when Pip would never forget that he had sundried tomatoes for the first time.

"The pizza is made with homemade ricotta and mozzarella," announced Peppina. She explained the correct way to pronounce the words ricotta and mozzarella. Even the usually quiet Emanuela couldn't control her laughter at that demonstration.

Pip took a liking to it right away. "Hmm, it's so good!" he chewed as he said it, but with his lips together, Pip was taught not to speak with food in his mouth, but he couldn't help it now. "The bread is always so good, too."

As the children continued eating, Luigi Massaro entered the dining area. He stretched his arms and yawned. Luigi dressed in dark trousers, a white dress shirt, and a vest as usual. He bore his shoulder holster with the larger revolver over his styled vest. The tired man was rising after working into the early hours of the day. He usually slept in one of the back rooms behind the 'gentlemen's smoking area,' the name given for the gambling area, so he wouldn't disturb his wife or children.

"So, who do we have here?" he asked, glancing at Pip as he walked toward where the kids were sitting.

"You know Douglas, Papa."

"Of course I do," laughed Luigi. "How are you today, young man?"

"Very good, sir!" Pip stood up as he addressed his friend's father, his eyes fixed on the pistol. The young boy was always a bit intimidated by the presence of the large, well-built man. Pip didn't see Luigi as often as he did Giulia. Peppina's father usually slept until the afternoon, then was busy bargaining with merchants and other businessmen.

Luigi smiled and held himself from laughing as the small, nervous boy stood shaking slightly. "Sit down, Douglas. Please relax." He patted the boy's blonde hair.

"Thank you, sir!" Still eyeing the gun, Pip secretly never understood why Giulia spoke with a heavy Italian accent, and Luigi spoke such good English. It was just one of those mysteries that children never ask about.

"Douglas, always remember to enjoy your childhood. You can never repeat it." Luigi smiled at Pip and raised his right hand with his forefinger pointed. "When you become a man, you will have many responsibilities and little time to enjoy yourself as you do now."

"Papa, we're kids. We do have fun!" intervened Peppina as she giggled, making her eyes twinkle.

Luigi couldn't resist his little firecracker and leaned over to give his eldest daughter a big kiss on her cheek. He noticed his younger daughter sitting quietly and walked over to kiss her, too. "Hey, Felo, how are you today?" he patted his son's head, seeing his face covered with the food he was eating.

Luigi wasn't earning enough from his small gambling operation in the smaller town, not as much as expected. Even though plenty of workers were anxious to gamble at the drop of a hat, he learned from experience to be more cautious. The robbery that nearly cleaned him out of money still rang clear in his memory. Operating his gambling skill at a slow pace was his only option, as frustrating as it was. He had less than half of his father's money left. Upon setting up his gambling lounge in town, the hotel, bar, and restaurant were initially only supposed to be a backup source of income for him. Now, he relied on the hotel's earnings but thought of it as scraps of money. There had to be a way to give a jolt to his gambling. Luigi pressured himself to work as hard as he could and spent time into the early morning hours, always focused on reclaiming his past grandeur. Luigi missed the better lifestyle he had in Italy as a child and as a younger man. Seeing his oldest daughter and her friend allowed him to reminisce about his youth with his best friend, Salvatore Giorgianni, and their adventures together as young men. Luigi recalled one trip in particular. They traveled together to Rome and climbed the stairs of the Trinità dei Monti on the Piazza di Spagna. And, of course, climbing the Spanish Steps, chasing beautiful young ladies as they did, listening to them giggle. Those days with Salvatore were now sacred to Luigi. He missed his parents and little sister. His father, Felice, had never sent anyone to find him, and he wondered if he was destined to remain in America his entire life. Luigi always worried about his father's troubles with the Mandanici family after his duel with their son. Now, in a small, remote industrial town, his mind drifted about living in the luxury of his past days.

At just twenty-seven years old, Giulia was still beautiful despite her hard work. She maintained her figure, probably from scrubbing, cooking, and cleaning. But disillusionment grew over the long nights her husband spent gambling, usually accompanied by pretty, nicely dressed young women surrounding him. She was jealous and forced to wear work dresses with aprons that had to be changed throughout the day to make herself presentable. It reminded her of those dreadful days in her parent's hotel in Little Italy. She missed dressing up and shopping with Maria Benedetto as she did back in Pittsburgh. Their lives were now so different from their time together there. Giulia began to resent Luigi for neglecting her and wanted those former days back when he craved her and gave her more attention. She swore she would do anything to get them back.

"Hey paesano, we speak the same dialect," an Italian immigrant in soot-covered clothes shouted to Giulia that afternoon. He was checking into the hotel and wanted to know the rate for long-term stays. He had heard the pretty young woman speaking and recognized her accent.

Giulia ignored the references to being his 'paesano' just because the grubby-looking man migrated from a region of Italy near where she was born. "I'll give you a special rate of three dollars and one free weekly bath," Giulia replied without making eye contact.

"That's the best a beautiful woman like you, with the face of an angel, can do?"

"The best," she replied, ignoring the foolish compliment and still not looking directly at him. "You want it?"

"Yeah, but I don't take baths; I just wash in a basin," he smiled, his mouth full of dirty, crooked teeth, with some missing. "I don't believe in baths! It weakens the body!" The 25-year-old short man looked older and was the type who always looked unkempt. He worked as a low-end laborer at the American Sheet and Tin Plate Company Mill, which was nearby. That plant produced the first tinplate in the United States. The vast complex began past Little Yellow Creek and ran far along the river. The immigrant man who recently arrived from Italy wore dirty, beat-up clothes as he usually did.

"Write your name on the line," said Giulia, pointing to the register ledger book. "Two weeks in advance."

"I don't write."

"What is your name?"

"Nicola Bucci," he replied in his crude dialect. "Hey, maybe you wanna give me a bath? Then, maybe I don't mind so much. Hey, whatta you say? I make wonderful things happen for you." He grinned, exposing that same dingy smile.

Giulia, who was also illiterate, put a mark for his name in the ledger. She was learning some basic reading and writing from Luigi but was not yet literate. "You wanna talk to my husband about me giving you a bath? He's the big man on the other side of the room leaning against the doorway." As much as she wanted to make her husband jealous, this was not the man. Nicola's odor and appearance repulsed her. Just the thought of what he said made her want to vomit.

Nicola didn't answer. He just slumped and blushed. Then, he reached into his pocket, pulled out some money, and handed Giulia six dollars in bills.

"I didn't think so! Here's your key."

Giulia couldn't be bothered with Nicola because of his crudeness and poor manners. He was loud and obnoxious, but something about his ruggedness secretly aroused her bodily desires. She wished she hadn't allowed the man in the hotel. She didn't need the temptation.

"Hey, take a bath sometime!" she told him in their mutual dialect the first time she served him in the dining area. "Maronna mia! I'll let you use one of the tubs for free anytime you want!"

Giulia usually seated Nicola near the kitchen to keep him away from the other people. 'Oh, my God! Do I want him to touch me because I pass here so often?' she thought as she struggled with that notion. 'I want to feel a rugged hand on my naked skin. Luigi is always busy, and I miss the touch of a man. No! I have to pull myself together. Nicola is nothing more than a measly ant. I could have any man I want! Dear God, what am I thinking; what am I doing?' Giulia fought these impulses she felt.

In the winters of 1890 and 1891, Peppina and Pip spent their time ice skating on small ponds. Sometimes, they bundled up in warm clothes and walked onto the frozen river, occasionally reaching the middle. Rollo joined them, skidding around on the shiny frozen water. The two kids often played board games of Parcheesi, Backgammon, and Checkers. They also played Traveler's Tour, usually with one of Pip's parents, since it was more of an advanced game for them. Luigi taught them card games such as solitaire and even poker in his spare time. Dice were not considered proper for children.

In nicer weather, they fished and swam or walked together in town. At Little Yellow Creek, Pip taught Peppina how to skip rocks along the creek and even at the edge of the Ohio River bank.

"You have to twist your wrist like this," Pip carefully instructed her.

"I think I got it!" Peppina was excited.

"It takes time, but you're doing real good for a beginner."

Peppina, in turn, taught Pip how to jump rope. She was quick and agile as she gracefully displayed her jumping skills. "Now you try."

"I don't know if I can do that."

"You can. Here, I'll show you." Peppina put Pip's hands in place. "Now jump while lifting your two feet at the same time. On the first try, Pip tripped and fell. Peppina knew he felt embarrassed. "Here, I'll do it real slow."

"You make it look easy." But after a few tries at doing it slowly, Pip caught on. "I got it!"

"Yes, you do!" Peppina clapped her hands with excitement. "Now, I'll teach you hopscotch. It's easy!"

The kids played together in front of the hotel or at Riverside in front of The Nicholson's home. Mrs. Heely, Pip's elderly next-door neighbor, always brought the kids glasses of freshly made lemonade. The two children even climbed trees together, smaller ones at best. Rollo accompanied them everywhere. "C'mon," said Peppina, "take my hand and let's skip!" Pip held Rollo's leash in his right hand and his friend Peppina's in his left. Together, they skipped along Riverside and Main Street.

One day in the late summer of 1892, Pip noticed General Reilly standing quietly at the Civil War Veterans Memorial. His head bowed as if he were paying homage to the valiant soldiers he had led in the battles of that war.

"He looks sad," Peppina said, holding tightly onto Rollo's leash as the kids walked along Riverside. "Why do you think that?"

As they walked, Pip explained the story of General Reilly, from his time as a congressman to serving as a colonel of a volunteer regiment and being promoted to general. "He works as a lawyer in town. My parents and most people in town have a lot of respect for him," Pip said. "There are other Civil War veterans in town. My dad explained that war to me." Pip bowed his head in a respectful gesture. "I think he's sad because of things he saw in the war, just like Bill Norton down near the end of Main Street. He's another soldier from that war in town. He lost one of his legs in battle and sits outside in the nicer weather. He says hello to us every time we pass his house. You know him."

"I learned a lot about that war from school and my papa. He went to university in Italy. He knows a lot about history."

"I know that he doesn't like Garibaldi," Pip laughed. "You told me that. We better leave the General alone and cross the street," Pip motioned as he observed General Reilly in deep thought. He didn't want to interrupt him at such a solemn time.

"Papa told me General Garibaldi was invited to be a major general in the Union Army during that war."

"Really?"

"Yep! I don't remember who, but some important American wrote a letter to ask him at the beginning. Garibaldi wanted to, but he only would if he could be in charge of the whole army, and he wanted to end slavery first. I guess they didn't agree to that. Papa says he was arrogant."

"Wow! I never knew that!" Pip stopped walking and stood surprised for a few seconds. Then, the children and Rollo resumed their stroll.

In the warmer weather, the two friends spent days searching the bottom of the Ohio River for various items and gadgets lost in past times over many years. They would take off their shoes and socks at the bank below a grassy slope and walk far out in the river, searching. The most precious commodity that eventually took precedence was their many discoveries of Indian stones.

"I found one! A nice one!" yelled Peppina. Pip and Rollo splashed through the water to see what she held. Rollo shook the water from his fur, splashing the kids. They laughed, enjoying the refreshing water on their bodies under the hot yellow noon sun as it blazed in the cloudless sky. The river was only about 12 inches deep in most places at that time. Some people walked all the way across, and others carefully drove their horse-drawn carriages or wagons to the other side.

"Oh! That's a nice one," Pip affirmed as Peppina handed it to him. "Look at the markings on it. Wow! I think this one's really old. I'll put it in the bag with the others." Pip carefully put it in the cloth bag slung over his left shoulder.

The kids found various types and shapes of river stones that the original natives used to inscribe different markings. Most of the rocks the kids were gathering were very old. Whenever they found one, they would excitedly shout out to the other, who would come running. Rollo always came charging over the shallow water, splattering it whenever he heard one of them holler. Then, he always shook the water from his fur, soaking both children as they twirled around to get all the revitalizing sprinkles of that cool river water they could. The two friends kept their collection of stones in jars at Pip's house to keep them away from Peppina's meddling younger sister.

Douglas and Peppina had already ridden on the new trolley with Mrs. Nicholson when she had to shop in East Liverpool, and she had taken the kids with her. The fare was five cents, and the children rode for free. Peppina and Douglas were in awe as they looked out the windows at all the sights as the moving trolley car traveled to the larger town and back to Wellsville.

Pip celebrated Peppina's tenth birthday on July fourth, 1892. Together, they made lunch from things in their homes. The two of them and Rollo walked down the slope of the river bank past the little shop houses across from the Third Street Station. Pip gave his friend a gift of a small ceramic music box he bought from one of the local shops on Main Street.

"Oh, Douglas, I love it! I'll keep it forever!" she gave Pip a small kiss on his cheek, which made him blush. Peppina giggled when he did.

They stood together that night, watching the Fourth of July fireworks display. Peppina jumped in joy, reminding Pip about the first time she saw the fireworks on her birthday and thinking the glorious show was for her. Over the noise, Peppina told Pip, "I love this holiday best of all!"

That's when Peppina noticed how much taller Pip was getting. By then, Pip had grown more than five inches taller than when he first met Peppina. Everyone told him he was growing like a weed. He also put on more weight, which filled him out. Peppina joked that it was from her mother's cooking.

Peppina bought Pip a beautiful large sterling silver crucifix and chain on his 11th birthday in early December 1892. "It will always help and protect you," she said as she placed it around Pip's neck and locked the clasp. "And it will remind you never to be afraid of anything ever again," Peppina added before she kissed Pip on the cheek, giggling. Pip blushed from embarrassment as he thanked her.

Probably due to her mother's growing reputation for serving

fine Italian food in her restaurant, a few folks in town made the connection that Peppina was the daughter of an Italian immigrant. There was no other way they could have known. The olive green-colored-eyed blonde girl who spoke perfect English hardly appeared to be the stereotypical image of what other immigrants expected an Italian immigrant to be.

The bullies at school learned one of the ethnic slurs for Italians: guineas. Both they and even Pip had no idea what it meant. One of the older kids heard the expression from a man talking outside a saloon one day. He was referring to an Italian coming into East Liverpool to work at one of the factories.

Then, it happened in the spring of 1893. Pip always tolerated bullying from the older kids. He grew to accept it, not realizing how much he was suppressing his anger. But, when they made fun of his friend Peppina, he snapped. But now, he was prepared.

"Hey, stupid! How are you and your dirty guinea friend doing today?" Erik Olsson yelled at Pip as he and his friends walked close to him, laughing. Sean McElhenny, Matt Carlson, and Filip Aries stood beside Erik, almost surrounding 11-year-old Pip. All four older boys were already in High School and still bullied Pip.

"Ignore them, Douglas. Walk with me," a teary-eyed Peppina asked softly. Pip had already handed Rollo's leash to her, and the little girl held it tightly. Pip had already told her how Rollo had worked his leash loose when the same boys harassed him. The dog ran wild, knocking over the boys and into the streets where a passing wagon could have hurt his dog. It was a funny story when she first heard it, but now Peppina didn't want anything bad to happen to Rollo, so she struggled to hold on to him by his leash.

"Yeah, Pip! Run away!" laughed Sean.

Pip glanced at Peppina, then turned back and stared directly into Erik's eyes. Pip had grown quite a bit over the last few years, but Erik still towered over him. He was the largest of the group and the most outspoken, with a body built like an ox.

"Don't call her names!" Pip answered in an angry voice. Rollo kept barking at the larger boys. He could sense his master's agitation.

"Please, Douglas," Peppina began to cry. She was frightened of the older boys and didn't want her friend to get hurt. "Come with me, please!" Rollo's barking almost drowned out her voice.

Erik noticed that Pip didn't run away as usual; he stood there, defiant. So Erik pulled his arm back to hit Pip. And by the length of his stretch, it would be a heavy blow. "You should have gone with the guinea dog," he yelled while throwing his fist. But Pip unexpectedly sidestepped the much larger boy's punch, forcing Erik to lose his balance. Then, to everyone's surprise, Pip punched the big kid hard and directly on his nose with a solid right. Then he punched Erik again, hitting him with a hard left in the pit of the bigger boy's stomach. Erik Olsson folded over and fell to his knees as blood gushed from his nose. All three larger boys stepped away from Pip, who formed a boxing stance and began bouncing while doing legwork. As Erik struggled to stand, Pip barraged the giant of a boy with a left-right combo firmly on his nose again.

"Stay down, you big ugly ogre!"

"You broke my nose!" cried out Erik. He began to sob. "I think you broke my nose!" he wept.

"Get up, you oversized pig! You want some more?" Pip screamed at the bigger kid. Salvia dripped from his mouth as he shrieked. "How about you?" he maneuvered to Sean. Then, still using his legwork, he faced Matt and, finally, Filip, asking them the same question. The older boys thought Pip went berserk. They backed up from the shorter boy, who kept bouncing on the balls of his feet with arms raised, ready to strike like a cobra snake.

"I'm getting out of here!" yelled Sean. "He's crazy!" he said while he turned to run. Erik got to his feet while holding his nose and followed his friends, who were already running away.

"My name is Douglas!" the boy screamed. "Anyone who

calls me Pip again will get worse!" Douglas turned back to face Peppina. He didn't even realize how much taller and stronger he had become. Peppina, who was always a chatterbox, stared back at her friend, speechless.

Douglas Nicholson Sr. was a good, God-fearing man but had grown tired of those older boys bullying his son. Martha and he had discussed the matter with the bullies for a while. Douglas Sr. wanted his son to come to terms with them by himself but realized he didn't. In the later part of the year before, he sat his son down for a talk.

"Son, I'm not one to encourage violence. God knows there's enough of it in this world. But there comes a time in everyone's life when you must stand against those who want to harm you," he began. "I think it might be time that you learn to defend yourself."

From that day on, for over seven months, Douglas Sr. began teaching his son the sport of boxing. His son was patient and willing to learn. Even though he was awkward initially, young Douglas didn't give up, a trait his dad admired. He learned footwork first, which taught him how to observe his opponent's moves and vulnerability. Maneuverability also helped him avoid getting hit and know when to strike. Douglas would practice his footwork around the house until it drove his mother practically crazy, and she insisted he only practice outside. Martha Nicholson wasn't a proponent of her husband's idea of self-defense. She didn't want her son to get hurt, but she didn't want to see her son bullied. Thus, she came to accept the idea, but with bitter-sweet feelings. Douglas obeyed the rule and practiced footwork at the back of their house and on outings with Rollo. He didn't do it in front of Peppina, only Rollo, who he considered his second coach. His dog would sit in front of him and bark back occasionally. Young Douglas gradually advanced to punches of different types but hitting without footwork. His father stuffed a large canvas bag and suspended it from a wooden beam in the cellar. His mother could feel the vibrations whenever her son hit it, and her eyes rolled back every time.

"Keep up your footwork, Son, but don't combine punches with it," his father advised. "You have to master all your punches first." The young boy practiced all angles of throwing: straight, uppercut, round, and hooks, one after the other, until he learned to hit from all directions. "Keep up your block, Son. Whichever hand does the hitting, the other arm blocks," his dad coached. "No low blows. I want you to learn to fight properly." In time, Douglas was ready to combine footwork with his punches. The first time he did, he became disoriented. "Now, you have to harmonize," his father directed. "Blend your footwork with all the punches you already mastered." Douglas Sr. noticed how his son was growing and his body was filling out.

Mr. Nicholson always had talks with his son, not just about boxing but about life in general. He taught his son always to eat right, exercise, and practice his boxing and any other sports he might be interested in. Douglas Sr. urged the young boy to always find a peaceful solution if possible and avoid violence whenever he could. And to find pleasure in whatever work or profession he chose later in life. "Life can be disappointing at times, Son, but these things will help you remain strong throughout rough times," he said, smiling proudly at his young boy. "But if you ever find yourself in a situation where you must fight more than one person, always go for the biggest first."

Then, the day of Douglas's first fight happened. Afterward, Mr. Olsson brought his son Erik to the Nicholson house. Martha greeted him calmly and invited them to sit. Mr. Nicholson and Mr. Olsson shook hands and began to speak. When Mr. Olsson learned that his son and his friends were bullying Douglas, he rose and looked directly at his son. "If I ever learn that you and your friends ever do that to any other boy, I'll break your other nose," he shouted at his son in a heavy Swedish accent. "Now apologize and shake hands with Douglas here, and that be the end of this nonsense."

The two boys rose. Erik had gauze in his nostrils, which affected his speech and made his voice sound somewhat like a honking duck. "Sorry, Douglas," Erik said, and the two boys shook hands. Douglas had to hold back a laugh or even a smile at the sound of Erik's voice.

"Now we'll leave these fine people alone and bid them a good night," Mr. Olsson addressed the Nicholson family before he and his son left.

One thing was sure: Douglas Nicholson II didn't want anyone to call him Pip again, and no one in town ever did after word got out about what he did.

Chapter Eleven

Wellsville, Ohio 1893
As Time Moves On

In 1892, the town of Wellsville accepted plans for a new city hall from architect W.G. Fraser. According to his figures, it would cost $18,000. Construction at the site at the south corner of Fifth and Main Streets was scheduled for completion in December of that same year. The town was growing.

Douglas and Peppina basted in the late afternoon sun lying by a slope at the river bank near the far end of the wharf on Riverside. Almost magically, the sounds of nature drowned out the noise of the factories and workshops in the town. Rollo lay on his back between them, sniffing the fresh grass of the latter part of spring 1893. Their friends lay beside Douglas, Peppina, and Rollo. Ever since word of the fight spread, Douglas became a local legend, and more and more of his classmates wanted to hang around with him. Margaret Myers and Jimmy Brier were among them. No one knew where Douglas's fishing spots were. That was a life-long secret between Peppina and him and, of course, Rollo.

A ruby-throated hummingbird balanced itself in midair directly in front of the children. The kids, amused by the sight of the bird busily collecting nectar from the sweet aroma of wildflowers spread along the grassy slope near the river, as mourning doves sat on the grass and wept their melancholy tunes. The talk between the kids was composed of the creative things formed in the minds of all children in prepuberty. And like most younger people, they had no appreciation of the majestic beauty of nature that spread before them. Taken for granted by the young, those perceptions are nurtured slowly and only live in the memories of older people reflecting on their childhoods.

Peppina began identifying the shapes of the moving cloud formations in the sky. "Look, that one looks like an angel," she said, and the other kids gazed in wonder.

"It does!" shouted Douglas. He pointed to the sky, "And that's God coming out of the clouds!" The configuration appeared like an old man, forcing him to yell, "See the beard!"

"Wow!" said Margaret, "it really does!" The other children pitched in with their versions of what they saw, all passing the time away until the sun began to set. Then, the sky rendered colors of dramatic and vivid swirls of orange and blue and blended in with the passing white floating clouds. Pastel colors reflected onto the flowing river and the children as the dense thickets surrounding them lit up bright green from the mirrored image from above. Rollo and the youngsters rested before God's presence in all his glory. The sounds of insects stirred around them, and birds chirped in their ritual of the end of the day as the sun slowly began to set in the valley. It marked the end of another happy time for the youngsters and unknowingly forever forged into their fondest memories. It was time to go home.

Nicola Bucci always tried to be around Giulia whenever Luigi wasn't present, hopelessly lusting after her voluptuous figure and the beautiful face that adorned it. She aroused him, and like a busy beaver, he worked to build a nest with which to bed her. He even bathed, though occasionally at best, as a show of his devotion to her. Then, one day, when Giulia was alone in the evening, Nicola made an advance on her.

"Hey, Bambina," he brushed closely against her and grinned, hiding his horrible teeth. "Your husband always leaves you alone," he kept the happy grin on his face. His manner of speaking frightened Giulia because it stirred a passion in her body like the devil tempting her. "I see he sleeps downstairs away from you at night. He's always too busy for you. You know there are a lot of pretty young girls here at night," he laughed as he gently put his right hand on her back and slid it downward. "Who knows, maybe he has a good time with those 'giovanna donne' while he works," his hand nimbly caressing her. "Why don't you have a good time, too," Nicola whispered, "I make you feel so good."

"Don't touch me," Giulia said quietly so that no one could hear, but allowing him to keep his hand on her as he slowly led her into a vacant room. Giulia hadn't had the touch of a man's hands on her body for a while, as her husband kept ignoring her, preoccupied with his work. She needed the feel of Nicola's hardened, calloused hands on her, permitting him to keep moving them lower. And she enjoyed the attention; it made her feel young again. Slowly moving her dress upward, he slid his hand underneath, feeling her warm flesh. Nicola massaged the creamy skin of her upper thighs. Giulia let out a soft groan as she allowed his fingers to caress the center of her femininity like a musician slowly stroking the keys of a piano until the thrill of it released a passion she hadn't felt for a while.

"Mmm, you like it. See, you need to have a little fun, too," Nicola whispered in her ear as his hand continued playing with that sensuous area that caused Giulia to melt in his arms as her feminine tears released onto Nicola's fingers as if her womanhood was crying from loneliness. "Mama mia, you feel so soft," his lips pushed against her ear as he gently whispered, "Let me have you," he pleaded, again like the devil. Kissing the inside of her ear, he softly continued, "I'll bet your skin is creamy white like mozzarella. Let me lose myself in you. It will feel so good."

Giulia could take no more, "Tonight, come quietly to my room tonight when my children are sleeping." Her shame wouldn't allow her to look into his eyes, "You can have me tonight." Giulia gracefully walked away from Nicola, purposely allowing him to admire her curvaceous figure, knowing that she would have the hands of a man on her once more. Nicola smiled like a demon, knowing he would be with the beautiful woman he lusted for so long. So aroused from the thought alone, he had to quickly sit at a table to hide the swelling in his trousers. His body trembled in anticipation of the coming night.

Luigi only left the smoking room at night at undetermined intervals to relieve himself of Giulia's homemade beer that he favored. He always focused on his games and never went upstairs. That night, as always, Luigi kissed his children downstairs when Giulia brought them to him before they went to sleep. He didn't even notice how nicely Giulia dressed, almost erotically. Giulia had prepared herself as she did in Pittsburgh when Luigi couldn't wait to come to her every night. She wore her hair down but styled. Her olive-green eyes glowed like a feline creature, complemented by the slight bit of powder on her face and rouge on her cheeks and lips, making them appear fuller and sexy. Intuitively, Giulia desperately tried to draw Luigi's attention to what she was about to do with Nicola and stop her. It was a subliminal plea to prevent her from the sin she was about to commit. Giulia sent her children to bed ahead of her and remained on the first floor, pretending to be checking on various things. She wanted Luigi and everyone to admire her beauty, not the hard-working woman in an apron they always saw.

Nicola was watching Giulia from a table as he sipped his beer. At first, he mistook her for a prostitute he hadn't seen before. When he realized it was Giulia, he was stunned, and her presence made her look like an angel from a painting. Nicola studied the way she gracefully moved about as if she was putting on a show. The demonstration excited him, as did the thought that he would be with this marvel of a woman in a short time. Then, impending doom swept over him. What if something happened that wouldn't allow him to be with her? Now, he had to have her if it meant breaking down her door. The vision of slowly removing her clothes and seeing her nakedness came to his mind, as did every step of what would follow. Then, Giulia gracefully and sensually climbed the stairway to her bedroom, her derrière swaying from side to side as if the angel was ascending to the heavens. Every man at the bar noticed how beautiful she looked except Luigi.

Nicola counted the seconds as he waited, watching the large grandfather clock beyond the stairway. He fixed his hair with his fingers and carefully looked around before he climbed the stairway that night. Luigi's attention stayed fixed on a card game, so Nicola softly crept up the stairs. Giulia heard the soft knock on her door, walked over, and cracked it open slightly. She gently pulled Nicola inside. As he remained standing there, she walked over toward her large bed. Wearing a tapered satin dressing gown, Giulia raised her hand to motion Nicola to stay there. Slowly, she removed the lush fabric belt, smiling at him before sliding out of the gown and letting it drop to the floor. After stepping out of her matching slippers with poms, Giulia stood before Nicola, completely naked. Tears formed in Nicola's eyes; his face was like a begging puppy's. Giulia left him standing there for a full minute; she could see the rise in his pants. Finally, she softly said, "Now, you can have me." Nicola rushed over to her. First, he touched the soft white skin of her shoulders. Nicola's hands shook from nervousness as he held Giulia's breasts together, kissing them, switching from one to the other. Nicola picked her up and put her on the bed. Giulia laughed as he quickly and feverishly undressed, tripping at times. Atop her soft, voluptuous figure, he began moaning while kissing her repeatedly. A few seconds later, Nicola was finished and rolled over. 'He's a wimp compared to my Luigi,' she thought while lying aside the puny man, unfulfilled.

Nicola had visited Giulia one more time. He knew he wasn't very bright, but felt proud thinking he was pleasuring a beautiful woman. Giulia expected more from Nicola the second time. Again, the experience was too quick, and the puny man rolled over after seconds. It was nothing like those magical days with Luigi. Giulia abruptly ended that fling with Nicola, admitting her enormous mistake.

In the early summer of 1893, Douglas's parents decided to have their family picture taken at the photo studio on the north part of Main Street. Mr. and Mrs. Nicholson became fond of Peppina over the years she spent with their son. In a way, they attributed his social development to her. So, several days before their appointment, they invited Peppina to have a few pictures of her taken with Douglas. That way, her mother could have time to prepare a lovely dress for Peppina for the photo.

"Oh "Maronna mia! You look so pretty, my little angel!" Giulia was almost in tears at the sight of her daughter all dressed up. Giulia didn't bother to dress her in her Sunday clothes. Instead, she took Peppina to the women's shop nearby on Main Street and bought her a new dress outfit and shoes.

Peppina stood before the wooden framed self-standing mirror in her parent's bedroom. Her blonde hair, parted and pulled back into a long braid, was tied with a medium blue colored large bow. The cream-colored dress she wore went down almost to her ankles. It had long, puffy sleeves and a wide, long white fringe around her neck, decorating her shoulders and complimenting the dress's color. A belt fitted the dress close to her waist and matched the color of her hair bow. Peppina wore new black stockings with matching black shoes. A bow the same color as the one binding her hair and waist adorned her new shoes. The young girl's olive-green eyes appeared as droplets from heaven as she stood wide-eyed and smiling in front of the mirror. "I look nice, don't I, Mama?"

"You look as beautiful as an angel from heaven!" Tears ran down Giulia's cheeks, the fingers of both her hands pressed on the sides of her face as she recalled her stolen youth.

"We have to have a new portrait done for our family," declared Peppina. The Massaros hadn't had a photo of their family since they were in Sharpsburg just after Felo was born. Now, the three-year-old was running about the hotel and in the yard. "Thank you, Mama," Peppina giggled with a wide grin. "I'm going to show Papa."

Luigi had risen earlier than usual from his nightly labor of gambling, drinking, and smoking cigars. However, he still did his daily exercise routine with dumbbells and calisthenics, maintaining the 35-year-old man's build. He heard someone coming after he finished working out and bathed in a back room on the first floor. Peppina walked past her father's office and to another back room, "Good morning, Papa."

Her father turned and faced his daughter. "Madonna mia!" he gasped. "This is surely a vision from heaven above!" Knowing his daughter was having her picture taken that early afternoon, he made sure he was up to take her. Luigi already had one of their horses hitched to an open carriage. The others were grazing in the large fenced-in yard behind the hotel, where a carriage house stood big enough for two coaches. Next to it was a small stable for the horses. "This can't be my little firecracker!" he laughed proudly at the sight of his oldest daughter.

"It is, Papa!" Peppina laughed. She was so happy.

"Come here and give Papa a hug." As his daughter ran into his open arms, he said, "Sei bellissima Figlia mia," in perfect Italian, telling her how beautiful she looked and embracing her tightly. Then he released the excited young girl and said, "Give me a couple of minutes to get ready. I'm taking my principessa to the ball!"

"Thank you, Papa!" Peppina did feel like a princess.

Luigi drove the carriage to Third Street. There was no train at the station, so without the excessive traffic there, he turned left and proceeded along Riverside, then turned onto Sixth Street and then Main. Luigi wanted to leave his little girl directly in front of the studio so she wouldn't dirty her new shoes. The father and daughter arrived promptly at their appointment time. The Nicholson family walked toward the studio doorway with Rollo by Douglas's side as Luigi pulled over. Luigi exchanged greetings with them and then leaned over and kissed his daughter. "You look beautiful, my darling Daughter," he proudly said.

"Thank you!" Peppina smiled again as she stepped off the carriage onto the brick sidewalk. She turned to her father and said, "Mr. Nicholson said he would take me home, Papa."

"I'll see you later. Have fun!" Luigi said before he drove away and headed back to the hotel.

Mrs. Nicholson looked beautiful with her blonde hair pulled back into a bun. She wore an attractive dark blue long-sleeved buttoned dress. The length went to between her knees and ankles. The lovely woman wore a beautiful cameo pinned below the split in the decorative white collar surrounding her neck. Mr. Nicholson wore a tailored dark suit. Douglas was dressed in a dark brown double-breasted suit with slacks and wore matching brown low-cut shoes.

Mr. and Mrs. Nicholson thought little Peppina looked stunning. Douglas agreed. He had never seen her so dressed up as much before. She, in turn, complimented how nice they looked.

"You look adorable, Peppina," Mrs. Nicholson repeated with a big smile. "We're so glad you came."

"Now you'll both have something to remember your time together when you were young," Douglas Sr. chuckled. "Someday, you'll be as old as us!" he laughed.

Martha Nicholson looked at her husband oddly. "Speak for yourself, Mr. Nicholson," she said and smiled.

After the studio processed the photos, the Nicholsons had a few beautiful family portraits. In one of them, Rollo joined them at young Douglas's insistence. Because of their fondness for Peppina, they had additional family portraits with her in the picture. There was a photo of Douglas alone and another with him and his friend, Peppina, with Rollo. Mr. and Mrs. Nicholson gave the young girl one of the family images. She also received one of the 6 1/2" x 4 1/2" glass framed Albumen print photos of her with Douglas and Rollo. Douglas received one of the same. The Nicholsons wanted the children to remember their childhood.

As the early morning river fog leisurely lifted, the sun slowly rose to the heavens, filling the sky with magical colors amidst some remaining spots and twirls of the rising river vapors. The vibrant hues contrasted with the bright white clouds of late summer just before school began. A soft breeze flowed over Douglas and Peppina as if God blessed them with a calm they had never before experienced. The two sat at the grassy slope near the wharf with Rollo by their side, waiting for their friends. The kids wanted a few more summer days before returning to classes and the doom of the cold winter days and nights when the sun set early and the fierce winds could be brutal. "I love days like this," Peppina finally said.

"I'm going to miss them," Douglas replied as if he was facing an impending catastrophe.

After everyone gathered, the small herd of kids decided to walk over to Fifth Street to see the construction site. In 1892, the town accepted plans for a new city hall. The site at the south corner of Fifth and Main Streets was under construction that day in 1893.

"The completion date is expected in December this year," Douglas announced. He became the untitled leader of the gang because he was usually informed of things and told the best stories—and, of course, because he could box well. Douglas had earned the respect of all the boys and girls. That day, the kids spread out on a patch of grass off the sidewalk across the street from the construction site. As they watched the workers on the scaffold, Douglas brought up the subject of two of Jules Verne's books. 'From The Earth to the Moon' and 'Around the Moon' were the topics that interested almost every boy at the time. They were stories about three Civil War Veterans who traveled to orbit the moon and return to Earth. The girls grudgingly merged into the conversation, though somewhat unwillingly.

"Maybe we can make a rocket," said Mike Walsh to all the boys' excitement. They always watched the moon at night and wondered if someone would someday land on it.

"I'll bet we could," added Felix Fischer.

"Do you realize how stupid you boys sound?" yelled Donna Madson so she could be heard over the boys' quibbling. "You sound like idiots!" Rollo barked at that statement, then lay back down in the shade and panted from the heat.

"C'mon, let's go to Bunting's and get something to eat!" Douglas declared when he realized the conversation was getting stale. "Let's go!" Everyone followed Douglas, Peppina, and Rollo. As they all walked, Douglas felt something was wrong with Peppina as she wasn't the chatterbox she always was. She didn't even ask to hold Rollo's leash like always. 'Maybe she's getting sick,' he thought. But he would ask her later, not in front of everyone. The group passed the United Presbyterian Church on their left on their way to Bunting's Confectionery. At that time, the kids had no idea that the church's bell tower hid one of the oldest bells in The United States. No one would learn about that until many years later.

Douglas was now popular with the younger kids who frequented the restaurant and ice cream parlor and had no inhibitions about going there anymore. Douglas tied Rollo to a streetlight. He sat with Peppina and asked her if she felt alright. That's when she told him for the first time. Peppina's pretty eyes teared, "Mama and Papa are arguing so much lately," she spoke her words, clearly showing that she was upset. "Papa used the word puttana. I never heard that word before, and I don't know what it means, but it wasn't good from the sound."

"Don't worry, Peppina, parents argue sometimes." Douglas didn't know what else to say. His parents disagreed at times, but nothing like what she was describing.

"I don't think as much as this," the young girl began sobbing.

Nicola sat at his table near the kitchen. Giulia bent over to place a food plate down. Nicola glanced around the room to see if anyone was looking. Then he slipped his hand under her dress.

"What's the matter with you? People are here, and I told you it was over."

"I'm in love," he said, exposing his terrible grin, "Nobody can see." He moved his hand around, hoping Giulia would succumb to him.

"You're sick," Giulia said, "you had your fun, and now it's over. It was a mistake—a big one!"

"You're gaining weight. I like it. There's nothing like a plump woman. Mmm, more to feel and love." He tried to touch her again, but Giulia moved away before he could.

"Shut up!" She stopped him. Giulia now had a problem—a serious one.

Giulia was pregnant but hadn't told anybody. She knew the timing was from Nicola's two nightly visits and now wore loose dresses to hide it. Being a petite woman helped. Her husband hadn't noticed, nor did her children. She glanced out the kitchen window and saw Luigi holding hands with Felo. They were walking together toward the back door. Luigi always took his son for walks in the afternoon and evenings in nicer weather. Sometimes, they went down to the Third Street Station, where Luigi bought candy or popcorn for his son. Now that it was getting cooler outside, the father and son took shorter walks. 'What am I going to do?' Guilia thought as she worried and pondered her dilemma of knowing it was Nicola's child inside her. 'If I tell Luigi it's his, and he finds out the truth, he'll kill Nicola, and maybe even me, with those Sicilian aristocratic ways of his.'

Emanuela never wanted to leave the yard. She would occasionally take a walk with her father. When she did, she stayed close to him. Always shy and quiet, the little girl, going on eight years old, seemed afraid of the outside world. Luigi always brought back popcorn or candy for his youngest daughter and Peppina whenever he took Felo for a walk alone.

A pregnant Giulia kept working even though she had a sufficient staff. Mrs. D'Angelo, her Italian immigrant helper, now did more in the kitchen. Luisa D'Angelo's husband, Marco, worked at Stevenson's factory. She was in her early thirties with two daughters and a son. Her eldest daughter, who was twelve, stayed home and cared for her younger siblings so Luisa could supplement her husband's salary.

Millie Brown, a negro woman in her early thirties, now managed the housekeeping. She had a son and a daughter. Millie's 11-year-old son watched his younger sister while she worked at the hotel. Her husband worked at the American Sheet and Tin Plate Company Mill.

Millie's husband, Hector Brown, was a proud man. He had had an excellent job in Pittsburgh, where he and Millie first settled. Derogatory names like 'nigger' rolled off his back as he focused on his work to build a family who could live as free people. Remembering the days of slavery when he was a young child, Hector worked his way up as a steel laborer, earning the job as foreman over a crew of immigrant Italian workers. They promoted him because he could speak English, and the Italians couldn't. The Browns had their first child, a boy they named Percy, in Pittsburgh in 1882. Everything was going well for the Brown family, and Millie became pregnant again in 1888. However, after several men attacked Hector at the plant, things changed for the family. A German worker wanted his job and felt the promotion should never have gone to a black man. Otto Hoffman got some of his friends at the mill, and together, they ambushed Hector while leaving after work one evening. They beat him mercilessly, leaving Hector in a puddle of mud outside the plant. A couple of his friends found him and carried him home. It took Millie a month to bring her husband back to health. She made soups and used herbs as they couldn't see a doctor. Slowly but surely, Millie mended his wounds. Hector was a strong man and recovered.

Both Millie and Hector were born into slavery in the South but in separate states. They escaped by the underground railroad. Hector arrived in Pennsylvania and eventually went to Pittsburgh to find a job. Millie came through Wellsville, Ohio, and then to Pittsburgh, where she met her husband while working as a housekeeper. Remembering the small town in the river valley of Ohio, Millie pleaded with Hector to take her there after his beating. She was pregnant at the time and didn't want a repeat of what happened to her husband. Hector agreed to leave the city, and they moved to Wellsville the same year, where their daughter Phoebe was born. Luigi Massaro hired her to work at his hotel a year after it opened. Hector eventually found work at the mill nearby.

Giulia usually worked in the restaurant while Millie and other hired people helped care for the rooms. Luigi managed all of the hotel business. Food, liquor, and other distributors preferred to deal only with men. He often hired Hector to do repairs at the hotel.

Luigi discovered that his wife was pregnant. He had sensed something was amiss because she didn't tell him about her pregnancy that he could now clearly see, and he had heard the whispers about her alleged infidelity. Luigi was no fool but never thought his wife would give herself to a slob like Nicola Bucci. Luigi deliberately walked into their bedroom to closely examine her body while she dressed. Giulia hadn't heard him enter, and he caught her off guard. Scrutinizing his wife's naked body and confirming the bulge of her abdomen, Luigi yelled in Italian, "Why did you allow yourself to lose your honor to a dirty buffoon like Nicola Bucci?" Luigi shook his head, "Now you've become like the whores that work downstairs!" Luigi usually remained calm, but now, with his suspicions confirmed, he became angry.

"To spite you!" she screamed, "You never wanted me like before!"

"I drained my body of all its energy by managing this place and then staying up into the wee hours of the morning to make money for you and my family. I had nothing left of myself to give you, only working toward the plan that you could once again live as a queen. You're the mother of three children. Now you ruined our family!" Luigi never hit his wife or children or lifted a finger to hurt them, verbally or physically. But now, he ferociously slammed the door behind him after calling her a 'puttana.' Giulia stayed in the bedroom and wept, her secret now revealed to her husband, wondering what he would do.

Not wanting to argue anymore in front of his children, Luigi never spoke to Giulia again. He had no choice, as his only concern was now for the welfare of his children, and he took the necessary measures to ensure that.

One week later, while Giulia served breakfast at the tables, a wagon pulled up at the hotel unbeknownst to her. Two workers picked up one trunk, loaded it in the wagon bed, and secured it tightly. They climbed back up on the seat and drove toward the train station.

Luigi had packed only his best clothes, shoes, and essential private items into his steamer trunk. He held the photo of him and Biaggio, which he kept on his desk. Luigi stared at it sentimentally, recalling those past days with Biaggio and when he met Giulia. Carefully, he packed the photo between his clothes to keep it safe. Already packed was another glass-framed family portrait taken in Sharpsburg, Pennsylvania, just before they moved to Wellsville in happier times. Luigi then hid the remaining money his father had given him years before in a small leather bag with handles.

His pistol was shoulder-holstered under his jacket. It was an emotional time for Luigi Massaro, the man who, 15 years before, had taken an adventurous journey from his wealthy life in Sicily to an unadorned country not yet built. A man who found fortune only to lose it twice was finally beaten. Admired by almost anyone who knew him, respected, and even feared by his workers with his extraordinary intelligence and talents in business and foresight, he found no other option. Now, he had to leave for reasons most Americans would not understand. How could they begin to comprehend the culture of a Sicilian aristocrat? But his plans were cast, forced upon him, as the mill-workers in the valley around him forged their steel, and there was no coming back.

Luigi, dressed in his finest vest and suit with a coat and top hat, held the handles of the small bag in one hand and his son Felo's in the other. Together, they walked toward the Third Street Station. "Papa has to go away, Son. I want you to be good."

"Okay, Papa." Felo smiled at his father as they walked together. "Papa going bye-bye?"

"Yes, Felo, I am. You'll be the man of the house while I'm gone," Luigi forced a chuckle. Heartbroken to have to leave his children, Luigi had to remain strong. As he walked, his only thoughts were of them. He would never be able to see his daughters marry or see his son become a man. No longer could he dream of their excited faces when they received the things he had planned to give them. Luigi Massaro had earned those dreams by the sweat of his brow, the calluses of his hands, and his precious time. Now, with no choice, he proceeded hand in hand, leading his young son to the station, never to see him again.

Peppina was already at the station with her sister. They each held a sign advertising the hotel. A train was already there, getting ready to depart for Pittsburgh. Wagons traveled in different directions as they did on the day the Massaro family first arrived in town over three years earlier. People were boarding the train while wagons loaded the freight cars. Luigi noticed his trunk loaded onto a luggage car. He already had a receipt from the workers. Luigi led his son to one of the vendors and bought him a box of candy corn. Peppina came walking to her father while Emanuela stayed with the signs. "Where are you going, Papa?" she looked puzzled. "You never told me you were going on a trip. How long will you be away?" Peppina suddenly appeared alarmed. She was old enough to know her parents had quarreled, and now her father was leaving without telling her.

Luigi just smiled at his little firecracker. Then, handing her a candy box, he said, "Tesoro, sometimes in life, things happen unexpectedly. All we can do is make the best of them. Papa made sure you will always have clothes, food to eat, and a bed to sleep in. I will love you always. You and your sister and brother will be fine." He bent and kissed his darling little daughter on the cheek, "Hold Felo's hand for a minute." Luigi walked over to Emanuela and hugged her tightly. "Goodbye, my baby," he whispered, holding her tightly. After he released his youngest daughter, Luigi handed her a candy box.

"Where're you going, Papa?"

"Papa has to go away. You be a good girl."

"Yes, Papa. I will," Emanuela answered, but bearing a look of terror.

Luigi walked back to where Peppina and Felo were standing. That distinctive-sounding whistle that all steam locomotives make tooted loudly and long. The engineer signaled the impending departure. "Papa, don't go." Tears began rolling down Peppina's cheeks. "I'll miss you. Please don't go away." Something within the child told her she might never see him again.

With tears forming in his eyes, Luigi fell to his knee and hugged his eldest daughter firmly. "I love you, my little firecracker," he whispered in her ear. "Be a good girl for me. Take Felo home." Remaining on bended knee, he turned and put his arms around his only son. "Goodbye, Felo. Papa loves you." He stood up and trotted to the train, which had started moving. Standing on the top step of the passenger car, Luigi held on to his small carry bag and waved to his kids from the moving train.

Peppina stood next to little Felo, and they both waved. Emanuela was behind them, also waving. Luigi remained on the step with his left hand held over his eyes to shield them from the intense morning sun. He waited there until he could no longer see his children. Then he entered the car. That beautiful autumn morning, the sun slowly rose above mixed-colored trees in the valley. It blended into the vivid tones of the sky as patches of white puff clouds leisurely passed.

Chapter Twelve

Wellsville, Ohio 1893
An End To Childhood

In 1893, women in Columbiana County, Ohio, still maintained few rights. Socially, they were still considered dependents of men. Though an 1887 law finally allowed women some property rights in Ohio, the wheels of justice always moved slowly. Implementing those female rights was moving forward unhurriedly. Women had difficulty managing their property, let alone owning and operating a business.

"What are you talking about?" Giulia had to sit as she was too shocked to stand. "Oh, my God," she said, her eyes tearing. She knew why Luigi left her, but now she had to explain it to her children.

"Why? Didn't you know Papa had to go away?" Peppina began crying again, seeing her mother in distress. She thought her mother knew her father was going on a trip. But now her suspicions were confirmed; her father left for good. Peppina still held onto Felo's hand. The little boy became upset and began to cry, too. He didn't understand what was happening.

Emanuela's eyes were wide as she stood by herself. The little girl appeared so terrified she couldn't cry from shock. "Mama?" was all she could say, waiting for her mother's explanation.

Giulia rose and went into Luigi's office downstairs. His things there were gone. She climbed the stairs, entered their bedroom, and saw that her husband had left only older clothes and unimportant things. She sat in a chair beside his armoire and noticed the edge of a piece of paper slightly exposed off the top of that piece of furniture. Giulia rose and picked it up. Sitting back down and looking at it, she could only distinguish the words 'document' in fancy scrip in the English wording.

"Mama, are you alright?" Peppina asked as she slowly crept up to where her mother was sitting. Giulia had been sitting for a while just staring.

Finally, Giulia said, "Tell Mrs. D'angelo to take care of the kitchen today." Sobbing, she added, "Peppina, take care of your sister and brother. See that they eat."

"Okay, Mama." Peppina quietly left her parent's bedroom; her eyes reddened from crying.

Giulia knew about the nobility and understood that Luigi would never return. He couldn't because the Italians in town would secretly refer to him with the horrible dialect slang word, 'cornuto' if he did. She betrayed her husband and now had to deal with the consequences. Luigi still loved his children and spared them the humiliation. He would solely harbor the guilt of abandoning his family so the community would scorn him but not speak badly of them. That would leave them with their 'onore,' their 'honor' while maintaining his own by doing so. It was the way of the aristocracy. And his legacy, the hotel, would shelter and feed his children for many years, so he thought. Giulia remained seated the rest of the day, not fully comprehending how much her life would change. 'Why did I allow myself to get involved with that idiot?'

Giulia traveled by trolley to speak to an Italian immigrant friend she knew in East Liverpool. Sofia Marino said she would have her husband, Nunzio, talk to a lawyer there who helped immigrants. Nunzio set up an appointment for Giulia so the attorney could direct her to get help managing the hotel. As an illiterate, and without Luigi, things could fall apart. Nicola also couldn't read or write and didn't have the brawn or brains to run the hotel. Giulia left Peppina in charge of the other children while Mrs. D'Angelo took over the hotel's operation with Millie's help. She put a 'no occupancy' sign on the front entrance to dissuade new lodgers until Giulia could resolve matters.

On the following day of her appointment, Giulia took the trolley to the attorney's office. Her friend, Sofia, met her there. The lawyer, Salvatore Moretti, spoke Italian but not all of the several poorer-class dialects of that language in the area, but he could understand most of them.

"Before I can speak with you, Mrs. Massaro, I must ask you for a retainer." He spoke the Italian that the educated used. Giulia could understand most of it. Aside from her dialect, she had learned to comprehend upper-class Italian from Luigi. But not being proficient in the entire vocabulary, she didn't know what a retainer meant, and her face expressed confusion. Sensing she didn't fully understand him, he said, "Money. You have to pay me before I can be your attorney."

"Oh!" Giulia pulled out several dollar bills and held them before Mr. Moretti.

He took the required amount from her hand, returned the rest, and asked, "How can I help you?"

Intelligent enough to know he would eventually learn the truth, Giulia explained to him her situation as humiliated as she was to mention it. She bowed her head in disgrace and said, "I'm pregnant with a baby who is not my husband's. My husband left me and my three children." She sighed, "I want to know where to get help managing my hotel. I have this document. My husband took care of all hotel business." She then presented the folded paper, opened it, and handed it to the lawyer.

The attorney glanced at the legal paper quickly but frowned. "Everything here is in order, Mrs. Massaro, but I'm afraid this is not a simple matter for you. Let me explain."

A distressed Giulia had to pay a fee, only to discover the truth about the law. Women still maintained few rights in Columbiana County, Ohio. Socially, they were still considered dependents of men. Though an 1887 law finally allowed women some personal property rights in Ohio, the wheels of justice always moved slowly. Implementing those female rights was moving forward unhurriedly and begrudgingly at the hands of primarily male politicians, even delaying the news of that law. Mr. Moretti explained the difficulty women had managing their property, let alone owning and operating a business. Then, there were social complications for both. Renting an appropriate apartment without a man representing her could also prove problematic. Women couldn't borrow money, which made landlords and business merchants skeptical of dealing with them. Her lawyer implied that Giulia needed a man to operate the hotel. Mr. Moretti gave her an overall picture of the adversities of hypothetically owning the hotel. However, there was more to her specific situation.

"Things are tough now with this depression. Unfortunately, that will worsen your matters, Mrs. Massaro. I'm so sorry." In 1893, an escalating financial crisis caused a major recession. It affected all the factories and businesses in town, even the railroad. Many banks were closing throughout the country. "Layoffs and harder times are coming, I'm afraid."

Giulia's first reaction was bewilderment. She remembered Luigi talking about the depression, but she had thought nothing about it. He handled all business matters, and his gambling earnings always supplemented their living expenses. Then she shouted, "But it's my hotel! Look! I have the document!"

Mr. Moretti raised his right hand and gently said, "I understand your frustration with this matter, Mrs. Massaro." He paused and looked directly into Giulia's eyes, "Technically, it's not your property and hotel. Your husband passed the hotel to your son, Felo."

"What does that mean?" she bore a look of shock.

"It means the hotel will become your son's when he is old enough to manage it. How old is he now?"

"Three."

"So, you can't sell it now." He hesitated, "It would be best to acquire a man to represent the hotel affairs for you until your son becomes of legal age." He shook his head back and forth at the injustice she faced. "You could lose everything. Difficulties could arise that might result in that. Do you have someone in your life, Mrs. Massaro?" He couldn't help but take a glance down toward her abundant abdomen. It was far too late even to suggest the subject of abortion. Then he raised his eyes to look into hers, "Is there a man in your life? A relative, per-haps?" Pregnant immigrant women were ordinary in his prac-tice. Many had relations with married or unavailable men. If they got pregnant, women usually opted for an abortion with a midwife's assistance. But that had to happen 'before the feeling of life inside,' as it was referred to then.

"No," replied Giulia, "I'm alone except for the fool who put the baby in my stomach."

"Is he available to help you?"

Giulia didn't answer; she only sat in deep thought. Then, the troubled 29-year-old woman left the office more upset than when she arrived. Sofia tried to comfort her but to no avail. Giulia finally understood that she was alone in the town. She wished someone or something could take her out of this night-mare. Giulia was a pregnant Italian immigrant who didn't speak English well. Luigi left the hotel to his son, but Felo was too young, and she needed a man to represent and manage it.

Luigi was an intelligent man, and he handled the matter as a Sicilian. Assuming Giulia would be with Nicola, Luigi didn't want him to have power over the property, thinking the fool would squander it. Felo would take over someday and abide by the Italian tradition of taking good care of his sisters until they were married. But Giulia didn't want to marry Nicola. She was sorry she had already let her bodily desires carry her away. Giulia could not read or write, and her family disowned her for running away to marry Luigi years before, remembering the letter her father's lawyer sent to Pittsburgh. Memories of what life was like in Little Italy surfaced. Giulia recalled that those who couldn't survive perished. Women who were alone had to find jobs. Immigrant women who couldn't find work had to face horrors like turning to prostitution. The women who worked in the factories in Wellsville made very little money. It wouldn't be enough to support her family. And what would she do with the hotel? She didn't know anyone capable of managing it, and she couldn't sell it. Giulia didn't know what to do. Who would marry her with three children and another on the way? Then, the nightmarish thought of Nicola came back to her mind.

"What you talking about?" Nicola stood shuffling his feet. "What baby?"

"The one you put in my belly. Do you remember the nightly visits to my bedroom? Well, now you have your prize. I must have been crazy to allow you to touch me." Giulia said it to justify her honor even though she was an adulteress. "I only did it to spite Luigi." That made her finally wonder why she did it. It was entirely her fault. Luigi was the best husband a woman could have. Why did she let her emotions get the best of her? She and Nicola exchanged their words in their crude native dialect, with some broken English spoken in between.

"I thought you were just getting fat. I don't know about any baby." Nicola sat down at the table where Giulia was sitting. "I like fat women, no babies!"

"Well, the baby knows about you." Giulia kept staring into Nicola's eyes.

"Okay, okay, let me think."

"Look at it this way," Giulia began, "You marry me and stay here for free with as much as you want to eat and drink! You like my beer, right? And, as husband and wife, we don't have to hide anymore. You sleep in my bed every night." She was tired of Nicola's disgusting habits, and that thought made her feel worse.

"I don't want to get married!" Nicola rose and left.

Two days had passed, and Nicola sneaked in and out of the hotel without Giulia noticing. He ate his meals at a different restaurant. Then, he approached Giulia on the third night when her children were asleep. "I have my answer." Nicola stood poised in his filthy clothes with his arms folded. He looked like a buffoon, Giulia thought. "I'll marry you, but your children must leave!"

Giulia's eyes widened. "What?" she thought she had heard wrong. "What did you say?"

"Your children have to leave! That's it!" Nicola bowed his head, then raised it and stared directly at Giulia. "I don't want them. I won't allow them to stay. It's too expensive now in this depression," he exclaimed, "especially with the girls if they can't find husbands later."

"But they're my babies. They're just little children." Giulia knew Nicola wasn't very bright but was a friendly and jovial man. How could he even think about something like this?

Nicola waved his right hand and shouted, "No!"

Giulia Massaro and her friend Sofia returned to the same lawyer. He could fit her in, but she had to wait two hours. Immigrants, mostly newly arrived Italians, filled the waiting area. When it was her turn, she entered the office of Mr. Salvatore Moretti, attorney at law. Giulia pleaded with him to give her other courses of action. She explained to her lawyer what had transpired between Nicola and her.

"I won't lose my children, Mr. Moretti. They're my darling, precious babies," she sobbed. Her eyes were tearing.

Salvatore Moretti felt her passion deeply inside him. He had seen such terrible things happen so often before. It was a cruelty of life that was so real for immigrants from all countries. "You couldn't give up Felo, actually," he said, trying to put forward some ease in a terrible situation. "Not while keeping the hotel anyway." Then he realized how undignified his remark was. "I'm sorry, Mrs. Massaro." He thought and then said, "If you have to forfeit the hotel, some charity organizations could temporarily shelter you and your children. But the better ones are in the cities." Giulia just sat motionless and said nothing as she was at a loss for words. She knew about what horrors took place at city shelters.

"Mrs. Massaro, it pains me even to suggest this," Moretti paused, "but I feel it's my obligation. If you can convince Nicola to allow you to keep your son, putting your daughters in an orphanage might be the right thing." Mr. Moretti raised his hand, "I know it might sound cruel, but a good one would provide for them," he sighed. "It might be the best option for you, Mrs. Massaro, under the circumstances. I'm afraid you don't have many choices," the grim attorney explained to the troubled mother. "They will properly attend to your daughters. They will feed and shelter them and continue their schooling," he sighed as he lowered his head. "Do you understand me, Mrs. Massaro? This way, you could at least keep Felo."

"Yes, I understand." That was all she said, tears rolling down her face while her thoughts raced. 'How was I so stupid? I lost Luigi, and it was my fault. A foolish mistake with a slob. What was I thinking? I should have been a better wife,' her guilt ruled her. 'Now I have to give up my darling babies,' Giulia thought remorsely. 'How can I do that and still live with myself? Maybe I should kill myself. I can't live like this, not with this torment. Luigi thought he provided for all of us. What a wonderful man he is. He would never allow this. I don't even know where he is now.' Giulia now cried out loud.

"I'm so very sorry, Mrs. Massaro. Do you want time to think? You could use my conference room."

"No. It has to be done. There is no other way," she sobbed.

The lawyer offered to arrange for the adoption of her two daughters at an orphanage in Cleveland, Ohio. "It's an excellent home, Mrs. Massaro," he explained to allow her to feel some comfort. The reality was that there were many such cases of child abandonment then, and it was the only one available.

Giulia was sobbing as she shed tears of despair. "I'll ask him," she replied before she left the office. When she arrived at the hotel, Nicola was returning from work. Giulia discussed the issue with Nicola, and he agreed to allow Felo to stay. He was getting a good deal: a place to stay and free food and drink. And

Nicola would sleep in Giulia's room.

'The slob gets what he wants,' Giulia thought in anger as she sat before the lawyer in his office the following day. Mr. Moretti informed Giulia of the amount necessary for his legal services rendered, and she paid it. Giulia had no emotion left. She cried them all away and sat before her lawyer like a zombie.

"You must understand that when you sign the papers from the orphanage, you relinquish your rights to knowing where they are if they become adopted or transferred to a different orphanage. Legally, they won't give you any information of their whereabouts." Mr. Moretti clarified in detail what that meant. "Do you understand that, Mrs. Massaro?"

"Yes," she replied despondently. "Will they both go to the same home together?"

"The orphanage tries to keep siblings together, if possible. But I want you to understand that there are no guarantees." Mr. Moretti thoroughly explained everything again to Giulia.

"I hope so," Giulia's eyes were red from so much shedding of tears. She told him, "My little Emanuela is afraid to be alone." She restrained from weeping. The mother had to be strong for her son.

"Someone from the orphanage will arrive at your hotel within the week to bring them. That person will have the necessary papers for you to sign." Mr. Moretti explained. "I'm so sorry for your situation, Mrs. Massaro. I will get word to you when the chaperone will arrive to accompany your daughters." Mr. Moretti had hardened from so many situations like this one.

"My Papa went away somewhere, and my mother is upset," Peppina explained to Douglas. They hadn't seen each other since Luigi left. "I don't know why, and I don't know if he's ever coming home." Peppina had walked over to his house that beautiful late autumn day. It was what people called 'Indian summer.'

Douglas could see that his friend was upset. He had visited the hotel several times, but nobody answered the door. After reading the 'no occupancy' sign, he assumed everyone was busy with work, so he and Rollo left each time.

"Do you want to go fishing? It's still early enough."

"No, I better not. Mama might send my sister to look for me. She knows I'm here."

"Okay! Let's play hopscotch!" Douglas declared to distract his friend from the subject.

"Okay."

It worked. Peppina giggled and played with Douglas as if nothing happened. That day, Martha Nicholson prepared fried chicken for the kids' lunch. The two children laughed and played with Rollo until the sun cast golden tones upon them and the valley about them as it slowly set, and it was time to go home. But that day, Peppina stayed and had dinner with Douglas's family. She had always enjoyed Martha's dinners, and Douglas thought it would cheer her up. He didn't tell his parents anything about Peppina's father; that was a secret between friends. Though typical, it was a memorable day for Douglas, one in time he would grow to treasure.

Giulia dressed Peppina in the outfit she wore for the studio photo. She brushed and fixed her hair the same way she did on that memorable day. Emanuela, already dressed in her best Sunday clothes, was ready. She stayed close to her mother while Giulia prepared Peppina for the trip.

"I don't understand, Mama. Why do we have to go away?"

"I told you," Giulia forced a smile. "You and your sister are going to a nice place for a while," she explained, not having the heart to tell her the truth. "It's a vacation for you both while the workers do repairs at the hotel." Giulia thought it would be better if the girls learned little by little about their fate. "Until Papa comes home." The thought of lying to her children bothered her, but she felt it best. Giulia had to hold back her tears to convince them everything was alright.

"Is Felo coming?"

"No, amore mio. He's too small. You and your sister are big girls now. Right, Emanuela?" she turned to her younger daughter and labored another smile.

"Yes, Mama, I am, but I don't want to go without you and Papa."

"Your sister will be with you, my dear. You'll both be fine and have a lot of fun." Giulia sincerely believed the lawyer in the idea that the orphanage was a nice place. She envisioned lots of kids playing and having fun. It's common for people to believe a lie when it makes them feel better.

"But I didn't say goodbye to Douglas and Rollo."

"Amore, you send them both a letter. I didn't know your chaperone was coming so soon."

"What's a chaperone?"

"A nice woman is coming to take you both where you will stay. You don't want to travel alone, do you? Now pack the things you want to bring."

Giulia packed two small suitcases of clothes for the girls. Peppina placed the small music box Douglas gave her between a dress. Then, she looked at the photo of her with Douglas and Rollo. Her eyes teared while admiring how nice they looked and how Rollo sat obediently beside her. She would miss them so much while she was away. The photo reminded her of all the happy times they shared. She didn't know where she and her sister were going, but the young girl would miss the beautiful sunsets in the valley and think of Douglas and Rollo when she did. Peppina couldn't wait to get back to see them and tell them all about her trip.

"Come along, children," the stern mistress commanded. Giulia held hands with both of her daughters and followed behind the woman. Millie Brown carried Felo as he couldn't walk as fast as the chaperone. Her husband, Hector, was working the late shift that day and was available to handle the girls' suitcases as they walked to the Third Street Station. The governess allowed no time for candy or popcorn when they arrived. "Say goodbye quickly," she ordered.

Peppina embraced her brother and kissed him, "I'll see you soon, Felo." The little boy just looked up at her, not understanding. He always felt a special bond with his older sister, and the thought of her leaving made him cry.

Emanuela stopped holding her mother's dress long enough to hug Felo and say goodbye. Then she went back to her mother's side. Peppina came to her sister and took her hand. Emanuela was afraid of the woman who wore a dark blue outfit and a small, pointed, matching hat with a feather sticking out of it. Giulia grabbed both her daughters and held them tightly while kissing them repeatedly. "My babies," she hoarsely said. Giulia had been crying all night, and her voice was rasp. She let go only when the unpleasant woman demanded her to.

"Come along now," the unsmiling, stony-faced woman directed the two girls. "We have to board the train now," she said as the mighty locomotive blasted its whistle for the second time.

When Douglas first heard the train coming into the station, he and Rollo had set out to see it. The young boy had no idea his friend was going away. He was arriving when he saw Peppina walking along the platform toward one of the passenger cars. Douglas held tightly onto Rollo's leash as they fought through the crowd. When he got close to his friend, he called, "Peppina!"

The young girl turned while climbing the stairs to the car. Firmly holding her sister's hand, she spotted her friend and Rollo. "Goodbye, Douglas. Goodbye, Rollo," she glumly said while beginning to cry. Douglas kept walking toward his friend, speechless and unable to understand what was happening. Rollo barked. Then, the chaperone pulled the two girls into the car. Peppina and Emanuela reappeared together in one of the windows. They were both waving to Douglas with solemn faces.

Douglas waved back as he felt the heavy silver crucifix under his shirt sway on the chain, remembering when Peppina gave it to him. 'So you'll never be afraid of anything again,' his friend explained at that happy time. He and Rollo waited until the faces of the two girls disappeared from his sight, the train only leaving a stream of puffy grey and white smoke. Giulia just stood motionless as her tears poured. That final image of her two daughters emblazoned into her mind would torment her for the rest of her life.

Giulia Pellettieri Massaro married Nicola Bucci shortly before delivering his baby daughter. Giulia Bucci loathed Nicola for making her lose her daughters and dreaded sleeping in the same bed with him. She would hate him for the rest of his life. Something deep inside Giulia happened to her that day when she stood at the train platform watching her daughters leave. Giulia vowed never again to allow herself to be in a position where she was dependent on a man. Never again, and she would do whatever it took—anything to prevent that. Giulia began her journey to licentiousness, unknowingly to fulfill the loss of her Luigi.

River Town
Wellsville Ohio

Book Two
The Town Grows

THE IMMIGRANTS OF AMERICA

The prehistoric tribes known as the Mound Builders were the earliest inhabitants of the region included in Columbiana County. Two petroglyphs, cut into the rocks bordering the Ohio River near the present town of Wellsville, are these inhabitants' most unusual records. The rock carvings were of crude objects and figures of animals, men, and snakes. A cemetery with a burial site in the remains of what was probably a village is also evidence of their primitive existence in the region.

The Wyandots, Mingoes, and Delawares were the principal historic Native American tribes in Columbiana County. These natives used marked trails that ran through many parts of the county.

The road to building America was paved with wars and discrimination of ethnicity, race, color, and creed. Foreign languages and cultures were among the factors that developed animosity after the colonization of America by the Dutch, French, and British Empires using their native tongues.

Africans came to America as slaves in the early 1600s. They are among the earliest immigrants. The Spanish word for black was 'Niger.' That and the word 'Negro' of the Negroid race gave the basis for pronouncing the term 'Nigger,' not an offensive term, but only to define them. After slavery, some negroes used that term as a prefix before their name as a title. It was a subtle terminology before it became a racially derogatory term.

The main Polish migration to America occurred from the British colonial era until 1914. A derogatory term for the Polish settlers was 'Polack.' Many Poles came with other Slavics, Germans, Russians, Austria-Hungarians, and Eastern Europeans. Much friction existed between many of these immigrants due to political and social issues between their homelands and was carried over to the immigrants in America.

One and a half million people left Ireland for refuge in America between 1845 and 1855. Disease had devastated Ireland's potato crops, leaving millions without food. Over four and a half million Irish people came to America. Those immigrants who came were poor and suffering from disease and starvation. The Irish immigrants who were well off were referred to as 'lace curtain Irish,' while those who were poor were called the 'shanty Irish' because they were presumed to live in shanties or roughly built cabins. Neither term was complimentary. They were considered insults from other immigrant nationalities and more established Americans. 'Micks,' derived from 'Mc,' name origins, was another derogatory term for Irish immigrants.

Though some came as early as the 1700s, it was during the 1880s that poorer Italians slowly began to migrate to America. The unification of Italy caused the breakdown of the feudal land system, heavy taxes, loss of their commodity markets, and resulting overpopulation. Eventually, The United States welcomed the Italian laborers due to the demands of American industry for more workers. The peak of Italian immigration occurred by the early 1900s. In total, four million Italians arrived from the agricultural sections of southern Italy in the United States, three million of them between 1900 and 1914. Some of those early 20th-century arrivers trickled into smaller industrial towns near larger ones. Upon arriving in this country, they settled chiefly in New York, New Orleans, Chicago, Boston, Providence, Philadelphia, and large cities of the East. Italians continued to come until the Quota Acts of 1921 and 1924 were passed. A derogatory term for Italian immigrants was Guineas, named after that part of Africa due to the dark sun-colored skin some Italian field workers developed. Other terms were Dagos, Wops, and White Niggers.

The German immigrants to America occurred between 1820 and World War I when nearly six million Germans immigrated to the United States. From 1840 to 1880, they were the largest group of immigrants. Many other Germans sought refuge in America before and after World War II. A derogatory term for German immigrants was Krauts because they consumed Sauerkraut.

About one and a half million Swedes left Sweden for the United States of America during the 19th and 20th centuries. Many settled in the Midwest and West. A slur was rutabaga.

About one-third of Norway's population, more than 800,000 Norwegians, left their country for North America Between 1825 and 1925 for religious reasons. The majority of them went to The United States. Slurs were fish-eaters and sea jews.

Between 1890 and 1917, about 450,000 Greeks arrived in The United States. Many worked as laborers for the railroads, and others went to The American West. Another 70,000 Greek immigrants arrived between 1918 and 1924, and about 30,000 arrived between 1925 and 1945. Racial slurs were Flease and Tufts.

Though there are records of Chinese people in New York City as far back as 1830, most arrived in that city in the 1880s. The Chinese settled in the West in search of gold. The racial slur for people of Chinese descent at the time was 'Chink' or 'Chinamen.'

The Spaniards settled in the southern territories of North America to southern California.

In the early development of America, languages and cultures varied. It was mainly between the British, French, Dutch, and Native Americans in the Northeast and The Spanish, British, French Canadians, and Native Americans in the Southeast. Even within the British language at that time, there were varied languages and dialects. Some Irish and Scots immigrants spoke Gaelic, a very different language than English. Many early American settlers used variations of the English language, like Cockney, for one example.

The area's early settlers who would establish Wellsville, Ohio, were of British ethnicity after the American Revolution. Mainly of English, Scots, Scots-Irish, and Welsh ancestry. Scots-Irish are descendants of Scots who lived in Northern Ireland for two or three generations but retained their Scottish character and Protestant religion.

As each wave of foreign-speaking immigrants arrived in America and other founded countries, it was common practice for those already settled to disassociate themselves from them. This happened with every ethnicity and race. Fear of change and the unknown was a human trait that extended globally.

Chapter Thirteen

Wellsville, Ohio 1901-1902
Life Changes

In April 1893, an attorney, J.E. McDonald, announced the forth-coming bridge construction between East Liverpool and West Virginia. There was only a ferry service at the time. The East Liverpool Bridge Company chartered in West Virginia, began work in January 1896. Approximately 475 acres in West Virginia formed the Chester Land Company, which McDonald and his associates founded to develop that land, which included Rock Springs Park. The Chester Bridge opened in December 1896. The town of Chester, West Virginia, was charted in 1899. McDonald also proposed trolley lines between East Liverpool over the bridge to the new town in West Virginia. In 1897, trolleys ran over the new bridge from East Liverpool to Rock Springs Park. Residents of Wellsville could now travel from their town and transfer to another trolley to Rocks Springs Park in West Virginia.

"Whoa, boy!" Douglas Nicholson steered Rollo back to Main Street. "We're not going there today, boy." Rollo still instinctively went in the direction of Peppina's hotel. After all the years that passed, the dog still had the notion to go there. "This way, Rollo!" Douglas noted the dissapointed expression on his dog's face and smiled, recalling all the long walks he and his best friend took years before.

Douglas was now a young man of almost 20 years old, stood

about six feet two inches tall, and had an excellent build from sports and boxing. He still took Rollo for longer walks whenever he could. That bright day at the end of summer in 1901, the two began their stroll from home and passed along Riverside. Rollo sniffed at places they both enjoyed in their younger years. Little Peppina always came to the young man's mind when they passed those places that reminded him of those magical days of his childhood. They passed the end of the train station, turned left onto Third Street, continued straight alongside the fence, and stopped just before the Hotel Metropole. That was the area of the earliest settlement of Wellsville in 1823. As Douglas turned to cross the street, Rollo fought him, but now the strong young man easily overpowered his sturdy dog. Gone were the days when Rollo led Douglas around town. "C'mon, boy, she's not there anymore; you know that. And you're too tired today to see Mrs. Buch."

It took Douglas a while to come to terms with the fact that his friend, Peppina, was gone for good. But he always wondered if he would ever see her again. A week after Peppina's departure, the young boy began to pass by the hotel often, not seeing signs of any of the kids. Finally, he knocked on the front door, and Nicola Bucci opened it. Douglas recognized the Italian immigrant from seeing him at the hotel often.

"Hello, sir," he politely said. "Is Peppina home yet?"

"She no live here no more!" Nicola said in his broken English. Then he remembered the boy who was always with Peppina. "She had to go somewhere else to live, son. Sorry." Nicola was somewhat impatient with the young boy. He was frustrated from living with a grieving wife, grew resentful of his new home life, and focused solely on work and drinking beer. Before his marriage, he knew little about supporting or raising a family. Work and a pastime at bars were his only activities and the pleasure Giulia had granted him. Now, he was raising a baby daughter and an adopted son.

Young Douglas Nicholson didn't understand and became somewhat disturbed by that news. He was waiting for the day when his friend would return. Seeing their son upset, Mr. and Mrs. Nicholson eventually learned what happened to the Massaro girls. It first came by way of gossip, as things are in every small town. Later, more reliable sources confirmed it. Douglas Sr. and Martha were devastated by the news and the loss of their son's friend, Peppina, whom they treated like family. They felt that the young girl was a blessing in helping their son overcome his prior introverted personality. After watching Douglas Jr. become increasingly withdrawn, Mr. Nicholas sat his son down for a talk.

"Son," he began. Douglas could tell from that introduction that he was in for some bad news, confirming what he already suspected, and just stared at his father. "Sometimes in life, bad things happen." He knew his son would take this badly but went on to explain what happened at the level of a young boy's comprehension. Douglas did take it badly. He stopped fishing, sat in his room with Rollo for most of his free time, and studied. He went to school but didn't socialize. His friends knew what happened but didn't mention anything, primarily out of fear of angering him. Douglas finally put his anger and sorrow into his boxing practice. The incident affected him and changed him. It was a point in his life that put forward an end to his childhood. The incident hardened Douglas to the realities of life. But such things remain with us, blend into our lives, and are never forgotten.

A few months after hearing his father's explanation, Douglas decided to attempt to see Peppina's mother. So he and Rollo walked over on a bitterly cold, windy, snowy Saturday in the winter.

"Douglas?" Giulia Buch was surprised but happy to see the young boy. "Oh my God, Mr. Douglas, how are you?" Tears began to form. "Hello, Rollo!"

"I'm fine," Douglas replied awkwardly. Knowing she was no longer Mrs. Massaro, he didn't know what to call her.

Giulia sensed his uneasiness, and she surmised it was because he missed her daughter, Peppina. That subject was indeed a sore spot for her, but she felt comfort in seeing her daughter's friend. Without knowing about Nicola's crude explanation to the boy, she assumed this was his first visit since losing her dear girls. "C'mon inside and get out of the cold. You too, Rollo. C'mon, I give you something to eat," she sobbed from the bittersweet feelings she harbored but smiled.

Douglas didn't know what to do, so he walked into the hotel clumsily. Once inside, he stomped the snow off his boots onto a mat. Then Douglas noticed a sign above the check-in counter that replaced Mrs. Giulia Massaro with Mrs. Giulia Buch. Now, he was relieved to know how to address her. However, he wondered why she didn't share the name Bucci with her new husband.

"You remind me of happier times, Mr. Douglas. I like that feeling," Giulia stated in her strong Italian accent. Sighing, she continued, "I'm glad my daughter was able to have nice times in the years she was here. Take your coat and hat off and sit down," she said, pointing to a table near the kitchen entrance.

Douglas had come to understand her accent well and became fond of it. "Thank you, Mrs. Buch," he replied before Giulia disappeared into the kitchen. Rollo sat by his side obediently. Douglas noticed a much smaller lunch crowd than before. 'It must be from that depression his father constantly talked about,' he thought. "Killing all the businesses, it is," his father would say. There was a small crib to the side of the doorway. A baby lay sleeping in it as Felo stood beside it.

"Hello, Douglas!" The little boy smiled, remembering his older sister's friend.

"Hi, Felo. How are you?"

Felo's name changed in late 1893. A German immigrant doctor who examined him didn't hear how softly Giulia pronounced the last two letters of their name–ci–as they were almost silent. He deciphered their name as Buch instead of Bucci. Thus, the little boy became Felo Buch. Giulia adopted the name as well. It was a small method of retaliation against the man who forced her to give up her daughters.

"Peppina, went bye-bye!" Felo was too young to know what had happened. "Anuela went, too." He used his own shortened version of his sister's name, Emanuela.

Giulia returned with a large tray containing a big dish, a smaller one, and a bowl. "Mangiare, Mr. Douglas!" she shouted as she placed the larger plate in front of the boy. "This is spaghetti alla norma! You too, Rollo! Eat!" She set down the bowl before the dog. Mixed jarred greens filled the smaller dish as it was winter and there were no fresh vegetables.

"Oh! I remember this! Spaghetti with eggplant. I love this." He recalled how Peppina explained all her mother's recipes to him, which brought back a sad memory.

"Bianca, take care of the kitchen. I have company."

"Okay, Giuditta!" she said Giulia's name using dialect. Bianca Gallo was another kitchen helper. She was a short, plump 35-year-old woman who lived nearby. She recently migrated to America with her husband and four children. Bianca was pleased that this young boy brought some happiness to Giuditta. It was one of the few times she noticed her show a sign of joy since both her daughters departed.

Douglas revisited Giuditta occasionally during his remaining years of grade school and through high school. He always felt a deep sense of peace in the presence of his friend's mother, who, in turn, was rewarded with cherished memories of her daughter.

High school sports were unorganized in the mid to late 1890s. Students would put together teams with other nearby schools to compete. Track, baseball, basketball, and football were coming into shape in the area. Most schools didn't condone them, and they went completely unsupervised, and some were brutal. Without uniforms or rules, Douglas participated in as many as he could in high school, which developed his muscular appearance. They helped toughen him to the realities of life.

Most considered bare-fisted boxing a bloody attempt at a

sport and was outlawed in 21 states. James J. Corbett, known professionally as 'Gentleman Jim,' changed all that in the early 1900s by fighting with gloves and abiding by the Marquis of Queensberry rules of boxing. He was one of the first sports sex symbols in the United States and made boxing popular among the female audience. Gentleman Jim was one of Douglas's heroes. Douglas trained with an Irish immigrant, Ronan Byrne, throughout high school. Ronan felt the towering young lad was a natural and had championship abilities. He called him the next Gentleman Jim because of his good looks and demeanor. Ronan encouraged the young man to pursue a career in the sport, but Douglas wanted to go to college.

Throughout high school, Douglas kept an eye on Felo. He acted as a big brother to him out of love for his old friend and her mother. The tall, well-built Douglas ensured no older kids bullied the young boy. His old friend's brother was small and puny, reminding Douglas of himself at those ages. "Hey, Felo, if anyone ever gives you a hard time in school, you tell me, okay?" he told Felo the day he began school, not wanting young Felo to endure those anxieties as he had while growing up.

"Thanks, Douglas," Felo felt some security in his sister's old friend. Most children have some anxiety about beginning school for the first time. Whenever any of the older kids attempted to bully Felo, the popular Douglas Nicholson ended it with just a look.

Midway through high school, Douglas had his first sensual relationship with a member of the opposite sex. Before then, he only saw girls as mere friends. Margaret Myers changed all that, bringing about those wicked temptations that his pastor preached to students.

Douglas always viewed Margaret Myers as a kid with knobby knees who hung around with the rest of his crowd of friends. But that knobby-kneed kid prematurely became a raving beauty with a shapely hourglass figure and a bit more advanced with the ways of young men than the other girls. And she had her eyes set on Douglas since her childhood crush on him. Now, the well-developed young woman would use her feminine gifts to take him, at least for a while. Many of the guys on Douglas's sports teams had fallen to Margaret's feminine wiles, and she wanted her childhood crush on that long list of male conquests she wrote in her diary.

Douglas finally noticed Margaret. Only he didn't know that her performances were baiting him. She did it slowly, like a spider weaving her web, and eventually drew him in. She poised gracefully, fixing her well-formed breasts or lifting her skirt enough to expose sexy hosiery, emphasizing her shapely legs, all the time pretending no one was watching her.

She worked on her prey until Douglas had strong temptations, especially at night. He resisted, not wanting to go to the fiery pits of hell that the pastor had warned all the boys about. She came to him in visions while he slept, releasing that suppressed lust by eruptions of nature in his dreams. Those nocturnal emissions weren't of his own doing, allowing him freedom from sin but forcing the young man to soak his night clothes out of fear of his mother finding them stained.

"Oh, Douglas!" Margaret called him over one day after school just before summer recess along Riverside Avenue when she felt he was primed enough for her full offensive. Now, as she called him, Margaret knew he was hooked. "Wait, Douglas!" she slowly trotted, pretending to be in pain but making sure her sizable breasts bounced individually to her stride.

Douglas turned, "Hi Margaret," hiding his bodily desire for her. She looked beautiful. Her lips had a little red lipstick, making them look full and voluptuous. The blush on her cheeks complimented her lips. But it was whatever that black stuff was around her eyes that made those pretty spherical globes of vision look wider and sexy that got to Douglas.

"Oh, Douglas. Thank God!" she smiled, her eyes widened. "I think I strained my leg. You're an athlete. Can you take a look?" Margaret stood on her tiptoes and leaned on him, her breasts purposely pressing against his body. At the same time, the long nails of her fingers gently caressed his upper arms as she accentuated the bend of her leg to show him. Douglas looked in awe. Smelling her perfume and feeling her soft bosoms and dainty hands on his body aroused him. She noticed the slight protrusion in his pants and thought, 'Success!' Then she seductively said, "Maybe I better sit down to show you," leading him by hand to a bench.

Margaret sat close to Douglas, her body touching his. After slipping her foot out of her heeled black shoes with tied floral ribbons, she lifted her dress high, exposing her legs all the way up to her thighs. Douglas was astounded. A proper lady never did such things. The black two-toned stockings embroidered with alluring floral designs were enticing. Then she slowly and sensually rolled down the hosiery on her supposed bad leg and removed it, revealing her naked leg up to her thigh. 'Oh, my God,' thought Douglas. Her naked leg was breathtaking, something he had never personally seen before on a young lady.

"It's here." Margaret took Douglas's hand and placed it on her leg. His eyes spontaneously widened as he marveled at how soft and warm her flesh felt. "No, move it further up. Over to the right," her voice became husky, "around here," she placed her hand over his and moved it higher, noticing Douglas's pants swelling marvelously and rapidly. "Oh!" she said, as she moved his hand even closer to the top of her thigh, "right there. That's where it hurts. Oh!" she said again but grimaced while gently moving his hand back and forth. "Oh!" she screamed, biting her lip.

Douglas felt moisture on his fingertips and then her pubic hair. He finally knew what he was touching. She wasn't wearing underwear, and he had dared to violate the most sacred of things that other boys only talk about secretly. That precious orifice only seen by him before in pictures boys secretly brought to school. Now, he had touched a real one, part of a living and breathing young lady. 'I am doomed to the pits of hell,' he pictured himself aside the devil holding a pitchfork and burst out saying, "Oh, we better go!" 'But she didn't stop me. Why? In fact, she put my hand upon that enchanting but forbidden 'jewel,' he pondered. Then he felt the toes of the temptress travel under the hem of his pants and onto his naked lower leg.

Ignoring Douglas's command about leaving, Margaret wiggled her toes along Douglas's shin, casually but alluringly sliding them around, and asked in a throaty voice, "Douglas, how come you never asked me out?"

Douglas was at a loss for words. He dreamed about her but never thought about asking her on a date. 'How stupid of me,' he mulled over how foolish he had been. "I-I don't know." 'Am I stuttering again,' he thought in nervous humor. "I guess it's because I'm always so busy."

"Never too late," she smiled.

That weekend, Douglas took Margaret on the trolly to dance at Rock Springs Park, the amusement center that had just opened a month before. Along the way, the assertive and experienced young lady aroused Douglas. By the time they arrived at the park, they were kissing, making an attractive couple to the amusement of others on the trolly.

The couple enjoyed dancing, eating, and going on several rides. All the time, Margaret worked her prey with the charm and proficiency of a much more experienced younger woman. On the way home, she whispered in her victim's ear, "Did you ever go swimming at night?" As Douglas sat dumbfounded, Margaret softly asked in her husky voice, "Please, for me?"

They hopped off the trolly near Little Yellow Creek. Margaret slid off her shoes as they walked along the grassy pathway deep into an isolated area. Lights from the mill gave Douglas enough illumination to watch Margaret disrobe until she stood in front of the gravely ill-looking young man completely nude. She led the love-stricken young man by the hand to the water and began seductively undressing him. As Douglas stood uncomfortably naked, Margaret glanced down and, with a big grin, declared, "Well, looks like somebody wants to play."

Douglas, being considerably taller than Margaret, went into the creek first. Then he reached out, and Margaret fell into his open arms. Carrying her into deeper water, she kissed him passionately with an open mouth, something Douglas had never before experienced. Margaret swung around, hanging from him with her arms around his neck and wrapping her legs around him. Nature took its course, and Margaret began moaning, then screaming, "Oh!" She squirmed and yelled again, "Oh, Douglas!"

Douglas panicked and asked, thinking she was hurt from stepping on something in the water, "Are you okay, Margaret? Are you okay?" he repeated.

"Yes! Yes!"

That began Douglas's first romance, and it was a whirlwind one. Douglas confessed his sins at least twice a week, but the relationship didn't last past the summer. In a way, Douglas was grateful, as Margaret was a wild woman who depleted him of all his energy. He couldn't take it any longer, even dropping out of summer football practice from exhaustion. Douglas was grateful when Margaret Myers moved on to another young man to prey upon. Douglas Nicholson wouldn't resume another relationship for quite a while.

After four years of high school, Douglas apprenticed at a lawyer's office his father knew in East Liverpool for a short time. After witnessing the loss of his childhood friend and her sister at the hands of what he felt was an injustice to them and their mother, the young man became interested in law. The same year, he decided to go to the University of Cincinnati to pursue a mandatory three-year course of study for a law degree.

Douglas was home on college recess that bright day at summer's end while walking his dog, Rollo, in 1901. He had one remaining year of law studies to complete. "Come on, big boy!" Rollo's walking pace had slowed. "Let's go back. That's enough for one day." They had visited Giuditta and Felo often before when Douglas was in town. But that day, Rollo seemed tired, and his master decided to take his dog back home and not visit the hotel on that particular day.

After Nicola forced Giuditta to give her two daughters up for adoption, she had two new daughters by him. The oldest was almost eight, and the second was five. Now pregnant, she also had a two-year-old son. Another baby boy had died at nine months old. Even as a young adult, Douglas didn't understand why Nicola made Giuditta give up Peppina and Emanuela for adoption. The young man always harbored animosity toward Nicola Bucci for the loss of his childhood friend. He felt the man who didn't want children was now being punished by God with more mouths to feed.

Rollo was indeed showing signs of getting old. It was one of the weaknesses of larger dogs, even those of mixed breeds. While his master was away, he missed him and would lie on Douglas's bed during the day, sniffing the scent of the one person who took him on daily adventures his whole life. Martha Nicholson walked Rollo in the morning across the street above the grassy slope and the railroad tracks where Douglas played with him as a child. Her husband gave the dog longer walks after he returned home from work. However, it seemed Rollo lived for the days when Douglas would return.

After the summer break, Douglas returned to his law school, which was located in Cincinnati, the second-largest city in Ohio with a population of about 326,000. The city's bustling lifestyle was a stark contrast to the quiet town where he had spent his childhood. Among his classmates, Douglas was popular, and he had the opportunity to meet a diverse range of people and experience things that were far beyond the scope of law.

Several months before graduating, Douglas met a young lady there who he liked, and she also seemed to favor him. However, the charming and adorable Gabrielle Delisle was still a high school student working in the university library and planning to study college-level economics. While maintaining a primarily platonic relationship, except for a few gentle kisses, the couple got to know each other well.

"How is the lovely Miss Delisle doing today?" his words flowed freely and naturally. Douglas always felt comfortable being in Gabrielle's company. Witty, outgoing, intelligent, and active, the blonde-haired, olive-green-eyed young lady seemed to be what Peppina would have been like at that age.

"I am doing well, Signore," she replied in perfect Italian. Gabrielle's mother had taught her daughter the language of her ancestors, and the young lady enjoyed speaking it so much that she perfected it. Douglas had told her many stories about his time with Mrs. Buch and Peppina while growing up, and she spoke Italian to make him feel at home.

"I was hoping you might accompany me to the Saturday dance?"

"Love to," Gabrielle's eyes widened. Her eyelids lowered, and the long lashes partially covering such beautiful-colored eyes gave her the appearance of sexy, lazy eyes, and Douglas couldn't resist them.

Over those months, their relationship became more serious, mainly because they both realized that Douglas would leave soon. They dated as much as they could and fit in short times in between, enjoying coffees with biscuits and sometimes lunch together.

"I'm going to miss you when I leave, Gab," Douglas began calling her that nickname right after she first referred to him as 'Doug.' He had succumbed to the charming and gorgeous young woman, "I don't suppose you would wait for me?"

Gabrielle practically leaped into Douglas's arms, saying, "Try to stop me!" They kissed passionately as they had never done before. She felt the bulk of his muscles, and her petite gazelle-like body melted as his hands felt the soft skin of her open back, gently sliding them lower to her waist. Gabrielle gasped from the erotic touches she had waited so long to feel, "I'll wait for you forever!"

Their final days drifted in the splendor of each other's company, enhanced by the flowery smells of those beautiful spring days. On their final day together before his departure by coach, Douglas told her, "I love you, Gabrielle Delisle."

"Oh, I love you too, Douglas!" tears filling her eyes, "You

will come back to me, won't you?"

Douglas kissed her lustfully with an open mouth and answered, "Does that seem like someone who won't come back?"

"I feel I'm going to miss you far too much, Doug," a teary-eyed Gabrielle forced a smile as she announced her sentiment to him as he boarded the coach.

"I'll come back to you, Gab, just as soon as I set up my law practice. You'll be busy with college anyway. The time will fly." Douglas smiled, "Say hello to Frenchie for me," he chuckled. They had exchanged information about their pet dogs. Frenchie was a medium-sized mixed poodle pup that Douglas got to meet before he readied for travel.

"And you say hello to Rollo for me!" she smiled at Douglas, who sat at the edge of his seat inside the open coach.

They had decided to write to each other often and already had exchanged addresses. Gabrielle stood on her tiptoes to give the man she loved one last kiss. Douglas made it a passionate exchange; he didn't care who was watching. "Til we meet again." He smiled, and the coach slowly moved to take him to the riverboat wharf. He waved back to Gabrielle and watched her wave until he could see her no more.

Knowing it would take longer, Douglas wanted to experience a voyage to his hometown by riverboat along the Ohio River. He and Rollo had seen so many boardings and arrivals throughout the years. Together, they smelled the rich, smoky aromas and heard the mighty blasts and toots of steam from the big boats. He and his dog had watched the facial expressions of passengers excitedly departing or arriving. So distanced they were from him as a child, only appreciating being aboard one in his dreams. Now, the young man wanted to travel on one as a passenger. His only regret was that Rollo couldn't accompany him or Gab, for that matter, but for entirely different reasons.

The town grew after Peppina left, and Douglas attended college. A few Italian immigrants arrived after the 1893 depression ended in 1897, and the economy picked up. The mills and factories needed more workers.

The Spanish-American War began in the spring of 1898. It was a relatively quick war that ended less than four months later, and the patriotic town of Wellsville participated.

By 1901, the Steubenville East Liverpool Railway & Light Co. trolley began replacing the East Liverpool line. The system started in Steubenville and ran through the smaller river towns to the many lines throughout East Liverpool. Work was ongoing to take it all the way to Beaver, Pennsylvania, with a completion date scheduled for 1905.

When Douglas arrived home at the riverboat wharf in Wellsville, his parents brought along Rollo. The large dog, confused at first, with some visual impairment and hearing loss, quickly sniffed his master. Mr. Nicholson fought to restrain the dog while Douglas bent slightly to hug Rollo, his first best friend. After Rollo calmed down a bit, Mr. Nicholson surrendered the dog's leash to Douglas. He looked fondly at his son and said, "Welcome home, Son. Or should I say, Attorney," his proud father smiled.

"Thanks, Dad."

"I'm so proud of you, Douglas," Martha declared. She had been crying since the riverboat first pulled into the slip. "And happy for you!" she continued, thinking, 'My little boy is a man now,' and remembering those days when her son couldn't defend himself from bullies.

"Wait, everybody! Douglas, get closer to your mother and pull Rollo next to you. Okay, everybody, stay still!" Mr. Nicholson had recently bought a Kodak camera and had waited for his family to be together. He pressed the shutter button. "Wait! One more. Everybody still!" He took the second shot. Douglas Sr. asked a bystander to take one with him in it. The friendly gentleman kindly agreed and took a photo of the Nicholson family with Rollo poised in the middle at the dock with the harbored riverboat in the background.

After a few days of rest and acclimating to his hometown,

Douglas decided to walk over and see Giuditta. "Come on, big boy, let's go over and see Giuditta," he somewhat loudly said as Rollo's hearing had failed, "You remember her. All those good meals we had?" The dog's eyes widened, and he stood like a soldier coming to attention. "That's my boy!" But as Rollo stood poised and ready, he suddenly keeled over. "Rollo?" Douglas didn't know what happened. He got down on his hands and knees and saw that his dog's eyes were open, but his breathing was labored. Rollo couldn't move; his eyes just stared at his master. "Dad!" he shouted. "Dad, come here!"

Mr. Nicholson ran up the stairs, fearing something had happened to his son. Martha followed quickly behind her husband. They entered their son's room and noticed Douglas sitting beside his dog. "What happened?" Douglas Sr. promptly asked. Then, he heard Rollo's heavy breathing. "I'll go over to Roger's; he's good with animals!"

"No, Dad," sobbed Douglas. "He's tired and wants to go," a teary-eyed Douglas said. "He waited for me to come home." Martha was already crying. Even Douglas Sr. had tears in his eyes. They knew Rollo was dying.

Douglas easily lifted his heavy dog and laid him on his bed. His parents quietly left the room so their son could be alone with his best friend. Rollo lay on the bed with his master holding him in his arms for two hours. When his dog's breathing began to slow, Douglas stared into Rollo's eyes and said, "Thanks, Rollo. Thanks for being my friend," he sobbed. "Thanks for everything, ole boy," Douglas cried, recollecting all the times they shared. Rollo's eyes closed as if he had gone to sleep, and then he passed away in the arms of his master.

Douglas wrapped his dog tightly in a blanket and brought him outside. With a shovel, he carried Rollo across the street above a slope on a grassy spot near the railroad tracks, where they loved to play together ever since Rollo was a pup.

"Should you help him?" Martha asked her husband.

"He has to do it himself, my dear."

The strong young man dug a deep pit while his parents

watched their son from the other side of the street. Douglas carefully laid his dog down into it and filled the hole with the Ohio River Valley's dark, rich river soil. Then Douglas knelt over the grave and reminisced about his happy childhood with his best friend, leading him about the town. Peppina came to his mind as he remained on his knees, crying.

A member of the Nicholson Family had died.

Chapter Fourteen

Wellsville, Ohio 1905-1906

Wellsville and The Area Around it Grows

James Newell and E.W. Hill mapped a town south of Chester, West Virginia, in 1901. Investors called the Lloyd Syndicate began selling lots at an encouraging pace. That land included the Wells farm. The North American Manufacturing Company was created in 1903 to develop the new town and build new industrial establishments. They also planned to construct a bridge and railroad yards to encourage iron manufacturing and other potteries in the area. In addition to the bridge, the developers outlined a streetcar system to connect with East Liverpool's transit system. The construction of the bridge and street railway system began in 1904. The 16-hundred-foot-long Newell Bridge opened on July fourth, 1905. The Newell Streetcar line opened ten days later. A bridge closer to Wellsville could now bring workers to the newly formed industries of the new area. In that same year, the post office began free mail delivery into the town of Wellsville.

Douglas mourned the loss of his dog, Rollo. His passing left a void in the young man's life. In some ways, it resurrected his childhood and the absence of his old friend, Peppina, who also loved Rollo. They were Douglas's only friends in the past days, which became glorious when a young boy called Pip came out of his shell years ago with their help. Those happy times led to that bridge from childhood, which all young boys and girls eventually crossed. As a man, Douglas had to put those days in that special place we all have to store our fondest memories.

Gabrielle plagued Douglas's mind until another letter envelope arrived from Miss Gabrielle Delisle, postmarked in Cincinnati, Ohio. There had been many since they decided to communicate after they parted. The news of Rollo's death was in the first letter she received just after Douglas returned to Wellsville. She conveyed her sincerest sorrow for the loss of his beloved friend. The two came to know each other well by their correspondence, and they often expressed their feelings. They exchanged portraits at times. Emotions became more passionate. Douglas opened the letter and smiled as Gab explained that she was getting ready to graduate college and decided to teach economics. From her photos, he could see that she had become an even more beautiful young woman. Douglas missed the petite Miss Gabrielle Delisle that he had gotten to know so well, and she longed for him as well. "I would love it if you could come and see me for my graduation," she wrote. "My parents are anxious to meet the mysterious young lawyer I write to so often."

Douglas had opened a small law practice in Wellsville. He overlooked offers to join larger law firms in cities and decided to remain in his hometown. Douglas was a man of principles, as was his father. He wanted to help all types of people. His practice was open to all townspeople of all ethnicities. Like many young people, he was a crusader. He did much pro bono work for those who couldn't afford good legal service, including newly arrived immigrants. Affluent residents also sought help from that reputable young lawyer with an excellent track record. Douglas became a prominent attorney and began making considerable money. But the thought of Gabrielle had bedeviled his mind far too long while he was so busy. He wanted to see her again; it had been too long.

Even though the years had passed, Douglas retained an image of Peppina parallel to his age. Our minds fool us with our memories. Only when he looked at the studio photo of her with

Rollo and himself from years before did he remember her as a child. As an attorney, Douglas knew the legality of adoption laws. However, he wanted to learn what happened to his old friend, Peppina, and her younger sister. She would now be in her early 20s, and Douglas decided to find her.

Mr. Salvatore Moretti, the lawyer who had handled the adoption of the Massaro girls, was initially hesitant to discuss anything about it with Douglas. "You know that it is considered unethical for me to explain anything about a client's case, don't you?" He sized up the handsome young attorney who had gained notoriety among his colleagues by winning so many of his criminal defense trials. But Douglas just sternly stared into the eyes of the aging immigration lawyer. "Okay, now I know why you win so many cases." Moretti smiled.

"So, where did you send them?"

"I honestly don't know where they ended up."

"Mrs. Massaro, now Mrs. Buch, told me they went to a very nice place," Douglas said coldly.

"I said that to ease her suffering. We never know exactly where they take these kids," he paused, "there are so many immigrant children put up for adoption."

Douglas remained staring at Mr. Moretti.

"I only know that a state official sent some spinster to take them to Cleveland. I don't know where they ended up, but I can give you the name of a man I know. He used to work for the Pinkertons." Salvatore Moretti scribbled a name on a piece of paper. "He occasionally does some investigation work for me."

"Thank you," Douglas said.

"Don't thank me." Moretti frowned. "I think it's going to be impossible, but if anyone can find out, it's him."

A few days had passed before Douglas met with Mr. John Rose. With a broken and twisted nose and swollen bags under his eyes, he looked like he had been in one too many bare-fisted boxing matches. "If they're out there, I'll find them. That I can tell you for sure!" John Rose's appearance alone showed Douglas he was capable. But his determination convinced him he was the right man for the job. Rose demanded a substantial down payment with no guarantees, only his promise to get to the bottom of the matter. "I leave no stone unturned!"

Before Douglas set out by train to see Gabrielle graduate, he decided to see Giuditta on a late spring day in 1906. Walking along Main Street, smoke stacks released plumes of grey clouds in the distance. The aromas of kilns burning from the potteries mixed with smells from the factories and scents from cooking foods from eateries. All formed the distinctive essence of the 25-year-old man's hometown. Things in Wellsville had changed so much since the days he, along with Rollo, Peppina, and the other kids, roamed the town. There were more buildings, and new stores had opened, with some replacing older ones. Everything seemed much more alive, with more trolleys running and horse-drawn wagons crowding the busy street. There were even occasional horseless carriages passing through town.

Telephone lines provided by Solon C. Thayer, who first brought telephone service to the town in 1899, were transferred to Columbiana County Telephone in 1901. The same year, the funeral train carrying the body of assassinated President William McKinley had passed through the town as Lincoln's did years before. The Catholic Church on Main Street was now the firehouse as of 1904. Douglas's hometown and surrounding area had indeed transformed since the turn of the century.

As Douglas turned the bend at the end of Third Street, he glimpsed at the old train station. The railroads recovered from the 1893 depression and were never busier. Flocks of people crowded the area around the Third Street Station building and faded memories returned. Douglas approached a vendor and bought some candy boxes from one of them. Then, he continued back along Main Street. As he came upon Guiditta's hotel, Douglas noticed that the hotel had recovered from the major recession referred to as a depression by the newspapers and townspeople. It looked good and well-kept, but not as nice as before. During the bad economic years, repairs waited as the occupancy and food and liquor service declined. There were also more Italian immigrant families, and some of their homes badly needed repairs.

Giuditta had toned down the obvious prostitutes who lingered around men. Now, they had to rent rooms upstairs for their services, dress nicely, and act inconspicuously in the hotel. Sandy, the young prostitute who fired her derringer at Enzo Ricci's hired thugs years before, remained. She was older now and looking for another line of work, though she still carried her small pistol in her garter belt under her dress. The young 'woman of the night' even considered marriage. Giuditta's new children now used two of the rooms Luigi had rented to prostitutes. Open gambling was no longer encouraged, though some men occasionally started a game or two. Liam Kelly remained as a caretaker and muscle, and still, sometimes, he broke up a fight or two. Liam still kept his club near him. However, he spent most of his time now reminiscing about the past days with Luigi Massaro and the adventures he had with that man he respected and missed. Roberto Barata moved to a larger bar in East Liverpool. He didn't like Nicola and wouldn't work for the dingy man after working with the legendary Luigi Massaro. He occasionally returned to Giuditta's establishment to speak with Liam and some of the older guys about the days with Luigi.

Felo appeared first, repairing the front door alongside Nicola. It was refreshing to see the teenager's stepfather giving some attention to him. Felo was nearing the end of high school, and Douglas always kept an eye on his surrogate younger brother whenever he could. They often discussed sports together, and the teen viewed Douglas as a hero. Felo, now 16 years old, filled out somewhat, probably from working around the hotel and occasionally at the mill. He was on the shorter side like his mother and apparently didn't inherit his father's towering height.

Douglas then noticed the other kids playing hopscotch on the brick pavement at the front left of the hotel. Millie Brown, who was supervising them, also joined in the game. The heavyset woman, now in her mid-forties, was light on her feet and agile as she gracefully hopped the chalked course, switching her feet. Giuditta's and Nicola's oldest daughter, Mary, was already 13 years old. Angela was 10, and John was seven years old. Giuditta's youngest daughter with Nicola, Telma, was now four years old. Memories of Douglas's youth re-surfaced while watching them enjoy the same games he played with Peppina.

"Hey, Douglas!" Felo shouted as he dropped his hammer and walked toward the man he considered an older brother. "How are you?" he asked, smiling. Nicola glanced, then walked away. He knew why Douglas didn't like him. It always resurrected thoughts of him forcing Peppina and Emanuela to go to an orphanage, a bad memory for all who remembered.

"I'm doing well, Felo. How's everything with you?" After some small talk, he heard Millie calling him.

"Hi there, Mr. Douglas!" Millie shouted with a big smile.

"Millie! How have you been?" Before Millie could answer, the other kids came running and interrupted them.

"Hi, Douglas!" Mary said first. She had a crush on the handsome young man.

Mary's sisters and brother all looked up to the charming man who always brought candy or popcorn for them. They crowded around him while the littlest, Telma, tugged at his trousers.

"Okay, everybody!" Douglas smiled while handing out the candy. "There's some for all! And even for kids of all ages!" he said as he handed Millie a box.

"Why thank you, Mr. Douglas!" she said before wrapping her arms around him in a bear hug.

Giuditta appeared at the front door. She had heard all the commotion from the side window. "Mr. Douglas!" she yelled, putting her hands to her face. "Come here and give me a kiss!"

Douglas walked over to embrace the woman who was still beautiful. She never got over losing her daughters and her anger toward her second husband. Now called Giuditta by all of the arriving new Italian immigrants. It was natural for them to use her name in the dialect of the region of her native country. She dreaded every night Nicola forced her to sleep with him. Giuditta referred to him as a dirty slob. He was the opposite of

Luigi. Compounded with the stress of running the hotel while caring for her new family, those things had drained her energy.

Giuditta often reflected on her younger years when she met the dashing young man she would marry and take her away on the adventure of her life. Those were joyous days in Pittsburgh and Sharpsburg when she longed to be in the arms of the man she loved at the end of the day. Memories of her family with Peppina, Emanuela, and eventually Felo always surfaced. She still loved Luigi and always would. 'He used to call me Giulia like the upperclass. I loved that,' she remembered. She also recollected the biggest mistake of her life made by cheating on him.

"What a 'presenza' you make! You get more handsome every time I see you, Mr. Douglas."

"You just say that because you want to feed me, Mrs. Buch!" Douglas said as he smiled. Giuditta had also changed the last names of her new family, as she had done with Felo after that German doctor's mistake. Only Nicola used Bucci.

"And you spoil my kids!" she laughed. "C'mon inside and eat!"

"Oh, boy!" he answered almost as a child once more.

Douglas enjoyed his lunch and his conversation with his old friend's mother. He didn't tell Giuditta about his search for her girls. He wouldn't tell her unless he could locate or bring them back. Even if they were married, Douglas would pay the expenses for them to return to see their mother. Douglas never told Giuditta that he chose to be a lawyer because of what had happened to her and her daughters. He never wanted to arouse her sentimental nature, which could perhaps upset her.

Nonetheless, it was Giuditta who brought up the old days when she spoke of Rollo's death with tears in her eyes. Douglas didn't tell her about Gabrielle. He planned to tell Giuditta all about the woman in his life when he returned from the trip.

On the eve of that day when Douglas visited Giuditta, the sun began to bow from sight. Dramatic colors that seemed rendered from an artist's palette formed. They mixed in with the heavenly white clouds that leisurely floated by as the sun slowly set in the valley. As a man, he still recalled those days when it was a sign that he, Peppina, Rollo, and his friends had to go home. The following day, he planned to move further into his adulthood.

Years after her marriage to Nicola, Giuditta realized what a mistake she had made by cheating on Luigi. Life with Nicola, whom she deemed a fool, became monotonous and senseless. "You move up and down like a little wind-up toy," Giuditta told Nicola as he feverishly tried to please her. "He'll be finished in seconds, as usual," she whispered, gazing impatiently at the ceiling, waiting for Nicola to finish what she considered an ineffective waste of her time.

Thirty seconds later, the diminutive man awkwardly gasped, his face contorted, swiftly concluding his rhythmic gestures. Then he rolled off Giuditta and moaned, "Maronna mia. That was good."

"For you!" Giuditta yelled, "I'll find myself a real man—one like Luigi." Then she shouted, "Get away from me! And don't sleep here anymore. You sleep downstairs from now on!"

"We made a deal. I'm your husband, and I forbid it!"

"What are you gonna do, you little monkey? I don't need you anymore! Felo runs the place now. Get out of my room!"

Over the years, Giuditta's past thoughts about her indiscretion plagued her, and it changed her. The sin she committed with Nicola drew her into a world of promiscuity with other men, thinking that she had already lost her soul for succumbing to Nicola's temptations long ago. That led to Luigi leaving and Giuditta losing her daughters. Subconsciously, she condemned herself, and her only avenue of escape fabricated in those far corners of her mind was to recapture Luigi in the arms of other men. Her moral descent had begun.

Chapter Fifteen

Cincinnati, Ohio 1906
Love Comes Quickly

Cincinnati thrived Along the Ohio River shoreline when steamboats first operated in 1811. It was nicknamed 'Porkopolis' since becoming the biggest meat processing center in the United States in the early 1800s. A popular spot of the Underground Railway because of its location, it also became the home of the Cincinnati Red Stockings, later becoming the Cincinnati Reds.

Martha and Douglas Nicholson stood together at their front door, watching their son board the carriage that would take him to the train station just blocks away. Mr. Causwell, their next-door neighbor, was taking him there on his way to do errands in town. "We're losing our little boy, honey," Martha said, teary-eyed, struggling to keep her composure, recalling days long ago and the cute ways of her fragile little boy.

Douglas Sr. smiled at his wife and held her close, "No, Martha, our little boy is a man now."

The evening before, Douglas told his parents he was considering asking Gabrielle for her hand in marriage. Knowing their son so well, they already knew he was more than considering marrying her. His every conversation with them lately included the young lady. The auspicious tones and descriptions Douglas always used clearly indicated his intentions. They were both delighted for their son but curious to meet the young woman who had stolen his heart.

Fragrances from budding flora and fresh grass along the slopes of the river filled the air as Douglas boarded the train at Third Street Station. He glanced through the window as he sat on the upholstered seat of the last passenger car, waiting for it to leave. Douglas wore his best suit: a dark grey single-breasted garment tailored from vicuna wool, with a matching vest and trousers. His crossed leg revealed one of the black laced leather shoes that complimented the suit.

Fog clouds floated slowly up from the river, resembling ghostly figures. Specks of orange and blue broke through the drifting shapes, revealing the bright celestial color-stained sky lurking behind them. The well-dressed young man removed his hat to view closer through the glass, exposing his wavy dark blonde hair. His narrow rolled-brimmed Alpine Fedora with a center dent now lay in his lap as he turned and looked down past the Third Street railroad shop houses below the slope. Reflections of pastel-colored hues covered his old favorite fishing spot, and he recalled when he and Rollo, along with Peppina, marveled in those sleepy days. Douglas often thought of Peppina at times like this when his mind was at ease, and he could imagine. And within that creative power at the center of his intellect, the wonder of what she would now be like as a young woman taunted him. He knew Peppina would be beautiful. Her magical olive-green-colored eyes that glistened when she smiled always revealed the loveliness of her nature. Would he now seek her hand in marriage instead of Gab if she was here? Should he wait for his investigator's report and find Peppina? Then he thought, 'No. I love Gab too much,' and he put his childhood behind him once more.

"Ticket, please." The conductor interrupted his thought process, as did the steam whistle blasting its last departure warning. The mighty 0-6-0 locomotive discharged spurts of steam before slowing moving, taking Douglas away from his hometown where his childhood memories lived. The uniformed man punched the ticket and handed it back. "Thank you, sir."

A smiling Douglas clapped loudly when he heard Gabrielle Delisle's name called from the dean at the podium. Mr. and Mrs. Delisle, sitting beside Douglas, also applauded as their daughter walked gracefully up to the stage, shook hands with the dean, and received her diploma. Claire, Gabrielle's mother, was crying, while Andre, her husband, kept a stern face but appeared to be holding back a few of his tears.

Douglas met Gabrielle's parents the day before upon his arrival at the train station. They welcomed him to stay with them at their charming home in a nice section of Cincinnati instead of at a hotel. The handsome, well-dressed, and gentlemanly young man made such an impression Mr. and Mrs. Delisle took an immediate liking to him. Even Frenchie, the poodle, remembered his scent and greeted him in her own way. Douglas presented Andre with a gift: a fine bottle of imported Château Margaux from the land of his heritage as they all sat in the Delisle family's formal living room after enjoying dinner.

"Thank you, young man," Andre expressed his gratitude with a smile, his appreciation for the thoughtful gift evident. Andre, a well-built man who had worked his way up in the meat industry, a thriving business in Cincinnati, to eventually own a store, was clearly pleased with the choice of wine. Douglas had learned from Gabrielle that Andre had a fondness for French wines, a detail he had carefully considered when selecting the gift.

France was the land of Andre's ancestry. It was natural he preferred the wines of that country. "It's my pleasure, sir." Then, Douglas carefully handed Claire a beautifully wrapped gift box that contained a hand-painted ceramic head of a princess made in Caltagirone, Sicily.

"Oh, my God! It's so gorgeous, Douglas!" exclaimed Claire, her hands holding her face, admiring the gift in her lap. "It's so stunning!" Claire was an attractive, slim woman in her mid-forties with fashionably styled black hair. Her eyes bore the same color as her daughter's. Claire's parents were Italian immigrants who migrated from Armento, in the Province of Potenza, near where Giuditta Buch was from. She was just three years old when they arrived in America, and her family settled in Cincinnati shortly after.

Douglas had captured both their hearts. Gabrielle proudly smiled as this young man she loved made such an impression on her parents.

"And last but not least, for you, my dear graduate, Gabrielle." Douglas formally used her birth name in the presence of her parents and placed a small gift-wrapped box in her hand.

Gabrielle's beautiful olive-green-colored eyes widened as that of a cat as she admired the contents of the small gift box. It was an exquisite European emerald cameo with intricate features of a woman's face surrounded by 18-carat gold trim. "Douglas! It's the most beautiful piece of jewelry I've ever seen." Gabrielle was ecstatic. "Thank you, Douglas," she used his full name in her astonishment. She handed it to her mother, who was already admiring it from her seat. Frenchie took one sniff of the cameo and also seemed to approve. Then Gabrielle arose and walked toward the man she loved, bent over, and kissed him on his cheek while touching his hand.

It was a long time since Douglas felt Gabrielle's warm, moist lips and the touch of her hand on his. It sent a chill up his spine, but her smile and the sparkle in her incredible eyes made him realize he loved her. "You're welcome" were the only words he could reckon to say, though his mind wished to convey much more to the beautiful young woman. Douglas already had another small box in one of his two large leather suitcases in the guest room upstairs. It was a platinum ring with intricate metalwork designs of scrolls, ribbons, and vines called filigree and a near-flawless Amethyst stone in the center. Amethyst was Gabrielle's birthstone. He had bought the engagement ring in Pittsburgh while on business, not realizing whether he would use it. Now, that desire awakened.

"It was so nice of you to take us to such a nice restaurant, Douglas," Mrs. Delisle commented over drinks in her parlor.

"A fine celebration for our daughter indeed," agreed Mr.

Delisle. "Thank you, young man."

The evening of Gabrielle's graduation, Douglas insisted on taking the family out to celebrate Gabrielle's landmark event. She had graduated second of a class of 50, mostly young men. Douglas insisted on the best champagne to celebrate before the four-course meal they all enjoyed. After conversing in the parlor for about an hour, Douglas asked Mr. Delisle, "May I have your permission to escort your daughter on a walk?"

"Certainly, young man," Andre smiled, as did Claire, "you may."

"Mademoiselle?" Douglas asked while extending his arm to an already chuckling Gabriele. He escorted her to the door, opened it, and allowed her to exit first. Then Douglas turned to where her parents were sitting, "We won't be long, folks," he said to assure them both.

Arm in arm, Gabrielle and Douglas went for an evening stroll. Aromatic smells from flowers, azaleas, and lilacs decorating the side of the walkway permeated the area. Blending into those fragrances was the scent of fresh-cut grass from the lawns in front of houses and along the sidewalks. "Where should I take you?" Gabrielle spoke first to break her awkwardness. She was finally in the arms of this handsome, sweet young man who overwhelmed her feelings. Gabrielle felt his muscular arms, which aroused her in a way she hadn't felt since he left. Gabrielle stopped and turned toward Douglas. Standing on her tiptoes, she pulled his face down to her level and passionately kissed him with an open mouth. Then her stunning eyes stared into his. "I love you, Doug. I think I have since the moment I first met you." Gabrielle smiled and remained looking into his dark blue eyes.

Douglas said nothing at first. He embraced her hard and leaned down to kiss her again. This time, it was longer, and he moved his hands about her body. His fingers explored the shape of her back and felt her petite waist while his lips remained engaged with hers. Displaying her deep affection, Gabrielle moved Douglas's hands onto her breasts, and she let out a sigh of ecstasy, feeling them. "I love you too," he whispered while kissing her ear.

"Maybe I should take you to the town fountain," she gently whispered as her eyes engaged his. Gabrielle privately humored she couldn't relinquish her virginity on a public street.

"That sounds good to me," Douglas replied, taking her dainty hand into his larger one. Holding hands, they continued their walk. Gabrielle played with Douglas's hand as they strolled. That mere touch of her aroused him. He had dated and passionately kissed and petted girls in high school. But it was Margaret Myers who took his virginity during high school when she seduced him. Douglas briefly recalled the weeks of that affair in a split second that shot before him. But no woman ever made Douglas feel the way he did now. They talked about feelings they shared while walking, subjects they both had felt were not permissible in postal letters.

After they rounded another corner, two strapping men dressed in working clothes, each sporting tweed caps, approached Gabrielle and Douglas. One of them was slightly larger than Douglas. "Spare the missus?" one asked in a thick Italian accent, "then give me all your money! Now!" The thug spoke threateningly, indicating they would hurt Gabrielle if he didn't. Douglas quickly surveyed the situation, then swiftly slid Gabrielle behind his body when he noticed one of the men pulling a knife from under his jacket. Guarding her, Douglas went into boxing mode. He skillfully struck the bigger one who held the knife first. Douglas hit him directly and hard on the nose, as learned from Ronan Byrne, his Irish boxing instructor. Then, he immediately landed a barrage of punches on the second man as the larger one spurted dark red blood from his broken nose. The shorter man's face was battered and bleeding from several places, and then his legs buckled, and he fell to his knees. Douglas used his legwork like a professional now. He didn't bounce but slowly moved around the beaten men, his arms slowly moving, observing their every move. Douglas's fists remained raised and poised, ready to strike as soon as either moved.

"Let's get out of here!" the taller man shouted in a muffled voice from holding his bleeding nose. "This guy's crazy!" The bigger man grabbed his accomplice by the arm and dragged him away. While pinching two fingers to stop the blood flowing from his nose, he shouted, "Pazzo bastardo!" in a voice that sounded like a honking duck. It reminded Douglas of Erik Olsson from his first fight years ago.

Douglas allowed them both to depart, as he didn't want to leave Gabrielle alone to chase them. He slowly turned to see his girlfriend shivering and in a gaze from the shock of the incident. Douglas was worried even though he knew neither of those bastards laid a hand on her. "Gab, are you alright?" Douglas put his arms around her body and gently glided them up and down Gabrielle's arms to prevent her from going into deeper shock. As he did, she kept staring into his eyes.

"I'm okay," Gabrielle said at last.

"Thank God!" Douglas kept massaging her arms until he slowly stopped.

"My God, I've never been so scared!" Gabrielle kept gazing into his dark blue eyes.

Douglas noticed a public bench and slowly walked Gabrielle over to it. The couple sat quietly; Douglas's arm remained around her shoulder. After some time, Gabrielle reached over and kissed him lovingly. "Thank you, Doug. They could have killed us," she said while holding his hand. "You mentioned you boxed but never said how good you were. Dear God, you looked like. . ."

"Gentleman Jim?" Douglas answered for her and laughed. He was happy to see that she recovered.

"Exactly! You looked like a professional!" Gabrielle appeared amazed. "Wow, I've never seen anything like that in my entire life!" She smiled now. "You were great!"

"C'mon, I think I should get you back home," Douglas said almost involuntarily, as he didn't want the evening to end. Gabrielle's only thought was for him to take her back to 'their' home. This was the man she wanted to marry.

"You should have seen Douglas!" Gabrielle shouted as soon as she entered the front door of her home amidst Frenchie's barking. Douglas slowly followed her while petting the dog to calm her, wondering how her parents would take this. Mr. and Mrs. Delisle sat in the same chairs as when they left. Frenchie returned to where she was lying down before the disturbance.

"What happened, Gabrielle?" Mr. Delisle asked first, fearing the worst. His wife's eyes widened as she noticed her daughter's excitement and pale face. Frenchie raised her head quickly and then set it back on the carpet between her arms as she remained sprawled on the floor.

"We were attacked!" Gabrielle excitedly explained how two big thugs attempted to rob them at knifepoint. Douglas fought them both, knocking one out and breaking the other's nose. "He was wonderful! Mom, Dad, you should have seen it!"

"Oh, my God!" shouted Claire.

"Are you hurt, young man?" responded Andre quickly.

"No, sir, I'm fine. More important, so is your daughter."

"Thank God!" Andre couldn't help admiring the young man who protected his daughter. "And thank you, Douglas!"

"Andre, you better call the police!" Then Claire turned to her daughter and her boyfriend, who remained close to the front door. "Are you sure you're both alright?" she appeared excited and worried. "Come," she pointed to a loveseat. "Come and sit down, both of you."

"They're long gone, but I'll call the police to make a report." Andre rose and walked toward the telephone at the other end of the parlor. "Good job, young man! Good job!" He patted Douglas's shoulder as he passed him.

Douglas's pleasant and assuring tone eased Mrs. Delisle's anxieties. It brought comfort to the panic-stricken mother.

"Thank God our daughter was in such good hands," Claire said gratefully to Douglas, who was a bit ashamed by where his hands were on their daughter not that long ago.

The following day, after breakfast, Gabrielle wanted to show Douglas the city. Mr. and Mrs. Delisle had absolutely no reservations about allowing their daughter to go out with the fine young man. He had proven he could and would take good care of their Gabrielle. So, the couple set out for the day to explore Cincinnati's sites. Gabrielle, however, knew where she would ultimately steer her gentleman escort. Even the thought of it embarrassed her. She had never before harbored such wicked thoughts. But she loved Douglas, and he had already returned that sentiment. 'He loves me. I know he does,' she thought.

Douglas put the engagement ring into his jacket pocket. Still contemplating whether he was being premature, he wondered if Gabrielle would even consider marrying him so soon. 'Gab said she loved me,' he thought, 'but is it too soon?' His mind wandered. Douglas wore a dark blue matching suit and sported the same Alpine Fedora hat. He decided not to be too aggressive with Gabrielle and see if they still shared the same feelings. Then, as he waited for her to finish dressing, he remembered how passionate she was the evening before.

As it was a warm day, Gabrielle wore a stunning light green dress with black floral designs. The flowery composition was lighter at the top and blended darker toward the full-length garment's bottom. A solid black fabric of about 12 inches high adorned her trim waist. The arms of the gown had sheer lace with smaller floral designs. White laced boots with brown soles and two-inch heels embellished her petite feet. The green emerald cameo with gold trim that Douglas gave her appeared at the base of the v-neck style of her dress. A fashionably pleated dark green and white decorative material surrounded the crown of her wide-brim hat. Douglas stared in amazement as he stood in the presence of the magnificently dressed and gorgeous young woman.

Gabrielle planned to take her man to the Cincinnati Zoo. They could stroll through the Botanical Gardens and see the animals. The grounds had a clubhouse restaurant where the couple could enjoy lunch. After that, she would set her bait. Gabrielle thought of that expression because she enjoyed fishing and knew Douglas did. With everything set, she had cast her net!

The couple held hands and walked along the garden's passageway, stopping at intervals to kiss in quieter places when alone. Gabrielle pretended to be alarmed by the chimpanzees only so Douglas would hold her close in his strong arms as he did the evening before. "Oh, my God, they're frightening!" Gabrielle said, snuggling close to Douglas. She did it seductively so he could feel her breasts on his chest. Gabrielle performed the same act at the bear pit; the newly erected elephant house called the Herbivora Building, and several other places. A burst of passion was building inside each of them.

While eating lunch, they stared at each other, learning the intricacies of the other's face. Douglas extended his arm, and his fingers gently caressed the sides of Gabrielle's face. "You're beautiful," he whispered. That erotic impulse aroused Gabrielle's libido, causing her to moan quietly.

"I'm ready to leave. Are you?" Gabrielle asked alluringly. "Perhaps we could go somewhere to rest for a while?" Her lascivious tone exhilarated Douglas.

"Waiter! Check, please." Douglas called out.

As their coach neared the corner where a large hotel stood, Gabrielle said while pointing to the building, "I think that would be a perfect place to relax for a time?" Her lazy eyes looked seductive as they stared directly into those of Douglas. 'I can't believe I'm acting like this. I can't help it. Doug will think I'm not a lady,' she thought.

"I think it would be perfect," Douglas answered her calmly, but his eyes conveyed the same sensual overtones as Gabrielle's. "Coachman, pull over!"

Moments after the bellboy brought them to the spacious room, Gabrielle turned and asked Douglas to unbutton her dress. She said it calmly and directly.

"Are you sure you want to do this?" At the moment, Douglas wanted this to happen more than anything else. But he adhered to his gentlemanlike behavior. However, he gently massaged her arms as a subliminal plea for her to say yes.

Gabrielle turned and faced Douglas. "For the third time, yes, I'm sure I want to do this." She hid her inner fright as she said the words. She had never done anything even close to this before. Gabrielle only allowed a fellow high school student to kiss her on the cheek, but that was before she met Douglas. 'Doug swept me away,' she thought. 'I only hope that he will marry me.' Gabrielle turned back to allow the man of her dreams to unbutton her dress.

Douglas nimbly slid one button out of its slit opening, then another. He bent and kissed Gabrielle on the nape of her neck, which drove her crazy, and she sighed. When he finished, she turned around, allowing her gown to slide down. She wore no corset, just a blouse bodice, which she removed, uncovering her shapely breasts. Gabrielle sat on the edge of the bed to remove her boots and slide down her stockings. She then stood up before Douglas naked, who stood admiring her ravishing body. Gabrielle approached Douglas and whispered, "Please be gentle; this is my first time." Then she stepped up on her tiptoes, put her arms around his neck, and began to kiss him seductively. It was something meant to be. Clearly, the young couple were in love.

Hours later, the exhausted couple lay under the sheets, embracing. "You made my eyes spin, young man," Gabrielle said, laughing before giving Douglas another enticing kiss.

Douglas reached over for his pocket watch on the table on the side of the bed. "Oh, my God! We have to go!" They hadn't realized how long they had become occupied. "It's close to dinner time!"

"My parents!" Gabrielle threw the sheet off and rose. Douglas couldn't take his eyes off her as she stood nude, washing herself from a water basin. His eyes remained on her while she began to dress. "Don't be a dirty boy!" she laughed.

At certain breaks and during their intimacy, they shared their most intimate feelings for each other. Gabrielle told Douglas she wanted to be with him for the rest of her life. He now knew with certainty that he wanted the same thing. He rose, washed, dressed quickly, and then walked to his jacket to remove the ring. It was gone. 'Oh my God!' he thought. "No! It's in the other pocket. There it is." He realized he was whispering to himself. In his nervousness, he forgot what pocket the jewelry box was in.

"Are you speaking to me?" Gabrielle laughed and looked at him. He was white. "Are you okay, Doug?"

"Yes! I'm more than okay!" He rushed to her and got down on bended knee. "I know we haven't been together long, Gab. That is, in the flesh." He thought. "Not the flesh. I mean in person." Gabrielle began to smile until she saw the little padded jewelry box he had in his hand. Her smile turned to tears. "But I feel like I've known you all my life," he said as he opened the box and presented it to her.

"Douglas! Oh, my God!" It finally registered that he was proposing to her, and she began to weep.

"Will you marry. . ."

"Yes!" Gabrielle didn't give him a chance to finish. "Yes! I will marry you!" She jumped into his open arms. "It's beautiful! Oh, Doug! It's so beautiful! It's exquisite!" Gabrielle whispered ever so softly, "When did you get it?"

Douglas explained how he bought it in Pittsburgh, hoping she would say yes. "I knew I loved you ever since we met." He smiled, "With each letter, I loved you more."

"That's exactly how I felt."

Douglas put the engagement ring on her finger. "It seems like a perfect fit."

"Yes, we are a perfect fit."

"Now I have to ask your father's permission."

"That won't be hard; my parents already love you. And besides, Daddy knows I always get what I want."

"Checking out so soon, Mr. and Mrs. Johnson?" the droopy-eyed hotel clerk wearing half-moon eyeglasses pleasantly asked as Douglas presented his cash.

Douglas had used a bogus name and was ashamed he did. It made him feel like a criminal. "Yes. I'm afraid I have urgent business I completely forgot about." Gabrielle had her right arm entwined with his left arm. Smiling, she tickled it as he lied.

"Do come and revisit us, Mr. and Mrs. Johnson." He smiled at the couple, "And enjoy your day. Our doorman will call a coach for you."

During the coach ride, Gabrielle remembered their time together at the hotel. "It was wonderful, Doug. When can we come back?" she asked as her lips reached closer and kissed his ear.

"As soon as you want," Douglas smiled. "We'll have wedding plans to arrange. After I ask your father, that is."

"You're wonderful, Doug," she said as her fingers glided over the back of his hand. "You're brave and charming," she smiled as her hand moved and gently caressed his wrist. She could tell it excited Douglas, whose eyes met hers. "I didn't tell you about how I really felt when you stopped those horrible robbers from hurting me. It excited me in a very peculiar way." Her lips moved close to his right ear. "It stimulated my loins," Gabrielle whispered. "I was ashamed to tell you then, but I'm not now. After this afternoon, I feel that I can tell you anything. I hope you feel the same way."

"I do," Douglas said softly. "I'll tell you something I never told you before." He kissed her on her soft lips and continued, "When I was a kid, I was smaller for my age. Older kids used to bully me. I had a stammer, and Rollo was my only friend." Douglas explained how he met Peppina and how the little girl 'opened the world for me to see.' He described how his father first taught him to box and his first fight, which led to his becoming the most popular boy in school and his neighborhood. He told the woman he now loved the story about what happened to his young friend, Peppina, and her sister and mother.

By the time Douglas finished his story, Gabrielle was crying. "How terrible for them." She reached over and embraced him. Then, with tears in her eyes, she chuckled, "Look how big and strong you are now. And such a wonderful man." Gabrielle pulled out her handkerchief to wipe her tears. Douglas gently pushed it aside and wiped away her tears with his finger. Gabrielle looked into his eyes and said, "That's why I love you so much."

Chapter Sixteen

Cincinnati, Ohio 1906

Gabrielle and Douglas

The charter of the Pennsylvania Railroad was expanded in 1853, which allowed it to buy stock and guarantee bonds of railroads in other states. Several lines were then aided by the Pennsylvania Railroad to secure additional railway traffic. The 'Pennsy,' as it was nicknamed, purchased stock in the Ohio & Pennsylvania, Ohio & Indiana, Marietta & Cincinnati, Maysville & Big Sandy, and Springfield, Mt. Vernon & Pittsburgh railroads by the end of 1854. The Steubenville & Indiana was assisted by the Pennsylvania Railroad in the form of a guarantee of half a million dollars in bonds. A controlling interest was purchased in the Cumberland Valley Railroad in 1856, and the Pennsylvania Railroad constructed lines in Philadelphia. Railroad travel became the primary means of travel. Still, some preferred the less chaotic ways provided by the paddle riverboats.

Martha opened the telegram, hoping it wasn't bad news. It was from Douglas, and it read:

Date: Thursday.June 14.1906

Dearest Parents.

I am marrying Gabrielle Delisle.

Wedding day Sunday. June 24. 1906 at the home of Mr. and Mrs. Andre Delisle.

Please come.

Your loving son, Douglas.

Martha ran to the telephone to call her husband at the Wellsville Shop. She had already prepared her gown, and her husband's best suit was also ready. 'I know my son better than he does. I knew he would ask her,' she thought while smiling.

Mr. Nicholson would get their tickets and prepare time off from work. He also confirmed their arrival via telegram. Martha had given him the Delisle address by telephone. Douglas Sr. told her they would arrive on Thursday, June 21, 1906, and named the hotel where they would stay.

The following day, another telegram arrived from Douglas stating that he would meet their train and take them directly to Gabrielle's parent's house. Her parents insisted they stay with them at their home.

Douglas's planned trip of a week to see Gabrielle's graduation turned into at least two additional weeks. After about an hour of the same practice rehearsal he did before a trial, Douglas Nicholson II gracefully and formally asked Andre Delisle for the hand of his only child in holy matrimony. He did so in the presence of Andre's wife, Claire, as Gabrielle just lovingly smiled, watching the man she loved go through the formality of the time. 'She had her man,' she thought while her eyes glistened and her smile widened.

Andre and Claire Delisle couldn't be happier. They were thrilled when their daughter first presented the engagement ring to them. Her parents were even more delighted that the young man had the respect to ask their permission. They liked Douglas immensely in the days leading up to his proposal. He was a well-mannered and respectful man who was handsomely and appropriately groomed and made a good living as a lawyer. They knew he would take excellent care of their daughter. However, they mourned their only child's relocation to another town, but they always knew that day would eventually come.

After much discussion and realizing that Douglas had an established law practice, Gabrielle decided to apply as a teacher in one of the schools in or near Wellsville as soon as she arrived. She considered an office job but felt a calling to become a teacher. Her plan depended on her poodle, Frenchie, coming along as well. Douglas had no intention of leaving Gab's beloved dog behind.

While discussing their forthcoming trip, Martha Nicholson told her husband, "The Delisles are Roman Catholic, dear. Do you know that?"

"My dear," he smiled at his wife, "you know me better than that." The Nicholsons were Episcopalian. Many people in the town of varying protestant faiths wouldn't even associate with Catholics at the time.

"I only wanted to mention it to you, sweetheart," she replied, smiling. "My parents weren't even strong churchgoers, but they raised me to be a better Christian than many of those who worship every Sunday."

"My only hope is that our son marries the woman he truly loves and is happy." Douglas Sr. leaned over to kiss his wife. "Like us, dear. I think we did a good job."

"We did indeed!" she kissed her husband again, looking into his eyes, "Yes, we did indeed!"

Douglas Jr. and Gabrielle met Mr. and Mrs. Nicholson at the Cincinnati train station. Douglas ran ahead to greet them. His lenghty arms held them both in a long hug. Then, he took his mother's hand as he walked his parents back to where his fiancée was standing.

"It's so nice to meet you, Mr. and Mrs. Nicholson," a smiling

Gabrielle said, curtseying in a sign of respect to her soon-to-be in-laws.

"Oh, Gabrielle, it's so nice to meet you finally!" Martha took the young lady into her arms, and they embraced. "You are so beautiful!"

"As are you, Mrs. Nicholson." Martha loved her from the start.

"You have fine taste, my son," Douglas Sr. said as he took Gabrielle's outstretched hand in his, bent and gently kissed it.

"Now I know where your son acquired his fine manners, sir." Gabrielle smiled widely.

Martha and Gabrielle sat side by side and spoke the entire coach ride. Douglas and his father sat discussing politics and local news of Wellsville. Both parents immediately liked each other when the Nicholsons arrived at the Delisle's home. Gabrielle winked at Douglas as a sign she was delighted that everything went so well. He winked back at her and remained seated, admiring the young woman he would marry. Douglas watched as she gracefully played hostess to his parents with the charm of a royal. Gabrielle Delisle was a beautiful, intelligent, outgoing, and remarkable lady. He loved her, and his plan in life was to make her happy in every way he could. 'She's too good for me,' he thought, smiling at the notion.

The Delisle's large home, adorned with flowers and decorations, was ready for the event. Gabrielle's extended family lived locally and were there to see her marry. Friends of her from school and work were also in attendance. Everyone had already met Douglas. Many of her girlfriends had complimented her taste in men.

Douglas now stood at the front of rows of rented chairs in the largest room in the house. Andre had opened the sliding wooden doors to the dining room to allow more space. Douglas's father stood beside him, acting as the best man for his son. Many men were standing. Facing Douglas was a Catholic priest standing behind a pulpit. As beautiful piano music began to play, 'Here Comes the Bride,' all heads turned toward the rear of the room. Gabrielle, dressed in a breathtaking white wedding gown with a covered veil, slowly and elegantly proceeded down the aisle between the chairs. One of her hands held a bouquet of fresh mixed flowers; the other grasped the arm of her father, Andre. Martha and Claire were already crying, seated at the front. As they reached Douglas, Andre removed his daughter's veil, took her hand, and placed it in Douglas's. He kissed his daughter and went to sit next to his wife, where Frenchie stood erect and observed the ceremony.

After Douglas kissed Gabrielle at the end of the heartwarming ceremony, the newly married Mr. and Mrs. Douglas Nicholson walked back down the aisle to the sound of 'The Wedding March.' They stood at the back of the room, greeting friends and family. Then, the new couple went upstairs to change their clothes.

Gabrielle threw her flower bouquet to the unmarried young ladies eagerly awaiting before she and Douglas trotted through the opened door to an awaiting coach, their packed luggage already stored in it. Douglas lifted his new wife onto the seat before jumping up to sit beside her. Frenchie stood on the floor on the opposite side of the coach, peering outside. The laughing couple waved goodbye to the small crowd of people cheering them. Bells, tied to the back of the coach, jingled as it slowly moved away.

Gabrielle and Douglas had said goodbye to their parents before the ceremony. The Nicholsons planned to stay another day before returning by train to Wellsville. Claire and Andre begged them to stay longer, but Douglas Sr. had to return to work. He had been promoted a few years before and had more responsibilities at the Shop.

"Andre, I want you to know that we would love for you and Claire to visit us as often as you can," Mr. Nicholson said the day they left the station.

"Thank you, both! We will! And we want you both to come

back and see us as well," Claire shouted over the noise as the steam locomotive began moving.

Gabrielle and Douglas were spending their honeymoon night at a hotel near the riverboat wharf. The following morning, they would take a relaxing trip to Wellsville, where they would stay in a fine room on a riverboat.

"How romantic!" Gabrielle told Douglas when he first mentioned the idea.

They planned a longer trip when Douglas found time to escape from work. By the time he returned, he would already be over three weeks behind. The new bride intended to help him in the office so he could catch up.

Chapter Seventeen

Wellsville, Ohio 1906
The Search Ends

One of the most popular security guard and detective agencies was the Pinkertons. Allan Pinkerton, a Scotsman, formed the Pinkertons around 1850 and ran the agency of his namesake. Pinkerton became famous for his claim of preventing the Baltimore Plot to assassinate President-elect Abraham Lincoln in 1861. The Pinkertons did espionage for the Union during the American Civil War. By protecting wealthy corporations and businessmen, they gained recognition from their brutal methods of enforcement by any means necessary, leaving their bloody mark on those who resisted them. The Pinkertons became the largest private law enforcement organization in the world. Many ex-Pinkerton agents went into other types of law enforcement, including the private sector.

"It will be temporary, Dad, just long enough for us to find our own home." Douglas didn't want to take advantage of his parents' generous offer to let him and Gabrielle live with them until they found an available house. They made that temporary arrangement while together at the Delisle home in Cincinnati.

"You and Gabrielle are welcome to stay as long as you wish," Martha Nicholson answered for her husband. "We're happy to have you. God knows we have the space here." Douglas Sr. shook his head agreeingly while petting Frenchie. "I already had the Causwell boy put all your things in the larger guest room," Martha explained. She smiled sheepishly, describing the room being a reasonable distance from her and her husband's. That would give the newly married couple the same privacy she longed for when she was first married.

"How old is their boy now?" asked Douglas

"Jack is already 13 years old," smiled Martha.

Gabrielle made herself useful around the home as soon as she arrived. Martha had to keep reminding her that they had someone who cleaned the house once a week, but Gabrielle still went about the house picking up after herself and her new husband. Frenchie was well-behaved in her new home. Martha did most of her cooking. At dinner parties and other occasions, she hired kitchen help. But Gabrielle became Martha's assistant in cooking most of the family meals.

"I'm dying to!" was Gabrielle's response to Douglas's question of when she might feel ready to help him with his office paperwork. She knew her husband had a lucrative law practice in town and had been away for weeks. "As soon as you need me!" Gabrielle also sensed her husband wanted her around him for a while. They both had to wean off of each other gradually. She hoped they wouldn't lose control of their intimate feelings during work and cause an embarrassing disruption among his employees. The newlyweds couldn't take their hands off each other.

"I think I might need your help now, honey." He used the new pet word they had called each other since their honeymoon. "I stopped in yesterday, and I'm swamped with letters, documents, court dates, and depositions."

"Good! we'll be a team!" Gabrielle's eyes twinkled at the exciting prospect. She was thrilled that her husband needed and wanted her.

Douglas marveled at how well his new wife took to the loads of papers. Intelligent, cordial, and charming, she jumped right into the work and quickly learned. Douglas had three secretaries and two legal assistants. There was an extensive library with a sizeable wooden table and ten matching chairs. Two offices were for his assistants, while a third one was available as an alternative meeting room.

Douglas occupied the larger corner office with four large windows. The bright room had a large oak desk with a highback padded armchair where Douglas sat. Three additional padded chairs directly faced his desk, with several others placed about the room. Framed paintings adorned the walls of his office, with wooden shelves that reached the tall ceiling and stacked with books and some ornaments between them. An oversized wooden globe secured to a polished mahogany base occupied one corner where a wall displayed personal, framed family photos. One at the center of the group was of Douglas, Peppina, and Rollo, taken at the studio years before. Another was of the Nicholson family with Peppina. There was also a photo of the day Douglas returned home from law school with his parents and Rollo with the riverboat docked behind them. That was the corner where Frenchie preferred to lie down on days when Gabrielle brought her dog to work with her. Gabrielle had already planned where their wedding photo would go.

Two secretaries had desks in the center of the large main room. The other, Mary, Douglas's private secretary, sat at a desk closer to Douglas's office. Everyone was ecstatic that their boss was back and that business would continue. They loved Gabrielle immediately and the help she rendered.

"I think you should sign this document promptly, Mr. Nicholson," Gabrielle whispered in Douglas's ear as her breast pushed against his shoulder. She had closed the door behind her, and they were alone. "Don't worry, I just want a kiss right now, honey. Tonight, we can finish," she softly said.

Douglas complied, slowly departing his lips from Gabrielle's, and gently said, "Behave, or God knows I won't be able to control myself." Then he noticed Frenchie sleeping in the corner and added, "Even if Frenchie sees us."

"Tonight, then," smiling delightedly at how so easily she had aroused her husband.

Martha and Douglas Nicholson arranged a party to celebrate their son's marriage, allowing Gabrielle to meet their family and friends. The date was set for two weeks after the couple arrived at their home in the river town after their voyage. Martha sent out invitations the day after she and her husband disembarked the train in Wellsville, days before the newly married couple returned.

The 74-year-old father of Douglas Sr. was traveling back to his old town for the event. It would be one of the few times James Nicholson returned after moving to Beaver, Pennsylvania after his wife passed away years before, and he went to live with his younger son, Robert. James Nicholson was born in the original settlement in town in 1832. After his wife's passing, memories of her were all too real, forcing him to leave Wellsville. James would ride with his son, Robert, his wife, Sarah, and their two unmarried daughters, Flora, 20, and Roberta,16. All would take a coach to the trolley at Beaver. The trolley line, now completed, ran all the way to Wellsville.

Martha's widowed sister, Ellen Brisco, never married after losing her husband, Leo, who perished in the War Between the States. She lived close enough to walk over to the event. Still, her brother-in-law, Douglas Sr., insisted on driving her over in his coach as other people would also need a ride. The Nicholson's 81-year-old next-door neighbor, Barbara Heely, said she wouldn't miss it for the world. "I watched that boy grow up," she announced when invited. Their other neighbors, Mr. & Mrs. Joshua Causwell, 'would definitely attend along with their son, Jack.' Other friends and neighbors from town were coming. The Nicholson's were glad to have a large and spacious home.

The party was a spectacular event. The large, high-ceilinged living and dining rooms accommodated many. Several friends and associates of Douglas Sr. attended, including Jack Carlson from the Shop. Local restaurants brought in delicious foods and treats. Giuditta Buch supplied several Italian delicacies as a wedding present for her, Mr. Douglas, and his new wife. She was invited but didn't attend. Giuditta explained that the restaurant needed her on that particular day. The reality was that she just felt out of place. There was now a lot of opposition and turmoil in town due to the significant number of Italian immigrants who had arrived in record numbers since the turn of the century. Also, the now promiscuous, attractive Italian woman had allowed an American man to 'have her.' She didn't know if that man would be in attendance. It seemed having romantic liaisons with Italian women wasn't prohibited. Still, Giuditta didn't want guests to feel uncomfortable at the wedding of the beloved young man she considered a son.

Aside from Nicola, the only other person who knew about Giuditta's rendezvous with men was Millie Brown. After seeing Giuditta secretly perform with an American laborer on a table in the laundry area, Millie confronted her with the notion that others might find out or see her in the act. Giuditta just waved her hand at Millie as if it was nothing. "You want your children to see you buck naked with a strange man?" she had asked at that time.

"Okay, okay, I'll be more careful. Okay?" Giuditta agreed at the time.

Some guests sat at wedding-decorated tables in the small yard at the back of the house. Margaret Myers and her husband were sitting out back. She finally married out of urgency when she became pregnant. However, her husband, Harry, wasn't the baby's father, though he thought he was. Margaret, who had lost count of how many men there had been in her life, would have to scour the town to find out who the real father was. She didn't have the time, so Margaret chose the gullible Harry, who made a good living.

The gang of kids who romped the town in those past glorious days all came. Friends Jimmy Brier, Bill Becker, Logan Conners, Mike Walsh, and Felix Fischer were there. Donna Madson never married. Word was that most men were afraid of her due to her temper. She now worked at a bar and couldn't leave work–or that was the excuse given.

As Douglas was now a prominent attorney, many old friends became clients. All his old foes also buried the axe and became friends over the years. Matt Carlson, Paul Schafer, and Filip Aries, all former bullies who terrorized Douglas, or 'Pip,' back then, came to the festive occasion. Even Erik Olsson, whom Douglas had beaten up long ago, was happily there.

"Ya was soo scared of me then, were ya?" Robert McElhenny laughed over the music as he brushed shoulders with Douglas. The 54-year-old guard had been transferred to the Twelfth Street Shop a few years before and was now under Douglas Sr's supervision. "Now look at ya standing there bigger than meself!" he laughed. His son, Sean, and his wife, Jean, were also there.

"Good to see you, Mr. McElhenny. We're glad you came," Douglas smiled and shook hands with his adversary of many years before. "Yes, those were the days, indeed. You had old Rollo and me scared, shitless," he laughed while his left hand covered his foul language and his right kept shaking McElhenny's hand. He stood erect. All the Nicholson men were tall, but now Douglas was the tallest.

Frenchie sniffed the gifts piled on a table in the foyer. Most guests gave the newlyweds quality presents, such as vases, fine crystal, china, and silverware, which were typical for a wedding—nothing of interest for the poodle.

Gabrielle presented Martha and Douglas Sr. with a large framed photo of the bride and groom and another with Douglas Sr. and her, with them together–all taken on the wedding day. Martha adored them. "It's a perfect likeness of us all," Martha exclaimed, her eyes glimmering as she placed them both on top of the wooden mantel of the living room fireplace with her husband's assistance. "I love them! Thank you so much!"

The day after the party was a Sunday. After church service, Douglas walked his parents and Gabrielle back home. While the women prepared Sunday dinner and Douglas Sr. occupied himself with his newspaper, Douglas walked to his office. He wanted to check the mail and the office's calendar of events for the forthcoming work week. When he arrived, Douglas noticed one large letter envelope sitting at the top of several others on his large oak desk. It was marked as hand-delivered by Mr. John Rose. Between his marriage and everything that followed, the investigation of his friend Peppina and her sister had fallen to the back corridors of his mind.

"He must have dropped it off on Friday," he whispered. "Hmm, I left early because of the party. He probably just missed me." Douglas began opening the letter slowly, anticipating the best. 'It's thick with papers. He must have found them,' he thought.

Douglas sat on his high-back padded armchair and viewed the surprisingly lengthy report. There were receipts, documents, and records. "Oh no," he muttered to himself. "Oh, God, no." John Rose's work was extensive. He had indeed found the orphanage where the girls ended up. Peppina and Emanuela had been to a previous location before that final one. However, while the sisters were there, the orphanage burned down.

'*All records were destroyed*,' wrote Rose, '*and it seems that both of the Massaro sisters died in the same fire at the orphanage, but there is no confirmation.*' He continued, '*My investigative search for the girls continued, but I can't find any other records of them after that point.*' His report mentioned the hope that one or both were adopted or alive, but there were no records or solid evidence. '*I am sorry, but all reason and investigations point to the reality that they are deceased. If they had been adopted, there would be some civil record of that apart from those in the orphanage. I am now on a dead trail. I will continue if it is your will, but I honestly feel there would be no additional outcome.*'

It was signed by Mr. John Rose, with sincerest condolences.

Mr. Rose had done his work as promised. All the enclosed papers had proved that. Douglas put everything back into the large envelope and slid it into a side drawer of his desk. He just sat with his forearms stretched on the chair's armrests, staring at a wall. There, his eyes focused on the photo of himself as a boy with Peppina and Rollo. He remained seated there, recalling the days when he was called 'Pip' and his only friend was Rollo until a little girl changed his life forever. Tears came to his eyes. His childhood friend was gone forever.

"My lady!" said Douglas, extending his arm and motioning for Gabrielle to take hold. Frenchie stood at the front doorway of the Nicholson home watching.

"Thank you, good sir!" his wife laughed as he helped her onto the carriage. They were on their way to see Giuditta at the hotel. After hearing all the stories, Gabrielle was anxious to meet the woman her husband thought of as a second mother.

Douglas showed Gabrielle some sights and explained things as they traveled down Main Street. "The firehouse is one block behind us. It used to be the Catholic Church." He pointed to a building as they approached Fifth Street, "That's City Hall. I watched with my friends when the workers built it!"

"My, aren't you a wonderful tour guide!"

"All to please, madame! The post office is at City Hall, Mrs. Nicholson. In case you're interested."

"Goodness, Wellsville has all modern amenities, doesn't it?"

"We've even had free postal delivery for a year now!"

"Good graciousness! Postmen! How wonderful," laughed Gabrielle.

"Never mind, city girl. Oh, that's Cooper's Opera House. And that's where all the kids hung around when I was little," Douglas said, pointing to Buntings. Douglas pointed to another building across the street before they came to the bend at Third Street. "That's the Fraternal Order of Eagles, and I am a proud member. It opened two years ago," Douglas smiled. "I'm also becoming a member of the Elk's Lodge 1040, which just opened this year."

"What kind of factory is that?" Gabrielle pointed to the complex of buildings, spurting smoke from several high chimneys.

"That's the Stevenson Company. It began as a foundry in 1836, making steamboat engines and machinery. Now, they also make other machinery, such as for brickyards and other types."

"That's the hotel." Douglas pointed up ahead. The area surrounding the hotel's location had changed. Douglas hadn't noticed the last time he visited; he was too preoccupied with his trip to see Gabrielle then. In 1906, the streets around Stevenson's and the Tin Plate mill were overcrowded with immigrants, mostly Italian.

Many working-class Italians from Southern Italy were a different breed of people. Vigor powered everything they did. They spoke and played their music loudly, their vibrant culture clashing with the more reserved ways of the Americans who had settled years earlier.

"The neighborhood's changed," Douglas told Gabrielle as he looked around, smelling the street scents of cooking food and piled garbage and outhouses. They mixed with the odors of the nearby factories. He had also noticed overcrowding starting around Commerce Street before as he drove the horse-drawn carriage around a turn. 'I didn't observe much since I had Gab on my brain,' he thought as his mind strolled back over the last few years. The peak year for Italian immigration was around 1901. But between being away at school and pining over Gabrielle, Douglas hadn't considered how many more immigrants had come to town. Most were Italian, but not all; other ethnicities were also coming.

"Well, we certainly needed workers to build the cities and towns of America," Gabrielle said as she assessed the area. "Well, here they are. Not really that bad." She could see that her husband looked a bit distressed. "It's quaint, actually," she said to raise her Douglas's spirit.

"Mr. Douglas, how good it is to see you!" Giuditta cried out as she walked out of her doorway. "And who is this beautiful young woman with you?"

Douglas walked over to Giuditta and gave her a warm embrace. "This is my new wife, Gabrielle." He turned and waited for Gab to reach them. "Gabrielle, this is Mrs. Buch," he promptly said.

"È un piacere conoscerla, Signora!" Gabrielle told Giuditta in Italian how nice it was to meet her. Gabrielle proudly spoke the language she had learned since childhood, when her Italian-American mother, Claire, taught her only child the language of her native country.

"Lodare Dio! She speaks my language!" Giuditta embraced the young woman. "I think I'm a gonna like her, Mr. Douglas!" Giuditta was in her glory. "She speaks the language like the aristocrats, the rich people," Guditta told him in her thick accent. She recalled her dear Luigi but said nothing. She missed him but didn't want to show her emotion.

"It looks like it," Douglas calmly answered. Then he turned to his wife, "I'm impressed!" he said and laughed. "You never cease to amaze me."

"You know I speak that language."

"I know, but I haven't heard you speak it for a while and so glamorously."

"Oh! You missed the kids!" Giuditta blurted out. "They've been waiting to see you and your new wife."

"Where are they?"

"Millie took them all to the park by the mill. My little Mary is supervising the crowd," she chuckled. "Quite the little lady now."

Douglas and Gabrielle thanked Giuditta for all the food she had arranged for their wedding. "It was so kind of you, and everything was so delicious," complimented Gabrielle.

"Now you both come inside and sit down and have something to eat," Giuditta said in her strong Italian accent. "C'mon! I have something nice!"

"I'll help you!" Gabrielle immediately said, walking alongside Giuditta into the hotel's kitchen. They were speaking in Italian the whole way.

"Hi, Douglas, how are you?" a voice behind Douglas asked.

"Felo. I didn't see you. I'm well. How's everything with you?"

"Congratulations on your wedding!" Felo smiled. "I was working on the side of the hotel. That's why you didn't notice me," he said as his eyes focused on Nicola sitting at the other corner of the hotel, sipping a glass of beer. "He says he hurt his leg," a smiling Felo said while nodding at Nicola. "He just doesn't want to work on the hotel anymore."

Douglas ignored the remark and asked, "How are things at the hotel?"

"We're doing very well, all things considered. We have a good cash flow and, more importantly, reliable help." Felo shrugged, "Everybody says it's not the same as when my father was here. but?" Felo shrugged his shoulders.

Douglas was impressed. Felo spoke and acted like a man now. He asked him, "How's everything at school?"

"I'm going for the fourth year of high school, mainly because they offer accounting," said Felo. "I want to be an accountant." He smiled. "I have to save up to get married, just like you."

Douglas wanted to do something to help out Giuditta's son. "I tell you what, if you have any free time, you can come to my office to work part-time. I'll pay you, and you can learn from real accountants."

"Really?" Felo was ecstatic. He had been working as a laborer at the mill to earn money, so this offer was a blessing.

"You bet! You're a fine young man, Felo," Douglas smiled and continued, "I'm proud of you. You always help out your mother, and you seem responsible."

That statement alone meant the world to the young man. "Thank you, Douglas."

Giuditta called for Douglas to come inside. "Well, it looks like it's time for your mom to feed me. You come over, and I'll set you up. I'm happy to help you, Felo." As he began to walk, he told Felo, "I can smell the wonderful aroma of your mother's kitchen from here."

Giuditta appeared coming out of the kitchen. Gabrielle was still inside. There was food already on one of the tables. "Douglas!" she beckoned him to follow her to the opposite side. "C'mon, just for a second."

Facing each other, standing at a quiet part of the bar, Giuditta said with her heavy accent, "You know?" she stopped. "This might sound crazy, but years back, I always thought maybe someday you and my little Giuseppina," she paused, smiling but with a tear in an eye, "that you might have married," she began weeping. "You both got along so well as kids. I remember Peppina and her sister every minute of every day of my life."

"It's okay, Mrs. Buch," Douglas embraced Giuditta and comforted her. "I miss her too. We might have married one day, who knows? But one thing for certain is I'll remember those happy times with her forever."

"Let me finish, my dear boy. I love you like a son, you know that?" Douglas noticed Guiditta's accent was getting a little better. 'It must be from living with her children,' he thought, 'they're getting older and three are in school, and she's hearing them speak better English.'

"Yes, ma'am, I know. I feel the same way toward you."

"I think you couldn't have picked a better wife!" Giuditta was sobbing. "She reminds me so much of my little Peppina that I feel like I have her again." Douglas just held Giuditta in his arms, consoling her.

Concetto Provenzano and Roberto Pugliano sat together eating lunch at a table next to where Douglas and Giuditta sat. As they enjoyed their food prepared by Giuditta with Gabrielle's assistance, Giuditta introduced both men to Douglas and Gabrielle. "This is my dear friend, Douglas Nicholson, and his beautiful new wife." Douglas and Gabrielle stood to make acquaintances.

Concetto stood first. A short man, he was a shoemaker in town. "I know, Mr. Nicholson," he smiled and said in his heavy accent, "He helped me with a business problem last year. How are you doing, sir?" he addressed Douglas with the respect of being an attorney. "A fine lawyer he is!" Concetto raised his right arm, made a fist, and pointed his forefinger upward to make his point. "And he wears nice shoes, a product of my work," the shoemaker proudly said with a smile. Concetto had learned his skills in Italy from his father. He arrived in America in 1887 and settled in Wellsville in 1895. Now, his 17-year-old son Carlo was working alongside him as an apprentice.

"It's good to see you again, Mr. Provenzano. Meet my lovely wife, Gabrielle," Douglas introduced his wife while holding her shoulders.

Concetto took Gabrielle's extended hand and kissed it, "It's good to meet you, signora," he announced in his hefty accent.

"Come lo sono io," Gabrielle replied, astonishing Concetto.

"She speaks my language! Maronna mia!"

Roberto Pugliano also arose. He couldn't yet speak English. Though he arrived in America in the late 1880s, he lived in Little Italy in New York City for several years, working as a barber. There, everyone spoke various Italian dialects and very little English. His 16-year-old son, Giacomo, was cutting hair alongside his father. Giuditta made the introductions for Gabrielle in Italian. Then, they both translated everything for Douglas.

"I'm a learning!" said Roberto with a thick accent. "My son. He a teach a mio." He made it clear that his son was going to school so he wouldn't be stupid like him.

During the carriage ride back home, Gabrielle seemed a little troubled. "I noticed you speaking to Giuditta, Doug. Why was she so upset?"

Douglas turned and said, "It's just she's very emotional. Giuditta likes you very much."

"Oh, that's sweet."

"She feels like her daughter, Peppina, lives again through you."

"Should I be jealous of Peppina?" Gabrielle smiled.

"I had an investigator check into the matter," Douglas said while looking straight ahead, driving the rig. "It's almost certain both her daughters died shortly after they left. There was a fire at the orphanage where they stayed." He turned back to face his wife. "I wasn't yet 12 years old the last time I saw her. I was just a mere boy. I didn't have dirty thoughts about girls back then like I do now for you."

"Oh, Doug, I'm so sorry!" her eyes began to tear. "What a poor joke I made. How terrible for Giuditta." Douglas leaned over and comforted her with a kiss. It seemed to work, but still, with eyes tearing, she asked, "Think you'll have dirty thoughts for me later?"

"I have dirty thoughts about you all the time." Then, on a serious note, Douglas said, "Don't ever tell Giuditta what I said about the fire. It's best she lives in hope."

Chapter Eighteen

Wellsville, Ohio 1910-1911

The Black Hand

One of the largest funerals in the history of New York City took place on April 12, 1909. Mayor McClellan, Police Commissioner Bingham, nearly every official in New York City, and almost two thousand policemen and firemen, marched behind the body of a slain police officer with 7000 people following, and 250,000 others lined the streets to pay final respects to Lieutenant Joseph Petrosino of the NYPD. Killed in Palermo, Sicily, Petrosino had been battling what became known as the Black Hand in America. Those thugs were mostly Italian Immigrants harassing their own people. They were gradually becomming more organized. Petrosino went to Sicily to determine if the Italian Mafia had connections in America. Coverage of the 1909 assassination of Lieutenant Petrosino was in both mainstream and Italian-American press. The event ignited a debate over the origin of the Black Hand and the dangerousness of the Italian community in the United States. In effect, to create a story, the media scared American citizens by putting erroneous ideas into their heads that led to the belief that all Italian Immigrants were a threat to their safety. To sell a story, that fabrication became the basis of animosity toward all Italian-American citizens in The United States.

"I remember exactly how she held me, the wide smile on her face, and most of all her eyes," Felo smiled while discussing a subject he had never before addressed with Douglas. Now 20, the young man was eager to know as much as he could about his sisters, Peppina and Emanuela. Felo vividly remembered Douglas always being with Peppina, whom he recalled best. Memories of her always haunted him. He never fully understood why she left when he was a child, so his mind manufactured different notions. However, seeing his mother always upset at mentioning her name, Felo stopped asking her questions. Nicola would wave his hand, refusing to address the matter whenever confronted. Felo had come to terms with the fact that the trauma of such an event was what allowed him to remember his sisters so well, especially Peppina.

Douglas was sitting with Felo in his office when the subject, a touchy one for him, came up. Douglas had tried to distance himself from that tragedy that ended his childhood. He was surprised that Felo brought it up after so many years. In time, Douglas discovered only part of the story of the Massaro sisters, but not what caused it and why Guilia, as people called her back then, was forced to marry Nicola. There were rumors only among the Italian community about Giuditta's sexual indiscretions. Then, Mr. Rose's investigation made what was a family's distressing event into an even more heart-rending one. Douglas couldn't tell the young man he sat facing the entire truth of what he knew. "I recollect everything from those days," he said, "just as if it were yesterday. And I reminisce about them often," smiling back at Felo. "They were some of the best days of my life," he happily added. 'Felo will learn the truth about his family's more personal matters in time,' Douglas thought, 'if not, then so be it.' "Tell me exactly what you would like to know."

Douglas sat telling stories about himself and Peppina for about an hour but bypassing anything too personal. As painful as those memories were for himself, he could see it brought happiness to the young man. Douglas mentioned Rollo in many of their youthful adventures. Felo remembered the big dog sitting on the restaurant floor beside him eating. Douglas explained a lot but never about the investigation by Mr. Rose. He also left

Nicola out of the tales, though he wanted to, never coming to terms with what that man did.

"So, Felo, are you courting a young lady on a steady basis?"

"Not yet, but I'm trying to find someone," Felo laughed. He had been busy working at the American Sheet and Tin Plate Company and Douglas's office to earn enough money to marry. Felo always found time to work at the hotel he now officially owned but left the profits and running of it to his mother. He managed the hotel's books and ordered supplies, freeing his mother to handle the day-to-day operations however she desired. Felo had $500 in savings.

"You'll find a wonderful woman. All in due time." Douglas offered his brotherly advice.

Douglas took time off from his office to stroll with his wife the following day. Gabrielle had recently had a miscarriage. She wanted to give Douglas a child terribly, so the incident became devastating. Gabrielle was still recovering on that spring day in 1910. Her husband asked his wife to walk with him to get her out of the house for fresh air. Frenchie took a look outside but turned away and walked to her favorite spot to lie down. Not as young as she used to be, she decided not to go out with Gabrielle and Douglas.

"Don't you feel a wee bit better out here in the fresh air?" Douglas asked his wife as they walked along Riverside's brick sidewalk. "Flowers are blooming everywhere." He sniffed, "Smell the aroma. Listen to the birds singing songs for you, my love."

Gabrielle could never resist her husband's charm and replied, "A wee bit better," she smiled.

Three years earlier, the couple purchased a beautiful large home further down Riverside Avenue, past where the street ended. It had spacious rooms and, most of all, a stunning view of the bend in the Ohio River going south. They both enjoyed being near to the river. The vitality of that natural wonder energized them. Gabrielle and Douglas often sat outside enjoying the views, fresh breezes, riverboat traffic, and the passing trains. Andre and Claire Delisle had already visited twice since their marriage: once at Douglas's parents' home and more recently at their new home. That visit reminded Gabrielle and Douglas that their home was the perfect place to raise a family of their own. The couple talked many times about losing the baby. Gabrielle knew that Douglas loved her and was always very supportive and sympathetic to all her needs. Still, she realized this was devasting to them both. Even so, Gabrielle knew her Doug was always there for her, holding and comforting the woman he loved it seemed almost like every minute he was with her.

"Well, the only thing I can think of is that we have to work harder," Douglas grimaced as he said it, his eyes peered at Gabrielle's reaction.

"Mr. Douglas Nicholson! Are you suggesting that you may have your way with me whenever you want?" Her eyes were stern at first, but then they relaxed as her face melted into a smile. "I think it's a wonderful idea, Doug," she said, rubbing her body against his.

"Just be gentle with me, please." Douglas laughed.

"You know, Doug, I am feeling better in the outside air," Gabrielle said as if the idea of taking a walk were hers. "Let's take a stroll along Main Street. Maybe we can do a little shopping," she merrily said.

Douglas rolled his eyes back and said nothing as he followed Gabrielle's arm, steering him toward Ninth Street. As they turned onto Main Street, the couple mingled with other pedestrians shopping or doing business on that bright, sunny day. Store awnings covered produce baskets and other merchandise. Two trollies passed each other in opposite directions as horse-drawn wagons followed. It was a busy day in town. The steam whistle blew from the direction of the Third Street Station. A train was leaving, reminding Douglas of the station and those days long ago when he and Rollo always ran to see them and all the activity.

"Did you know that as of 1908, the Pennsylvania Railroad operated 256 miles and carried almost two million passengers?" Douglas asked his wife.

"I love it when you speak romantically to me," Gabrielle twinkled her eyes in amusement.

Douglas ignored her and continued, "It has provided a valuable western connection for both the railroad and Cleveland. That's historic, Gab!"

"Yes, darling, but do you remember the great flood of 1907 right after I came here?" Gabrielle smiled at Douglas. "It damaged the Third Street Station so much that Mr. Beane closed his restaurant inside the station." Her face changed to an angry child's as she continued, "I was just beginning to love his veal cutlet sandwiches. News of his food traveled along the rails throughout the country." Gabrielle frowned, "That's history, Doug!"

The flood of 1907 also damaged much of Wellsville's low-lying areas. Everyone in town hoped that the Ohio River Lock No. 8, just east of the town, would forever resolve the floods. The expected completion date was sometime in 1911.

"How do you do today, Mr. Nicholson?" a middle-aged man asked in a strong Italian accent as he tipped his homburg derby hat when he saw Douglas.

"Mr. Quintania, I'm well. Thank you." Douglas reached out his right hand for a handshake. "Gab, this is Mr. Fabio Quintania. He's a friend of Giuditta. And this, Mr. Quintania, is my wife, Gabrielle."

"A pleasure to meet you, Mr. Quintania," Gabrielle said smilingly, extending her right hand.

Fabio removed his hat and swayed it before him as he gallantly bowed before the young lady. "The pleasure is mine, Mrs. Nicholson," Fabio said in crude English. "Your husband is'a the bestest lawyer inna the world!"

"Give my regards to your wife, Teresa. Oh, and to your son, Giovanni, and his wife."

When her husband finished his chat with Fabio, Gabrielle

asked, "Who is that man over there?"

"Where?"

"That man with the terrifying face standing at the corner. He looked at me."

"That man you don't want to meet. He's Matteo Fontana, a criminal and a thug. I represented him once for theft. I told him I would never help him again," Douglas curled his lip in disgust. "Don't make eye contact with him, honey."

"Oh, my God, he looks so mean!"

"He is. Stay clear of him. He's a bad apple. An overabundance of immigrants has been coming here in the last ten years, most recently Italians. Matteo Fontana is one of those who makes it difficult for the other hard-working Italians. That's why established townspeople here are beginning to treat them so poorly–because of people like Fontana."

"Most of us were immigrants at some point or another," Gabrielle reminded her husband. "And look at all the criminals who aren't Italian immigrants?"

"That's the Gab crusader I know and love. You should study law. You'd make a wonderful criminal defense lawyer."

"I am studying law, honey," she laughed, "with you."

"I should let you make the opening and closing statements in my next trial."

"Oh, please do. It would be so much fun," Gabrielle laughed.

Logan Conners passed the couple. He was hurrying for a meeting, so he quickly tipped his hat to Gabrielle and told Douglas, "I'll see you at the club on Friday." He referred to the Elks lodge, where they had to induct a new member.

In late January 1911, Gabrielle announced that she was pregnant. She was hoping and praying for a birth sometime in August. Douglas was ecstatic, as were his parents, Martha and Douglas Sr., and his in-laws, Andre and Claire. The very likable Gabrielle had made many friends since her arrival and became active in women's affairs in the community. When not helping at Douglas's office, she volunteered at the library sponsored by the local Women's Christian Temperance Union on Main Street. Gabrielle also acted as a substitute teacher at the Central High School, where her husband attended when he was a young boy. But now Gabrielle decided to take things slower. Following her doctor's advice, she stopped working and spent time relaxing. Gabrielle wouldn't allow the same thing as before to happen again; she wanted this baby badly.

Gabrielle had also visited Giuditta at the hotel often. There, she learned many new recipes from her. Among them were the popular style of pizza and other homemade kinds of pasta served at the hotel. Giuditta loved Gabrielle's company, and ever since her husband told her that she felt as if her daughter was living in her, Gabrielle made a point of going there. It was one of the few places she still went after learning of her pregnancy. In a way, speaking Italian with Giuditta reminded her of Claire, her mother she missed so much.

Giuseppe Seggiano stood observing Giuditta's establishment. "Nice," he whispered to himself. The traveling harp player often frequented the restaurant whenever he passed this area. While patrons dined or drank beer and whiskey, Giuseppe played soft background music, sometimes singing. While packing his harp, which he had used the previous evening, he was in deep thought, pondering an idea that might resolve a personal problem at home.

"Signora Buch, may I have a word with you?" Giuseppe's grin displayed a mouthful of long yellow teeth beneath his handlebar mustache as he called Giuditta, sitting with Gabrielle and talking.

"I already paid you, Signor Seggiano. Bella musica, grazie." Giuditta went back to her conversation with Gabrielle.

Giuseppe widened his grin, exposing even more smoke-stained elongated teeth. "No, no, signora! It's a personal matter, if you will."

Giuditta blocked her mouth with her right hand so the harp player couldn't hear her, "Let me go and see what 'Signor Faccia di Cavallo' wants," she smiled at Gabrielle.

"Mrs. Buch, it's not nice to call him a horse face," Gabrielle whispered back, but she couldn't help laughing.

"Your husband is like a son to me, so you're my daughter," Giuditta smiled, "You call me Mama Buch, no more Mrs. Buch. And with such a long face and teeth to match, what else should I call this guy? Something about him bothers me."

Giuditta seated herself across the table from the harp player, "What can I do for you, Signore Seggiano?" she asked in her regional Italian dialect. Her eyes quickly glanced and smiled at Gabrielle, still sitting at the other table. Gabrielle grinned back, holding herself from laughing.

"I have a proposition for you, my good lady," Giuseppe spoke a better version of the Italian language than Giuditta. That same smile returned as he resumed, "I met your son outside. A fine young man." The smile continued, "You see, my wife has a beautiful sister." He gestured with his hands, "Just from Italy, almost eighteen years old. She would make a suitable wife for your son, Felo."

"Can she cook and clean?"

"More than that! Not only does she make the most delicious meals, but she's impeccably clean. And!" Giuseppe stood to finish his sentence. With his right arm extended and forefinger pointing upward, he declared, "She can read and write Italian!"

"Hmm," Giuditta sat thinking. She noticed Felo had come indoors and stood by the front door.

"This is her!" Giuseppe pulled an albumen photo print from his inner jacket pocket and showed the picture to Giuditta. "Beautiful, eh?" The smoke-stained teeth reappeared. "Felo is interested in marrying her, but I wanted to mention this to you out of respect."

"Oh! Beauty leaves quickly when a woman works hard. Well, my son's a man now. If he's interested. . ."

Giuseppe interrupted her, "This all depends on my wife. I must discuss the matter with her first. The young lady is her sister, after all." Giuseppe arose and said, "I will contact you as soon as possible." Then he took his harp, already in its case, and asked Felo to help him carry it to his carriage waiting out front. After carefully placing the harp in the carriage and climbing aboard, Giuseppe told Felo, "This might be your lucky day, young man." Giuseppe Seggiano then took the reins and drove away.

As Felo returned to the hotel's main door, he spotted Gabrielle and called to her, "Gabrielle! Tell Douglas I might be getting married!" Then he stood chuckling.

Gabrielle couldn't help but overhear the conversation between Giuditta and Giuseppe. Gabrielle was a romantic and had mixed feelings about arranged marriages, though they were customary among immigrants and the wealthy. She smiled back at Felo while replying, "I'll be sure to let him know!"

Later that afternoon, a well-built, average-sized man who appeared to be in his late thirties approached the check-in counter of Giuditta's hotel. He appeared to be a fine man with strong facial features, clean-shaven with a trimmed mustache, and neatly dressed in dark belted dress trousers. A white dress shirt with thin black pinstripes appeared underneath his overcoat. The man put his only suitcase beside his black leather hand-made laced boots before ringing the desk bell.

Gabrielle walked outside the kitchen to the check-in counter, leaving Giuditta to work some dough on a giant wooden board with her hands. "Yes, sir, can I help you?" asked a smiling Gabrielle while accessing the man who seemed to be a gentleman. Noticing that he didn't acknowledge what she said, she repeated her words in Italian.

"Oh, Sí Grazie! I am Senore Francesco Trieste." He introduced himself while removing his derby. Then he explained that he had just arrived in town and needed a room. Someone at the Third Street Station had recommended this hotel to Mr. Trieste.

Gabrielle began chatting with Mr. Trieste while she checked

the room occupancy log. Giuditta appeared from the doorway and introduced herself to the stranger.

"Where are you from, Mr. Trieste?" Giuditta asked in her dialect.

"I'm from Aguila, Senora," Francesco replied with his hat in hand. "I just arrived in New York in December. He explained how he was looking for a job and a place for his family, who would arrive in about seven months. "I have three children and a baby coming," Francesco smiled.

"I was born in Laurenzana but taken to America when I was a bambina," Giuditta smiled. She immediately liked this man. He was a clean, well-dressed, handsome man with manners, reminding her of Luigi. "You stay here until you find something. I give you a good rate." His prior statement about being married dissuaded Giuditta from any wishful notions of using Mr. Trieste for more personal reasons. 'He's a nice guy with a family like I had with Luigi,' she thought regretfully, 'I won't ruin that. I'll wait for another.'

The newcomer had $40 to his name. He wore most of his money in a money belt. Though he tucked some cash in his socks, Francesco pulled some bills from his pocket to pay for his room.

"No, put your money away. You pay me at the end of the week. I trust you, Mr. Trieste. You have an honest face. You'll find work very soon. Maybe at the Tin Plate Company. My son works there." Francesco Trieste expressed his gratitude.

"Actually, I could ask my husband about a job," Gabrielle added, speaking Italian. "He knows a lot of people."

Francesco extended his derby to the two women before placing it on his head. "Grazie to you both." He took the key Giuditta handed him, reached down, picked up his valise, and said, "I am so very appreciative to you both," he repeated his sentiment. Then, he headed up the two-section fruitwood stairway next to the check-in counter to find his room.

"Something about him I like," Giuditta told Gabrielle, "I'm a good judge of character."

Later that evening, Matteo Fontana sat at the bar drinking his fifth shot of Overholt since arriving just fifteen minutes before. Matteo had been drinking the same rye whiskey at other saloons since the afternoon before arriving at Giuditta's. Neil Watson, a regular there, sat next to Fontana at the bar and sipped his bourbon after enjoying one of Giuditta's meals.

"Where's the whores?" Matteo shouted into his empty shot glass. "Can't be a bar without whores!" he called again, hardly understandable between his slur and heavy Italian accent.

Everett Holt, the bartender, glanced down to the other end of the bar where Liam Kelly, the giant Irishman, stood, his big oak club aside from him. Liam clutched the end of what was a heavy weapon rather than a baton and began slowly walking toward the commotion. Matteo Fontana was a known criminal, troublemaker, and very dangerous man. Liam moved cautiously.

"This one's on the house," said Everett as he poured another drink for Matteo. "Would be nice if you kept it down a little. Others are trying to enjoy their drinks," Everett smiled as he spoke in a mild German accent acquired from his youth in Germany.

Matteo stared into the light blue eyes of the bartender for about five seconds. Then he motioned him to come closer by crooking his forefinger. When Everett stood before him, Matteo said in his crude English, "Com'a little closer. I don't wanna shout an'a disturb these'a nice'a people," he smiled, an open mouth full of crooked, dark brown stained teeth. As the bartender leaned closer, Matteo drank the filled shot glass in one gulp. Then he grabbed Everett by his shirt collar and smashed the empty glass against Everett's nose and face. Matteo kept crashing the glass repeatedly, then took Everett by his hair and banged his face on the polished hardwood bar over and over until he saw Liam coming closer to him. Neil Watson was knocked off his bar stool by Matteo's swinging arm. Blood spurted from

Everett's nose as he fell away and onto his knees behind the bar, feverishly trying to stop the flow of bright red blood with his bar apron in his stunned stupor.

"Get away, you dago bastard!" yelled Liam in his thick Irish brogue. At a close distance, he reached his extended right arm over the bar to take hold of Matteo.

Matteo quickly reached under his heavy winter coat and pulled out a large and heavy Smith & Wesson .38 caliber revolver. Liam stopped at the sight of the gun. He was older now, his reflexes had slowed, and his eyesight wasn't as good as it used to be. "Make'a me! You big'a fu'kin leprechaun!" He smashed the butt of the gun against Liam's forehead repeatedly until Liam fell beside the bleeding bartender. Matteo climbed over the bar in his drunken state and continued pistol-whipping Liam until the big Irishman stopped moving. Then he began hitting Everett again but with the pistol butt this time.

The inebriated Italian immigrant rose with blood spatter on his face and yelled out, "Never get'a involved with'a woman when'a you're married. Buy whores instead! less'a problems." He staggered and said, "Should'a have'a whores here!" Matteo headed toward the front door, his pistol still in hand, and fired a shot upward, hitting the ceiling. He swayed and wobbled all the way to his house on First Street.

When she saw his face, Matteo's wife, Rosa, ran over to her husband. "What happened? You have blood all over your face!" The blood wasn't his but of the men he had beaten.

Matteo replied in the same Italian dialect, "Get away from me, puttana industriale!" Rosa kept coming to help him. Matteo went crazy. He made a tight fist and punched her hard on her right eye. Rosa fell back, crashed into a glass table, and then rolled onto the floor, sobbing and struggling to get up.

"Papa! No!" screamed his 17-year-old daughter, Alessia, as she ran from her bedroom toward her father.

Matteo used the same bloody knuckles of his closed fist to punch his daughter solidly and severely on her nose repeatedly, and she fell hard onto the floor. He slid off his heavy leather belt and curled it around his hand; his gun fell from the waist of his trousers and onto the floor. "Figlia di puttana," he yelled while whipping Alessia's face and body with the heavy buckle until blood showed through her nightgown, her face in tatters. Pieces of flesh hung from what was once a face as lovely as an angel. Matteo bent down, and with his tremendous upper body strength, he lifted Alessia's cut and battered body and hurled her. The petite body of the girl crashed onto a heavy marble-topped chest, and she once again landed on the floor. He staggered to her and kicked her body hard over and over with his boot.

Matteo's heavy leather belt was still wrapped around his hand, the weighty metal buckle swaying. He turned and thrashed Rosa repeatedly with the heavy belt buckle. As the beaten woman desperately tried to lift her head, Matteo kept kicking her with his boot until she passed out, her face now covered with blood.

The ghastly sight of mother and daughter lay on the floor unconscious, dark blood from them both soaking the carpet as the drunken man staggered to his bedroom and fell face-first onto his bed. Matteo Fontana's 16-year-old son, Luca, peered through the slightly ajar door of his bedroom. He had witnessed the entire incident. It was one of many, but this beating was far worse than any other.

Chapter Nineteen

Corleto, Italy to Wellsville, Ohio, 1910-1911
Lucia Antonietta Ducatelli

Completing the north river tunnels under the Hudson River allowed electrified lines to run from the newly built Pennsylvania Train Station in New York City to New Jersey. Traveling by boat was no longer necessary to reach New Jersey as it had been for Luigi Massaro and his new bride, Giulia, years before. Passengers could now board in New York City and go directly to New Jersey, where a train would take them to Philadelphia and Pittsburgh, Pennsylvania.

Lucia Antonietta Ducatelli opened the wooden shutters of the full-length window in the grand parlor. The petite 17-year-old woman stepped out onto the limestone veranda, her small hands clutching the heavy wrought iron railing of the balcony. She stood between the two long lantana flower boxes that hung from the rail. Lucia looked below, observing the circular cobblestone street and the stone houses built around it, all owned by her father, Biaggio Ducatelli. There, the day before, a grand funeral procession followed the horse-drawn hearse carrying the open casket of her uncle, the priest who raised her.

Lucia Antonietta Ducatelli was born on February 20, 1893, in Corleto, Italy. Her grandfather, Pasquale Toci, owned much land and prospered from sending all his wheat and vegetable harvests to Naples. Due to his alliance with the aristocracy,

Pasquale's son, Leonardo, was granted the honor of becoming a priest. As a young man, he studied in Rome and, once ordained, served there. After several years of duty at the Vatican, Leonardo requested permission to return to his hometown after the passing of the priest who ministered there. The Church gave him the title of 'Archiprete,' an Archpriest of the area surrounding Corleto, Italy.

Leonardo's sister, Eleanora Toci, married Biaggio Ducatelli in 1873. Together, they had two sons, Antonio and Leonardo, and three daughters, Giulia, Teresa, and Lucia. Eleanora died during the childbirth of her fourth daughter, named Eleanora, in her memory. After her mother's death, her father, Biaggio, gave custody of three-year-old Lucia to her grandmother, Teresa Toci, who lived with her son, Leonardo, the Archpriest.

Lucia's father, Biaggio, a wealthy man, did so that Lucia was educated, appropriately treated, and given to a suitable man in marriage. As the people in Italy at that time treated positions of Catholic clerics akin to royalty, Lucia grew up with housekeepers and servants. She had tutors for literature and other studies. As a young girl, Lucia formally learned the social etiquette of a lady. When Lucia was ten, her grandmother passed away, leaving her in the care of her uncle, the priest, and his staff.

A church bishop conducted a grand funeral after Archiprete Leonardo Toci's death. Crowds from all over the region attended the funeral mass, some standing outside the beautifully designed church.

When Archiprete Toci died, Biaggio Ducatelli decided it would be best that his 17-year-old daughter, Lucia, be sent to America and stay with her sister, Giulia, who was already living there. Lucia would remain at her sister and brother-in-law's home until they arranged for her to marry an appropriate husband. Had her uncle, Archiprete Leonardo Toci, lived, Lucia might have been among the few young women attending University the following year. Now, her older siblings would decide her future. So, on that beautiful spring day in 1910, the pretty, petite, blue-eyed, blonde-haired Lucia Antonietta

Ducatelli stood on one of the home's balconies where she was raised and educated. She wondered what life would be like in a country where 'the streets were paved with gold,' as many Italians believed.

Lucia readied the final things for her journey that early December, her steamer trunk already packed. Biaggio had arranged for a married couple, Mr. and Mrs. Giovanni Desario, to act as chaperones for his daughter's safety on her long voyage. After Lucia bid her family goodbye, she traveled to the Port of Naples with her escorts. She stayed in a private room at a hotel adjacent to the Desarios. The following day, they would be sailing on the oceanliner Santa Lucia. Biaggio arranged for Giovanni Desario to purchase a separate second-class room for his daughter on the ship.

While at sea the evening before Santa Lucia's feast day, someone knocked on Lucia's cabin. The young lady opened it, and a handsome uniformed ship's first officer stood with his white peaked hat in hand. "Signorina, it is at the captain's request that I am here," announced the young man.

"Yes?" replied Lucia.

"He extends a warm invitation to you to dine at his table tomorrow," the officer smiled, "for the feast day of Santa Lucia, the namesake of you and this ship," he spoke the perfect Italian of an educated person, as did she. Lucia had never been asked out to an occasion, especially by such a handsome young man in a striking navy blue uniform. She stood before the man still, almost in a daze. "Signorina?" the first officer asked, "may I please have your reply?" Lucia just gazed into the man's eyes.

"Tell the captain, yes," she smiled as her deep blue eyes met his, "I would be honored to dine at his table."

"Thank you, signorina." He smiled again and bowed before her, swaying his white peaked uniform cap. "I will relay your response to the captain immediately. Good evening, signorina." Lucia remained in the cabin doorway, watching as the young man walked away, her heart pounding.

The next evening, Lucia dressed in a white wide-brimmed evening hat with a center fold and pink roses that complimented her floor-length, white belted blue satin gown. She looked stunning, gracefully walking to her table, her dainty figure catching the eye of everyone in the dining room.

"You look remarkably well this evening, Signorina Ducatelli," the captain said, rising from his highback chair like all the other men seated. "So glad you could join us," he smiled, pulling out the chair next to him for her to sit.

"Grazie, Capitano," Lucia said with just a hint of a smile as the captain seated her. The other men waited and then sat back down.

A couple of the women at the table showed their jealousy by questioning the young lady. But Lucia politely engaged in all conversations, speaking her pleasant Italian and charmingly displaying her knowledge of other countries and cities—the people seated at the table, especially the men, were fascinated by the delightful young lady.

As the small orchestra played soft music, several single men lined up to ask Lucia to dance. She smiled as she danced with one young man after another, noticing the Desarios watching her from a distant table. Lucia Antonietta Ducatelli was the bell of the ball.

The Santa Lucia docked at the West Side piers of Manhattan along the Hudson River in the latter part of December 1910. First and second-class passengers were given a brief onboard examination before disembarking. Small boats took the steerage passengers to Ellis Island to be processed and have more thorough interviews and physical examinations.

Mr. and Mrs. Giovanni Desario accompanied Lucia from New York City to Pittsburgh from the new Penn Station. Completing the north river tunnels under the Hudson River allowed electrified lines to run from New York City to New Jersey. Traveling by boat was no longer necessary as it had been for Luigi Massaro and his new bride, Giulia, years before.

Antonio Ducatelli, Lucia's older brother, met her in Pittsburgh. He mentioned that it wouldn't look proper for a young single woman to stay as a visitor in his home. The reality was that Antonio was a 'lady's man' and often entertained young women in his house, and his sister, Lucia, would interfere with those arrangements. The following day, he took Lucia to the home of their sister, Giulia, and her husband, Giuseppe Seggiano, in Wheeling, West Virginia.

Giuseppe Seggiano hated doing labor of any sort. He was employed as a labor foreman when he first came to America and prayed for rain so he wouldn't have to go to work. Now, he traveled playing his harp at social occasions in restaurants and saloons. In his spare time, he would polish his imported Italian harp.

While living in Wheeling, West Virginia, with her older sister, Giulia, and her husband, Giuseppe, Lucia helped out by taking care of their two daughters. Lucia didn't like America; her hometown in Italy afforded her a better lifestyle, which she missed. In early 1911, Lucia met a local mailman named Leon Bauer, who was from Germany. The young woman waited for him to come every day. She would carefully watch for the handsome young man, and they grew fond of each other. Leon wanted to marry Lucia and even offered to send her to school to speak better English before they did. The young man came from a well-to-do family, and Leon had saved considerable money. However, her sister would not hear of such a marriage; her father insisted Lucia marry an Italian. Her fate was in the hands of her older sister and her brother-in-law. Then, one evening, Giuseppe Seggiano returned home grinning, exposing his long, smoke-stained teeth. "I have good news, my dear." He noticed Lucia listening, so he pulled his wife into another room. Softly, he said, "I found the perfect husband for Lucia!" He chuckled in his merriment.

"Who?" asked Giulia in an untrusting tone. She knew Giuseppe wanted to get rid of her sister. "Too many mouths to feed already. We don't need another," he would always say, but privately. Now, he had a chance to unload her.

"A nice young man! His family owns a prestigious hotel in the town of Wellsville, Ohio," he exaggerated the truth. The hotel was slightly more than acceptable now that Luigi was gone. "They do very well." He rubbed his thumb and forefinger to indicate money or 'soldi' in Italian. "I play beautiful music in their dining area. They love me." Giuseppe glanced at his wife, who didn't look entirely convinced. "And they're 'Pisanos' of us. Well, at least his mother is." Still, Giulia had hesitation. "Hey, you keep a pretty, unwed young woman around a man like me for too long, and you don't know what might happen," insinuating Lucia might fall passionately in love with him.

"You? Ha!" Giulia laughed loudly. Then she composed herself and asked, "Do you really think he would be a good husband?"

"Perfect!"

"Well, Papa wants her to marry an Italian, and he has money to support her so. . ."

"Good!" Giuseppe cut off his wife. "I'll make arrangements and send for Felo Buch! He is most certainly a suitable husband for Lucia!"

Lucia was heartbroken when she found out. "I would rather marry Leon Bauer," she pleaded. But, one look at her sister, and she knew they had already settled the matter. Her father's wishes sealed her fate.

Later that week, Felo rode on horse and buggy to Wheeling, West Virginia. A small church ceremony took place at the local Catholic Church. Lucia looked radiant as a bride. After the ceremony, the Seggianos served coffee, cake, Italian biscuits, and other cookies. The newlywed couple left for Wellsville by the same horse and carriage in the morning. It was a beautiful day, unseasonably warm for the time of year. Lucia saw Leon Bauer in the distance, delivering his mail. She turned away and looked straight ahead to face the new reality forced upon her.

Chapter Twenty

Wellsville, Ohio, 1911
Origins of The Black Hand

The Black Hand in America grew in the larger cities after the mass Italian immigration of the early 1900s. It was comprised of individuals who hired small groups of Italian immigrant thugs to prey on other Italians. Their success was based on the fact that Sicilians knew the brutal methods of the Sicilian Mafia in maintaining power over the peasant class. Though these gangs had no ties to the Sicilian Mafia, they sent notes to immigrant merchants with pictures of a black hand or daggers and other such frightening things to extort money, making threats that they would hurt their victims or destroy their property. Some of these gangs succeeded, others didn't. Like most things, the Black Hand toughs eventually spread to smaller cities and towns where immigrant Italians lived. Many of these small-time hoods failed, but someone usually filled their place.

Matteo Fontana woke up in the late morning, still dressed in the same clothes as the day before, except for his heavy leather belt. He sat at the side of his bed, rubbing his eyes while the world seemed to spin around him. Matteo pulled out the chamber pot from under the bed and vomited bitter-tasting bile into it. He kept his head positioned there for a full minute until he finished. Matteo then rose and urinated into the pot, his flow missing at times. He hobbled over to a piece of furniture where his wife, Rosa, kept a cleanly prepared floral ceramic wash basin and matching water pitcher. After splashing his face several times, he wiped it dry with a fresh towel Rosa always left for him.

"Rosa! Come here," he yelled while looking for his belt, stinking of stale alcohol and body odor. "Rosa!" Matteo saw the belt lying on the floor in the next room alongside his Smith & Wesson .38. He strapped the belt around his trouser loops. Then he slid the revolver into the shabby, weathered holster. "Rosa!" he called again.

"She ain't here, Papa," his son, Luca, quietly said. The 16-year-old boy was small for his age, both in height and build.

"Where she go?" Matteo used broken English. His head pounded like someone was hammering it with a railroad spike maul.

Luca was beginning to realize his father had no recollection of what happened the night before. Memory lapses were common after Matteo sobered up. "I don't know, Papa."

Matteo beat his wife and daughter so severely that it took the short, thin-framed Luca over an hour to get them both up off the floor. The boy wasn't crying, even though his mother and sister couldn't wake up and might have been dying. When they awakened, he saw how disabled they were.

Rosa had asked her son in a bearly understandable whisper, "Is the tethered horse-drawn wagon still outside the door?"

"Yeah," was all he answered.

His mother told him, "Carry us and put us in the back of the wagon one at a time. Take us to Giuditta Buch's hotel." Rosa waited to regain her speech and said, "Pack your clothes to stay with us."

Luca complied with his mother's request and put her and his sister in the wagon, but he didn't pack his clothes to stay there. He knew he had to return when Matteo woke up. Luca would try to calm him down. Similar situations had happened before, but not nearly as bad as this one.

Luca carried his mother first inside the Buch hotel. Then he went back and brought in his sister. He noticed what was going on at the hotel bar. Giuditta and another black woman were helping the big Irishman who worked there. Another man was lying beside them, bleeding profusely. After a short conversation with Giuditta Buch, Luca ran outside and drove the rig the short distance back to his home, worrying that his father might awaken.

"Whatta you mean you don't know?" Matteo finally replied to his son's answer about not knowing where Rosa was. He had absolutely no recollection of what he had done.

The 16-year-old thought that if he told his father he brought them to the Buch's place, it would be his turn to get a thrashing. Luca instead said, "You beat them both pretty bad. Maybe they went to get a doctor."

"Whatta you talking about?"

"You did, Papa. They both looked pretty bad." Luca knew he was safe when his father wasn't drinking.

Matteo shrugged, "If they don't come back soon, I'll go looking for them," he said in his Sicilian dialect. Then he turned to his son, "Luca, get me something to eat. Just some bread and olive oil. It's good for my stomach."

"Okay."

Matteo Fontana arrived in New York City in 1901. His wife, Rosa, and his two children accompanied him. Alessia was seven at the time, and Luca was six. Rosa was a slightly plump woman, customary for a wife in Palermo, Sicily, where the importance of eating became a tradition. Years of invasions and fighting in Sicily caused suffering and starvation for the people who lived during those times. The mafia compounded those problems. That made eating food–actually overeating when it was available–a way of life. Rosa had a pretty face and had always been a good mother to her two children. However, she lived in constant fear of her husband's temper. Matteo Fontana was a product of the Sicilian Mafia and a hothead since his marriage. After consummating his matrimonial duties years before, on the night of their wedding in Palermo, Matteo beat Rosa to show her who was boss.

Sicily's culture was always apart from mainland Italy. The same brutality that placed such importance on food by the lower classes of that country was a basis for building Sicily's history. Peasants represented the majority of Sicily's population before and after Italy's unification. Historically, Sicily was considered 'the pearl of the Mediterranean' due to its luscious fruits, vegetables, ancient olives, and other commodities. The island came under the influences of the Catholic Church and the aristocracy, literally or figuratively, depending on what era. The mafia also became part of the ruling class of Sicily. It had existed for centuries, and the unification of Italy empowered omertà, the secrecy of the society of the Mafiosa, even more by expanding its reach. Initially helping the former serfs, they immersed themselves in land management for the aristocracy.

The methods employed by the mafia became brutal and feared by all there. The poor farmers worked from dawn to the setting sun but had to surrender most of their crops, which left them in starvation. They bowed to the mafia's will; saying no to them was not an option. Out of fear of the mafia, women obeyed their male protectors: husbands, fathers, uncles, and brothers. The men of the Sicilian Mafia didn't dress lavishly. They blended into the commoners. When foreign invasions occurred, they hid amongst the people who feared them so much they would never expose them. Then, they resurfaced to rule again with ferocity.

Matteo Fontana had worked for the Sicilian Mafia in Palermo alongside Casio Ferro. The two men were involved in the kidnapping of the Baroness of Valpetrosa in 1898. Released from custody after two years, Matteo and Casio escaped the Sicilian police scrutiny by leaving the country together in 1901. Matteo considered leaving his wife and family behind. However, a shrewd way to obtain citizenship was to present himself as a married man entering America. The two immigrants went to work for the Morello gang in the Harlem section of New York City. Matteo worked with Casio Ferro in a counterfeiting ring, but both men escaped conviction using fake alibis.

Joseph Petrosino, an Italian-American sergeant of the New York City Police Department at the time, eventually targeted the partners, Fontana and Ferro, for barrel murders. Barrel murders were the act of murdering and disposing of enemies of the Black Hand gangs. It sometimes required the murder victims to be decapitated or completely cut to pieces to avoid identification. The remains were stuffed into barrels, dropped off at inconspicuous places, or dumped in the rivers or the harbor bay. Matteo Fontana escaped to Pittsburgh in 1904 with his family to avoid conviction. Eventually, he moved to the small town of Wellsville to use his skills of intimating Italians for profit. Casio Ferro returned to Sicily and the mafia there.

Matteo carried with him vivid memories of the horrendous things he had done in Sicily and America. They always haunted him, especially in his dreams, where his mind re-enacted those evil deeds repeatedly, disrupting his sleep. His life began to fall apart, and he resorted to booze to force back the hideous acts he had committed in his life. Matteo could no longer hold a decent job, only as a Black Hand thug, and resorted to violence while under the influence of alcohol. Being drunk was the only way to battle those ghosts of his past, and by attacking and brutalizing innocent people and even his family.

When Luca Fontana dropped off his mother and sister at Giuditta's hotel, he told her he had to get back home to make sure his father didn't wake up and come looking for his mother. Giuditta glanced up while she tried to stop the bleeding from Liam's face and head. The boy looked terrified at what had happened. "Did my papa do this?" he asked.

Giuditta didn't want to blame the boy for his father's actions. "Don't worry, Luca. This is not your fault," she simply replied. "You go home! The doctor is on his way. Everything will be okay."

While upstairs preparing to go to bed, Giuditta had heard the gunshot fired from Matteo Fontana's pistol. A small group of men surrounded Liam Kelly and Everett Holt as Giuditta ran toward the bar. She couldn't find Nicola. 'Where is that idiot,' she thought as she spotted Sandy.

"Sandy! Go over to get Millie on First Street," she hollered. Millie and Hector didn't yet have a telephone. Giuditta knew that Millie was good at using herbal remedies. Millie had long ago told her about what happened to Hector and how she treated him with natural remedies. "Somebody call the doctor! I no speak so well in English."

"I did already, Giuditta," Sandy shouted back as she fought through the crowd to the door to go and get Millie Brown.

"Okay!" Giuditta pointed to two men, "Pick them up and lay them on the floor over here!" Giuditta pointed to where she was standing. "Bring them here! Carefully!" Mrs. D'Angelo and Bianca Gallo had already left earlier, so Giuditta called her dear friend Sofia Marino. After that phone call, Giuditta knelt and began to help Liam first; he seemed much worse than Everett. 'This would never have happened if my Luigi was here,' she thought, quickly putting him out of her mind. She had work to do and needed to concentrate. After about ten minutes, Millie Brown was down on her knees beside her, huffing and puffing. The short, heavyset woman ran the whole way from home. That's when Luca Fontana arrived, bringing in two more patients.

"Mother of God, have mercy on us!" Millie yelled. "This is bad. Okay, Giuditta, you take care of Everett. I'll take care of Liam. We need blankets and clean towels," Millie shouted, taking charge; her bag of herbs and other things lay beside her.

"I'll get them!" shouted Sandy. As she did, the doctor arrived.

As the doctor assessed the two men, and the two women, Giuditta stopped for a few minutes to check on her children sleeping in their rooms on the first floor. They were all sound asleep and hadn't heard a thing.

Matteo leaned forward into his walk. The gruff man didn't reply to friendly townspeople who passed him along the sidewalk; he merely grunted. Matteo hadn't heard from either his wife or his daughter all morning. His son, Luca, begged him to remain home, afraid he would get into another fight if he found them at Giuditta's Hotel. Rosa was always punctual and prepared his lunch on time. 'Puttana!' Matteo motioned his hand while he thought about how he would give it to her when he found her. 'I'll show her who's boss!' He made a fist with his hand, the knuckles of that hand already forming scabs as the blood began to dry from the beatings he had given out the night before. 'Those two idiots at the Buch bar,' he remembered. 'The Buch bar! Yeah! Rosa is friends with that Puttana, who's married to that cornuto over there who lets her sleep with other men. Maybe she went to see her. That's where she is! Maybe I'll give her a beating, too. It's her husband's job, but he's a weak dope. I'll smack Giuditta around a little. That will teach her to stop interfering with my wife's business. Rosa didn't make my lunch because of her.' Matteo turned and headed in the direction of Giuditta's hotel.

The doctor had stabilized Everett and Liam, as well as the mother and daughter. "Liam has what's called a brain concussion," the doctor explained as he worked. He didn't know if they understood the seriousness of that. "That's a severe injury to the brain." Dr. Falco looked up at the staring faces and said, "He might not make it. If he does, he'll have several side effects from it. Some might last the rest of his life." The doctor shook his head back and forth and added, "The man who did this beat him very badly. He'll need a lot of bed rest." Dr. Falco also explained that aside from all the cuts and abrasions, there were also several fractures in different parts of his face. "The other guy, Everett Holt, fared better. He has a broken nose and a couple of broken teeth. The cuts on his face are mostly superficial, but it'll take time for the swelling to go down." Sofia Marino was translating everything the doctor said to Giuditta. Millie stood beside her, listening attentively. She didn't understand all the technical jargon. But at least she admitted it. Most people surrounding the doctor as he spoke didn't either; they just pretended to follow.

"Now! as for the women. What are their names?" Millie told him their names. Dr. Falco bowed his head, shaking it side to side. "What kind of man would batter women like this?" He shrugged, "Rosa has so many facial cuts and bruises. . ." He stopped himself and shrugged again before continuing, "She appears to have a brain concussion as Liam has. She also has several fractures, too, again, like Liam. It appears she was kicked and hit with a heavy object. Maybe a large belt buckle because she also has strap marks." The doctor looked at Millie because it seemed she had become the official spokeswoman in the group. "Rosa's going to need a lot of time to heal. I have no idea what her outcome might be. Only time will tell. But her body injuries could have been worse; her being a little chubby helped her a bit with that," the doctor spoke bluntly. "Alessia has a badly broken nose and severe facial and body lacerations," Dr. Falco paused again in disgust. "Many of the cuts are deep. I temporarily wrapped her face, but I'm going to sedate her so I can set her nose as best as possible and suture her face. The extent of the wound to her nose and the deep cuts on her face will disfigure her appearance. But there's worse. The young woman was lashed with a heavy strap so savagely that I will also have to suture all of the wounds on her body, and she'll always have bad scaring." Dr. Falco noticed most faces in the group didn't comprehend. "I have to stitch them with thread," he clarified himself. "An even bigger problem is that she appears to have a broken hip." The doctor shook his head again, "She probably won't walk correctly again." Dr. Falco turned to Giuditta and asked, "Do you have a room for me to work?" Giuditta nodded and brought the doctor to Luigi's old office on the first floor.

"My son uses it sometimes but can work elsewhere now."

Sandy served drinks to some of the men who returned in the morning. The crowd grew and became angrier by the minute, learning the fate of the four people. Some men and women stayed into the night, helping as much as possible. "I like Liam, always have," a well-built man called Hank shouted from the group. "To Liam!" he toasted.

People of mixed nationalities still came to Giuditta's hotel to enjoy her fine Italian meals and pizzas. Some stopped by to pick up a freshly baked loaf of Italian bread. Her homemade beer was popular and had been selling for years. However, due to the constant flow of Italian immigrants, they became the primary ethnicity that frequented her establishment. People sharing the same foreign language and culture always feel more comfortable together.

So that day, many Italians, especially Sicilians, gathered at Giuditta's. The Sicilians had lived under the mafia control of their former country. A hardened people, they knew the brutality of retaliation, witnessing it so often there. Many felt that Sicilian justice would be appropriate for the man who had done these despicable deeds.

"Everett is a fine young man, too. What that Fontana guy did is wrong! Never liked him!" A laborer named Vito delivered those words. The speeches continued as the lunch crowd began to arrive. More and more strappy laborers came and the mood grew angrier, fueled by disgust at such an awful story and the power of booze. They learned what happened to Liam and Everett and the two women. Their voices grew louder, as did their anger.

"Let's find Matteo Fontano!" Vito shouted to the workers.

"Aye to that," roared one man, and the other men agreed as the crowd grew.

The only man who tried to reason with the angry horde was

Francesco Trieste. He had seen mobs form before. He advised, "Make sure you get all the facts together before you go to the police." But, he noticed he was in a losing debate since only the Italians could understand his language, and they didn't care. Most of them were the ones firing the flames of that angry crowd.

"Police?" asked Marco, an Italian worker. "We don't need 'la polizia' for this. We need to hunt down that bastard, Fontana, who did this! Let's go!" Most working-class Italians from Southern Italy never trusted the police. So many of them worked or took orders from the mafia there. So feared in Sicily was the mafia that nobody ever mentioned the word, La Mafia. Instead, they used replacement words such as 'friends' or 'guardians.' But the immigrants from that country knew well how to handle men like Matteo Fontana. Going back to the ancient civilizations that conquered that country inbred survival into those people.

"But this way, he goes to prison. A good lawyer would see that he'll do hard time in prison with solid facts," Francesco responded in Italian, "and we have facts!" Before Francesco finished his point, the front door flew open forcibly. Matteo Fontana stepped into the hotel.

"Anybody sees'a that puttana Giuditta?" Matteo looked around the room filled with angry men. "Caus'a her I no have my breakfast or'a my lunch!" He folded his arms together and stood waiting for an answer. "Where is'a my Rosa? I gotta eat!"

The group of men grabbed hold of Matteo Fontana and carried him outside. Francesco Trieste stood with Giuditta inside the hotel. He told her, "No good will come from this. I know; I've seen it before. They should have called the police."

"La polizia?" Giuditta nodded in disgust, "You'll learn the ways of this country soon enough. As far as the guy who did these things? The nature of the beast! I saw things like this when I was young in Little Italy in New York. But you seem like a good man, Francesco. You remind me of my first husband, an honorable man."

Giuditta went back to attend to her children. She put her older daughter, Mary, already almost 18 years old, in charge of the others to ensure they ate and did their chores. Mrs. D'Angelo and Bianca Gallo arrived for work earlier, and both were attending to the four patients Giuditta had inherited. Giuditta had put her four children into one room to allow the other available rooms for the victims of Matteo Fontana's rage. Liam and Everett were in one, and Rosa and her daughter, Alessia, were in the other. Liam and Rosa were still unresponsive. Everett wanted to get up, but the doctor ordered him to bed rest, and Millie or one of the other women stood guard to see that he did. Even with the heavy drugs the doctor administered, Alessia sobbed throughout the remainder of the night into the morning. Millie had rested in one of the rooms upstairs for only about an hour and then returned to her duties.

Francesco Trieste passed by the mob outside while on his way out, looking for work. The men were already beating Matteo savagely. One man in particular, Marco Gullo, was leading the angry crowd. He was from Sicily and had worked for an old-time mafia boss before coming to America. Everyone feared Marco because he often spoke about the brutal ways of his old country.

Before Francesco left the ghastly site, he noticed one of the laborers beating Matteo's face and head with spiked brass knuckles. The indignant Matteo cursed him through his broken teeth while his face dripped blood, mumbling, "bastardi." The mob of men had already stomped his head into a pile of horse manure repeatedly, seemingly causing damage to his neck because of the way it swelled unhuman-like.

The crowd was relentless, driven by Marco, the liquor, and the madness of revenge. Matteo's bloated head hung to one side. His left eyeball had popped out of its socket. He looked hideous, his head leaning to the side and his eyeball swaying, held by the stretched thread of the optic nerve. Rich blood streamed from Matteo's face as he struggled to curse the men through his swollen, cut lips, but now only mumbles came out. He dangled from the arms of the men like a broken marionette on strings as they kept beating him.

But when Marco Gullo began to unbuckle Matteo's belt and pull off his trousers, Matteo squealed as loudly as a pig going to slaughter. He knew what that meant. The Sicilian Mafia had done such things as punishment to men who offended them, though Matteo's pleads went unheard. Blood filled Matteo's remaining eye, and with blurred vision, he watched as Marco snapped open a sharp switchblade knife. Matteo fought to hold his legs together tightly, howling like a wolf, trying to prevent what they were about to do to him. Another worker picked up a heavy river rock and slammed it against Matteo's knees, one at a time, over and over, until his legs were lifeless. Now, as Marco held the sharp knife, he easily grabbed Matteo's scrotum and quickly sliced it off with the skill of a surgeon, Matteo screaming like a wild animal as he did. Marco dangled the bag of skin containing his testes before Matteo's remaining eye before stuffing it into the swollen lips of his victim.

Matteo's lifeless body lay for about 15 minutes in the cold, damp night, the wind from the river making it feel more frigid. The hardened man tried to drag himself by the fingertips of one of his shattered arms, moaning as his broken, numb legs and battered body slid behind him just an inch before the abomination of a man fell unconscious. A policeman spotted him on patrol. A funeral hearse took what remained of Matteo Fontana to an infirmary.

Chapter Twenty-One

Wellsville, Ohio, 1911
Changing Times

The Black Hand came to the town of Wellsville, not as a great squall like those barrages of wind that swept through the valley but as subtle as the blades of grass that rooted and sprang there in spring. Matteo Fontana was only one of the first. He tilled the ground and led the way for other thugs to follow, and more would come.

For over ten years, cars had been passing through Wellsville. By 1911, several people in town had owned motor vehicles for a few years, especially after the Ford Model T arrived on the scene. But Douglas, a creature of habit like his father, preferred to use a horse-driven carriage or wagon. "Reliability is what you want in a means of transportation. You can't beat a horse for that," Douglas Sr. would constantly say every time he saw a motorized vehicle pass by. However, the adventurous Gabrielle persuaded her husband to consider one.

The petite and feline body of Gabrielle Delisle Nicholson was now showing her pregnancy, but as with all things, gracefully. Her morning sickness was long gone. Many a morning, Douglas had helped by holding her head over the new gravity-flush toilet they had installed when they moved to their new home four years earlier. She arranged a wardrobe of lovely but loose-fitting dresses that she could alter as her belly grew. Gabrielle adhered to her doctor's advice to manage her activity to prevent the misfortune of a miscarriage from reoccurring. However, she maintained her childish curiosities and enjoyed delving into innovative notions, especially gadgets. And those innocent, adolescent fancies awakened every time a motorized vehicle passed by their horse-driven carriage.

"I want one of those!" Gabrielle laughed as a Ford Model-T passed them by one day.

"Not practical, Gab!" Douglas answered her quickly, fully aware of her urge to drive one, let alone own one.

"They are! Everyone's getting one!"

"I see a lot of them by the wayside blowing off steam, with men waving their hats for help. You don't see too many broken carriages anymore." He turned and smiled at his wife, "Problem is you're too daring."

"It must be that French pioneering blood from my father's side." Gabrielle smiled back, "I vote we buy a horseless carriage! You see, this way, you still have your carriage but not the horse! It's a compromise!"

"Do you really believe your husband to be a dummy?" Douglas asked, smiling but looking straight ahead, watching the road.

Gabrielle always drew upon her olive-green colored eyes and long lashes, creating that lazy-eyed appearance that made her husband melt, especially when she wanted something badly. So, a short time later, Mr. and Mrs. Douglas Nicholson were the proud owners of a 1910 Cadillac Model 30 Tourer. Gabrielle's logic of comfort during her pregnancy persuaded Douglas and ended the debate.

It was five days after Matteo Fontana was beaten to near death by the angry mob that Gabrielle and Douglas drove up to Giuditta's hotel, bestowing upon the entire block the distinctive honk of the motorized vehicle. There was chaos when Giuditta's children wanted to ride in the car. Even her older daughters, Mary and Angelina, now young ladies, wanted to be seen riding in a Cadillac. John, also a teen, took to the car immediately, making Douglas wonder why men and boys coveted mechanical things more than women. John held nine-year-old Telma in his lap, and Douglas drove them and their sisters around the town. Then, Millie wanted a turn, but Douglas practically had to drag Giuditta inside the car. Millie laughed during the whole ride while Giuditta braced herself in fear the entire time. "These things are against the laws of God!" she shouted in her dialect when she stepped out, waving her hands high in the air as Gabrielle laughed along with Giuditta's children.

Douglas had heard about what happened at the hotel the day after that incident occurred, and he rode over on horseback to see if there was any way he could help. Knowing Gabrielle would have wanted to come along, he hadn't told his wife because he didn't want to upset her. But Gabrielle found out from other sources and became upset just upon hearing the news, let alone being there. Douglas reminded her of the man they saw on Main Street the year before. 'Oh my God!' she thought as that memory came alive, "That scary-looking man! Yes, I remember!" Gabrielle told Douglas as she recalled that time when they strolled outside after she had her miscarriage. "He looked like someone who could do something so horrific as that."

After she found out and unbeknownst to her husband, Gabrielle rode by horse and carriage to help the men and the mother and daughter beaten so severely. Many women in the surrounding area did the same. Together, they prepared a small infirmary in the back rooms, better than the one where immigrants went to die. Giuditta and Millie confined the pregnant young woman to do seated jobs, nothing that required physical activity or stress. Gabrielle folded clean clothes and bandages and prepared the medicines the doctor brought over on his daily visits. They also used some of Millie's potions and other concoctions. Gabrielle sobbed while working, still not recovered from seeing what that man had done to his wife and daughter.

The gossipers and busybodies came to the hotel from town after hearing about the incident. Many people always crave to see a place where tragedy occurred. It brought crowds of customers to the hotel. Giuditta had to hire substitute bartenders she trusted; Sandy was among them. A female bartender who happened to be a prostitute wasn't a common occurrence. Still, Sandy was capable and stood her ground. With her regular kitchen help, Giuditta managed the food service without additional workers.

After a few days of feeling a little better, Everett Holt rose from his bed and wanted to help. He had bandages on his face from the broken shot glass Matteo slammed against his face so many times, and he walked around with wads of cotton shoved in his nose. The young man knew he would have scarring from the attack. Everett wasn't ready to tend the bar yet, so he helped out by bringing food and beverages from the kitchen to the injured. Liam Kelly awoke to a great deal of pain around the same time as Everett left his bed. The big Irishman couldn't remember anything; his memory was gone. It was one of the reasons Everett got up, feeling guilty lying down and wanting to help his friend.

Nicola was at a different bar the night of Matteo's assaults. When he came home and saw the turmoil, he sneaked upstairs to hide in his bedroom; he didn't want to get involved with Matteo Fontana. In the following days, Nicola worked at the mill occasionally. When he returned to the hotel, he sat quietly in a corner, sipping beer, reaping the rewards of marrying a woman who owned a hotel.

As Giuditta prepared dinner for her family in the evening, her children still talked about Douglas's new car. Gabrielle rose to help Giuditta but succumbed when Giuditta raised one hand without saying anything. The intelligent young woman knew from experience there was no way to subdue that sign.

While Giuditta was preoccupied with dinner, Felo Buch, returning from Wheeling, West Virginia, with his new bride, steered his buggy toward the side of the hotel. He secured the wooden block brake and then tethered the horse temporarily to the tree. As Felo helped Lucia from the carriage, his eyes spotted the brand-new car. Parts of its dark red color and the two golden-colored lanterns that hung from each side at the front of the vehicle glistened from the lighting at the front of the hotel. The new groom carefully guided Lucia to the hotel door, peering at the car's interior as he did. 'The upholstery alone is better than anything I've ever seen,' Felo thought as he opened the front door for his new wife.

It was late in the day, and they were both tired from traveling. Lucia yawned slightly, then excused herself as her eyes surveyed the interior of the hotel's first floor. Douglas Nicholson quickly walked over, Gabrielle trailing him to congratulate Felo and meet his new bride, distracting Lucia from assessing her new home.

Upon hearing commotion in the dining area, Giuditta rushed out, embraced Lucia, and kissed each of her cheeks, the traditional Italian greeting. Lucia's ears ached, not only from the crude dialect but also from how loud Giuditta spoke. 'A peasant woman,' she thought. However, she was respectful and pleasant to her new mother-in-law and friends. Lucia was always cordial to new acquaintances. She especially liked Gabrielle and Douglas, who seemed to go out of their way to make her feel more comfortable in her new home. They did so more than anyone else. She also appreciated that Gabrielle spoke her language and translated what her husband and others were saying.

Finally, after the excitement ceased, Lucia could evaluate the hotel. Her eyes scanned the bar and dining area. The vulgar language and offensive behavior of men drinking alcohol and the way they carried on with women repulsed her. Some of the men were gambling. The hotel was not the type of establishment her sister and brother-in-law told her about. It was not the kind of place she envisioned from all the compliments her 'scoiattolo' (squirrel) brother-in-law, Giuseppe Seggiano, raved about. Lucia felt betrayed and wanted to leave immediately.

As Lucia's anger brewed, two town policemen entered the hotel as people introduced themselves to her. The officers wanted information about Matteo Fontana's beating. "Anyone here knows anything about what happened that night?" bellowed one of the policemen.

The police usually didn't bother too much with incidences in the Italian community. Gossip was circulating about the town regarding that brutal occurrence that brought them to Giuditta's hotel. The police decided to ask questions to get facts about the vicious manner by which the mob of men had beaten Fontana and mutilated his body. Even that thought made them sick to their stomachs, and they wondered how someone could do something like that to another man. "This is felonious assault! Attempted murder! We will treat any man harboring facts as an accomplice!" one policeman threatened as the men at the bar looked in different directions. "You went too far this time. We won't take this type of crap in this town!" The police knew about how some of the Italian immigrants in the cities were forming larger gangs, bringing with them the violent ways of their country. Everyone, frightened to death of Marco Gullo, never said a word.

Lucia was shocked that she would have to live in a place raided by the police. 'What kind of hell am I in?' she wondered; what type of place did that scoiattolo get me into?' She felt weak at the knees and asked her new husband to take her to their bedroom. Felo complied, picked up her luggage, and escorted his young bride to a room in the hotel. Alone in her room and teary-eyed, Lucia began putting paper on furniture before placing her personal items. Even though the room was spotless and Giuditta kept a clean hotel, Lucia was immaculately clean and didn't want to take chances.

Matteo Fontana sat on a plain wooden armchair in the center of his living room, his head tilted to the side, a black patch covering the socket of his missing eye. The stench of the air was putrid as his son was late in arriving home to change the chamber pot below where he sat. The result of his injuries was devastating and caused severe neurological damage to his spinal cord. Matteo Fontana never received any medical care. Matteo's son, Luca, converted the wooden armchair to a potty. He put a simple, large, round hole in the seat as Matteo could no longer control his bowel and bladder functions. As he now wore no pants or underwear, a blanket on his lap covered the grotesque deformity done to him.

In addition to being paralyzed in most of his body, the man who had committed such ungodly undertakings in his life now had some blurred vision in his remaining eye. Heavy scarring and indents from cuts and fractures appeared all over what no longer resembled a face but an ugly mask. He lost all his teeth in the beating, and the scarring to his lips, tongue, and throat made him mute. His only method of communication was mumbling while moving his fingers, as he couldn't move either of his arms.

Luca Fontana had to attend to his father even though he couldn't stand the stench of him. Out of repulsion, Luca never washed his father. He fed him mashed foods and liquids and changed his chamber pot only when he could. Luca quit school ever since the other boys started making jokes about him and his father's disfigurement. "Hey, Luca, is your father singing in the girl's choir?" Or, "Does your father sing soprano?" Those kids threw even worse insults his way. Quitting school made Luca change. He was now on a journey to becoming an angry young man filled with hatred. He began socializing with a criminal gang of younger men in East Liverpool. Luca needed money to get away from his father's stinking house. He started robbing storefronts at night and hijacking wagons and trucks with other young thugs.

After Rosa and her daughter, Allessia, slowly recovered, they lived together at Giuditta's hotel until they were strong enough to work and afford an apartment.

When Rosa felt able to travel the short distance, she returned to her home. Millie took her by horse-driven wagon to get some of Rosa and Alessia's personal things.

"Boy, it stinks in here!" Millie said as soon as she walked in. Rosa feared for her life as she remembered that awful night, so Millie held her steady and took her by her arm, escorting Rosa inside.

Millie ignored the monster sitting on his potty, but Rosa almost lost her mind when she saw him. "You rotten son of a bitch! Look what you did to me!" she screamed as loud as she could. "You crippled your daughter! I hope you rot in Hell for all eternity!" Rosa was out of control. Crying, she looked for a sharp object or something to hurt him. "Bastardo!" she yelled with a kitchen knife in her hand." Matteo farted, then began to have an uncontrolled bowel movement.

Millie grabbed the small knife from Rosa's hand. "You don't want to go to jail for killing the likes of him." Millie couldn't understand Italian that well. She learned some from Giuditta but couldn't make out what the angry woman had said; she only knew it sounded terrible, and Rosa wanted to kill him. "C'mon, Rosa, come outside in the fresh air. I'll get the rest." Millie escorted the hysterical woman outside. Then, Millie held her nose as she went back inside and took the remaining things with her other hand. She wouldn't look upon the wicked man, worrying she would be turned to stone if she did, just like in the Bible.

Alessia never returned to see her father. Matteo stayed in the stiff wooden armchair potty day after day, where he would be for the rest of his life. His only remaining ability was harboring the ghosts of his past who tormented him every passing second of every day for his evil deeds done over the years.

Chapter Twenty-Two

Wellsville, Ohio, 1911-1914
The World War Begins

On June 28, 1914, a Bosnian Serb named Gavrilo Princip assassinated Archduke Franz Ferdinand, heir to the throne of the Austro-Hungarian Empire, and his wife, Sophia, Dutchess of Hohenberg, as they drove through Sarajevo. Their deaths were blamed on Serbia, and as a result, Austria-Hungary declared war a month later. Russia supported Serbia, prompting a 'war of alliances' as France, Great Britain, and Germany entered the war. The Ottoman Empire joined the war late that same year. Horrendous fighting began confined to a series of trenches spanning from the English Channel to Switzerland, referred to as the Western Front. The geography of the Eastern Front was different but no less dreadful, with Bulgaria, Romania, Italy, the Ottomans, and Greece joining it. The Great War had begun, and newspapers worldwide filled readers in daily.

In June 1914, Douglas stood by the river alone. A breeze from the hills, cool and refreshing, flowed down and softly touched his face, allowing him to remember. He had just read an article in the East Liverpool newspaper describing how the completion of a chain of dams would raise the level of the Ohio River. That flowing body of water would forever cover the precious Indian rocks he collected as a child. Douglas chose to be alone that evening as he reflected on the days when he and

Peppina walked barefoot out in the low water, searching for stones with Indian markings as Rollo shook off the water from his fur, soaking them as they laughed from the refreshingly cool river water. He still had that collection of their rocks at home. They were sentimental memories he shared with no one else, not even his wife, so he chose not to display those tender emotions that day but to harbor them privately.

Gone were those days of laughing and having fun in the simplicity of children's play. Douglas was now a father and a pillar of society in the area. But when he recalled those uncomplicated times, they reminded him of his little friend. Douglas finally came to terms with the fact that Peppina had probably died in that fire. She would have contacted him if she had lived. Whether or not she was angry at her mother or Nicola for what they did, Peppina would have certainly gotten in touch with her old friend; that was for sure. Those thoughts saddened him and brought tears to his eyes as he reflected on those past times. The sweet aroma of jasmine rose from the foliage as the golden sun weakened and slowly set in the valley. It was time to go home to his wife and daughter, who was almost three years old. Gabrielle was expecting another child in five months. Douglas bent down and picked up a small, flat stone. He held it slanted, flung it into the river, and watched it skip across the top of the shallow flowing current six times, a perfect throw. "That one's for you, Peppina!" he whispered, misty-eyed but smiling tenderly.

Back in August 1911, Gabrielle had delivered a healthy baby girl. She knew that if she eventually gave birth to a boy, it would undoubtedly have to be named Douglas, not to disrupt that name's tradition. So, following tradition and her husband's influence, they named their first child Claire after Gabrielle's mother.

"He's a very protective father," Gabrielle told Giudetta laughingly as she explained why her husband, Douglas, forbade his infant daughter from leaving the house until he felt she was of a certain age. "Too protective, maybe. But he loves that child to death. Even when he's busy at work, he takes time off and drives home to see 'the apple of his eye' as he calls her. You must come over to see her! Please do?" Giuditta's former husband, Luigi, used the exact phrase, 'the apple of his eye,' when he referred to his daughter, Peppina. It brought back sentiments about Giuditta's first daughter, who was born many years ago.

Giudetta was anxious to see the newborn of the young woman she considered her daughter, Peppina, living through her. However, she didn't usually leave the hotel unless it was absolutely vital. Her hotel was her castle, and she had earned it. The only exceptions were few and far between. But for the man she thought of as a son, she would take the trolley to Ninth Street and walk along Riverside, which led to the Nicholson house. She obstinately refused Gabrielle's offer to send Douglas with the car. In autumn, Giuditta, dressed in her best attire with a wide-brimmed black feathered hat, a gift in hand, boarded the southbound trolly to see the baby Claire.

Andre and Claire Delisle came to Wellsville to help their daughter before the birth of their first grandchild. The Delisles were ecstatic when the baby was born and again to be reunited with Douglas and Martha Nicholson, who had become so endeared to them over the years. They remained for over two months and were present the day Guiditta visited. It was the first time they met Giuditta, and Claire was thrilled to speak her native language to this woman she had heard so much about. Giuditta and Claire made dinner, sharing recipes while everyone laughed at Giuditta's humor. It was a wonderful day and a memory that would last a lifetime.

Shortly after she arrived in 1911, word spread that Giuditta's daughter-in-law, Lucia, could read and write in Italian. People of the Italian immigrant community longed for someone who could fluently read the letters sent from their families in their native country and even write back to them. Lucia Buch attained popularity by providing that only form of communication for them.

At first, people walked over to Giuditta's hotel, bearing gifts of bread loaves, candies, homemade cookies, and other food-stuffs. Then they invited Lucia to their homes, primarily in the area extending from First to Third and down Commerce Street. In the process, Lucia learned many personal things about those families and gossip from around the community. However, Lucia kept all of the information she learned secretly. She never discussed what she knew, even with her husband, Felo. When-ever asked what she learned or knew about particular things, she answered in broken English, "I don't a know nothing." Lucia eventually learned just about everything going on in the town of Wellsville. That made her trustworthy, and she became a confidant of many. It also put her in many personal, some-times precarious situations.

Francesco Trieste became good friends with Giuditta and the Buch family. Together with Douglas and Gabrielle, they enjoyed hearing about his exploits. Francesco was an adventur-er. As a younger man, he had traveled to various parts of Italy seeking employment and the possibility of fortune for his wife, Colomba, and his family. Douglas especially enjoyed hearing about Francesco's exploits in Africa, 'the dark continent' as it was known at that time. "Italy was one of the European coun-tries colonizing Africa beginning in 1890," Francesco had ex-plained. "I took a job aboard a steamship that sailed to Africa to earn money for my family," as everyone sat interested. "From the port, we ventured into Eritrea, north of Ethiopia, and then progressed south and inland over the following months." As Francesco told his tales, he kept everyone in suspense with ex-aggerated encounters with thieves and murderers, fighting them off with pistols and rifles.

The natives proved to be less harmful than the mixtures of Arabs from the north and white fortune hunters. An Italian friend had offered Francesco a partnership in a rubber plantation. Ex-citedly, he traveled back to Italy to bring his wife, Colomba, and daughter, Nina, the only child they had at the time. Colom-ba refused to go to Africa, where there were dangerous native tribes that ate people, as she had heard. And she didn't want to bring her daughter or raise a family in such a dirty place. What Colomba didn't tell her husband was that she had his child in her womb at the time.

In the summer of 1911, nudged by his ever-persevering wife, Gabrielle, Douglas Nicholson found a good job for Francesco across the river at a shop in one of the newer industrial areas that had begun developing just six years earlier. It would be a trolley ride away with the system now running over the Newell Bridge. Francesco had worked at the nearby mill for one month and quit. Dirty laborers weren't allowed to ride on the trolleys; they had to walk. Luckily, Francesco only had a short walk from the mill to Guiditta's hotel. They gave lower-level jobs to the Italians who couldn't understand English. Francesco had so much dirt and soot covering him that he could hardly breathe on his short walk back.

Francesco began searching for an affordable home for himself and his family. He found one on Third Street next to the Metropole Hotel. As soon as Francesco received the good news, he sent a transatlantic telegraph message to his wife in Italy.

Francesco Trieste's family arrived in Wellsville at the end of the first week of October 1911. They had traveled with a group of others from near her village aboard the vessel 'Taormina' and, after passing the Statue of Liberty, docked in New York City earlier in October. Once in New York, they reunited with Francesco, who traveled there to meet them. From New York, they went to Pittsburgh and then to Wellsville. Colomba held one-year-old Louise tightly in her arms. Nina guided her sister and brother, all holding hands, following their mother as Francesco took care of the luggage and personal items.

In early 1912, Lucia announced that she was pregnant. Lucia grew more and more discontent about living in a place where men drank and spoke vulgarities. Observing the bar in the evening, she heard men making lewd remarks to women, some of whom she believed to be prostitutes. "I won't bring up my child in such a place," Lucia declared one evening when Felo returned from work. Arguments broke out between her and her husband and persisted, but they never resolved them.

"When we save enough money, we'll leave, not before!" Felo quietly commanded. Felo had developed into a personable young man and was respected by everyone he met. He was even-tempered and never raised his voice but was firm in his convictions. Although Lucia didn't like Felo confining her to such a place, she held in her hostility out of respect for her husband. However, the young woman's mind began formulating a plan.

During the summer of 1912, the newspaper published a photo of Giuditta's son, John, with his friends at the river bank in Congo, West Virginia, directly across from Wellsville. It was titled 'Good Old Summer Swim in the Ohio.' The ferry boat Mr. Johnson of Congo operated was in the picture's background.

The day after the excitement of John's photo in the newspaper, Lucia gave birth to a baby daughter. She named the child Giulia after her mother-in-law, according to Italian tradition. It was also the name of Lucia's grandmother. She used the Italian spelling of the name Giulia, not the dialect Giuditta.

Lucia was relentless in her bickering with Felo about wanting to leave the hotel. She spent her time caring for her baby, mostly remaining in her room. Then, one day, she took baby Giulia and left the hotel and Felo to stay with a friend and her family from Sicily. Felo had no other option but to leave the hotel and rent an apartment nearby for his wife and baby. Giuditta was furious that this 'primadonna' didn't like her hotel. She couldn't understand that Lucia had social graces and was brought up by a priest; the things that took place at her hotel were sacrilegious.

Douglas Nicholson used his influence to get Felo a job as a bookkeeper for the Pennsylvania Railroad later that year. Not realizing he was of Italian descent, he became the first Italian-American white-collar worker in that railroad's division. Felo could then afford to rent a home located on Broadway and furnish it as well. It became Lucia's pride and joy.

Felo now had an excellent job and could buy Lucia the furniture she desired. They purchased a large wooden bed, armoire, and mirrored dresser for the bedroom on the second floor. A three-piece wooden table, buffet, and glass-door china closet adorned their dining Room. The living room was comfortable, with a hardwood rocking chair for Felo and a matching wood smoking stand to the side of it. There was a gramophone with a cylinder cone, the predecessor of electric record players, to play music. To the side of the gramophone was a fruitwood-framed couch with pleated dark red velvet material. A matching loveseat graced another wall of that room. Lucia was now in her glory, keeping her new home clean and spotless. She was out of the hotel and felt comfortable entertaining guests. It was a short period of vanity on her part and a reminder of her lifestyle in Italy, nothing a trip to the Catholic confessional couldn't cure.

In 1913, Francesco and Colomba Trieste welcomed another beautiful baby girl, Maria. Their family was growing closer to the Buch family. Even in the busy Trieste household, Colomba always sent one of her older girls over to help Lucia with her baby, Giulia, whenever she needed a helping hand. Lucia reciprocated by watching Colomba's children whenever necessary.

Felo's new excellent job also came with benefits. He now had a railway pass for him and his wife to travel free. Felo used it for many sporting events in other cities besides Pittsburgh and Cleveland. Before he received his pass, Felo had to pay to travel to sports events and other places he loved, like when he went to see Buffalo Bill's Wild West Show seven years before. Felo took his wife to New York, but Lucia's main interest was to use her free pass to visit her sister and shop in Pittsburgh. There, she could buy the Italian delicacies she cherished, only found in cities.

As Douglas walked back home at that sundown on June 22, 1914, he left his childhood memories at the riverbank only to retrieve them at a later time when such recollections echoed in his mind.

Gabrielle delivered her second daughter in November 1914. "You're going to have to work harder if you want a boy," Gabrielle whispered to her husband, struggling to display her humor as Douglas held his new daughter. Gabrielle knew her husband wanted a boy; all men did, she thought.

"She's beautiful, honey," the smiling, proud father replied. "I love my girls. I'll take another anytime, "But I will work harder anyway Gab!" he laughed.

Gabrielle and Douglas named their new child Martha after Douglas's mother. Andre and Claire Delisle traveled again from Cincinnati to meet their new granddaughter. In time, Giuditta traveled the short distance by trolley to see the baby, somehow feeling like they were her grandchildren. As everyone reunited, they feasted and laughed and built another lifelong memory.

Chapter Twenty-Three

Wellsville, Ohio, 1915-1917
The Foreign War Lures America

In the snows of winter, trolley cars used snow sweepers in front. The clearing devices were usually made of circular stiff bristol brushes around three or four feet in diameter and rotated by a motor to blow the snow into the air, where it was whisked away, clearing the tracks. The brushes were attached to both ends of the trolly for operation in either direction. Some trolleys also kept hand shovels aboard in case of severe blizzards. People would pitch in to help clear the tracks of accumulated snow in those exceptional situations. Plows were less popular because they were noisy when they touched the rails and incompetent if they didn't.

Millie Brown left the Buch Hotel on a cold January evening in 1915. She walked along the snow-covered sidewalk toward Lisbon Street. Millie didn't usually like to walk down by the Stevenson Plant, where workers hung outside, and drifters lingered behind the Third Street Station after getting off trains. She preferred the longer alternate route in the early darkness of winter months. Millie heard muffled footsteps on the snow behind her as she stepped along. As she increased the speed of her steps, trying not to slip, the ones behind her hastened, longer strides and heavy, like those of a man. Knowing she couldn't outpace the person behind her, Millie stopped, almost slipping on the snow, ready to face her follower, her arm ready to swing the heavy shopping bag filled with groceries she carried. She turned abruptly, ready to clobber whoever meant her harm, only to stop as she recognized a somewhat familiar person.

"Are you Luke?" she used the English version of Luca Fontana's first name.

"Yeah," Luke said gruffly. He had changed since the last time Millie saw the boy after bringing his mother and sister to the hotel after Matteo beat them. Luke Fontana had grown taller, and his body had filled out and had become more muscular. Now 20, Luke was a man. "I gotta talk to ya," again, speaking bluntly, his dark eyes squinting. Even his voice had changed; it was now deeper and throaty. His overall appearance gave Millie a chill; she was scared. "Don't worry, I ain't gonna hurt ya." Even the way he spoke was frightening. He talked like a tough guy.

"What you want from me?"

"I gotta propa-sition for ya," Luke said, using his poor pronunciation. That scared Millie even more. "I want ya to watch my fadder," Luke said.

"Well, Mr. Luke," as Millie addressed him, frightened, "I can't do that. I got a job and a family." Her eyes widened, "Surely you can get someone else?"

"No! Gotta be you!" Millie could see that Luke was getting angry. "You know 'bout that herb stuff. People call ya a healer of some type. Gotta be you!" he demanded now, not asking anymore.

"Well, I can't."

"Don't sass me, nigger! You'll do it 'cause I said so, and I'll pay you good! You be at his house in two days on Thursday at 10 AM, or else!" Millie ignored Luke, who had stopped walking but was still watching her as she continued home.

Millie never wanted to go to that man's house after what he did to his wife and daughter. "No, sir! I want no part of him," she whispered to herself as she walked, "I don't know what I'm gonna do, but I ain't gonna go over there! No, sir, no way!"

Then Millie realized she shouldn't speak to her husband about what happened. "Hector, he'll get riled up and go over there. No, sir, I can't let him do that. He'll get himself beat up all over again. No, sir, I can't do that. The man's 57 years old now; He's too old!" Millie kept whispering to herself as she struggled with the problem. "Mr. Douglas! That's who I'll talk to! Yes, sir, Mr. Douglas can help me. I'll pay him officially like. Yes, sir, Mr. Douglas is an answer to my prayers. Thank you, Jesus! Mr. Douglas is the answer. I best not say anything to Hector." Millie composed herself. Hector always knew when she was upset and wasn't getting him involved. Millie waited until she stopped huffing and puffing. When Millie had calmed herself completely, she stomped the snow from her boots and opened the door as if nothing had happened.

Luke Fontana had traveled with the young gang of hoods in East Liverpool to do their dirty work in the cities. There were far more opportunities among the crowds of people and an abundance of stores to rob. They began in Youngstown and worked there for a while but never lived there; it was wise never to live where you did robberies. The group always traveled home at night. Luke managed to find a woman desperate for money to clean his father's chamber pot and feed him, but that immigrant woman was moving. He wanted no part of his father or his stinking house. Luke lived with a girlfriend who was slightly older than him in Wellsville.

As things progressed, Luke got involved with a more prominent Sicilian gang in Cleveland and left the small-time one. The young man was impressed with how organized the group was. They referred to themselves as a family. No member could speak face-to-face with the boss; they had to go through his subordinates. That way, the police could never pin anything directly on the head of the family. Luke observed them closely while doing small jobs for them. One of the lower-ranking leaders took a liking to Luke and gave him larger jobs, but scrutinizing him keenly. This gang had only professionals working for them. They knew the response time of the police to a burglary scene and, from experience, developed elaborate backup plans in case something went wrong, such as problems with a getaway car, for example. They used beat-up Model Ts and always had extras on reserve. Luke was amazed at how much jewelry, fur coats, and other valuable things they could steal in one night. And this gang worked all over the city doing other more profitable things like gambling and prostitution. Luke had already killed another human being, so whenever he received an order to 'knock off' someone, as they called it, he didn't hesitate. In early 1915, they asked Luke to join them. Although they had other ethnicities working for them, you had to be a Sicilian to become a member. Luke was all in; he just needed to find someone to care for his father. Luke couldn't care less about his father. But his new family abided by a Sicilian code of honor, which came first among old-world Sicilians. Luke had to find someone to care for his father and adhere to that Sicilian tradition, or his boss would view it as disrespectful. However, the immigrant woman he had hired couldn't always go there.

One day, that woman left Matteo for three days without food. When Luke stepped into the fowl-smelling house, his father's chamber pot was overflowing and spilling to the ground, causing even more stench. His father struggled to mutter, saliva dripping from his mouth. He tried to bang his hand but couldn't. He was only able to tap his fingers of one hand on the wooden armrest. Matteo's throat made animal-like shrills from hunger.

"Shut up, you bastard!" Luke shouted at his father, "Or I won't feed you at all!" He looked around the kitchen but couldn't find anything to feed him. 'That bitch didn't even leave any food around.' Luke resented the infringement of time this duty put on him, and he dreaded seeing the grotesque creature that was once his father. Luke walked outside and picked a bag of garbage from the next-door neighbor's metal trash can. They were poor immigrants, so whatever they threw out was nothing more than scraps of food the neighborhood dogs didn't even want. While quickly mixing the garbage in a large bowl until it was mush, he noticed a pitcher of stale water sitting on the table, invaded by roaches and other insects. He added some to the bowl of slop. After stirring it, Luke grabbed a large spoon and fed his father. The smell was atrocious.

"Ugh! Ugh!" Matteo grunted and refused it at first, keeping his lips tightly closed; his neck hung in that hideous way it would remain for the rest of his life.

"It's this, or you ain't eatin nothin at all, ole man!" Matteo was so hungry he began eating. As he did, he started gulping the mashed garbage like an infant sucking on its mother's breast. Then he started retching from devouring his meal too fast. Gurgling, his one remaining eye looked at Luke angrily. "I don't care if you choke to death!" Hearing his own remark fostered an idea. "Not today. I'll wait," he whispered. Then he thought of that black woman who took care of his mother and sister with her bag of medicinal tricks. 'Maybe I won't need her after all.'

On the day and time Millie was supposed to be at the Fontana house, Douglas showed up at the door instead. Luke Fontana seemed bewildered at first, then grew angry. "Where's the black woman?"

Douglas looked disgusted at the sight of what he used to think was a nice, respectful boy. Now, he resembled one of the gangsters he had read about, and Douglas effortlessly pushed Luke aside. Luke might have gotten bigger and heftier, but Douglas's strapping and powerful body towered over Luke. Once inside, he immediately smelled the putrid odor. It smelled worse than an animal lying dead for weeks. Douglas surveyed the place. The interior of the house was filthy. Spilled food spread all over the floors. Cockroaches crawled everywhere, even all over Matteo's head, which appeared to be worse than that of Frankenstein, the book by Mary Shelley he had read years before. "Do you live here like this?" he asked Luke.

"Of course not. I got a nice place somewheres else." Luke didn't want to give Douglas too much information.

"What happened to you? You used to be a good kid." Douglas stood looking baffled. "When was the last time you saw your mother and sister?"

"None of yeh business, Dr. Freud!" Seeing Douglas's surprised expression that someone like Luke would even know about a brilliant psychoanalyst like Sigmund Freud, Luke said, "Yeah! I got smarts, too. I hear things! You ain't the only one with brains. As for my mutter and sister, I'll take care of them. Don't you worry!"

Douglas, disgusted, shook his head. "Stay away from Millie!"

"What you gonna do?"

Douglas walked right up to Luke's face. Luke was intimidated by Douglas, though he didn't show it. Everyone in town had heard of Douglas's boxing achievements. "I'll tell you what I'm 'gonna do' you punk," imitating Luke's poor speech, "I'm going to set hell on you. I'll use the full power of the courts to track you down and bring you in, even if I have to hire the Pinkertons!" His association with John Rose came to mind. Douglas's face was only inches from Luke's as he continued, "You would think someone like you would want to stay in good grace with me because when you get arrested, no other lawyer will want to represent you." Douglas thought, 'Not that I would represent a piece of shit like this.' "Your ass will just stay in jail and rot, I guess! Yeah, you got smarts! Your smarts are going to get you killed!"

"Okay, okay! I'll stay aways from 'er . I'll find somebody else!" Luke was biting his lip in anger. 'This bastard don't know I got connections in the city now,' he thought, 'and I got no use for the black woman no more anyway.'

Douglas pushed him aside and walked out the door. "You better, Luca," Douglas used his Italian name.

"I don't need her anyway," whispered Luke as he watched Douglas leave. Then he turned back to where his father sat on his hardwood potty. Luke's eyes seethed with murder as he crept up on Matteo slowly. Matteo glanced at his son with his one eye. He knew that expression well and bore it often in those times before he slaughtered someone. Matteo broke his wind and began to clear his bowels as he waited.

The day after Millie's encounter with Luke, she took the trolley to Douglas's office. It was the first time she was there. Douglas's private secretary, Mary, came to the waiting room and told Millie, "Mr. Nicholson is meeting with clients. Would you like to make an appointment?"

"No, ma'am. I'll wait. Tell Mr. Douglas that Millie is here. I'll wait as long as it takes."

"Okay." The secretary knocked on the conference door before she opened it. Peeping inside, she said, "Mr. Nicholson, there's a Millie here to see you?"

"Millie? Millie Brown? A black woman?"

"Yes, Douglas."

"Please put her in my office." He turned to his clients, "Gentlemen, how about I send out for lunch? I think it's about time we take a break." Douglas headed to his office, where he saw Millie Brown seated across from his desk. "Millie! Is everything okay?" Douglas was worried that something terrible had happened at the hotel.

"Oh! Mr. Douglas! It's kind of you to see me. Yes, I'm afraid I do got a personal problem." Then Millie looked around the room and said, "Nice office you got here, Mr. Douglas." As Douglas smiled at her, she explained what had occurred between her and Luke Fontana as Douglas listened attentively. Millie held out cash in her hand. "Whatever it takes, Mr. Douglas! I don't want nothing to do with that man! Please, Mr. Douglas."

Finally, Douglas rose. "Put your money away, Millie. You're a friend. Don't worry about anything. I'll take care of this myself."

Millie already felt relieved by the tone of Douglas's voice and his comforting words. "Thank you, Mr. Douglas. Now, you be careful, Mr. Douglas. Something not right with that guy."

"Don't worry, Millie. You go back to the hotel. Everything will be alright. I always thought Luke was a good kid, the opposite of his father. But, I guess the apple doesn't fall far from the tree."

"No more, Mr. Douglas. He's rotten to the core," Millie said as she left the door. "Thank you, Mr. Douglas."

Two days later, on Thursday, Douglas phoned the hotel and told Millie she no longer had to worry. Luke Fontana wouldn't bother her anymore.

A week later, 62-year-old Douglas Sr. stood before his family at dinner. "I've decided," he hesitated, "that I will be retiring from the railroad." Douglas Jr. was in shock. He couldn't remember a time when his father didn't work for the railroad. A self-made man, Douglas Sr., in the true pioneer tradition, had worked his way up the ladder, which made his son proud.

Douglas stood erect, holding his wine glass up. He said, "I propose a toast to the railroad's greatest employee and the best father there ever was!" Then he embraced his father. Douglas Sr. appeared touched and showed it.

"Here, here!" declared Andre Delisle, speaking while he rose to stand. He and his wife, Claire, had been invited to stay for Christmas after their granddaughter was born in November. Martha started to cheer, and Claire and Gabrielle joined her from where they sat. Gabrielle got up and trotted over to where Douglas Sr. was standing, stood on her tiptoes, and kissed her father-in-law on his cheek.

"What will you do with all your time now, Dad?" asked Douglas.

"Oh, I have plenty of things for him to do," announced Martha. Everyone, now seated, laughed. Douglas's mother, Martha, was still a pretty woman at 55. Her dark blond hair only hinted at greying, and she still maintained her small-framed body.

"I think maybe sometime in the future, we'll take a riverboat to Cincinnati to visit some dear friends who live there now that we have the time to travel leisurely." Douglas Sr. smiled.

"A wonderful idea," Clair and Andre shouted almost simultaneously.

Douglas and Gabrielle threw Douglas Sr. a grand party at their home on Riverside Avenue to celebrate the event of his retirement.

In August of that same year, Lucia Buch delivered her second daughter. Felo and Lucia named the baby Eleanora after Lucia's mother. Felo already had the extra room upstairs in their house prepared for the new baby. Colombo Trieste sent one of her older daughters to help Lucia whenever possible. Nina was already 14 years old, and Modesta, who was called Maude ever since going to school, was 12. Either one who wasn't busy with homework or helping their younger sisters went over.

Francesco Trieste worked steadily at the plant across the river in West Virginia. When Colomba heard the whistle blow from the other side of the Ohio River, she knew it was time to prepare the evening meal. All the daughters, except Maria, pitched in to help. Seven-year-old Anthony did chores around the house. He always swept outside the door to the building after he heard the whistle so he could be outside to greet his father.

Later in the year, the newspaper had a small article on page two. It described an immigrant plant laborer in Wellsville, identified as Marco Gullo, found shot to death. Allegedly a murder, the bullets hit the man's lower abdomen and groin area, and he bled to death. Police found no motive in the shooting, though echoes of gossip spread that Luke Fontana might have had something to do with it.

Toward the end of 1915, Douglas read an article in Collier's magazine. It was entitled The Plattsburg Idea and written by Richard Harding Davis. The article encouraged the spread of voluntary training camps, of which Davis was a graduate of one. The camps were becoming one with elites preparing to become officers to build America's military and to lead men in the war the United States could undoubtedly become a part of. Many men from prominent families attended, encouraging the idea of appointing more officers to lead an eventual Army of the United States, whose numbers had been significantly low for years. America was now committed to building large armed forces, especially for the Navy and Army, and an air wing. They needed experienced men Douglas's age to train for senior officer positions, as very few existed then. Douglas had been reading the continuing news of the war daily. When the RMS Lusitania was sunk by a German U-boat and over one hundred Americans perished, many viewed the Germans as the aggressors. Regardless of their justifiability, Douglas realized the Germans crossed the line in the sand, and his country would enter the war. After many conversations and debates with Gabrielle, Douglas planned to attend the officer's training school.

In October 1916, Douglas, now a second lieutenant in reserve, was offered a partnership with a prominent law firm in neighboring East Liverpool, Ohio. Douglas accepted the offer because it was a good and reputable establishment.

"If America eventually enters the war, we would have an income to keep the law office open while I'm away. It's an excellent opportunity, and the location in Wellsville would become a branch office." He stopped speaking once he observed his wife's lifeless expression. "What is it, Gab?"

"It's the first time I actually envisioned America going to war. When you said those words, I realized you would have to go overseas."

"Gab, I'm only preparing in the event of that likelihood. This way, my employees could keep their jobs. And you and the children would also receive an income while I'm away—if I have to go." 'And in case of my demise,' he thought. Of course, he would never tell her that. Douglas had told Gab that he would be on light duty to spare her the burden of worrying.

Tragedy struck later that same month as the Nicholson family lost James, the father of Douglas Sr. The 84-year-old man passed away in his sleep while fighting a severe case of pneumonia. Douglas would use his new Packard for this trip. He had traded in his older automobile earlier in the year. Gabrielle was now driving occasionally, and Douglas wanted to leave his wife with a newer, safer car if he had to go overseas. Even the thought of that gave him a chill. The reality of war never really hit him before he began making preparations.

Following the bad news, the Nicholsons left for Beaver, Pennsylvania, early in the morning. Douglas drove, and his father sat in the front passenger seat. Gabrielle held tightly to Martha, who was almost two, while her mother-in-law's arm held her five-year-old granddaughter, Claire. They arrived in Beaver in a much shorter time than the trolley and an even much faster time than a horse-drawn carriage, a fact that he reminded his father about as he sat beside him.

After they entered the home of Douglas's brother, Robert, Douglas's family reunited. Robert's wife, Sarah, had grown older, and her daughters Flora and Roberta were now married with children. James lay in a casket filled with ice, an Episcopalian minister in attendance. Gabrielle reintroduced herself to the family she had last seen at her post-wedding party in Wellsville. Then, she and Martha took her children and sat on the arranged seats in the large room. Douglas Sr. took his son by the arm and led him to a secluded spot in the back. "I'd like to have a few words with you," he said as they walked together.

"Am I in trouble, Dad?" Douglas used slight humor to relieve his father's grief, which clearly showed on his face.

"No, son, you're not." Douglas Sr. smiled back, remembering when he had to speak to his son over a reprimand. "Times like this make us," Douglas Sr. hesitated, "I don't know the right word. I guess it's appreciate what we have while we're alive." He bowed his head. "I'm worried about you, Son."

"The war, Dad?"

"Yes, Douglas, the war. I'm proud of what you're doing, but America will enter. You know that, don't you?"

"Yes, Dad, I do. I'm beginning to think we'll enter it."

"Of course you do. You're an intelligent young man. I'd be doing the same thing if I were younger. A Nicholson fought in every war America was in since the American Revolution, except for me. I was too young for the War Between the States and too old for the Spanish War." Douglas Sr. pointed, "Your grandfather, lying up there, fought in what is now called the Civil War." Douglas Sr. smiled, remembering, "I packed up my things and went to join my father," he chuckled, "got only a few miles before your grandmother came riding after me on horseback. She was some woman. I wish you could have gotten to know her. She did the work of a man and could ride like the wind; a true pioneer woman if there ever was one." Realizing he got sidetracked, Douglas Sr. continued, "The thing is, son, you're going to see things in battle that you can't even comprehend. My dad told me stories, horrible stories about the atrocities of wartime. 'Man's inhumanity to man,' he used to say. I don't know where he heard that."

"I think it's from poems from the old country, Dad."

Douglas Sr. looked admiringly at his son, "You see. You're educated, Douglas. I grew up when this town was coming into shape after the riverboats began stopping here to port. First, they built the wharves down on Riverside by seventh and eighth, and then they worked together with the old railroad center up on Broadway. That's where they had the first turntable. Then they began making riverboats in town." Nodding to his father's corpse, he continued, "He was born in the first settlement in town back in 1832 when people were still living in tents and cold wood cabins. Some of them were dilapidated," Douglas Sr. chuckled again, "They were just like slums. My dad said it was almost like war. It was hard living, hunting for food, fighting stray or drunk Indians occasionally; they had to cross the river to escape them sometimes. It was a cruel place at first. 'Man's inhumanity to man' existed here as well. It's hard building a town from scratch. There were no doctors at first until some veterinarians served as human physicians. My dad told me stories about people being hungry in that filthy, disease-infested place. Finally, ministers came and brought God's words and his peace." Douglas Sr. stopped speaking for a few seconds and turned to face his son, "When the time comes, just be careful over there, okay? Keep your head down, and don't try to be a hero."

"I will, Dad, I promise. We're building a strong Army. We'll be prepared, but I'll keep a keen eye open."

"Okay, son, Okay."

America declared war in April 1917. On May 16, 1917, the United States Army promoted 35-year-old Douglas Nicholson to the rank of first lieutenant. Douglas, a highly regarded officer, was selected among 179 other men to leave for Europe as part of General John J Pershing's advance party. He had to report in New York City by May 28.

Gabrielle hid her hysteria about her husband leaving for war. She knew nothing she could say or do would change his mind. When Douglas said the words, "The countries of our family's ancestors are at stake," Gabrielle understood. But like so many other wives and girlfriends, she didn't want her husband to be in a war so far away. 'A positive mind,' she thought, 'I must keep a positive mind if I'm going to survive.' Then tears poured from her eyes, 'I don't even know what to pack for him.'

Martha related to her daughter-in-law's grief; she felt the same way. When she was alone with Gabrielle, she told her, "We'll get through this together, sweetheart. You're not alone. You're a big part of our family," Then they embraced.

Douglas went through his things, selecting only essential items he might need. He admired the selection of river stones he and Peppina had collected so many years before. He put the jars aside, thinking they should be in a museum someday. While going through other personal items, Douglas came upon the large sterling silver crucifix Peppina gave him on his 11th birthday. Smiling, he remembered the day well. "It will always help and protect you," Douglas recalled her putting it around his neck and locking the clasp. He put his hands on his neck, remembering the feel of her touch. "And it will remind you never to be afraid of anything ever again," she said before she kissed him on his cheek and giggled. His sentiments surfaced. Douglas hadn't worn the cross for years as it drew upon too many memories. "If ever I needed this, I most certainly do now," he placed the crucifix on his neck, securing the clasp.

"I want you to be a good little girl for mommy, sweetheart," Douglas whispered to his daughter Claire. "You're almost six; a big girl now." Douglas had both his daughters in his lap. When he whispered the same sentiments to Martha, the two-year-old just played with his nose. He kissed them both and held them tightly. Gabrielle was watching them through the small opening of the door ajar. Tears flooded her eyes as she watched her husband with their daughters. Throughout that last week, he spoke to them and subtly explained his departure, hugging them and softly talking to 'his girls.'

Later that evening, Gabrielle showed Douglas one of his photos in uniform and another in his civilian suit with his daughters. "These are the pictures I plan to show the girls at least five times daily." Gabrielle forced a smile. "They won't forget their daddy, not for a minute."

Douglas stood in uniform at the Third Street Station without fanfare. His parents, Gabrielle and his daughters, accompanied him. Douglas carried Martha to the train station, holding hands with Claire. He had just finished hugging them both and finally let them down to be with their mother. Gabrielle felt so proud of Douglas but so afraid. However, she held in her emotions and presented a brave appearance, though hysterical inside.

After the locomotive blasted its loud whistle, they noticed Giuditta and Millie running in their direction. Douglas had already embraced his parents and Gabrielle and their daughters repeatedly. Then, after both Giuditta and Millie finished huffing and puffing from running, they hugged Douglas at the same time, almost harmonizing, "You be careful over there, Mr. Douglas!" Millie told him she would pray for him every day. Felo ran down from his office to shake hands with Douglas.

Gabrielle followed her husband to the passenger car, his gear already packed onboard by Felo. "I'll be back in no time!" Douglas declared as Gabrielle remained hugging him and trying to smile.

Finally, as the mighty locomotive tooted its final departure warning, Gabrielle whispered into his ear, "You come back to me, Douglas!" As the train slowly began moving, Gabrielle followed it, her hand throwing kisses at her husband until she could no longer see his face. Douglas Nicholson II was off to war over there.

Chapter Twenty-Four

France and Belgium 1917
The War

After America entered the Great World War in 1917, John J. Pershing became the Commander of the American Expeditionary Force on the Western Front. Pershing established an advance party of 180 American men consisting of officers and non-commissioned officers to train troops and learn tactics from American Allies who had been fighting the war since 1914. They departed for Europe in May of 1917.

"This way, sir!" the sergeant spoke in a cockney English accent. Lieutenant Douglas Nicholson followed behind the short, stocky man walking through the maze of trenches on the Western Front; wooden planks clunked and moved under their feet, spouting mud and water in places. "Aye, sir, you're doing fine. Not much longer. Watch yeh feet, sir, so's that ya don't slip. Many a man sprained or broke thar bloody ankles falling between them, sir." Sergeant Walter Clark tightly held his Lee Enfield rifle as he guided his superior officer. They passed other soldiers with drawn faces and eyes petrified. Unshaven and unkempt, they clung to their rifles, all bearing terror-stricken looks and distress. Readied with straightened bodies as they stood behind the piled sand-filled bags for protection. Wooden beams kept the woven canvas bags supported and, in places, strands of barbed wire strung atop them.

"Keep yeh head down, sir!" Then, the two men felt a massive tremor shaking the wood-planked earth under their feet. It rattled Douglas so much that his head ached as if a bolt of lightning hit him. The trench wobbled and swayed, spewing dust and dirt covering them and all the nearby soldiers. Shrapnel from the explosion overhead pierced one man's helmet, and it flew off his head, breaking the strap that held it on. He instinctively stood erect, blood sprouting from large holes that soaked his hair, and the soldier marched like an electrified man for several seconds before falling over. Instantaneously following the havoc came a short whistling and then the blasting noise of the cannon that fired it, making Douglas notice that the damage had arrived before the sound, allowing for no warning. "No worries, sir! Missed most of us!" Sergeant Clark said, his face covered with dirt and smut.

Douglas realized his face must look the same as he followed behind his subordinate on his way to see the regimental commander, Colonel Reginald Hughes. Douglas had left New York Harbor on May 28, 1917, and arrived in Liverpool, England, on June 8. As part of the advance force of Americans, his particular job was to learn as much as he could about the war, leadership, and military tactics to be ready to lead American forces when they arrived. The best way to do that was from the soldiers fighting for the last three years. He was assigned to the British troops to learn to lead a platoon or, eventually, a company, as the British forces were beginning to dwindle and badly needed replacement officers.

The head of the American expeditionary forces, General John J. Pershing, was adamant that he didn't want his men to fight under the ranks of his allies permanently, but this was only a temporary measure. He knew his officers weren't ready to lead soldiers into battle. So, he agreed to allow some of his officers from the advance group to study the tactics of the more experienced British and French until American forces had landed and formed. Some Americans had already volunteered to fight under the Allies before 1917. More Americans were flying in

British flying services than the famed Lafayette Escadrille of United States pilots in the French Air Service.

Less than two weeks after he arrived in England, Douglas was on the Western Front, walking along the trenches with Sergeant Walter Clark. "Keep yeh head down, sir! You're a large man, sir. Ya must remember that!" Clark stopped his advance to turn to Douglas, "No offense intended, sir, but there are snipers out there always." Clark wiped his face with the cuff of his uniform jacket, "The blimey Huns just luv to kill officers, I'm afraid, sir." The sergeant went back to leading Douglas to headquarters.

The first thing Douglas perceived was the horrendous odor of mud mixed with rotting, mutilated human bodies and lingering tear gas. Those things overpowered the other causes of the overwhelming stench of the Western Front, like open latrines and unbathed men, some of whom soiled themselves from fear. He recalled Matteo Fontana's house, but this was far worse. He never even imagined so many human remains piled in what they referred to as 'No Man's Land,' the area between the Allied trenches and those of the enemy. It looked like a surreal human junkyard. Some figures seemed almost comical in the frozen positions where they died. Broken vehicles, tires, and other equipment were mixed in with the carnage. A few puny trees and bushes survived as a solemn testimony of the war.

"Err, we are, sir! Just up ahead!" Sergeant Clark stopped and pointed. "I'll be ya batman, sir, take care of yeh things and the like—arranged by the colonel himself, sir, it was. I'll wait inside the doorway to escort ya back to yeh quarters when yeh ready, sir." The sergeant saluted Douglas one last time. With mud and soot on his face and his eyes widened, Sergeant Clark appeared like a raccoon, his nose wiggling, shifting the whiskers of his mustache as he spoke. Douglas returned a salute to the sergeant and then walked inside the building.

The regimental command headquarters was behind lines in a building dug much deeper than the trenches. In addition to the wood-planked floors, the walls and ceiling were of the same material. Lights held by wire hung from above, though the rooms still appeared dinghy, eerie-like. Douglas walked up to the first senior officer he saw. "First Lieutenant Douglas Nicholson, sir!" Douglas gave his American military salute. "Reporting for duty."

"At ease, Lieutenant."

"I'm here to see Colonel Reginald Hughes. Are you he, sir?"

"No Lieutenant, I am not. I am Lieutenant Colonel Fergus Bastings." Bastings was average-sized and well-built for a man who appeared to be in his early fifties. Smiling slightly, he said, "I see you haven't got your British officer ranks in order yet. No worries, Lieutenant. You will in time." He pointed to a seated officer at a table speaking on a field phone, "The Colonel is over there; I'll take you to him." Lieutenant Colonel Bastings waited for his senior officer to finish his call before making introductions. "This is the American officer we've been expecting, First Lieutenant Douglas Nic. . ." he couldn't remember the surname.

Douglas stood erect, coming to full attention. "First Lieutenant Douglas Nicholson, sir!"

"At ease, at ease, Lieutenant." Colonel Reginald Hughes struck Douglas as low-keyed, the type of senior officer who wasn't looking for fanfare, only results. He sported a thin grey mustache and stood at an equal height as Douglas but was very thin and appeared slightly older than his subordinate, Bastings. "Good to meet you, Douglas," he said, using his first name while extending his arm for a handshake. "Jolly good!" Observing Douglas closely, he told him, "Have a seat," motioning to a chair at his table. "Join us, Fergus."

After they were seated, Colonel Hughes, looking directly at Douglas, declared, "Maybe you Americans will bring us some luck," smiling, he added, "After all, you brought us Coca-Cola!" he laughed at his joke, as did Fergus Bastings, so Douglas joined in laughing also. Colonel Hughes scribbled something in writing, and while handing it to Bastings, he told Douglas, "I'm assigning you to Captain Silas Williams, a fine officer, jolly good indeed. He'll give you a complete orientation, explain the ropes to you, so to speak. The captain will show you your quarters, and you'll work alongside him.

Before Douglas parted, Colonel Hughes looked at Douglas with a somewhat cynical smile and said, "I'll see you at the briefings, Lieutenant." Before he finished speaking, the whole building shook. Dust and dirt appeared as evil clouds, slowly settling and seeping between the wooden planks. Then, they immediately heard the slight whistling followed by the sound of the artillery canon.

The point of the blast seemed more distant, and everyone in the building completely ignored it. A boyish-looking, blonde-haired subaltern walked up to the colonel, saluted, and then respectfully told him that they were ready. The colonel rose, saying, "Gentlemen, It's time." Colonel Hughes led Bastings and Douglas outside. "Lieutenant Nicholson, I wanted to meet you personally, as with all my officers. I'm afraid my duty as senior officer compels me to preside over an unpleasant requirement presently. Please join us."

A soldier tied to a wooden post in front of a partial brick wall, probably the remains of a building, immediately caught Douglas's eye. He could clearly see that the man, who appeared to be only about seventeen or eighteen, had already urinated in his uniform trousers. His legs shook uncontrollably, almost unable to support his body. It seemed the ropes that bound him to the post held him upright. The young man's eyes, reddened, probably from crying, were wide and had a look of fright so severe, Douglas had never before seen any expression so terrifying. Colonel Hughes walked up to the soldier and began reading from a piece of paper held in his hand. As the colonel spoke, Bastings whispered in Douglas's ear, "Charge of desertion. Most unfortunate, but it has to be done." Bastings watched Douglas's expression closely. Knowing that a superior officer was evaluating him, Douglas displayed no emotions, standing strong and firm. Desertion had become an increasing problem for both the Allies and Germans of such near-suicidal and devasting conditions of war. The British Army was forced to take strict measures to prevent it.

A small contingent of eight soldiers marched up to take their places in front of the young man about to be executed. When the colonel finished his short address to the man, he marched back to where Bastings and Douglas stood. The boyish-looking subaltern handed each rifleman of the firing squad one bullet, one purposely being a dud, no shooter knowing who received it. A blindfold was tied over the young man's eyes by his request. The young soldier whispered something illegible when asked if he had anything to say before carrying out the sentence. The subaltern looked at the colonel, waiting. Colonel Hughes nodded, and the subaltern cried out, "Ready!..Aim!..Fire!" Eight guns blasted in unison. The young soldier's lifeless body hung by the ropes that bound him, his uniform so bloodied, making a hideous sight. There were still signs of blood pumping through the bullet holes in the front of his uniform jacket, flowing downward from the position of the drooping body. A uniformed physician walked from behind Douglas, Bastings, and Hughes. Douglas hadn't noticed him standing there. The doctor approached the dangling body and checked for a heartbeat with his stethoscope. He nodded to the colonel, who barked, "Dismissed!" The soldiers of the firing squad went into formation and marched away. Colonel Hughes turned to Douglas, "Welcome to hell, son."

The French had launched an offensive in April 1917 before Douglas arrived at the war. Although the British cooperated with their plan, it was a complete failure. Many French soldiers mutinied in objection to the suicidal frontal assaults ordered by their superiors. By July, Douglas and Captain Silas Williams found themselves in battle to control ridges near the city of Ypres. It was part of a strategy decided by the Allies.

Douglas and Silas were sent to the last ridge of Ypres, Passchendaele. It was near a railroad junction, a main supply route of the German 4th Army. Earlier that year, the British command wanted to seize control of the area. Attached to the 15th Welsh Regiment, Douglas witnessed his worst experience of the war. Before that, it was fighting closer to the trenches, where wave after wave of Germans attacked their position.

Douglas had killed his first man defending the trenches before he went to Passchendaele. In those deadly trenches, Douglas tasted the blood of killing men one after the other. "Why do they pour their men at us? It's so futile!" Douglas yelled at Silas while firing his Lee Enfield rifle. He hit one German directly in his face. As the blood poured from that victim's eye, he quickly rechambered twice and hit a heavyset soldier first, followed by a smaller one. The second German's helmet fell off, revealing the wavy blond hair of what seemed like a boy of no more than 17 years old. The golden locks of the boy soldier were soaking with dark blood as he struggled to crawl before succumbing to his fate.

"It's the way they do things," Silas hollered back, quickly reloading another clip, "Napoleonic style, the old generals prefer!" He fired his weapon into the cloudy, cordite-smelling smoke. Glimpsing back at Douglas, he yelled, "Why, I'll never know!"

Douglas continued firing upon the stampede of enemy infantry, hitting one after the other, all repulsive mutilations from his large caliber rifle. "Why?" he whispered, "why do you still come?" But the enemy rushed forward in a fury of frightened young men with terrified expressions. "Stop! Damn it! Stop!" he now hollered, but they still advanced. Over and over again, the charges and artillery shellings continued until He and Silas were rewarded with long-awaited but short rest periods.

After a short rest period the columns of Germans advanced again. Douglas became a machine. He could no longer assess or pity those who fell by his hits; it was too hard and ate at his soul. Douglas never pictured war to be like this. As a patriot, he wanted to honor his country. However, the killing was getting to him, haunting him in the short amount of sleep afforded in the trenches.

Douglas kept the 1903 Springfield rifle issued to him by the American Army at his quarters because of its longer bullet length. He used the Lee Enfield due to its faster firing speed and available cartridge size. In the trenches, Douglas had seen poison gas used. None of the men knew what it was as a near luminescent greenish cloud slowly and silently drifted to his far right, away from the trench where he and Silas hunched positioned. They watched the vile plume move. The men far to the right began coughing blood and screaming from pain as they grabbed their faces, not able to see. Those who survived felt that wrath inside for the rest of their lives.

When Douglas and Silas went to the last ridge of Ypres, Passchendaele, fighting was different from defending the trenches. When the whistle blew, Douglas regularly engaged in hazardous, sometimes desperate, frontal assault offenses.

"Follow me!" the now-hardened Douglas yelled when leading his first infantry charge. A broad wave of his men beside him and rows behind followed his lead. "Let's go, men!" Douglas fired his Colt 1911, the sidearm he preferred, hitting a German with a fixed bayonet heading toward him. The man was shot in his chest and somersaulted, dropping his weapon. Douglas didn't evaluate his adversaries' age, shape, or weight any longer. He only confirmed his gory hits and the sound bones made when breaking from falls nearby. Dropping to his knee, Douglas reloaded a clip. He fired from that low, steady position, killing four German soldiers in a row. Douglas stood erect and fired from his hip, hitting another enemy who charged at him. Dropping the empty clip and reloading, he continued his charge. Craters opened in the field grounds around him, and then he heard those dastardly whistling sounds before hearing the canon that made those wide and deep holes. "C'mon!" Douglas yelled as he ran further into the face of death, with no other thought than to kill. Stopping to aim with two hands, Douglas picked off four men, one he noticed was hit directly between the eyes. He couldn't help but notice the surprised eyes of that man as if he was wondering what had happened to him before he fell to his knees. As Douglas stopped to quickly snap another clip into his Colt, a bullet that seemed to come from nowhere grazed the upper part of his left arm. Then he heard the whistle blow, signaling retreat.

A member of the RAMC (Royal Army Medical Corps) tended to Douglas's wound. "Only a scrape, Mate," he told him, "thank the Lord above, Lieutenant." The corpsman wrapped the wound in gauze and left quickly to attend to other wounds.

"I'll mend it up bloody good as new, that rip in your field uniform, sir, I mean!" Sergeant Walter Clark, Douglas's 'soldier-servant,' affirmed. "I've got yeh dress uniform and shoes all spiffy in case ya got to go to headquarters," Clark smiled. "And yeh shaving kit is set up on the table inside yeh quarters, sir." The sergeant smiled again. "Oh! And yeh washing tin is ready," his voice lowered, "put some steaming hot water in it, meself, I did." Back in full voice, he told Douglas, "The Dhobis have your laundry; those blokes should have them back in a blink. Yeh camp bed's made up to yeh liken, Sir. Will ya be fancying me any longer, sir?"

"No. Thank you, Sergeant."

"Jolly good, then," Sergeant Clark saluted before leaving the tent. He peeped inside two seconds later, "You're knackered, sir. Get yeh self some rest. You'll be in spitting shape in no time, sir."

Douglas took a cat nap in his quarters as soon as Sergeant Clark left. He grappled to separate himself from the horror he faced in war, just long enough to think of Gab and his kids and parents back home. "I love you, Gab," he whispered before falling into a deep sleep.

The ground shaking under him quickly woke him up. Then, he heard the dreadful sound of whistling before hearing the heavy shelling around him. Surprise attacks were typical. The Germans used light-shell rockets suspended from parachutes to illuminate an area in darkness. 'There was no safe time or place on the front,' Douglas thought as he speedily got ready to battle again.

Douglas always wore the silver crucifix Peppina gave him long ago. Before going into every charge of battle, he pulled it out from his undershirt and kissed it fondly, then placed it back under next to his dog tags. If there ever was a time to be close to his maker, these were the times.

In July, while leading a platoon alongside Silas, Douglas continued leading his men bravely, guiding them around the large water-filled holes in the ground from artillery shells. The Germans fired everything they had at them. Artillery shells raged overhead, pouring deadly shrapnel down upon them—constant machine gun and rifle fire directed at the advance of the ensuing British soldiers who charged through the muddied grounds.

Douglas shouted, "Get shelter!" the incoming barrage was too intense. "Find a hole!" Douglas directed the frightened men under his command to get positioned behind something. His adrenaline rushed, caught in the momentum of combat, fearing for them more than that of his own life. "You there!" he pointed to a young subaltern, "get those men inside that hole until the canons give way some!" Douglas noticed a German sniper on the field emerge from behind dead bodies and barbed wire. Holding his gun steady with two hands, he carefully aimed and shot the man with his sidearm before he had the chance to fire on his men. Kneeling behind a tree trunk, its battered branches spread about the field, Douglas watched a doomed cavalry charge riding directly into a barrage of rifle and machine gun fire at his right flank; a sad sight, but no time to grieve. "You men!" he hollered as loud as he could, "get behind that vehicle! You there, jump into that hole over there! Quickly!" Douglas leaped into a giant crater, still smoking from a gigantic 17-inch German shell that had exploded moments before. Two dead men hung down from the ground around it; their heads dangled from the vibrations of the shaking earth. Douglas yelled as loud as he could from behind the hanging dead men, "Fire men! Keep firing your weapons! You two set up your Lewis Gun behind that cover over there!" A riderless horse passed him. Another one was bleeding, struggling to stand before being shot by a passing bullet. It let out a terrible hissing sound from its foaming mouth before the stallion folded its body and fell to the ground, spilling frothy red blood. The sound of the dying animal overpowered by the cries of the wounded and dying spread throughout that deadly place. Then, they heard the signal to retreat.

Heavy rainfalls began, unseasonable for August, and turned the fighting area into a muddy quagmire—the trenches filled with water well above the wooden planks. Men were slipping everywhere; their feet soaked through their poorly made boots. Finally, the command ordered a halt. It didn't last long, but Douglas learned the value of leadership on the field by such battles—and the terror of war. He had never been so afraid in all his life. This horror was truly terrifying and real, unlike when he was a small child and scared of bullies.

Captain Silas Williams was slightly shorter than Douglas, thin, and peaked from fighting for almost three years. They served on the front line for usually four to five days at a time, which was a nonstop, harrowing, and sleepless experience. But they became friends during their reserve duty stationing and rest periods, sharing many common interests. "I can't believe your wife allowed you to leave her and two children behind to join us in this shite world," Silas smiled after calming down from days of fighting. Silas wasn't married. "My lady gave me a hard time, and we're only engaged."

"I had a hard time leaving them, much more than I showed."

"I was watching you out there today. You're a good leader, but don't try to win the war all by yourself. Don't try to be a blimey hero," Silas laughed. "We want to get you back to your wife and daughters, hey?"

"Yes, sir, Captain Williams," Douglas laughed back.

After a few days, Douglas and Silas returned to the fighting, climbing, and running through heavy fire. The two officers fought apart, dividing their leadership among the men who sought direction in No Man's Land. As officers became extremely scarce during the bloodbath of Passchendaele, First

Lieutenant Douglas Nicholson took charge of two dwindling platoons. Captain Silas Williams commanded the rest of his company until another lieutenant became available. "Take charge of those men there, Sergeant!" Douglas yelled, almost drowned out by the blasting cannon shells hitting the ground and those that exploded overhead of the attacking men, raining loads of heavy shrapnel upon them. The roaring of heavy machine gun fire and rifles and pistols was unceasing. Those mightier sounds overwhelmed the feeble cries for help, the misery of men sobbing, the pious prayers to the Lord above, or any of the many pathetic echoes of men dying. "Move along quickly, men!" Douglas shouted even louder, "Follow me or die where you stand. Move swiftly!" He realized his men's feet were sinking in the mud of the past rains and slowing them down.

Douglas held tightly to his handgun, firing the weapon at Germans as he went deeper into that place of hell called No Man's Land. He watched as one of his men was speared by a bayonet, squirting blood where the shiny, sharpened metal protruded from his back. Douglas immediately fired upon the butcher, hitting him twice in his throat. The German fell hard and bleeding as he lay next to the man he had killed. Douglas finished him off with a crack of one bullet. While dropping a spent clip and sliding in another, Douglas glanced far across the field, looking for his friend, Silas. He couldn't find him or his men through the heavy plumes of dark and white smoke. For a split second, the fuming clouds reminded him of the locomotives leaving trails like these flowing puffs when departing the Third Street Station in those days long past when he and Rollo stood watching them together. As he snapped out of that half-second of bliss, Douglas noticed a man lying on the ground wounded. There was a British tank partially sunken in mud near the injured man that would make a good cover from everything the Germans were firing at them, seemingly heavier on that day. Tanks could no longer maneuver in the mud; he keenly assessed that the allies abandoned that armored vehicle, now partially devoured by terrain before the rains. Douglas had to make a move before one of the advancing enemy soldiers finished off the injured man. He waited, carefully listening for a let-up of opposing gunfire and watching for a wide enough space to go through the lines of the Germans pressing onward. With his fully loaded pistol in hand, Douglas saw a spot, and the gunfire had mellowed. He dashed across the open field like a sprinter, the tattering of machine gun fire following him as he slid beside the wounded soldier. The trail of those same bullets bounced off the heavy metal of the sunken tank as he stayed low to the ground. Douglas felt the soldier's chest, and there was a heartbeat; he was alive. Douglas had to quickly get him behind the tank. Hardened by his time in battle, Douglas was in tip-top shape. He grabbed the man with his muscular left arm, his right held his Colt, ready to fire at any enemy soldier who tried to stop him. He began dragging the wounded man until he got him safely behind the tank. "Thank God," he whispered. "Wounded man here!" Douglas shouted to a passing stretcher-bearer. "Here!" he kept yelling until the stretcher-bearer heard him.

After the wounded man was carried away, Douglas waited a minute in the still of calmness until he regathered his thoughts. He had to rejoin his troops. Quickly standing to his feet and ready to run, he felt something like a big punch, but much more forceful than his boxing days. Then, something knocked him off his legs. As he bled profusely, Douglas realized that bullets hit his chest and leg. His head turned to the side, and he lay in shock, thinking of home, Gab, and 'his girls.' The soldier he had saved was probably already receiving medical care. That gave him a gratifying thought, granting some comfort but still reflecting on Gab and home. Douglas's eyes closed like a tired little boy, remembering when his mother made him take an afternoon nap.

"Get up, Douglas!" Peppina called. "Don't go to sleep!" she shouted as she stood by the river holding Rollo's leash, dancing around the big dog, trying to restrain him. He could smell the fragrance of the budding spring flowers below them on the grassy slope before the railroad tracks that followed the river's flow. In his stupor, he knew his mind was playing tricks on him. His last coherent thoughts were of them, and Douglas decided to join them.

"Hi, Peppina!" Then, looking at Rollo, he called, "Hi, boy! Come here, boy!" Rollo came close, licking him. "Oh, I missed you, big boy!" He was back home and reliving his childhood. The experience was authentic in every detail but surreal.

"You can't come here. We don't have time to play anymore. It's dusk." Peppina and Rollo began fading as the sun set in the valley, vividly displaying its magical orange-tinted hues, "Goodbye, Douglas! You have to go!"

"No, I want to stay here with you and Rollo. We still have time to play."

"You can't, Douglas, you have to go home. You have a family now." She and Rollo had completely disappeared.

"Gab? Is that you?" Douglas felt a soft hand on his arm. "Help me get back, honey. Please help me. I have to see you and 'my girls.' Gab, please help me!"

Chapter Twenty-Five

Wellsville, Ohio October 1917

Letters Home

During the Great War, letter writing was the main form of communication between soldiers and their loved ones on the homefront. Soldiers wrote their deepest sentiments while in trenches or during rest periods. Writing letters to family, friends, and sweethearts back home helped keep the troops' morale overseas. It allowed loved ones to feel connected to those fighting far away.

Gabrielle Nicholson's letter began with 'My dearest Doug,' just like those days years before when she and Douglas corresponded by mail and fell deeper and deeper in love. Gabrielle had only received two letters from her husband since his departure in May. 'He's busy,' she thought. And she rested somewhat in the comfort of his departing words, "I'll do everything I can to avoid the battlefield. Knowing I'm a lawyer, they'll probably want to confine me to an office overseeing legal matters. The worst I'll be doing is probably training troops." It eased some of her mental trauma.

Gabrielle had just lost her precious pet, Frenchie. As devastated as she was, she would never dare mention it in her letter to Douglas. Gabrielle didn't want him to feel any remorse; it would upset him and might make him lose his concentration. But her dog reminded her of those early days with Douglas when he first met Frenchie. 'How much time had passed,' she thought. And that upset her most. Frenchie had lived a good life longer than anyone expected, but she still missed her tremendously.

Her letter described the 'happenings' of the town, her daily routines, and how much she loved him. 'I put a Blue Star outside on the front door in your honor. Your mom and dad put one also. It's rather nice. It has a rectangular red border surrounding a white box and a blue star in the center. I'm beginning to see them all over.' Gabrielle always put a dab of her perfume on her letters as she did when they first communicated. She also included how his parents were doing, fully aware that Martha sent her own letters expressing her sentiments and those of Douglas Sr. Giuditta and Millie often requested to mention them in her letters as neither of them could read or write. They always sent their love and prayers. Felo occasionally sent his big brother figure letters using the train station's letterhead. 'His girls' were mentioned in every letter; Claire usually made a drawing, and Martha doodled something. Gabrielle concluded her letters with a hand-drawn heart with the words, 'I love you' in the center. Then she sealed the envelope and kissed it.

Gabrielle also sent packages to Douglas. She worked with Martha to send two packages at a time, one from her and the other from Martha and Douglas Sr. There was a ten-pound limit on packages. This way, they knew there were no duplicate items. Giuditta sent over the sun-dried tomatoes that she knew Douglas loved so much. Giuditta also carefully wrapped and sent the type of soppressata that he favored. Other items included chocolate, candies, and other tins of foodstuff.

Gabrielle received a substantial monthly income from Douglas's partnership, allowing her to understand how clever her husband was. While consumed by near hysteria before his departure, she never fully understood that Douglas agreed to the partnership if anything happened to him overseas. She didn't grasp it then and certainly wouldn't dwell on it now. Gabrielle's policy was one of only positive thinking with absolutely no negativity allowed. She adhered to that every day from sunrise to sunset. Douglas had prepared his 'Last Will and Testament' for her and their daughters, but Gabrielle thought it sweet that he arranged the supplemental income for them.

One month after Douglas's departure, Gabrielle discovered she was pregnant again, expecting in January of the following year. She didn't know if she should tell Douglas; he might get excited and accidentally shoot himself. That thought alone made her hold off until she could consider the matter through. Yes, Gabrielle would definitely hold off telling him the news—or anyone else for that matter—until a future letter. Her husband had the right to learn about it first. After all, positive energy filled her body.

Gabrielle heard the mailman and trotted to the door to hand him the letter she had just finished. "Take special care of that one, Kevin." She knew the mailman by name.

"I certainly will, Mrs. Nicholson, and do send my best to your husband next time you write to him. The missus and I are proud of the men going overseas," he said, tipping his hat to her.

The doorbell rang as Gabrielle prepared to check on her daughters in their playroom.

Chapter Twenty-Six

Belgium 1917
The Reality of War

Fighting in fully mechanized battles of the Great War dwarfed previous wars in casualties. It is estimated that over ten million military men perished, and about 21 million were wounded. Advanced artillery, fully automated weapons, and newly introduced types of gas warfare caused gruesome and lifelong wounds to the body and mind.

Douglas's head twisted back and forth abruptly from the powerful chemical odor that filled his nasal passageway. He kept turning his head repeatedly until his conscious mind slowly refocused. His eyes opened but squinted from the harsh overhead lighting. As he adjusted to them slowly, Douglas's tender eyes cautiously stared straight up, his throat scratchy and sore, and he heard a man's voice saying, "He's awake."

"The salts always work when they're ready to come back," answered a woman.

"Welcome back, Lieutenant." Douglas rolled his eyes slightly, seeing the man who spoke was coming from a doctor. "Don't try to speak." The surgeon took Douglas's hand. "If you understand me, just squeeze my hand." Douglas did, and tightly. "Good, bloody good." 'A British physician,' Douglas thought. "I'm going to leave you with a very competent nurse. I'll be back to check on you. No worries, you're doing very well."

"So you're a Yank, hey mate?" The woman stood before the white-railed bed, her plump but pretty face beaming with a smile, wearing a white starched nurse cap.

Douglas glanced up, not able to move his body. He wanted to say something. The heavy sedation and pain drugs caused his euphoric but low, raspy response, "Yes, ma'am. A red, white, and blue Yankee doodle I am," he whispered; his voice barely heard, and it hurt him to speak. Smiling in his drug-induced mood, he softly muttered, "mate."

Douglas heard the nurse chuckle and then laugh. "I'm joking!" She kept laughing and said between pauses, "I'm an American volunteer nurse!" She reverted to chuckling, "That's my imitation Brit accent. How do you like it?"

"Marvelous, simply marvelous!"

"How are you feeling? I'm just trying to lift your spirits." The nurse also maintained Douglas's attention so he wouldn't fall back into unconsciousness.

"Marvelous, simply marvelous!" Douglas hoarsely whispered again.

"I see the drugs I gave you took effect," her smile was a welcome sight. "We were worried about you, but I told the doctor: a big guy like that! He'll pull through! I'm Nurse Bank." Quickly, she said, "Please, no jokes about lending you money or such. I've heard them all." The nurse was busy checking the IV drip attached to Douglas and ensuring his bandages were clean. "Your throat will be sore from the surgery they did. It will come back soon. You lost a lot of blood. You're lucky." She tapped the glass IV bottle and continued, "It was touch and go for a while, but you'll be okay soon."

"What happene. . ."

"Who's Peppina, by the way?" her curiosity interrupted what Douglas was trying to say. "You were calling her name when you first got here." She smiled, "Is that your wife's name?" She knew from his records that he was married. "And who is Gab? You kept calling both names while the doctors were struggling to bring you back to us."

Douglas vaguely recalled seeing Peppina as a little girl, his old friend Rollo, and the calming comfort of being back by the river. Then, his wife, Gabrielle, was with him. But he didn't feel up to explaining such a bizarre experience. "Gab is short for Gabrielle, my wife," he swallowed, trying to regain his voice, "What happened to me?"

"Well, part of the puzzle is solved."

"What happened to me?" Douglas struggled to repeat his words.

"Let me give you a swallow of water first." Nurse Bank reached to fill a glass. She put a straw in it and placed the water glass close to Douglas's lips. "Here, drink something first."

'She's stalling me,' Douglas thought, 'maybe I lost a body part, or I'm crippled for life,' he worried.

"You don't remember, do you?"

"No. Well, a little, but it's fuzzy."

"You were shot," the nurse put her hand on Douglas's arm.

"That touch. I remember it." Douglas said as he recalled the soft touch he thought was his wife, Gabrielle.

"Yes, when you were coming to," said Nurse Bank, smiling. The nurse looked pridefully down at her patient. "You're a hero, Lieutenant!" she said boldly but proudly. "You saved the life of a very important person, the son of a British noble, and you saved the lives of many of your men. Another officer spotted you leading and said you were gloriously leading and protecting your platoon. It's on record!" she beamed from ear to ear. Douglas listened, trying to remember, but still worried that he might be disabled. Continuing to smile proudly, she whispered, "You didn't hear this from me, but I think a high-ranking British officer is coming here to present you with a medal." The nurse's face lit up.

"Thank you, Nurse Bank. I'm beginning to remember now. It's foggy, but I do recall. Yes, I do call to mind that there was a wounded soldier," he whispered, "I dragged him behind a tank stuck in the deep mud." Speaking agitated his throat even more. As he summoned his thoughts, it seemed like a lifetime ago.

"What is today's date?"

"Now, Lieutenant, try to remain calm." Nurse Bank could see that the memory agitated him. "I'll call a doctor to explain everything to you."

The nurse's demeanor indicated something was wrong. "No, please. You tell me. Tell me everything, please?"

His nurse hated to leave someone she considered a fine man and a hero in the dark. "Well, Lieutenant. . ."

"Please call me Douglas."

"Okay, Douglas, we don't know how long you were lying in the field bleeding, but a Royal medical team arrived on the scene. It was a stroke of luck for you, Douglas. You had already called a stretcher-bearer for Captain John Hemsworth. He was leading another company well ahead of you, the man you saved. You know, many men lay unnoticed in the field and usually bleed to death. The stretcher bearers first took you to a casualty clearing station. Thanks to you, Captain Hemsworth was already there." Nurse Bank paused to assess Douglas to see how he was taking the news. "Doctors stabilized you both there, transferring you and Captain Hemsworth here at the Base Hospital."

Douglas lay among rows of white-railed beds. The hospital appeared to be an evacuated hotel with nurses and doctors running up and down the elegant stairway or taking the small, slow lift when not so hurried. The entire first floor was the area where patients received medical care. "You see, Douglas, you were in a coma, then you've been in and out of consciousness for over two months. It's mid-November." To change the subject, Nurse Bank said, "The Americans have an army here already. They're still building a large Army back home and expect to get many more troops here soo. . ."

Douglas interrupted her, "Oh, my God! My wife!" He moved his right hand to hold his throat. It hurt him tremendously to move even slightly. "She'll be worried sick not hearing from me for two and a half months!"

"There's another problem, Douglas." Nurse Bank said softly, almost sympathetically. Then, she paused, seemingly thinking of the right words to use. "Your friend, Captain Williams, didn't make it and. . ."

"Oh no, poor Silas!" Douglas remembered his friend, Silas, who patiently helped him train and offered him his friendship. Flashes of the young officer's face went through his mind. But Douglas could tell that the nurse wanted to say more to him. "What?" Douglas whispered hoarsely. "Please tell me everything?"

The nurse felt obligated to tell him, "Your company assumed you died in battle when you didn't report to your unit for over a month. They didn't know a medical team had taken you to the hospital. Bombs incinerate many men in No Man's Land with no trace of them left. You know that." She shook her head. "Headquarters sent your next of kin a letter stating that you are missing and presumed dead. I didn't know until recently, Douglas. Headquarters had a mix-up and never checked the hospitals for you, being an American, I mean."

"Oh God, no! No, no." Douglas's eyes began tearing.

It hurt Nurse Bank to watch Douglas so upset. Especially after all he went through. "You know what? And I never said this, but if that officer comes to give you that medal," she looked around, then whispered, "You ask him to notify your wife. That's the least they can do! I see them all the time using telegraphs for personal things. You ask him. That's what I would do." Nurse Bank felt nothing but sorrow. "Please try to stay calm, Douglas. You don't want a relapse. I'll be back later to check on you." She knew he wanted some privacy. All the nurses got to know their patients' reactions well.

"Nurse Bank?"

"Yes?"

"How badly am I hurt?" Douglas began worrying that maybe he was permanently disabled.

"You were shot with a rifle bullet twice, one in your upper chest and the other in your leg. You're okay!" the nurse immediately added, assuming he might think he had lost his leg.

"You'll walk again in time. The other injury was more serious. It was close to the spinal cord and a major blood vessel. You've had two surgeries, but now the doctors say you'll recover well." The nurse, now smiling, looked at him, "You are a very fortunate man, Douglas. The doctor said it must have been that big crucifix you were wearing. The doctor who performed the first surgery said that the bullet hit the crucifix first and deflected it just enough to keep it away from a more vital area. Would you like to keep it?" she reached over to a table near his bed. "There's not much left of it now, just this odd-shaped piece of silver." Nurse Bank held it up. "It was dangling on its chain when they brought you in. They had to cut away the chain quickly to treat you." She held up the mutilated piece of silver, no longer resembling a cross with what remained of the chain.

"Yes. I want to keep it." Douglas began sobbing. "Thank you, Nurse Bank." Douglas took the remains of that gift given to him many years before. He held it tightly, remembering his old friend's words.

Douglas lifted his head slightly; that petty movement sent a piercing shot of agony throughout his upper body. Struggling to keep his head up, he noticed quite a few amputees; bandaged stumps replaced where arms and legs once were. One poor soul was armless and had his eyes wrapped. Another soldier was apparently suffering from the effects of mustard gas, Douglas reasoned. He had witnessed poisonous gases used on the battlefield and knew that Phosgene was used in 1915 and was more deadly than chlorine. But mustard gas had just been released by the Germans. That new type of gas damaged the skin and blinded its victims. The gas masks used by the Allies were useless against it. The man in the bed next to him had lost both his legs above the knees. He spotted Douglas watching him and said, "Charlie Troll here."

"I'm Douglas Nicholson."

"Both me legs blown off in a bloody instant." Charlie let out a hideous laugh and continued, "All I can remember as they dragged me away was watching me own legs with boots still on 'em standing straight up, smoking. Funny thing is they appeared like they was getting ready to walk!" He laughed that same grotesque howl, allowing Douglas to believe the man was somewhat mentally deranged.

As Douglas looked around the ward, he noticed burn victims; bandages almost engulfed one soldier's whole body. Other burn victims bore horrible open sores and were covered in salve, making the wounds look worse. Douglas knew about 'trench foot,' as doctors came to call it, and he saw many cases of it around him. The design of the boots worn by soldiers in the trenches didn't protect them from the constant wetness and moisture. It rotted the flesh, and when some men removed their socks, their toes and some flesh slid off with them. Others had to have their feet amputated. Some men screamed commands of 'duck!' or 'run!' in horror as loud as they could; others wrapped themselves into a ball, fearing everything around them. They were diagnosed with what was called 'shell shock.' Like the man next to him, nurses sedated them before transferring them to psych hospitals elsewhere. Douglas lay in the center of the exemplification of war, allowing him to reflect on his father's words at his grandfather's funeral service, 'Man's inhumanity to man.' Now Douglas knew what war was like.

Regimental Commander Colonel Reginald Hughes himself showed up to see Douglas at the hospital about three days after he awakened. He had received word that Lieutenant Nicholson was out of his coma. He came by motor vehicle with none other than Sergeant Walter Clark at the wheel. Captain John Hemsworth, the young officer Douglas had saved, accompanied the colonel sitting by his side in the back seat. An escort troop vehicle with a small contingent of soldiers for protection rode ahead of them.

Nurse Bank had propped Douglas up on his bed, trying to help him finish his bland meal, when Colonel Hughes appeared, facing him with another younger officer he didn't recognize.

"Alright! There you are!" the colonel spoke with a smiling face. Douglas instinctively tried to salute. "There, there!" chuckled the colonel, "Please stay at ease, Douglas," he said in a fatherly manner. "How are you feeling, then?"

"Very good, sir!"

"Well, I have to disagree by the looks of you," he joked. Then Colonel Hughes's voice became more serious. "Exemplary service, young man, exemplary." Looking proud, he continued, "Lieutenant Douglas Nicholson, I am truly honored to present you with this token of appreciation from the United Kingdom for gallantry during active operations against the enemy." He bowed down and pinned the Military Cross decoration on Douglas's hospital shirt. "Congratulations, son, on a job well done!" shaking Douglas's hand as he spoke. The colonel noticed Douglas glance at the young man next to him. "This here is Captain John Hemsworth, whose life you saved." His left arm extended, with hand open, he introduced the captain. The colonel pulled up a chair, allowing the younger officer to speak.

"It's a pleasure to meet you, Lieutenant; it truly is," the young officer said, smiling. Captain Hemsworth was a tall, handsome, and well-groomed man. His diction was perfect, like that of an educated elite. "I wish to thank you very much for your gallantry and for saving my life. I saw you on the battlefield earlier that fateful day. You were positively magnificent."

"Thank you, sir! I appreciate you coming here."

"Please call me John. Ironically, I fared better than you." Smiling, he said, "I've been here often to visit you. However, you were in a coma each time I came. Did you, for an instant, think I wouldn't want to meet the man who saved my life?"

The colonel and the captain, now both seated, remained for over an hour. They discussed battlefield policy and other military jargon. They went on to talk about their families, the places they lived before the war, and prospective plans. John Hemsworth was married just before he was deployed and learned months later that he was the father of a baby girl. Douglas liked John, and it seemed that the feeling was mutual. They shared similar interests, but John was an aristocrat and lived a privileged life, though he didn't flaunt it.

"I'll be back to see you again," John said, shaking Douglas's hand. "Do take care, Douglas."

"Thank you for visiting me," Douglas responded.

Colonel Hughes declared, "Douglas, do come and see me after that ghastly wound heals. Beastly experience it is, I verily believe. I've been in one of those beds myself more than once," he chuckled.

"Sir! May I ask a favor?"

"Name it!"

Douglas explained his predicament about the letter sent to his family claiming he was missing, presumed killed. The colonel appeared horrified. Before Douglas could say another word, Colonel Hughes exclaimed, "By God, I'll get behind this immediately! No worries. I'll take care of this myself the second I get back to headquarters!" Then he thought and said, "Better still! I'll shoot a telegram across the pond right from here. And I'll indicate it as a priority! I'm sorry about this, Douglas. I truly am."

Before the colonel and the captain left the ward, Sergeant Walter Clark sneaked over to Douglas. "Just wanted to wish ya the best, sir." The sergeant stood at attention, offering the wide British salute. "A noble deed, sir! A bloody noble deed for certain! God bless ya, Lieutenant!" Then he hurried out to be ready at his vehicle.

Chapter Twenty-Seven

Wellsville, Ohio October-November 1917
Dreaded Telegrams

Though soldiers wore ID tags, there was no official way or system of notifying next of kin at the start of the Great War. It was a war of alliances that escalated. Neither side ever expected fatalities and wounds of such a magnitude. As the war progressed, governments often used telegrams to send notifications of death, capture, or wounding. In some cases, friends of fallen soldiers wrote letters to inform their families. Soldiers sometimes used telegrams home to let their families know that they survived noted battles or where they were fighting.

Douglas Sr. stood facing the open doorway of his home. Gabrielle was a few feet behind him. It was nearing the end of October. Colorful orange and yellow leaves paraded the hills across the river, showing evidence of the season's passing. Reverend Hansley from the Nicholsons' church and Father King from the Catholic church stood before him. Gabrielle saw them and didn't need to wait to hear what they said; she immediately knew something was wrong. "No!" she screamed. "No! Nooo!" she hollered again before putting her hand to her lips and going into shock and denial.

Douglas Sr. quickly walked over to Gabrielle and embraced her. "There, there. Everything is going to be okay." Gabrielle remained shocked, but her eyes teared while in his arms. "I received a telegram from overseas," Douglas Sr. whispered. He was a broken man; his voice gave way, which wouldn't allow him to continue. After a moment's pause, he said, "That's why I asked Jack Causwell to bring you and the girls here today, to be with family when you heard the news."

He and Martha had received the telegram every family dreaded during World War One. Douglas Jr. had put his parents as next of kin as he didn't want Gabrielle to be alone with the girls on the outside chance she acquired news that he was hurt or killed in the war. Written by a company commander, it explained that Douglas was missing and that a man of his caliber would indeed not desert his men. 'After such a long period, we must assume he was killed in action. He was an extraordinary man, and we all mourn his loss,' it read.

Douglas Sr., still holding Gabrielle, forced himself to continue, "He's missing, honey. We must pray for hope. There's always hope when we don't know for sure." Tears filled his eyes. His voice went hoarse for a few seconds, and then he resumed, "But we also have to prepare ourselves for the worst. That's why I asked the clergymen to be here to explain that to you when you heard the news and to give us all some comfort."

"He's not dead, Dad. I would know it," she sobbed, "I still feel him. I know he's alive!"

Martha, crying since the telegram had arrived, had been hiding upstairs since Gabrielle's arrival at her home. She didn't want her daughter-in-law to see her tears. Now, she took Gabrielle, and they embraced. Then, Martha took Gabrielle by the hand to a couch. "Sit down here, dear. I'll sit beside you. I don't believe my son is dead, either." She fought to force a slight smile, "We women know," she sobbed.

"Oh! The children are playing. Let me get them."

"No, honey. Let them stay; they don't need to know right now."

Gabrielle remained in denial. The Nicholsons allowed her

to accept the news at her own pace. None of them wanted to believe the news. However, after the passing of some time, it would be easier for them to realize that their beloved husband, son, father, and friend to all was gone.

Now seven months pregnant, Gabrielle went about her business in a zombielike state, taking private moments when needed. Tears poured from her eyes when she recalled her husband's bright, cheerful, handsome face. Memories flashed in her mind. There were days when she wanted to cry; other times, she tried to fight it with her positive energy. Overall, she was a mess. The Nicholsons helped out with the girls, explaining versions of where their daddy was. Andre and Claire Delisle came from Cincinnati to be with their daughter and grandchildren.

Giuditta, Lucia, and Millie brought food almost daily, unable to control their tears from the prospect of Douglas's survival. Felo helped out around the house in any way he could. There were so many people whom Douglas had helped in some way; they all showed up to ask if they could help. It was touching for Gabrielle to see how many men and women loved her husband.

In mid-November 1918, Gabrielle began thinking she was being unfair to her in-laws and friends. She concluded that she must face the inevitable truth of her husband's death. And Gabrielle hadn't honored her husband by providing a funeral mass for him. The thought overwhelmed her as she sat crying by herself in her bedroom. Gabrielle couldn't bear the thought that Douglas, still so youthful, would never be with her again in that room. She remained crying until she heard her mother's voice shouting from downstairs. Gabrielle rose to see what the problem was.

As Gabrielle descended the stairs, she noticed Claire crying while holding a telegram shaking in her hand. 'The official proof of his death,' Gabrielle thought. 'I must be strong.' She composed herself and took the envelope from her speechless mother. As Gabrielle read it, her legs wobbled, causing her to seek a place to sit. She began crying uncontrollably. "He's alive!" She screamed, "He's alive!"

Andre and Douglas Sr. rushed to her side, their faces etched with worry. They held their breath, waiting for Gabrielle to find her voice. "Douglas is. . . he's alive," she murmured, her eyes swollen from weeks of tears. "My dear, dear, Douglas is alive," she repeated, her voice filled with a mix of hope and disbelief.

"May I read it, dear?" a shocked Douglas Sr. asked in disbelief. Gabrielle remained seated and said nothing. She handed the telegram to her father-in-law. Douglas Sr. read the words aloud:

Regimental Commander
Fifteenth Welsh Regiment

It is my sincerest happiness to inform you that your husband First Lieutenant Douglas Nicholson is alive
STOP
He was wounded though recovering well. I am at the hospital with him
STOP
Douglas distinguished himself exemplary in battle. A hero I personally awarded him the Military Cross Decoration for gallantry during active operations against the enemy
STOP
Once in tip-top shape, I will personally see he is discharged and returned to you safely
STOP

Regimental Commander
Colonel Reginald Hughes

Chapter Twenty-Eight

France to Wellsville, Ohio 1918

Memories of War

Older Generals of all the armies that fought in the Great War used the same Napoleonic tactics taught them before mechanized warfare. Due to exceptional horrors of fighting a war of direct assaults against the trenches of opposing forces, horrible wounds resulted. Men ran in plain sight against heavy machine gun fire while artillery canons exploded overhead, dropping clusters of shrapnel. Some soldiers took direct hits from exploding shells and were torn apart in pieces or dissipated into clouds of dust. Among the wounds was psychological trauma inflicted upon exorbitant numbers. Many succumbed to what was called 'shell shock,' or catatonia. Most veterans of the war bore mental memories of the war for the rest of their lives.

Douglas sat peacefully on a chair, his arms resting on an outdoor table of a café, watching the arriving ships at the French port of Saint-Nazaire. It wasn't until well into 1918 that Douglas fully recovered. He had seen the bombed and broken buildings in Belgium and France and the mutilation of human and animal bodies spread across the battlefields. Douglas had taken other human life; he had killed. Douglas Nicholson had experienced man's inhumanity to man. Now, as he sat, he relived all of those horrors in his mind.

One week earlier, an American full colonel from the 33rd

Division of the American forces sent orders to see First Lieutenant Douglas Nicholson. Douglas was expecting to command a company within a regiment of that division, though mentally dreading it. When Douglas arrived at the American headquarters, Colonel William Wilson saw him immediately without any wait. A reception room filled with many officers who outranked Douglas waited while the colonel's secretary escorted Douglas into the regimental head's office.

First Lieutenant Douglas Nicholson stood at attention, saluting the superior officer behind his desk. "At ease, Major Nicholson, sit down," he pointed to the chair before the desk.

"I'm a first lieutenant, sir, not a major; pardon my interruption, sir."

"You're a major now. We were supposed to promote you to the rank of captain already," the colonel raised his arms, "Another mishap, I suppose, probably because you were attached to British command. We're proud of your service representing the American Army. Colonel Hughes speaks very highly of you," he smiled. The colonel appeared in his late fifties, probably tall from a sitting position and in excellent shape.

While assessing Douglas, he spoke. "Colonel Hughes mentioned how bravely you fought under his command. 'Exemplary service,' he phrased it. It seems he's a very influential man, too. We heard about the miscommunication that occurred regarding your family." He shook his head, appearing aggravated. "You would have made a good company commander, even battalion leader. However, due to your injuries and the recommendation of Colonel Hughes, we're sending you home as a major in rank. You already did your duty to God and your country. America is proud of your performance in representing your country. I put you in for a Citation Star. It's a new military award for gallantry in action against an enemy of the United States. You will receive it after Congress ratifies it, which should be soon."

"Sir, but I can still. . ."

"No buts, Major!" Colonel Wilson stood; he was even taller than Douglas thought. "We want to send a true American hero home." He smiled, "We still need heroes to sell liberty bonds around the country. You'll travel with your wife and family to some events, that's all. You'll still be serving your country. Thanks to officers like you, we have about two million trained American soldiers over here." He looked at Douglas proudly and said, "If you need anything, contact me directly." Colonel Wilson smiled again, "Now, I'd like a handshake," he said while taking Douglas's hand. "I wanted to meet you personally. Excellent service, Major Nicholson. You'll be returning home on the next available return transport ship. "That's an order, Major."

"Thank you, sir!" Douglas saluted before he turned to leave.

"Oh, Douglas," the colonel used his first name.

"Yes, sir?"

"Send a telegram to that family of yours before you leave," he said, smiling.

"Gladly, sir!" Douglas beamed.

While Douglas waited at the port in France, he bumped into John Hemsworth among those returning home. Like Douglas, John was a very philosophical person. "A chance meeting this is," John declared. "And a happy one at that!"

"It is indeed!" Douglas said as the friends shook hands. John and Douglas had spoken often while Douglas was in the hospital and as he recovered in a convalescent infirmary. They both enjoyed their conversations. "How about dinner this evening before we both part?"

"Splendid idea, old man."

The two young men dined on fresh fish and meats, no longer limited as much to rationing as the allies were being supplied regularly from both Great Britain and America. The German U-boats had been weakened the past spring by several Allied attacks and by the use of new equipment. Douglas had escargot for the first time and enjoyed other foods from his wife's heritage on her father's side. Instead of discussing world things and philosophies, this time, the two men discussed their families and friends at home while drinking delicious French wines. John seemed interested in small-town life, and Douglas inquired about the life of a royal.

"What's your choice for an after-dinner drink?" asked John.

"I'll gladly take a brandy."

"Good choice, as will I. Waiter! Two brandies. Make them doubles."

"At least you get to go back to practicing law," John explained, referring to the boring life of a royal in England. The men bantered as they enjoyed their drinks.

"Yes, I work while you play," Douglas replied, causing John to laugh hysterically at that remark.

They noticed both were promoted in rank and congratulated each other. "They'll parade me through streets like other unlucky returning military men," Douglas remarked.

"And what do you think I'll be doing? Now you'll get a taste of being a royal!" They both laughed at that irony. "Waiter!" John held up his empty glass, "Two more!"

The two men drank their brandies with fresh oysters on the side throughout that last evening before they were both scheduled to leave. John was to go first as he had only a short trip across the channel.

"Well, I'm a bit tipsy," John announced. "I guess I should call it an evening. I have a daughter to see that I've never before met." The two young men embraced. "Always remember that you have a friend in England, Douglas. Do come and visit with your wife. My family would love to meet you, and you can see the land of your heritage."

"I might take you up on that, old man!" Douglas spoke like an Englishman; the alcohol influenced his speech.

"Please do!" they embraced again. "Well, it was destiny, our meeting. It was a fortunate one."

"I'm glad we did. If you ever decide to bring your family to the States, please visit my family and me. It won't be a royal reception, but it will indeed be a loving one!"

"It would be great!" John and Douglas shook hands. "Farewell, my friend," said John before turning toward the harbor where his ship was docked and readied.

"Farewell, John! My dear friend," Douglas called out.

Douglas waited on a chair at the outdoor table of a café, preparing to board in an hour. He had already sent the telegram directly to Gabrielle, explaining he would arrive in New York Harbor in about a week and a half. Douglas told his wife he loved her and couldn't wait to see her. Douglas would telegram her again when he left for Pittsburgh and again with his expected arrival at the Third Street Station in Wellsville. Major Douglas Nicholson was on his way home.

Douglas rode the train from Pittsburgh. It came around the same bend that he and his dog, Rollo, had watched years before, waiting for a train to appear. As a young boy, he remembered how excitedly he walked with his dog to see the people and all the commotion when a train entered the Third Street Station. Douglas peered out his window as the train approached and saw a massive crowd. Inductees from the Draft Board at City Hall on Fifth and Main stood lined up waiting for the train as a railroad band played music and people cheered. Gabrielle had told him in a letter how the inductees marched from City Hall following the band. America was still sending thousands of troops overseas.

Douglas had had enough of bands, music, and people cheering at uniformed men and women and the military in general. Fighting in battles had changed him. Now realizing the horrendous things he had done, he recalled that line from a poem, 'man's inhumanity to man,' when he conversed with his dad before he left. As a soldier, he had done the unthinkable and witnessed atrocities that made him ashamed. Of the men in the crowd, he saw the faces of those he had killed in battle and remembered those poor souls in the hospital with despicable wounds they would bear for the rest of their lives. During the time of his recuperation, Douglas Nicholson had indeed changed. He could only confide his true feelings to men like John Hemsworth. But now he was departed from the only ones who could understand his sentiments, soldiers who had witnessed the same frightful horrors.

As the nose of the giant locomotive blasted its steam and then slowly came to a stop at the end of Third Street, the locomotive's wheels squealed as it did. Douglas could now clearly see those happy young men, jubilant to be going 'over there' as the band gloriously played the same song written by George M. Cohan. As if a kaleidoscope blurred out all the others surrounding her, Douglas spotted Gabrielle. She looked beautiful, dressed meticulously with a green pastel-colored gown and wide-brimmed summer hat; she radiated while searching for someone in particular. Douglas knew 'his Gab' was looking for him, but how could he face her after all his despicable actions overseas? And who was the baby she was holding so lovingly?

Gabrielle Nicholson had spent the entire morning dressing and then changing her clothes. She wanted to appear her best for her husband, Douglas, whom she hadn't seen in over a year. As Gabrielle glanced at herself in the mirror image, she wondered if she had done the right thing by not burdening him with the news of the birth of his new child. At first, she thought it best to spare him the worry of her pregnancy with all else he had going on, fearful things probably, she thought. Gabrielle had read a lot about the war and had seen horrible photos. She knew that returning servicemen were having trouble re-adjusting to civilian life as they did in all wars. But Gabrielle also sensed that if anyone could help him, it was her, and prepared herself. She was ready to bring her husband, the man she loved, back to her. Gabrielle finished dressing Martha and Claire and put the finishing touches on her baby's outfit.

Douglas saw his parents in the crowd as he stood on the passenger car's stairs. Then he saw Giuditta with Felo and Lucia. Felo held tightly to his two daughter's hands. Francesco Trieste and his wife, Colomba, stood with their six children. Giuditta's daughters and son were there; Mary and Angelina were now married with children. And 16-year-old Thelma looked radiant, no longer a child. Millie was with her husband, Hector. Then he noticed friends, old school classmates, neighbors, and other people he knew from business, even acquaintances. His entire office staff was at the station. Politicians were present, probably to make speeches before their constituents. Douglas couldn't have known that his stories and exploits were widely known and had leaked to the newspapers. Douglas didn't know what to do; there was no escaping, and he dreaded being in the limelight, especially with the gruesome memories he harbored.

"Welcome home, Major Nicholson," the train conductor proudly smiled. "You have quite a crowd waiting for you. We put your steamer trunk in your father's wagon." 'Dad still hasn't got a car yet,' Douglas smiled for the first time. The band played 'Over There' even louder as the crowd began cheering and yelling his name, Douglas.

73-year-old Bob McElhenny, the long-retired station guard, was the first one near the stairs to greet Douglas. After a quick hello, he sidestepped him and ran into the waiting arms of his teary-eyed wife, Gabrielle. "About time you got back, soldier!" she whispered in his ear, "or should I say, Major!" Gabrielle was crying, and her grasp held passionately to the man only months before she thought dead. "I love you, Doug." She wouldn't let go, and Douglas didn't want her to. It was his daughters who fought their way through.

"I love you too. I missed you every day. I thought of you always. Always," he repeated himself as his daughters tore him away. Douglas knelt and embraced them securely, saying, "I missed you both so much! My God! How big you got, both of you!"

"I go to school now, Daddy!" Claire told him.

"I know how to fish!" Martha exclaimed. "Grandpa taught me!"

"I'm so proud of you both!" Then Douglas looked up at Gabrielle from where he kneeled and asked, "Whose baby were you holding?"

"Oh! That's your son, Douglas Jr.," she giggled at her husband's expression. "Mom has him now. I didn't want to drop him running to you." She pointed to where Claire and Andre stood, waving.

Friends and loved ones gradually departed later that evening, leaving only close family members. A tired Douglas pulled his trunk over to where he sat next to Gabrielle, laid it on the floor, and opened it. Douglas had left his large canvas pack back in France. He bought a small steamer trunk for his uniforms, souvenirs, and other things, including his smaller duffle bag, now folded, a memory carried in most of his battles and engagements. He also kept his two sidearms, a British Webley Mk VI and a Colt 1911. Then Douglas began passing out gifts and souvenirs.

Douglas gave Gabrielle, his mother, and his mother-in-law new dresses he had bought in France. They marveled at the delicate styles of fabrics.

"They're so splendid, Douglas." Martha beat Claire in saying her compliment. Claire said almost the exact phrase a second after Martha.

The French berets he selected for his dad and Andre and the stylish European shirts suited them well. He brought back beautiful souvenirs for his Aunt Ellen and the Causwells next door to his parents. Barbara Heely had passed away at 92 years old in the autumn of 1917 while Douglas was overseas. Douglas remembered Giuditta, Millie, and others and left those gifts in the trunk until he saw them.

Then, Douglas looked at the bemused expressions on his daughter's faces and said, "Let's see if there's anything else in here?" He reached between his carefully folded uniforms and quickly pulled out two hand-crafted porcelain dolls and two Kewpie dolls.

The girls' faces beamed as their father kept pulling toys and games out of his trunk. Among them was a miniature tea set. "Oh! Thank you, Daddy!" the girls harmonized as they began playing, not knowing which to try first.

Douglas sat beside his wife and took his baby son in his arms. "I didn't know about you, little guy." He kissed his son's cheek, "I guess I have the rest of my life to get to know you." That brought a tear to everyone except 'his girls,' who were too busy to notice. Douglas remained seated, one arm holding Gab, the other holding his son. Relaxing in the comfort of his home, Douglas was finally home.

River Town
Wellsville Ohio

Book Three
America's
Greatest Generation

Chapter Twenty-Nine

Wellsville, Ohio 1918-1919
Back Home in The USA

After homecoming ceremonies, parades, and political speeches, the returning American soldier had to readjust to becoming a 'civvie' once again. For all, it was a period of mental adjustment after fighting in the first worldwide war using mechanical warfare. For many of those wounded, it was a long period of physical and occupational rehabilitation. Using new weaponry, the injuries and mutilations were more profound than in previous wars. The term shell shock originated in the Great War and was treated as a medical condition. Anyone who witnessed the horrors of that war experienced mental trauma for long periods afterward.

It took Douglas Nicholson a while to get back to work full-time, slowly like a swimmer putting his toe first into the water, gradually letting his body acclimate to the temperature change by splashing water onto it. The wounds to his soul were deep, and he needed time to heal as best he could. A year and a half didn't seem long to most, but that span to him was a lifetime. His time overseas, divided between struggles of battles and then the grueling recovery, was over. Going through the process of metamorphosis into a fighting man, one who lives in the fear of constant death and fights to exist, was unavoidable. The 'fight to survive instinct' occurs when stress hormones develop from perceived danger and create physiological changes in the human body to either face danger or flee from it. Now, he had to endure the transformation back into the man he was before he went overseas, a journey that would take time. Some nights, he woke up in a sweat, screaming until Gabrielle gently calmed him down. Slowly, he regained his position as a loving husband, father, and son to his family. Douglas's saving grace was that he had fought in a world war so that his son would never have to. 'Thank God, I spared him from ever knowing that savagery,' he silently prayed.

Douglas also had to readjust to his profession and the changes in town since he was away. Some days, it felt like he was a stranger in his home and town. But he gradually eased back into his office environment, and Gabrielle accompanied him there at first. She helped him reorientate. Slowly, his life changed from keeping his guns clean, preparing assault strategies, and huddling under a rain cape to stay dry and warm to organizing and preparing his legal trial cases. Together, he and Gabrielle went to lunch and ate finely prepared foods and desserts. It was a drastic change for Douglas, who was used to eating from a mess kit, drinking from a canteen, and occasionally eating bland meals at officers' quarters. But in time, Gabrielle brought him back to his family, little by little.

"I see they finished the library," commented Douglas as he and Gabrielle took an evening stroll, hand in hand, passing Ninth Street and Main.

"See how nice it is to get outside in the open air." Gabrielle smiled at the man she loved walking beside her. "You need to socialize again. Go back to your clubs. Your 'brothers' at the lodge miss you; they keep asking for you."

"I will in time, Gab." Douglas walked around town, gazing at the changes since he had been away. "I just want to spend some more time enjoying you and the kids first," he smiled back at his wife. Then his face became serious. An instant change he now became capable of ever since he was in Europe. One moment over there, he would be joking with a fellow soldier; the next, he witnessed that man's head was shot to a gruesome pulp by a sniper. His expressions changed often when on the front lines. "Why didn't you tell me about Frenchie in your letters?"

"I didn't want to burden you with grief."

"So you bore it all by yourself? My words, though distanced, could have helped comfort you."

Gabrielle held her husband tighter, "I know you loved Frenchie, Doug. You're here now; that's all that matters."

Police had found Matteo Fontana's dead body weeks after his son, Luke's, final visit. The wicked man, tormented by deeds of his past and the booze he used as a cure, had been one of the early predecessors of the Black Hand. Fontana terrorized fellow Italians and Sicilians by using the same methods as the old-school mafia in Sicily. Simply by hiring a man or two, he gave the appearance of many to instill fear into those whom he abused and robbed.

Neighbors notified the police after smelling the robust, putrid odor from the Fontana house. He had been dead for a very long time. The doctor diagnosed his death as choking. "He must have swallowed his tongue, so badly torn in that beating," the doctor said. Privately, he suspected that someone had strangled the wicked man. And he was right. His son Luke did it to put his father out of his misery—and because he didn't have the time to keep replacing caretakers who didn't want to be in that house for a minute. Luke had closed all the doors and windows directly after killing his father so as not to draw attention to the odor immediately.

Matteo died a horrible death after sitting in his hardwood potty chair, suffering day after day for years. From being dead for so long, his head leaned slightly forward and swelled, his body bloated and stiffened, adding to the already ghastly sight it was before. Matteo's one remaining eye had bulged and dried, making him appear like an angry cyclops right out of 'Homer's Odyssey.' Dried blood appeared on his nostrils and mouth.

Almost as a homage to that departed soul, a band of crooks with a leader formed in Wellsville whom townspeople referred to as Black Handers, like those gangs in the larger cities. And now Matteo's son, Luke, was advancing through the ranks of a much more organized and significant family of criminals in Cleveland.

Rosa Fontana mostly recovered. Her head wounds left her with some brain damage, and her face and body remained severely scarred from the beatings. She was able to get a job sewing in town. Rosa never returned to see Matteo since that one time with Millie before his death. Alessia never went back to that house, though she wanted to see his mutilated body and scream into his grotesque face. However, she still feared the horrible man who crippled her even after his death.

"Rosa, I'm gonna charge you a small fee for room and board at my hotel, just enough to cover expenses. This way, you save your money and rent or buy something someday," Giuditta told Rosa privately, speaking in half Italian and half English. "And your daughter can work for me, something not so hard. She saves some money, too." Giuditta employed Rosa's disabled daughter, the once beautiful Alessia, out of sympathy. Alessia's nose was severely disfigured, her face gravely scarred, and her left eye drooped, giving her a hideous appearance. Her father's attack also left her with long and repulsive body scarring and pain. Originally sowed with fabric thread, the wounds got infected and required repeat surgical work. She needed special shoes because her broken hip made her left leg shorter than her right. The shoemaker, Mr. Provenzano, made her a specially designed pair free of charge. Alessia never went outside. Young children were frightened of her face and gait the first time she did, and older ones made fun of her and called her names. When not working, the young woman mainly stayed in the room at Giuditta's hotel, which she shared with her mother.

Luke Fontana tried bringing money for his mother and sister. Rosa refused because of the rumors about how he earned it. She wanted nothing to do with someone who made his money like Matteo did. Rosa told him, "The way you talk now is like a tough guy, just like one of those gangsters from the city, like a thug!" she cried out. "What happened to you? You're getting just like your father! Look at me! Look at what he did to me! I can't even chew my food anymore." She began to sob, "Look what he did to your beautiful sister!"

A spurned and angered Luke replied to his mother, "Ya wanna know sumtin? I learned things from when Papa used to beat you. It taught me how someone could have so much power over another person, and that gave me satis-factien!" He told her in the street language he now used and watched the horrified look on his mother's face. "Yeah, I liked it! Whataya think a that?" Rosa was now crying uncontrollably. Luke was firing her emotions and seemed to enjoy the suffering it caused. "Ya don't want my money? Good! Keep watching my sister walk around like the 'Hunchback of Notre Dame' for all I care!" His face contorted with glaring eyes. For a split second, they appeared to Rosa as reddish pupils with yellow-colored eyeballs, like a wild animal or a grotesque monster. Rosa jumped back, shocked at the sight of her own flesh and blood.

"You're evil!" she shouted, "Satan himself possesses you!" She made the sign of the cross and began mumbling prayers.

Luke waved his hand at her, gesturing mockery at everything she said. "Have it your way, ya bitch!" Rosa ignored her son's words and kept muttering her prayers, not making eye contact with him. Luke turned and walked away.

Liam Kelly died from his head wound shortly after Douglas Nicholson left for overseas duty in the spring of 1917. The doctor said it was probably from blood leakage in the brain. Giuditta paid for his funeral and burial. Many people of varying ethnicities attended his mass at the Catholic Church and burial out of respect for an old friend. Everett Holt, the German immigrant thrashed with Liam by Matteo Fontana, went back to bartending. However, he still bore the many scars from Fontana

344

that fateful night years ago.

The teen prostitute who turned into a woman before the eyes of everyone at Giuditta's hotel, Sandy, was married in the summer of 1917. Sandra 'Sandy' Bursky, now 40 years old, married an Italian worker named Lorenzo Ajello. She still worked as a waitress, but her body was off-limits. And she still carried her Derringer pistol to enforce that policy.

Lifelong friendships begin naturally with no memory of time or place. Such was that of Eleanora Buch and the Trieste girls. Only the older sisters, Nina and Maude, vaguely recalled how Eleanora merged into their family as a toddler.

Even at such a young age, Eleanora and Julia reminded Felo of the memories and stories he harbored for his older sisters, only in reverse ages. Eleanora, the younger sister, was a 'firecracker,' active and talkative like Peppina. Julia was quiet and kept to herself like Emanuela. To Felo, his older sisters lived on through his daughters.

After Lucia Buch arrived, when Italian immigrants came to town in much greater numbers, one woman stood out among the rest in and around the Italian settlement centering on Commerce Street. The widow, Adelina Rampucini, beheld the power to cast the 'evil eye' or 'mal'occhio,' feared by all the poor, working-class Italians. To those illiterate immigrants, the 'mal'occhio' was the most dangerous weapon known to them. Greater than canons, bombs, rifles, or la pistola, anyone who indeed possessed this power was feared and obeyed. Before her arrival, fate spared the Italian community and some settled Americans those great and evil powers. Viewed as a 'zinchera,' or gypsy, Signora Rampucini was a practicing 'strega,' or witch, and she made a good living in town as a 'cartomande,' a reader of cards and palms. She only spoke in sessions. Whenever anyone greeted her in public, her stone face ignored them. Always wearing the widow's black dress, stockings, and veil, Adelina Rampucini was thin in build and had completely grey hair. The only exposed skin of the woman, who appeared to be in her mid-50s, was her face and hands, which were pale white. The dark shadows under her deep eye sockets added trepidation to the thin-lipped woman's expression.

The inside of Adelina's home was dark, with curtains closed. Candles provided the only source of light, and incense always burned. Lines formed in front of her house in all weather conditions with anxious people wishing to know their future or that of a loved one. Many came to speak to dearly departed friends or relatives. Among them was Nicola Bucci, who held his pants tightly in the groin area where his 'coglioni' were, as other men on the line did the same. Some men thought of it as a remedy in case the widow cast the mal'occhio upon them.

Adelina Rampucini's daughter, Ginevra, played a pivotal role in this enigmatic setting. A seemingly unremarkable yet courteous young woman, she served as the conduit between her mother and the outside world. She would engage in conversations, at times deciphering her mother's enigmatic messages into comprehensible words. The house had a strict policy of admitting only one person at a time unless they were a relative or a close family friend. As each visitor departed, their head lowered in reverence, Ginevra would welcome the next, guiding them to her mother.

Adelina Rampucini was a woman not to be trifled with. If anyone dared to fault, disrespect, or hurt her, they would face the wrath of her power. She would close the two middle fingers of her right hand tightly under her bent thumb, her forefinger and pinky pointing outwards. With a forceful and repeated motion, she would cast her evil spell, her piercing eyes adding to the intensity of the moment.

"Come this way," Ginevra said to Nicola Bucci, next on the line. She led him before Signora Rampucini in the darkness of her home and seated him across from her mother. The one candle on the table reflected onto Adelina's face, accentuated her facial features, and transformed her into a sinister sorceress.

Nicola rose quickly and bowed, saying, "Forgive me for my

manners. May I sit?"

Signora Rampucini had seen Nicola holding his crotch and said, "That won't help you, Signore Bucci," pointing her pale, bony finger to his groin as he stood before her. "Be seated," her thin, colorless lips squeezed together. Her chilling eyes glared at him, "Nothing can help those who scorn or ridicule me," she spoke in an Italian dialect understood by Nicola.

Nicola squirmed in his chair, almost wetting himself from fear. "May I speak?" Adelina nodded her approval. "How do you know my name?"

The Signora replied nothing, only her stern expression. "Go on."

"What is my future?"

Signora Rampucini spread some cards on the table and carefully observed them. "There are tragedies in store for your family," the widow kept looking at the cards. "Some bad things will befall your family soon, other things later."

Now, Nicola had to hold his coglioni to prevent himself from urinating from fright. "Will I have a long life?"

"Give me your right palm." Nicola promptly complied. Adelina Rampucini looked closely at the calloused hand and said, "Give me your other hand." After observing both his palms, she declared, "Your life will not be a long one," her eyes glared at him, causing an eruption inside his pants. After quickly paying Ginevra, who handled the money for her mother, Nicola scurried out of the room, now holding his coglioni so the waiting people in line couldn't see his wet trousers.

Nicola raced back to the hotel, and when he entered, he began screaming, "I'm gonna die! I'm gonna die!"

"What are you talking about, you idiot?" Giuditta yelled back. "People are gonna think you're crazy!"

"The widow Rampucini told me!" he ran to his room, repeatedly yelling the phrase, "I'm gonna die!"

"I don't believe in that stuff!" Giuditta whispered.

When Nicola told Lucia about his fortune, she renounced it as a sin against God. "Una disgrazia!" Lucia yelled at Nicola,

forcing him to make the sign of the cross. "It's ignorant super-
stition, nothing more!" But her words couldn't convince Nicola.

Chapter Thirty

Wellsville, Ohio 1920
The Volstead Act

In January 1919, Congress ratified the 18th Amendment, which banned the manufacture, sale, and transportation of alcoholic beverages. In October 1919, Congress passed the Volstead Act, which would go into effect on January 17, 1920. Most people knew it was coming, just a matter of time since 1917 when it was proposed to the Senate. Many prepared for the loss of their precious booze by hoarding it since there was no actual law prohibiting drinking it. Other more scrupulous characters, depending on which way you viewed it, prepared to manufacture it. It was a point in time when more criminal activity than at any other time before began from one source. The exorbitant amounts of money acquired transformed small-time hoods into millionaires and ultimately turned the more organized Sicilian Black Hand gangs into the American mafia. Most law enforcement forces across the American Nation succumbed to the temptations of bribes.

"Aunt Bert! Customer, Aunt Bert!" the parrot cried from the wooden perch, flapping and expanding its colorful wings. The store door had a bell attached, and whenever someone opened it, the parrot yelled his warning when he heard the jingling sound. It was the third time Mary, Eleanora, and Annie opened and closed the door to hear the bird repeat those words.

"Okay, Polly!" Dora said to the bird as she came from the store's back room. Children always wanted to hear the bird talk, and sometimes they opened the door to listen to the colorful and funny-looking bird speak. After doing it three times, she wanted to reprimand them, but they looked adorable. "So, girls, what can I get you?" Mary, the oldest of the group, was in school and prepared a list for her mother, Columba, and one for Lucia Buch, who couldn't write in English. She handed it to Dora, who went about the store plucking things from different places.

Dora's husband had worked on the Panama Canal. Working conditions while building that waterway were so bad that many American laborers deserted their positions within the first year. They lived in barracks like the military. Her husband brought back the bird and some disease that his doctors thought was the cause of his premature death. That left Dora Brick as a widow who worked the store alone, with the bird as her sole company.

After the girls left the items they bought from the store with their parents, Eleanora said, "Let's go to my grandma's. We can have something to eat."

"Good idea," Mary answered. "I put our things by the door so my mama wouldn't see me. She probably has work for us to do." Mary took the smaller girls by the hand to cross Third Street. From there, Eleanora and Annie held hands and skipped ahead of Mary to the hotel.

"I'm getting sick and tired of you!" Giuditta yelled at Nicola, who simply returned a smile, exposing his dirty and crooked teeth. Giuditta had long ago outgrown Nicola and regretted the day she allowed him to touch her. Already bedding a tall, Italian man, she couldn't care less if Nicola knew. "Yeah! Walk away from me, you dirty slob. You don't even bathe anymore, for God's sake. What's wrong with you?"

"Nothing wrong with me, woman! You don't want me in your bed anymore, so what do I care about taking a bath? I told you years ago that they're unhealthy!" Giuditta was about to throw another crude remark toward Nicola when she heard her granddaughter coming into the hotel with her friends. Nicola was closer to the door, so he spoke to them first, "Hi, kids! Everybody good today?" He was always kind to his grandchildren and their friends, and they loved the man who was always jolly in front of them. The Trieste sisters returned his greeting, Annie standing slightly behind her older sister. She was a little afraid of the man.

"Hi, kids!" Giuditta called. "C'mon, I give you something to eat." She turned back to Nicola and, in a whisper so that the kids couldn't hear, told him, "You go away now. Get out of here!" Nicola rose from where he was sitting and said goodbye to Eleanora and the Trieste sisters before walking out the door.

As the children were eating, George Bamarra descended the stairway. Born Giorgio Bamarra in Sicily, George boarded in Giuditta's hotel. Though stern, quiet, and intimidating, Giuditta liked the 27-year-old man. She appreciated his strong workman's body—like a bull. Some rumors floated that the promiscuous woman liked him a little too much, and by his performance in that carnal area, combined with his being a good earner, decided that he would make a suitable husband for her youngest daughter, now called by the English version of her name, Thelma.

Giuditta knew George was involved with the Black Hand doing bootlegging in town. She even let him hide liquor under the hotel and realized he would soon make a lot of cash. Money became everything to her after she lost her daughters; never allowing herself to be in a position of dependence on a man again, she would do anything for money. George and Giuditta had a plan for George to marry Thelma against her will.

George had already built a liquor still on a farm up on one of the hills, even though prohibition hadn't officially begun. Salvatore Gusto, the head of the local Black Hand, also liked and trusted George. Bootlegging was about to be the most significant commodity for Salvatore Gusto, his crew, and almost every criminal in the country. Salvatore had already planned his operation and depended on George and other small-time hooch makers to produce what would sell mainly in gallon jugs. Up to that time, the Black Hand's income in America limited their evil deeds to things like extortion, gambling, and prostitution. Prohibition was about to open new avenues for making illegal money.

Thelma Buch was a beauty at the age of 17. Her face was immaculate, with delicate features, and her body was petite but shapely. She didn't like the crude, vulgar, and older George Bamarra. The young woman was madly in love with Barney Allen, and the feeling was mutual. Barney was a hard-working 20-year-old man with a good job at one of the banks, saving all his money to marry Thelma. Together, they counted the days when he would have enough. "It will be soon, baby. I almost have enough saved," he told her one beautiful day. It was in 1919, and the couple sat together, sprawled on a blanket over fresh grass, enjoying a picnic lunch. "Do you think your mom and dad will approve of me?"

"I can't wait to tell my mama and papa. They'll love you. Why wouldn't they?" She giggled, "My God, you have a good job, you're a good man, handsome," she blushed, "and, well, everything any parent would want as a husband for their daughter." They kissed with the fascination of youth, yearning to explore the core of each other's bodies and souls. Barney and Thelma were young, in love, and foolish enough to think the world was that simple. Even in a small town, there were complications with many things. That reality was about to dawn on that young couple.

One day, Nicola sat at a table drinking the homemade beer he favored even more than his wife, pretending not to listen to the discussion between Giuditta and George. They spoke softly, which was quite a change for Giuditta, who was always loud, but Nicola could make out what they were saying. "Don't worry about nothing!" George began in his crude vernacular, "Salvatore Gusto will stop by and pick Thelma up. I know she'll go with him, thinking that Barney guy is there. Gusto's doing me a favor. I'll be hiding behind the old stable next to my still."

"Do what you have to do, but don't hurt her too much," Giuditta said coldly without any emotion, "just get the job done and make sure she knows who the boss is. I don't want her running away with that American."

"I'll get it done. Don't worry."

"I know you will, and you'll enjoy every minute," she smiled. "You better leave now to get there before Salvatore comes by." Then, as a bid of farewell, Giuditta put her hand on George's bulging upper arm. George faced her and held Giuditta's shoulders, massaging them as his calloused hands slowly slid down her arms. The touch of those hardened hands on her flesh gave Giuditta a rush, and she stood in awe before the muscular man who caused it. "Maybe I should keep you for myself," she whispered, kidding George.

George spanked Giuditta's behind before leaving the impassioned woman who was desperately trying to replace her lost Luigi. "Maybe you should, bad girl," he laughed wickedly. His laughter continued as he walked to the front door.

Nicola knew about his wife and George always petting each other, though questioning how far it went. 'She's just a big tease,' thought Nicola. But at that moment, Nicola couldn't believe what he heard about what would happen to his youngest daughter. The panic-stricken man quickly walked over to his daughter-in-law Lucia's house, now called Lucy by most people she knew in town. Along the way, he thought about his poor baby, Thelma. He remembered her sweetness even as a child, how he held her on his knee and bounced her, and she laughed in return and wanted him to keep doing it. Tears came to his eyes as he thought about how useless he was. "How could I defy a Black Hand boss?" he whispered along the way to Lucy's. "I know I'm dumb, but Lucy is intelligent; maybe she might have an idea," he began walking faster.

At four months pregnant, Lucy was in shock, her hands covered her mouth, when she learned of this evil plan. "Veni´ca! Get your coach!" 'Something snapped in that woman's brain when she lost her two daughters,' she thought. "We have to go there before it's too late!" Lucy read and wrote letters for

Salvatore Gusto. Maybe he would listen to her. "I never liked that George." Lucy knew everything, from reading and writing letters for Italian Immigrants. She knew information about the Italian community and some things about Americans. Nicola returned with the horse-drawn coach about 15 minutes later. Neither he nor Lucy knew Thelma was already on her way.

George Bamarra promptly left when Giuditta told him. Ten minutes later, Salvatore Gusto came by with his Cadillac. "Hi, Thelma!" he called to the beautiful young lady sitting in the sun on the hotel's steps. "How are you this beautiful day?"

"Hello, Mr. Gusto, how are you?" she replied, shielding her eyes from the bright sun with her right hand. Thelma was a little intimidated by Gusto, knowing his affiliation with the local mob.

"I'm going up to the farm. Hey, maybe you'd like to come. Barney Allen is up there. He's doing some side work for me." Gusto smiled, "Probably wants to save his money to marry a special someone, huh?" Thelma blushed at that comment, but she loved every minute she spent with Barney and loved just seeing him. Sometimes, she would go to the bank just to watch the handsome young man. Now, he was working to save more money to marry her; she couldn't wait for that day.

"He is?" She sat erect, contemplating, then happily said, "Okay, I appreciate it, but can you give me a few minutes to change?" Thelma wanted to look especially beautiful for the love of her life. "I'll just be a minute." Gusto smiled in agreement. She hurried to her room.

Thelma quickly undressed and admired her body in a mirror. "What should I wear?" she whispered. Her red dress! That was it! It was one of her best and made her look sexy. Barney would love it. She put on her bra and used panties instead of bloomers. Then she slipped into her bright red dress with a length that ran just above her knees, displaying her shapely legs. A plain white stripe sewed at the hip of the garment accentuated the contour of that part of her body. A small white bow stitched at the V-neck gave some purity to the above-average size of her breasts. She wore black open shoes with ties at her ankles and no stockings. She quickly descended the stairs and headed for the door.

"Where are you going?" asked her mother, smiling and knowing exactly where she headed. "You look beautiful, Tesoro."

"Thank you, Mama. I won't be too long. Bye, Mama."

"You'll be there as long as it takes," Giuditta whispered, smiling. She knew George would take care of everything. She chuckled, knowing her youngest daughter was about to become a woman.

Gusto's Cadillac slowly crept along the stone path off the main road that led to the farm. From his peripheral vision, he admired Thelma's shapely legs where she sat beside him. The way she crossed them made her dress rise to her thighs, exposing a hint of her panties. The perfume she wore permeated throughout the interior of the vehicle. 'George is a lucky man,' thought Gusto. 'Maybe I should have taken her for myself.' It was simply a daydream, as Gusto already had a mulatto mistress, Mrs. Loretta, who was married to a white man. He also had a wife and family in Italy and was in no hurry to bring them to America. He kept his eyes on the pathway, following it to a remote stable where George's liquor still stood camouflaged, hidden behind.

"I don't see Barney," Thelma sat poised, her long, elegant neck bent, peering at the structure, looking for him.

"Let's get out and look." Gusto faked being concerned.

Thelma removed her shoes, exposing her delicate, perfectly shaped feet; she loved the feel of fresh grass on her bare feet. "I hear something," she called.

At that remark, Gusto quietly stepped back to his automobile. "Maronna mia!" he mumbled, "I wish it could be me!"

Thelma didn't hear George's footsteps pressing on fresh, soft grass, only the sound of the door of Gusto's Cadillac closing. It was too late. As she turned, she felt a hard, calloused hand grab her thin wrist. She turned to the horror of seeing George Bamarra smiling while holding her wrist tightly. "What are you doing here?" her voice was tense and unsuspecting. George kept smiling as he pulled the terrified girl closer to him. Trying to wiggle her arm away from his, she screamed, "Leave me alone!"

George put his other large paw firmly under her jaw, holding her neck tightly, "Listen carefully to me: we can do this the easy way or the hard way," he stared like a lion looking at its prey. "Why don't you just surrender yourself to me? Either way, I'm going to take your virginity." His gaze filled her with horror.

"No! N-o-o-o!" Thelma screamed as loud as she could, fighting George's hardened body with her dainty fists. The thought of him doing something as grotesque as what he wanted to do repulsed her.

George smacked her face hard, putting her in a daze long enough for him to lift her frail body and lay it on the grass. He pulled and ripped at her red dress as Thelma struggled to fight back in her stupor. George finally tore it off. His mighty, calloused hand swiftly ripped the undergarments off her body and flung them to the side. The force of his heavy body atop her figure sobered the young girl. The feel of him disgusted her. Thelma grabbed at his back with her hands, clawing at him. His pants pulled down to his ankles, her toes clutched at his bare thighs, trying to scratch them with her toenails. George hit her again to stop her, harder this time. She used all the might she had to try to stop him, but he forcibly entered her roughly, pushing his body weight against her. Thelma screamed as he did, "No! No! N-o-o-o!" The sound of her screams so loud penetrated the quiet area. With its motor running, Gusto sat in his automobile and turned his head to watch. Smiling, he leered like a hawk as George battered and raped the young woman. Then Gusto turned away, put his car in gear, and drove back down the path to the main road.

George's thrusts were painful, and his victim began to vomit and started to choke on her void. Then, her body eased to the rhythmic motion as George softly told her, "Now, you're mine!" He lifted himself off the now passive body; the arms and legs of the young woman lay spread to her sides as she lay in shock. Thelma appeared like a broken doll, her torn clothes sprawled around her. The vivid colors of the red and white mutilated garments seemed like tattered flowers, sorrowful and growing amid the bright green grass. As George stood up, he noticed a carriage riding up the pathway. He lifted his pants and returned to his Packard, hidden behind the stable. George drove past the coach, not glancing directly at it but seeing the horrified faces of Lucy and Nicola with his peripheral vision. Before leaving the road, he stopped his automobile, turned, and looked back as Lucy and Nicola comforted Thelma. George glanced at his hand, holding the little white bow from Thelma's dress. Smiling, he kissed it, put it into his pocket, and then rode off.

"It was the evil eye!" Nicola's voice cracked with fear, tears streaming down his face. "The widow Rampucini must have put the mal'occhio on me!" he bellowed, his voice filled with anguish, to Lucy.

Lucy waved her hand at Nicola and told him, "Silenzio!" as she tended to the shattered and sobbing Thelma.

Nicola immediately began the coglioni remedy again to ward off any further harm. "Tragedy would befall my family she said to me," Nicola wept like a baby as he spoke.

Lucy Buch gave birth to a son in March 1920. Felo and Lucy named their baby son Nicholas, the American version of Nicola, after Felo's surrogate father. Felo wanted to name his son after Luigi but realized that would disrespect his mother and Nicola. Felo was always quiet and didn't indulge in unnecessary chatter. When he did speak, it was softly, in sharp contrast to the woman who bore him, Giuditta. He usually bore the image of sadness, probably from the loss of his sisters and how his mother conducted herself after they left. His wish in life was not that of wealth but only to have known his natural father. From the stories he had heard about him, he knew he was an honorable man. Now, Felo finally had a son who would share his interest in sports and already planned which events he would take his son to when he was of age. He promised never to forsake his children and teach them to become honest, hardworking Americans as he was.

When Thelma returned to her home after her rape, the broken toy doll's clothes were in tatters, hanging from her partially naked body. The side of Thelma's face was bruised, her lip swollen and bleeding, and she had a blackened and puffy eye. The young woman, silent from shock, had tears in her widened eyes. Lucy and Nicola held her at each side, practically carrying her inside the hotel. Giuditta ran to her daughter, crying, "Figlia mia! Figlia mia!" She pretended to comfort her.

After Lucy put Thelma in the comfort of her bed, she walked down to the first floor and calmly told Giuditta, "I know what you did! I know how you set up your own daughter! I could hear her screams from a mile away. Una disgrazia! May God forgive you!"

Lucy left the hotel, and Nicola stood before his wife, shaking his head as his eyes teared. He walked away, leaving Giuditta standing alone. "What did God ever do for me?" she mumbled.

Thelma had to marry George Bamarra. It was scandalous in the Italian community for a young woman who lost her virginity to do otherwise. To those people, she had given herself to George, and now she must become his wife. It was a quickly prepared wedding; Thelma remained unemotional and distanced throughout the ceremony. She no longer appeared vibrant and beautiful, as if George had stolen those attributes from her along with her virginity. Her face was sullen, still showing bruises, and some blackness around her eye remained to mark that fateful day.

George happily greeted guests and members of the Black Hand, including Salvatore Gusto, the boss. Thelma sneered at him especially. On her wedding night, as George ruffly forced himself upon her, she had no other option but to allow him. Her silent screams were always quieted by her fear whenever George grunted over her. Just like when she had childhood nightmares, Thelma agonized in her fright, alone without anyone to comfort her. Thelma hated him and dreaded each time he touched her, cringing from the feel of him and the sounds of his pleasure. She wished George was dead. Thelma became pregnant soon after the hastily prepared wedding. She bore a daughter the same year that Nicholas Buch was born.

Barney never understood what had happened. Thelma didn't know how to tell him what George had done to her; she was ashamed of herself for what that monster had done. When Barney asked certain people who happened to be George's associates, they angrily told him to back off or else. He mourned her marriage alone until his sorrow eventually turned to anger. Barney began to hate Thelma, believing she had betrayed him by marrying George for his money.

Thelma took care of her baby daughter but didn't allow Giuditta near her when she found out her own mother was involved in such a diabolical plan that destroyed her life and happiness.

After Nicholas Buch was born, close friends of Lucy and Felo, Giovanni and Louisa Demarco, became the proud parents of a new baby girl named Elena. They had prepared an extravagant party for their new daughter's baptism. Eleanora Buch, along with Mary, Annie, and the rest of the Trieste family, laughed and danced. Colomba held one-year-old Clara in her arms. Thelma didn't accompany George; she stayed home with her baby daughter. But George laughed, joined in the fun, and danced the Italian tarantella with Giuditta like there was no tomorrow.

Chapter Thirty-One

Wellsville, Ohio 1922-1925
Prohibition

During prohibition, many prospered. Booze was smuggled inside coffins of funeral hearses, by truck, and wagons. Some reaped hefty amounts, bringing it into the country by boat or crossing the borders. Most sheriffs and police in cities and towns turned a blind eye and cashed in, as did politicians and others holding power. Masses of people prospered during the sale of illegal liquor. Prohibition gave birth to the American Mafia. People wanted their booze, and they would get it any way possible.

Nicola now slept downstairs in the room his daughter Mary once used before she married. He couldn't sleep, so he rose from his bed to siphon a glass of beer from the keg in the basement that ran to the bar. As he passed the stairway to the second floor, noises came from upstairs. Not knowing exactly where they were coming from, Nicola slowly climbed the steps, listening. The sounds became clearer as he came closer to the upper floor. Groans, crying, and moans came from Giuditta's room. Nicola put his head to the door to better listen. The babble was coming from Giuditta, sounding as deep as a man at times, and she seemed to be shaking from torment, bouncing on her bed. His poor wife sounded like she was sick, probably going through convulsions from her sounds and the vibrations.

'Maybe she's swallowing her tongue like Matteo Fontana did or drowning in vomit,' he thought. Quickly opening the door, Nicola saw a large, muscular man lying on top of his naked wife, her legs high and apart in the air. They both profusely sweated as if exercising intertwined and bouncing to the same rhythm. Neither the big man nor Giuditta noticed Nicola standing there, watching what appeared to be a wrestling match from the dim light in the hallway. Finally, Giuditta turned her head to see the dumbfounded expression on her husband's face. She smiled at Nicola, trying to laugh, but her pleasure wouldn't allow laughter, only cries of titillating satisfaction. To spite her husband, Giuditta used the toes of one of her feet to grasp the edge of the door and slammed it shut. Nicola stood in the hallway listening to his wife's cries for a full minute before slowly descending the stairway.

The following morning, while Nicola sat eating his breakfast before going to work, Giuditta passed by him holding a food tray and laughed at Nicola, "Did you like my performance, Marito?" She proceeded to another table where her lover sat, waiting for his breakfast. Nicola heard her whisper to him fondly, "Amore." Giuditta didn't touch the big guy in public. And Nicola noticed the man's muscly arm reach under her dress while Giuditta giggled. Nicola knew who his wife's lover was. Marco Pilato was a strapping laborer at the mill and had to be over ten years younger than her. He reminded Giuditta of Luigi in body only, though his brainpower was that of a child. Nicola only cursed Marco under his breath as the large arm worked its way further under Giuditta's dress until her embarrassment forced her to leave to go back to the kitchen. The much smaller and slimmer Nicola didn't have a chance of picking a fight with such a huge man. But he was still Giuditta's husband, and he reaped his rewards of free room and board, especially the homemade beer he loved so much.

In the late summer, Douglas Nicholson, carrying a small

fishing rod, took his five-year-old son, Douglas Nicholson III, to the driveway behind his house. A smiling Gabrielle waved goodbye to her men from the back porch of their home, where she preferred to do her sewing to avoid the hot sun.

Gabrielle's father, Andre Delisle, passed away unexpectedly from a heart attack over a year before. It was a shock to Clair, Gabriele, and the Nicholsons. Together, they trekked to Cincinnati to mourn the loss of the remarkable man loved by all. A self-made man, he started at the bottom of a business and rose to the top. Douglas was especially comforting to Gabrielle, and although she still grieved at times, her family brought her slowly back to them. Andre's wife, Clair, came to stay with her daughter for a few months but returned to the home she shared so long with her dear husband. That's where her fondest memories resided.

Now, seeing her little boy about to embark on his first official fishing venture, Gabrielle felt a rush of happiness. "Goodbye, Dougie!" she yelled to her son as her husband opened the door of their automobile. "Good luck!"

"Goodbye, Mommy!" Little Douglas looked so excited and eager. He gave a big wave and grinned from ear to ear.

"Goodbye, Dougie! Have fun!" Gabrielle knew her husband had waited for this day, probably ever since their son was born.

Although Douglas's father took little Martha fishing when she was three, she gave up the sport quickly. Now nine, she focused on other forms of amusement. Claire, now 12, never even tried to fish; she thought it was disgusting for a young lady, as she thought of herself now.

Douglas thought it was too far of a walk for the little boy, so he put his son beside him in his automobile, and they drove off together to the Third Street Station, where Douglas pulled aside a parked truck. There was no activity at the station. Douglas had checked the schedule first to safely take his son across the train tracks. He told the young boy, "You must never cross the tracks without Grandpa or me, okay?"

"Yes, Daddy, you told me that a thousand times," he laughed.

The boy was beautiful, with blonde hair like both his parents and the olive-green colored eyes of his mother.

"Okay, Son, and I'm probably going to tell you again," Douglas smiled at his only boy, "I don't want anything bad to happen to you, ever," he smiled again as he picked up little Douglas and kissed him. "Now, I'm going to take you to a very special place." Douglas couldn't wait for the day when he could take his boy fishing at the same places he did as a child. "C'mon, let's go!" Little Douglas carried the small rod his father bought specially for him.

The father and son walked across the tracks further down the river. Douglas, his heart heavy with nostalgia, remembered Mr. McElhenny, who had passed away two years before and smiled at his memories. "Now," Douglas looked into his son's beautiful eyes, "You must promise never to tell anyone about this spot. Remember, it's special." Douglas had a few seconds of sadness, recalling telling Peppina the same thing many years before as Rollo sat by his side.

"I promise, Daddy, cross my heart and hope to die."

"Okay, then, let's go!" he said as he guided his son down the slope to that magical, memorable spot from his childhood.

A few moments later, little Douglas excitedly shouted, "Oh boy! Golly! I've never seen so many fish!"

Later that year, right before the winter frost, Giuditta had her fill of Nicola. No longer needing his name to run her business for a while, she wanted to throw him out of the hotel. One evening, upon returning from work, Nicola found his bags packed at the side of the front door. Giuditta was waiting for him. With his powerful arms folded, her enforcer, Marco Pilato, stood behind her. "Get out!" Giuditta pointed to the front door. "Get out and stay out, you poor excuse for a man." She turned slightly and put her left hand on Marco's arm, gently massaging it. "Get out, or I'll have a real man throw you out," she told Nicola. Marco proudly smiled, unfolding his arms to hold Giuditta's shoulders while gently rubbing them.

"Where am I supposed to go? It's freezing out there!" Nicola's voice was tinged with desperation, and his words were a plea for mercy.

"I don't care where you go. Just get out of my sight!" Giuditta looked at Marco and pointed to Nicola's two small suitcases. Marco picked them up, opened the front door, and threw the suitcases down the few stairs onto the sidewalk. Nicola watched them tumble over several times until the battered old luggage toppled over and opened, spilling all his things onto the street.

Nicola's eyes teared as he looked at Marco and then Giuditta. "I'm the father of your children!" Giuditta said nothing, only looked the other way. Nicola turned and slowly walked out the door, muttering "la puttana" under his breath.

The only place Nicola could afford was at the Morelli's home. They were the poorest Italian immigrants in the town. The entire family's wardrobe were almost rags, and their children didn't have shoes in the cold of winter. So, the father, Nunzio, was glad to earn extra money by allowing Nicola to board in his home. It was nothing more than a wreck where no other boarder wanted to stay. They had little heat, sometimes none. When able to afford it, Nunzio lit a small coal fireplace downstairs that could not fight the valley's cold and windy winters. They were so dirty that when Nunzio's wife, Maria, went to the doctor, he sent her home, telling her, "I can't examine you until you take a bath."

Nicola was forced to share a room with another poor worker from the mill. No longer could Nicola Bucci indulge in the comforts of the hotel. The delicious food, beer, and warmth were gone forever. However, Giuditta stayed warm in Marco Pilato's arms every night, begging for more from the bull of a man who never stopped or refused to satisfy her undying desires.

Lucy Buch felt terrible for her father-in-law, who was always kind to her. "Here, Suocero, mangiare." She brought food over for Nicola every day. "I brought your clean laundry." Lucy gathered Nicola's dirty clothes, saying, "I'll do these tomorrow." As she walked to the door of the filthy room, she told Nicola, "Suocero, I'll see you tomorrow." It repulsed her to see him in such a filthy place, though he refused to leave and stay in Felo's home.

"You see my wife lately?" Nicola asked Lucy one day.

Lucy looked upon that woman with contempt but forgave her. She knew Guiditta had struggled with the loss of her daughters and the man she once loved and was somehow reliving those days with him through other men. "No," Lucy simply replied. She didn't go to the hotel after what happened to Thelma, and Giuditta took it as a personal insult. "I don't see her anymore," Lucy honestly replied.

Months later, during the cold of winter, Nicola became ill from the poor living conditions at the drafty and cold Morelli house. Felo sent for a doctor who diagnosed Nicola with pneumonia. Lucy went over during the days when her daughters were home from school to watch little Nicholas, whom they called Nicky. Lucy cared for Nicola, kept him clean, and put compresses on his forehead to help relieve his fever. However, Nicola passed away alone during a cold winter night. The man who shared his room found him dead in the morning. Giuditta had no idea as she lay in the warm arms of her lover.

Nicola's body, prepared by a town mortician, arrived later that day at Felo's home on Broadway. They put the open casket on the right side of the room near the front doorway. That way, visitors could pay their respects as soon as they entered the home. Nicola's face appeared stern, with a specific look of dignity as his body lay over ice.

"I'm so sorry about Nicola," Sofia Marino offered sympathies to Giuditta at the hotel. Sofia knew Giuditta hadn't yet learned about Nicola's death but didn't want to embarrass her friend. She also knew of Giuditta's liaisons with other men; most of the Italian community did. But Sofia had personally seen the torment of that woman when taking her to the lawyer in East Liverpool. She understood why her friend had resorted to men after losing her daughters and the man she really loved.

Upon hearing of Nicola's death, Giuditta donned her black dress and telephoned the florist. "Marco! Not now! I'm on the telephone," she brushed away his roaming hands. "Do something useful. Hand me my shoes!" She returned to her conversation with the florist. Giuditta ordered two huge and extravagant porcelain vases in the figures of doves filled with flowers. A purple ribbon spread across both dove vases, spelling the words: 'To my darling husband.' "I want the biggest and best flowers you have! Only fresh ones!" she demanded in her broken English.

Later that day, Giuditta walked the short distance to Broadway to see Nicola. Before opening the front door, she readied herself for her theatrical presentation, as an actor does. She burst through the door crying, sobbing, and screamed as loud as she could, "Nicola mio! Marito beddo!" 'My husband, my beautiful husband.' Kneeling before the man she threw out of his home, she sobbed and softly repeated those words while patting his forehead.

Giuditta rose and turned to see her doves standing beside the other flowers, dwarfing them, which made her proud. Two female paid mourners who sang lamenting songs at intervals sat, each at opposite sides of the floral arrangements. They were heavyset women from which the saying, 'It's not over until the fat lady sings,' was derived. As Giuditta left to go to the main room where people sat, one of the paid mourners rose and began bawling loudly while the other one whimpered where she sat. Occasionally, one of them sang or spoke bible verses. They took turns keeping the mood of the house somber. Giuditta mixed in with her family, continuing her performance. Everyone knew she threw Nicola out to live in a horrible place that killed him. Thelma wouldn't even look at Giuditta.

People kept arriving throughout the day and night, bringing food and beverages. Nicola's daughters and son sat grieving amidst the other mourners, including the Trieste family. Annie sat next to Eleanora. The other Trieste sisters sat together with their mother and father. Lucy put Nicky to bed early after she fed him. She made Julia, now spelled the American way, and Eleanora rest for some time around midnight.

The following morning, the undertaker arrived to take Nicola to the church. The plump ladies sang together at the funeral mass for Nicola as Giuditta cried the loudest in the front pew. Nicola Bucci was laid to rest later that day next to a plot already marked for his loving wife, who promptly returned to her bed with Marco.

Giuditta danced the tarantella, shouting "Hey-hey-hey" to the loud music at a Christening one week later. She dressed in the colors of a grieving widow. Yet, she raised her black dress to expose he legs, laughing and having a merry time with Marco. To her, Nicola was just a bad memory.

One week later, Lucy Buch noticed one particular letter in her mail. Felo went through most of the mail as Lucy struggled with English, but this one was addressed to her. As she opened it, a check fell out onto the table. Though the letter was in English, Lucy could understand the amount inscribed. Nicola had left Lucy substantial money from a life insurance policy.

"Ciao, Lucy! How are you today?" Maria Rispola took the chair offered to her by Lucy at the dining room table. "Come sta, Felo, and the children?" she asked about her family.

"Busy, Maria. You know he has a big office job at the Railroad," the proud wife replied in her native language. "He's too busy sometimes. Julia is a big help to Nicky, but Eleanora?" she grimaced and gestured with her hands. "She always wants to go outside. Would you like a coffee?" Lucy asked as she placed a plate of biscotti in the center of the table.

"Yes, grazie. That's how some kids are." She spread her arms wide with the palms of her hands open and nodded with a smirk, "What are you gonna do?"

Lucy returned from the kitchen with a small tray containing an espresso pot and two small coffee cups, which she also placed on the table and then filled each cup. "So, how can I help you?" she asked as she sat across from Maria.

Maria pulled a letter from her purse and handed it to Lucy, who sat back and read it. It appeared poorly written, and then Lucy's eyes widened in surprise. "What is it, Lucy?" Maria immediately asked as she saw the look on Lucy's face.

"Is this a close friend of yours, Maria?"

"Yes, why?"

Lucy explained the news of her friend's village in Sicily and how she and her husband were doing. Then Lucy told her, "She writes about a Valentina. Do you know her?"

"Yes, she's a friend from my village."

"Oh, well, she had twin baby boys," Lucy smiled, "imagine that." But Maria looked in shock and turned pale before Lucy. "What? That's a good thing."

"Her husband is here in Wellsville, Marty Gallo. He's been here for two years, saving money to bring Valentina over here." Maria put her hands to the sides of her pale white face. "Maronna mia!"

Lucy realized that her friend had twin illegitimate babies. She knew of Marty Gallo. 'What a small world,' she thought. Marty was bad-tempered and worked with the Black Hand. This situation was the worst thing a woman could do and the most horrible thing for an Italian man to endure, especially a Sicilian. Lucy thought quickly, wondering if Maria would tell Valentina's husband. Finally, she said, "Maybe you shouldn't tell anyone, particularly the husband."

Maria's face remained white, and she lifted her eyes to stare into Lucy's. "You know how these people are, Lucy." She meant the Black Hand. "If Marty found out we know and didn't tell him, he might hurt us." Lucy shook her head, regretting she read the letter. How could she have known the husband was a local man? Maria rose and walked over to Lucy, who was now nervously standing beside her chair. Maria took Lucy's hand and kissed each side of her face, the traditional Italian gesture. "Don't tell anyone, Lucy. I'll think about what I should do."

"I'll never say anything," replied Lucy while making the

sign of the cross.

Maria Rispola made one of the biggest mistakes of her life when she told her husband. He promised to keep quiet about it, but the temptation was too great. He told an old friend from Sicily, Gregorio Musto, but didn't know Gregorio also worked for the Black Hand in town. The next time Gregorio saw Marty Gallo, he laid in with the jokes. "Hey, Marty, I heard you got a bargain, two kids for the price of one!" he laughed.

"What are you talking about?" Marty raised his shoulders, questioning.

"Your wife; she had twin boys! Auguri!" he congratulated him.

Then Ricardo Molto, another Black Hand associate, approached the two men. "Hey, Cornuto! Auguri! Nice job!" Calling an Italian man a cornuto was the worst insult you could make. Marty Gallo pushed Ricardo hard, making him trip. Ricardo regained his balance and pulled a .38 pistol from under his jacket, "Do that again, and I'll kill you!"

Gregorio Musto told Marty Gallo it was true. A letter from Italy arrived for his friend's wife and explained everything: "Your wife, Valentina, had twin boys. Ricardo's right, you're a cornuto! Accept it!" He laughed in Marty's face. "Come, we're going to the bar. We'll help you come up with two names for the boys." He laughed again, but Marty Gallo left for his house in a fury.

An hour later, Marty's anger was still festering. He had to regain the honor that 'puttana wife' of his stole from him by her actions. He imagined planning to send for her only so he could kill her and her two bastards; he had to vent this madness that now possessed him. Marty took his .45 caliber handgun from the closet, tucked it into his waist belt, and slipped his jacket over. Any rational thoughts had left him; only rage guided the man now as he quickly walked, trotting at times, to the bar where Gregorio was.

Ricardo Molto stood outside the tavern, talking to another man. As Marty approached, Ricardo saw the dazed face that was no longer human but that of an animal, eyes glaring like a wild beast. A somewhat frightened Ricardo told Marty, "If you're looking for Gregorio, he already went home." Marty didn't care about anything, his mind only flashing the image of his beloved wife Valentina being with that animal who impregnated her. Marty imagined her delivering 'his' babies and the look of contentment on both their faces as she proudly displayed those bastards. Marty pulled the heavy revolver from his waist, seeing the horror on Ricardo's face, and blasted the gun three times. Ricardo's body folded from the force of the large caliber bullets, his feet danced on tiptoes for a few seconds, and then he fell to the sidewalk. His body lay there folded, his limbs twisted, giving the appearance of a puppet that fell from the strings that held it. The man who was speaking to him had already run into the bar, fearing for his own life. Marty Gallo walked in a trancelike state to the home of Gregorio Musto on Broadway.

The house that Felo rented on Broadway had a large piece of property extending all the way to the next block, Commerce Street. They had a sophisticated, as little Eleanora called it, outhouse directly in the back with a self-flushing toilet seat. A neighbor asked Felo if he could plant a garden in the space that Felo didn't use, and he agreed. The deal was that Felo and Lucy received half of everything produced, a good deal for the Buch family.

As Julia gave Nicky a bath in the kitchen sink that late afternoon, her family was shocked to hear three consecutive blasts. "Boom-boom-boom," one after the other, the loud and penetrating gunshots rang out for everyone on the block to hear. Then Julia looked out the window and noticed the figure of a man who seemed to drop something. The young girl didn't think much about it at the time. The following day, Eleanora found a pistol lying next to the outhouse. She glanced at it, surprised, and then ran inside to call her mother.

The day before, Marty Gallo knocked like a madman on the door of Gregorio Musto's house on Broadway. He fired his .45 immediately as soon as the door opened. Marty kept pulling the trigger on the empty chambers of the gun after he had fired the last three remaining bullets. In his rage, he didn't realize that he shot Gregorio's wife by mistake. Loretta Musto, a large woman, fell further backward by each of the bullets fired in swift succession. Blood spurted from each hole thrust into her body. With time only for a dazed expression on her face, the big woman dropped to her knees, looking into the eyes of Marty Gallo, and then her head dropped, and Loretta's corpse fell forward. Her large posterior remained raised, and she appeared to be kissing the feet of the man who had mistakenly killed her. Marty ran four houses down Broadway and cut across a yard with a garden he knew led to Commerce. He dropped his revolver and fled home. A little boy by the name of Wilbur Cambell, playing across the street from the Musto home, saw the entire murder.

After Eleanora found the gun, Lucy knew she couldn't call the police; that meant death by the Black Hand. Instead, she telephoned Salvatore Gusto, the godfather of the Black Hand. He sent over someone to get the revolver.

Later that afternoon, Mary, Annie, and Eleanora walked down the steep hill, returning from a farm. Eleanora excitedly told them the story of the shooting the day before. Giuditta sent them to bring George Bamarra the lunch he had forgotten at the hotel. Even though he bought a beautiful brick home near the corner of Third, George always picked up his lunch from Giuditta's hotel. Thelma avoided that place at all costs, but little by little, like a spider, her mother was luring her daughter back to her with her magical skills, her psychological manipulations, and the comforts of money and clothes. She told George to give her none of these things so Giuditta could win Thelma back by providing these specialties for her daughter. Little Clara Trieste desperately wanted to come along with her sisters, but her mother didn't think the six-year-old could yet manage the long walk up the hill and back.

"Boom-boom-boom!" Elenora described the loud sounds of the blasts that pierced her ears and penetrated the area surrounding her home on Broadway. "I was scared to death!" The Trieste girls listened attentively with widened eyes. "Mom told my dad that she wanted to leave the house."

"Where will you go?" asked Mary. She and her sister looked terrified by the story and the possibility of Eleanora leaving.

"I don't know, but she wants to get away from the large, secluded backyard after that man ran through it. He could have shot one of us!" Eleanora explained with a serious expression. Annie walked over to the side of the road and casually grabbed a bunch of cardone, called 'cardoon,' by the Italians. Seeds of the vegetable that was a cousin of the artichoke spread from the farms where Italians planted them and grew wild. Anytime the girls spotted them, they plucked them to bring home to their parents, who prized them as a delicacy.

"I hope you stay close to us," Annie said, clutching the vegetable. "You don't think you'll leave town, do you?" Mary, Annie, and Eleanora were still in grammar school at the East End School on Lisbon Street. Annie's older sister, Louise, would start high school on Center Street, where her brother, Anthony, would begin his senior year. Both were a little older and acted somewhat as authority figures to the younger girls.

"I don't think your parents will leave town," Mary said confidently, "Your dad works at the Third Street Station."

"I hope so," Eleanora agreed. "Oh! There's another." Eleanora trotted over to the side and picked another cardoon. Just then, all the girls heard the loud clang and clatter of an older motor vehicle from behind them, chugging along and coming down the road. It was Mr. Hanley driving his old Ford Model T one-ton pickup truck. All the girls knew Jim Hanley. He was a friendly man who helped Eleanora's uncle George with deliveries. They didn't precisely know what he transported, only that he was always nice to them. The truck came to a slow stop, its brakes squealing like a railroad train as it did. The motor idled in the middle of the road and clattered as it let out occasional bursts of steam and hissed.

"C'mon, girls! I'll give you all a ride to town! Jump in the back!"

"Thanks, Mr. Hanley!" the girls yelled simultaneously and with a harmonious beat. The three of them fit themselves behind some canvas covers obscuring the contents beneath them. Eleanora, the nosiest of the three girls, slightly moved the canvas cover to reveal wooded crates. Peeking through the spaces of the crates appeared to be large ceramic jugs. She quickly dropped the canvas, realizing what they were. The girls sat and enjoyed the bumpy ride, laughing all the way to Third Street in town. "Thanks, Mr. Hanley!" the girls yelled out again simultaneously to that same harmonious beat.

Chapter Thirty-Two

Wellsville, Ohio 1926

The Klan and A Town Tragedy

The Ku Klux Klan began in the post-American Civil War era. Former Confederate soldiers put white sheets over them and rode on horseback to commemorate the ghosts of their brave brothers in arms who perished in that war. Eventually, it grew to oppose, harass, and hurt freed slaves and the Republicans who freed them and were helping them merge into the society of the South. That original movement was crushed but replaced by a wholly different type of Klan many years later.

The newer Ku Klux Klan rose after the Great War and began wearing white pointed hoods with only round holes for their eyes and white open-fronted full-length robes, some with rope ties. Attached to the robes were round red patches with white and black crosses and a tilted black-bordered white rectangle with a sewn symbolic drop of red blood in its center. The patch was worn on the left side of the uniform over the men's hearts. By the mid-1920s, it became more of a fraternal organization of White Anglo-Saxon Protestants. Members paid dues, and the Klan flourished nationwide. Wellsville was close to the heart of the densest membership in Indiana. The Klan rose to oppose the rising number of Jews and Catholics, mainly Italian Immigrants. It endorsed a white Protestant America and prohibition and fought against the sale of illegal liquor. The Klan paraded in towns and cities and burned crosses to display a show of power and frighten those who didn't adhere to their values.

After 1922, the Mingo railroad yards, distanced from Wellsville, expanded. Simultaneously, construction of the river's half-mile-long mainline connection began at Yellow Creek, became known as the Wye, and finished in the mid-1920s. That bypassed the mine runs that had made Wellsville's railroad significant. The glorious Shop where Douglas and Peppina once romped as day-trippers, guided by Douglas's father, was gradually downsizing. The railroad relocated workers and foremen and laid off some. Slowly, the railroad dismantled much of the Shop, leaving only remnants. The newer roundhouse and turntable that replaced the older ones remained. They had been built during the Great War when the government ran the railroads but now dwelled in a more ghostly vacancy that was once great.

Hooded ghostlike figures assembled and prepared for their parade along Main Street near that spectral area. The intimidating, spooky figures, five abreast, slowly marched in rows on their long trek past the corner of Third and Lisbon Street.The ghostly shapes of about 40 to 50 men followed a Klan member holding an American flag as another carried a cross. They followed the trolley tracks along the town's main and most frequently used street. Creating an eerie mood as they stepped, evenly paced like soldiers, people of all ethnicities came out to see them, forming crowds along the sides of the street. Out of that horde of people on the sidelines, some cheered, others yelled sentiments of reinforcement. Many women clapped and rallied the men. Only in larger groups did any opposers make negative comments, and even then, they did so while hiding their faces in the mob, where they blended in.

Immigrants from the Italian community came out at the corner of Tenth Street, some bringing their families with them. Remaining quiet, they observed closely. Oppression was nothing new to many of them, especially the Sicilians. Harassed, ridiculed, and persecuted from both sides of the great ocean by brotherhoods like the mafia or royals, which made up part of the ruling class of Italy, they knew that type of treatment well. Now, in this part of America, it was the Klan. However, the children were terrified and cried from the spine-chilling cavalcade of men in ghostly garments. "Hey!" one father told his son, "look at me!" The little boy wiped his eyes and tilted his head to see his father's. "Never let anyone try to scare you! You're going to be a man someday. Start acting like it now, okay? Crying is for girls and ladies and those fat women who sing at funerals. Let them do the crying!" The boy nodded his head at his father in approval. The man gently patted his boy's crop of plentiful light brown hair and said, "That's my boy! See how stupid they look; men dressed up like children." The man and his son laughed together as the procession passed them.

There appeared to be a formal delegation standing near City Hall at Fifth Street. All prestigious men holding their right hands over their hearts in admiration. One block and a half away began the point on Main, where most Italians from town who had come out flocked together to stay safe in case something unexpected and threatening happened to them. Among them were the shoemaker Concetto Provenzano and his son, Carlo, who blended into the mass of Italian immigrants. Concetto was nearing retirement and cut back his hours, leaving most of the work to his capable son, who was now married and had his own family.

"Carlo," Concetto whispered to his son in his native dialect, "Allen Brown in front of that short guy."

"Pop," Carlo whispered back, "Bill Johnson, behind the fat guy."

Concetto and Carlo could identify almost all the men by their shoes. As the only shoemakers and repairmen in town, they either made or repaired most of the shoes and boots that now marched past them. "Hey, Pop," Carlo whispered in between putting names to the footwear, "They don't like us, but they sure love our shoe handiwork," he laughed, putting his hand over his mouth to hide his amusement.

"We should have left a few nails sticking up inside the insoles before their parade," Concetto replied. That made his son laugh even harder.

After the shooting near their home on Broadway, Felo and Lucy bought a lovely house on Commerce Street. Lucy's precious furniture and ornaments were carefully moved to the next block under the scrutiny of Lucy's adept eyes. The Trieste sisters were happily secure in the knowledge that their friend, whom they treated as a fellow sister, would not be moving far but actually closer.

As the Ku Klux Klan marched, the Buch and Trieste families stood together at the turn to Third Street, near the boarding house of Colomba and Frank. The Trieste sisters, as well as Eleanora and Julia, were frightened. Lucy noticed that the girls were terrified and almost crying, and she told them, "Hey! They just'a dress up lik'a Halloween! No you be afraid of these idiots in'a clown costumes!" The words and the way Lucy pronounced them made all the girls chuckle.

The robed and hooded figures trudged past Third Street and around the bend to Lisbon Street. There was a path that led to the Indian Stone face. They burned a much larger cross on that hill, and the shooting flames brightened the darkening sky. Julia and Eleanora stayed up most of the night watching the blood-curdling firey cross from their bedroom window burn, watching as the hooded men encircled the large burning cross like pagans worshipping a god. The two young girls lay awake, afraid of what might happen.

"Yeah, you can use the boat, but you have to promise me that you all be careful."

"Thank you, Mr. Clary!" Mary, the oldest of the small group of girls, excitedly replied. "Okay, girls, let's push her out."

"Wait!" Mr. Clary yelled out. Mary and the others thought he was going to ask for money. "The rowboat has a leak. Be sure to use that small can there," he said, pointing to an old paint bucket at the stern of the boat. "Use that to scoop out the water."

"Okay, Mr. Clary, we will!" Mary waved back. "Eleanora, you help me shove it off. Annie, you and Clara get in," the older sister directed, "Clara, you get all the way back and use the can. That's your job." Clara, the youngest sister, went aboard first. She was already tall for her age of six. As Annie sat at the bow of the old wood, dilapidated rowboat, Eleanora and Mary pushed it out into the river, quickly jumping aboard to sit together at the center wood-planked seat. As soon as they did, they each grabbed one of the oars lying on the floor of the small watercraft. Mr. Clary watched from a distance, smiling and shaking his head.

"We'll take turns rowing, but Clara, you gotta keep the water out." They all noticed that water was already seeping inside.

"Okay!" Clara feverishly labored to empty the accumulated water. But the little girl was having fun with the responsible task the older children had delegated to her.

Annie jumped down to take a turn at the oars to give her older sister a rest. As Mary rested, Eleanora, and Annie sat side by side. All the girls laughed and talked about what they would do with their lives. Not knowing what the future had in store for them, the young children sailed together along the Ohio River, laughing as if searching for some hidden meaning to their existence. As the girls rowed, fighting the slight current of the river on the calm, beautiful sun-filled day, they all began singing, "Row, row, row, your boat, gently down the stream, merrily, merrily, merrily, merrily, life is but a dream, row, row. . ." Clara kept up with the water leaking and filling the bucket.

That Sunday in mid-May was a special occasion for Mr. and Mrs. Alberto Albino. They were celebrating the Baptism of their baby daughter, Maria. After the christening ceremony, they held a party at Frank DiLino's home on Commerce Street between 12th and 13th Streets. As the Albinos had only a small apartment, Frank offered them his yard for a party to mark the blessed occasion.

Mr. and Mrs. Albino invited many from the Italian community, and even one of the Catholic priests made a short appearance. They extended an invitation to Salvatore Gusto; it would have been deemed an insult to do otherwise, especially since Carmella Albino was a second cousin to Gusto's wife. The so-called Godfather of the Black Hand gladly accepted the somewhat dubious invitation on the part of the Albinos. He brought along a few of his cronies.

Eleanora Buch was friends with the baby's older sister, Dorothea, and her mother, Lucy, knew the mother, Carmella Albino. Eleanora's older sister, Julia, came along as well. At first, she didn't want to, but she knew there would be dancing, which she loved. The Trieste family couldn't attend the occasion. However, they allowed their daughter, Annie, to accompany Eleanora since she was also friends with the baby's sister. Giuditta was there but stayed apart from Lucy and close to her unofficial boyfriend, Marco.

In the Italian tradition that marked such a noteworthy time, festivities of all types took place. The Italian women prepared scrumptious foods and delicacies of various kinds as some of the men played musical instruments. Two women banged and shook tambourines as men and women danced the tarantella to the music of men playing a mandolin, guitar, and banjo. Some men sneaked liquor from flasks as they enjoyed the merriment, which the booze intensified.

As the afternoon festivities extended to early evening, Lucy Buch decided to bring the girls home against their wishes. "Oh, please, Mom! Let us stay a little bit longer," Eleanora pleaded. "We're having such a good time!" She, along with Annie, Julia, and Dorothea, had been dancing and laughing the afternoon away, not realizing how fast the time flew, as all young girls and boys do. But Lucy's keen eye noticed the slurred words the men spoke and the erratic way they were acting, most likely from liquor.

"It's time to go home, girls," she said, offering no other reason. Eleanora and Annie pouted but followed Lucy as she bid everyone a fine good night and congratulated the baby's parents one last time. A friend's husband drove them to their home further up Commerce, closer to Third Street.

The gaiety continued well past midnight. Men spoke loudly in their piercing Italian operatic voices, from soprano and baritone to bass. The music, singing, and dancing continued until only a skeleton crew of the original crowd remained. Neighbors became annoyed, shouting out their windows for quiet. With their pleas to end the noise ignored, two neighbors wanted the police to end the celebration that had become an annoyance.

A figure emerged out of the shadows to approach Salvatore Gusto. The man wore a dark grey silk shirt and black dress trousers, the front rim of his Fedora hat partially concealing Luke Fontana's shifty and wicked eyes. Luke, now in his early thirties, had been rising up the ranks of his now fully organized family in Cleveland. His only reason for seeing Gusto was to initiate the sale of bottled liquors of various types smuggled into the States from Canada. He had an appointment to see Salvatore Gusto at midnight, but Gusto didn't realize the time and missed the meeting place. Now Luke, very perturbed, angrily told Gusto, "I'm doing ya a favor!" Like a mountain lion ready to pounce on its prey, his eyes glowed with hostility.

Gusto guided Fontano to the side, not wanting his men to see this man degrade his power and manhood. "I'm sorry, Luke. I completely forgot," he said, waving his arms. "With all the festivities, I lost track of time. We can talk now." As they spoke, a young uniformed policeman approached the yard.

Officer James Renny addressed the first man he saw, 28-year-old Nick Salerno. "Are you running this ruckus?" The music gradually stopped upon seeing an officer of the law so feared by Italians in their home country. Nick could hardly speak English and didn't understand what the policeman was saying. He stood dumbfounded. Frank DiLino spotted him and rushed over. Officer Renny smelled liquor on Nick's breath but ignored it as he saw DiLino standing before him. "Is this your house?"

"Yes, officer, it is."

"We have several complaints," the policeman told him. Officer James Renny worked as a fireman and an officer of the law, which was common then. He looked around and continued, "I want you to shut down your party now. Your neighbors are complaining, and I don't blame them. Do you realize what time it is?"

Frank surveyed the houses surrounding his home, wondering who the complainers were. He angrily thought about his retribution when he discovered who made them. "Yes, Officer, right away!" He politely replied, maintaining his composure but still adhering to his revenge.

"Okay. You know I can cite you for disturbing the peace. I'll let you go this time, but put an end to the noise." Renny spoke firmly, as a peace officer should, but in no way disrespectful.

"Yes, officer, I'm sorry, very sorry," Frank answered. Gusto was observing Frank and the patrolman speaking. Gusto was getting angry as he stood in the distance, first for Luke humiliating him. Now, by not hearing the conversation, he assumed the cop was asking for a payoff for the liquor that was there.

A furious Gusto turned to Rocco Brocella, one of his men, "Didn't you pay them this month?" Gusto was fuming, not knowing that Officer James Renny was an honest policeman and didn't take bribes.

"Yeah, boss, I did, as usual." Rocco tried to calm down Gusto as Luke Fontana shoved his way over. Officer Renny had left and was already half a block away.

"Don't ya guys know how'ta control the cops around here?" Luke dripped what looked like foam from his mouth, so annoyed. "Are we gonna talk business or not? I got crates of fine Canadian booze that you can make a fortune by distrib-atin in the area. Are ya in or ain't ya? Tell me now, or I walk!"

Gusto shouted out, "Play back the music! Now! This is a party, for God's sake! Everyone, have fun!" trying to show his power and authority to surpass that of the law. Frank DiLino was so scared of Gusto's sudden fury that he didn't dare suggest that it might not be a good idea to resume the noise. Seeing the malicious looks of Gusto and Fontana, he kept his mouth shut. The musicians reluctantly began playing. From a block and a half away, Officer Renny could hear them start the music again, completely disregarding his warning. He immediately headed back.

Emotions were tense between Luke and Gusto when the officer returned. Gusto still thought he was looking for money and lost control. Before the officer spoke, Gusto shouted out, "Son of a bitch!" he reached under his light jacket and pulled out his .38 revolver. The young officer quickly spotted the gun in the poor lighting outside and reached for his service revolver. Rocco Brocella tried to stop his boss from making the mistake of shooting a police officer and grabbed Gusto's arm. "Boom!" The sound of his gunshot was like a cannon in the dead of night. But the sudden movement as Rocco grabbed Gusto's arm forced the shot to fire low, and the bullet hit Officer Renny's right foot. From surprise and pain from the wound, Renny's arm jerked, and his expended bullet cracked loudly but ricocheted. It hit Nick Salerno's foot in the crossfire. Officer Renny's revolver blasted again but missed. Still struggling to stand from the pain radiating in his right foot, he fired again; the deafening blast hurt the ears of the scattering people still close by.

Luke Fontana pushed Rocco and Gusto aside, making Renny's third shot also miss. "You bunch a pussies!" Luke shouted as he fired his weapon, the lead trajectory traveling faster than the speed of sound, hitting Officer Renny's right arm before the sound blared, forcing his body to turn. Luke fired again, and the piercing bullet hit the turning body of the policeman in his back. "Take that copper!" Luke walked up and shot the policeman in the face as Renny's body fell backward toward a fence, bleeding, his arm lowering, still with his gun in hand, and firing the last three remaining bullets. One of the officer's shots hit the ground, and the other two bullets hit Nick Salerno in his leg and groin. Then Renny's spent revolver dropped aside his body.

Everyone had ducked or ran off. A mandolin remained on the ground, left in the musician's haste. "Rocco!" Gusto shouted to his man, "Take Nick to my house!" Rocco obeyed, quickly put his arm around Nick, and dragged him over to his boss's home on Thirteenth Street. Officer James Renny lay bleeding to death in a puddle of blood. Luke Fontana headed back to Cleveland to sell his liquor elsewhere.

Salvatore Gusto had one of his men call in an anonymous tip to the police that the murderer of the police officer was at Gusto's home, and he had broken a window to get in. Nick Salerno lay with makeshift bandages, not understanding anything when the police arrived. The police arrested Nick and took him to the hospital in East Liverpool. The prosecutor questioned Nick Salerno in his bed, who didn't understand anything he was saying. The only thing that Nick Salerno did understand was what Gusto told him in Italian, "Don't say anything!"

The Black Hand told the innocent man to take the blame, and they would get him off. People went from house to house for donations. Nick's sister told him in Italian, "Fratello, tell them who did it," but he knew that if he did, the Black Handers would kill him.

Nick Salerno stood in the courtroom facing the judge who sentenced him. His mother screamed at the top of her lungs, "Mio figlio e innocente! Innocente e mio figlio!" 'My son is innocent!' over and over until Gusto's men dragged her out before the officials did. The innocent man spent 45 years in prison as a model prisoner and was released, dying two years later.

Officer James Renny left behind his widow, two children, brothers and sisters, and others in his family, and the town and surrounding area mourned his death. The honest young officer died a hero; outnumbered by the Black Hand, he stood his ground enforcing the law. The mayor announced a $1000 reward leading to the murderer's arrest. The town formed a lynch party targeting all Italians, not just the thugs of the Black Hand who perpetrated the murder; they roamed free. The mayor asked Chief Shultz, already suspended and pending trial, to assist in the investigation.

Chapter Thirty-Three

Wellsville, Ohio 1926
The Feast of San Rocco

On August 12th, the Feast of San Rocco was celebrated in Wellsville. It was a sacred time for the Italian American community. After a mass in honor of the saint, a procession began. Afterward, festivities continued with a tremendous fireworks display.

Giuditta held a dress against her nude body. Turning slightly, she viewed her mirrored reflection carefully, wanting to look her best for the trip. It was the third outfit she tried, and she decided it was the one. She flung the black dress on the bed and continued admiring herself.

For her age, she was still a well-formed and attractive woman. The slight bit of weight gained over the past few years only added more shape to her legs and to those other parts of her body men relished, namely her derriere and bust. Her few grey hairs added a dignified look. Hard work had maintained her figure all these years, and her face remained stunning as it did years ago. One would have to look closely to see the slight crowfeet and wrinkles around her eyes, nothing a little makeup couldn't easily hide. She stood pleased and then sat to dress, all of her clothes readied on her bed.

Lying back on a cushioned chair, she slowly rolled the flesh-colored silk stockings up her shapely leg, wiggling her foot to make a tight fit without bunches. After repeating the process for her other leg, Giuditta stood to attach the stockings to her skimpy garter belt. Pushing her body back on the chair, she lifted her legs and gently massaged the silk stockings of her left leg with the toes of her right foot, feeling invigorated. Observing herself in the mirror, she whispered, "No, I want him to see my naked legs."

After removing the garter and nylons, she rose, nude again, and appraised her soft, creamy, ivory-white shapely legs. Standing on her tiptoes accentuated her lower limbs and gave them more form and sex appeal, she noticed. "When I slip my heels on, they'll remain like that," she whispered, "He'll love the feel of my naked legs more than those heavy stockings."

Giuditta didn't wear undergarments and slid the black dress she had chosen over her body, shaking it so it fit snuggly. Glancing again in the mirror, she was pleased with the fit, accentuating the shape of her figure, and turned to each side to better appreciate it. The top of the dress's design was cut low, exposing the cleavage of her large breasts, and black transparent silk mesh material covered her naked upper arms. The one-piece garment ran down her body and ended well above her knees. The newer styles exposed much more of a lady's legs for the first time, finally allowing Giuditta to display her beautiful limbs in public. Stylish matching black fringes hung at the bottom of the garment, covertly revealing her curvaceous naked legs and providing an overall image of appeal. Giuditta intended to look younger, and with the finishing touches of makeup, she did by at least 15 years. Delighted with herself, Giuditta slid her petite feet into open black dress shoes, having two-and-a-half-inch heels and a strap around her ankles. "Yes," she giggled, "My legs do look sexy. He won't be able to resist me."

Her boyfriend, Marco, entered the bedroom and put his arm around her waist. "Not now, tesoro," she smiled as she removed his hands. "How do I look?" She twirled so he could see her entire body.

"You look nice," he tried to slip his hand under her black dress to feel her naked thigh, but Giuditta pushed it away.

"Where are you going all dressed up?"

"I have to go away on business," she smiled with one eye still admiring herself. She knew Marco wasn't too bright and served only one purpose for her, and she realized the mindless man wouldn't suspect anything.

"Where?"

"I have to go to New York City. I want you to take care of the hotel while I'm gone, knowing fully that her business would take care of itself. Everyone who worked for her knew how to do their job, and her son, Felo, always took care of the books and counted the money at the end of the day.

"Okay," Marco replied.

'What a dumbbell,' thought Giuditta as she continued admiring herself. "Carry my suitcases," she pointed to them next to the door. "Put them in the coach waiting in the front," she demanded, finally leaving the mirror.

As Giuditta boarded the passenger car at the train station, she checked her ticket and looked around for the private compartment of the man she was meeting. Smiling, she noticed the well-dressed gentleman quietly standing in the corridor, waiting.

"Hi, Johnny," Giuditta said in her heavy Italian accent.

John Kenworth walked toward her and kissed her on her cheek. "So glad you were able to make it." He appeared slightly nervous as he took Giuditta's hand and led her to his door. After Giuditta settled in, she sat close to John and began rubbing her leg against his. Then she took his hand and put it on her leg, slowly moving it higher and up to her thigh to allow him to feel the nakedness of her flesh. For her own amusement, she moaned very low in a husky voice, watching his reaction from the corner of her eye. 'I set my trap and caught a wealthy man,' she thought, 'I'll never let him go. Whatever he wants, I'll do,' she smiled at him, 'anything for him,' recalling her pledge to never be in a position like she was when she had to marry Nicola, 'anything at all to make him happy.'

Johnny was a wealthy American businessman a few years

younger than Giuditta. He had lusted after her ever since she was with Nicola, constantly offering to take her to the big city with him. Finally, she succumbed to him after tasting the gentle manner in which he made love to her one afternoon when Marco was working. Marco was a rough lover, and this was a change; it reminded her of the way Luigi maneuvered around her body slowly, managing to set off sparks in her she hadn't experienced since he left.

In the private compartment, Giuditta maneuvered Johnny's hand around her body. Her dress rose high as she sat poised like a kitten, her throaty moaning low. "You look remarkable, my dear," John softly whispered in her ear, feeling her soft skin with his hand.

John rose abruptly and locked the door; he could wait no longer, and Giuditta stood prepared to please him. As John slowly slid down Giuditta's black dress, the one she had chosen to seduce him, he stood admiring her beautiful body. "How beautiful you are, my love," he whispered into her ear, exciting Giuditta even more.

Giuditta was thrilled to go to the city with such a refined and handsome gentleman like John. It reminded her of the days after Luigi took her away from the slums of Little Italy and showed her a new life. Now officially a widow, why shouldn't she have fun? That muscle-bound idiot's body would be waiting for her when she returned. All her attention was now on this man she hoped would take her on many more trips. And Giuditta meant to please him to earn that reward, already purring in his ear and rubbing his thigh. She smiled and kissed Johnny full on his lips as the mighty locomotive blasted its last departure signal.

In August, the Feast of San Rocco occurred on the 12th, as usual. Most Italian immigrants were illiterate, so Salvatore Gusto finagled and appointed Frank Weise to manage the affair. Frank Weise was a good-looking man with fine German facial features, as was his brother, Bill, a known playboy and womanizer. He also managed most of the gambling in the area with a major operation on Fourth Street, at the square. Their well-furnished gambling parlor was lovely, with beautiful velvet drapes and decorations. Anyone who had money was welcome to gamble, no matter what ethnicity. Therefore, on those grounds, Gusto persuaded the Italian committee to use a man who could count and manage the money well, and Weise certainly did.

First, there was a holy mass at the Immaculate Conception Church, which stood below the school on 11th Street. Even the unlawful Black Handers attended the mass with their families, spoken entirely in Italian. Then, men would remove the statue of San Rocco from the church and place it on the carrying platform with two protruding handles on each side so that six men could carry the revered saint. A musical band played pious music with brass instruments of higher-pitched trumpets and midlevel trombones, capped off with the lower bass tubas and a drum pounding to the same rhythmic beat. Behind the band marched young Italian girls and boys wearing their white First Holy Communion outfits with matching shoes, some faces glowing with happiness, others bore looks of ceremonious solemnity. All the young girls carried bouquets of fresh flowers. Following the children was the sizable statue, well over five feet in height, displaying the saint with a staff in his arm, an open sore on his leg, and a dog beside him. Venerated in the Roman Catholic Church as a protector against contagious diseases and plagues, the Italian Catholic townspeople prayed to him for cures for themselves and their families. San Rocco rose in popularity among those in southern Italy and Sicily during the reign of the Kingdom of the Two Sicilies.

The parade began marching, carrying the statue of San Rocco. People followed the statue and formed a procession. The march stopped in places where townspeople would pray for a particular intention or a cure. Then, as a tribute, they pinned paper money of different denominations to a dark purple ribbon strapped over the shoulders of the saint. Some Italian Black Hand members posed for a few seconds so everyone could see the large amount they contributed. Giuditta Buch had no use for the Catholic Church or Saint Rocco. When the saint jounced slightly from the tired men who carried it, Giuditta bounced higher to the melody of bed springs in Johnny's arms in a far-off luxurious hotel in New York City.

As the procession passed, several Ku Klux Klan members from the sidewalks heckled, cursed and made fun of the Catholics. Along Main Street, the procession led by the musical band marched as people came up to pray for a special request and then pinned their hard-earned money onto the ribbon. Eleanora spotted Salvatore Gusto ceremoniously pinning a large amount of money onto the statue's ribbon, smiling at the bystanders who stood in awe. The thoughts running through their minds were what a noble and generous man he was to donate so much. Salvatore waited, his posture straight, until all the admiration and applause subsided. "Probably for all his sins," Eleanora Buch whispered her sentiments for the Black Hand leader as she walked with her family in the procession. She was by far the feistier of the two sisters walking behind their parents.

"Quiet!" Felo whispered as he turned, revealing a stern expression. Felo was a kind and generous father but firm. He only had to correct his daughters once. Eleanora obeyed immediately, and Julia glared at her sister for getting her in trouble even though she had said nothing.

After the procession, the feast continued with festivities and a generous display of fireworks presented to commemorate San Rocco in an open field near 14th Street.

Felo Buch didn't associate with many Italians, not by his intention. Aside from his extended family, most of his friends were original Americans from the railroad or one of the clubs he frequented. Most people in town, even some Italians, assumed Felo was German or British by the sound of his name, light complexion, and perfectly spoken English. Born in Sharpsburg, Pennsylvania, he was an American. So, it wasn't unusual for

Frank Weise to confide in him the day following the feast.

"Hey, Felo, my gambling parlor took in a bundle of cash from the feast yesterday—a lot of money. Most of the cash had pinholes," he laughed. The Black Hand boys had gotten their share of the stolen blessed donations and contributions and gambled them away at Weise's place. Those paper bills spread through the town, most not realizing the tiny holes where people had pinned their donations.

Giuditta returned three days later wearing a red dress of the same girlish style as the one she left in. Enjoying herself so much, she stayed an extra day, easily persuaded by John Kenworth, who promised his lover they would do the same thing again in a month. He would see Giuditta sooner, probably sometime during the week when Marco worked. Her daughter-in-law, Lucy, knew what Giuditta was doing. That younger woman knew most of the goings on in town, including the scandalous affairs of her mother-in-law. Though she told nobody, she viewed Giuditta as 'la disgrazia,' a disgrace, even though she knew the reason.

Giuditta continued making her beer during prohibition, and George Bamarra provided illegal liquor and paid the police to leave her alone. George kept a horde of his prepared booze under the hotel, often stopping in for one of Giuditta's specially made meals.

After the war, Douglas Nicholson didn't socialize as much as before, not seeing Giuditta, the motherly figure he had known since childhood, as often as before. His family commanded most of his free time now, enjoying that time off, having picnics, and fishing with his son. Gabrielle missed her father, Andre, and Douglas wanted to spend quality time with her. Their eldest daughter, Claire, would begin high school in the new school on Center Street. "Times are passing us, Honey," Gabrielle asserted herself, making Douglas realize they never took that honeymoon he promised years before.

"How about taking a trip to England?" Douglas recalled his wartime friend's fond invitation. He and John Hemsworth continued corresponding by letters. What better time than now to go? He wanted to ask his parents if they would babysit his family before he made final arrangements. Gabrielle sat poised like a graceful cat, smiling as if he had told her a joke. "I'm not kidding, Gab; let me ask my parents or Aunt Ellen if they're up to the task of watching the kids."

The following day, Douglas had a meeting scheduled for his conference room, which he didn't look forward to. After the shooting of a police officer in their town, a small group of about four or five men wanted to speak together about the rising problems of the Italian Immigrants, especially the Black Hand.

Douglas began the meeting by welcoming the men to his office and thanking them for coming. Then he casually asked, "What's on your minds, men," fully knowing what they were there for.

Larry Johnson was older than the rest. He began first, "Well, Doug, I'll be frank. We wanted," he waved his arm to include all the men sitting around the large conference table, "to discuss the growing Italian immigration problem in town after the tragic death of Office Renny. We. . ."

"Excuse me, Larry, I'm sorry to interrupt," Everett Long stated, "but I want to include the Black Hand problem when you refer to the growing Italian crisis. Sorry again; please proceed, Larry." The man in his mid-forties gracefully returned the floor back to Larry Johnson.

"Yes," Larry put his hand to his mouth and cleared his throat with a slight cough, "We feel that the Italians bring a bad influence with them." He used the Black Hand as proof and glanced back at Everett with a look of approval as he spoke. "In addition to the violence, the Italians are bringing an influx of Roman

Catholics to town. Did you see how many of them there were at that feast?"

"We're trying to retain the purity of our race and ethnicity. The original town settlers chartered Wellsville as such, Doug; look what's happening now." Michael Walsh voiced his opinion.

"Here, here," Felix Fischer agreed, shaking his head with approval.

"Everywhere they live turns to shambles," Harry Belmore remarked, spreading his arms as if to signify the whole town. Harry Belmore was married to the former Miss Margaret Myers. 'What a cornuto,' Douglas thought. Giuditta had taught him that word. 'The man is already raising one child who, unknowingly, he didn't father. His wife runs around town with other men he doesn't know about. I wonder who fathered his other children? And he has the right to criticize the morals of other people?'

"Gentlemen," Douglas smiled, "I know that most of you belong to the Klan," he calmly said, leaning back in his finely upholstered high-back chair, "Is it those values you propose here today?"

"Frankly, yes, Doug, and why don't you join the Klan?" asked Felix. "We went to school and hung around with each other, Doug. I remember little Peppina in our group. But that was different. I never even knew she was Italian with her blonde hair. For God's sake, I recall her father. He looked more American than you and me. But that was different; they were the only Italians then. The Massaros were clean and ran a business. But now the real dagos are taking over!"

"Well, Italian immigration stopped two years ago, so no more Italians will come from overseas. Those few who are coming now are from cities and looking for work. Second, our constitution gives the right to freedom of religion, along with life, liberty, and the pursuit of happiness," Douglas reminded them. "How do you elect to oppose that?"

"Look, Doug, if we don't take a stand and eradicate this here and now, the blacks will be taking over before you know," Larry interjected, "If not all the dagos. We have to throw the Black Hand the hell out of town!"

"I agree," answered Douglas. "It was the Black Hand that killed that young police officer, not the Italian community. And, from what I hear, the police in town, including the chief himself, are making a lot of money from the Black Hand bootleggers. That's happening in every village, town, and city all over the country." Douglas kept his temper and spoke skillfully and peacefully, "They're not going to want to throw out anyone who blesses them with such supplementary income, and I think they might stop any of you men who try to halt their gravy train, for sure." All the men in the room were wide-eyed as if they had awakened from a long sleep with that realization. They might be the ones to get prosecuted for violence or tampering with the law on trumped-up charges. Douglas knew by their expressions that he got through to most of them. He raised his hand to stop Everett from speaking, "Please, let me finish. Gentlemen, my dad told me stories about the first settlement in town. As you might know, my granddad was among them. Those people were dirty, lived in shacks, wore dirty and smelly clothes, and were starving at times. They lived in what we now call slums, or worse."

"But they were pioneers! They were building a town!" cried out Larry, passionately attempting to adhere to the memory of those patriotic ancestors who struggled to bring a wilderness space into a solid town.

"So give the Italian immigrants a chance to build a bigger country! Because that's what all the immigrants are doing. Every time steel, bricks, or any of the other commodities we produce board trains, they're traveling to make our cities greater. Bring in health codes and home inspections to deal with those who are living in dirty conditions. You're right about those things. They have to change. But many of those immigrants suffered cruelties in their home countries beyond our comprehension. That's why they came to America: for freedom. The Black

Hand persecutes the poor working-class Italians, not original Americans. It's the bootlegging that's the problem. That made the Black Hand grow and, let's face it, it's not only the Italians involved in that. Why not give those Italians who live in clean houses, wear nice and carefully pressed clothes, and lead respectable lives the opportunity to live in better neighborhoods? People like Felo Buch."

"Felo is Italian?" Everett burst out in surprise.

"He's American. He was born here. His parents were from Italy. You, Felix, just said you remember his father, Luigi, right?" Douglas smiled.

"For God's sake, I invited Felo to join the Klan," laughed Everett.

"Forget about the Klan. Their days are over in our area after that scandal with D.C. Stephenson. The Black Hand is certainly bad, and I'll join you in any lawful method of getting rid of them!" The men gradually lost interest in why they called for a meeting. They began to worry about the uncertainties associated with forcibly removing people and the remote possibility of losing their honorable reputations. They didn't want them tainted in any way. The subjects changed to sports, politics, pool, and the railroad, and Douglas Nicholson joined in with those discussions.

"Nice catch you made today, Son," Douglas said as he closed the refrigerator door, noticing the fish in a large bowl. "Good job!"

"Thanks, Dad."

"Okay, Dougie. It's time for you to go to bed. I let you stay up to see Daddy, but now it's time," Gabrielle said, pointing to the electric kitchen clock. "Time for beddy-bye."

"Please don't baby me, Mom."

Douglas glanced at his wife with that particular look he used when she did something he considered wrong.

"Okay, Son," Gabrielle amusingly stepped back, extending

her arm for a handshake.

Dougie ran into his mother's arms, laughing, and said, "Nah, not like that, Mom."

"Remember, no matter how big or old you get, you'll always be my little boy," Gabrielle fondly kissed her son.

After watching their son walk to his bedroom, Douglas told his wife about the meeting. "I'm so proud of you, honey. I couldn't have done it better myself," she said, pecking him on the cheek just as she did with her son. "In fact, I might just have a special something for you upstairs," Gabrielle guiltily giggled and blushed while taking Douglas by his hand and leading him upstairs.

Chapter Thirty-Four

Wellsville, Ohio to England 1926
A Jolly Good Trip

The RMS Olympic was the leading luxury ocean liner in the White Star Line, serving 24 years from 1911 to 1935. A sister ship to the ill-fated Titanic, the Olympic served as a troop transport during The Great War. The Great Depression caused failing profits, forcing the White Star Line to halt the RMS Olympic's operation. It was sold for scrap in 1935.

Eleanora, Annie, and Clara carefully crossed Third Street in front of the Trieste boarding house, anxiously waiting for the trolly, automobiles, and wagons to pass. They held each other's hands and dashed to the other side when they found their chance. They waved to Bill Norton, sitting out in front of his home as usual. "Hi, Mr. Norton," the three girls vocalized almost entirely in harmony.

"Hello, young ladies," Bill answered with an enduring smile. Bill Norton lost his leg in the American Civil War. Following that horror, he turned back to God, appreciated his family and friends, and had an optimistic outlook on life and the beauty of it and all nature. After his recovery and return to town, he worked in his family store. But as the years progressed, and now over 80 years old, spending lovely days sitting outside and enjoying the town's growth, remembering the early development of Wellsville, was his sole satisfaction. Bill initially rode in an open carriage in the town's patriotic parades, eventually in convertible automobiles. So, with that unyielding grin, he addressed the three young girls, the future of his country, in the same manner as he had done with Douglas Nicholson and Peppina Massaro so many years before.

The three girls usually romped around town doing errands for their parents, extending that time to do those things young girls enjoyed. Eleanora spotted Jim Hanley's old pickup truck at the corner of Third and Broadway, where the girls were headed. Jim leaned against his old truck and spoke to Eleanora's Uncle George Bamarra. Jim was explaining how the police were constantly stopping him, threatening to arrest him if he didn't pay money. "No need to use the truck for such a small delivery," George told Jim, "I'll take you." Then he spotted the three girls approaching them and nodded at Jim. "I'll bring these girls along; that way, nobody will stop us," he laughed.

"Hi, Uncle George," Eleanora cried out. Annie and Clara were always a little intimidated by the rugged-looking man.

"C'mon, girls! Jump in the back," he bellowed as he slid open the rumble seat. "Squeeze together; I'll take you for a ride in my new car."

Eleanora and the two Trieste sisters couldn't resist a ride in a new car, so they cuddled together in the back, laughing and chattering as the Packard sped off. They called to people they knew as they held each other, teary-eyed from their bursts of laughter.

Ellen Brisco, Martha Nicholson's older sister, passed away earlier that year in the winter from an infection. Douglas's parents held the wake in their home on Riverside Avenue. Aunt Ellen didn't have many remaining relatives left, but friends and associates of both Douglas and his father filled the house. Douglas's mother, Martha, showed signs of aging gracefully. Though her hair was a golden grey, the crow's feet encircling her hazel-colored eyes enhanced them, and her petite framed body remained. She was still an attractive woman at the age of 67 years old.

Her 74-year-old husband had aged. Douglas Sr. had a head full of grey hair, and his body was slightly hunched and somewhat frail in appearance, probably from all the hard work he had done throughout his life. Gabrielle sat with Martha, holding her hand as the older woman mourned the loss of her sister. Gabrielle's older daughter, Claire, attended to her younger sister and brother. Martha was too young to remember her great-grandfather's wake, and Dougie wasn't born yet. Both children were a little disturbed as neither had seen a corpse before.

As Douglas Sr. sat with his son, he asked, entirely out of the blue, "Think you can take me down to the Shop in that fancy automobile of yours?" Douglas turned to see his father with a grin on his face.

"Do you think it's a good idea, Dad?" asked Douglas.

"Your mother doesn't think so; she thinks it will be too upsetting for me, but I'm going either way."

Douglas, thinking the same thing, knew nobody could stop his father when he set his mind to something and said, "I'll take you, Dad."

"Thanks. I should have learned to drive one of those darn contraptions when I was younger." Douglas just rolled back his eyes at that comment.

It was sad to see his father's mournful expression as he walked like a zombie into the once mighty Shop where the old man had spent his career. Douglas remembered how proud his dad had been of his workplace as if he owned it himself. There was still activity there. The track lines held freight cars, and the station building still stood, as did the roundhouse and turntable, but Douglas wondered for how long. It was a ghost of what it used to be.

"I didn't have the heart, or I should say, guts, to come down here before now. But it's time I came down to say goodbye to the old place," Douglas Sr. declared, his voice a little shaky, and Douglas knew his father was extremely upset. "At least the roundhouse is standing," he paused, "for now."

"Everything passes in time, Dad; you taught me that. You taught me a lot of things, just about everything I know." Now Douglas was saddened. Burdens of memories surfaced, including the day he and his friend, Peppina, had spent such a wonderful time exploring the Shop. "C'mon, Dad, Let's go home. Mom will be waiting."

"I'm sure she's waiting by the door, Son."

In the spring, Douglas fulfilled his promise of a second honeymoon. He arranged to take time off from work to travel to England to see John Hemsworth and his family. The delighted Gabrielle wasted no time preparing for the trip abroad; it was the first time she would travel so far. "Doug, you said they're royals? How should I dress?"

"John is the eldest son of an earl; he will inherit that title someday when his father passes. He's a fine man and not snobbish in any way if that's what you're thinking, Gab. And from what he told me, his wife is also a wonderful woman." Douglas knew Gabrielle well and expected her to have some self-doubt and even awkwardness about meeting British bluebloods. "Buy yourself whatever gowns you wish, Gab; I'm sure you'll look like the belle of the ball in whatever you choose." Gabrielle smiled at that compliment, but it didn't relieve her unrelenting tension.

"Oh, Doug, but this is different. Please come with me so that I can choose the right apparel for the occasions we'll encounter. I'm completely lost."

Douglas thought quickly as if he was cross-examining in one of his legal bouts. Accompanying his wife in one of her anxiety-ridden clothes-shopping sprees would be nerve-racking for him; he knew from experience. It was the one thing he must avoid at all costs. There had to be other options. He kept thinking. Yes, there were, he finally realized. "I'd love to, my dear, but don't you think you'd be better off if a woman accompanied you?" 'Prepare names, counselor, hurry, prepare names,' he thought. "Someone like John Causwell's wife, Gloria Causwell. She'd be perfect!" He admired himself for thinking of a perfect example of someone who could accompany Gab. "She's young and has been abroad, and you're always complimenting her dress outfits."

"Hmm." Gabrielle was in deep thought as her eyes rolled back.

"Gloria and my mother would compliment each other's taste. Mom is well-read and up-to-date on styles." He was exhausting himself, but they were good choices, and he couldn't possibly go with Gab; he knew it would be much too stressful. Gabrielle squinted her cat-like olive green eyes in that lazy position that made him melt into a puddle of helpless horse poop. At first, Douglas suspected she was on to his attempt to avoid going with her until she spoke.

"Yes! I think that would be a wonderful idea!" Gabrielle smiled at her husband, "How clever of you! A younger and older woman's opinions. Yes!" Then her eyes fell back into that sexy glare, "You're off the hook, dear." She knew Doug was scheming, but it was actually a good idea.

On Saturday, June 18, 1927, the couple left New York City on the RMS Olympic, the long-lost Titanic's sister ship. Gabrielle's new wardrobe was carefully packed in steamer trunks. Douglas brought his finest suits and even purchased a new tuxedo for the occasions he would encounter.

Gabrielle walked about the ship like a princess. She fit the part in one of her stylish new outfits, seizing young and older gentlemen's attention. Inside, she felt like a child at a carnival. Sometimes, unable to resist her enthusiasm, she lifted her long gown and anxiously trotted in her high heels. At dinners, Gabrielle occasionally dressed in the newer styles of the roaring 20s but maintained her elegance. Wearing evening gloves that rose above her elbows, trendy open high-heeled shoes, a dress with sparkled designs, and sheered in places that exposed her upper arms and the lower parts of her shapely legs, Gabrielle looked seductive. The pearls around her neck and matching long earrings were stunning, and they complimented the decorated headband with a feather protruding and accentuating her stylish shorter hairstyle. Her makeup made her lips appear more voluptuous and her eyes even more bewitching. Mrs. Gabrielle Nicholson looked 15 years younger than the 42-year-old woman she was, and her husband savored every minute of being with her on their second honeymoon.

The ship had the same elegant stairway as her sister ship, the Titanic. Gabrielle loved to descend the elegantly carpeted stairs with her arm locked into her husband's. In the evenings, after they mingled with other first-class passengers at their table, they would stroll along the corridors, stopping at lounges or the veranda café decorated with palms. They sometimes danced to the orchestra in the ballroom or listened to concerts. They roamed the outer decks when the ocean was calm and offered them that solitary tranquility that only those deep blue waters could, and they kissed under the stars. "This is beautiful, Doug!" she told her husband.

"You're beautiful, my lovely wife." As the honeymooners they were, the couple remained in their splendid, 'deluxe parlour suite' often.

The RMS Olympic docked in Southampton, England, where John Hemsworth awaited them. "I'm so glad you came," John told Douglas, teary-eyed as the two men embraced after nine years. "You look jolly well, my good man." Turning, he asked, "Is this beautiful young woman your daughter?" Gabrielle loved John already.

"Allow me to introduce my lovely wife, Gabrielle. Gabrielle, this is the legendary John Hemsworth, one day to be an earl."

"No, no, none of that between friends," John replied, taking Gabrielle's gloved hand and bending to kiss it. "It's lovely to meet you, Mrs. Nicholson. May I call you Gabrielle?"

"Of course you may, John. It's so nice to finally meet you. I feel I already know you from all the wonderful things Douglas has told me about you."

"My wife, Isabelle, wanted so much to be here to greet you, but regretfully, with preparations and the children, she couldn't. Please come this way." John pointed to the two Rolls Royce vehicles parked aside from each other, chauffeurs standing beside them. They had already loaded their steamer trunks into one of the luxury cars without Gabrielle or Douglas noticing. "Please," John gestured for them to enter the back as a chauffeur held open a door. "I'll ride up front so you can be more comfortable," he quickly opened the door himself before the chauffeur had a chance to. "And I can be a better tour guide on the way," John, already seated, turned and smiled. "I think we're ready, Webster," he addressed the driver, and the Rolls began to move. The other followed. Gabrielle clutched Douglas's hand firmly, an expression of her delight and anticipation.

Isabella Hemsworth waited anxiously in the immense foyer before the large wooden double doors at the front of the stately Hemsworth Mansion. When she heard the automobiles pull up, she called her servant, Alastair, to fetch her 11-year-old daughter and five-year-old son. Now, with her children at each of her sides, they waited as Alastair opened the giant portal.

"Ah! There you all are," said John, smiling, upon entering first, leading his guests. "Gabrielle, Douglas, please meet my wife, Lady Isabella Hemsworth."

"No! None of that, John, no formalities," she declared as she gracefully rushed up to Gabrielle first, embracing her, then kissing her cheek. "Please call me Isabella or Izzie, as my other friends call me. I already know you and Douglas from all the letters," she laughed delightedly. "Though it's so wonderful to meet you both in person." She then put out her hand, and Douglas bowed and kissed it.

"The feeling is mutual," Douglas answered first as Gabrielle stood in amazement at how down-to-earth Isabella was.

"My husband and good friends call me Gab; I wish you also would," a smiling Gabrielle told the woman she immediately liked.

"It's a deal!" laughed Isabella.

"And this must be Amelia," Douglas walked up to Isabella's and John's daughter.

"Yes," said John proudly, "This is Amelia," as the young girl curtsied."

"It's lovely to meet you, Amelia." Douglas gave a friendly smile, fondly recalling how little Peppina had curtsied and presented herself similarly years before when Douglas's father had introduced her to his assistant at the Shop.

"It's very nice to meet you also, sir, and so good of you to come," she proclaimed in a ladylike manner. When John introduced his five-year-old son, the little boy blushed but presented himself formally. Isabella interrupted John and made the same introductions of her children for Gabrielle. Both children responded in the same manner as they did with Douglas to Gabrielle's enjoyment.

"Children, you may play now. I'll have Alastair call you at teatime."

"Yes, Mum," both shouted harmoniously and then scurried off to do those things that all young children do.

"Our John is the fourth; it's so confusing with all the Johns in our family." Isabella took Gabrielle by her arm and led her as they spoke. Gabrielle laughed while explaining how she had the same problem with the name Douglas, and the two women wandered away, happily speaking together.

"Well, I see the ladies hit it off jolly well. How about something to wet the whistle?" John asked, "Still brandy, is it?"

"You remember well, my friend."

"How could I forget? I was a bit wankered in France that last night of our parting," John chuckled. "How did you fare that fine night?" John spoke as he filled two glasses with his top-shelf brandy.

Douglas laughed wholeheartedly and loudly, "I eventually found my ship and boarded," remembering how difficult it was for him to walk a straight line.

The two friends drank their brandy and smoked Cuban cigars that Douglas brought as one of his gifts for his friend. They spoke of world affairs, enjoying each other's opinions and exchanging phrases of 'They made a mess of that' with a reply of 'A dog's dinner they certainly did' and 'It would have been a doodle' followed by 'Yes, an easy task' only stopping at times to hear the laughs and amusing screams as their ladies spoke loudly in the background of another room. "Sounds like they're having a jolly chinwag in there," John mused at one of their pauses.

The next few days were spent sightseeing in London, the Nicholsons enjoying first-class touring of the significant places of the city, and dining in only the very best restaurants that London had to offer. Then, the two couples traveled in a caravan of chauffeured Rolls Royces to the Hemsworth Manor, their country home in Berkshire. John and Douglas rode together in one, and Isabella and Gabrielle rode in the other, all luggage packed into the spacious boots of the luxury vehicles. There, the couples went horseback riding together. John gave Douglas lessons in Polo while the women laughingly cheered. They all played golf on the estate's generous grounds surrounding the manor and engaged in tennis on the court, where Isabella furnished Gabrielle with a fashionable outfit. John and Douglas shotguned pigeons and quails on the grounds or in the woods nearby. On rainy days, the couples played billiards indoors or board games. They walked together in the extensive outdoor spaces some afternoons, stopping to have a prepared picnic with brollies nearby in case of rain. Dinners were either in the dining hall of the manor, eating scrumptious feasts of prime meats or fish specially brought in on ice, or in the finest country restaurants or pubs.

The two weeks in England went as the wind, and the couples stood together at the harbor, saddened by the departure. They had all expressed their regrets the evening before and repeated them often and into the following morning as they left the mansion in London. The two women held hands in one of the automobiles as they rode to the dock, crying and promising to write often. John and Douglas solemnly spoke of the joys they shared together in that time, which went so quickly.

"Well, I've been faffing about with the likes of you for too long. Begone with you then," John tried to joke at such a sad time to lighten the mood. Then John and Douglas embraced for a last time, "I'll miss you, old friend," a teary-eyed John spoke first.

"Come take a trip across the pond," Douglas used the British terminology, "Please, do visit us."

Isabella and Gabrielle clung to each other for a final time. "Thank you both for such a wonderful time," Gabrielle's voice crackled as she spoke.

"You both must have thanked us a hundred times at least," claimed John. "We'll get together again, dear mates. It's our destiny!"

"Still a very philosophical person!" Douglas shouted back as he and Gabrielle walked up the gangway, Gabrielle waving robustly.

Gabrielle and Douglas enjoyed their trip home as much as when they came. It temporarily eased their sorrowful sentiments. Only in time do people separate themselves from such sadness, but the good memories always live on. Upon their arrival in Wellsville, Gabrielle relived her time in England by using the British terms she learned there: 'Cheeky of them' or 'Full of beans' and 'Better use a brolly; it might rain,' all to the elder Nicholson's and her children's entertainment.

As she spoke to Douglas Sr. and Martha, she told them, "My humble husband never told me whose life he saved in the war was of royal blood. I had to hear that from Isabella." She smiled, "My hero husband, that is." Then she added, "We were treated like a king and a queen," Gabrielle curtsied in humor as she spoke.

Chapter Thirty-Five

Wellsville, Ohio 1927-1929
Before The Crash

The 1920s, called the 'Roaring Twenties,' brought in a new era. In the earlier part of the century, a great panic developed: rumors rose that women were being forced into prostitution by the great amount of Italian immigrants. Though "white slavery' was a myth, the 1920s brought in a time of more rights for women. Higher-paying jobs became available for women, and so did privileges. Many women chose to work as prostitutes as a slap in the face to the stigma of pre-marital sex. Black Handers did have much control of prostitution in New York and other larger cities, but many brothels became owned by females.

"My God, that horn sounds like someone's strangling a duck," Mary Trieste turned and noticed Eleanora's Uncle George driving down the hill toward town. "Eleanora, your uncle's a coming this way," she mused. Annie and Eleanora were in such a deep and engrossing conversation that neither remembered what they were talking about once they were interrupted. Now, all their attention was on getting a ride back to Wellsville. Clara was already waving at George's Packard to stop.

Again, George blasted that fowl-sounding horn, "Do you girls need a ride?" All the girls quickly responded in a chorus of mixed tones that they did. "Okay, Mary, you're the oldest, so you get in front; the rest of you open the rumble seat and climb in." As they often rode in the small pull-out upholstered seating accommodation, Clara knew best how it operated. She beat the others and opened it. Annie and Eleanora crammed in beside her.

The girls had walked up the hill, past the cemetery, to view the sights on that warm, beautiful Saturday just before school ended. They could climb a tree, sit on a branch, and talk for over an hour. Nina Trieste was already married to Charles Obiso, living in a home near the foot of State Route 45, one of the other hills. Maude was engaged to Giacomo Bozzi, now called James, and Louise was a senior in high school, all of them now too old for such trivial girlish fun.

George left the girls next to the fruit wagon near Third Street. "Thanks," they all shouted in unison for the ride and began walking down Commerce Street.

Giacomo Baggio, an immigrant from Sicily, sold fruit from his truck in town. Giacomo, or Gio, as he was often called, was a top distributor for George Bamarra and also made his own hooch. "Hello, girls!" he greeted them as they passed his parked truck.

"Hello, Mr. Baggio!" Eleanora and the Trieste sisters shouted back one at a time as they hurried by.

After the girls passed, Gio looked both ways, reached underneath the fresh bananas, oranges, lemons, and other delicious produce, and pulled out two hidden gallon jugs of his finest brew. After Giacomo made that delivery, he drove to his next customer.

As Eleanora and the Trieste sisters walked along Commerce, they heard what sounded like an explosion nearby. It was loud even among the clatter of the nearby factories and traffic. Following the blast's location, the girls noticed a commotion at Giovanni Quintania's home. He was the son of Fabio Quintania, who knew Giuditta and had occasionally used Douglas Nicholson's attorney skills. Giovanni was a huge man, both tall and wide and round. Following the lucrative practices of many in town, Giovanni built a still in a cellar next to his home with his partner Rocco Delmare. There was only a trap door to access their secret apparatus. However, it couldn't fully accommodate the enormous man. Giovanni had to squeeze through every time he wanted to enter and leave.

"Damn it to hell, John," Rocco called him by his American name, "you have to make a bigger entrance," Rocco told him earlier that day.

"Hey, it will draw too much attention. If the police see me working here, what will I say? Then they want to go down and look, and we're both in jail. Huh?" Giovanni raised his big arms and spread them apart, questioning his accomplice. Rocco just shook his head and went down the hatch first, then helped Giovanni get in.

The still was a work of genius by the craftsmanship of the two men. The confined area was well-ventilated with a wood stove pipe that ran up to the ground and was hidden by a tree, so no fumes were visible. The men heated the elevated pot with a coal fire beneath it. They prepared everything, waiting for the pot to heat. Once the proper temperature was reached, the vapor rose to the cap and headed to the arm, from there to the doubler barrel, where extra water condensed to double the vapor's purity, and then to the coiled copper tube condenser set in another barrel with cool running water that the men piped in from an outside spigot. The alcohol condensed, and liquid moonshine dripped into a small collection bucket. As usual, everything was working fine until Giovanni spotted a problem.

"Hey, Rocco. Look at that arm," Giovanni motioned to the copper pipe. "Something's wrong. It doesn't look right; I think it's clogged. Damn it, give me a hand. Hurry!" In his haste, Giovanni accidentally kicked the coal burner, causing a flame to shoot up. That created one gigantic boom heard throughout the neighborhood. The liquor still exploded into flying pieces of metal from the burst. It spread like shrapnel throughout the hidden, concealed area as the fire spread. The inground vent blew into the air, taking a portion of the surrounding ground. The pressure buildup propelled the trap door and the concrete that held it in place up in the air like a colossal cannonball. Rocco, his clothes in tatters, covered his face from the flames and the heavy smoke. He noticed Giovanni lying on the brick floor and desperately tried to drag his large body to get him out, but he couldn't budge the heavy man. Rocco climbed outside to get help.

Eleanora and the Trieste sisters arrived at the same time as the police. It took two policemen to push John's body up through the open torn space where the hatch had been and another man to lift it from the outside with the help of Rocco. Annie, Eleanora, and Clara sat atop a wooden fence as Mary stood leaning, all watching in horror as they laid the burned and half-naked body of Giovanni Quintania on the partially grass-covered ground as the skies darkened. A soft drizzle began in the gloom of the forming fog. Giovanni died on the spot, and the police arrested Rocco. The policemen broke up the still before leaving. Then they led Rocco away in handcuffs, the soot-covered man in torn clothes trying to glance at his dead friend as they did.

Giacomo Baggio asked George Bamarra to supply the widow since the now-deceased Giovanni had worked for him. She could feed her kids by selling glasses of liquor and, of course, paying protection money like everyone else had to.

If Lucy or Colomba had known where their kids were, they might have killed them. But Eleanora, like the aunt she never knew, Peppina, was as curious as a cat.

During Giovanni's funeral, a band played while people sang 'Nearer to God.' Eleanora didn't attend but could hear from her classroom in the school above the church. People marched in procession to Giovanni Quintania's funeral behind the hearse.

Lucy busily prepared her crochet pieces, watching the large clock as she did and remembering the first time she met Nora four years before. "Julia, you and your sister stay with Nicky. I have an important person coming here soon," she called out to her eldest daughter.

"Who, Mama? Who's coming?" Julia was inquisitive, but not as much as her younger sister.

"Never mind, just do as you're told." Lucy glanced at the clock once more.

"But Eleanora's getting ready to go out, Mama she. . ."

"No!" her mother interrupted, "You tell her to stay inside until I say so."

"Yes, Mama," Julia walked quickly to stop her sister. Julia wasn't one to go out that often, even now that she was in high school. Ever since the Black Handers killed the policeman, parents forbid their children to socialize with Italian immigrants. But things like that just bounced off her sister like rubber bullets. Eleanora was out the door at the drop of a hat.

All of the crochet pieces were ready except the last one. Lucy, who learned to weave her beautiful designs in Italy, had outdone herself. Almost done with her labor, she glanced up to see the time again, recalling the first time she met Nora.

Frank and Bill Weise had an aunt who was a Madam of a brothel on Broadway, a large and beautiful house painted exceptionally with vivid colors and magnificent designs. The inside was even more exquisite than the exterior. Shellacked floors with splendid Persian carpets in places and varnished oak woodwork graced the interior. Glamourous paintings, some refined of nude women, adorned the walls and created an atmosphere of sensuality. The furnishings were nothing short of marvelous: several luxurious upholstered cushioned chairs, two large matching loveseats, and a couch, all embellished with feathery pillows, each having floral painted renderings. The comfortable seating was for gentlemen callers, meeting or waiting for their 'dates.' Gilt chairs filled most of the empty wall space. Nora insisted that her girls wore the best garments that money could afford. Corsets fit snugly, accentuating a trim waist and full buxom. But she wanted something sheer over the laced corset cover worn by her women. She heard that a sweet Italian immigrant woman did beautiful crochet work and laid eyes on a sample worn by someone she knew. Nora had to meet this woman and immediately had someone make an appointment to do so for her.

Lucy waited impatiently for this appointment; extra money was always welcome to supplement her husband's handsome salary as an accountant for the railroad. Lucy always dressed her children nicely and could use the money to buy new outfits. She didn't know the woman coming to her home was a madam; that would be 'vergognoso!'

A lavish double-sided open carriage appeared in front of Lucy's house as she peered out a window. A beautiful woman wearing a stylish wide-brimmed hat and holding a parasol sat waiting for the gentleman driver to open her door. Lucy remembered the ladies in the cities in Italy using their daytime umbrellas when it wasn't raining, but those were the extremely wealthy. The driver wore a black wool creased Stetson Homburg dress hat, a white shirt with bow tie, and a dark maroon three-piece striped suit. He opened the woman's door and helped her out of the carriage by taking her arm. Holding her parasol, the woman's shapely hips swayed to a lively beat as the driver escorted her to the front door of Lucy's home. Lucy quickly looked in the large mirror in her foyer, fixed her hair, and fluffed out her dress. She waited beside the front door until the doorbell rang. Upon opening the entrance of her home, Lucy stood gracefully and asked, "Yes? May I help you?" innocently pretending she wasn't expecting anyone.

"Yes, I am Madam Nora Weise. Are you Lucy?" The woman folded her parasol and smiled charmingly. Lucy could see that the woman wore lipstick and makeup that allowed her eyelashes to look longer, accentuating her beautifully colored eyes. The blush on the woman's cheeks was done tastefully and enhanced her soft white skin. Lace gloves covered her dainty hands and arms past her elbows, and her extravagant dress was the most elegant Lucy had ever seen.

"Yes, I am. Please come in." Lucy motioned with her hand, struggling to speak in English. Nora nodded in return, smiling as her gentleman escort bowed and walked back to the carriage.

Nora was a shapely, full-figured, and tall woman. Lucy had to look up as she asked, "Would you like an espresso or tea?" thinking carefully if she had any tea left. She only used it for her family when they were ill.

"Espresso. How charming. Yes, I will have an espresso, thank you." Lucy thanked God in heaven and his angels above for her choice.

"Please be seated." Lucy motioned Nora to her finest chair as she went to the kitchen to prepare the coffee. She selected some of her freshly baked biscotti as the espresso brewed.

"Lucy, I've seen some of your crochet pieces, and I must say they're marvelous, simply stunning," Nora stated between sips of coffee and small munches of the homemade cookies. "These are so delicious," she held up one of the biscotti cookies, "you are indeed a very talented woman."

"Thank you," Lucy spoke in her heavy accent, always loving to hear compliments for her labors.

"I was wondering If you could make me a sheer crocheted blouse to go above a corset?" her hands spread over her shoulders and sizable bust to indicate the area as she spoke. "If I like them, I have several other women I would buy them for. It would be an ongoing task I would ask of you." Lucy assumed the lady was a clothing business owner, never in a million years thinking of the actual type of establishment Nora conducted.

Lucy told the woman, "I can do it, but it will cost ten dollars for the one sample piece."

"Certainly," Nora agreed.

"I can have it ready in a couple days."

"That's fine; I'll be back then," Nora smiled and left.

When Nora Weiss returned two days later, she was astounded by how beautiful the sample was. "Oh, Lucy," she kissed her cheek. "They are exactly what I wanted, so elegant yet transparent. Yes, they're lovely." Nora beamed from cheek to cheek.

"Thank you." Lucy was relieved the woman liked them. She desperately wanted the extra ten dollars regularly.

"Lucy, I like them so much I'll pay 20 dollars a piece and

take 12 to start. Let's talk about colors." Lucy was in shock and could hardly concentrate. It was the beginning of a profitable business relationship that she told no one about, not even her husband, Felo.

Now, four years later, Lucy rushed to finish her work; soon, Nora would be arriving to pick up her latest batch, watching the large clock as she worked.

Luke Fontana arrived back in town the same day Lucy raced against the clock to prepare Nora's sheer, laced blouses. Salvatore Gusto waited patiently at his small mob's club hangout for the appointment with Luke, hating the arrogant but dangerous man every second as he did. Luke hadn't given Gusto any reason for his visit, and his imagination ran wild as he waited. But Gusto couldn't show fear to a person like Luke Fontana. Too many men succumbed to fear, especially to one as powerful and evil as Luke. He would detect any anxiety or trepidation whatsoever and eat such a man whole. Luke Fontana had built a dreadful reputation that all Black Handers throughout the valley feared. His association with the large and powerful organized crime family in Cleveland was legendary for gruesome acts of violence that surpassed any that the small-time local Black Hands ever did. Nobody crossed Luke Fontana.

Luke entered the club cautiously, with a bodyguard on each side. He was now a capo in the Cleveland crime family. Luke Fontana had made many enemies working his way up that ladder of corruption. His dreadful eyes squinted, casing the joint as he set foot inside. "I don't need ta sit!" he shouted as Gusto offered him a chair, "I come here ta do business, not lounge round like you and ya men." He turned his body to look closer at the place, "if ya wanna call dem men!" Salvatore Gusto was so angry he wanted to pull his revolver and shoot Luke and his cronies dead, just like Luke did to the policeman.

"I need booze, good booze. We're having some tempa-rary problems in the city right now," he spoke in his slang American

English, wiping his mouth between his sentences, "nuntin we can't take care of."

"I got it, but you have to pay." Gusto knew about the issues the mob was having in the larger cities.

Luke walked right up to Gusto's face, his eyes glaring an inch away from Gusto's, "Don't try ta muscle me!" he shouted; drool began to slide down his mouthline, and some salvia spattered onto Gusto's face. Luke was furious instantly. Holding all his anger, Gusto didn't want to further Luke's frenzy, noticing his men already with hands reaching under their suit jackets. This meeting could go bad by one wrong move or word, and he didn't want a shootout or have to answer to the Cleveland mob.

"There's no problem. I can get as much liquor as you need." Luke backed down at Gusto's words.

"I'm collectin from all yoo guys in da valley 'cause we need a lot! And I know I gotta pay. I just don't like your att-a-tude!"

"Hey, Luke, I ain't got no attitudes, okay?" Salvatore Gusto knew the police were pinching the more populated areas of larger cities. They paid too many payoffs, which lessened the profits of the mob. Some illegal brewers of alcoholic beverages in the cities across the states were using wood alcohol, which was toxic to people. By the end of prohibition, about 50,000 people died from tainted liquor. Gusto knew Luke and his mob were desperate for wholesome booze and not the type that blinded or killed.

"You should a bought those crates of labeled bottles I offered ya a year ago. Now, dere worth dere weight in gold. I got a hard time getting 'em now; everybody wants 'em. How many gallons you got for me now, and how many can you get?"

"I'll have to check with my people and get back to you. George has some let me. . ."

"George who? Bamarra?"

"Yeah, but I got to see how much he has stashed away." George Bamarra did a big favor for Gusto back in 1923. Gusto had him take a train all the way to New York City to bring his wife and family back to Wellsville when they first came to

America. George was reliable and obeyed; he'd hurry and get together as much as possible. But he didn't like to wholesale at low prices; Gusto would have to lean on him a little.

"George makes good hooch. Get dem to put tagetha as much as dey can. Call me, and I'll send as many trucks as ya need. But hurry!" Luke waved for his men to follow him out. They immediately obeyed but keenly watched all of Salvatore Gusto's men as they departed, hands still remaining under their jackets, ready to grab their guns.

When Luke Fontana left the building, Gusto commanded one of his men, "Get George now and all the others! Tell them to come here!" Then he thought and added, "Take any liquor you can get your hands on from his suppliers. I gotta have a lot!"

A few days later, Wellsville and the surrounding area were short on booze. Salvatore Gusto had squeezed all the liquor makers in and around the town, including all their suppliers. It became a dry area for a while until the bootleggers made new moonshine. The only person George didn't take any from was Giuditta Buch.

John Buch was a friendly man like his father, Nicola. He had an excellent job with the Standard Oil Company of Ohio and was always ready to spring for drinks for his friends at the bars he frequented.

"Hey, John!" men would yell out whenever he entered a tavern. John loved that attention, and unknowingly, it propelled his generosity.

At other times, "John! How about joining us for a drink?" all of the group, knowing that John would pick up the tab.

The kind, big-hearted, and gentle John also had the misfortune of falling in love with a married woman. She was the daughter of a popular American doctor in the area. And even though John was born in the grand old USA, locals still deemed him an Italian since his parents were born in Italy. He didn't inherit the same qualities of his half-brother Felo, who acted more German or British, anything but Italian. Evidently, Felo had inherited those characteristics of his natural father, Luigi Massaro.

Mrs. Betty Harrison, his lover, didn't care what nationality he was. She lusted for the pleasures that only a man could satisfy her with. Betty's husband was stricken with tuberculosis, and he couldn't provide her with those carnal delights. Mrs. Harrison hand-picked John because of his philanthropic traits. The beautiful and eager woman rewarded him with an abundance of ways of physical gratification, which John had never before known of, let alone experienced, until he met her. John was a happy man and always yearned for the benevolent and satisfying joys Betty Harrison offered him, endowed with those skills from personal adventures.

"Come by the restaurant after I close it tonight," Betty brushed up against John and whispered in his ear in that distinctive way she knew he couldn't resist. "I'll cook up something special for you," her husky tone and mannerisms wouldn't allow John to do anything but graciously accept. "I'll be in the back room waiting for you. You can use your key to get in."

Mrs. Harrison operated a restaurant given to her by her father as her husband couldn't work. Mr. Harrison had no clue his wife was unfaithful to him. But she seemed to him to be very happy and always joyful. She told him, "You shouldn't exert yourself, dear," whenever he attempted to touch her. "You remember what happened the last time you tried." The truth was he repulsed her, constantly coughing up phlegm, sometimes bloody, and he was skinny as a bone. John took care of those husbandly duties for her just like a little worker bee. Usually, John labored his passions with his lover at his apartment, where Betty sneaked in or pretended to be delivering food if anyone saw her. But, several times, John serviced her in her home, pretending to be a worker or painter. Her husband, lying sick upstairs, barely had the strength to call down, "Are you alright, Honey?" anytime he heard grunts and moans from his wife.

416

After catching her breath, she usually called back, "I'm fine, dear. I'm just working hard." Then, she would go back to her labor of love. Sometimes, she was so engrossed in her efforts that she completely ignored her husband Robert's calls, making him feel guilty that his wife was working so hard. No matter where or when Mrs. Harrison called, John was immediately on his way. It was the only time he was abrupt with people, as he pushed his way through anyone in his way on the street to get to his destination. John even left work if Betty called him in her particular way.

Douglas Nicholson walked home from the Elk's Club, where he had attended a birthday celebration for a fellow member. He was eager to get home as he had a critical fatherly duty at hand. There weren't as many people out as in the daytime, but being a Saturday, there were more than usual. He always took Eight to Main Street so he could walk in the back entrance of his home on Riverside Avenue. As Douglas turned the corner to Main, John Buch whizzed by, nearly knocking him over. "Where you going in such a hurry there, John?"

"Uh, nowhere," John yelled back without turning, "I'm in a hurry, that's all." John was trotting now.

"Walking pretty fast to get to nowhere," Douglas whispered curiously.

As soon as Douglas entered his home, he called, "Gab?" Then again, "Gab? Is she here yet?"

"In here, Doug," Gabrielle called back. Her husband followed her voice to the living room. "I'm finally relaxing," Gabrielle lay on the couch; her silk bathrobe exposed her legs past her knees and her petite bare feet. She looked lovely lying there reading a book and listening to a record playing soft music. Once she noticed Douglas's eyes staring at her in that manner she knew so well, Gabrielle declared, "Not now, big guy," smiling, pointing to the clock, "We're expecting someone, aren't we?" Watching Gabrielle lying there had broken Douglas's concentration. "And Martha and little Dougie are upstairs."

"Yes, of course we are," he said, fixing his collar and clearing his throat, Gabrielle smiling as he did.

She sensually wiped her lips with her tongue, knowing it would further arouse her husband. "Later, dear," she said in a throaty voice, her eyelids lazy in that way that drove him crazy. After so many years, having a husband who still wanted her as much as he did when they first met was wonderful.

Douglas warded off any wicked thoughts, reached into his vest, and pulled out his pocket watch. Gabrielle noticed him doing it for the second time since he had arrived. He popped it open and quickly closed the flap. "Relax, honey, she'll be here on time," she said, smiling. Their daughter, Claire, was a senior in high school and went on a double date. Gabrielle smiled as she watched her husband pace the floors.

"What time did you say the dance was over?"

"For the tenth time, ten o'clock, dear. But you know all the kids go out and have burgers and malted milks afterward."

"I'll bet she'll eat those French fries too. They're too greasy for her stomach."

"You told me you ate them in France during the war, dear. In fact, you said you liked them. Honey, come here; sit with me." Douglas slowly walked toward her timidly, afraid that his attraction might resurface. In a way, it reminded Gabriele of her dear French poodle so many years before. "Oh, Douglas!" she held her hands to the sides of her face while jokingly proclaiming, "You look so much like Frenchie," she laughed, "poor little doggie can't have some fun right now," her voice cracked from laughing wholeheartedly.

"A dog? Now, I remind you of a dog?" Douglas shook his head.

Gabrielle tried to compose herself, but she burst out laughing again, her eyes teary-eyed, "No!" she gasped from her hysteria. "Wait!" trying to speak, she giggled, "It's just the way you're walking," her words broke up in laughter, "sad face and all," her hysteria continued. She sniffed, "I'm trying to stop laughing, Doug. I am; forgive me," but she couldn't stop. Gabrielle said, looking up at Douglas's face and howling again. "I'm sorry!" she was crying now, hysterical and snorting, "excuse me."

"Well, I'm glad someone's having fun," Douglas took out his watch again, popped open the lid, quickly glanced at it, and shut it. As it snapped closed, their youngest daughter, Martha, entered the room.

"What's going on down here?" she smiled when she saw her mother laughing hysterically. "What happened? I can hear you clear up to my room."

"In three years, it will be her!" Gabrielle burst back into her laughing fit, then wiped her eyes and raised her arm. "I'm okay, I'm okay." Finally, though gradually, she began to calm down.

"Oh pooh! I thought something good happened. I'm going back upstairs." Martha headed back to her room.

"Make sure Dougie is asleep and not reading," Her father called back.

Gabrielle cuddled up with Douglas, massaging his arms to relax him. "You know Doug, someday we're going to lose them all. Well, we can never really lose them, but our children will marry and move on." She smiled at the man she loved, "It will be just the two of us, like the way we started."

"I know, I know," Douglas smiled, "I just want to enjoy the time we have left with them. They're growing up so quickly."

"Our daughters are beautiful," she tickled her husband, "I did a pretty good job."

"I had something to do with that, too, you know."

Gabrielle whispered in Douglas's ear, "I know; I remember well," her voice was husky. Then she added, "Just because you were a bad boy in high school doesn't mean all boys are," she began laughing again. That thought brought back vivid memories of him and Margaret Myers in high school, and Douglas took out his pocket watch again.

In August 1929, when Eleanora Buch began high school,

she was happy to have the opportunity that many women and men before her didn't have. Her father, Felo, firmly believed in education and insisted that his daughters continue theirs. His daughter, Julia, was already a senior in high school. Some immigrant parents only wanted their children to learn to read and write in English and then get jobs to earn money. But Felo was privileged in that sense. Having an excellent white-collar job allowed him advantages others couldn't afford.

But Eleanora didn't know what was coming; nobody did, not even the father she revered. He was one of the few people she looked up to in the small range of vision she harbored then. The town, the country, and the world, for that matter, didn't know what lay waiting like a coiled snake preparing to spring and leash upon the population, a wrath that was not seen even though the signs were there. People usually live in denial during shaky times.

About two months later, the stock market crashed on October 24, 1929. It was called Black Thursday. About 14 billion dollars of stock value was lost. It was the basis for a depression that spread like wildfire around the globe. Hard times were in store for the town of Wellsville, Ohio.

The widow, Adelina Rampucini, and her daughter left the town of Wellsville shortly before the crash, as mysteriously as when they first appeared. Nobody ever heard about them again. Many missed the widow's telling of fortunes; others didn't and were happy she was gone. One thing was sure: the Italian community was grateful that they no longer had to live in fear of the strega who could cast the evil mal'occhio.

Chapter Thirty-Six

Wellsville, Ohio 1930-1934

The American Mafia

Salvatore Maranzano is known as the father of the American mafia. Ironically, he once studied to be a priest with an interest in the Roman Empire's structure of hierarchy. He formed a relationship with the Sicilian mafia boss, Don Vito Ferro, and emigrated to America with his assistance during prohibition to seize control of what was becoming an organized effort of riveling Black Handers' enormous profits made from illegal booze. The Roman Empire inspired him to create the confidential and organized ranking of the American Mafia. Maranzano enacted the secret ritual of induction: burning a picture of a saint to signify that a new member of his family would burn as so if they betrayed their new family in any way. Based on the omertà he knew from the Sicilian mafia, he also initiated the term 'cosa nostra,' the meaning of the American mafia. After the elimination of rival Black Hand bosses Giuseppe Morello and Joe 'the boss' Masseria, Maranzano rose to become the boss of all bosses, or 'capo di tutti.' Charles 'Lucky' Luciano had Maranzano killed by his henchmen. Instead of replacing Maranzano as the boss of all bosses, knowing he would eventually be killed the same way, Luciano formed 'the Commission,' a central organization of all mafia bosses nationwide, each having a vote.

Douglas and Gabrielle Nicholson took their son Douglas for a walk on an unseasonably warm day in early spring. Young

Douglas's sisters were busy, and his mother felt he was too young to stay home alone. Therefore, all three of them walked to Giuditta's hotel to pay their respects to Millie, who had lost her husband, Hector. Since it was such a beautiful day, they walked along Riverside, passing some of Douglas's old childhood haunts.

General Reilly had long ago passed, as did the widow, Mrs. Heely. Mr. and Mrs. Causwell sold their house in the 1920s and moved in with their son, John, and his wife, who now lived outside Wheeling, West Virginia. The infamous Whitacre House, where three United States Presidents spoke, including Abraham Lincoln, and where the Confederate General Morgan was held prisoner, had burned down years before and stood no longer. The old wharf was still there, and as they passed it, Douglas told his family, "I read somewhere that they may consider building up the riverboat traffic. People are looking for less expensive ways to travel, with the price of fuel and everything. Good old steam might come back to save the day." He reminded himself of the way his father spoke.

Douglas survived the Depression well. Before the market crash, he had diversified his money by granting business partnerships to people who proved honest and their propositions worthwhile. He also bought any available property. In a way, Douglas helped people while making money. His investments were always in solid, tangible things. He actually made money from his gold investments during the crash. And he was still a practicing attorney. However, at the beginning of the Depression, most other things declined somewhat.

"You don't have to hold my hand at every corner, Mom," complained Douglas Jr. The sun beat down a golden cast upon the boy's face as he spoke. "I'm 12 now, Mom." Gabrielle had immediately taken her boy's hand out of force of habit. Douglas Jr. had already complained about it two times that day. His father looked at his wife with that 'The boy's right' expression. Too often did he tell Gabrielle that she shouldn't baby his son, recalling the years of his bullying. But Douglas Jr. wasn't bullied like he had been. The young boy already had a good build and was much taller for his age. 'Not a runt like I was,' Douglas thought and smiled as he did. However, Douglas taught his only son how to box if the need for self-defense ever occurred. He also fished with his son sometimes, but the boy had taken to fishing like flies to honey. He loved it and often brought catches of his day back, reminding Douglas of the days when he did the same.

Gabrielle and Douglas had long ago resolved how to address their son with three Douglass in the family. His friends sometimes called him Dougie, which Gabrielle finally adapted only privately. The resolution was that he should be referred to as Douglas Jr. and assume that title from his father. When in the company of his grandfather, all would be called by their sequence of order of rank: Douglas one, two, and three. Only in private would they call him Dougie.

"Mama Giuditta!" Gabrielle called out as she saw Giuditta on the side of the hotel, coming out of the bakehouse, as she called it. "Do you have fresh bread for me?" laughed Gabrielle. Gabrielle and her husband didn't know about Giuditta's indiscretions with men or the real reason for her travels; they weren't in the Italian loop of gossip. When Giuditta went to New York, the Nicholsons assumed they were the innocent excursions of a lonely woman with her female friends. Though by that time, Giuditta's amorous entanglements had stopped.

"I have fresh bread inside!" Giuditta shouted back. C'mon inside, we have something to eat." She pointed to the front doorway to signal them to go inside. "I was cleaning the shelves in the bakehouse," she said in her crude use of the English language.

As the three Nicholsons ate, Gabrielle and Douglas noticed that the hotel didn't have anywhere near the regular crowds as before. Giuditta picked up those sentiments from their expressions. "Yeah, not too many people as before, ever since the Depression started," she frowned, "nobody has money anymore. A lot of the people who get off the trains aren't looking for rooms," she opened her arms in a look of appeal, "they just look for free food. They sneak on the trains and go from town to town. The few with money don't get off in town; they keep riding elsewhere."

"How's Millie doing?" As Gabrielle asked, Millie walked through the door from the kitchen with a boy around the same age as Douglas Jr. Gabrielle got up and rushed into Millie's arms, "Oh, Millie, we're so sorry. We just heard about Hector." Millie sobbed in her arms until Douglas came up to her.

"He was a wonderful man, Millie, a hard worker and an excellent provider. I'm so sorry." Douglas held her tightly. He knew about the struggles Hector had throughout his life, losing his crew manager job in Pittsburgh and the beating he took.

"Yes, sir, Mr. Douglas, he was at that!" Millie stepped back and wiped her eyes with the handkerchief she removed from her pocket. "Seems all I've been doing is crying." Then she declared, "Hector was born a slave, but he died a free man and proud." Acknowledging the young boy beside her, she asked, "Do you know my grandson? This is Hector Allen; he's my daughter, Phoebe's son. He's staying with me for the day." Hector stepped up and smiled.

Douglas and Gabrielle said almost in unison, "It's nice to meet you, Hector," Douglas shaking Hector's hand. At the same time, Douglas Jr. nodded, as children do.

At almost 70, Millie still worked in the hotel but had slowed down since the old days. Since the Depression started, the hotel hadn't had as much work. Bianca Gallo and Mrs. D'Angelo had left town a few years before. Sofia Marino, Giuditta's friend, still stopped by on occasion. Sandra 'Sandy' Bursky and her husband, Lorenzo, also moved away; Lorenzo got a job in Steubenville. Rosa Fontana and her crippled daughter still kept a room at Giuditta's hotel. An older Everett Holt still worked the bar occasionally; faded scars showed upon his face as memories of the beating he took from Matteo Fontano years before.

Eleanora and Annie entered the hotel as Douglas and his family prepared to leave. "You know my granddaughter, Eleanora, and her friend, Annie," Giuditta grinned, always proud of all her grandchildren.

"Of course we do," Gabrielle quickly answered, smiling as she did.

"We always see them romping all about town," laughed Douglas, "Just like I did when I was a kid," remembering his old days with Peppina and the gang, walking the streets and running through alleyways for shortcuts. As his eyes glanced back to Giuditta, he saw the look of remorse on her face, realizing she was also recalling those days of long ago, and he felt some regret for resurrecting that subject.

But Giuditta quickly rebounded and asked, "Where are you girls off to?"

"We're going to the drug store to get milkshakes, Gramma," Eleanora happily answered. Giuditta was already reaching into one of her dress's deep pockets as she listened.

"I'm having a malt," Annie laughed, "with extra chocolate."

"Here, girls," Giuditta pulled out a handful of quarters and gave them three. "Buy some candy, too, girls."

"Thanks, Gram!"

Thank you, Mrs. Buch!" Annie and Eleanora rushed out of the hotel, quickly exchanging their goodbyes with the Nicholsons.

Giuditta always gave all of her grandchildren money, and they knew it. "That's why they stopped here," Giuditta laughed, explaining it to Gabrielle and Douglas. "They're already in high school. Pretty soon, the boys will be coming around," she chuckled, waving her right hand. "Let them have fun while they're young."

As Gabrielle and Douglas stepped outside the hotel's door, John Buch brushed by them, quickly greeting them, and then ran up to the room he still kept at the hotel. He lept back down the stairway and out the door where Giuditta and Millie were saying their final farewells to the Nicholson family. Gabrielle asked the question everyone was wondering, "Where is he going in such a hurry?"

Giuditta raised her shoulders, indicating she didn't know. But Millie, standing closer to Gabrielle, whispered into her ear, "A woman," Millie's eyes widened and hinted at a smile as Gabrielle turned to look at her. Gabrielle got the message and didn't say anything in front of Giuditta.

Millie tended tables after Giuditta lost so many of her workers during those hard times of the Depression. Being disgusted by the decline of the hotel she had protected as her own for years upset Millie. When an older couple asked for one of Giuditta's Italian recipes, which had been offered for years, she answered, "We have a limited menu, folks." Recalling all the delicious Italian recipes that made Giuditta so popular saddened the woman, now Giuditta's friend, more than a worker. Millie grimly explained what was available. After the couple decided, Millie said, "Hmm, good choice," and her face merged into a big smile.

In high school, there were students whose families came up the valley from Kentucky. Many of the other pupils called them 'Kentucky Wonder Beans.' Those who came down from the hills in the high country of West Virginia and Ohio were referred to as 'Hoopies.'

Between the two friends, Annie and Eleanora, Annie was the more attractive and outgoing one, already catching the eyes of many of the boys, even as a younger teen. At the same time, Eleanora considered herself a wallflower who hadn't yet come out of her shell. When Eleanora was young, she had an infection that caused her eye to begin to turn. A doctor corrected the eye problem, but it diminished the eyesight of that one eye, requiring Eleanora to wear glasses. She was also puny and became a target for bullies at school. On the other hand, Annie, who otherwise was a sweetheart to her sisters and friends, especially Eleanora, shot directly from the hip whenever anyone taunted her or anyone close to her; she was the spirited one.

One boy in particular, Charles Boyle, or Charlie as his

friends called him, was exceptionally adept at making fun of other kids, especially those who couldn't defend themselves as bullies usually do; he was a 'smart Alec.' Charlie was a handsome teenager and popular among those he selected to be in his inner circle. Always nicely dressed in cuffed dress slacks, a pressed collared shirt, and a necktie, sometimes wearing a sports jacket or paisley sweater, he was a year higher in grade than Annie and Eleanora and teased Eleanora unrelentingly. Until Annie had enough of it one day while overhearing him tease her friend, Eleanora.

"Hey, four-eyes! How you doing today?" Charlie shouted with a big smile as other teens in the hallway laughed. That's when Annie released her fury upon the unsuspecting tormentor.

"Hey, Charlie!" Annie stood poised with her left hand on her hip and her right one with her forefinger pointing directly at him. "Your father's a cop, isn't he?"

"What about it?" Charlie looked down on her with a look of superiority plastered on his face.

"Well, you think you're the 'cat's meow.' But your dad's a crook! That's what it's about!" Charlie blushed with a shocked expression. "He's a corrupt cop, even more than all the others!" Her smile made Charlie look furious.

"Is not!" Charlie looked around to see that other students were eavesdropping, which embarrassed him.

"Oh yeah?" Annie walked up closer to him and told him, "My friend here, the one you were just harassing, she told me a little story. Wanna hear it?" Charlie's demeanor clearly showed that he didn't, but Annie pursued, her thumb indicating Eleanora standing behind her, "Eleanora's Uncle George. . ."

"Oh, Annie, don't. We'll get in trouble," Eleanora was worried, but Annie ignored her friend's remark.

"Her Uncle George was stopped by your father. Your daddy told him, 'George, I know you have liquor there. Now, you can do one of two things: Give me $100, and I'll let you go, or I'm turning you in.' That's what he said." Annie seemed to enjoy that moment in the sun and continued, "You know what else?

The chief didn't know. Your father is supposed to share all the money they take from shakedowns of bootleggers with the other corrupt police officers." Eleanora had her hand on Annie's shoulder, trying to quiet her, but Annie rolled on, "The chief is crooked too. He. . ."

"Enough!" cracked Charlie, almost blue in the face.

"No!" John Aliotta spoke for the first time. He was one of the students standing around listening. "I want to hear the rest." John was a football player, bigger than Charlie, who then shut up. Eleanora's sister, Julia, was going steady with John.

"Jiminy, I want to hear more, too," another student named Kevin cried out, "Sounds good."

Annie had the green light to continue, "The chief lives in a nice home high up on the hill, with beautiful furnishings, and even has a nice organ. How do you think he got all those things?" Annie was unstoppable. "He even takes money from a poor widow who lost her husband in the Great War. She's only trying to get by and earn food by selling some measly liquor. George Bamarra pays the chief off every month. But your father even steals from the other police. Everyone knows."

Eleanora nudged her, "Annie, we have to go!" Eleanora saw the principal turn the corner, probably to see what the gathering was about. "C'mon, let's go."

Annie slipped in one last comment before Eleanora almost dragged her away, "The chief called her Uncle George once and said, 'George, hide everything. The state officials are in town.' That's what he said." The state officers would break open beer, wine, and hard liquor barrels into the street. Annie finally left, thrilled at her avenging performance, walking away like an attorney leaving the courtroom after giving a successful closing argument.

When the Great Depression began, Lucy still made crocheted sheer blouses for the brothel's madam, Nora. Even that type of business didn't escape the wrath of those bad times.

As men wanted those pleasures as much as ever, many didn't have the money to spend on such luxuries. But Madam Nora remained insistent on providing only the best for her girls. She would not cut down on their attire or the atmosphere of her workplace. That meant prices remained the same; she preferred to have fewer customers but provide the same service as before. So Lucy still produced her beautifully crocheted pieces, but her workload decreased slightly.

Lucy continued writing and reading letters for the Italian illiterates, where she inadvertently learned so much astonishing gossip but never said a word about anything she learned to others. Lucy wasn't as privileged to hear American gossip in town as her husband, Felo. That's why she never knew where the items she produced were going. She found out only when an incident occurred at Madame Nora's bordello. While Felo casually flipped through the local newspaper at dinner, he came upon an article that mentioned a physical altercation between a former patron and a prostitute who worked for Nora. Felo knew that place existed from a fellow member of one of the clubs he attended. He whispered aloud at the dinner table, "Well, I'll be," his face turning to a smirk, "they finally caught up with Nora Weiss." Lucy's eyes widened, exposing the entire rim of white that encircled her rich blue eyes, her face flushed red.

Felo couldn't help but notice her expression and asked her, "Something wrong, dear?" But Lucy pretended to have swallowed her food wrong and said nothing. Learning that her precious work would aid and abet a house of ill repute almost choked her.

Both her daughters and Nicky noticed their mother's reaction, all suspecting nothing.

Only Eleanora, the inquisitive one, asked, "Are you alright, Mom?" She knew her mother well and suspected something. Eleanora, like always, would persist until she found out what happened. Julia didn't think anything about it at all; she just twirled her food and sat dreamy-eyed over John Aliotta, her boyfriend.

Later that night, Lucy confessed to her husband, who she worked for, to buy such nice things for her children. Felo didn't seem to care much. In fact, he thought it was a good thing. His wife wasn't doing anything wrong and making some extra money. But he didn't know how much Lucy had made over those years.

Lucy went to confession to pray for forgiveness for her sin. The Catholic priest told her in the confessional, "Lucia, you did nothing wrong. Take the money. In these troubled times, you'll need it." She couldn't see that the priest was smiling from behind the screen. Lucy would also learn a short time later how correct his prediction about needing the money was. Lucy made the sign of the cross every time she began working on one of the blouses and prayed for penance.

Nina and Maude were already married but wanted to take their younger sisters and Eleanora to Rock Springs Amusement Park across the bridge in Chester, West Virginia. Louise attended Geneva College in Beaver, Pennsylvania, and was home on a break. The older sisters wanted it to be an all-girl event with no husbands or boyfriends. The same trolley line company that ran cars from Steubenville, Ohio, to Beaver, Pennsylvania, purchased Rock Springs Park in 1900 after J.E. McDonald built up the Chester, West Virginia area. However, the park officially opened after the East Liverpool trolley line crossed the Chester Bridge and entered the park. Rock Springs Amusement Park offered something for people of all ages, from rides like the Cyclone roller coaster to bands playing music while people danced under the stars. Douglas Nicholson had taken Margaret Myers there right after it opened years before.

Eleanora just about ran all the way home to get permission. She loved that park and was overwhelmed with excitement, as were Annie and the other younger Trieste sisters. Even Nina, Maude, and Louise were thrilled but hid it remarkably well, as older sisters usually do with childlike events.

As soon as Eleanora ran in the door, she asked her mother, "Mom, they want to take me. Can I go?"

"Take you where?" Lucy was startled since Eleanora didn't even explain who wanted to take her or where she wanted to go. This wasn't unusual for her daughter, Eleanora, who was ready to go anywhere at the drop of a hat.

"Oh!" Eleanora laughed, realizing her absentmindedness. "Nina, Maude, Louise, and the rest of the girls are going to Rock Springs Park. You know, the amusement park over the river in Chester."

"If the older girls are going, it's okay with me, but you have to ask your father," her mother's customary reply whenever Eleanora or her sister asked to go somewhere ever since they became teenagers. Felo had just taken a cigarette from his silver case and was prepared to sit on his rocking chair, searching for the newspaper to read before dinner.

Eleanora spotted the paper first, grabbed it, and gracefully walked over to her father. "Hi, Dad; did you have a nice day at work today?" she asked, handing the paper to him. Felo was immediately suspicious as he smiled at his daughter.

"Yes, dear, I did. How was school?" He smiled because Eleanora always resurrected faded memories he had, as well as stories that others had told him about his older sister, Peppina. She now lived again in his heart through his daughter, Eleanora, even though she didn't physically resemble her. The spirit of the happy, bubbly little creature that Peppina was, he now saw again in her. On the other hand, Julia looked almost exactly like Emanuela, his other sister who was also separated from him long ago.

"I did good in school today, Dad," she stood next to the rocker as Felo sat himself down for a leisurely read. "Dad," she looked down at him appealingly, "Nina and her sisters asked me to go to Rock Springs Park tomorrow. You know it's a Saturday, and I have no school." Felo always admired the socially spirited and extroverted manner by which his younger daughter conducted herself. It was a trait he never acquired. Having more of a laid-back personality, Felo had high hopes for his daughter and always thought those same characteristics would take her far.

"Yes, dear, you can go. Here," he reached into his trouser pocket and pulled out his money clip, "Here's three dollars. Have a good time."

"Oh, thank you, Dad!" Eleanora ran into the kitchen and asked her mother if she could call the Trieste home. Then she ran to the telephone to tell the girls she could go and asked what time she should be at their house.

That day when the girls thrilled themselves on the roller coaster, rode the carousel and the Ferris wheel, traveled the scenic railroad, boated on the lake, dropped from the shoot-the-chutes, watched a stage show, visited the old mill and the zoo as well as other amusements—all would be repeated in the coming years with Eleanora's friends who were more like sisters. Eleanora would dance under the stars with her boyfriends in those years ahead when she became pretty.

As the Depression progressed, further potential tax from liquor revenues began to look attractive to the government. Repeal of prohibition was one of Franklin D. Roosevelt's campaign promises of 1932. People wanted their liquor, and illegal operations and crime rose because of it. An amendment to fully ratify the repeal of prohibition went into effect by December 1933. Gangsters had made a fortune during prohibition. Al Capone's enterprise in Chicago earned about sixty million dollars annually during that period. Importation and sale of illegal alcohol propelled the small-time Italian gangs of the Black Hand into the organized crime families of the American Mafia.

After prohibition ended, local profiteers of that era, including Black Handers and bootleggers, used their illegal earnings to buy taverns and make other investments in Wellsville. The Weiss brothers' gambling ventures boomed, and Black Handers, like the Brocella brothers, served as enforcers to those who didn't pay their debts. "Suckers one and all," laughed Joe Brocella to Frank Weise, who chuckled in response.

"It looks like everyone wants to be a millionaire. They don't know that they can't beat the house," Frank declared, "Every now and then, we let one of the chumps win," he was now laughing along with Joe. It seemed that even in hard times, people wanted to take a chance at making money, a philosophy that Luigi Massaro and Biaggio Giglio had adhered to years before.

George Bamarra financed several bars in town with some of the money he earned. He didn't know that his wife, Thelma, who despised him for what he did to her, secretly stole money from him. Acting kindly to other children, George ruled his household with an iron fist. He made his young daughters dress like Amish children in plain clothes, probably thinking someone might do to them what he did to their mother. Thelma still dreaded the touch of him whenever he forced himself upon her and wanted to hurt him in the only way she knew how. Little by little, she stashed a fortune of cash in glass jars throughout hidden places in the house. "Take that, you son of a bitch," she whispered every time she took his money. One time, Thelma, always called Aunt May by her nieces and nephews, staged a robbery in their home. She messed up the house to make it look like a break-in had happened and stole six thousand dollars of George's money. George was furious, on a rampage, suspecting and threatening everyone except his wife. Thelma was thrilled at his performance, laughing on the inside. She smiled when George wasn't looking and softly said, "You son of a bitch, and you too, Giuditta." Aunt May was very generous to her nieces and nephews who visited her, always sneaking some of George's money to them from one of the jars.

John Buch kept rushing about town in his eagerness to be satisfied in the arms of his lover, Mrs. Betty Harrison. To please her and to encourage her to maintain the abundance of pleasure she rewarded him with, John began gambling to take her out and buy her lovely things. Living beyond the limit of his income now, like the little worker bee John was, he labored passionately to receive the satisfaction only the experienced Mrs. Harrison could provide him with. He was living the high life that Betty enjoyed until his gambling debts rose far too high for Frank Weise's liking.

Rocco Brocella, the taller brother, approached John on Frank's behalf one day as John was rushing over to Mrs. Harrison's house for some of her delightful pleasure. Rocco abruptly stopped John and told him, "You gotta pay up, John."

"I'll pay Rocco, don't worry. Tell Frank I'll pay him in no time," the amicable, much shorter, and thinner John smiled.

"You gotta pay now," Rocco said, not smiling. A look of malice quickly appeared on his face, which frightened John. "Frank wants the money now. Do you even know how much you owe?"

John rolled his eyes back briefly, thinking, "I owe Frank about seventy, maybe just a bit more." John was now scared by Rocco's frightening expression. He had completely forgotten how much he owed.

"You owe four hundred dollars!" Rocco barked, "And Frank wants it now!"

"What? My tab isn't that high." John thought in his fright, 'It's not that much by a long shot,' but he was too scared to say it aloud.

"Interest!" Rocco was getting restless.

"Well, that's a lot of money. I don't have that kind of money," John gulped. His fear was getting the best of him. 'Get hold of yourself,' John thought and tried desperately.

"Get it!" Rocco demanded, pulling a switchblade out of his trouser pocket and snapping it open, "or else," Rocco sneered, standing firmly and looking down directly into John's scared eyes with a look of evil that caused a tingle to penetrate up and down the puny man's spine. His legs buckled, and he almost wet himself.

John was speechless but somehow brought himself to say, "Okay, okay," but timidly. Rocco's knife snapped back inside, and he turned and walked away. John stood thinking about where to get that much money in such a short time. He began to sweat as he drifted aimlessly along the sidewalk. Finally, he whispered, "That's it," he thought again, "It's the only way. God forgive me, but it's the only way," John began to shed tears, "I'm sorry. It's the only way," he repeated.

John didn't go to Betty's house that day; he couldn't even think about her at such a time. He couldn't sleep that night, with the next day so foreboding, fear and embarrassment lingering in his mind.

"Mom, just sign here," John instructed his mother after they had their breakfast together. He couldn't look directly at Giuditta's eyes.

"What's this for," Giuditta smiled at her son, happy that he was responsible enough to step up and take over for Felo, who was now busy with his prestigious job and family. Giuditta had been proud of John working so hard at his job and still finding the time to manage the hotel for her. She had no idea she was signing ownership of the hotel over to John. Giuditta had learned to write her name for business purposes but always had her son, John, check everything she signed since she never learned to read.

"Business, Mama, just business," he answered, lying and about to do something that would change their lives forever.

John planned to get a loan using the hotel as collateral so he could pay off his gambling debts. He used a town bank but tried to keep it quiet from the locals. As long as he paid the monthly payments, everything would be fine. John would stop gambling and toe the line. No more extravagant spending, and he would work extra hours to meet those payments. 'Straighten up and fly right' was his new motto. Yes, everything would be okay. That worked for about three days.

"Can I come over in an hour, honey?" Betty's voice sounded so refreshing after three days of not seeing her.

"Well, I have to work late." John cleared his throat.

"Oh, honey pie, mommy's lonely," her voice became husky. "Well, I said. . ."

Betty cut him off, "Mommy has something special for her pussycat," she whispered alluringly. Moaning, she added, "It's what you like, mmm."

"Okay, in an hour."

While John rested in Betty's arms, she asked him, "Remember that coat you wanted to buy for me, honey pie?"

"Yeah," John dreaded ever mentioning that.

"I saw one in the window on Main Street today," she brushed her toes along John's shin, knowing how much he liked it. Then she giggled, watching the sheet covering John's lower abdomen begin to rise. "It's really nice, pussycat."

"Okay, I'll give you some money." John lost control.

"Oh, you sweetheart!" Betty cried out and crawled over him. "Looks like little Johnny boy wants to come out to play again."

After Mrs. Harrison left a few hours later, John needed a drink to steady his nerves. As soon as he entered the bar, a group of men called him over. One drunken man said, "Here's our friend, Johnny!" Several rounds later, John picked up the tab as usual.

As the months went by, John couldn't change. He tried, but it was a lost cause; he was what he was. He couldn't meet the mortgage payments and tried his hand at gambling again. His tab there rose, and John didn't pay the loan payments. Every time the bank called the hotel, using sophisticated words alien to her limited English vocabulary, Giuditta told them in poor English, "My son takes care of business." Even when a bank representative came to the hotel, Giuditta ignored him and directed him to her son, who never seemed to be around. John also hid all the hand-delivered notices that arrived.

John's haphazard and extravagant lifestyle went on for months. When Giuditta asked her son why the bank was calling so much, he told her, "It's business, Mama, just business." Giuditta always rested assured that her son knew as much about these things as Felo. John was always a good boy.

John's loan remained remiss until a sheriff's deputy came over in the late afternoon one day. He entered the hotel as Giuditta served lunch to a small group; her business had shrunk even more from the hard times. "May I see the owner, please?" he asked Millie, who pointed to a startled Giuditta next to her. "You have to leave the premises."

Giuditta looked at Millie, "What does he mean?" she asked in her heavy accent.

The sheriff's deputy answered for her, "It means you were served several foreclosure and eviction notices, and you ignored them. Now you have to leave this place. You're being evicted. I'll give you some time to gather your personal belongings. You have three hours, then the bank gets the building and everything in it."

"But I live here!" Giuditta was startled. "What are you talking about?" The deputy only spread his arms apart, not fully understanding Giuditta's accent. "Maronna mia!" Giuditta screamed at the top of her voice, startling the deputy, who instinctively hopped away from the hysterical woman, now crying and stomping her feet. Giuditta raised her hands to the heavens, whimpering, "What am I gonna do now?"

"C'mon, Giuditta, I'll help you pack. Ain't no fighting the law. We'll think of something." Millie assumed John was behind this. 'That woman and all,' she thought. Millie had heard talk around town but didn't believe it as Giuditta always paid her bills. 'It had to be that no good son of hers,' Millie reasoned while preparing to help Giuditta with her things. Trotting to the telephone, Millie tried to call Felo at his office, but the lines were busy every time she called. 'Just upset him anyway. Too late for anyone to help.'

The deputy stood guard at the front door as people left. He prevented anyone who wasn't a hotel boarder from entering the building. Millie asked the deputy, "Will lodgers who ain't here right now get their things?"

The deputy shrugged, "My job is to evict the owner, John Buch and his family. Maybe the bank will keep the hotel open.

They sent out too many prior warnings, hand-delivered, and mailings. One was an order of eviction signed by Mr. Buch. He should have contacted them; all this might have been avoided."

"But where am I gonna go?" tears streamed down Giuditta's cheeks. "This has been my home for over 40 years," she said in broken English. "Everything I own is here."

"You stay with me until we find out what happened." Millie was now also crying.

As she walked the hotel floors for the last time, Giuditta remembered herself and Luigi as they surveyed it for the first time years before. She reflected on the happy times she and her family had while fixing it up. All the memories she had long suppressed resurfaced as did the tremendous security she once had with Luigi. All those years of using men as the only method of healing the pain she couldn't deal with after losing Luigi, Giuditta now reckoned. Her memories took her back to Douglas when everyone called him Pip. With Rollo faithfully at his side, he played with her long-lost daughter, Peppina.

Those recollections took her back to the beginning of her life with Luigi and every wonderful thing that followed. Every second of those remembrances flashed before the distraught and repentant woman as Millie slowly led her to a loaded wagon with all that remained of her life's work. Ironically, Giuditta indirectly suffered the consequences of gambling, as did her first husband, Luigi, years ago.

After graduating high school, Eleanora wanted to go to college. Felo always knew his daughter had what it took to go far, and he wanted her to go. She did well in school, which made him proud of her. Nicky would have enough money to go to school if he wanted when he graduated in five years.

"Hard times now, Eleanora. You'll have to do your share by improvising," He knew his daughter liked nice things and spent money on going out with her friends. "I can help you set up a budget for you."

"Thank you, Dad, I will. I'll follow any budget you set up and do well in school. I can even get a side job while I'm there." Felo smiled; it was Peppina speaking.

Later that fall, Eleanora began college. She lived up to her word and studied hard while working a few hours a day helping take care of a professor's children, where she boarded. She also did errands for him. Eleanora took a train home every recess. She limited her spending and only went places that didn't require much money, mainly with Annie and the other Trieste sisters. She even got a summer job. Eleanora adhered to her part of the bargain until circumstances changed toward the end of her second year of college.

Felo had received notice that the Third Street Station would cease operations. The old building was closing after so much damage from past flooding and the railroad's slowdown. He hadn't mentioned anything about it because he was still employed when the station shut down. Closing a railroad station required an accountant on the premises throughout the process. Felo hoped the railroad would find a position for him elsewhere, but they didn't. The Shop on 12th Street was a shell of its former place, and the Depression was causing layoffs everywhere. The railroad gave Felo a pension, and he could keep his railway pass, but his position was gone.

Eleanora had to come home from school right after finishing her second year of college. Felo felt devastated that his daughter wouldn't be able to finish school. As disheartened as Eleanora was, she understood how hard things were becoming for everyone and accepted the bad news. The Depression was changing the way people lived. When families defaulted, the banks recalled their mortgages and repossessed farms and homes. Eleanora saw photos of people in the big cities living on the streets, some in cardboard shelters, sitting outside on a chair reading the newspaper. People in the cities had it harder. Many ate meals in soup kitchens, while others starved. Living in a small town where people planted mutual vegetable gardens and shared and bartered with each other was somewhat better.

Eleanora learned to appreciate the gifts she had.

Douglas and Gabrielle had visited Claire Delisle, Gabrielle's mother, several times since the death of her husband. Their older daughter, Claire, lived with her grandmother while attending the same college her mother had years before. Gabrielle urged her mother to move to Wellsville to live with her family, as her daughter, Claire, was leaving as soon as she graduated. "God, we certainly have enough room." However, though she occasionally visited to see the Nicholsons she loved, Claire wanted to remain in Cincinnati, where she settled with her late husband, Andre, so many years before.

Douglas and Gabrielle left their other daughter and son in the care of their housekeeper to visit Clair, who was now in her early 70s and had a bad hip.

They stayed a week, and before they departed to go home, Gabrielle and Douglas tried one last time to persuade her to come and live with them. Though Claire appreciated it, she wanted to remain where her memories resided.

"This is where you and Douglas were married," Claire said with a tear in her eye. "I can't leave my home."

"I'll hire a nurse to care for you then if you're certain you won't come to live with us," Douglas told her. He knew his mother-in-law well; she had a strong attachment to her home in Cincinnati.

"You are a wonderful man, Douglas," she answered him, "and you've been such a good husband and provider to my daughter. I liked you from the first moment I met you so many years ago."

Felo didn't know what had happened at the hotel until he received a phone call from a friend, but too late to be of help. Embarrassed to show his face, John was hiding. Felo wanted his mother to stay with him until he could get information. But

Giuditta preferred to be with Millie instead of Lucy, though she didn't tell her son it was for that reason. Felo contacted Douglas Nicholson to see if he could do anything legally.

Douglas seemed annoyed at John, "Why didn't he come to me when the problem began?" he asked Felo. "I didn't know anything about this. I would have helped out. Let me look into this right now."

When Douglas quickly got to the root of the problem, he phoned Felo back later the same day. "Felo, I'm afraid it's too late; your brother ignored several foreclosure warnings. Your brother kept this quiet. I can only surmise he wanted to keep a low profile. Your mother put her signature on all the hand-delivered documents, not knowing what they were, and it seems your brother signed the eviction notice. The bank already repossessed the hotel and property; it's in their hands. It's complicated, but because of the Depression and all the banks' failures, there are now government-issued regulations. There's nothing we can do. Felo? Are you there?" The line was quiet.

Felo was despondent, "Yes, I'm still here. I just don't know what to say."

"Felo, did you know your mother is not feeling well?"

"Well, with all that's going on, I expect so."

"No," answered Douglas. "I spoke to Millie Brown, who told me she thinks it might be more serious. Millie went with her to a doctor before all this happened. I'm sending her to my doctor, and I'll try to find her a better apartment. It's all on my tab. Maybe the hotel will remain open, and she can get a room there? I don't know. Her ownership and business is over.""It's very generous of you, Douglas," Felo's voice cracked, "You always were a good friend to us. I'll pay you back."

"No need. Your mother was wonderful to me when I was a boy. I have fond memories of that hotel. I wish there were something I could do." Douglas thought quickly, "By the way, I can throw some bookkeeping jobs your way. There are a lot of business owners who can't afford accounting firms anymore." He sighed, "You'll have to charge a fraction of what they were paying, I'm afraid. All businesses are suffering to some degree. I'm doing more pro bono work than ever before."

"Thanks, Douglas. Thanks for everything."

Sofia Marino and Millie took Giuditta to Douglas's physician. After examining her, Dr. Edwards ordered a test to confirm his suspicions. The doctor first gave the bad news to Douglas Nicholson. Giuditta had cancer and he didn't expect her to live long.

"My God," Douglas was shocked, "She looked fine the last time I saw her. How long do you think she has?"

"Not long, I'm afraid. Sometimes stress or aggravation can trigger illnesses faster," Doctor Edwards answered solemnly. "We've been living in hard times."

"Can you do anything at all for her?"

"I'm afraid not. Mrs. Buch is beyond help. There's nothing we can do for her." Doctor Edwards sounded apologetic. "I'll give her medication to make her feel more comfortable. She should stay in a warm dwelling and rest."

Douglas was in shock. It was as if his own mother was dying. "Thank you, doctor." Douglas took a short mental stroll down memory lane as he hung up the telephone. He remembered the first time he met Giuditta. 'She said I was too thin,' he smiled, thinking. 'The first time I had pizza and sundried tomatoes. And all the delicious foods she introduced me to. She was always so generous.' It was too hard to go further down the deep corridors of his mind. 'The memories buried there should remain as happy as the times I enjoyed them,' Douglas thought.

At the end of her life, Giuditta turned to God. She sent for Lucy, who graciously intended to see her mother-in-law anyway.

"I'm so sorry for how I treated you, Lucy," sobbed Giuditta, her face drawn and pale from the disease eating away at her inside. Giuditta had aged immensely, making her look haggard. The woman who had taken pride in her beauty her whole life now appeared a sickly creature but repentant.

"Niente," Lucy softly answered while wiping Giuditta's

forehead with a cool, wet cloth.

"I was a horrible woman," Giuditta whispered hoarsely. "I treated Nicola so badly." She waited to regain enough energy to speak again. "All those men I sinned with. . . I wanted my Luigi back so much." Giuditta was crying. "I used them all by pretending they were him. It was all my fault. May God forgive me."

"You had ghosts of the past, as we all do. God will forgive you," Lucy said kindly and softly. "Look at all the good you did. You were generous to so many people. You helped Rosa and Alessia Fontana when they needed help. You helped others without even knowing. The eyes of God see all things, not only the bad things we do."

"Where did Rosa and her daughter go after the hotel closed?" Giuditta could barely get her words out.

"They're safe. They live in a nice clean apartment." Lucy kept wiping Giuditta's forehead to make her comfortable. Millie Brown was sitting in the corner weeping.

Gabrielle and Douglas Nicholson had visited often since hearing about Giuditta's incurable illness. Felo was by his mother's side on her final day. Her daughters visited every day. Thelma came to say goodbye to her mother and forgave Giuditta for what she had done to her years before. Eleanora and her other grandchildren cried when they came, remembering how generous she was. A priest came to hear her confession.

Minutes before Giuditta passed, she asked, "Lucy, please come closer," and her daughter-in-law complied. "Take some of my money for my funeral," Giuditta stopped to compose herself, then whispered the rest to Lucy. Giuditta muttered something softly before slowly closing her eyes; her labored breathing stopped. Giuditta Buch passed away one day before her 70th birthday.

Giuditta's last words to Lucy were that she wanted three priests to attend her funeral Mass and requested paid mourners. She had felt that no one else would shed a tear for her. But she was wrong. The church filled with people crying for the woman they remembered fondly in their hearts. Among them were her family, Millie Brown, the Nicholson family, Sofia Marino, the Triestes, the Provenzanos, the Puglianos, and most of the Italian community and so many others who remembered Giuditta Buch's generosity and kindness over the many years. Even Luisa D'Angelo returned for Giuditta's funeral.

Giuditta Buch was laid to rest beside her husband, Nicola. The last words she had muttered the night she died were about how much she regretted losing Luigi Massaro, her greatest sin. The woman who escaped the wrath of New York's Little Italy by eloping on the adventure of her life with the man of her dreams, who lived a life of luxury in Pittsburgh and Sharpsburg, Pennsylvania, set up a small hotel to her satisfaction, was gone.

The hotel deceitfully put in her son John's name before she passed, didn't sell due to the Depression and many floods in town. In 1938, it was auctioned at a sheriff's sale.

Chapter Thirty-Seven

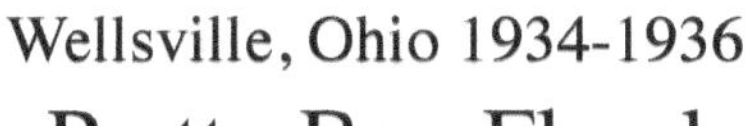

Wellsville, Ohio 1934-1936
Pretty Boy Floyd

The aftermath of the stock market crash spawned the Depression-era criminals, most of whom robbed banks. During that period, average people blamed the banks for causing the Depression and their bad times by overinvesting in the market in their eagerness to make money. Then, as the government helped restore stability to the banks, they foreclosed on working-class farms and homes. Many bank robbers bred into a life of crime during that time took mortgage loan documents with them and destroyed them, making them heroes and legends amongst those hurt by the severe situations of that era.

In 1924, a young, ambitious man named J. Edgar Hoover became Director of the Bureau of Investigation (BOI). He aggressively promoted that organization as a personal career move through the success of the BOI. Hoover was a man looking for power. When the Depression-era criminals began making headlines, he appointed Melvin Purvis to take the lead in tracking down John Dillinger, the most wanted man then. After the outlaw John Dillinger was killed in July 1934, Charles Arthur 'Pretty Boy' Floyd became Public Enemy number one by the G-men (government men). They assumed Vern Miller, Adam Richetti, and Charles Floyd orchestrated the Kansas City Massacre and killed four policemen there. It made headlines, and

Hoover pressured Melvin Purvis to hunt down Floyd. Already criticized for his mistakes made in the Dillinger case, Purvis had to get results quickly. Hoover demanded that the BOI get credit for the killing of Floyd and not some local police force or deputy.

Melvin Purvis, a short man who some said had a short-fused temper, was a lawyer trying to make a reputation for himself. While on the run from the law, Charles Floyd and Adam Richetti were traveling with their girlfriends and passed through the town of Wellsville, Ohio. The heavy lingering river fog that Pip and Rollo walked through on their morning fishing expeditions years before rose so heavy it blinded them and forced their car to hit a telephone pole. Floyd and Richetti sent their girlfriends to get a tow truck while they waited, as they didn't want anyone to recognize them from their wanted posters. A townsperson spotted two unfamiliar men sitting on the side of the road, which looked suspicious to him. He immediately contacted the police chief. As the chief casually approached the men, Floyd saw the bulge of a pistol in his waist under his jacket. He opened fire, thinking the police were zoning in on them. Luckily, the chief was only hit in his foot with a flesh wound by a ricocheting bullet, and he sent officers to pursue them. The Wellsville police captured Richetti and locked him up in the city hall jail on Fifth Street. In a suit and dress shoes, Charles Floyd attempted to evade the police by way of the wooded hills.

Floyd was trying to get to Youngstown, Ohio, where he could blend in with a city crowd. First, he tried to go up the hilly road of Route 45, close to where Nina Obiso lived at the time. That place proved futile, as roadblocks barred that way. His only option was to climb the hill off-road, desperately trying to avoid the police, not knowing that a posse was pursuing him. He needed to hijack a car somehow.

After spending two days lost in the shrubs and tree-lined high grounds between Wellsville and East Liverpool, the cold and hungry Floyd approached a farm above the rock-bouldered hills of East Liverpool in the afternoon.

"I'll gladly pay you for some food," Floyd smiled at a woman who opened the backdoor of her farmhouse. As Ellen Conkle, the owner, viewed the stranger, her skepticism grew. His clothes, torn from tree branches and shrubs and unshaven, Floyd appeared like a man running from the law. When he pulled out a large roll of money, her suspicions were confirmed: this man didn't look like the typical hobo who traveled from place to place looking for food. Without even seeing the two .45 caliber automatic pistols tucked in his belt under his jacket, a chill ran up and down her spine.

"Sit here while I prepare something for you," she told him, pointing to a porch chair. She quickly surmised it would be better to feed him and let him be on his way rather than risk his anger by turning him down.

Floyd nodded and smiled in appreciation. While sitting, he picked up a copy of the East Liverpool newspaper and read about the manhunt underway to find him. "Feds," he mumbled quietly before walking to the road to see if anyone was coming to the farm. When he returned to the back porch, Mrs. Conkle called him to go inside and sit at the kitchen table to eat his meal. The hungry man gobbled down his food, which consisted of spare ribs, potatoes, rice, and pumpkin pie with coffee, muttering in between gulps, "This is so good." Waiting patiently for him to finish eating, the 41-year-old widow hoped this strange man would be on his way. Finally, when he finished, he told Ellen, "This was a fine meal, one fit for a king!" Floyd placed down a one-dollar bill near his dish. "I insist," he said as he saw her hand wave to indicate she didn't want any money.

As Floyd rose from the table, he asked Mrs. Conkle, "Can you get me to Youngstown?" He offered one of his smiles and said, "I'd be happy to pay."

As was normal, Ellen was a bit frightened and answered, "I can't," she hesitated while thinking, "But I could ask my brother when he comes out of the fields. He shouldn't be too much longer. He and his wife are husking corn for me."

Pretty Boy Floyd took that as a yes and asked, "Is that his

car?" he pointed to a Ford Model A.

"Yes," Ellen shook her head.

"I'll wait in the car." Another smile appeared, albeit a nervous one now.

A few minutes later, Ellen's brother, Stewart Dykes, and his wife returned from the field, noticing a man sitting in their automobile. Stewart could hear the ignition sound as if this guy was trying to start his car up. Mrs. Dykes walked toward Ellen as Stewart, her husband, quickly went to talk to the stranger. "Can I help you, friend?"

"Yeah. Can you get me to Youngstown? I'm happy to pay you."

"Well," his eyes rolled back, thinking. "I can't go that far, but I can take you to Clarkson. You can get a bus from there."

Floyd answered, "Okay, that'll be fine." Dykes waved his wife over. Floyd went to sit in the back seat as Mrs. Dykes sat in the front next to her husband. As soon as they pulled out, two Chevrolets came up from Sprucevale Road, blocking Stewart Dyke's Ford. The four-man posse from East Liverpool sat in the first car, and three BOI agents, along with Melvin Purvis, sat in the second one.

"Drive behind that building over there," Floyd shouted to Stewart Dykes, "they're looking for me," pulling out two .45 caliber Colt automatics as he spoke those words.

Officer Montgomery of the East Liverpool Police Department, a posse member, spotted Floyd first, "He's over there!" he yelled. Floyd danced like a boxer doing footwork as he hurried, moving side to side along the back of the 15-foot-long shed, deciding which way to go. The posse and the federal agents could see his feet through an opening along the bottom of the building. Knowing that if the police captured him, he would be executed, Floyd had to make a break. His only chance of escaping was a wooded area about 200 yards away, but he had to cross an open area to reach it. He went for it.

Chester Smith, a decorated veteran of the Great War and a sniper, was the only one of the posse and the federal agents who had a high-velocity rifle capable of shooting at a long distance. The police and agents only had pistols, shotguns, and one .45 caliber Thompson submachine gun, all incapable of accurately reaching the distance where Floyd already was.

Chester Smith shouted to Floyd, "Stop! Police!" As Floyd continued running, Smith raised his 1892 Winchester lever action rifle and fired a .32/20 high-velocity round and hit Floyd's arm, forcing Floyd to drop one of his pistols. Chester had seen enough violence in the war and quietly said, "I want to bring Floyd down without killing him," as he aimed his second shot, "I got him sighted!" That round hit Floyd in the shoulder, causing him to drop. The posse and agents trotted to where Floyd lay bleeding. Chester Smith asked the bank robber, "Why didn't you stop when I warned you?"

"Damnit, you never would have gotten me if I got to those woods!"

"You're Charles Floyd, right?" Purvis asked, confirming his identity. He didn't want to kill an innocent man.

"Yeah, I am, but I ain't telling you sons of bitches anything else!" which irritated Purvis. As his temper flared, it showed on his face, recalling how Hoover demanded he wanted a BOI agent to get Floyd.

Chester Smith and the rest of the posse turned around to walk back to the farmhouse. They heard a pistol crack, seeming louder in the open country space as they did. They all abruptly turned back to see one of the federal agent's pistols with smoke dissipating from the barrel. Melvin Purvis had what appeared to be a slight grin on his face. The BOI did get their man; J. Edgar Hoover would be proud to know.

Melvin Purvis resigned from the Department of Justice's Bureau of Investigation (BOI) the following year, 1935, after tracking down Baby Face Nelson. J. Edgar Hoover's BOI became the Federal Bureau of Investigation (FBI) the same year. He became one of the most feared men in politics and society in the United States, attaining the power he craved.

The widow Ellen Conkle became somewhat of a beloved

local hero. She packed away the plates Charles Arthur 'Pretty Boy' Floyd, Public Enemy number one, had used to eat his last meal and framed the one dollar bill he gave her along with the copy of the newspaper he was reading before he died. Nicky Buch and his friends were hanging around city hall when the law enforcement officials transferred Adam Richetti from the Wellsville jail to federal prison. Richetti was found guilty and executed by gas chamber in 1938 in Missouri State Penitentiary in Jefferson City, Missouri.

The police chief of Wellsville also became a local hero, and he redeemed himself to those who questioned any of his prior misdeeds. The Wellsville police force, as displayed by their steadfast hunt and capture of Adam Richetti, proved their capability to protect the citizens of their town.

Eleanora was initially a little withdrawn when she had to return home from college. Many of Eleanora's friends were attending college or had already graduated. Knowing well that times were tough and that she and her family had it better than many in town couldn't prevent the reality that her dream bubble had burst. Louise Trieste had graduated from college and began teaching in town. Annie attended the same college in Beaver from which Louise graduated and planned to become a teacher like her sister.

Eleanora had stopped wearing her glasses when she went out ever since high school. Her skinny body filled out, and the fine features of her face matured. Eleanora became pretty, and many of the young men were in pursuit of her. However, Eleanora didn't want to marry and settle in a small town. Ever since she was little, she had visions of traveling to distant places and seeing the world. Her sister, Julia, was the complete opposite. She was already engaged to John Aliotta, her high school sweetheart, and John worked in the mill to save enough money.

Eleanora found a job at a large florist in East Liverpool. She had a ride to and from the large complex but could take the trolley or bus whenever necessary. Buses were already replacing trolleys in East Liverpool. The complete transition would take time, but the larger sister town of Wellsville had begun removing trolley tracks; it was a sign of the time.

Loving the beauty and sweet smell of flowers made that work enjoyable. All the greenhouses filled the air with fragrances that reached into the offices. Eleanora excelled in both helping to make arrangements and doing paperwork. The owner, Mr. Allan Johnson, took a liking to her capabilities and efficiency, promoting her, which made other workers envious. The way they expressed that jealousy was by tormenting Eleanora with ethnic slurs. That began a series of events that became ongoing and somewhat comical.

"Where's Eleanora?" Mr. Johnson asked one of the workers, puzzled by not seeing her at work.

"She quit yesterday," replied John Moody, one of Eleanora's harassers, not looking directly at his boss.

"What?" Johnson's face reddened, and he looked annoyed, "Why?" John only shrugged his shoulders in response, pretending not to know why.

Allan Johnson immediately went to his automobile and drove to Eleanora's home in Wellsville. When Eleanora opened the front door, surprised to see her boss standing there, he told her, "You have to come back to work. I need you."

"I'm sorry, Mr. Johnson, I won't work with people who disrespect me," she said, shaking her head in a no. She didn't want to single out the few who made her days there miserable.

"I'll talk to the staff. Don't worry." Realizing it was late, he said, "You be at the office tomorrow, and everything will be okay. I'll see to it." He waved goodbye from his car, "Tomorrow."

Eleanora returned to the florist the following morning, and everyone focused on their work, not bothering her at all. The small handful of those who constantly badgered her now completely ignored the young woman who returned. It only lasted a couple of weeks before one person slipped out a nasty remark, and Eleanora quit again. Mr. Johnson appeared at her door again, pleading for her return, finally convincing her.

That same scenario lasted several months. Eleanora would quit, and Allan Johnson would return, asking her to come back and offering her a raise each time until she began applying for work elsewhere; she had had it. That was it! Eleanora became employed at the courthouse as a clerical in Lisbon, Ohio, the capitol of Columbiana County. A young gentleman admirer in town who also worked there gave her a ride each way. A heartbroken Mr. Allan Johnson lost one of his best employees.

During their high school years, Elena Demarco and Douglas Nicholson III began dating. Nicky Buch was in the same class as Elena, but she only had eyes for the tall and handsome Douglas, who was two years ahead in class. Even as a sophomore in school, Elena was already stunning with lavishly styled dirty blonde hair and wide, piercing brown eyes. Her graceful and shapely body was always nicely dressed, and her facial features were immaculate; she looked ravishing. And even more, Elena was a wonderful and pleasant person. Douglas had the same chiseled facial features as his father. He also inherited blonde hair and his mother's beautiful olive-green colored eyes, making him the target of many girls in school. But it was love at first sight for Douglas and Elena. Everyone thought they made the perfect couple.

Logan Conners, Douglas Nicholson's friend from one of his clubs, had four daughters and three boys. Logan owned a farm outside of town. His son, William, or Bill as everyone called him, excelled at sports. He played end on the football team beginning in 1932 and became captain of the Tigers football team in 1935. He also played on the basketball team alongside his friend Douglas Nicholson and captained that team from 1934 to 1935 as well. Everyone in school cheered on Bill Conners, and the girls adored him.

Clara Trieste was now a junior in high school and a friend

of Elena's, whom she had known before she could remember. Eleanora's family was close friends with the Demarcos. Clara and Elena double-dated together, often going to Rock Springs Park. Usually, they met Eleanora there, sometimes with one of her young male admirers. Together, they all laughed and had a good time. Dancing to the music of the swing band era was a main attraction in the evenings. Annie, busy with her college studies, joined them on weekends whenever she could.

In the early fall, Douglas Nicholson Jr. stood at the passenger train station at 12th Street with Elena Demarco in his arms. After graduating high school, he planned to follow in his dad's footsteps. During that past summer, his relationship with Elena had taken on a seriousness that neither could deny. They had already committed themselves to each other, both body and soul. The couple planned to get engaged when he graduated college and established himself in his father's law practice.

Douglas Jr. stepped back a few inches, only enough to hold the sides of Elena's face with his open hands, "I love you, Elena," he smiled and kissed her gently, "I'll be back soon," he smiled.

"Oh, Doug, I'm going to miss you so much," a tear rolled down her cheek. She found no other words than to say, "I love you too."

"I'll see you at summer recess. We'll spend every day together," he kissed her open mouth longer. Her eyes closed as she savored the moment. The mighty locomotive spit a burst of steam and hissed loudly, indicating it was readying.

"Ahem," Douglas cleared his throat to signal he was there. Gabriele stood beside him, her arm interlocked with his.

"Remember when we courted, dear," she whispered closely into her husband's ear, her other hand gently massaging his still-muscular arm. Douglas turned to look into his wife's beautiful olive-green colored eyes, her eyelids lazy in the way he cherished them, and he thought about how much he loved her even more now. At almost 50 years old, she looked to him as beautiful as she did the day he married her.

Another 'ahem' broke the couple up, and the distinctive sounding steam whistle tooted loudly and long as the conductor yelled, "All aboard!" checking his pocket watch as he did.

Douglas Jr. ran to his mother and embraced her, "I love you, Mom. I'll see you soon." He turned and embraced his father, "I love you, Dad."

"I love you too, Son," Gabrielle and Douglas said in unison, tears rolling down Gabrielle's eyes as her son ran and jumped onto the moving train. Smiling, the tall and handsome young man was the spitting image of his father but with the beautiful green-colored eyes of his mother.

Douglas Jr. was going to attend the University of Cincinnati. He would stay with his ailing grandmother, Claire. Gabrielle felt secure that a close family member would be with her mother, who insisted on staying in the large house with only the care worker her husband had hired for her. All three watched the train in the distance until it became a blurred speck between the luscious rolling hills, now just succumbing to the change of early autumn colors.

Douglas's sisters weren't at the train station, nor were his grandparents. Martha and Douglas Sr. had a small sendoff party for only the immediate family. At 81 years old, Douglas Sr. had physical difficulty getting around. However, his son surmised he didn't want to revisit his old place of work, now mainly a passenger station. His granddaughter, Claire, now engaged to be married, had a prior commitment. She was attending the wedding of her fianceé's sister in Cleveland but was heartbroken to be absent from her brother's departure. And young Martha stayed at home. She was the closest sibling to her brother and knew she would embarrass him and herself by breaking down in tears at the station. Martha hated to see her brother leave her.

Harry Martin, Claire's fianceé, formally asked Douglas for his daughter's hand in holy matrimony, as Douglas had done with Gabrielle's father, Andre, so many years before. Gabrielle and Douglas knew this day was coming. As much as Douglas wouldn't admit it, he was saddened to lose his daughter; his little girl was leaving the nest. But he could see that Harry was a good man, and Claire had completed her education and received her degree. After he wholeheartedly granted his blessing for their marriage, Douglas took his daughter to the side. He asked her, "Why did you pick Harry to marry?" He hoped it was for love and not from his pressuring her to finish college, and she might have passed up other opportunities while at school.

Claire smiled at her father and calmly said, "I was waiting for a man just like you, Daddy." She offered another of her smiles that could break his heart, and they embraced.

"I know I don't have to worry about you, honey," he sentimentally said while he held his eldest child firmly in his arms. "Maybe I should worry about Harry," he chuckled.

"Oh, Father!" she laughed.

By the time police found Luke Fontana's body stuffed in the trunk of a '32 Ford Coupe in Cleveland in the summer of 1936, he had been dead for at least a week. Several people passing by smelled a putrid odor from the vehicle's trunk and notified the authorities. As an officer lifted the hatch, he immediately dropped it from the odor and the sight of the gruesome contents inside. "Oh, my God," he called to his partner as he vomited the lunch he had eaten just a half hour before.

Bobby Clark was an older policeman and a twenty-year veteran of the force. He casually strolled over to his rookie partner, assuming what it was. "Another mob hit, Johnny?" he calmly asked, waiting for the younger officer to finish spewing his lunch all over the sidewalk until only bile dripped. Johnny Blampied finished wiping his mouth with the sleeve of his uniform shirt and shook his head in a yes. "Come back to the car with me." Once there, Bobby handed his partner a bottle of clove oil. "Rub some of this under your nose; it might help." He waited patiently and said, "Now be a man and help me do our job. First, bring that fingerprint kit the FBI gave us. For some reason, they like to keep records of all these guys. Me; I couldn't care who they were as long as they're just gone." Both men walked back to the rear of the automobile. Bobby didn't need any odor ointment; he was used to finding dead bodies from various circumstances throughout his career.

Rope bound Luke by his arms and legs in a most gruesome form of mob execution. A dead canary was sticking out of his mouth, indicating that he somehow 'talked' or betrayed his family, probably trying to rise in power. The Cleveland mob used 'incaprettamento,' which tied a slipknot around the victim's neck, and the other end bounded his bent legs from around his back. As it is impossible for a person to maintain such a position without eventually causing self-strangulation, Luca 'Luke' Fontana died a slow and painful death. The extreme heat of summer advanced the decomposing of the body, offering an even more horrific sight.

"See the way his head swelled?" Luke's distorted head resembled the same bloated and grotesque appearance of his father's after he strangled him years before. "He suffocated slowly and painfully. See his eyes. They're dried now, but see how they popped," Bobby explained to Johnny, who kept turning away as he did. "Look and learn! Don't turn away!" Johnny forced himself to watch as his partner described every aspect of the crime scene. "The canary means his own people killed him."

"Why?" Johnny asked hesitantly but with curiosity.

"Because he talked. It's a message sent as a warning to other members of his organization." Talking about secrets in what was now the American mafia was the ultimate betrayal of a family member. The penalty for such a violation of trust, the basis of the mafia family structure, was death in the most gruesome form to send an extreme message to other family members.

"How do you know all of these things?"

"Because every time I catch these sons of bitches, I beat the hell out of them to learn about them. Some talk, others don't."

456

Bobby shrugged, "You'll learn. If you want to stay alive, that is. Always know your enemy." Bobby accessed his partner, "Now, you take the prints off each of his fingers." He could see from his peripheral vision that Johnny looked horrified. "Don't touch anything else. I'll be in the patrol car; I'm calling this in. The station will tell us if they want anything else except for the coroner."

The coroner's attendees pulled Luke's stiff remains out of the small trunk. Rigor mortis had long before set in, allowing the partially decomposed body to appear as that of a rigid but broken and folded mannequin. A city detective came to the location to ensure nobody tampered with evidence since the FBI had expressed an interest as soon as the police notified them. The detective checked the fingerprints and had to redo a couple. The rope used to tie Luke in that deadly position had to remain for further forensic investigation by the FBI.

After placing the bent body on a stretcher, they immediately threw a cover over it, creating an unhuman geometric figure. People had already crowded in visual distance of the Ford Coupe to see the grisly exhibition, but away from the odor that penetrated the humid air of that hot day. With looks of horror plastered on their faces, some moaned while others wondered and chatted—all in awe but drawn to the atrocious spectacle. A newspaper reporter and a photographer stood among them, taking notes and statements from police and bystanders for the next newspaper edition. The two attendees slid the stretcher onto the closed-panel ambulance. The police directed them as they pulled away the remains of Luke Fontana.

It took a month for the authorities to track down Luke's mother after police identified his body. Since Giuditta lost ownership of her hotel, Rosa and Alessia Fontana rented a room close to Millie Brown's house. A local police officer knocked on the front door, and as the landlord opened it, he asked, "Is this the residence of. . ." he had to glance down at the paper in his hand. . ."Rosa Fontana?"

"Yes, it is," the man answered in a heavy Italian accent, "Is something wrong?"

"I'd like to speak with her if you don't mind," the officer said, giving the immigrant a stern look.

"Rosa! Alessia! Vieni qui!" he yelled up the stairway in Italian for one of them to come down.

Rosa appeared at the foot of the stairs, and Alessia remained a short distance behind her. "Yes?" Rosa asked.

The officer observed the disfigured face of the woman standing behind her and abruptly turned away and looked directly at Rosa. "I'm Officer John McRoy," he said as he again glanced down at the paper he held. "Are you the mother of Luke Fontana? Do you understand English?"

"I understand," Rosa spoke in her heavily accented English. She knew Luke would someday bring trouble to her and coldly asked, "What did he do?"

"Are you his mother?" Rosa didn't answer, only nodded yes. "I'm afraid to inform you that your son is dead." Officer McRoy hated doing this part of his job, but he knew someone had to do it.

Rosa didn't budge, nor did her facial expression change. She stood firm, and her eyes glared into those of Officer John McRoy. "Thank God," she said, looking up to the heavens. "Finally, it's over."

"Where do you want us to send the body?" the policeman was confused. Usually, these Italians went wild whenever one of their kin died, but this woman didn't seem to care.

Rosa wiped her hands twice as if shaking dust from them, "You tell them to throw him in the river for all I care!" Then she turned and walked back up the stairs, making the sign of the cross as she did. Alessia remained looking at the policeman as she shed her first tear. It was she who was upset; her only chance of getting enough money for proper surgery for her face and body died with her brother. Officer McRoy turned and left the building, shutting the door behind him.

Chapter Thirty-Eight

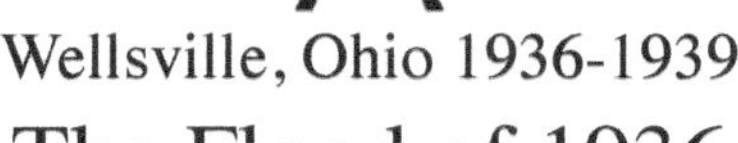

Wellsville, Ohio 1936-1939

The Flood of 1936

In 1936, the town of Wellsville experienced its third financial crisis of a series which would further weaken the economy of that community. First, the Shop at 12th Street was downsized, and the various shop buildings moved, as did the mine-run crews. That compelled many workers to move away from town or lose their jobs. Second was the devastating effects of the stock market crash that led to the Depression. Everyone felt the impact of that catastrophe one way or another. There were massive layoffs and food shortages, though the town pulled together and planted gardens people shared. Third, on a cold day of March 19, 1936, fifty-one and a half feet of water finally peaked off and submerged most of the town. Wellsville experienced the most damaging recorded flood in its history, one of the worst blows of all.

A small motor-driven boat, sounding like a stifled motorcycle, skated over the water and steered around the corner of Third Street onto Commerce. The man operating the small craft cut the outboard motor and drifted toward a rowboat. "How goes it, Henry?" Officer John McRoy shouted through his megaphone as Henry Oliver pulled the oars of his boat and laid them inside, his right hand reaching out to pull in the port side of McRoy's boat to stabilize it as it came alongside his. The officer was one of many officials and volunteers assisting people with the higher levels of accumulated water. He knew Henry and many like him were rescuing people all over town under the constant guidance of a coordinated effort of police and firefighters like John McRoy, using megaphones to alert the townspeople. About 150 Works Progress Administration (WPA) workers assisted in the rescue operation.

"I've taken dozens since this morning," Henry answered in a lower voice since he was aside John's motorboat. "Thank God the water capped off. As bad as it is, it might have been much worse. I've never seen anything like this before." He pointed down Commerce Street. Household goods and some furniture floated along the slow current. Families were sitting on rooftops or looking out of second-floor windows, waiting for someone to take them to one of the makeshift rescue camps. "I'm going down there and begin getting those people. Nice water cycle you've got there, by the way," he chuckled.

"I'll send more rowboats your way. God bless and stay safe." John shoved his craft away and kicked in the motor. It sputtered and then hummed smoothly. He steered his 'water cycle' back to Main Street to get more rescuers, smiling as he thought of the new term Henry had given his motorboat that now hummed along Main Street. The seamless coordination between the officials and volunteers was a testament to the effectiveness of the rescue operation.

Heavy snow and some rain forced the elevation of the river tributaries of the surrounding areas of Wellsville. By March 18th, the Ohio River towns were already flooding with water, but Wellsville seemed worse. The streetcar bridges over Yellow Creek were already underwater, and the flooding water level was still rising.

Wellsville was cut off from its sister town, East Liverpool, which was also flooded and underwater in many areas. Transportation to and from Wellsville: trolley service, buses, railroad trains, and road vehicles had ceased. The riverway was the only means of passage. The Third Street Station building was gone, but the tracks along where the building once stood were covered entirely with water, forcing the trains to a halt. The town was without heat and lights as workers shut down all gas lines and electricity. Many recorded floods had occurred in the small town since the early 1800s, but this one was by far the worst. Usually, floods centered around Third Street and down to Commerce. This time, most of the town of Wellsville was under flooding water. Automobiles, wagons, and other vehicles had floated along the current until they filled with water and sank. High water lifted a stranded trolly off its track. Rescue boats had been taking victims to schools and churches at higher elevations. Red Cross workers administered food, clothing, sleeping cots, and medical aid, allowing stricken people to rest in the warmth of potbelly stoves.

Other rowboats now followed Henry Oliver down Commerce Street. Sam Tamini was among them. "Hey there!" Sam shouted to Felo Buch, who leaned outside a window on the second floor of his house. "How many are you?"

"Me, my wife, and two daughters. Four altogether," Felo yelled back. Sam rowed the boat closer until it was level with the window.

"I can get you all in this boat. Help me. Pull the boat against the window and hold it steady while your family comes aboard." Felo complied and shouted for Lucy to board first.

"Take the girls first," Lucy said placidly. She was never one to yell, especially now, as devastated as she was. All her precious furniture and decorations, always meticulously cared for, were ruined and floating downstairs. "Eleanora, Julia, vieni qui," she calmly told them to come and go into the rowboat. "Julia, you first, you're smaller. Eleanora, you get ready."

Sam had immense upper body strength for a shorter man. He used his right arm to help Felo steady the boat against the window and his left arm to help the young lady climb into the boat. When Julia was seated at the back, he helped Eleanora, the taller sister, sit beside her. Julia's sole thought was her new wedding gown, which the water ruined and was now inside her bedroom in the flooded house. She was engaged to be married to John Aliotta that coming May.

"Lucy!" shouted Felo, "come on!" Lucy took one more look around her. Water had crept up to the second floor, ruining her carpeting and rising above the base of her furniture. With tears in her eyes, she complied with her husband and left behind everything she owned. Sam's boat departed for one of the rescue centers.

When the water finally receded, the cleanup of mildewed homes and businesses began. The strong water current uprooted, ruined, or swept away many structures and homes. Hundreds of homes were destroyed. Furniture, clothing, appliances, and other personal or household goods floated and lay strewn about town. Many of these items blocked main thoroughfares and presented additional problems. The Board of Education of Wellsville closed schools for the rest of March 1936 to use them as housing for all the people who were now homeless. The MacDonald School at Ninth Street, formerly called Central School when Douglas Nicholson was a student years before, was included.

Less than a year later, the town received federal funding to erect a floodwall. During the wall construction in 1937, two more floods hit Wellsville: one in January, totaling 44 feet of water, and the second in April, totaling 43 feet. The floods hit the small town of Wellsville hard, but it survived. However, the once mighty and significant industrial river town had begun to decline.

Julia Buch had married John Aliotta in May after the flood. That was the last straw for her. She never forgave what she called viciousness toward the hard-working, clean, well-mannered Italian immigrants like her ancestors had been. As her father, Felo, was born in America, she considered herself a third-generation American. But that's not how her classmates, some of whom were the children of earlier settlers, viewed it.

That animosity extended down from those parents to some of the children of her generation. She wanted to leave Wellsville and never look back. The newlywed couple moved to Steubenville, Ohio, where John got a good job at a mill in the heart of the steel-making industry.

Felo and Lucy lost their home and most of its contents in the 1936 flood. They bought a small house on 11th Street across from the Catholic Church and School. Several people learned that Lucy was an Italian and objected to their family living near Riverside, which was off-limits to immigrants from that country. It was by the good graces of Felo's interaction in the town that those objections ceased. Though their new next-door neighbors, Mr. and Mrs. Beckle, who were German immigrants, sometimes enjoyed taunting them. When they first arrived, Henry Beckle told Felo, "You have a nice fireplace in your home," referring to the polished fruitwood mantle, framed mirror, and surrounding legs and plinths, "Give it a try." Felo opened the flue to humor his neighbor and threw on a few large coal chunks. When he lit the fire, all the dark smoke and soot didn't rise through the chimney but instead began to fill the living room. In a fury, Felo smothered the fire as Lucy ran to open the windows and doors to vent the smoke.

Mr. Beckle knew the flue was broken and began to laugh at the sight of Felo's face colored with soot. Laughing fanatically, Mr. Beckle became hysterical, "I heard some of you guineas were dark, but you look like a nigger!"

The ever-calm Felo quietly responded, "I was born in Pennsylvania, Henry."

Mr. Beckle ignored the comment and continued laughing as he walked next door to his home.

That began an era when Lucy Buch started to make cookies for passing students when they left school. Some kids would stop and draw fresh water to drink from the well at the end of the mansion on the river side of the Buch home. Lucy would offer them a cookie. Soon, kids would be waiting for the nice woman to feed them her delightful sugar-coated biscotti.

Just as she had done on Commerce Street when the Third Street Station existed, Lucy also left a drinking glass and a bottle of water at the side of her home facing the railroad tracks; it was for the hobos who still passed frequently looking for food and water. Sometimes, she fed them a meal, and they sat on a chair and table she had set up for them outside. Lucy also sent food for the priests in the rectory across the street a couple of days a week.

Annie Trieste met a young man after she graduated college whom she took an immediate liking to. He was handsome and charming, but it was his eyes that took her breath away. They dazzled her and deepened her affection for him. Born James Bassino, his family name was shortened either by the port of entry of his parents or local authorities at some point, just like so many other Immigrants. Now called Jimmy Bass, his feelings for Annie were mutual. Jimmy was brought up by strict Italian American parents who wouldn't allow him to date in high school. Annie was his first girlfriend.

Jimmy was already an excellent musician. After studying piano as a child, he advanced to the saxophone and clarinet, a perfect combination of musical instruments for the popular sounds of the time. While he and Annie dated, Jimmy began playing in local bands, including some gigs at Rock Springs Park.

Annie and Eleanora decided to see Jimmy perform on a weekend evening at Rocks Springs Park. The high school student who couldn't get a boy to notice her now had several young men after her, but Eleanor played the field and selected one to escort her to the park. Louise Trieste had recently married Anthony Nash, and those newlyweds came along. Clara was dating Wilbur Cambell. Now a young man, he was the child who witnessed the shooting of Gregorio Musto's wife on Broadway years before. Clara and Wilbur came as well. Mary, now married to John Venezia, couldn't come since Mary was pregnant and expecting soon.

They all listened to the music at Rock Springs Park and danced under the stars. Other girls closer to the band had their eyes attached to Jimmy's as his nimble fingers danced along his saxophone keys. He lured them into a daze like a pungi player charms a cobra.

Lucy nicknamed her daughter 'Toot Toot Eleanora' since she was always on the go at the 'toot' of an automobile's horn. Sometimes, it would be a date, a double date, or a group. Cars would honk their horns to signal they were there, and Eleanora was quickly out the door. Lucy always waited up late anxiously for her daughter to come home. Whenever Eleanora would sit in a parked car speaking at the end of an evening, Lucy would run outside in her bathrobe, calling, "Eleanora, hurry, come inside; your father will be home," biting the forefinger of her right hand after she spoke. Lucy would repeat that routine until her daughter came inside.

Another place Eleanora and the Trieste girls frequented was Craig Beach on Lake Milton in Milton Township, Youngstown, Ohio. They enjoyed sitting at the beach and swimming or taking boat trips in the summers of their youth. There was an amusement park with a roller coaster and other rides. The east side of the lake had a dance hall and skating rink with taverns to mingle while enjoying a drink. Craig Beach was where 17-year-old Dino Crocetti debuted his singing career in 1934. He took to the stage for the first time, using the stage name of Dino Martini, singing 'Oh Marie' to the music of the George Williams Orchestra. He was later known as Dean Martin.

Douglas Nicholson's daughter, Claire, married in 1938, with her family in attendance. Shortly after, her brother, Douglas, returned to school in Cincinnati. Claire had planned her wedding when her brother would be in town on semester break. The day after he returned to his grandmother's home, her caretaker told him that his grandmother, Claire, was wheezing from her chest. Douglas immediately called a physician to examine

Claire against her will.

"I'm fine, Douglas," she smiled at her grandson, but in a raspy voice, "You're a good young man just like your father and the spitting image of him," a sentiment she often told him. "Don't worry about me. Study hard so you can become a lawyer like your dad."

But Claire wasn't fine. The doctor diagnosed her with a severe case of pneumonia with an extremely high fever, probably from being bedridden so much from her bad hip. He took Douglas aside and told him, "Notify your family; your grandmother doesn't have long to live." He observed the young man's distress, "I'm sorry to be so blunt, young man, but it's best they know so they can make arrangements." Douglas knew the doctor meant funeral arrangements. Douglas believed it would be best to mention the bad news to his father first, knowing how emotional his mother was. He looked at his watch, saw that his father would still be at work, and telephoned him there. After bypassing all the well wishes of his father's secretary, he explained the sad news that his grandmother was on her deathbed.

"Alright, Son. I'll explain everything to your mother," Douglas said, dreading how much it would hurt Gabrielle. "We'll catch the soonest train we can." Douglas turned to see Gabrielle standing behind him, her beautiful olive-green eyes tearing. He didn't hear her soft footsteps enter his office. Gabrielle knew it was bad news about her mother. Douglas held her tightly, reinforcing his love and devotion to her first. Then, he explained the situation to his wife and comforted her throughout the night. The next day, they were on a train to Cincinnati.

Gabrielle was satisfied that at least she had enough time to say goodbye to her last remaining parent. She spoke to her throughout the night Claire passed away, telling her the things a daughter tells her mother before she will never see her again. Within that final conversation, Gabrielle thanked her for being such a good mother and always providing her with the best things when she was growing up. "Thank you, Momma," she kissed her forehead after she passed. Douglas, as always, was beside her.

After the funeral, they decided to keep the house until Douglas Jr. graduated. Gabrielle's beautiful memories came to life whenever she was in her old home. Among the indelible recollections laid deep in her heart were those of growing up and playing dolls. Her father, Andre, kneeling next to the doll-house he built for her with his own two hands and pretending to drink tea with her make-believe friends. She remembered those days when her mother spoiled her by always buying the finest clothes for her and afterward enjoying ice cream sodas after eating lunch together and laughing happily at the simplest things. Gabrielle also recalled how both her parents supported even her craziest notions, those things only a child's mind can manufacture. Gabrielle resurrected those precious memories of her parents supporting and encouraging her to excel at college at a time when only the strongest women did. But her beautiful wedding day in that loving home was at the forefront of her mind. Glancing at the photos on the mantle of Andre and Claire, smiling proudly on that day as Gabrielle stood beside the man she loved, Douglas. Her darling poodle, Frenchie, poised herself with elegance. So many other echoes of happiness from years gone by flooded her heart. Most of the older people who had attended were now gone and passed into those same recollections. Now, Gabrielle was shaping new memories with the family she had built: her ever-faithful husband, her daughters, and her son. This collective commemoration of her life made Gabrielle realize how successful she was.

As the decade came close to ending, the Black Hand in town had already faded into legitimate businesses. Salvatore Gusto marched in the San Rocco Feast on the stump of his ankle; his foot lost to diabetes. He did it for repentance. What Eleanora had whispered to her sister, Julia, when they were children and marching in that procession years before came true: 'Probably for all his sins,' she had whispered. And now he repented.

Millie Brown also succumbed the same year. The Nicholsons didn't know until Douglas Jr. bumped into her grandson, Hector, on Main Street. Douglas expressed his condolences and said, "We didn't know. How did it happen?" Douglas assumed from her age that she was vulnerable.

"She caught pneumonia," Hector raised his arms, "She was close to 80 years old."

"My parents loved her. Geeze, my dad remembers her from when he was a kid." Douglas began telling Hector stories his parents had told him over the years. He laid out tales extending from the days of Peppina and Giuditta, the adventures of Luigi Massaro, Matteo Fontana's brutality and punishment, how Millie had defied Luke Fontana, and more glimpses into the past. Hector seemed fascinated by all those things that had happened in town. "We all thought she was indestructible."

"I know my grandmother was a slave from the South who passed through this town by way of the underground railroad as a little girl and later convinced my grandfather to move here. And I know about her magical herbal cures. Hell, she used a lot of them on me," he smiled. "I'll always remember her."

"So will a lot of other people. I know my parents will be upset when I tell them. She was some woman." acknowledged Douglas and bid Hector goodbye.

Adolf Hitler had already manipulated his way to power in Germany. In 1934, he began building a military violating the Treaty of Versailles. Ironically, that treaty, considered unfair by many, created the need to fulfill the sentiment of the German people, thus allowing someone like Hitler to rise to power. As his military grew, a small army of Germans invaded the Rhineland in the spring of 1936. England and France did nothing, though they could have crushed the small German army. Both countries were depleted of men from the Great War and didn't want to stir the sparks of another war. Next, Hitler had his army march into Austria while England and France again did nothing. Hitler was gaining ground, and with his prosperous country rallying him in the same year, he took the Sudetenland (the northern part of Czechoslovakia of German ethnicity) and, the following year, the remainder of Czechoslovakia. Now, England's Prime Minister Neville Chamberlain realized his weakness in handling Hitler and knew there could inevitably be war. He drew a line in the sand in Poland, unaware of the secret alliance Hitler had with Stalin.

In the fall of 1939, Hitler invaded Poland on September 1, 1939. Guaranteeing Poland's protection, Great Britain and France declared war on Germany that day. The battle for Poland lasted until October 6, 1939.

Annie Trieste and Jimmy Bass were married on September 4, 1939, three days after the declaration of war. Eleanora stood in as Maid of Honor for her best friend. The newly married Mr. and Mrs. James Bass beamed with happiness on that special day they shared with their family and friends.

Douglas Nicholson Sr., adhering to his lifelong addiction to reading news and discussing politics, absorbed every step the Germans took with interest. Slapping the armrest of his upholstered chair, he shouted, "Stop them, you fools," as the Germans took the Rhineland, now listening to the living room radio with newspapers strewn about him.

At first, Martha was amused by his banter, as she had been for years. But she became concerned when Hitler took Czechoslovakia. Now, her husband was getting much too upset, especially at his age.

"Do something, you idiot," he yelled at the radio when Neville Chamberlain gave a speech. "He spoke about 'peace for our time' after the Sudetenland and did nothing, just like he's doing now."

"Calm down, dear," Martha said softly, trying to mollify her husband's temperament. "Let's listen to something else. How about some music?" But Douglas Sr. just waved his arm as if to make her silent. Martha shook her head and continued crocheting.

When Hitler attacked Poland in 1939, Douglas Sr. was in a fury and screamed, "You see what happened!" He rose from his chair to raise the radio's volume but fell back into his seat.

Martha glanced up to see her husband grasping his chest. "Douglas? Douglas!" she ran to his side, "Are you okay? dear, are you alright?"

"Pain. Left arm," was all he could struggle to say. Martha ran to call the doctor, then rang her son's line.

"Please tell Douglas to come over, dear," she replied after Gabrielle pleasantly answered.

"Okay, okay," Gabrielle knew something was wrong. Her mother-in-law had never been even remotely abrupt with her before. "We'll be right over."

Gabrielle and Douglas arrived at the same time as the doctor did. Douglas opened the door to his childhood home and ran inside. Martha was kneeling next to her husband's chair, crying. "He was listening to one of his programs," she sobbed.

"Politics, I'm sure," Douglas said as he gently lifted her from kneeling at the side of the chair to allow the doctor to examine his father. He knew it was from his excitement about politics.

Gabrielle quickly intervened, "Come, Mom, let's go inside the kitchen and sit. I'll make us a cup of tea." Martha followed like a zombie, extremely upset.

"Douglas, call an ambulance; your father has had a heart attack," Doctor Edwards directed without looking up, his stethoscope attached around his neck. Douglas was shocked but quickly responded. "I've given him something to stabilize him," the doctor added. Douglas was already dialing the telephone and could only offer a quick peek back at the doctor.

Douglas Sr. returned home after a week in the City Hospital. In a weakened state, he remained bedridden. Douglas took off from work and visited his father for hours daily to give his mother some respite. Privately, he couldn't wait until his son was ready to take over his position at the law firm.

One day, Douglas and his father reminisced about the old times, anything other than politics or the impending war many people thought America would eventually enter. Douglas recalled when his dad taught him how to box, and they shared a good laugh about the days when Douglas was a scrawny kid.

"I'm proud of you son. I never get to say it enough," he smiled.

"You tell me all the time, Dad." Douglas lowered his head and thought. "It was all because of everything you and Mom did for me, Dad."

"No, Son. It wasn't just us. You had it in you all along. You remind me so much of my dad, a man of great strength and character," he said, his voice filled with admiration and belief in his son's natural potential.

"Hey, do you remember when I came to the Shop with little Peppina?" Douglas held that thought, "I was so proud of you; I always was. You were a big and strong guy everybody admired and obeyed."

"Oh yeah, I remember that day. I was proud of you, too. You were always a good and respectful boy." Then his face went solemn, and he said, "Sad what happened to her. . . and her sister."

"It was. I still remember Peppina," Douglas mused, searching those recollections of his simpler life as a child. "It's funny; I know she was a little girl, but my memories of her are like speaking to someone today, as a peer. Our brains play tricks on us, I guess."

"It certainly does." Then Douglas Sr. said something unexpectedly, one of those things that comes out of a person at times. "Shame we'll have to fight another war. I was so proud of you when you returned from the war as a hero, the band at the old Third Street Station playing for you," he smiled. "I still have that shirt and fancy French beret you brought back for me," still grinning. Then his voice became serious, "From what you told me about the horror of deadly mechanized warfare from that war, this one might even be worse. Industries always grow during wars. They'll have bigger, longer-range canons, better tanks, and faster machine guns." Douglas Sr. shook his head shamefully and asked the rhetorical question, "When will we ever learn?"

"Don't worry about it, Dad." He could see that his father was getting upset. "I think I'm going to call it a day and let you get some rest. I'll see you tomorrow, Dad." He turned back and told his father, "Thanks for everything, Dad." His father didn't answer, but he could see that Douglas Sr. had a tear in his eye. Douglas left the house thinking of another war, one where his son might fight. It worried him for the first time since hearing of the war. Douglas never got to speak to his father again; he passed away in his sleep that cool fall night.

The remains of Douglas Nicholson Sr. lay in his coffin at the front of the viewing room in the Haugh Funeral home on Main Street. For a man of his age, he looked well. The undertaker's work renewed the fatigue and drawn features of his face from sickness and age. Martha sat in the center of the front row with Douglas on one side of her and Gabrielle on the other. Douglas Jr. sat next to his father with Elena beside him. Douglas's daughters sat beside their mother with young Claire's husband and Martha's new fiancée. Their family patriarch was gone, and all their eyes teared.

People from the town and east Liverpool flooded in to pay their respects. Many of the surviving retirees from the former Shop were there. Douglas couldn't believe how many of his friends, associates, and clients came to express their sympathies. He stood to greet each of them when they came to him, proudly introducing his son, who would eventually replace him at his law firm, standing beside him.

After the crowd diminished, Douglas got up and moved to a chair in the back row. He needed to compose himself from the outpouring of love and the memories of his father each person bestowed upon him. It seemed almost everyone in town had love and respect for his father, and he learned new stories of how much he had helped other people.

As he sat in the back row, his son came to sit next to him. "How are you doing, Dad?" Douglas Jr. asked him with concern, knowing his father was emotionally drained. He was watching as his dad greeted everyone who came.

Douglas smiled and answered proudly, "Fine, Son. I'm fine," he observed his son and realized how much he reminded him of himself. A son to be proud of: intelligent, well-mannered, and most of all, kind and caring. He had already instinctively chosen his future career and was with the woman he loved. Father and son began small talk and exchanged their opinions about the town. Douglas Jr. explained his school curriculum and his study of law cases. Then, the subject of the war arose; they couldn't avoid it at such a crucial time in the world.

"Dad, I don't know if this is the right time," he began while thinking about the war and forced himself to continue, "Some of the fellows at school are leaving to go overseas to fight with the British," carefully watching his father's change. "I'm thinking about leaving school to do the same." He quickly added, "I can finish when I return." He smiled, "You went and came back a hero."

Douglas's mind traveled back to when his dad tried to explain the reality of war to him at his grandfather's wake. How hard he attempted to make the horrors of war clear and understandable. His dad had told him how he tried to join his father in the Civil War, and his mother, her legs astride on her horse, rode after him as he was far too young to go. Douglas Sr. had never personally experienced war, though he had heard so many horrific stories about it. He used his grandfather's stories of Wellsville's first settlement and paralleled those harsh conditions and encounters with war. Douglas Sr. was born in that settlement and knew well about it. Now, Douglas was confronted with his only son wanting to go to that evil place he understood all too well, and he had to try to dissuade him, at least for now.

"Douglas, I didn't know what war was like when I left to fight. That man lying up front there," he nodded to his dad, "tried as best he could to explain it to me." Douglas tried to find the words but fought himself with those horrors and grotesque memories now resurrected. As painful as it was for him, he had to make an effort, and he began. "I saw things that no person should ever see. There is a side of humanity that only comes out in one's battle for life. My father called it 'Man's inhumanity to man; I remember that day so well."

"From the poem?" his son quickly asked.

Douglas recalled his father's use of that passage on that day. "Yes, from the Robert Burns poem. War is like someone suffocating you, and you grasp onto anything to stop it, but you can't. It turns you into a primal creature, inhuman and brutal." Douglas told his son of the smell of rotting flesh mixed with human bodily odors and the crying at night as soldiers feared rising to fight again. As Douglas continued his dissertation about 'man's inhumanity to man,' he noticed the terrorized expression that was now upon his son's face, and he stopped speaking.

"I didn't know, Dad. I didn't know how hard it was for you over there."

Douglas's voice now became strained. "I never told you because I never, in a million years, thought you would have to fight in one. They told us it was the war to end all wars. Now, it seems they're putting numbers on them. I read this is expected to be called World War Two." His eyes were now glassy, and he spoke to his son, "All I ask, Son, is that you wait and see if America does enter it. Maybe the British and French can handle it on their own this time. Finish getting your degree; you're so close. Let's see what happens."

Douglas Jr. was taken back. In that short appraisal of war, he learned a lot, especially from a decorated war veteran. "Okay, Dad, I will. I'll do what you say. I'll wait."

"Thank you, Son," Douglas said while remembering John Hemsworth and his family in England and wondering how he was doing. He and Isabelle were supposed to visit them in Wellsville before Germany's rise to power. 'I guess now they won't be able.' He thought. Douglas hadn't heard from John since Poland was invaded.

Chapter Thirty-Nine

Wellsville, Europe, The Pacific 1940-1943
Wellsville Goes To War

After Germany defeated Poland, Hitler was unstoppable. The two world powers, the British Empire and the Second French Republic had given Hitler too much leeway and were now poised to suffer the consequences. In 1940, as Poland was occupied, Germany spread its armies in every direction. They quickly attacked Denmark and Norway in April. Luxembourg was overrun by tanks in one day. German troops advanced into the Belgian forest and broke through the Maginot Line in Belgium, where it was undefended. By May, the Netherlands had fallen, Belgium surrendered, and then German tanks entered France, forcing allied defenders to Dunkirk, where the Germans stopped their advance to surround the British allies and thus prevent a breakout. About 300,000 British allies were surprisingly evacuated by boat, a blessing to the Allies by that grave mistake of the Germans. The German army entered Paris nine days later. France surrendered on June 24th. By April of 1941, the Germans were in Greece and Yugoslavia. Then Germany made what was considered its greatest mistake by launching an invasion into the Soviet Union in June 1941.

A militaristic dictatorship began in Japan during the 1920s and throughout the Depression that hurt them and most countries worldwide. Japan's militaristic and older faction always resented the Westernization of their country. They hated Caucasians and feared the blending of their blood with the West through interaction and trade. A thirst began for expansion of Japan to provide themselves with the resources they needed to be self-sufficient. By resurrecting ideals such as the Bushido and the Samurai for the recruitment of young men, the country had become militaristic and aggressive by 1930. In the fall of 1931, Japan invaded Manchuria, inflicting barbaric cruelty upon those people, thus establishing a basis for developing some of the materials they needed. That was the beginning. In 1937, after the invasion of Nanking, 'The Rape of Nanjing' by the Japanese was a massacre of grand proportions inflicted upon the Chinese. For approximately six weeks, the Japanese Imperial Army exterminated Chinese men, women, and children and raped women in masses before they killed them, as they looted and burned the city. Missionaries stationed there warned the Western countries, but they again did nothing, allowing the Japanese to further build and train a barbarous and merciless military. Their plans were in place for expansion to develop a means of supplying the resources needed, especially oil. In early December 1941, Japanese aircraft launched from their carriers hidden out at sea systematically attacked the United States Naval base at Pearl Harbor without warning or provocation. The Japanese ambassador was still conducting negotiations with the Americans over an oil embargo on Japan due to their aggressive behavior in China. The attack on Pearl Harbor created such animosity toward the Japanese that most able-bodied Americans scrambled to join a branch of the military to retaliate. Japan had awakened a sleeping giant.

After Felo Buch and his wife and daughter returned from Sunday Mass at the Immaculate Conception Catholic Church across the street, Felo turned on his living room radio to the Brooklyn Dodgers football game, which was already in progress. Sitting on his wooden rocking chair, smoking a cigarette, he listened intently to the game as Lucy and Eleanora prepared

Sunday dinner.

Less than an hour later, the radio broadcast the first news of the surprise attack on Pearl Harbor. Felo got up from his rocker and raised the volume of the radio. Hearing the news from two rooms away, Eleanora and Lucy rushed into the living room and began asking questions. Felo waved his arm to silence them so they could hear. "Wait a minute," he said, "Let's hear the rest." A narrator was explaining only some facts as the attack was still raging. Felo and his family were in shock. Hearing about America's ships exploding, they all became speechless. The always curious Eleanora was silent, listening as the devastation unfolded. She had never heard of Pearl Harbor before. To her knowledge, the Japanese people were a peaceful country whose women wore beautiful costumes and distinctive hairdos. She had seen exotic paintings and drawings of geisha girls but didn't know much about that country. Most Americans were focused on the war in Europe then, and not that many were interested in the politics of the Japan oil embargo. An attack on an American naval base from a country so far away was akin to being attacked by Martians, so it came as no surprise when the attack jolted Americans into a nightmare.

The telephone rang, and Eleanora ran to answer it. "Yes, we just heard. Really?" Eleanora spoke casually and calmly as always. "Okay, we will. Okay, goodbye." She ran back into the living room to see her parents, who had inquisitive expressions as if Eleanora had heard something important. "It was just Julia," she quickly answered their bewildered faces. "She told me she heard that people on the California coast were preparing for an attack." Her parents' faces went back to face the radio. Eleanora had always mused that when narrators broadcast something important, people had the notion of facing the radio as if they could see the person speaking. It was a nervous thought that raced through her mind.

Throughout the day, friends and relatives phoned about the attack. All the Trieste sisters called at different times. Their oldest sister, Nina Obiso, was now a widow. She had lost her husband to cancer in 1940. Frank Trieste had passed away earlier in 1941, leaving his wife, Colomba, also a widow. She had spoken to Lucy often, worrying about their homeland in Italy ever since Mussolini had sided with Hitler. Before the attack on Pearl Harbor, Colomba came to Lucy's house. "I'm worried now that the 'Niapponese' is with Hitler and Mussolini!" she said, expressing her fears about the Tripartite Pack her daughter, Nina, had told her about. In her native Italian dialect, she said, "I think America is going to be in this war."

Lucy shrugged her shoulders and answered, "What can we do?"

After the attack, Colomba telephoned Lucy, "See? Now, we will probably go to war. Thank God my Francesco isn't here to see this."

Lucy answered, "I don't think there will be fighting in Italy. I pray there won't be for my family's sake."

The following day, President Roosevelt stood before Congress and stated, "I ask that the Congress declare that since the unprovoked and dastardly attack by Japan on Sunday, December 7, 1941, a state of war has existed between the United States and the Japanese Empire." War was declared on America by Adolf Hitler three days later, drawing America into what was beginning to be called the Second World War. The sentiment toward the Japanese by Americans was anger to the highest degree. Immediately, young men from cities and towns throughout the country, like Wellsville, East Liverpool, and all other surrounding river towns, came forward to volunteer for active duty in the military.

In the late fall, before Japan's attack, Douglas and Elena, planning to get married soon, bought a puppy from a farm up on the hill of Route 45. Elena chose a golden Labrador Retriever pup because she couldn't resist his wide, beguiling eyes that reminded her of Douglas. "He's our first step toward building our family," laughed Douglas as he put the pooch on Elena's lap after she sat in the front seat of his automobile. "Now all we have to do is finish our wedding plans," he continued as he sat behind the driver's wheel.

"He's a little Romeo with those eyes of his," declared Elena.

"Then that's what we'll call him: Romeo."

"I like it," Elena laughed. Hey there, Romeo," Elena cuddled with the pup; it was a blissful time. The thought of war felt distant and unspoken in their idyllic world. However, uncertainty existed in the corners of their minds.

Douglas had given up any notions of fighting with the British. As Americans were apart from the war and did not witness the violence firsthand, many young men in the US used wishful thinking to believe the British would handle the war. After all, they had valiantly won the Battle of Britain, and Great Britain was the most prominent world power. Also, America had enacted the lend-lease program to supply the British war effort. Most didn't realize England's military was holding on by their fingernails.

The Nicholsons had just celebrated Douglas's 60th birthday two days before the Pearl Harbor attack. Gabrielle had a restaurant prepare a small gathering in their home on Riverside for their immediate family. Memories of Giuditta preparing many dishes for her wedding party years ago flooded her mind with deep and loving sentiments as she made the arrangements. Gabrielle recalled how the Italian immigrant woman didn't appear at the party. Shaking her head, she thought, 'So long ago. How things had changed since then.' The generation of Giuditta's grandchildren was mixing with the offspring of earlier American settlers. Gabrielle's mother was an Italian immigrant, and now her own dear son was marrying the daughter of an Italian immigrant. Italian Americans were becoming respectful citizens of the community, though harsh feelings still lingered by some.

Martha baked her son's favorite chocolate layer cake with seafoam icing. The dainty, small-framed woman, now 81 years old, moved slowly but maintained her regular daily routines.

Grey streaks prevailed through her remaining blonde hair. The wrinkles on her face and the crow's feet under her eyes told the story of a once beautiful woman.

Gabrielle's and Douglas's daughters honored the present family patriarch. They brought their families to pay homage: Claire and her husband, Harry, and their two children, Gabrielle, the oldest, and Marissa, the youngest; Martha and her husband, William, and their son, Jeffrey.

"To my father," Douglas Jr. raised his glass of wine for a toast, "A wonderful dad, granddad, husband, and a pillar of this community." The proud son finished as the entire family, from elders to children, joined in a unified applause.

"And to a great father-in-law," added Harry with a 'Here, here,' from William.

Though it was a grey day in the Ohio River Valley, everyone had a wonderful time. Gabrielle ordered the adults to refrain from conversations about politics and the possibility of the United States entering the war. The children played with Douglas's puppy and follied together throughout the house as children usually do. All merriness subsided that following Sunday as America became propelled into another world war.

Douglas Nicholson turned off the radio that had brought about his worst fears. America was entering the war. Gabrielle gently rubbed his shoulders to relax him; she knew he was as worried for their son as she was. Douglas hadn't been as excitable about news and politics as his father had been until now. His recollections of the Great War lay buried in that part of his mind all people reserve to hide dark memories, where the horrors and trepidations of the past can find solace and heal. Gabrielle had helped her husband rehabilitate and reconcile in the months following his return from war. And now the sanctuary hiding his trauma was unfolding, releasing that world of hell he once knew all too well.

After hearing that America was going to war, Douglas rose,

faced his wife, and was about to speak, but Gabrielle spoke first. "I know, Dear; I know. I'm worried about him, too." A tear ran down her face. "I'm worried about his friends and all the young boys. I know all too well about the horror of war. I know you bore the brunt of it as a soldier," she paused, remembering, "but it was also terrible on the home front, with shortages, worrying, and help for the war effort from the people in towns and cities across the country. I don't think I can endure the suffering of waiting and feeling unable to do something about it again."

Douglas listened and grasped her hand lovingly. But he knew she couldn't understand what might be in store for their only son, the little boy he taught to fish and how to defend himself. His mind resurrected past thoughts of helping his boy with baseball, football, and basketball since he was old enough to run, as were memories of taking him to his first movies in the Liberty Theatre on Main Street. He recalled how little Dougie liked Peter Pan best of all. Douglas pictured his boy, now a man, facing the dread of war.

Their son, Douglas, had completed his law degree earlier that spring and planned to marry as soon as he had made enough money. Like his father, he wanted to earn his own way. Already working with him, Douglas was thrilled to have his son beside him at his office, now 60 years old. He was grateful that his son would probably be ready to run his branch by the time he retired, which he planned to do in two years.

But that day, he and Gabrielle waited for Douglas Jr. to stroll through the door to tell them he was joining the military; they both knew their son well. All the young men were driven by their animosity toward Japan after their sneak attack, and their son was no different. They waited anxiously, already devastated that he would be in harm's way as Douglas himself had been in what was now beginning to be labeled as the First World War. He had experienced the horrors of that bloody struggle.

"Let's get married before you ship out," Elena almost pleaded, illogically feeling more secure that it would be better and even safer if Douglas were married if he went overseas. The thought of their separation was enough, yet to have him go into harm's way was intolerable. "We can have a small ceremony, even at the justice of the peace, if it's the only way. I don't care." She held herself closer in his arms.

"No, Dear," Douglas looked into her alluring wide eyes, filling with tears not yet shed, "We'll have the biggest wedding in the county as soon as I get back," he smiled wide. It made his expression change and offered an appearance even more seductive to her.

"But, I love you, Douglas and. . ."

Douglas held her face between his hands, stopping her words, "I love you, too, Elena; you mean everything to me." Elena's tears rolled down her cheeks; she buried her head in his chest. Douglas brushed her dark blonde hair with his hand and softly told her, "I won't be long. We'll whip those Japs and Krauts in six months. You'll see. America will be unstoppable. I'll be back by summer, and we'll get married—no need to rush. I told my dad to keep his eyes on a piece of property for us. I have the money saved for a down payment." Douglas gently held her face toward his and kissed her.

"Douglas, promise me that if you go overseas. . ." she hesitated, then continued, "you'll keep safe and won't try to be a hero like in one of those war movies."

"I will," he offered another one of his smiles that made her tingle inside.

"Promise me."

"I promise."

What most eager young Americans didn't know was that their country didn't have a large army. The considerable Army raised for the Great War years before was depleted after that war and during the Depression years. The United States had less than 200,000 Army troops and ranked 19th compared to other countries of the world. The American Navy, severely hurt after the surprise attack at Pearl Harbor, their battleships destroyed, left only three aircraft carriers in that area, two of which were older designs. Another carrier from the Atlantic was on the way. One US Army ground force and Filipino troops, some ill-trained, defended the Philippines without necessary armaments and supplies. American-occupied islands in the Pacific fared no better. All were wide open to a Japanese invasion so brutal as the likes never before experienced by the Western Allies. In the Pacific, the US was holding on by its fingertips.

Jimmy Bass's strict upbringing suppressed his natural desire to be among young women as a teenager. As much as he loved Annie, even after his marriage, he was tempted when many female fans were lured to him in a daze as his agile fingers gracefully floated along his saxophone or clarinet keys. Eventually, he succumbed to the lust; he could no longer contain himself from the flirting of women and the propositions made to him by them, especially in the alcohol-infested environments where he worked.

In the summer of 1941, Annie delivered a healthy baby girl, joyously passing the newborn into her husband's waiting arms. Colomba, all the Trieste sisters, and Eleanora were there to see the baby for the first time. The proud father, Jimmy, beamed with joy as he later passed cigars to his friends.

At the Christening, Eleanora served as Godmother, and Jimmy's best man and friend served as Godfather to the baby, now named Laura. It was another happy occasion. Jimmy and his friends played musical instruments at the small gathering to celebrate that sacred day of Christening.

A few weeks later, Colomba was helping out with the baby at Annie's home. Two women, an older one and a younger one, showed up at the front door. Colomba recognized the older woman.

"Signora Macelli, come va?" asking how she was while greeting Maria Macelli, whom she knew from town.

"Not so well, Colomba; may we come in?" Maria replied in

the Italian dialect of her region. "I have something to discuss with you and your daughter."

"Oh, okay, come inside." Then, Colomba noticed the younger woman was carrying a baby.

"This is my daughter, Carla." The younger woman held her head down and only nodded.

"Sit down," Colomba pointed to a loveseat. Overhearing the conversation, Annie put her baby, Laura, into her crib and came over as her mother readied to call her. Carla sat down and put the baby on her lap. Annie immediately noticed that the baby's face looked familiar as she prepared to sit across from the mother and daughter.

Then tears poured down Maria's cheeks as it seemed only Italian women could force upon themselves. Raising both her arms into the air and looking directly at Colomba, she cried out, "Look what your son-in-law did to my daughter." She put her arm around the infant sitting on Carla's lap. "She has no husband, and he put this baby girl in her belly!"

Eleanora put her arm around Annie and comforted her best friend, who was now crying in her lap. Eleanora, who was like a sister more than a friend, was the first one Annie called after her shock of hearing the news. Colomba was upset, but differently. She was angry at that 'Bastardo' as she addressed her son-in-law while fuming. Colomba paced the floor in her rage, unable to afford any consolation for her daughter at those moments, as people usually express trauma in different ways.

"I don't know what I'm going to do," sobbed Annie, her voice muffled in the lap of the woman she had been friends with since before she could remember. "I hate him!"

Eleanora, also in a state of shock, came over as soon as she heard Annie crying uncontrollably on the phone. She didn't know why; only the young woman she loved like a sister was extremely distraught and rushed over. But what words could Eleanora have, knowing that Annie didn't hate Jimmy? She loved him, and that was the greater tragedy. It would take time, Eleanora knew. She brushed Annie's hair with her hand and softly said, "I'm here for you, Annie. I always will be."

Young men were leaving town by the day. Douglas, surrounded by his family, waited as the train loaded and prepared to depart from the 12th Street Station. He had exchanged farewells with Elena the night before at a small family party in his honor at his parents' home. But Douglas felt the first chill of reality hit him while standing among his family and the woman he loved. Before that day, a planned act of patriotism and duty to his country propelled him, partially built on the camaraderie with friends also preparing to depart. Now, he faced the actuality that, unlike leaving for school, an unknown destination lay in store for him. Douglas faced his family, seeing the tears in all their eyes, not knowing when they would be together again as he didn't know when he would return. There were no semester breaks in war.

Hector Allen was already seated by a window, waving to his mother, Phoebe, his father, Nathan, and sister, Ruth, who watched and waved as they all shed tears at his departure. Hector had volunteered for the Army and was leaving on the same train. "Bye," Hector whispered while waiting for the steam blast to signal the train leaving the station.

As the whistle of the mighty locomotive blasted its loud steam, signaling departure, Douglas hugged his parents and then his sisters without exchanging words. All sentiments were clearly on their faces and by their body language. It was the hardest with his mother, Gabrielle, and Elena. As they cried uncontrollably, he didn't have time to console them; the train had already begun the strenuous labor of pulling out of the station, wheels squeaking while spurts of steam blasted between them. Douglas again held his mother and Elena tightly and whispered to each of them, "I love you. I'll write you every chance I have." He threw his long canvas bag onto his shoulders and rushed to the last car of the departing train, yelling, "I'll be back in no time!" as he ran. "Take care of Romeo until I get back, Dad." Bill Conners, already standing on the deck at the end of the passenger car, waved to his parents, sisters, and two brothers who hadn't left yet to serve. Bill reached down and gave Douglas his arm to help him aboard. "Thanks," Douglas smiled at his friend and stood next to Bill, waving and getting a last glimpse of their families and girlfriends. Together, they watched their loved one's emotions flare until all that remained was the distance that separated them. Among the crowd separated by the accumulating space as the train chugged along, Douglas could only see the white handkerchiefs Elena and Gabrielle used to stop the flow of their tears. All the brave young men left chatting together, not knowing where they were going or their fate.

After Pearl Harbor, America was losing ground in the Pacific by the day. The ill-supplied American and Filipino troops in the Philipines struggled to hold off the Japanese invasion. General MacArthur and his family escaped to Australia by a PT boat, leaving Major General Wainwright in command of a starving and disease-stricken Army with malaria, dengue fever, and other sicknesses. After finishing the few food supplies MacArthur had taken during his retreat to Bataan before he fled, his men lived off of jungle animals like rats, monkeys, and birds. The Americans survived for over three months on a starvation diet of diseased foods.

Bataan fell in April of 1942. The Soldiers of the Imperial Japanese Army forced thousands of American Army, Naval, Marines, and Army Air Force personnel and a majority of Filipino prisoners of war to a horrific 65-mile march on foot. For one whole week in the grueling tropical heat, beaten and tortured by Japanese soldiers, they marched to an internment camp on the Luzon plains, all of them already suffering from starvation and sickness. The militaristic government hated the Western white race and considered anyone who surrendered to be unsuitable to live. Japanese Colonel Tsuji's hatred for the prisoners ran so deep that he issued orders to execute all prisoners of war; many Japanese soldiers complied, but some didn't. However, they treated all brutally physically and mentally. Any prisoner who fell was bayonetted or decapitated. Japanese soldiers beat prisoners along the way and cut fingers and hands off to get rings from them. West Point and Annapolis rings were prized souvenirs. Anyone who asked for water was shot. Only one cup of muddy water, drawn from stagnant pools that caused dysentery, was allocated at the end of each day. About 20,000 prisoners of war died at the hands of the Japanese during the march. An official broadcast only told a portion of that story to the public, but not until later. They didn't divulge all the atrocities. Only escaped Filipino prisoners spread that news among their people, who had resorted to fighting the Japanese in the hills. Americans knew nothing about Japan's immense and explicit brutality during the Bataan Death March and in the prisoner-of-war camps until after the war.

As bad as things were in the Pacific theatre of war, America's main focus was stopping Germany's advance into Great Britain. Therefore, most supplies and weaponry went there first. If England, which had been holding off the Germans since 1939, fell, it would be difficult to gain a strong foothold in Europe. The Soviets, which had sided with Germany, now joined the American allies. At the time, it was unknown that Stalin was a greater monster than Hitler. And, even though most allied generals didn't trust Stalin, they had to use him to keep an offensive on the Eastern Front, which began in the summer of 1941 when the Germans invaded Russia. Many American generals and citizens felt that Roosevelt gave Stalin far more military aid than the Soviets needed.

In May 1942, the Japanese launched an attack on Port Moresby in New Guinea, a move crucial to their plan of gaining control. This strategic location would serve as a launching pad for land-based planes to bomb Northern Australia and potentially pave the way for an invasion. However, the naval Battle of the Coral Sea marked a significant turning point. It was the first instance where American carriers successfully repelled a Japanese advance, thwarting their plans for an Australian invasion. This victory was a testament to the strategic importance of the Battle of Coral Sea.

After the Americans broke the Japanese secret coded messages, they knew where the Imperial Japanese fleet was. Along with some of the same aircraft carriers that had attacked Pearl Harbor, they headed to Midway, an American Marine-held island situated about halfway between Hawaii and Japan. Having a chance to prepare, the Americans sent planes, searched for the fleet, and found it. After naval air battles in the sea near Midway and heavy bombing and strafing of Midway Island itself, the Americans defeated the Japanese in that carrier battle of June 1942. Japan lost four aircraft carriers, and it was a turning point for the Allies in the Pacific, causing the Japanese to abandon efforts to invade Port Moresby by sea. The Japanese Army moved further into the jungles of New Guinea.

American forces, initially marines, made their first strategic landing after the Battle of Midway. They landed on several islands: Guadalcanal, Tulagi, and the Floridas in early August 1942. As the Battle of Guadalcanal still raged, Eleanora Buch realized that all her male cousins, boyfriends, and husbands of friends were already in uniform. A banner with four blue stars proudly adorned Eleanora's Aunt Angelina's home. She had four sons who joined the military: Dick and Andy joined the Army; John was in the Navy, and Carmine was already in the Marines and saw action first. Carmine fought at the Battle of Midway and became partially deaf from the heavy bombing as the Japanese attacked. Wave after wave of Japanese planes flew over Midway Atoll, bombing, and strafing as the marine ground forces dug in and fought back. Obsolete Marine fighter planes, like the Bruster F2A Buffalos, took off, most being destroyed by the superior and faster Japanese aircraft. Only a few US Marine

Wildcats could fight in the air combat longer. But, firing their 90mm M1 antiaircraft guns and Browning M2 aircraft heavy machine guns, the Marines held their island, but with heavy casualties. Eleanora's cousins, Dick, John, and Andy, waited to find out where fate would take them after their basic training.

After hearing such stories, Eleanora wanted to do her share of service. However, older men on the home front and officers and soldiers overseas expressed resentment about women serving in the military. Many called them prostitutes and feared that women wouldn't provide the same results as men, especially overseas. The American high command disregarded such notions, as British women had served meticulously in the armed forces since the war first broke out in Europe in 1939. And by doing non-combat jobs, they freed up men to fight. The Queen Alexandra's Imperial Military Nursing Service, called 'QA-IMNS,' also provided an invaluable service and had already been overseas with the British Expeditionary Force in France.

Eleanora pursued her desire to serve. "What do you think?" she asked Annie and her sisters when discussing the Women's Army Auxiliary Corps (WAAC) together.

"I think it's a good way to serve," Annie said first, holding her baby daughter against her body and burping her. All the sisters, Maude, Louise, Mary, and Clara, shook their heads in agreement, knowing Eleanora would probably stay within the country in the WAAC. Even if women were allowed to go overseas, Eleanora couldn't possibly go because of her eyesight and being so thin. Their mother, Colomba, overheard the conversation from the kitchen. All the sisters were married except for Nina, a widow, and Clara, who was engaged to Wilbur Cambell.

Then, the senior sister, Nina, spoke. "You know what? I might join you, Eleanora." Tired of being a widow at a relatively young age, Nina thought it would be an excellent way for women to help with the war effort. "I have to get my affairs in order first."

Like the Trieste sisters and Eleanora, most women in town were resilient and hard workers. They had braved the difficult years of floods and a major depression. These patriotic red-blooded women were ready to step up and do their share, whether in the military or at the home front.

When Eleanora returned to her home and walked through the doorway, Lucy said, "Goodbye," and put the phone receiver on its hanger.

"Hi, Mom," Eleanora put her purse on a chair.

"Hello." Lucy always used that English word as a greeting, but this time, she looked sheepish and returned to rolling dough on a large wooden board.

"What?" Eleanora knew her mother well and recognized she was hiding something.

"I have nothing to say," Lucy replied, raising her arms as she spoke. Eleanora had a knack for pulling information out of her mother. However, she was a patient woman who would wait until later to find out what was on Lucy's mind. At that moment, Eleanora wanted to rehearse her speech with her father about joining the WAACs. Even though she was in her twenties, she had the respect to get her father's approval first. But like Felo's sister, Peppina, Eleanora inherited the personality of the aunt she never knew and used that ability to convince her father.

Lucy went outside to burn off some nervous energy after dinner by sweeping leaves off the walkway along the side of the house and then the front stairs on that warm autumn evening in 1942. Colomba had told her on the telephone about Eleanora and Nina's mention of joining the US Women's Army, which caused both women to worry.

Two of Lucy's next-door neighbors, Emma Beckle and her daughter, Sally, passed by. Sally said, "Hello, Mrs. Buch," and bid her a good evening. Lucy smiled quickly at Sally, but Emma stopped.

"Why are you outside doing that, Lucy?" Mrs. Beckle could see that something was driving Lucy to work so hard. She was also looking for a good gossip story. "Get somebody else to do that."

"Ah," Lucy stopped and stood with the broom beside her.

"What's wrong, Lucy?"

Lucy knew Mrs. Beckle was nosy and a gossiper, but as a good Christian, and to unburden the weight she was now carrying, Lucy answered, "My daughter, Eleanora. She wants to join the service."

"No, Lucy!" Emma looked terrified. "Don't let her! She'll be with men. You know what happens then."

"My daughter's a good girl."

"It doesn't matter. The radio said they make them prostitutes." She whispered, "They force men on them."

"No! Shame!"

"You'll see. If you let Eleanora go, she'll come home pregnant."

"I gotta go!" Lucy shrieked and ran along the side of the house to the kitchen door, her heart pounding hard all the way.

"You'll see!" Mrs. Beckle shouted after her.

While her mother had been outside, Eleanora sat beside her father and explained her plan to serve her country. Though listening attentively, Felo held back some smiles at times, recalling again those faded memories and the stories people had told him of his lost sister and how his daughter reminded him of her. When Felo asked Eleanora questions, he was impressed with how Eleanora responded intelligently but passionately. "When would you plan to leave?"

Eleanora, delighted she had made headway in the conversation, replied, "I would have to go to Pittsburgh. That's where the headquarters are. I'd like to leave next week." She smiled at her father, knowing he couldn't resist her charm. "But I wouldn't be posted until after the first of the year," she quickly added.

Felo was proud of his daughter. She was bright, outgoing, and had a wonderful personality. He always felt terrible she couldn't finish her third and fourth years of college; he knew that Eleanora could have gone far. "Eleanora, you're an intelligent young woman. Do you know what you're in store for?" Eleanora was beginning to answer, but Felo put up his hand to pause her, "All these stories I hear on the radio and read in newspapers about women in the military. . ." Felo watched as Eleanora sat back in her seat, thinking she had lost her case. "I don't believe them. As I said, you're intelligent enough to know what to expect," he watched his daughter rise back erect in her seat and continued, "And most of all, I trust you."

It was one of the few times Eleanora was speechless and could only muster up the words, "Thank you, Dad."

The WAACs (Woman's Army Auxiliary Corps) was proposed to Congress in May 1941 and passed after the Pearl Harbor attack in May 1942. Shortly after Eleanora went to Headquarters-Pittsburgh Joint Army and Navy District and became a WAAC, the Auxiliary Corps merged into the WACS (Woman's Army Corps) in early February 1943. Nina Obiso also joined the WAAC a month before it changed to the WACs. Both women were among the first WACs and were stationed stateside. Lucy worried every day as Mrs. Beckle constantly bombarded her with warnings.

Things moved quickly for Eleanora. She became secretary to the colonel who headed the prisoner-of-war camp at Camp Wheeler, Georgia.

"Achtung!" the German officer shouted to his assembled lower-ranking prisoners of war, and they stood at attention. "Vormarsch!" he then yelled, and the German prisoners began to march in formation inside the yard of the prisoner-of-war camp, protected by a high chain-linked fence with barbed wire atop it.

Eleanora, beside a fellow WAC, watched together as the Germans goose-stepped across the field to their daily drills. The German prisoners-of-war were well disciplined, but not the Italians. The Italian prisoners sat or lay with their bodies spread out on the opposite side of the yard, relaxing or playing cards, not exerting themselves in the least.

An officer of the prison guard asked Eleanora if she spoke any Italian, assuming from records that her mother knew the language. When she answered that she did, she became an unofficial translator for the Italian prisoners.

"Amica donna!" they would whistle to Eleanora and call, "Madonna mia! Bambina, vieni qua!" calling her over to flirt and admire a woman as only an Italian man could.

A short time later, Eleanora was promoted to corporal. "I earned those stripes," she told her friend, Gloria.

"What do you mean?" Gloria asked.

"By having to deal with all those Italian Casanovas," she laughed.

"To tell you the truth, I wouldn't mind it," Gloria laughed back, "Some of those guys are pretty cute."

Eleanora stood at attention and saluted before the desk of the head colonel. "At ease, Corporal." The head of the prisoner-of-war camp, a man about her father's age, closely observed Eleanora. "I'm impressed with your performance here, Corporal." He offered a slight smile, remembering his own daughter back home. "Higher ranking officers have been asked by the top brass to look for men and women suitable to go outside the states," this time his eyes faced down as he scribbled something on a piece of paper. "I'm recommending you for overseas duty, young woman. You did fine work here." Eleanora was shocked at the idea of going overseas. Everyone considered her unfit, but she didn't mention a word about her eye problem. "Dismissed, Corporal, and good luck," the colonel glanced back up and smiled again.

Eleanora rattled off every line of the eye examination chart before proceeding to her next exam. She had devised a plan to overcome the one thing that could prevent her from going overseas. Eleanora's ace in the hole was that she had a photographic memory. Eleanora memorized the entire chart on a prior walkby with her glasses on. She was now fit for duty overseas.

Eleanora advanced to Daytona, Florida, to receive advanced overseas training with the Fifth Training Regiment. By early

May 1944, she was on a troopship headed to Australia. Unknowingly, the young woman from the small town of Wellsville, Ohio, was on a voyage to experience things that would change her for the rest of her life.

Chapter Forty

Wellsville, Europe, The Pacific 1943-1944
The War Years

Unlike previous wars, during World War Two, V-mail was be-coming common. A person wrote a letter normally but with-out an envelope. After military censors read the letter, it went through a photographic process and transferred to microfilm. After transit to whatever overseas theatre it was addressed, it was printed back into letter form. This freed up valuable space for the transport of precious cargo of military weapons and supplies. The process was reciprocated by overseas troops to their families back home.

Elena Demarco smiled as she folded Douglas's letter and put it in her personal diary book with the two others she had received. "I love you," she whispered before releasing it. There, her love correspondences remained concealed from the roving eyes of her younger brother and sister and especially hidden from her parents. She and Douglas expressed loving and senti-mental things that no one else should be privy to.

Donning a light jacket suitable for the early evening in the spring of 1943, Elena set off for the Nicholson's home. Her heart was heavy with the need to update them about their son in case they hadn't received a recent letter. Douglas had written about how busy he had been, and she wanted to ease their wor-ries. She also longed to see Romeo, their 'first child,' as Douglas fondly referred to their dog, as he reminded her of Douglas. Elena walked along Riverside, smelling the fresh scents of early blossoming flora as life resurrected around her after the cold and windy gusts of the passing winter. Douglas's letter was still fresh in her mind, and she couldn't help thinking about him.

Douglas had completed his Army basic training at Fort Benning, Georgia. When he finished, his commanding officer noticed his educational level, and he was transferred to OCS (Officer Candidate School) there at Fort Benning. The Army desperately needed officers, and Douglas fit the bill. He mentioned in his letter that he had completed his OCS training and was now a Second Lieutenant. He also informed her that his schedule was to train in a newly formed army sector called Rangers. Elena, with her limited knowledge of the military, was intrigued by this new term. Her only recollection of the word was of the Texas Rangers she had seen in films.

"Come in, my Dear. Let me take your jacket," Douglas Sr. smiled at his future daughter-in-law. Romeo heard her voice and came charging into the foyer.

Elena got down on her knees to hug Romeo as he licked her excitedly. Giggling, she said, "He gets spunkier each time I come. There's a good boy," she calmed down the dog; his big eyes widened as he waged his tail. "You smell what I have for you, don't you, boy?" Elena unwrapped a folded piece of writing paper from her purse, revealing a piece of bacon she had saved from her breakfast. She always brought over something for Romeo.

"Hi, Dear," Gabrielle quickly came inside after hearing the commotion. "Come inside, Elena. Let's compare notes," she anxiously said while laughing, wanting to know what each had heard. It had been their new routine since Douglas left.

Elena began by telling them about her most recent letter, which she had received earlier that day. "Oh, we didn't know where he was being transferred. Last we heard, he had completed OCS," Douglas explained.

Then they compared everything they learned from their letters from the young man they all loved. They scrutinized the little things like the names of his fellow soldiers, where each was from, what they did before the war, the food he was eating, and all the simple things that made them all feel closer to Douglas. Elena left out the juicy parts Douglas told her, knowing his parents would understand that certain romantic tidbits in her letters were confidential.

Gabrielle had mentioned to Elena some, of course not all, sentiments she had expressed when her husband was overseas years before. Gabrielle gave Elena the tip of putting a smidgen of perfume on her letters. "Men love things like that," Gabrielle had winked at Elena when she advised that bit of information. "I used it with my husband during the First War." At the time, Gabriele didn't know that things had changed and that V-mail was becoming common. It was a letter without an envelope, read by military censors and then transferred to microfilm. After transit to whatever overseas theatre, it was printed back into letter form. The process freed up valuable space for precious cargo transported. Overseas troops reciprocated the process to their families back home. But it left out the human touch of things like a hint of perfume or a lipstick mark from a kiss.

"His friend, Bob, seems so funny. I'd like to meet him someday," Elena laughed.

"So he's going to join these Rangers, is he?" Douglas Sr. said proudly. "Hmm, I'll have to read about this."

"I'm sure you'll get a letter from him soon. You know how the mail has been since the war," Elena quickly interjected. "He just wrote that it was a Ranger Battalion and going to train at Camp Forrest, Tennessee."

The winds of war were moving quickly, and they all agreed.

As those winds of war brushed America after Pearl Harbor, Bill Conners joined the US Army. He was assigned to the 145th Infantry Regiment of the 37th Division, comprised of a National Guard Division from Ohio, nicknamed the 'Buckeye Division,' that had seen action in the First World War. In May 1942, Bill left America from the San Francisco Port of Embarkation and headed for Viti Levu, Fiji Islands, in the Pacific Theatre. The 37th Division was among the first American Army Divisions in the Pacific.

"Not like that! Like this, Private!" Sergeant Sean O'Brien shouted at the PFC standing beside Bill in the work line digging ditches and foxholes. The sergeant was a hardened man of the 'old school' Army, one of the regular Army, and a veteran of the Great War. "Figure out if you guys want to live or die, damn it!" he screamed. "The Japs want to kill you, and they ain't that particular! Learn that now, or you'll be living on the end of a Nip's bayonet!"

"Yes, sir!" PFC Ryan shouted.

"I'm not a sir!" Sergeant O'Brien sneered as he barked at Private First Class Toby Ryan. "I ain't no damn officer! You call me sergeant! You should have learned that in training."

Due to the possibility of invasion, Conner's battalion was helping to reinforce the island of Fiji in the early summer of 1942. He was going through advanced island training there with the likes of the hardened Sergeant O'Brien shouting in the faces of all the troopers in Bill's platoon.

"Good thing I don't have a rifle right now; I'd shoot the son of a bitch," whispered Bill's friend, Tony.

"I might just help you with that," Bill whispered back.

As Sammy shoveled on the other side of Bill, glancing at him, he added through his labored huffs and puffs, "I'll bet you wish you could go back to your sports years in high school. And those cheerleaders dancing around in those short skirts and all." Then he stopped long enough to smile at Bill, "I know I do." Sammy had played quarterback in school deep within the state of Indiana. He played center on the basketball team there. A tall guy, He and Bill often reflected together on their sports achievements and life in good old American small towns.

"To tell you the truth, I wish I was back home on my family's farm. It was nice and quiet up there," Bill ended the short conversation when he spotted Sergeant O'Brien returning.

Bill Conners and his platoon headed to Guadalcanal after severe fighting ended there in the spring of 1943. After several conflicts in clearing Guadalcanal from remaining Japanese infestations, they continued training on that island. Then, they readied for Munda in New Georgia, where the Japanese held an airfield. They assisted the 43rd division in heavy fighting during the sweltering heat of July and August and finally secured Munda Airfield. After finishing the mop-up of New Georgia, Bill and his platoon returned to Guadalcanal by the fall of 1943 for long-needed rest and rehabilitation. The Allies had begun to break the backbone of the Japanese-held Pacific Islands.

Hector Allen was in the 92nd Division, an African-American division nicknamed 'Buffalo Soldiers' from the African-American cavalry days of the late 1800s. That division fought in the First World War and wore the insignia patch of a buffalo on their arms. Sent to different posts in a segregated South, he faced hostile racism. The officers were white and made what they referred to as 'colored troops' do degrading jobs to humiliate them. The townspeople there heckled the black soldiers, referring to them as nigger soldiers or Darkies.

While stationed at Fort McClellan, Alabama, Hector had maintained a friendship with Isaac Williams. Isaac was an exceptionally tall, well-built black man who worked as a cook. He had worked in the kitchen of a restaurant in New York City before the war. Hector enjoyed hearing stories about the big city and wanted to visit it one day.

"You got to be careful where you go there, man," Isaac always told him, "ain't no different than any other city, but lots different than small towns like where you's from," he preached as he prepared grub for the mess hall. Hector always offered Isaac companionship and help sometimes as Isaac labored in the even hotter kitchen of the already intense Southern heat. In turn, Isaac gave Hector a share of the choicest pieces of meats and foods he secretly reserved for himself. "You come over and visit me there after the war," Isaac laughed, "I'll see you don't get into any trouble," always remembering Hector was from a small town.

As Isaac and Hector spoke, a white lieutenant burst into the mess hall kitchen and abruptly interrupted them, and they both stood at attention. Short and puny, Second Lieutenant Mitchell Barlow had to bend his neck far back to eyeball the much taller Corporal Isaac Williams. With his swagger stick tucked under his arm, he shouted his order into Isaac's face, "Corporal Williams, the captain and I want a hamburger each, one medium and the other well done, and French fries on our plates." The lieutenant's eyes remained fixed on those of Isaac, "Pronto! Deliver them to Captain Hendrick's quarters. I'll be dining with him. Do you understand me, boy? You darkies have hard heads, so make sure you do it right!"

"Yes, sir!" Isaac responded, still at attention, sweating profusely from the kitchen's heat.

"At ease, boy!" the lieutenant turned and paraded out of the heated kitchen.

"I hate that guy," Hector frowned as he watched from the window as the lieutenant walked away.

"Thou shalt not hate. Leviticus 19:17-18," or something like that," Isaac corrected Hector. "My momma made me read the bible when I was a kid." Then he walked to the large refrigerator, took out two beef burgers, and threw them on the grill. After dumping the French fries container into the hot oil, the thin-cut potatoes began to sizzle along with the burgers. He continued, "I loved my momma and always obeyed her." Isaac flipped the burgers over. "It's hot in here, isn't it?" Isaac asked as his strapped undershirt soaked through with perspiration. "Hey man, hand me a couple of those rolls," he pointed to where they were.

"It's as hot as Hell. Amen to that," Hector answered as he handed the rolls to Isaac. You're sweating like Hell, too. I don't know how you take it in here all day long. They make me march all over the place, but this," Hector shook his head, "is much worse." He watched Isaac lift the potatoes out of the oil.

"I probably stink like Hell, too. I got to wait until I get off duty to take my shower." Isaac cut open the rolls and placed them next to the French fries already on the plates. He scooped the hamburgers off the grill and onto the open rolls. Isaac waited a minute; then, he took one burger in his hand and placed it under his left armpit, allowing his sweat to soak well into it. Issac turned it over to drench the other side of the burger under the same armpit. "Gotta let it marinate good." Then Isaac did the same with the other burger under his right armpit. "Mama never told me not to do this, though," he laughed.

Hector's eyes widened in shock. He slowly began to laugh, and next, he was roaring hysterically.

"Excuse me, Hector, this stupid nigger boy has to make a delivery," now he too was roaring with laughter.

Hector had grown into a strong, muscular man like his grandfather and namesake. And military training had kept him fit. But Hector knew how to hold his temper. He learned about injustices early in life from his mother, Phoebe, and grandmother, Millie. Hector also experienced the kindness of white people, such as the Nicholsons and Buches of his hometown of Wellsville. As a grandson of slaves, Hector wanted to make his family proud by serving in the US Army, honoring his grandparents he remembered fondly. Racial slurs rolled right off Hector's back while focusing on his training. Finally, he and Isaac settled at Fort Huachuca, where his division battalion began preparations for overseas duty in the European Theatre with the 92nd Division of the Fifth Army.

Around the time of Pretty Boy Floyd's capture in the 1930s, Nick Buch, just beginning high school, worked as a water boy for the rail workers to earn money. He watched the coordination of the men hammering in spikes. By the time Nick finished school, he had advanced, working at hammering spikes on the railroad lines. Money was scarce, and like the other hard workers of Wellsville, he wanted to earn his share.

Nick developed his upper body strength on the railroad line, and for a short man, he toed the line with the much larger men.

"Faster, men," the foreman roared as he walked along the rails, trying to get his workers to perform even more. Most laborers whispered back profane expletives and vulgarities, with a few hexes mixed in, but the boss didn't hear them, drowned out in the clatter of hammers on spikes.

Nick tried to join the Navy before the war but didn't meet the height requirement. He would have most likely been stationed at Pearl Harbor at the time of the devastating attack if he had. After the war began, the Army welcomed him, and he shipped out to the Pacific Theatre of War.

After General Douglas MacArthur was appointed Supreme Commander of Allied Forces in the South-West Pacific Area, he established his headquarters in Brisbane, Australia. Eleanora Buch was stationed there and worked in G-2 Army Intelligence. She was over 9,000 miles away from her hometown of Wellsville, Ohio. For a young woman who had never traveled past Craig Beach near Youngstown, being 'down under' was indeed an experience in itself. So was the appreciation of the Australian people that rallied around the American Military, or 'Yanks' as they were called, for being there to help them. As bad as things were during wartime Australia, they had narrowly averted a Japanese invasion. The Australian Military was fighting in various areas of the war, including New Guinea, pushing the Japanese further back.

On her day off, Eleanora was strolling through Brisbane in uniform, visiting as many sights as possible, when an elderly couple made eye contact with her. The older gentleman tipped his hat as his wife smiled.

Then, with his hat in hand, the gentleman introduced himself, "Good day to you. I'm John Clarke, and this is my wife,

Edith." He spoke in a perfect British accent, not the Australian dialect she had been hearing. "We couldn't help but notice you're an American," he smiled, not using the word Yank as most Australians called her up to that point.

"Yes, I am," she answered, "my name is Corporal Eleanora Buch," she laughed. "You can skip the corporal. I've become so used to using it."

"Lovely to meet you, my dear," Edith answered. "We're so glad you're here in our country, and as you must know by now, we all appreciate it."

The well-dressed, friendly couple continued their conversation with Eleanora, discussing issues from the war to personal things. In the short time they spoke, Eleanora felt she had known these people all her life. They had moved from England years before. Their son had gone to college there and was now an officer in the Australian Army stationed in New Guinea.

"Why don't you join us for dinner this afternoon?" Edith asked.

"That's a jolly good idea. It will allow us to show our gratitude," John intervened. "Have you the time? We live just outside the city. We can drive you in our motorcar and bring you back."

"Well, yes, I'd love to. As long as it wouldn't be an inconvenience for you."

"Not at all," John smiled, "We'll get you back before lights out. You see, I know a bit about Army life. British Army though back in the Great War."

"We're parked just over there," Martha said, pointing to their automobile and taking Eleanora's arm with hers as she spoke.

While driving, Eleanora saw koala bears and kangaroos in the wild for the first time. The WACs played with the tame baby koalas and fed some very young kangaroos, but that was in captivity. Seeing them in their natural habitat seemed amazing.

When they arrived, Martha served Eleanora tea. Then she enjoyed a home-prepared dinner, the first one Eleanora had in a while. "To the American Military!" John toasted during dinner.

To show her gratefulness, Eleanora began corresponding with the elder couple. She exchanged addresses with her new friends, the Clarkes, and added them to her list of letter recipients. She would never forget the fondness of their generosity and that of the Australian people.

While on leave, the ever-friendly and inquiring adventurous young woman, like the aunt she never knew, Peppina, took the tram from Brisbane, trying to see as many of Australia's cities as possible. She traveled from Brisbane to Sydney and then to Canberra and Melbourne, visiting cathedrals, museums, and other beautiful attractions Australia had to offer. The war was going well for Eleanora. That was about to change.

Eleanora didn't stay in Australia long; she was selected for the medical corps of the chief surgeon's staff in New Guinea. Eleanora would now see the effects of the brutality of war. Recently promoted to sergeant, she boarded a C-47 troop transport once again. Her previous transport flights were stateside and one in Australia. This plane headed to headquarters in Port Moresby, New Guinea.

Aside from the few WACs she was traveling with, it was a mixed-passenger-filled transport: WAC nurses, GIs, army officers and NCOs, and some naval personnel. Everyone sat side by side on long, plain metal seats that ran the length of the inside of the plane. After a few wolf whistles and other forms of flirting from the soldiers onboard, Eleanora settled in between two women she had recently met, Rebecca 'Beckie' Langford and Laurie Giulio. Now stationed together, they expected to see a lot of each other.

"Where you from?" Beckie struck up the conversation. "I'm from Texas," she was pretty and seemed charming. She had a big smile and chuckled as she spoke, ignoring the wooing from gentlemen admirers as she buckled her canvas seat strap.

"I'm from Pennsylvania," answered Laurie, who could never resist a good conversation.

"What part?" Eleanora quickly intervened, "I ask because I'm from Eastern Ohio."

"I'm a ways off from you. I live in Central PA, near Lancaster."

"I've heard of that. The Amish live there, don't they?" Beckie chuckled again.

"Yeah! And they ain't doing that much for the war effort," a gruff sergeant shouted, facing them from across the aisle. "Easy stuff, stateside, no fighting. I've been fighting in the jungles since we got here."

The young ladies just nodded and smiled in appreciation, then returned to their conversation. They were so engrossed in speaking that none even heard the two robust airplane engines start up. Before they knew it, they were taxiing and tilting sideways as the plane lifted off the ground.

"Whoa! That's fun!" Beckie delighted in her deep Texas accent, "like an amusement park ride."

"You can have it. My stomach gets queasy on those rides," Laurie looked slightly pale.

Eleanora didn't have a care in the world. Flying didn't bother her at all. As it was a military direct route, it took only a little over two hours. Laurie spotted the cloud-filled mountains of the Papua Peninsular in the distance. It was a beautiful sight, and the plane had cooled down somewhat at higher altitudes. But as they descended, that changed. The air became stifling while taxiing along Jackson's Airfield runway in Port Moresby. Then, when the hatch popped open, the tropical humidity of the coastal area plunged into the seating area of the plane like a sauna.

The three women looked around as two tribal natives loaded their footlockers onto a truck. "My God, we're in Hell," Laurie said in a daze, her uniform already inundated with the tropical rainy mist, humidity, and perspiration from heat.

The surgical clericals' eventual goal was to work their way through field hospitals and evacuation medical facilities all the way to the 99th Evacuation Hospital in Hollandia, Dutch New Guinea. This hospital would become operational after the fighting ended in Hollandia and the area was secure. The WACs were on their way, ready to visit other field hospitals and temporary emergency surgical units along the way to their destination.

"When do you think?" Bob asked, but Douglas only shook his shoulders. Both men stood poised, facing the waters of the English Channel. The entire platoon knew it would happen soon; it was in the air. Everyone was instructed not to speak to anyone outside the American Army about any personal information, or 'intel' they called it, a soldier might have—and that included girlfriends most of all; they had a way of whittling things out of the GIs. 'Loose lips sink ships' was one of the biggest mottos then. Bob asked the question out of force of habit. He knew Douglas would tell his second in command as soon as he found out.

The 5th Rangers became activated in September of 1943. By early 1944, Douglas traveled to New York and boarded the HMS Mauretania for Liverpool, England. The Army promoted Douglas to First Lieutenant and was in charge of a platoon assigned to C Company of the 5th Ranger Battalion. In England, the five Ranger battalions deployed in Europe continued specific training, each practicing different assignments.

"It's going to be soon, Bob, real soon," Douglas displayed enthusiasm or trepidation. It was hard to tell under such strenuous circumstances. But Bob knew Douglas had overheard something from the expression he now exhibited. There was a lockdown, and there would be no cancelation. First Lieutenant Douglas Nicholson dreaded his promotion to captain and company leader. He and his men had trained hard and long for an invasion, not knowing where or exactly when it would be. But Douglas intuitively knew that if he survived, there would be several vacancies for a captain, and he didn't know if he was ready to lead so many men. Douglas's platoon was large and commanded by Douglas with his friend, Second Lieutenant Bob Licasi, as second in command.

In the early morning of June 6, 1944, the Allied forces finally received word of what they had trained so vigorously for in a letter dispatched to them:

'Soldiers, Sailors, and Airmen of the Allied Expeditionary Force!

You are about to embark upon the Great Crusade, toward which we have striven these many months. The eyes of the world are upon you. The hope and prayers of liberty-loving people everywhere march with you. In company with our brave Allies and brothers-in-arms on other Fronts, you will bring about the destruction of the German war machine, the elimination of Nazi tyranny over the oppressed peoples of Europe, and security for ourselves in a free world. Your task will not be an easy one. Your enemy is well-trained, well equipped and battle-hardened. He will fight savagely. But this is the year 1944! Much has happened since the Nazi triumphs of 1940-41. The United Nations have inflicted upon the Germans great defeats, in open battle, man-to-man. Our air offensive has seriously reduced their strength in the air and their capacity to wage war on the ground. Our Home Fronts have given us an overwhelming superiority in weapons and munitions of war and placed at our disposal great reserves of trained fighting men. The tide has turned! The free men of the world are marching together to Victory!

"I have full confidence in your courage, devotion to duty and skill in battle. We will accept nothing less than full Victory! Good luck! And let us beseech the blessing of Almighty God upon this great and noble undertaking.'

With the word given, Douglas stood at the bow of an LCA Landing Craft Assault boat as it lowered into the water. His ranger company chose that model because it had metal bulkheads and sides and was efficiently manned by four British crew members. As the LCA floated in the water, Douglas ordered the pilot to remain until he watched the rest of his platoon lowered in a second craft commanded by Bob Licasi. As that vessel readied for launch, Douglas saluted Bob and forced a smile. "Good luck, Bob," he whispered, knowing his friend couldn't hear him with the sounds and commotion of the largest amphibious assault ever assembled. Douglas noticed Bob formally saluted and saw his mouth word something, probably a gesture of good luck. Douglas sat beside Staff Sergeant Mike Peterson for the ride ashore. Sergeant Ron DiMico, Sergeant Bart Harrison, and Corporal Peter Lioni, all friends of Douglas since he began with the Rangers, boated with Bob Licasi.

The waters on the Channel, from the weather, were rough that morning. Douglas stood up to observe the shoreline still in the distance. He wondered why Command decided to go on such an awful day. But he never questioned authority or what drove it. Most of his Rangers hadn't eaten a hearty breakfast earlier; Douglas learned about nausea from others in the Italian landings. However, as they delved further toward the shoreline, his men were getting seasick from the heavy seas caused by strong winds. Sturdy waves splashed against the seacraft, soaking him and his men. He lost sight of Bob's LCA in the heavy fog. Douglas sat back and tried to rest for what lay ahead. His only thoughts were those of home, the soft reflections of fading light onto the still Ohio River, the quiet times, his friends there, and, of course, Elena, his parents, and his sisters.

It wasn't until Douglas heard a ping sound that he realized his landing craft was coming into waters close enough to be hit by enemy fire. "Keep low, men!" he yelled, lifting his head quickly to get a spot visual. Then, the roar of rattling machine guns and loud blasts from explosions began. The cloudy fog obscured the other landing crafts, lifting over them and making them appear like figures out of an Edgar Allan Poe novel. Throughout the sounds of devastation, Douglas's platoon circled the beach at 0630 hours. Shortly after, three waves of Rangers hit the beaches. Companies A and B, immediately demolished by the unrelenting havoc the Germans dispensed, lay strewn about on the sandy beach or floated in the shallow waters. Douglas's company and the platoon he led had been ordered to establish, at all costs, a beachhead at Dog White and Red Beaches near Vierville-sur-Mer.

Douglas watched a boat ahead of his LCA get bogged down on a sandbar. Heavy bullets riddled the men with direct hits of machine gun fire. A thunderous burst erupted. Its impact jolted the men in Douglas's LCA and hit the stranded boat nearby, causing a massive fire. As those men, some burning from fiery flames, jumped into deep waters, they couldn't swim and splashed around, trying to unload their backpacks but only drawing more enemy fire. Then, that landing craft blew apart; the sound of it was deafening. Douglas whispered, "Shit!" He thought quickly and instinctively shouted orders, "Listen up!"

As he gave that order, his pilot yelled, "We're beached. We can't move!" Douglas realized they were too far from shore and would become sitting targets.

"Ditch your backpacks!" Douglas hollered.

"But, sir?"

"Shut up and listen!" bullets spurted the waters about his boat, and the horrible sounds of explosions and German machine gun fire continued, "There'll be plenty of supplies on the beach. You want to end up like those poor souls?" Douglas pointed to the men now floating around the disabled and smoking LCA. "You take the ammunition, and you try to take the BAR," he pointed to each man in turn, "you guys take the Thompsons and ammo. Everybody else, take your M1s, check your magazines and grenades, and follow me!" Douglas, his Colt 1911 attached to his side, strapped an M1 over his shoulder and jumped over the side, and began to swim, doggie paddle style, to the rear of the crippled landing craft. Pieces of that LCA floated around what remained of it.

Staff Sergeant Mike Peterson yelled to the frightened men, "Let's go!" and jumped into the chilled early morning water, following Douglas. Everyone followed, all drifting toward the fuming pieces of wreckage.

As the platoon threaded water behind the largest pieces of

the torn LCA, Douglas directed, "See all that floating debris and those bodies floating around? Grab hold and secure yourself to one of them." He watched the horrified expressions on his men's faces. Only the deceased that were fully intact without backpacks stayed afloat; the mutilated ones sank or drifted in pieces. Blood colored the murky, sandy water around the sandbar. "We're going to drift ashore when I give the order," Douglas waited until the fortified enemy machine gun fire preyed on another incoming craft. There were so many of them. He knew all his men wouldn't make it to shore, but hiding behind fallen brothers or debris was their only chance. "Go now! As soon as your feet reach the ground, run like hell!"

Five of Douglas's men were killed, and four wounded coming ashore. The tattering of the machine guns followed them as they ran, and hidden landmines exploded, killing several more of them. Once on land, they joined other disorganized troops. Douglas took command until he could find a superior officer. Most of the German gunfire directed its fire at landing crafts. They apparently couldn't see his men wading ashore between all the floating corpses. The first order Douglas gave as they assembled below the safety of the higher terrain of a bluff was to the medic. "Take care of the wounded." Douglas then assessed his situation while the sounds of German gunfire and explosives shook the earth around him. The odor of death was atrocious.

The 29th Infantry Division remained pinned down by the enemy's strong fortifications, manned by the German General Rommel's toughest troops. Douglas didn't know, but General Bradley was considering abandoning the beachhead to prevent more men from dying. Douglas found a captain who ordered his platoon to help blow holes through the wire that trapped the army forces on the beach. Under heavy fire from German pillboxes, Douglas complied. Mike Peterson stayed by his side to distribute any orders to his men. The man in front of them took a direct hit; his brains smeared onto Douglas and Mike. The noises from gunfire were dreadful. Douglas ordered his men on their elbows and knees as they moved positions away from enemy fire. Still, he watched some of his men get violently hit one after the other, he and Mike miraculously avoiding gunfire. Now, they were crawling over blood-soaked grounds filled with the remains of American soldiers: spilled intestines, body parts torn off by mines or gunfire, and men crying for help. His only orders were for medics as he focused on breaking through the heavy wire that separated him and his remaining men from life and death.

Finally, after several hours, the Rangers opened the wires, allowing the infantry and the Rangers to break through. They reached the top of the bluffs, hidden under heavy smoke, and took the Germans by surprise. By late afternoon, the 5th Rangers occupied Vierville-sur-Mer.

"Yes, sir! They're making every effort to get letters home as quickly as possible." The staff sergeant saluted as he replied to Douglas's question of how soon his letter would reach the home front.

"Thank you, Sergeant." Douglas returned the salute and turned back to his temporary headquarters.

The morning after the landing, Douglas set up his headquarters in an evacuated damaged church, completely demolished on one side by an apparent bomb. Sitting on a stool next to a bed in his private quarters, which had probably been a rectory of sorts, he recounted the last days as his men searched for Germans in the area and took prisoners. Douglas had received a field promotion to captain and a company commander, one of several available that dreadful day.

Douglas's friends on the other landing craft, Sergeant Ron DiMico, Sergeant Bart Harrison, Corporal Peter Lioni, and Second Lieutenant Bob Licasi, all perished the morning of the invasion. Their LCA had taken a direct hit.

In deep thought, harsh pictures and recollections echoed in his mind, things too horrible to realize at the time they happened. Douglas and his men had responded in battle like robots, feeling little in an instinctive quest to stay alive. It was all coming out, little by little, every detail. Douglas began to chuckle at the horror and absurdity of it all. It was a grotesque laugh, dreadful and devilish. His body began to tremble and shake as that wicked laughter quickly turned to sobbing. He felt he was losing his mind, never being able to take the time to realize all he had witnessed, now finally sinking in. All his efforts had been in ordering his men and making judgment calls, with no time allocated for his personal feelings or the trauma he had witnessed until now. Douglas had to pull himself together. He remembered what his father had tried to tell him. How foolish and young he was then. Now, he was old; that battle had aged him, and he understood his dad's advice and warnings. Douglas had seen 'man's inhumanity to man.'

Douglas's letters were to Elena and his parents. He couldn't tell them exactly where he was; he could only mention he was in France and made it through. He was safe. Douglas also noted, 'Word is that after a while, when we finish cleaning up this area, the Rangers will drive back the Germans in the same direction they came from. I couldn't give you specifics if I knew, which I don't.'

Douglas pulled himself together and stood up. He put on his helmet and proceeded to a meeting with a regimental commander who summoned him that afternoon.

Chapter Forty-One

Wellsville, Europe, The Pacific 1944-1945
The War Years

Japan signed but never ratified the 1929 Geneva Convention. Anywhere they waged war, they attacked anything with an Allied flag attached to it, including hospitals and temporary medical facilities. Japan's leadership knew that America had the resources to build a massive war machine and realized they had a short window of opportunity to defeat America by attacking them while they were unprepared. Their hope was that the American people would shy away from such brutality and allow the Japanese to keep their conquered islands. However, by 1943, Japan had lost its aerial superiority. Their faster and better climbing fighter planes at the start of the war were beginning to be outclassed by American ingenuity. The vast industrial capabilities of the US started building better-designed fighters and bombers, ships, and aircraft carriers. By 1944, Japan's air forces, navy, and supply shipping, as well as its economy, were severely crippled. However, the Japanese armed forces, still conditioned by a militaristic government with no negotiations offered, were ready to fight to the last man.

Douglas Sr. opened the door for Elena, who had phoned a half hour before, telling him she was coming over. Walking excitedly under the hot sun that stood high that sunny summer afternoon in the Ohio River Valley, she could hardly contain herself while stepping into the house. "He's safe!" she burst out, sobbing from relief, ignoring Romeo's banter to get her words out. She couldn't say it over the telephone since she had to say news like this in person and because the operator usually listened to all the wartime news.

"We know! We know, dear." a tearing Gabrielle ran toward the door ever since she heard the front doorbell ring, beating Douglas to confirm the news. The two women, their eyes filled with tears of joy, embraced tightly. "We just received a letter." Then Elena turned to hug Douglas Sr., sobbing with joy as he held her in his arms.

Douglas had asked everyone he knew, from work to his social life, to phone him day or night with important war news. A night clerk at the local newspaper called him at half past three on Tuesday morning, June 6th, saying that scratchy information about a European invasion had begun. He and Gabrielle had rushed to their radio to listen in. Thinking it could be a trick, several of the allied news reporters were skeptical to report transmissions from German radios announcing that bombing had begun along the French Coast and paratroopers were filling the sky. Finally, the Allies transmitted General Dwight David Eisenhower's recorded message to the American people:

Supreme Headquarters
Allied Expeditionary Force

'Soldiers, Sailors, and Airmen of the Allied Expeditionary Force!

"You are about to embark upon the Great Crusade, toward which we have striven these many months. The eyes of the world are upon you. The hope and prayers of liberty-loving people everywhere march with you. In company with our brave Allies and brothers-in-arms on other Fronts, you will bring about the destruction...'

It was the same announcement Douglas and his men had

read before the landings, ending with: *'Good luck! And let us beseech the blessing of Almighty God upon this great and noble undertaking'*

Elena and the Nicholsons had lived in fear every day since, as did most American and Allied families who had relatives stationed there. Now, Elena sat playing with Romeo, comparing letters with the Nicholsons, and knowing Douglas Jr. was safely in France and the war would soon be over.

Douglas didn't acknowledge the portion where his son mentioned that he now understood what he tried to tell him. It was too painful for him to know that his only son had experienced that brutality of battle he once knew himself. Nor did he speak about the tone of his son's writing. It seemed to come from an older man, not the young fellow, so excited and assured that 'the war would be over in no time at all.'

Elena and Gabrielle only focused on the fact that he was safe, and from all news accounts, it would be easy sailing from here to Germany. They both attributed the hurriedness of the letters to the fact that he was tired and pointed out the parts in both their letters where he mentioned, 'sorry to be hasty, but I'm a bit tired and need some sleep' and when he told them. 'I love you, and I miss you.' He ended each letter by saying, 'I'll write soon.'

"Well, I think this calls for a toast!" Douglas announced. "Let me get my best bottle of French champagne!"

"I'll get some cheese and crackers to go with it!" Gabrielle joyously announced.

"I'll help you," Elena followed her future mother-in-law into the kitchen.

When Douglas popped the bottle, he toasted, "To Captain Douglas Nicholson, now safely in France." His memory quickly took him back to those dreadful days he was over there. But he held that sentiment deep inside him, as he had learned to do with his wife Gabrielle's help years before. "May Douglas join us for a glass of champagne on his arrival home soon."

"Here, here!" Gabrielle and Elena smiled as they each held their glass high.

"And to our dear daughter, Martha, who will bring a new member to our family next month!" Gabrielle proudly toasted Martha's pregnancy.

"Here! Here!" the three of them rang out almost simultaneously.

Douglas turned to face the living room window as he sipped his champagne. Next to that window was a red-bordered banner with a blue star, representing their son serving overseas. The sky had darkened since Elena's arrival; clouds were forming, making him wonder if they were in store for a rainstorm. He glanced at his wristwatch, "Still too soon to tell," he whispered.

After the WACs left Port Moresby, they saw their first horrors of war as they passed and stayed in WAC encampments along the way. The Allied workers were still clearing the war-torn areas from the Battle of Buna-Gona at Buna. They feverishly labored in the deep holes of dried mud. The weather conditions in New Guinea were horrible and fickle. Just being on that enormous island was a nightmare. Rains were heavy at times, then dried, leaving thick humidity throughout the tremendous island. Bombed-out areas demolished most of the former colorful foliage, leaving only a few coconut palm trees, most of their leaves withered, some dead on their stumps. Ossified animal and human corpses and body parts, mostly all Japanese, lay strewn about. Some remained in the morbid positions as when they met their fate. Cadavers of Japanese soldiers burned alive, poised as grotesque statues amidst the terrain. The women were appalled as they watched GIs mount skulls and bones of Japanese into neat racks and pyramids.

"Trophies." The driver of the truck troop carrier, or 'jimmys' as the soldiers called them, shouted back to the WACs.

"How horrible!" Laurie shouted back over the rattling noise of the jimmy bouncing and the loud motor as it traveled. She,

Beckie, and Eleanora were sitting closest to the driver.

"War, ma'am," the driver, Sergeant Ed Haggerty, told her. "Payback for what they did. Now, everyone wants a souvenir," he glanced over at Laurie and quickly focused back on the bumpy and dried-muddied road and avoided some water-filled holes along the way. "Some guys even send them to their girlfriends back home."

"Is it safe here?" Beckie asked.

"The Japs evacuated to the jungles and mountains after the Allies first pushed in," he pointed to show them where. "Some raiding parties now and then. The Japs are living off the land. They even raid the natives and steal their food. Hope they choke on it!"

"They told us this is a safe area," it was more of a question than a statement from Eleanora.

"Oh, yeah. The fellows in the jeeps will ward off anything. Don't worry." He referred to the jeeps with .50 caliber machine guns mounted on them. One rode up in front of the small convoy, the other in the back. "Of course, if we don't hit a land mine, that is," he chuckled.

"Now you're toying with us, Sergeant," Beckie laughed, exposing the white teeth of her merry smile. The sergeant didn't answer, keeping the women wondering.

The WAC accommodations in parts of New Guinea were primitive at best in many places. Most were like prisons. With the higher ratio of men to women, soldiers had to guard the WACs. Unlike in the European theatre of war, there were no cities to visit and no socializing whatsoever. The women slept in field tents, eating in larger tents serving as mess halls. The WACs used latrines just like the men. The portable field hospitals they temporarily worked in had dirt floors and basic cots for the wounded, with tree poles supporting grass roofs. They showered behind quickly built wooden stalls with rain water pouring from buckets when there was water. The comfort of Australia lay behind them. But it was the wounded lying in the field hospitals that got to the WACs the most.

The women in the corps volunteered to assist the nurses during busy times. Also, they helped by providing morale to the wounded military men. However, most weren't men but boys, averaging around 18 years old. They lay there, cots aside each other, suffering from gunshots, open wounds, and single, double, and quadruple amputations. Many, almost completely bandaged from severe burns, lay under cloth tents. Several of them had facial scars and burns that disfigured them beyond recognition. Then there were those with the wounds of mental trauma, those of combat fatigue and shell shock. Some were bound for their own protection, waiting for transports to take them to hospital units when there was room and time. Those young men would most likely go back to the States, many of them spending their remaining days in psychiatric institutions.

Eleanora took the dandling hand of an amputee's remaining arm. She noticed by the sheets that covered him that he had also lost a leg. The boy looked straight up at the grass-covered ceiling, his eyes in a glaze. "Hi, soldier, what's your name?" Eleanora spoke in a low voice.

"I'm sorry, ma'am, I can't turn my neck," he seemed troubled that he couldn't twist his neck for the kind woman who greeted him. "The doctor thinks a bullet hit my spine. My name is Alan, Private Alan Barker, ma'am."

"I'm Eleanora. Can I get you anything? A Coca-Cola?"

"No, ma'am, but thank you." His voice reminded Eleanora of a high school student, high pitched at times and respectful. 'That age between boyhood and manhood. So young and marred for life,' she thought.

"How about I read something to you?" Eleanora tried to seem cheery, which was difficult to do at such a time.

Surprisingly, the teen answered, "Oh, would you? I'd love that."

"What would you like?"

"Oh, anything, ma'am. Anything at all."

"I'll be right back." Eleanora hurriedly looked around until she found a stack of outdated magazines. She searched for something pleasant and not war-like. Also, her training taught her not to show the wounded GIs anything with pictures of girls from back home. Eleanora pulled out some she felt appropriate, including a July 1943 edition of The Saturday Evening Post. It had a cartoon of Adolf Hitler, illustrated by Ken Stuart. It was perfect.

Eleanora read Alan an ordinary story, but she read it slowly, even spiced it up in places to make it more interesting. After a short while, she noticed Alan smile. It expressed passion, interest, and appreciation, all from a simple magazine article. After a little less than an hour, Eleanora had to report back to duty. She had spent her lunch break reading to Private Alan Barker and was glad she did. She felt she had helped someone with a simple mercy for the first time since the war began.

"I'll be back tomorrow, Alan. See you then."

"Thank you, Eleanora. Thank you so much. I'll never forget you," he whispered back.

Eleanora noticed complete chaos while returning to report to her superior officer for duty. At first, she thought an attack or an emergency of some sort had occurred. About 15 WACs in uniform, including Beckie and Laurie, were running from the building. Stopping an NCO trotting toward the large hut, Eleanora asked, "What's going on?"

"Look up, Sergeant." He stopped and stood beside Eleanora. The tall, thin, young sergeant pointed to the top of the front tree pole that supported the building.

Eleanora shielded her eyes from the sun with her right hand as if saluting the American flag atop the hut. Then she noticed it. "What is that?" Then she realized what it was. At first sight, it looked artificial, but as her eyes adjusted to the lighting, she gasped. "Is that a h. . .?"

"Yep. It's a head. A Japanese one," the thin sergeant rubbed his chin as he spoke, now appearing like a young Jimmy Stewart. "The Papuan natives bring them to us as gifts now and then. They hate the Japs." The head still had a Japanese uniform hat attached. Its dead eyes were swollen, probably from exposure to the sun and the climate, making the bloated morbid decoration appear hideous, like the face of a gargoyle peering down. "Yeah, we call the natives Fuzzy Wuzzy Angels after the Aussies began calling them that because they're so helpful a. . ." The young 'Jimmy Stewart' glanced over and realized the young woman wasn't listening to him. Eleanora was long gone, running after the other WACs.

Eleanora and a group of WACs walked in the drizzling rain along the twisting, muddy pathway to their tent after eating dinner in the mess hall. Their fatigue-uniform pant legs were soaked with the wet soil well past their boots, making their feet squish with each step. Daylight dimmed from seasonal fog and the time of day. Carefully, they strolled amid the only assisting lighting coming from torches. Approaching the side of the tent up ahead, Beckie shrieked, "Get down, Girls!" The other women glanced and saw the figures moving around inside their tent. Backlite from torches on the other side, they could clearly see the shapes of men moving around.

"Do you think they're Japs?" whispered Mary Sigford, recently assigned to Eleanora's quarters.

"How come the guards didn't spot them?" Eleanora sighed.

"I'm going to get help!" Beckie reached down to a squat position and began waddling. Then she got up and ran back to the mess hall. Within a few minutes, she returned to the women huddled together and anxiously waiting.

"Wait here!" a burly sergeant told them as he took out his Colt 1911 and carefully walked toward the tent. A few minutes later, he came outside and stood beside the tent. He held a woman's fatigue uniform in each hand and undergarments thrown over his shoulder. "Is this what you're talking about, ladies?" A smile plastered across his face.

"Oh, my God! Remember we did the laundry early this morning?" Beckie was embarrassed.

"Oh, no! How humiliating!" Laurie remembered, "We hung them on a line inside because we thought it would rain."

"But look! They do look like figures moving, don't they?"

Eleanora looked sheepish. Then, the other girls burst out in laughter.

At breakfast the following day, the women assigned to Eleanora's tent were the butt of many jokes. Word had gotten around about their mishap. They became known as the 'laundry quarters.' But the girls of the laundry quarters took it on the chin. "Ain't no Japs around here, ladies," a young WAC shouted laughingly from across the mess hall.

At lunch break the next day, Eleanora returned to the field hospital, still fuming from the stupidity of herself and the women in her tent. How ridiculous it seemed that they could all forget about their laundry. And then for some soldier to discover it, especially their personal items. Eleanora had collected several magazines from a recreation hut and the mess hall. Holding them under her arm, she strolled along the muddy pathway that led to the hospital. Humidity filled the air that afternoon, so thick she felt she could cut it with a knife.

The usual musty, medicinal odors filled the confined spaces inside the field hospital. Eleanora looked among rows of cots, noticing the sad faces of the boys who filled them. She spotted Beckie and waved to her. Beckie was always a big hit with the men, and she decided to see if she could administer some of her cheer among those poor, wounded souls.

Eleanora couldn't spot Alan Barker, so she asked a nurse who was taking a break; it seemed from her facial expressions it was a long-needed one. "I can't find a young patient I spoke to yesterday. Do you know where he might be?"

"Do you know his name, dear?" the nurse was a little older than the rest. She looked experienced and hardened but was pleasant.

"Yes, I do. His name is Alan, Private Alan Barker."

As soon as Eleanora mentioned the name, the nurse's eyes lowered, her face filled with despair. She looked up at the bright, genial demeanor Eleanora bore and thought, 'So many of them. They come to help with their kindness, and they do in so many ways. But they're so naïve with their mercy and of war.' Finally, the nurse slowly answered as she had so often done before, "I'm afraid we lost him early this morning. He passed away just after I came in for duty," watching Eleanora's expression change as she had seen others do so many times before.

"Oh, my God! He was only a boy." Eleanora's eyes teared.

"Some advice?" the nurse looked into Eleanora's eyes as if she could see her soul. "Try not to get too close. Help them, but help yourself too. We lost four young boys like Alan already today. We're losing young boys every day in this bloody war," Eleanora finally connected the accent; the nurse was an Australian. In her shock, she didn't recognize it.

"Go back to your quarters and come back when you feel better. I can tell this is your first time," the nurse smiled.

"Thank you, ma'am," Eleanora turned for the door. She was crying.

While dining at the mess hall that evening, thoughts of the young man and his short life still ruminated in Eleanora's mind. Then, suddenly, the air raid siren rang. It was the first time the WACs and Eleanora heard it. The noise was loud and shrieking, shrilling over and over again. Part of the WAC's overseas training was a reaction to an impending attack. They all responded swiftly, strapping their issued helmets securely while running toward the nearest foxholes. The whining sound of a plane quickly descending forced Eleanora to dive into a dirty, wet, muddy foxhole. She got to her knees to peek out; her heart was pounding. A Japanese fighter dived down at full speed and dropped a bomb near the gas tanks, causing the sky to erupt in a yellowish-orange explosion. The ground shook under Eleanora, and dirt from the bomb blast hit her in the face. A second plane descended as the first circled the hospital encampment and strafed one of the machinegun-mounted American jeeps. It blew up and raised from the ground like an invisible rope, pulling it up high. The aircraft continued roaring its machine guns as the American anti-aircraft guns blared. Their Ack-Ack filled the skies. The second Japanese fighter swept down just enough to drop its bomb onto an ambulance truck, then blasted its two

20-millimeter cannons, blowing up transports and jimmies that parked about before the Japanese Zero swiftly rose toward the sky. The Ack-Ack continued filling the sky with black puffs of smoke as the air raid siren shrilled. Eventually, the sound faded like someone pulled its electrical plug.

Eleanora remained in shock, kneeling in the dugout hole. She didn't even realize she was beside Mary Sigford. The two women looked at each other as Mary's mouth spit out some dirt and said, "They told us we would be safe."

Eleanora remembered Sergeant Ed Haggerty, the truck driver. 'Maybe he wasn't kidding, after all,' she thought.

The following day at breakfast, while the girls of the 'laundry quarters' sat eating, Beckie yelled out across the mess hall to the woman who commented the day before, "Yeah! There ain't no Japs here! That's for sure!" More air raids continued before the WACs left that area.

From that post, the WACs passed through Wau to Lae. Then Finschhafen, and Saidor to Madang. They saw where the heavy bombing had been in Hansa Bay on their way to Wewak, New Guinea, after the Aitape-Wewak campaign. After the victory at Aitape, the Allied command sent the Americans who fought there to a different war sector. The Australians mainly fought at Wewak, with some American air support provided. It was a place Eleanora would never forget for the rest of her life.

As the Allies advanced into New Guinea, many Japanese troops that fell outside the perimeter became abandoned and resorted to guerrilla fighting from jungle locations. Many of them went deep into the bush and higher terrain areas. From there, they launched quick assaults on allied troops, taking any supplies, food, and equipment they could manage and retreat back into the jungles.

Ever since the Japanese invaded New Guinea, their brutality reined even amongst the native tribes living there. They requisitioned all their food supplies and left the natives to starve.

Enslaving many of them, they shot natives dead for not obeying even though most of them couldn't understand what they were saying. After Japanese troops spread throughout the jungles, things got worse for the natives. The Marind-anim were among several tribes of headhunters in New Guinea and sought after the Japanese. Cannibalism existed among some tribes of New Guinea. Many of the isolated Japanese also resorted to cannibalism. Japanese soldiers consumed the flesh of allied captives taken prisoner, many bailing out of flaming US planes.

There had been a Catholic missionary in Wewak, New Guinea, along with protestant missionaries spreading God's word to the natives and setting up hospitals and care facilities. After the Japanese occupation, they marooned all clergy, nuns, priests, and some children on Kairiru Island off Wewak. Eventually, the Japanese viewed these missionaries as threats. They transported them to the Japanese ship, Akikaze. Afterward, the Japanese trucked soldiers to Wewak to destroy all churches, mission plantations, clinics, and houses. They bayoneted to death all converts and made sure they obliterated the Divine Word Missionaries from the face of the earth.

Japanese High Command then ordered all those prisoners aboard the Akikaze executed. First, they tossed the children overboard. The Japanese took the men and women on deck and hung them by their wrists, shot them, and threw their bodies overboard just like it was a sport or a contest. One by one, the Japanese murdered sixty people within hours.

As the WACs settled into Wewak, they noticed an absence of natives as they had seen before. They had no idea just how much the natives had been traumatized by the Japanese. As a result, they feared all those who moved in after the Japanese vacated. Even though they were unsheltered and starving, they sought no help and stayed away from the American and Australian encampments.

While Eleanora was preparing for lights out one late evening, she heard sounds from outside. Beckie was awake, so she motioned her with her right forefinger over her lips to signal quiet. She whispered directly in Beckie's ear, "Someone's outside."

"We should call someone."

"Remember the last time we asked for help? The laundry?" Eleanora reminded her. "No, we have to take a look ourselves."

The two women crept quietly to avoid waking anyone or alerting the guards. Eleanora grabbed her friend's arm and pulled her down. They waited behind a paperbark tree until a jeep patrol passed by. Slowly and cautiously, they continued the trek toward the mess hall where the sounds came from. When they arrived behind the mess hall, young children were hiding there. The oldest looked about nine years old, and the youngest was a toddler. They filled the area behind the hall, pulling scraps of garbage from the trash containers and taking bites before handing them to others as they ate the trash. The stink of the open containers was enough to make Beckie and Eleanora nauseous, and they both stood gagging.

"Oh my God, we have to do something about this." Eleanora gasped.

"We sure do," Beckie agreed. "And I know what."

It took the ingenuity of the Women's Army Corps to resolve this problem. Beckie led the way, using all her charm and skill to maneuver the men on KP duty to hand out food. In no time at all, she took charge. "Not so many cans; they're too hard to open so many. More meat," Beckie pointed as if she were shopping in a market back home in Texas.

All the women pitched in and codenamed that duty 'Operation Foodstuff' to feed the starving natives. That night, they all sneaked back, prearranging where they would position themselves earlier in the day. They had to wean the children from eating garbage. As they squatted in place, they watched as the children arrived. They were so emaciated that it brought tears to their eyes.

Beckie excitedly threw out the first small package as if she were throwing the first pitch in a major league baseball game. The women neatly wrapped the fresh foods in tin foil for preservation. A little boy was startled initially, then slowly crept up to the shiny bundle. Smelling the aroma, he quickly opened it and indulged himself. Whispering something in a language the women couldn't understand, others approached the boy. They flung a small package one at a time, as planned not to frighten them. Now, the native children abandoned the trash containers and sat on the ground eating the wholesome food provided by the WACs.

That's how it all began. Eventually, adults accompanied the children. They knew these people were not oppressors like the horrors they had witnessed at the hands of the Japanese. Before long, the Allies set up a clinic, and then a missionary returned.

That same ingenuity laid the groundwork for an even grander WAC secret operation in World War Two. 'Operation Ice Cream' was a collaboration of several WACs. It began when Eleanora and two other medical clericals volunteered to visit a remote surgical hospital in a mountain above Wewak. The military built it there to treat injuries and post-surgical patient cases so severe they couldn't transport them. Considering themselves accomplished veterans after their earlier experiences, the WACs quickly offered their services and moral support. But they weren't prepared for what they saw atop that mountain. It was much worse than anything they had seen before.

The place's isolation presented far too many challenges to the doctors and nurses who treated them. The difficulty of providing a constant flow of medical supplies and equipment was harrowing. Getting through the muddy trails to the facility required four-wheel-drive vehicles, which were in short supply in that area. They also had to contend with heavy rains at times, which left mud far too deep for any four-wheel vehicle to climb.

Eleanora, Beckie, and Mary hitched a ride in a 'beep,' a small light cargo variation of a jeep and a truck. Laurie had a tropical fever and couldn't make the trip. Dressed in fatigues and boots, with their helmets on, sitting amidst the cargo of medical supplies and other small boxes with paraphernalia, the three women were off. They clung onto side straps while riding the journey's bends, curves, and bumps as the beep skidded the entire ride.

It was almost a horror scene from a movie when they entered the hastily built shack that served as a surgical hospital. Every case was critical, but it was the sounds of young boys whimpering and crying that bore a hole through the hearts of the three women. They had already seen wounded young boys and amputees, but here were types of wounds they hadn't ever witnessed. It was hard to believe that a human body could remain alive enduring such conditions.

"You can speak to them," an American nurse greeted them, "it's okay," she smiled. However, she appeared to be exhausted, probably running on adrenaline.

Stunned at first, the three women walked up, each trying to comfort a patient. The odor in the shack was sickening.

Beckie stood before a boy. A transparent sheet tented him from under his neck to just below his abdominal area. She could see that his body below his lower abdomen was gone. "Hi, soldier. How are you feeling today?" She forced the words and avoided showing her horror.

"Fine, ma'am," he whispered so softly that Beckie bent to hear him.

"That's good to hear," she said softly. Beckie took a wet washcloth from a basin on a folding stand beside the cot and began wiping the young boy's sweating forehead.

"Where do you come from?"

"Oklahoma, ma'am."

"Well, I'm your neighbor. I'm from Texas," she smiled. "I hope you get back there real quick."

"Thank you, ma'am. I'm one of the lucky ones. I'm still alive."

While Beckie tended to her patient, Eleanora stood beside a soldier in an entire body cast, several tubes running from the molded plaster that entombed him. There were only holes for his eyes, ears, and mouth, and just his fingertips revealed themselves. She thought, 'How horrible it must be to be trapped like that,' but questioned, "How old are you, soldier?" not knowing if he could speak.

Two syllables slowly sounded from the mouth-hole: "eighteen." Listening carefully, Eleanora heard a third: "miss." His words were soft and feeble.

"Well, we're gonna see these fine people fix you up good, or they'll answer to me!"

"Thanks," he could barely answer.

Mary was feeding another boy, a quadruple amputee, and speaking to him as she did. "Where are you from, soldier?"

"Brisbane, miss." One of his remaining stumps had blood and yellowish pus seeping through the bandages. Surgeons removed that last limb, leaving only a minimal amount of thigh. It led Mary to believe it was a recent surgery, and maybe the surgeons had to take more off after the first amputations.

"Oh, I loved it there. It's a beautiful city. You'll be back before you know it."

"Yes, miss," the boy answered as if in a daze.

As the three demoralized women quietly traveled back to their post by a returning beep, Beckie was the one to break the silence, "We have to do something for those boys," she had tears in her eyes.

"Something special," Eleanora agreed.

"I got it!" Mary's eyes lit up. "What's the one frozen, refreshing thing you miss from home?"

The two other women didn't have to think for long. Almost in harmony, they rang out, "Ice cream!"

"I haven't had ice cream in ages. The sailors offshore have it on their ships," Beckie remembered.

"I know. They're always flirting that they'll get us some ice cream," Mary added.

"Let's work on the officers to get some ice cream for those boys up there," Eleanora began the plan.

After several negotiations, the navy agreed to allow the army a ration of ice cream for the wounded atop that mountainous hospital. The outcome was that the same three WACs had to deliver it, and they considered it an honor. Operation Ice Cream was on.

The ice cream was packed in ice and coordinated with a beep to deliver it before it melted. There was enough ice cream for all the coherent patients, and the women left some of the precious frozen treats for the nurses. The three WACs went from cot to cot, administering the delicacy to the severely wounded. The young boys wept with appreciation; some nurses cried at the kindness.

Eleanora slowly and patiently fed the boy in the body cast. She could see a movement of his tongue as he savored the refreshing, creamy treat between each small spoonful. Eleanora took her time, allowing him to enjoy it thoroughly. When he finished, he softly and slowly whispered, "God bless you, ma'am. I'll never forget you." It brought back Eleanora's tearful memory of Private Alan Barker, who expressed the same sentiment.

A short time later, now veterans of war's devastation, the WACs proceeded to Hollandia General Hospital, Hollandia, Medicine, New Guinea. The Australian Women's Army Service (AWAS) was there first. The WACs joined with the AWAS women, assisting in the larger field and evacuation hospitals there.

Douglas sat in a makeshift command headquarters, conferring with a regimental commander. "Last evening, there was a skirmish with the Germans about a few miles or so up from the beaches," the colonel who spoke looked weathered and tired. "Some soldiers from the First Division were resting in a hedgerow when the Krauts opened up with machinegun fire."

"How many casualties, sir?"

"Seven. But seven too many, Captain." Colonel William Martin was an older man of about 50. He reminded Douglas of his father at that age: tall, strong, and in good shape. "Before you leave for your rest period, I'd like you to take a reconnaissance to look around there."

"How many men, sir?"

"A platoon strength to be safe. But don't interact with any enemy troops. I only want a report about the terrain the men will be encountering," the colonel hesitated. "You'll be shoving off in the other direction soon, I know. But I need someone I trust to give me a report about those hedgerows the First Division was talking about. Aerial photos aren't that clear and only show the hedgerows from a higher perspective. I want to make sure there aren't any German strongholds."

"When do we leave, sir?"

"At dawn. And remember, Doug," he used his first name, "don't encounter the enemy. If they attack, retreat. Try to get a good look around and report back directly to me. Oh, by the way, I see you're not wearing these." He handed Douglas a pair of captain's bars. "They were mine. It seems not too long ago."

"Thank you, sir." The colonel could see that Douglas was fatigued, but everyone was, and he needed someone reliable, like Captain Douglas Nicholson.

By morning, Douglas and his selected men were trekking through the areas well past the beaches. They took transport vehicles to get them well away from the shore area. Douglas left them and assembled five squads with a sergeant leading each. There were no available lieutenants, and Douglas still needed to configure his company. Staff Sergeant Mike Peterson walked beside Douglas.

"You'd think they'd give us a break," chuckled Mike.

"Mike, you're in the Army now," Douglas laughed back. Neither knew that the Germans had built strong defenses behind the hedgerows. It was the perfect way to hold off forces and delay the invasion into Normandy.

Douglas spotted a hedgerow a little over 50 yards ahead, not far from their transports. He took out his binoculars to get a better look. Though it seemed quiet, Douglas had a bad feeling and had Mike send the signal to hit the ground. It was a good call because a German machine gun began blasting as soon as he did.

"Mike!" he yelled, "Set up the BARs to give cover fire as the men retreat." The four Browning Automatic Rifles began to spew their earsplitting, large 30-06 caliber ammo at over 600 rounds a minute. But Douglas knew they couldn't hold off so many Germans for long.

"Get the men out of here! Back to the transports!" Douglas screamed. He waited as his squads began to run back one at a time. When safely out of the German fire, Douglas told Mike, "Come on, let's go!"

The squads up ahead dropped down and took positions to cover Douglas and the remaining men with him. As they reached the trucks, Douglas watched two of his men get hit. The Germans had sent out a small detachment of infantry to follow them. Douglas ordered Mike to set up the BARs again to take out the few Germans remaining following behind them. "Put the wounded in the Trucks! Hurry!" Douglas yelled. He turned back to assess any enemy troops behind them. As he did, a force hit him in his chest as if a gorilla had punched him. Falling to his knees, Mike swooped him up and speedily carried him to the last transport. As Mike laid him beside the other wounded men, Douglas tried to speak. Blood spurted from his mouth. Struggling, he whispered, "Tell the colonel. Tell him." Douglas thought of home. "I have a wonderful family and fiancée to get back to. . ." his whisper faded off. Mike could see the beginning of a smile before Douglas's eyes rolled back.

Chapter Forty-Two

The War Years

The WACs and nurses in the Pacific encountered entirely differ-ent difficulties than their European counterparts. Not until the end of the war would they see civilization or socialize. Many WACs fell ill solely from the humidity of the jungles. Dehydra-tion, heatstroke, rashes, and cramps were among them. Tropi-cal sicknesses of yaws from natives became rampant, requiring immediate antibiotics. Dysentery swept through New Guinea, killing thousands of the Allied military and natives. Mosqui-to-born diseases from swamps and puddles caused unprece-dented cases of filariasis, malaria, and dengue fever. Just being in the Pacific for long periods seemed like a hellhole.

After Hollandia, the WACs' next stop was the Philippines. Many of the WACs had suffered from dermatitis and Malaria in New Guinea. The Army administered Quinine pills, but in many cases, the Japanese cut off supply lines, which led to an epidemic in many places. The excessive heat and humidity and the heavy uniforms they wore caused dermatitis. Cases of bron-chitis that led to pneumonia had intensified from the climate and the constant wet footwear from puddles and swampy areas.

Unlike the WACs in Europe, the women in the corps serving in the Pacific had stricter rules. Due to the overwhelming ratio of men to women, headquarters enforced isolation regulations.

Also, due to the possibility of Japanese attacks from split-up forces after the Allied invasions and roaming natives, some of whom were cannibalistic, WACs were confined to armed-guarded base camps without leave. They spent their only leisure time on base, mainly in the mess hall, which also served as a recreation area. They felt like prisoners, remembering being in Australia, where they could visit places in the cities.

Already seated side by side on the long metal seats of the C-47 troop transport plane, Beckie, Laurie, Mary, and Eleanora reflected on New Guinea. As they waited for liftoff, they recalled all the horrors associated with that time. Eleanora had become a name too long for her closest friends to pronounce, so they nicknamed her 'Buchie.'

"Ready for the Philippines, Buchie?" Mary asked, smiling.

"Can it even be worse?" Laurie answered the question.

"We won't know 'til we get there, will we?" Eleanora replied to the question initially intended for her.

"Oh, Girls, hush. They locked us up like prisoners in New Guinea 'to protect us from all the men,' didn't they?" Beckie vented her opinion, and her voice had a facetious ring. "Now we'll get to meet all the GIs we want."

"There were Japs and natives back there too. Maybe it'll be worse where we're going," Mary said, adding to the conversation as the C-47's twin engines burst to life.

There were other WACs, a few GIs, and a couple of Marines on the flight. Among them sat several civilians, probably contractors. They all sat along the sides of the plain metal seats that ran the plane's length. The C-47 taxied along Hollandia airfield. Once on the main runway, the aircraft gained enough speed, lifted its nose, and ascended into the sky. The girls tilted sideways as the plane lifted off Hollandia Air Strip, headed for Morotai to refuel and then to Tacloban on Leyte Island, now under Allied occupation.

"Whoa! That's fun!" Beckie again enjoyed the liftoff, reminding her of an amusement park ride. This time, it reminded Eleanora of Rock Springs Park and the fun she had there.

It seemed like a lifetime ago that she and the Trieste sisters frequented that place. Eleanora was getting homesick, missing everyone, and wondering how Annie was doing with Jimmy. Eleanora didn't get mail often in the Pacific, moving around as much as she did. It was in Hollandia where her dated mail waited for her. Last she heard that Jimmy had joined the Navy and was a radioman. Nina was in the WACs and working in Washington, DC.

The transport took a direct route to Morotai, flying over the northern tip of New Guinea and then over part of the Pacific. It was a clear day, and as they came close to the island over three hours later, the four women turned to view the beautiful greenish-blue tints of the tropical water of the beaches. Then came the reminder of war as they saw the devastation of battle in that place that seemed so peaceful from the sky.

Later, when the plane descended, Laurie announced, "My stomach feels queasy."

"Well then, you better complain to the stewardess, first-class accommodations and all," Beckie laughed. Laurie didn't find the comment amusing.

"Put your head between your legs," Eleanora advised as the C-47 dived into the short runway.

"I'm okay now, Buchie, thanks."

After the plane landed, the women and the passengers left the transport to stretch their legs while the fueling took place. The pilot ordered all passengers to stay close.

"Prisoners again," Beckie got some chuckles from the others as the WACs and other passengers walked around the airfield.

An hour later, they were airborne again on their way to Tacloban. There was a noticeable bump as they passed the northern coast of Mindanao. The passengers thought it was just an air pocket, but the pilot knew differently. "What was that?" Captain Bob Nicastro asked the copilot. "We're losing altitude. Take a look, quickly."

"I see some smoke coming from the right engine," Rick Miller answered. As soon as he finished those words, the engine burst into flames. "Fire, Bob!" Rick Miller tried not to shout so as not to alarm the passengers.

"Were we hit?" Captain Nicastro urgently worked the rudders and the throttle to slow the plane without going into a spin.

"I can't tell!"

"Mayday. Mayday, mayday," Captain Nicastro radioed as he tried to stabilize the C-47 transport.

Rick Miller was out of his seat but could hear the emergency landing instructions from the radio as he left the cockpit to do a spot check on the plane's body. By then, plumes of thick black smoke filled the sky, trailing the yellowish-orange flames from the right engine. Miller ran back to the cockpit, shouting, "Shut down the right engine immediately!"

The men and women passengers were already screaming and crying. One of the civilian contractors hollered, "We're all gonna die!" Lieutenant Miller stood at the front and yelled to everyone, "Heads between your knees. You there, buckle up," repeating those instructions to anyone who wasn't wearing a strap. "We're preparing for an emergency landing! Helmets on!" Rick returned to his co-pilot seat. Bob was turning the wheel and working the wings' and rudder flaps as the plane took a steep nose dive. American Navy F4U Corsair fighters, called bent-winged birds by the marines and navy men who flew them, appeared on each side of the transport plane, offering support for the landing.

Beckie was screaming, "I don't want to die!" Laurie was dazed, and Mary had tears in her eyes and appeared to be in shock. But Eleanora was calm, her tranquil demeanor suitably helping to calm those panicking. Others turned in horror and watched out the windows as the black smoke turned grey and streamed from the right wing. They could see the fighter plane's pilot to the right giving the thumbs-up sign, signaling he was there. However, the right engine was off; its propellor turned slowly, moving solely from the wind that forced the yellowish flames against the plane. The pilot had to land with one engine.

A sudden calm came over the aircraft as if everyone was

making peace with God and preparing to die. There was no more fight inside those screaming just minutes before. Everyone had resolved to their fate as the C-47 descended over the military airport in Tacloban on Leyte Island. Emergency ground crews were in place as the aircraft still discharged smoke from the flaming engine as it came in. The seconds seemed like hours until the noise of the landing wheels sounded that they touched down with only one engine. The C-47 bounced high and swayed from side to side as it slowed down, all passengers aboard tightly grasping the edges of the metal seating as they hunched forward as instructed.

As the passengers raised their heads, the transport still rolling along the runway, Lieutenant Rick Miller stood outside the cockpit. The ground crew was preparing to spray the flames from the right engine. "As soon as that hatch opens," he pointed, "jump immediately. Quickly line up!" Emergency vehicles were waiting alongside the transport as everyone jumped to the ground. Rick Miller jumped off after the passengers, followed by the captain, who was last.

As the women gathered far from the transport plane, calming down, Mary asked, "My God, Eleanora, how did you stay so calm?"

Eleanora thought, then quietly replied, "Well, my father always taught me that a good Indian never runs in the rain."

Leyte Island had swampy terrain. The Allied landings there had been difficult. The Japanese used Kamikazes for the first time in the Battle of Leyte Gulf. The suicide pilots used their own planes as bombs to cause as much havoc for the Allied ships. The disillusioned WACs that flew in by emergency landing sat quietly on a transport truck that took them to their base on Tacloban. They jumped off the vehicles and marched like zombies to their quarters.

On Leyte, they saw and witnessed the same horrors as they did in New Guinea. They worked their shifts and visited the wounded in the field hospitals. Still treated as 'prisoners,' as they called it, they had become hardened to the savagery of

536

war; they were now veterans of it. But, seeing those soldiers so young and mutilated for life was something a human could not become accustomed to. Like all the troops in the Pacific, they had seen enough of war and wanted to go home. But the war wasn't over yet. Their next stop was Manilla.

In late July, Douglas Nicholson stood in a daze before the same living room window where he had sipped his champagne just a month before, celebrating his son's safety after the Normandy invasion. Now, he stood like the ghost of a man watching the Ohio River flow by through the glass separating him from that mighty body of water as the late afternoon heat simmered into the evening. Still in bereavement for the loss of his mother, Martha, who had passed away at 88 years old just a few weeks before, he now faced his greatest fear.

As soon as Gabrielle had spotted the vehicle approaching from her sewing spot on the back porch, she sensed danger. It was an intuitive feeling only a mother could harbor. When a chaplain and a military officer appeared, she shrieked, "No! N-o-o-o-o-o!" so loud that her husband came running down the stairs to the sound of his wife screaming. Upon seeing the two men approach, Douglas immediately realized what was happening as Gabrielle screamed, "It's a mistake! It happened before!" Douglas held her tight as the two men walked closer. "Tell them, Doug!" she was hysterical, "Tell them about you! Remember? When they came to tell me about you. . . ," her words were mumbled, then faded off to the silence of her broken heart.

Gabrielle remained silent from shock as she sat beside her husband, who was now crying. The officer was graciously explaining the circumstances of their son's death as their minister comforted an unresponsive Gabrielle. The officer presented Douglas with a Silver Star, a Purple Heart, and an American flag.

Colonel William Martin, Douglas's regimental commander

who had assigned him for that fatal mission, had called in a favor to dispatch a military escort. He also sent a hand-written letter from their son's friend by military mail, now promoted to Master Sergeant Mike Peterson. It was a short note and read:

My words cannot express my gratitude for having served under your son. I know there is nothing I can say or do to relieve your grief but know that your son was a wonderful man and a born leader. He died saving his men. Every one of them that survived was because of his actions, both on the beach and inland. I saw to it personally that his body was turned into the Army's graves registration unit for documentation and I attended his burial. Know that his last thoughts were of his beloved family and fiancée.

My condolences for your loss,
Master Sergeant Michael Peterson, Fifth Rangers

Gabrielle remained in denial. Douglas had contacted his daughter, Claire, who arrived and attended to her mother. He didn't call his daughter, Martha, yet as she was expecting her baby any day, and he didn't want to upset her suddenly. Douglas planned to tell his daughter, Martha, appropriately that her younger brother, the boy she cared for when he was a child, was killed in action. It would be especially hard for her as she and Douglas always remained close. Claire also had the sad task of contacting Elena.

Douglas's eyes were red and swollen from crying as he stood at the window, Romeo whimpering at his feet. Watching the river flow, he faced the reality that the blue star on the red-bordered banner would be replaced with one of gold.

Bill Conners put down his M1 Garand next to the stump of a blasted coconut tree and sat to take a short break. Next to the tree stump was a rigid figure of a Japanese soldier burnt by a flamethrower as he came out of a hole. Frozen in the same position that he perished, only his upper body was exposed. His arms rested on the ground around the pit. The man appeared to be checking outside when the torch burned him alive.

Bill Conners and the 145th Infantry Regiment of the 37th Division had been in Bougainville alongside the Marines, patrolling the beaches and training for the Luzon Campaign. In January 1945, he landed on the shores of Lingayen Gulf in northwestern Luzon in the Philippines. His battalion then went to fight at Clark Field and Fort Stotsenburg against fierce resistance until the end of January. Bill Conners and his platoon continued to the hills of Northwest Luzon, enduring heavy fighting until they captured Baguio toward the end of April.

"Heads up!" A coconut landed next to Bill. His friend, Roger Dolan, had climbed up a coconut tree and began dropping them beside Bill as he sat beside the statuesque figure of what once was a Japanese soldier. The men of the 145th Infantry Regiment rested that day in May near Baguio.

"Easy there, Sergeant," Bill quipped in half jest. Now a Lieutenant, Bill had received a battlefield promotion for his excellence in leadership. American forces had encountered heavy casualties in the months before and were short of officers and men. He was leading a platoon and took that responsibility seriously. The old-school soldier, Sergeant Sean O'Brien, met his fate just days before, ironically serving under Bill, a soldier he had trained. His friends from the beginning of the war, Tony Amico and Toby Ryan, had also perished.

Bill rose, took his weapon, and headed to his tent. Roger Dolan remained on the tree, dropping coconuts. Soon after, Bill and his troops were setting off again to face action in the Cagayan Valley as the Japanese forces lingered. The 37th Division took heavy casualties again as they pushed down toward Manila.

American and Filipino forces first encircled Manila. Then they drove onward, fighting on the outskirts of Manila, then entered the city and fought in the streets. Along with Filipino troops, the Americans cleared Manila at the beginning of March.

Eleanora and the WACs traveled through the Philippines to Manila after its liberation, where the women finally saw a civilized city after many months—or the remnants of a city. Much of Manila lay in devastation. Sergeant Buch made a friend in Manilla who served in the Filipino Women's Auxiliary Service (WAS). Hiding in the hills at times, Isa Caras had served in the medical corps of the organized Philippine guerrilla groups ever since the Japanese invaded her country. The Americans supplied them by submarine at first before they came ashore in the Philippines.

Isa Caras and Eleanora became close friends while serving together in Manilla. Isa explained untold stories of horror and degradation about Filipino women during the Japanese occupation of the Phillippines.

"My God, Isa, we never knew about these things." It was the first time Eleanora heard first-hand accounts of the atrocities committed by the Japanese in the Phillippines.

"Yes, Eleanora. It was terrible. We learned about these things from some who escaped," Isa explained. "They made the women sexual slaves. The Japanese called them 'Comfort Women' during that time."

"Oh, my God," was all the horrified Eleanora could repeat, thinking about such horrible things.

"Yes, while the Americans were circling the city, the Japanese slaughtered over 100,000 Filipinos." Isa's eyes filled with tears as she went on, "They're calling it the Rape of Manilla. They killed them in the most gruesome ways. Women were raped in public before the Japanese executed them," a tear ran down Isa's cheek, causing Eleanora's eyes to tear. "Some of the Japanese soldiers even had sexual intercourse with the dead bodies."

"Oh, no," Eleanora was disgusted and angered at these terrifying things she didn't know. The US Army hadn't yet released such information.

"The Japs even killed members of the Red Cross in Manilla. Eleanora, they killed everyone in sight before we could stop it. They even smashed babies' heads against tree trunks." Eleanora could only shake her head back and forth in disgust, as these things were too horrible to picture in her mind.

After the Allies secured Manilla, the WACs finally received time off and, eventually, short leaves. These liberties came with strict rules and included places that were off-limits and curfews. The heavy WAC uniforms required when off base added to their discomfort in the tropical humidity.

Many military men were lonely without their wives or girl-friends back home. Knowing that few women were available, Eleanora believed most men were looking for a quick night with a lady. Prostitution flourished in all wars, but more so in Europe than in the Pacific. But Eleanora met a boyfriend, Sid, in the Philippines. He was an officer who worked as a lawyer before joining the Army and loved Eleanora.

"Thanks for a wonderful evening," Eleanora kissed Sid before rushing into her barracks before lights out. Sid always took Eleanora to lovely places, as best he could find in a war-torn city. Always commandeering a jeep, he took her to sights around Manilla, explaining things to her as he drove.

"You're welcome," answering before she broke his embrace and left. Sid waited in the jeep until he saw her safely enter her quarters.

Eleanora was at headquarters in Manilla. Unlike New Guinea, there were buildings requisitioned for the military. She slept in barracks and not grass huts. One day, while strolling the halls of a large building, Eleanora heard piano music in the distance and followed the sounds. She came upon an open doorway of a large room. A man was playing an upright piano in the large, empty room. Eleanora just stood there in a trance-like state. It was the most beautiful piano music she had ever heard. She leaned and accidentally creaked the door, making that familiar eerie sound of a haunted house, not wanting to disturb the piano player. He turned from his piano and faced Eleanora, "C'mon inside," he waved.

"I wouldn't want to disturb you."

"Nonsense, c'mon in."

As Eleanora stood beside the man, he told her, "Sit down next to me." He slid over on the long piano seat, making room for her. "What would you like to hear?" Wearing a plain uniform, Eleanora assumed the dark-haired man, who appeared to be in his late 50s, was a private.

"Oh, anything. You play so nicely. It's been a long time since I heard live music." She remembered those days when she danced under the night sky at Rock Springs Park, listening to live bands, including Jimmy Bass.

"Thank you, young lady. How about I play, 'You're Laughing at Me?' Do you like that one?" He began playing that song to Eleanora's enjoyment. She watched how his nimble fingers worked along the keyboard, playing the piano so beautifully. She observed that he appeared to be a shorter man, reminding her of her father back home, Felo.

Eleanora sat in awe as the dark-haired man played many tunes that Eleanora knew so well. After playing 'Easter Parade,' he capped it off with 'God Bless America' before someone interrupted him. The person seemed like an organizer, conversing with the piano player about preparing for a show. Eleanora realized it was time for her to leave. She had been there for nearly an hour, rose, and told the dark-haired man, "Thank you, sir. Thank you so much for the lovely music."

The older, dark-haired man smiled back, "Oh, you're very welcome, young lady. You have a nice day."

Two other WACs stood by the door, watching inside, and asked Eleanora, "Wow, do you know Irving Berlin?"

"No, is he in the Philippines?" Eleanora answered.

"He's the man who was just playing the piano for you."

"Oh, my God!" Eleanora had unknowingly been listening to a private recital from the infamous Irving Berlin.

The once beautiful city of Manilla lay devasted by battle. Many buildings miraculously stood untouched among those utterly ruined. Eleanora again saw men, women, and children eating out of garbage cans. As it was within city limits, WAC special operations could not help them. It would take time to rebuild Manilla and the Philippines.

As Eleanora and Sid dated, she came to believe he indeed loved her. Before he left the Philippines, Sid proposed to Eleanora.

Flattered, and as much as she liked Sid, she knew marriage was out of the question. Hesitantly, she answered, "I can't, Sid," as he held her in his arms after his proposal.

"Why?" he was bewildered. "You said you love me."

"I do, Sid, but it's like we talked about before," Eleanora turned down her head and separated from Sid's arms.

"Oh, that."

"You don't know my mother and my family." Sid was Jewish, and Eleanora was a Catholic. Lucy would have died if she knew her daughter was seeing a Jewish man.

"I just don't understand," but realizing his parents would feel the same, it was how it was.

Before parting, a dispirited Sid gave Eleanora a book about the countryside of England as a parting gift; it was about one of the subjects they talked about during their romance.

Beckie, Laurie, and Mary all dated while in the Philippines, dancing at clubs and seeing entertainment provided by the military. The WAC women visited the hospitals in the area, some outside the city, offering morale to the sick and wounded. Isa Caras took Eleanora on tours of Manila to get her mind off Sid. She explained how beautiful Manila once was. Eleanora could tell from the layout and architecture that it must have been much more glorious than it now looked. They talked about their futures and vowed to remain friends after the war.

On Okinawa, a fortuitous meeting occurred. Nick Buch crossed paths with Giovanni Quintania's son, John, whose last name was now Quinter, who was also serving in the army. Together, they explored the secure bases, sharing experiences and camaraderie, creating a bond in their short time together.

While on Okinawa, they unexpectedly met Tyrone Powers, the film star. Marine First Lieutenant Powers had been trained as a pilot at Corpus Christi, Texas, and was flying planes. With an excellent physique, bright white teeth, and wavy hair, the dark-complexioned Powers maintained the image of a Hollywood elite. Though trying to keep a low profile, he was friendly and invited John and Nick to sit at his table for a drink. Chatting with Tyrone Powers was one of the highlights of Nick Buch's and John Quinter's lives. Nick and John were separated and returned to their regiments before being shipped back to the States after the end of the war.

In 1944, Hector Allen and Isaac Williams went with the 92nd Division to fight in the Italian Campaign. Isaac was no longer a cook but a fighting man in the infantry. He did, however, manage to rustle up some good grub in the fields for his fellow soldiers at times. Their division faced the same racism on the battlefields as they did Stateside. He and his fellow Buffalo Soldiers fought vigorously for five months in the Apennines and the Italian Alps. By the spring of 1945, they were fighting on a mountain stronghold in Viareggio, Italy, before the war ended in Europe.

The US Army discharged Hector as Staff Sergeant Hector Allen with several commendations, a bronze star for helping storm a Nazi machine gun nest, and a Purple Heart. Before being discharged, Issac, now also a staff sergeant, made plans to meet Hector in New York City, as they had always discussed, even on the battlefield. They exchanged addresses and vowed to meet again in New York City.

"You be a good boy now!" Issac laughed as they parted for their homeland.

"Don't you boy me, nigger!" They laughed together, recalling all the racism they had encountered throughout their war years together and how they eventually became respected soldiers. Then they embraced and parted.

While in Manilla, Eleanora and her fellow WACs picked up a radio broadcast regarding a bombing. The Allies had repeatedly carpet-bombed Mainland Japan with incendiary explosives in an effort to end the war. Still, the Japanese people obeyed and adhered to their militaristic leadership, where surrender wasn't an option. Brainwashed Japanese citizens preferred to jump off cliffs in captured islands rather than face American capture. Their government had convinced them that the Allies would conduct themselves in the same vicious manner the Japanese had done on their bloody quest throughout the war. Japanese citizens and soldiers were surprised by the kindness and care provided by the Americans. But now, the narrator speaking on the radio was referring to a super bomb the American Army Air Force dropped. It was part of a secret mission where pilots had been training isolated and under the strictest security. An American B-29 bomber named the 'Enola Gay' dropped this super bomb on Hiroshima, Japan, at 8:15 AM on August 6, 1945. Sporadic reports were coming in with vague information. No one understood what a super bomb named 'Little Boy' was.

Three days later, a second super bomb, named 'Fat Man,' was dropped on Nagasaki by a B-29 bomber named 'Bockscar' at 11:02 AM on August 9, 1945. These became known as Atomic bombs and brought an end to World War Two in the Pacific.

Finally, on August 14, 1945, President Harry S. Truman announced that Japan surrendered unconditionally. However, the Americans secretly accepted many conditions from Japan to end the war and prevent the complete annihilation of Mainland Japan. Like V-E Day months before, Americans everywhere celebrated V-J Day or Victory over Japan Day.

On August 15, Japanese Emperor Hirohito told the Japanese people on the radio that their enemy had employed a most 'cruel bomb' capable of doing incalculable damage to innocent Japanese people. Completely disregarding the unspeakable cruelty his military had inflicted on innocent lives throughout the Pacific Islands, China, the Philippines, Dutch East Indies, Malaya, Singapore, and Burma, he announced that the war was over. It was the first time his people heard his words on a radio. Japanese Emperor Hirohito escaped imprisonment and execution.

Eleanora celebrated with her friends who remained stationed in Manilla. She and her closest WAC friends, Beckie Langford, Laurie Giulio, Mary Sigford, and Isa Caras, remained in that city until the formal Japanese surrender ceremony on September 2, 1945. Afterward, they all made a pact to stay in contact after returning home, exchanging addresses and writing notes to one another.

One of the last orders the WACs received from their superiors in The US Women's Army Corps was to take an oath not to expose what they were about to see to anyone. As they stood in formation, the few remaining prisoners of the Bataan Death March slowly walked in a line before them, returning from their inhuman treatment in captivity. Many people bowed their heads, and most were crying. The men appeared like marching skeletons before them.

It was an emotional day when the wartime friends hugged each other before parting. As anxious as they were to go home, it was difficult after experiencing so much grief, along with happy memories and camaraderie. They referred to themselves evermore as sisters.

Eleanora was the last to depart. She hugged Isa before boarding the transport plane, the first step on her voyage back to the small town of Wellsville, Ohio.

The Battle of Luzon ended with the Japanese surrender on August 15, 1945. Now a captain, Bill Conners had fought to the end. His only remaining friend was Bob Chipwick; all the others had died in battle. Bill and his company helped process prisoners of war after Japan's surrender on August 15. It wasn't until November of 1945 that he left for the States.

Chapter Forty-Three

Wellsville, Ohio 1945

Coming Home

The American military, who returned directly after World War Two in Europe, received great fanfare on the home front. Parades and special celebrations were common. Soldiers were granted free drinks and other courtesies just by wearing their uniforms. Towns and cities all over the US rewarded the valiant victors who came back first from Europe and the Pacific. It seemed there was little fanfare left for those who fought to the end. By the time they returned, America was already moving on, giving jobs to the first who came. At the end of World War Two, high-ranking officers praised the role of American women in the military. General Douglas MacArthur called them 'My best Soldiers.' Aside from serving as nurses and surgical aids, the military recruited women for positions often filled by men. Women served in the American Army, Navy, Marines, and Army Air Force. They drove trucks and buses and repaired vehicles and planes. Women learned to fly heavy bombers and other aircraft and ferried them while in overseas positions. Many were killed and wounded, and others became prisoners of war. There were also deaths from diseases and illnesses caused by harsh conditions.

Eleanora's cousin, Rocco, picked her up at the train station around the corner on 12th Street to help her with her foot locker. She had wired ahead about which train she would be coming home on.

Annie was the first to hug her before she walked into the door, "Oh, Eleanora, I'm so glad you're back," Annie held her close; they were both crying. "I was so worried about you over there in the jungles. Thank God you're home."

"How's Jimmy doing?" Eleanora wiped her tears. After that last incident, after her first daughter was born, she worried about her best friend's marriage. Eleanora knew Annie and Jimmy had another daughter while she was overseas. Eleanora finally understood how cut off she was from civilization, too busy to realize it during her time in the service overseas. Eleanora missed Annie most of all.

"We'll talk. We have a lot to catch up on," Annie said, her eyes widened. Her daughter, Laura, was already five years old, and her new baby, Maryanne, was an almost two-and-a-half-year-old toddler running about the house. "Jimmy was just discharged from the service. He went back to his band, and he left for work before we got here." As Eleanora and Annie walked into the living room, Colomba Trieste got up from her chair to grab the wandering baby and greet Eleanora.

Eleanora was surprised to see so many people. Felo rose from his rocker to welcome home his daughter. There was a house full of family, relatives, and friends. She was glad to finally be home among all these folks. Eleanora had dreamed of sleeping in her own bed after all the different types of uncomfortable military cots she had used in the service.

Eleanora's Aunt Thelma was there with her two-year-old son but not her daughters. George still ruled his daughters with an iron fist, even as adults. They remained home with George.

All of Eleanora's cousins who had served survived. Carmine, who was at the Battle of Midway, remained partially deaf from the intense bombing by the Japanese on that island he helped defend. Her cousin Andy had served valiantly in the US Army. Dick had been a soldier of the infamous special operations 'Merrill's Marauders.' Always outnumbered by the Japanese, Dick fought behind enemy lines. He was a survivor of the Marauders who fought relentlessly during the monsoons in Burma's mountains, swamps, and jungles without heavy weapons. John distinguished himself as a hero by volunteering for a dangerous rescue mission of a US Navy vessel stranded at sea. During a fierce storm, John boarded a rubber raft, fought heavy winds to help secure a tow line to the abandoned ship, and remained aboard until it reached a safe harbor. The US Navy cited John for courage, devotion, and meritorious performance. Eleanora was so happy that all her cousins were safely home and able to reunite with them. It was only her brother Nick, who hadn't yet returned home from the Army.

As Eleanora mingled with her aunts, uncles, cousins, and friends, she noticed Henry Beckle, their next-door neighbor, sitting and talking to one of her cousins. She looked around but couldn't spot Mr. Beckle's wife, Emma, or their daughter, Sally. Shrugging it off, she went back to answering all the questions people were asking her about the war and hearing all the experiences of her cousins who served overseas.

Later, when she went to the kitchen to help her mother and sister, Julia, prepare some desserts, she asked Lucy, "Mom?"

"Hello," Lucy went about her work, giving her routine response to a question.

"Where's Emma and Sally Beckle? I see Henry inside, but not them."

"I don't know nothing." Lucy didn't lift her face to answer; she just went about preparing her homemade cookies.

When Lucy walked outside to throw something in the trash, Julia walked close to Eleanora and whispered, "Sally got pregnant while you were away," Julia stood with a sinister grin. "No husband."

"Oh, my God," Eleanora blushed, then began chuckling. "I can't believe it," she said quietly. "They gave Mom such a hard time, telling her I would get pregnant if I joined the WACs, and she. . ." Eleanora broke up laughing. After she composed herself, she asked Julia, "Who's the father?"

"The bread delivery man," now Julia was also laughing. "He's married."

The following morning at breakfast, Eleanora questioned Lucy, "Mom, what's this I hear about Sally Beckle?" Lucy remained silent while eating. "All that time they worried and bothered you about me getting pregnant if I joined the Army, and she got pregnant?"

"I don't know nothing," Lucy waved her hand. Felo smiled behind his newspaper.

Eleanora wore her full uniform, with ribbons and three bronze battle stars pinned to it for several days. She had lost so much weight from the stress of activity and the extreme conditions of the jungles overseas that she needed a new wardrobe. Eleanora also faced other adjustments after her return. Memories of the hardships she encountered, especially the young wounded boys, plagued her. Those harsh recollections of war would haunt her for the rest of her life.

Chapter Forty-Four

Wellsville, Ohio 1951

Wounds Heal

It is said that time heals all wounds. The truth is that the loss of an endeared person never fully heals. The struggles at first gently subside like the soft breezes that float from the Ohio River at sundown. When those superb skies boast beautiful golden hues that only God can create, he allows our minds to process them in ways until we find special places for them in our lives. The loss of a younger person still blooming is never fully healed. They are stored within us every second of each day through our memories of them. Our hearts always carry them with us until we meet them again beyond those vast, vivid clouds.

Elena had a mild breakdown from the shock of hearing about her fiancé's death. She vowed she would remember Douglas Nicholson as the love of her life until the day she died. Elena moved on until she would one day again reunite with him.

Douglas was in the driveway behind the back porch, preparing to take his grandson, Douglas, fishing for the first time. Their daughter, Martha's six-year-old son, she and her husband named Douglas after the uncle he would never meet, was excitedly helping his grandfather. Romeo, now an old dog, was forcing his eagerness, a trait all loyal canines possess, and shuffling between the man and the boy.

"Like this, Pop-Pop?" The boy stood like a soldier with his

fishing rod poised against the front of his body.

Douglas smiled, "That's fine, Son. Are you ready?" He grabbed his bag and slung it over his shoulder.

"Yes, sir!" Young Douglas began walking, "Bye, Meemaw!"

Gabrielle sat on her back porch, enjoying her sewing. "Aren't you fellas taking the car?" Her blonde hair was now completely grey and complemented her wide olive-green eyes. She was still attractive but bore the crow's feet and wrinkles of her age and tragedy.

"We're walking!" her husband answered for them.

"Are you sure you're up to it, old man?" she giggled.

"Gab, this old man still has some skin on his butt!" Then Douglas grinned, offering that look he knew his wife loved, "See you later, dear," he said as he led his grandson past the porch along the walkway at the side of the house that led to Riverside.

"Good luck, fellas!" she told them as they passed her on the porch, "Hope you catch a lot of fish!"

"Thanks, Meemaw! We will!" little Douglas shouted excitedly.

Gabrielle smiled as she remembered her little boy leaving for his first fishing trip. It seemed like yesterday, and a tear rolled down her cheek as she returned to her sewing.

Douglas Nicholson walked along Riverside with his grandson to where the road began. Romeo, the Golden Labrador Retriever, proudly led the way, reminding Douglas of Rollo so many years before, those fond recollections when he and his faithful companion led mighty forces against hordes of enemies in his childhood imagination. They crossed over to the side of the road, little Douglas walking along the grass above the slope to the railroad tracks.

Douglas showed the boy the house where he grew up as they passed it, remembering his mother and father fondly. Then they walked by the Elks Lodge, where he was still a member. Memories poured as they came upon his church on Riverside, rebuilt with stone in 1916 before Douglas left for that dreaded war. He pictured Rollo waiting outside under the shade of a tree until services ended on Sundays.

Romeo persevered along Riverside Avenue, struggling to act like a younger dog. He reminded Douglas again of those glorious days with his loyal sidekick, Rollo, his only friend at one time when they romped together through the small town.

General Reilly's home on Riverside had become MacLean's Funeral Home since 1937, and Douglas recalled the general fondly. Douglas couldn't stop at the War Memorial. It would be too hard with his son's nephew and namesake with him. He only pointed and said, "That's a memorial that honors great men."

The wharf was gone, and the three figures headed for the empty lot beside the flood wall where the old Third Street Station once stood majestically. Douglas smiled as he remembered his and Rollo's terror of Robert McElhenny.

Reflecting on his happy days as a child, Peppina rose from the buried corridors of his mind and those magical childhood days with her and his friends. 'Sundried tomatoes,' he smiled at his private thoughts, recalling how often he ate at Giuditta's hotel. A vision of the day he waited anxiously on the train at that station before he left to go and see Gabrielle, knowing she was the woman for him, resurfaced within him.

"There was once a huge building here, Douglas," he pointed to the lot, "before they built that floodwall," recalling the days of the great floods.

"Really? Why did they knock it down?" asked young Douglas as Romeo sat patiently, listening with a puzzled expression.

"Well, Son," Douglas contemplated, his eyes gazing into the distance, "all things come to an end, like the setting sun on a summer's eve." The boy, captivated by his grandfather's words, pondered quietly. "Now, are you ready to make a promise?"

"Yes, Pop-Pop."

"You must promise never to tell anyone about the secret place I'm about to show you, only those you truly love and trust. Okay?"

"Okay, Pop-Pop. I won't ever tell anyone that I don't trust," young Douglas excitedly answered, "I promise! Cross my heart!"

"Then take my hand and let's go. C'mon, Rollo!"

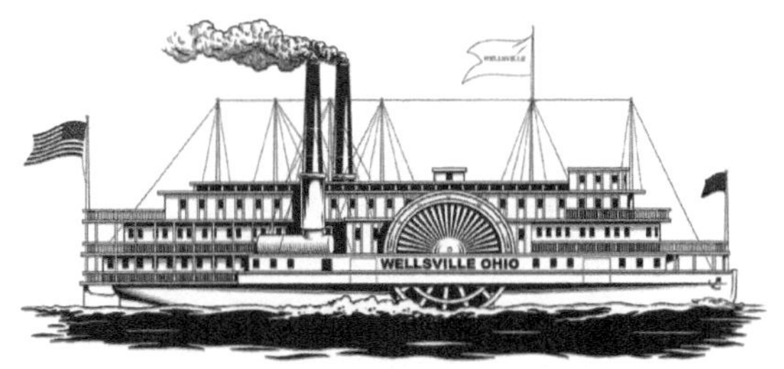

River Town
Wellsville Ohio

Afterword

The town of Wellsville came together during and after the Second World War. People of all ethnicities and races worked together on the home front. US Soldiers, Sailors, Marines, and Airmen didn't care what country their ancestors came from; they welcomed anyone fighting with them in the foxholes of the battlefields, at sea, and in the air.

Douglas Nicholson passed away from a heart attack a few years after his first fishing expedition with his grandson. His doctor thought it was a complication from his war injury to the vascular area of his chest. Those who knew him felt it was from a broken heart after losing his son in the war. A few years after the death of Douglas, Gabrielle moved to Cincinnati to live in her old home owned by her daughter, Martha, and her husband, William. They had bought the Delisle home to keep it in the family. Gabrielle lived her remaining days there. Her cherished photos of Douglas and her with their parents and Frenchie on her wedding day remained on the fireplace mantel. She added pictures of her and Douglas taken in England and those of her children, grandchildren, and other family images. Framed photos of her husband and son in uniform stood side by side. The photo of Douglas and his childhood friends, Peppina and Rollo, was among them. Gabrielle knew her beloved Douglas would want them there.

Elena Demarco remembered Douglas Nicholson Jr. as the love of her life until the day she died. She told my mother that.

Bill Conners returned to Wellsville as a war hero. He joined the Army as a private and returned as a captain. Bill married his girlfriend and raised two boys and a girl. Bill had several jobs throughout his life. He settled in Savannah, Georgia, for a few years but returned to Wellsville. His eldest son became a priest and then a monsignor. Bill's daughter became an officer in the Navy. Later, she joined a convent as a nun.

Nick Buch returned home from the war in 1946. He got a job in a steel mill not far from Wellsville. He played the field and waited until 1970 to get married. Nick died in 2006 at the age of 86.

After visiting his wartime friend Isaac in New York City, Hector Allen decided to move there. He married, raised a family, and died there as a resident.

After the war, Beckie Langford worked at an army hospital in New York City and invited my mother to visit her. Eleanora not only visited but also took a job there. My mom met a young lady who would become a dear friend and introduced her to my father. Eleanora married my father in Wellsville at the Immaculate Conception Church in 1947, with Annie as her matron-of-honor. They moved to a mixed-ethnicity neighborhood in New York City, where my father's family lived. My grandmother Lucy was heartbroken; she had arranged for her daughter to marry a local man.

Anthony Trieste passed away mysteriously in 1948, preceding his mother's death. There was talk about the Brocella brothers' involvement in his death, but there was no solid evidence.

Colomba Trieste passed away in 1955. Her family and the many friends she had throughout the town mourned her loss.

My mother, Eleanora, brought my older brother and me to

Wellsville by train before I was one year old. That was my first visit to the town. My grandfather, Felo, passed away in 1955, the same year as Colomba Trieste. My parents booked a plane to go to his funeral. It was my first air flight. We visited my grandmother, Lucy, and other family members and friends every summer vacation in Wellsville.

After several matrimonial indiscretions, Jimmy Bass finally deserted his wife, Annie, and left town with another woman. Annie had to return to work to support herself and her remaining family. Jimmy died in Florida not long after leaving Wellsville. Still loyal to her marriage, Annie paid to transport Jimmy's body back to Wellsville for burial.

The Trieste sisters were like family to my mother. I remember all of them well. They were wonderful and loving people, as were their husbands. When I was a child, I thought they were blood relatives, and I continued to address all of them as aunts and uncles until they parted this world. Aunt Annie was my older brother's godmother, and Aunt Nina was my godmother. Aunt Louise was the first to pass away in 1981. Aunt Nina followed her passing in 1983, and Aunt Maude in 1988. My mother lost her dear friend, my Aunt Annie, in 2001. Aunt Mary lived until 2006; Aunt Clara, the youngest sister, died in 2011.

My grandmother, Lucy, lived to be 100 years old. My Aunt Julia passed away three months after her mother died.

As a child, I remember my mother faithfully sending a monthly check to a missionary in Wewak, New Guinea. She made that donation every month, no matter what financial restraints she was under. I only understood why once she explained that story to me for this book.

My mother's three best WAC friends, Beckie Langford, Laurie Giulio, and Mary Sigford, stayed true to their word and often corresponded by mail. On the way home from one of our trips from Wellsville, my family visited Laurie Giulio at her and her husband's home in Lancaster, PA. They were lovely people. While looking through my mother's things after her death, I came upon a letter from Becky written before she died. Among

other simple things, Beckie mentioned that she was having dinner at a veteran's affair near where she lived in Texas. She was
a widow and seemed lonely.

Isa Caras married an international banker and visited New
York City once a year. Isa and my mother reunited for lunch
whenever she was in the city until her husband retired.

Unbeknownst to me then, my mother's old boyfriend, Sid,
phoned her one day while my brother and I were at school. Sid
had also married and had become a successful attorney, but
wanted to see my mother. They met for lunch in the city.

At the time of the memorial's opening in Washington, D.C.,
dedicated to American women in the military, a local New York
newspaper interviewed my mother, Eleanora. As she was in
Ohio then, they interviewed her by telephone. I was living in
New York and couldn't be present. After reading the article, I
asked my mom why she didn't detail all the stories I knew from
our collaboration for this book. She answered that she didn't
want to take away the glory from 'the boys' who fought in those
gruesome battles. I explained how she also was in harm's way
and should have told more about her and her fellow WACs. With
a tear in her eye, my mom merely replied, "You can't know, David; You had to have been there to understand. Watch the kids
leaving any high school, laughing and carrying on. I saw boys
the same age dying in field hospitals, some mutilated beyond
comprehension. It was a sight I can't get out of my mind, and
I won't ever be able to. How could I take anything away from
them?" I never questioned my mother about that article again.

In the mid-1990s, when my mother was in her 80s, I went to
pick her up at the airport. She was returning from visiting a relative in Florida. While waiting, I noticed her flight number flashing until it read: canceled. I learned that the flight had to land
in Virginia, and my mom wouldn't come in until the next day.
Upon arriving at the terminal the following day, I noticed my
mother surrounded by many people. I could hear them thanking
and praising her for helping them as I approached. I learned
the jet hit a heavy wind pocket, lost power to one engine, and

went into a temporary nosedive. It had to make an emergency landing in Virginia. As I stood waiting with my mom's luggage, strangers introduced themselves. They complimented me, telling me how calm and wonderful my mother was to the panicking passengers and helping them recover from their anxieties. It reminded me of my mother's accounting of flying into Leyte during the war many years before. She was indeed a remarkable woman.

—*David Navarria*

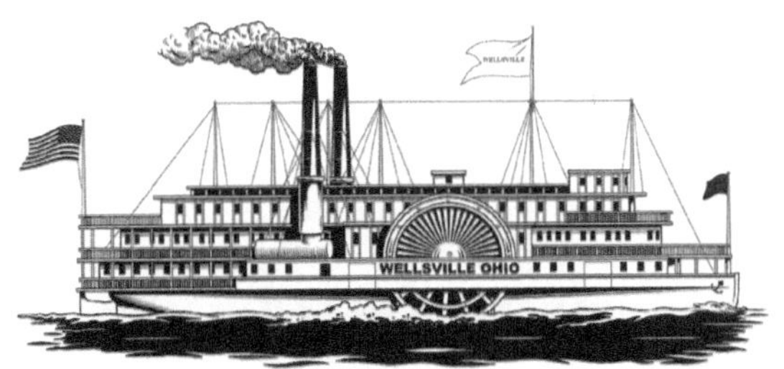

River Town
Wellsville Ohio

The End

From the poem: Man Was Made To Mourn
by Robert Burns

Many and sharp the numerous ills
Inwoven with our frame;
More pointed still, we make ourselves
Regret, remorse and shame;
And man, whose heaven-erected face
The smiles of love adorn,
Man's inhumanity to man,
Makes countless thousands mourn.

Recommended reading about the history of Wellsville, Ohio from 1795-1950:
BEFORE THE MEMORY FADES
Published by The Wellsville Historical Society

More About the Book, River Town Wellsville Ohio and Author At:
www.DavidNavarria.com